Richard Hooker Wilmer, Alexander C. Branscom

Mystic Romances of the Blue and the Grey

Masks of War, Commerce and Society

Richard Hooker Wilmer, Alexander C. Branscom

Mystic Romances of the Blue and the Grey
Masks of War, Commerce and Society

ISBN/EAN: 9783337346836

Printed in Europe, USA, Canada, Australia, Japan

Cover: Foto ©Andreas Hilbeck / pixelio.de

More available books at **www.hansebooks.com**

MYSTIC ROMANCES

—OF THE—

BLUE AND THE GREY:

MASKS OF WAR, COMMERCE AND SOCIETY.

PICTURES OF REAL LIFE SCENES ENACTED IN THIS AGE, RARELY
SURPASSED IN THE WILDEST DREAMS OF FICTITIOUS
ROMANCE.

⬥

BY ALEXANDER C. BRANSCOM,

Author of "An Improved System of Self-teaching the English Language," etc., etc.

— ⬥ —

"Try not the pass," the old man said;
"Dark lowers the tempest overhead;
The roaring torrent is deep and wide;
     *   *   *   *
Beware the pine tree's withered branch;
Beware the awful avalanche."
—LONGFELLOW.

—⬥—

MUTUAL PUBLISHING COMPANY,
45, 47, 49 & 51 Rose Street,
NEW YORK.

Press of David H. Gildersleeve, 45-51 Rose St., N. Y.

PREFACE.

The writer has known nearly every vicissitude in the scale of fortune, through a long career, in peculiar relations with the characters, or their intimate friends, portrayed in this volume.   Thus, through nearly a quarter of a century of active and thrilling experience in daily life has the foundation for every chapter been obtained.   The mystic influence which the actions of characters exercise on one another are masterful and incomprehensible lessons of life worthy the attention of mankind.   AUTHOR.

December, 1883.

CONTENTS.

CONTENTS.

MYSTIC ROMANCES

BLUE AND THE GREY.

CHAPTER I.

INTRODUCTORY.

" Down came the storm, and smote amain
   That vessel in her strength.
 She shudder'd and paused, like a frighten'd steed :
   Then leaped her cable's length.
      *   *   *   *
 Through the midnight dark and drear ;
   Through the whistling sleet and snow,
 Like a shrouded ghost that vessel swept
   Towards the reef of Norman's woe.
      *   *   *   *
 She struck where the white and fleecy waves
   Looked soft as carded wool ;
 But the cruel rocks, they gored her sides,
   Like the horns of an angry bull."
                  —LONGFELLOW.

MYSTERY veils many details of our gigantic civil war, the greatest conflict, when the issues at stake are contemplated, that has ever convulsed a nation. Strangely interesting vicissitudes have grown out of the obscure circumstances of individual contact, among antagonists who met on the outposts or beyond; on the field of battle, in the hospital—minutiæ too insignificant for the perceptions of the historian—concealed, as they were and are, in the shadows of great events.

Writers of romance ransack the legendary lore of the Old World, and dive into the musty halls of palaces, or the beaten tracks of court routine, amid the regal shades of despotism, to locate their plots and to arouse their characters oftener from the sleep of many centuries than to portray them from animate life; forgetting that the most intensified romances of earth are to be found in real life in this fast age and country. The war of the American rebellion, and the years following in its wake, created and have developed many genuine heroes and heroines who have lived and moved in the mystic spell of fairy romance, the centres of magnetic attractions swaying and influencing numbers of other characters and lives in masterful degree, yet all unknown to the great and heedless world, because eclipsed by the effulgent radiance of the leaders of legions, and corps, and armies, and the sheen of beauty in the brilliant circles that throng the gilded saloons of aristocratic mansions. With these the historian has acquainted the world; and the exploits of some of them are too romantic for the grave professor of history to credit with confiding alacrity. But what made them ideal heroes? Was it alone all but matchless talent and transcendent genius? Did these clothe Lee and Jackson with the insignia bearing the imprint of heroism and immortal renown? No; they were essential elements; but without the unyielding chivalry and indomitable, self-sacrificing devotion of the Southern masses, their bright names would not shine in their towering niches in the temple of Fame.

To Grant and Sherman the same truth applies. What laid the foundation of their successful triumphs in the South-west, and brought them from obscurity to stand forth the pillars of hope to support a tottering and despairing empire? The sturdy pioneers of the West, with their unerring rifles and indefatigable zeal. These developed commanders who inspired national confidence that rallied to their support the waning wealth of the North and the East. Had their early campaigns been prosecuted with less efficient troops.

they would not now be the adored of the nation, as the commanders who saved the Union.

Amid the rank and file must the makers of commanding and historical heroes be sought—amid the rank and file must the typical heroes of life be sought. Here have we looked for and found characters with strange features of interest clustering about them, to rival the war scenes of the Arabian Nights; the loves of Petrarch and Laura, in the famous romance located in the fabled vale of Vaucluse; the story of Enoch Arden's long absence and mysterious return; the woes of the unfortunate merchant of Venice, had they remained unabated; the tragedy of Romeo and Juliet; the sleep of Rip Van Winkle; the ghosts of Banquo and Hamlet; the Pandemonium of Milton and the Inferno of Dante.

Although not portrayed with the pleasing colors of an Addison, the unique genius of a Scott, nor yet with the matchless grace of an Irving, our life sketches, if not well, shall be truly delineated. These shall embrace every phase of its shady and bright side that pervades the middle and upper ranks of American society. We have learned this through peculiar relations maintained with the characters themselves, under singular circumstances arising from conditions in which we have been placed with them, and which we never could have known by other means. All of our leading characters, together with their parts, even to details, have been and are intimately known to us, while the parts of other characters have been supplied by the parties themselves, or by those who were well acquainted with the facts.

We find in them many startling surprises and thrilling developments in the highest ranks of both cosmopolitan and rural aristocracy, as well as from the middle marches of life; in the mountain cabin and the metropolitan palace; the fierce and fickle love of the Northern Lily, and the wild and passionate devotion of the Southern Rose. How each in turn was swayed by war's tempest, and tried in the ordeal of that social pestilence which followed in the wake of bloody strife, together with soldiers of fortune and business men as portrayed in wonderful careers. We shall present a number of characters just embark-

ing, and continue to exhibit them as they progress, either cautiously or recklessly, on the voyage of life, buffeted by the boisterous, inconstant waves, as they are thus impelled toward the breakers, in the dangerous surf, fringing the margins of that dreary, desolate strand of the rushing, soothing, destroying sea of Time, strewn far and wide with numberless wrecks of hope.

Deign to accompany us to the great theatre where may be witnessed some almost unique acts in the drama of life—that prolific and inexhaustible play where develops all that amuses, shocks and instructs the mind of mankind. There we shall unfold to your view some mystic and some shady realities that are untold—swiftly shifting and wildly varying scenes. You will see actors and actresses without one moment to rehearse their parts, rushed as though it were by mysterious and supernatural managers upon the stage, and bid to play. We shall show you acting required of them, so fierce and so precipitate, as the great curtain rolls up, disclosing their destined parts so rapidly that they appear to be too much occupied to reflect, or too indifferent to care, what new wonder next awaits them.

Among our characters there are some mask-wearers whose complications present interesting and instructive features, which clearly demonstrate that the course of life pursued by these indiscreet ones has cost and is ever costing confiding, imprudent, deluded, unfortunate, despairing men and women, and those who are near and dear to them, unnumbered cruel and undying heart aches. The sequel will show, however, that most of those who assume the mask in the commercial or in the social world, do so at first, actuated by no unworthy motive, but by what they at that time regard as a laudable desire to protect an interest or a reputation from some apprehended danger. But thus seeds of infection are planted in a fertile soil and matured by a congenial clime, where they germinate, rapidly attain dark luxuriance, and soon mature their bitter fruits.

Few, very few, are securely exempt from becoming exposed, at some period of life, to the baneful allurements of the beguiling mask; for strange circumstances, peculiar associations, mysterious influences, terrible misfortunes, in a word, any precipitate revolution in the affairs and relations of life, in the social compacts of earth, may bring any one face to face with this diabolical generator of ruin and woe. By the fickle capriciousness of fortune, either gradually, by slow decay, or with the precipitation of "a giant powder explosion," possessions slip or are wrenched away from the wealthy and from the independent; and unnatural calamities, unforeseen and unavoidable disasters overtake and crush the prosperous with a pitiless, unsparing hand.

In and throughout these thrilling acts, the true, the pure and the good will intermingle or be inextricably blended with the false, the treacherous and the evil, as though by some envious, even malicious, hand of destiny; and these conflicting influences will continually struggle, each seeking for the mastery.

Out of consideration for the relatives and the friends of the wayward and those of the good with whom the wayward were associated, we shall disguise the true names of characters and the location of two or three scenes; but with these exceptions we shall reproduce realistic vicissitudes through which actual flesh and blood characters have passed. We shall not draw on the imagination except in a few instances, when we may presume to bring the supernatural to the surface, merely for the reason that the predominating force of such controlling influence and presence is so unmistakably perceptible as clearly to demonstrate that chance never produced many things which will be portrayed; that like the ghost at the banquet, the shadowy phantom "will not down;" hence this becomes a mysterious personality we cannot utterly ignore.

We promise to offer nothing unworthy to enter the purest and the most sanctified precincts of the home circle or the church, as moral lessons commendable as models to be followed by struggling and friendless youth in the lone cheerless battle of life, or as warnings against the dangers and snares ever lurking or concealed about the pathway of the heedless, prepared for their destruction; to present the sentimental and

the sensational only where they belong to and are inseparable from true life-pictures.

Our early scene will be located under the dark shadow of the rising cloud, in the gathering tempest of war, and amid the shocks and the tumult and the carnage of contending hosts on the blood crimsoned and ever memorable fields of Virginia.

From the war scenes we shall follow in the commercial wake of subsequent years, often wandering amid the bubbles of the social cauldron.

CHAPTER II.

GARLAND CLOUD.

"Alas! our young affections run to waste,
Or water but the desert; whence arise
But weeds of dark luxuriance, tares of haste;
Rank at the core, though tempting to the eye,
Flowers whose wild odors breathe but agonies;
And trees whose gums are poison; such the plants,
Which spring beneath her steps, as Passion flies
O'er the world's wilderness, and vainly pants
For some celestial fruit forbidden to our wants."
—BYRON.

WHAT startling memories run back to cluster about the May-day of 1861. Prattling children of that historical time have its memory seared into the tablets of their hearts. May-Queens who were not crowned recall that cruel day of disappointment with rankling bitterness; and it is associated with shadows of sadness that older people do not forget.

Admirers of Nature in perfect loveliness may find their imaged beauty enshrined in a thousand spots—as fairy enchantresses—in the blue-grass region of South-western Virginia, so calmly serene as to impress one with the idea that agitation, tumult, passion and sorrow never invade these sequestered haunts of tranquil blissfulness. Amid the blue hills, the rippling rills, and the crystal streams of this picturesque country, and high up among surrounding mountain-peaks to the East and West—to the North the lovely blue-grass country rolling away in undulating waves far beyond the vision of the eye, and South the pine forests, the fields and the villages of North Carolina spreading out before the wondering gaze until the horizon veils the view—lays a broad, level tract of glade land known for many miles around as "the mountain meadows," one of its margins resting on the very summit of the abruptly precipitous steeps of the Blue-Ridge Mountain. On this vast tract stands a desolate homestead, the reputed scene of a horrible tragedy, where it was believed the owner murdered a traveler for his money: hence the house was said to be haunted. Many people in the neighborhood gave it a wide berth in daylight, and few of the most daring hunters would have visited it at night; no one could be induced to live in the "haunted house." Thus it was in May, 1861; it is much the same in May, 1883.

It is a May-day scene in 1861 which we are to present on this stage—a scene not much out of harmony with the ghostly legends of the spot; a scene such as never had been witnessed before in this peaceful region, and such as the advancing centuries may not unfold again.

Usually, the traveler journeying along the highway that lies in a lane through this tract, would not see a human being anywhere within the bounds of the vast meadows. But how changed was the aspect of the spot on that bright May morning, when charming Nature smiled on those desolate fields! Could some one of the numerous octogenarians of that vitalizing clime and neighborhood, utterly ignorant of the maddening agitations of the day, have looked upon the meadows in the yet early morning of that day, he would have been struck dumb with amazement.

The sun rose bright and gloriously; not a cloud spot or mist of haze obscured the cerulean dome of the smiling horizon. Young Nature, but lately freed from the icy chains of winter, bounded with exuberant gratitude, and danced in rapturous ecstasy before the King of Day on his Oriental throne of transcendent brilliancy and matchless splendor. Sun-rise, on a morning such as we have just described, in those vast mountain solitudes, impresses the stranger who first beholds it with a thrill of emotion, and awakens in his being a sense of reverential admiration ever to be remembered. Already flowers were blushing in the dells and on the hill-sides, and exhaling their sweet perfumes. Budding Nature beamed on every twig. The gentle zephyrs were redolent

with her fragrance, and replete with the dulcet notes of the warbling songsters of the forest. What a fearful contrast of sombre gloom was shed upon this peaceful scene from that dark political cloud looming up the northern sky; smoke from the wasting fires kindling by wicked man.

The dew was not yet dry on the tender grass and young leaves, when scores of people were on the meadows, and every road or pathway, for miles and miles in all directions, was thronged with men, women and children, all eagerly hastening toward the meadows, clearly indicating that intense excitement was raging at fever heat among the children of the mountain. Before ten o'clock thousands of people were on the ground, and yet they came. Never before, not within twenty-five miles of this spot, had there been one-fourth as many people collected together. But now, something extraordinary was on hand.

It was expected that at this place and on this day, the second company of volunteers called for in the county would be enlisted and organized. Speeches were made, urging all who wished to share in the honors and the glories of the war to embrace this, the last opportunity, as peace would be made before another company would be organized in the county. Old men—veterans of the war of 1812-14—hung their heads and assumed an air of gravity, women wept.

Just as the music was ready to start as the signal for volunteers to fall in line, all eyes were turned in the direction of a solitary traveler, coming from the north, on the Court-house road. He was young, tall, rather prepossessing, and clad in the uniform of a volunteer, the only one who would be there, the first upon whom the eyes of nine-tenths of that assembly had ever rested.

Farmer Moore was the only man on the speaker's stand able to recognize the young man.

"There is coming yonder," said he, "young Cloud, one of the Guards. We shall now get the news from H——."

"Let us have the music delayed until we learn what news he brings, and, in the meantime, tell us who this young man is, friend Moore," was the rejoinder of Judge Carter.

"He is," said Mr. Moore, "a son of the mountain. Yonder stand his grand-parents, parents, sisters and other relatives, under the cedar-tree, admiring him; and well they may admire him, for he is a young man of whom any family might justly be proud. The family belongs to the middle class, and has since Yorktown was first colonized; they are all respectable, sober and honest people, with no stain on the family name. Four years since, when the lad was only thirteen years old, he had committed to memory all the meagre studies taught in our schools. Because no others are introduced, he never goes to school, and his father would not send him to a higher school. He is rather awkward, taciturn, and extremely backward and bashful in the company of ladies. He is the best shot with a rifle in the county, and nothing excites him. He was the first volunteer in the county. But he will pass us. I must hail him. Say, Cloud, what is the news?"

CLOUD: "Not a word, Mr. Moore, except that the Guards have received marching orders, and will leave H——to-morrow morning at ten o'clock for the tented field."

Then this object that attracted so many admiring eyes, hastened to join his family group, where he was quickly surrounded by friends and strangers. Old and young ladies of the first families in the land, regardless of etiquette or ceremony, eagerly vied with one another to grasp his hand and bid him God's blessing. But his own family —mother and sisters—greeted him with quivering lips and moistening eyes.

The musicians also came up and stood by young Cloud. But soon they received the signal from the speaker's stand to proceed. At once the shrill, stirring notes of the fife, and the tumultuous roll of the drum, were echoing and reverberating from the craggy mountain-spurs, down among deep and cavernous ravines, and floating away on the mild and balmy breeze, laden with odoriferous perfume from the dogwood, the laurel and the honeysuckle.

The father of young Cloud and his mother's brother were the first men in line behind the music. In five minutes double the number wanted were in line; and they had to be rejected by lot.

The uncle was elected captain, the father first-lieutenant by acclamation; then young Cloud's name was mentioned in connection with the next nomination.

Promptly this young man, manifesting painful embarrassment, stepped in front of the line and said:

"Schoolmates, companions, neighbors and friends, I entreat you not to nominate me for any office. I could not accept, because I do not merit such a gift. I thank you, my friends, those of you who called my name; but think no more about it. My position has been chosen. I shall die in the ranks, or rise from them, should I ever rise, on the scale of merit. To-morrow I depart for the front. To-morrow morning there will be more than one hundred sad families in this county. Ten days hence the number will double; there will be vacant places at the table, empty chairs in the home circle; some of them—God only knows how many—forever. Do not grieve that lot has rejected many of you. It is but for a few days. Many may get an opportunity to hear their names called from the muster-roll who are not anxious to have that distinction before the end comes. Our enemies have the flag and the constitution of our forefathers. Would to God that we had them. There is a magic in their name that will be a greater power against us than half the legions of the North. You have a hundred worthier than I from whom to select. Please proceed with your organization."

CHAPTER III.

ADIEU TO HOME.

"Perchance my dog will whine in vain,
'Till fed by stranger hands;
But, long ere I come back again,
He'd tear me where he stands."
—BYRON.

THOUSANDS remember to this day, in mournful despair, the agonizing anguish of those sad days of farewells, when fair cheeks were wet with tears; rosy lips kissed for the last time; receding forms watched by eyes—tear-dimmed eyes—gazing with longing fondness after loved ones until these disappeared round the street corners, the turn of the road, or over the brow of a hill, to return—nevermore. Oh, alas! for the broken hearts these partings have since wrung.

Seated in the home-circle with the family, the grandfather and some other friends, on the same evening after the Mountain Meadow scene, the grandfather was the first to address young Cloud with reference to the momentous questions of the day.

"Garland," he said thoughtfully, and with manifest reluctance, "you do not know how it pained me to see you so abrupt with those gentlemen as we were leaving the Meadows this evening."

"I could not help it, grandfather. I hate them with all the intensity of my passionate young nature, and I could not dissemble."

"Why, Garland Cloud! you amaze me, boy; but for the uniform you wear, I could scarcely refrain from striking you. Foolish boy! They have been Assemblymen, Congressmen, Senators, and are likely to be generals; probably over you; they might then remember this occurrence."

"Hum! Those politicians? You are as likely to wake a young man to-morrow morning, my grandfather, as you are ever to see one of those oily-tongued public distracters in a soldier's uniform. They have made the war, and are little, if any, better than John Brown was. Was the same fate meted out to some thousands of them, both North and South, to-morrow, that would put an end to all this disturbance for the next hundred years, and save the country ten times as many and by far more valuable lives, besides all the other undreamed-of desolation and miseries which war must bring. Why don't they prove their professions? Why have they not stepped first, somewhere, to the notes of the music, as they saw my father and uncle, their dupes, step to-day? Where does the country need them? Is it to go from place to place exclaiming—'Go on, boys; we will meet you there,' when ere many days or weeks the thunder of cannon and the smoke of burning homesteads, as it ascends heavenward, will make this appeal more eloquently and more forcibly than any words these demagogues can utter, as those tocsins and emblems of danger and desolation are wafted Southward from the banks of the Potomac? Let them do their duty, grandfather, and I will respect and honor them; but until then I cannot."

The grandfather sat mutely gazing at the rosy face of this youth, now in an unusual glow from the ardor of his earnest zeal in the subject upon which he had been speaking.

The early breakfast was eaten amid the silence that pervades the mourning group pending the solemn services of a funeral—hearts were full to overflowing.

The farewells were the silent pressure of hands, the mute sealing and severing of lips. Thus quitting the threshold of his mountain home, young Cloud was met by his two little hounds, the companions of his youthful sports. In a choking voice he said, "Stay here, my good boys." The little brutes, seated on the ground, looking wistfully through the yet grey twilight after his receding form, raised a mournful howl—something they had never done before—which was regarded as ominous of evil to come. Garland Cloud was gone on his tidal wave of time, out into the tumult, the storms and the darkness of the mad and thundering sea of life, and into the valley and shadows of death.

CHAPTER IV.

BLACKBURN'S FORD.

"But hark! that deep sound breaks in once more—
To arms! to arms! it is, it is the cannon's opening roar."
—BYRON.

In Prince William County, Virginia, there is, and was at the time of which we write, a railway junction on the Orange and Alexandria R. R. known on the maps as Manassas Junction. This now is known in history as a tragic stage, a military depot, a strategic point, associated with the manœuvring of grand armies and sanguinary battle-fields. Here the Confederate forces selected their early rendezvous from which to watch and guard the approaches leading to Washington, where it was known the Government of the Union was collecting an army to invade Virginia. Between this spot and Washington a narrow, sluggish, but crooked and deep stream slowly meanders along the base of steep and almost perpendicular hill-sides and precipices, and through swamps covered with dense forests, with only occasional places that are fordable; and few approaches available for armies to move to other points where bridges might be thrown across; or, such is true of the topography of the stream and its banks from Stone Bridge on down toward the Potomac below, where it would be desirable for an army to cross in an advance on Manassas Junction. Above Stone Bridge a skillful general would not attempt to make the detour necessary to reach the crossings and return to the objective point, as such a move would expose his column to direct attacks, on the march, and his baggage and communication to seizure by the enemy in the vicinity of Centreville, near which point the Confederates were posted, guarding the fords of this stream, known as Bull Run. The most critical points were from four to eight miles from the junction. One of these heads this chapter— Blackburn's Ford.

The night of the 16th and the morning of the 17th of July, 1861, contained moments of intense excitement for the Confederate army of, observation, then for the first time drawn up in line of battle, face to face with the grim realities of war —the marshaled hosts of the enemy; the antagonists were hovering near the margins of Bull Run, which flowed between them. The few fords and the railroad bridge were alertly guarded by the Confederates, some bodies of whom were in motion so constantly as to catch not even broken moments of sleep on the night of the 16th. .

Col. E——'s brigade of Virginians, one such a body of vigilant troops, was constantly in motion or under arms until nine o'clock A. M. on the 17th, when arms were stacked in the piney shrubs with a corn-field in front, about five hundred yards in rear of Blackburn's Ford, then held by Gen. Longstreet.

But a few moments elapsed before the men were generally asleep. One private sat bolt upright with no symptoms of sleep in his restless blue eyes. This individual was watching clouds of dust rising up on a high plateau across the corn-field, and about one mile distant. He did not know how far it was to Bull Run, and was unable to tell whether friends or foes were raising the dust; yet, at all events, natural instinct enabled his untutored mind to determine that it was no small scouting party, be it which side it might; and he watched it with deep interest.

This unsophisticated person was Garland Cloud —the child and boy-soldier of the mountain, wrenched away from his home of purity and the innocent joys of his tender years, objects and scenes he loved so well, and launched out on that rising sea of fire and blood to be all but a lone and friendless wanderer.

The family of every other member of his company was regarded as being above his in the social scale. Because of this he had often felt that he was slighted. Some of the ranker members of the blue-blooded aristocracy had attempted to make him the drudge of the company, while others had tried to humiliate him by offering to hire him to do little acts of menial service, all of which he treated with dignified and becoming contempt. For these reasons between him and his comrades there was little sympathy and no intimate companionship. Off duty he was rather morose and retiring.

Seated as we have described him, his thoughts were rambling; they wandered back home; then back into history,—to the bridge of Lodi; to Austerlitz; to Waterloo; across to the rising clouds of dust; then to his sleeping companions. He concluded that their advantages of birth and social position would avail them nothing in the great lottery of life and death in which they were about to be played; that they could not endure hardships and exposure with him; that many of them had already been in trouble for infraction of discipline; and that upon the whole they were more truly objects of pity than himself.

Suddenly amid the clouds of dust his eye caught a whiff of smoke; in an instant a bomb-shell came crashing into the corn-field; in less than another minute one came tearing through the pine saplings. The first one had startled several sleepers; the last one aroused Col. E—— and the entire brigade to a man.

Col. E—— was a veteran of the Mexican and Indian wars, and as profane as his Satanic majesty could wish.

He was a member of the Virginia Convention, where his extraordinary powers of forensic eloquence were employed in opposition to secession, in course of which he demonstrated, in terms that could not be gainsaid, and were virtually unanswerable, how futile were the hopes that there were any chances for the Southern Confederation to succeed; and portrayed the picture of devastation and ruin which would inevitably entail on the Old Dominion, his beloved and native land, in colors of fire, blood, desolation, poverty and mourning, which made the fiery blood of those intoxicating times run cold and curdling in its feverish veins. To the last and final ballot he voted against the act of secession, asserting that the blood and tears of his country should not be on his head. The act of secession having sealed his prophetic doom of Virginia, as one of her true, chivalrous, obedient sons, he meekly bowed his head to the decree which he had in vain so valiantly battled to defeat; and without a moment of hesitation or delay, buckled on his sword with a soldier's experienced hand, and hastened to where the infernal machines of war would first hurl and explode their missiles of death.

The curtain had been rolled up while he slept; he awoke to find the bloody scene before his open eyes, merging forth upon the stage.

On lying down to sleep he had unbuckled his sword and placed it by his side, where the pine leaves covered it up. Garland Cloud was not ten feet from his veteran commander, who was both his colonel and brigade commander *pro tem.* The young tyro at this moment was intently watching and noting the coolness and apparent unconcern of the old soldier while searching for his blade, but was much shocked when the old officer turned to his adjutant and said:

"Capt. G——, where in h— is my sword?"

Very soon the four regiments were under arms. Col. E—— in front of the centre, gave the command: "Load at will, load!" Instantaneously the commanders of regiments repeated this order, and it was in turn as quickly reiterated by the commanders of forty companies.

Capt. H—— was a West-Pointer of high honors, but was, for the first time, under fire. He was Col. E——'s townsman, and belonged to his regiment. Facing his company with a graceful precision that no one but a trained soldier could imitate, yet so far influenced by the prevalent excitement as to forget the order he had just received, in a clear, stentorian voice, he gave the command:

"Company ——, load in nine times, load!"

Col. E—— was a considerable distance from this officer, but his experienced ear caught this bungling blunder from among the forty voices with which it mingled, and standing straight in his stirrups, he exclaimed at the top of his voice:

"Capt. H——, load in h— fire and d—nation; load as quick as you can, and shoot the same way."

By this time the clear, sharp report of now and then an out-post rifle was heard. This gradually increased to the desultory rattle of the skirmish lines. A temporary, but to those whom experience had taught its import, ominous silence followed; Longstreet's skirmishers had retired to their regiments. This suspense was soon broken by a volley of musketry, followed in rapid succession by another and another, until, in a few moments, the firing deepened into one steady continuous roll.

The peculiar sensations which thrill the being, and the unique impression made upon the mind of the uninitiated, the first time one hears the incessant, unbroken roll of musketry, in actual, hostile combat, has never yet been described by words. No language in this world, no combination of words ever constructed by man, has in any degree, even approximately approached towards doing the subject justice. To be understood fully, and to be appreciated duly, these emotions and impressions must be experienced; and those only who have thus learned them can imagine what they are like, because there is nothing to present as a parallel illustration with which the reality might be contrasted. Hence it is needless to attempt a description, for no matter howsoever earnestly and intelligently the effort might be made, the result would inevitably be a miserable failure.

Quickly Col. E——'s command crossed the corn-field. In a narrow skirt of pines beyond, it began to meet Longstreet's wounded; some were walking, some were borne on litters, while others were in ambulances. There was both the dripping and streaming life-blood of mortal man visibly and unquestionably ebbing out.

Emerging from the pines, the advancing column came into an open field extending, with considerable down grade, to the banks of Bull Run, in full view of the Federal batteries posted on the opposite heights, and exposed to their fire.

A double-quick-step movement promptly placed Col. E——'s column in position on the left of Longstreet's hotly engaged line, just as the Federal infantry was finally repulsed.

For some hours, a spirited artillery duel was maintained, but the sun went down on a scene of apparently perfect tranquillity. Col. E——'s command remained in line of battle on the bank of the stream.

When it was quite dark, the immediate comrades of Garland Cloud observed him with his bayonet in hand, actively gouging into the ground.

"What are you doing, Cloud?" came from several mouths.

"Preparing to build breastworks. We have no picks nor spades, yet we can, however, loosen earth with the bayonet and throw it up with the hands, so as to make some protection long before day, which we are likely to need to-morrow," was the reply.

In less than twenty minutes every man in the brigade was at work like a beaver. Before midnight a line of earth had thus risen to defy musket-balls or grape-shot. Behind this improvised protection the brigade remained exposed to the burning sun of July by day, and the chilling dews of this flat and boggy locality by night, until the afternoon of the 20th of July, as quietly as if participating in some solemn or sacred ceremony; then it was relieved, and retired to the rear for a night of much-needed repose.

CHAPTER V.

THE PLAINS OF MANASSAS.

"Cannon to right of them;
Cannon to left of them;
Cannon in front of them,
Volleyed and thundered."
—TENNYSON.

PURE, consecrated and holy day, ordained for piety and devotion; as bright, as lovely, and as glorious in its transcendent brilliancy and perfect endowments of Nature, as any that ever

2

burst forth from the Oriental realms of morning upon a strife-rent and sin-stricken world, since the first dawned in its rare and radiant beauty upon innocent, semi-Heavenly Paradise! Such was that Sabbath morning of July 21st, 1861, as it broke upon sweet, serenely sleeping creation, in the beautiful and yet tranquil plains of Manassas.

All Nature was perfect in her appointments; the trees and the fields were adorned with the most gorgeous apparel from the brightest textures of summer splendor. The canopy of Heaven was clear, without a cloud or haze spot anywhere visible. Not a breath of air stirred the most delicate leaf. Scattered far and wide, was to be seen here and there the smoke from homesteads of the early-rising tillers of the soil, or those whom the stirring events,—anticipated in their midst, but yet held in appalling suspense—had caused to quit restless beds earlier than their wonted Sabbath morning hours. In two particular localities, smoke rose high up as from two huge cities; spread out and hung like a pall suspended in the elements, as slowly gathering, sluggishly moving, yet blackly portentous clouds—threatening harbingers of a coming storm.

Far away in the back-ground, rose up in bold relief, the huge, dimly-defined outlines of the Alleghany Mountains, yet partially obscured by streaks of grey twilight. Back in the rear the shrill scream of the locomotives occasionally rang through the still dewy air. Besides this, " the cock's shrill clarion " was the only sound to be heard.

The sun rose bright and glowing, his first rays transforming the myriad dew-drops to silver and pearl; for all things were

"Dewy with Nature's tear-drops,
Weeping, if aught inanimate ever weeps,
For the unreturning brave."

The Confederate camps were quiet. The early repast was over. Conversation, whenever any occurred, was carried on in subdued tones. Occasionally a man could be seen with the head bowed in mute but meditative prayer; another reading the Bible. But the heart—ah, where was the heart? Far away on the Sabbath of other days, amid scenes the moistening eye of the pensive one, yet kept bright by the labored pulsations of that wildly throbbing heart, might behold never more.

And those away there, among those distant scenes of yore, what of them? From Plymouth Rock to the Gulf of Mexico; from the base of the Rocky Mountains to the Atlantic, oh merciful God! what a day of agonizing suspense and bitter anguish of mind and of soul this was destined to be for thousands and thousands of families all over this broad and distracted land!

Such was the situation, and such was the scenery which surrounded and decorated the stage of this Sabbath day's theatre, when Nature's grand curtain rolled up and disclosed the same in the early morning, before the mad actors appeared to trample it under foot, begrime it with smoke, scorch it with fire, and deluge it with blood.

The sun was scarcely up before the boom of cannon on the turnpike leading from Stone Bridge to Centreville, announced that the anticipated event,—the struggle which for three days had been suspended in abeyance, the day of destruction and carnage,—had come.

At an early hour, it was evident to those miles away, at Blackburn's Ford and the railroad bridge, along the Confederate centre and right, that their companions in the vicinity of Stone Bridge, on the left, were being steadily beaten back, and that there would be the scene of the terrible conflict. On the centre and right, column after column was put in motion, and made forced marches for the field of battle.

Col. E—— arrived on the field at a critical moment. Just before his command took a position, preparatory for the reception of the now triumphing, exultant onslaught of the enemy the announcement was made to each regiment that one man from each company was demanded for detached duty, to be furnished voluntarily, or by special detail, should no one in any company feel disposed to volunteer.

Instantly the tall form of Garland Cloud stepped forward and stood a few paces in front of his company, a shade paler than usual, yet manifesting that determination which meets death unmoved. Thirty-nine other men stood on the same line with him, each a solitary figure, alone in front of his own company. Quickly they

closed together, and under charge of special officers, moved rapidly away into the smoking, flaming jaws of death. At this moment there were more admiring eyes following and more kindly feeling cherished in his company for poor lowly born Cloud than his aristocratic comrades had ever before deigned to bestow upon this boy of the mountain. Secretly, each one felt that this child of humble parentage had voluntarily put his body in the place in this over-hazardous duty, which the impartial casting of lots might have fixed on an aristocrat, perhaps himself. Gen. Beauregard strictly enjoined Col. E—— not to fire on some South Carolina troops in his front as they were retiring on his position. This order was duly communicated to commanders of regiments.

Now Col. E——'s long and final opposition to secession caused him to be regarded rather in the guise of a traitor than that of a Southern patriot, by a large element in the army. Col. K——, also a member of the convention, and a zealous and uncompromising advocate of secession, and commanding one of the regiments in Col. E——'s brigade, mistrusted his loyalty. Through the smoke a dense body of troops could be discerned cautiously advancing. Both officers and men were restless. Col. E—— rode back and forth along the line, entreating his men not to fire, as those men were retiring friends.

Col. K——'s eye in the meantime had detected the regulation blue and the stars and stripes, and he shouted: "Col. E——, they may be your friends, but I will be d——d if they are mine. Fire on them, my men!" The fire was answered by a withering volley; the South Carolinians had fallen back on some other point.

The day soon grew desperate for the Southern arms. Bee, Bartow, and many other gallant officers and brave men were dead on the field. The Confederates were defeated and forced back at all points. According to all laws of war, they were, in the middle of the afternoon, hopelessly beaten. Some bodies of troops rallied and faced the enemy; but the general tendency was toward a retrograde movement in bad order. Some troops from one of the cotton States were thus moving past another body in good order and facing the enemy, when the commander of the former suddenly exclaimed:

" For shame men, rally ! Just look there at Jackson's men standing like a " *Stone Wall !* "

About this time a body of troops were discovered debouching from a dense wood on the Confederate left rear, and bearing directly down upon it: The stoutest heart quailed. There could be but one conviction: the Federal commander had detached a heavy column, which, by a detour under cover of this wood, had gained the Confederate rear, and was moving down to complete the annihilation of the discomfited and disheartened Southerners. Gen. Beauregard's dark, swarthy features paled. It was a moment of intense and painful suspense bordering on desperation. But suddenly as a flash of lightning Beauregard's countenance fired up as he shouted: "It is E. Kerby Smith! The day is ours! Forward!" The effect was magical and instantaneous.

An Alabama regiment wavered as its colors went down again and again. Beauregard urged his horse forward, seized the flag, whose folds partly enveloped his body, while the clarion notes of his voice were heard above the surrounding tumult:

" Follow your general ! Victory is ours ! "

And an irresistible wave rolled forward that, had they not been thereby surprised, would have overwhelmed the Union troops. They have been unjustly censured for flying so ignobly from a but late victorious field. Had they been expecting this assault, and fully prepared to meet it the result would have been the same. No troops could have withstood that mad torrent in the open field. It was the result of a sudden reaction, an outburst of enthusiasm that sprung wildly and spontaneously from stifled despair, such as transforms mankind to superhuman beings. This was an avalanche that swept all before it.

The plateau of the renowned Henry house was cleared. The result of the day was no longer doubtful. A page of history was written in letters of mingled tears and blood.

" The thunder clouds close over it, which, when rent,
The earth was covered thick with other clay,
Which its own clay shall cover, heap'd and pent,
Rider, horse,—friend,—foe in one red burial blent."

After the terrible conflict had spent its fury and ceased to rage, Garland Cloud and one companion of the day were still together without an officer, amid the pitiful, heart-rending scenes of that ghastly field, rendering such assistance to their suffering and dying friends as their untutored mountain hands were able to perform; and at every step, on every hand, they met sights to wring their yet pure and tender hearts.

They halted at one spot where the ground was literally covered with the slain who fell in the last stubborn and desperately contested struggle. Some lay with their hands folded across their breasts and a sweet smile on their lips. The first impression on a person ignorant of the situation would have been that these forms were a large number of men in peaceful and healthy slumber, as

" He who hath bent him o'er the dead,
Ere the first day of death is fled,
And marked the mild, angelic air,
The rapture of repose that's there,
And, but for that sad, shrouded eye,
That fires not, wins not, weeps not now,
So fair, so calm, so softly sealed.
The first, last looks by death revealed !
So coldly sweet, so deadly fair,
We start, for soul is wanting there."

Passing on, they soon reached a point where none of the badly wounded had been removed; and the groans and shrieks were heart-rending.

Cloud and his boy companion, rude and unskilled ministers of mercy, bandaged wounds with handkerchiefs and any other material to be had; gave a sip of water, and helped men to points where ambulances could reach them.

When they could do no more good at this point, and were moving away, they came upon a silent, fair-haired, smooth-faced, rosy-cheeked, Union lieutenant. A handsome boy, beautiful as a lovely girl in her teens, bleeding to death from a wound in the leg. Hearing the sound of footsteps and voices, his face brightened for a moment, until his eye caught the grey uniform advancing toward him, when a dark scowl passed over his lovely features as he turned his head away with an air of despair. Garland Cloud's heart was touched to the core. "Can we do something for you, poor boy," he said in kind and sympathetic, almost sobbing tones.

At the sound of this expression the poor sufferer turned his large, dreamy, deep-blue eyes up to the speaker's powder-begrimed face bending anxiously over him, and gazed at him, then at his boy companion, for a moment in mingled doubt and astonishment; then said slowly and hesitatingly:

"You are enemies and offer me kindness; or do I dream?"

"This morning we were enemies; this evening the cause of humanity makes us friends. Fear us not. Tell us what we can do for you, and we will help you as brothers," Cloud answered.

"Oh, may heaven bless you! I need a kindly voice and a friendly hand now. I am bleeding to death from a wound in the thigh. My hours are numbered and few. If not too much to ask, and possible, I beg that one of you may stay by me until I am gone, close my eyes, wrap me in my blanket, put me in the ground deep enough so the rain won't uncover me, and write to mother."

The poor boy paused, choking with sobs. By this time Cloud was ripping the pant-leg, and instantly had the wound naked. Then jerking the suspenders and shirt from a dead man, these were quickly slitted and ripped into bandages and cords; a silk handkerchief torn up, the leg corded, the wound plugged and bandaged before another word was uttered. Then Cloud said:

"We must save your life, Lieutenant. After this fails it will be time to attend to your request. Take courage. Now we must carry you in a blanket to a surgeon."

"Oh! forgive me for coming to fight you. You are too kind to me;" and he wept like a child.

It was not long before a kind-hearted old surgeon was bending over the wound. Soon the artery was taken up and tied, the wound dressed, and the young soldier pronounced out of immediate danger. Then he slept for an hour. Cloud watched beside him while his companion slept, for it was raining, and too dark for the two boys to seek their regiments until morning.

The wounded boy awoke, drank some water, expressed a few words in acknowledgment of his gratitude; then for a few moments his lips moved as though in silent prayer, until finally he murmured aloud:

"Mother, poor mother; it will kill her."

Then he fell into a deep and prolonged sleep. When he awoke again day was breaking, and Cloud and his companion standing by the lowly cot to bid him farewell.

CHAPTER VI.

LAWRENCE PLEASINGTON.

"Wounded and sorrowful, far from my home,
Sick among strangers, uncared for, unknown."

LAWRENCE PLEASINGTON was the name of the wounded captive beside whose feverish form Garland Cloud and companion stood, in the dim grey twilight on the gloomy morning after the stormy July Sabbath recorded in the last chapter, to say farewell. The sun was mantled with a thick black veil, refusing to look upon the ghastly and sickening scenes still scattered all over that ensanguined field. All Nature seemed to be in sympathy with the mourning throughout the land so wide-spread as to merit the appellation of "a nation's woe." The dark clouds and big rain-drops harmonized with the gloomy distress and tears of despair which on this morning wrung and convulsed so many human hearts. Among, and one of those sad and disappointed spirits was that of young Pleasington, the poor wounded captive. The thought of the cruel anguish and hopeless despair which his poor mother would suffer was more to his sad soul than anything that could be in store for himself. It was of her, and not of self, that he thought.

Just now, too, the two rude, uncouth mountaineers, whom a few hours before he had hated so cordially, were about to leave him. They had been kind, humane and sympathetic; for these reasons, in the absence of anything more cheerful, it was a comfort to the poor sufferer to look into their frank and generous faces; and what assurance had he that he would fall into similar hands after they were gone? Certainly there could be no eye to watch over him; no hand to minister unto him, to soothe his aching brow or smooth the rude, hard pillow; no voice to greet his ear: none of these for him but such as enemies might bestow. To him, everything, from all other sources, "was baned and barred, forbidden fare;" and this might be bestowed harshly and unkindly and cruelly.

With two great pearly tear-drops starting

from the grand and winning eyes, and a quiver on his lip, he clung to Cloud's hand as he falteringly said:

"Mr. Cloud, we were arrayed as enemies; from you I hoped for the harshest civilized treatment; this was all. But you have treated me as a comrade, a brother. I want your full name, regiment, company, and your home post-office. I want to write to mother and Effie, so they may know what you have done for me, should I not live to see them again. Effie is the young lady most dear to my heart. To-day, oh cruel fate! they will mourn me dead; and there is no means by which I can let them know that I yet cling to life by a feeble, uncertain thread. I want to write to you from the hospital and the prison if the authorities and you will permit me; and if you are in reach and can find me, please come and see me some time this week, if possible. And I want the address of your young friend."

"Lieutenant, every thing in my power I will do for you. Give me your poor mother's address. Probably I can get word sent to her. There must be some flags of truce passing soon. I will see what can be done. Some time, to-morrow, perhaps, I may be in the same fix," was Cloud's reply.

"May heaven bless and shield you from harm," was the wounded soldier's sobbing response.

At this moment the surgeon came along looking at the condition of the numerous sufferers under his care. Cloud addressed him:

"Dr. Chamberlain, this is the young prisoner we brought you last night in such a critical condition. Please care for him, in the name of humanity, for his mother and his Effie, to the very best of your ability; and please let me know where you place him, until he is able to be transferred to the interior."

"Garland," replied the doctor, "be assured this shall be my special care. I am proud to see such fine and commendable manifestations of magnanimity and humanity among our young men."

"Farewell, Lieutenant; you are in good hands. We must hasten away," was Cloud's parting salutation. His young comrade was met the first time on the battle-field, but was a mountaineer

from his neighboring or adjoining county; a member of another regiment in the same brigade, and a volunteer in the detached service with Cloud. But he will appear again, and be more closely defined.

Cloud found his regiment just moving, to go to outpost duty, well down toward Alexandria.

From the outpost he went away to a homestead near by, ostensibly to get some canteens of water for the company, but in reality to see an old colored man with whom he was already on intimate but somewhat mysterious terms, known as Uncle Jake.

UNCLE JAKE: "Well, for shure, young massa Cloud, you not killed, bress the Lawrd for dat."

CLOUD: "No, uncle Jake, they missed me this time. But I am delighted to find that you did not run off with the Yanks."

UNCLE JAKE: "What for I run away? Old Jake not gwine to turn fool dis late in life, when he is freer dan de white folks."

CLOUD: "Well, that is all right, Jake. But I want a little job put right through. Here is a despatch to be at the office in Alexandria to-night, to which an answer will be received by the operator, by mail, day after to-morrow morning. That answer must be here and in my hands the same evening before our relief comes. No mistakes for money, now mind you. I want to let a wounded Yankee's mother know he is not dead."

JAKE: "Dat's shure, ceptin' Jake and de oder mail-carrier dies."

Cloud drew his memorandum book and wrote:

"MAUD PLEASINGTON,   R——.
    "Am wounded and prisoner; well treated. Wound not fatal. Tell Effie. Don't worry. Write to-night, sure, care operator, Alexandria.
                                    "LAWRENCE."
"OPERATOR:
    "Please send immediately and arrange with bearer about mail answer, when you receive it, so as to forward without delay.
                    "LAWRENCE PLEASINGTON.

CLOUD: "Now, uncle, here it is. You understand that this is more sacred than regular business, and not to be breathed to our safest friends."

JAKE: "Bress your soul, honey, dis old nigger's head not white for nuffen; dis spatch gwine shure, and nobody but Jake de wiser."

The two strange characters parted. Cloud was as confident the dispatch would go and the answer come as though he was relying on the United States mail, in time of peace.

Not one event of interest transpired at the outpost.

Late in the afternoon of the appointed day, Cloud was at the well. Jake came out of his cabin grinning with the expected letter in hand, for which he received some silver pieces.

CLOUD: "This has been admirably done, uncle, and may not be the last service of the same nature. I expect soon to see you again."

JAKE: "All right, young massa; ole Jake powerful glad to see you any time. Ize gwine to de Junction for young missus to-morrow."

CLOUD: "All right. I may see you there."

Garland Cloud cordially grasped the hand of the old man, and then left him bowing and courtesying as few but the genuine, olden-time, Virginia darkey could thus manifest the supreme superiority of nature's politeness.

In this old man,—as his wonderful fertility of resources, and tact of manipulating them with his own race and the white people (both of whom esteemed him without measure, and many idolized), enabled him to wield a peculiar force of influence that rendered him something approaching a type of indefinable genius,—the people of his immediate section of country and the Confederate army had an invaluable factor, a strangely mystic agent—an element of action that enchants the superstitious mind of the colored race everywhere. To deal out the enigmatical, and surround himself and his actions with an air of profound and incomprehensible mystery, at once became the ruling passion of the old darkey's life, the centre-head and main-spring of his joy and pride. Nature had wonderfully fitted him with the requisite endowments for playing this rôle. The intoxicating excitement of the stirring scenes, in the midst of which he lived and moved, operated to develop these latent powers, and afforded masterful opportunities for their employment. And people were not slow in perceiving

their value, nor dilatory about putting them into requisition. Hence, within a short time after the Federal outposts were advanced any distance from the suburbs of Alexandria, Uncle Jake was a general agent for the underground mail and secret-service bureau of the border; and he had his net-work of connections extended in all directions for many miles around, through the colored race, with whom he was a famous character many years before the war.

His half a century of virtual emancipation from the oppressive feature of human bondage—that broken yoke of his slavery which he no longer wore—his many accomplishments and the latitude his immunity from restraint allowed him to parade before admiring multitudes, together with his snowy locks and beard—were well calculated to inspire veneration, and transformed the otherwise common-place old darkey into an object of boundless popularity with all classes of people; but with his own race shed about him a halo of magic mystery, and clothed his name with an awe-inspiring grandeur.—For Jake to be a traitor to the cause of the South was not within the harmony of things—the strongest ties which bound him to the earth. With his own idolizing race the question of his loyalty entered not into the scale of estimation. He loved his own people with the deep devotion of a true child of Nature; they adored him. That he was a traitor to them, he never dreamed.

There was not the slightest difficulty about the old man's ability to abuse the credulity of the Federal troops,—an art in the practice of which he was a consummate adept. As to the part Jake's assistants took in the enterprise of which he was the moving spirit, they were as true as Jake himself; but actuated by no principles of fidelity to any interest involved, save alone to that indefinable one concealed in the old man's personality, and the instinctive fascination for the proud distinction of being the faithful bearer of any communication. This is an incomprehensible characteristic of the colored race, that excites a spirit of zeal and enthusiasm in an undertaking of this nature, sufficient to induce a colored person of either sex to endure cold, hunger and fatigue, and to brave dangers—often walking many miles through the worst weather of winter and crossing swollen streams at the peril of life—a greater peril than the bearer of the National mails is required to hazard—and without the least definite assurance of reward—in order to forward a non-important letter to its destination. We may venture the assertion, with confidence, that a price-list on a postal-card will travel to its destination one hundred miles, anywhere in the Southern States, if its transmission be but intrusted to the care of the colored race, and that scarcely one in a thousand would miscarry.

In addition to this actuating incentive, ample by itself to prompt the colored people to carry letters, regardless of their character, anywhere through or within the Federal lines, it was an easy matter for Jake to infuse into the beings of his simple-minded race a love for the air of mystery within which his own existence was so amazingly shrouded, and to induce them to adopt most skillful methods to conceal letters while in transit, and to frame the most plausible pretexts to pass the lines. Very small children were sometimes sent on ostensibly different pretenses—the most natural neighborly errands.

But all these things were wonderfully facilitated by the unbounded confidence reposed by the Union troops in the unswerving fidelity of the colored race,—an element prized for its intrinsic value, without estimating the detriment of its probable dangers; an oversight originating on the part of the Northern people in their ignorance of the true character and swaying impulses of the colored people—lessons that the lapse of twenty years has not sufficed to inculcate.

But not so with the people of the South, with whom the advantage was thus poised. They knew alike the valuable and the dangerous element of the colored population to their cause —used the one and guarded against the other. Time has not changed the situation very materially, when the relations of the colored race to politics are viewed from the same standpoint of Southern interest. The Southern people still understand the freedman, because they knew his predominating characteristics as a slave—and these neither the boundless privileges of freedom nor the elevating influences of education possess

any power to change. The Northern people understood not these in the slave character; no better do they understand the same elements of the freedman's composition. The interests of the freedman are inextricably blended with the interests of the white people of the South; and the more enlightened the former becomes, the more firmly are his relations cemented to the common weal of his own fair, sunny land.

Garland Cloud understood Uncle Jake, and properly appreciated his peculiar merits.

The love of adventure acquired in early life by the hardy mountaineer or the venturesome frontiersman, tempts him to pass the neutral ground of war's critical domain, and to tempt fate beyond the limits of the dead-line; and to this rule young Cloud was no exception. Beyond the picket-post there was a luring fascination for him. The stealthy creeping of the still hunter enabled him to evade the lax vigilance of the inexperienced volunteer vedette or picket-sentry almost with impunity, and often in broad daylight.

The charming courtesy and witching flattery lavished upon one who thus presumed to defy danger and cross the lines of the enemy, by the fair daughters of Dixie, constituted, it must be granted, a strong temptation to pass the confines of mortal danger, in order to enjoy the raptures of the clandestine ovations and delicate luncheons from the mystic treasures of the Virginia mansion, that nothing but consuming flames seemed able entirely to deplete. Such ever awaited any one who took the chances to call where the grey uniform of the Confederacy was rarely seen, and had much to do with Cloud's early ventures. These he made without the permission, or the knowledge even, of his commanders or comrades. Being a good soldier he had no difficulty to procure a pass to be absent from roll-call for twenty-four hours any day when he was not on duty. This he invariably used to make excursions beyond the limits of the territory scoured by the foraging individuals and parties of his friends, where smiling hospitality, dispensed by the charms of beauty's sheen, lent to danger a fascinating enchantment. Thus encouraged, he yearned to link duty with pleasure, which would become trebly enhanced, and blossom with new delights, as they grew to be promoting factors auxiliary to the public service.

In these early rambles Cloud made the acquaintance of Uncle Jake; always met him after the first contact—sometimes by special appointment, and learned from his young mistress, and other people in the community, the character and the capabilities of the old darkey.

Already mutual confidence and reciprocal bonds of interest had been established and sealed between the young mountaineer and the old darkey of the aristocratic mansion.

CHAPTER VII.

THE CONTRABAND LETTERS.

"The violet still grows in the depth of the valleys,
Though withered, thy tear will unfold it again."
—BYRON.

LIEUTENANT PLEASINGTON lay rather restless and impatient, with his face to the wall, on a rude but clean cot, in a hospital ward at Manassas, on an oppressively hot July afternoon, the fourth day after he was wounded—his fourth day of suffering and captivity.

Hearing a cautious footstep approaching, he turned his head. Garland Cloud stood beside his cot.

CLOUD: "Lieutenant, before asking how you are, I will give you a soothing opiate."

He handed the wounded boy a letter. When the poor sufferer's eye caught the post-mark, together with the well-known characters of the address, his astonishment and joy were boundless. Nothing, but for his mother to have been bending over him, would have more surprised him. Eagerly he broke the seal, and found under it two inclosures. One was:

"MY POOR, DEAR BOY:

"Your shocking telegram relieved our cruel suspense; and humbly do I thank God that it is no worse. I shall most earnestly pray for your recovery and safe return home. This was our first tidings of you. Everything here is mingled confusion, suspense, distress and mourning. Nothing definite has been heard concerning our boys, except some who were killed or

wounded early in the day—Sunday. We hope soon to receive a letter from you, telling us more fully your condition. Every one thinks it so strange that we should have heard from you so promptly, and you wounded and a prisoner. Perhaps your letter, when it comes, will explain this mystery. Please try to write soon. Be patient, and trust the good Lord. We shall hope for the best. Much love from your loving mother.

"M. P."

The other letter was yet more eagerly read, without remembering even the presence of the bearer; it was:

"MY ESTEEMED FRIEND:

"I write in haste to assure you of my deep sympathy for you in your terrible misfortune. How kind to remember me in your short dispatch to your mother. I appreciate those two words, under the painful and trying circumstances in which you wrote them, more than a long letter when you are well and free. If you can, write a line to your little friend   "EFFIE."

Lieut. Pleasington turned his welling eyes up to Cloud's face interrogatively; for the moment his heart was too full to speak.

CLOUD: "Don't ask me how it is, Lieutenant. You have the result of your commission; that is the extent of your interest in the matter; the means is my affair."

PLEASINGTON: "My gratitude to you no words can express; and nothing in the bounds of human possibility can ever pay you my debt."

CLOUD: "Your extreme youth and lonely, friendless situation on the bank of the dark river, in the midst of the shadows of death, aroused my pity and created uncontrollable sympathy for you; and your maternal devotion stirred the soul within me. Thus was I impulsively prompted to do the trifling favors which seem to have so overwhelmed you with gratitude. Well, and with your armor buckled on, no man under our colors would fight you with more desperate determination. Disarmed, wounded and helpless, we have very few men who would not treat you as I have treated you, under similar circumstances and with the same opportunity. The only debt you owe me is to treat the poorest soldier lad in our ranks the same as I have treated you, so far as you are able, whenever a wounded one falls into your hands. The doctor tells me you are safe to get well. He will now find you much better. To-morrow my command moves far over near the Potomac. I shall see you no more until we meet on the battle-field. I have some little matters to look after for an hour. During this time prepare answers to your letters, and they will reach your mother and Effie. After this you may not find it so easy and quick to communicate with home. Mention no names in connection with the transmission of letters. As to the battle-field and hospital, I do not care what you write; but this letter business might compromise me unpleasantly. Here are all the materials for writing."

Without waiting for a reply, Cloud walked rapidly out of the building, leaving the wounded officer to write his letters to mother and Effie. Cloud returned just as the envelope covering the letters was addressed, which had been left unsealed for him to read the contents.

CLOUD: "Seal it up securely, Lieutenant; I have no desire to read it. Your family and private matters are sacred. It is not in your power to write a word detrimental to our public interest."

PLEASINGTON: "It repents me that I have fought your people. I shall not again enter the service."

CLOUD: "Yes, you will. National pride and popular pressure will speedily cure this weakness. Young men in your section will have no option, any more than those with us will have. Going into the army will be a necessity, no matter how much inclination rebels against it. You must be either against, or for us. There is no neutral ground for you. Rather than array yourself against your own section and people, you will go with them; and this means against us to the bitter end."

PLEASINGTON: "Perhaps you may be correct. If you are, I much regret it. I am a poor boy, the son of an humble mother, who has been a poor, lone widow ever since I was one year old.

Really, I do not know for what I am fighting. I have nearly lost my life, and now owe it to the very people whom I raised my hand to smite, on their own soil, as its invader. God knows that if there is any honorable way out, I shall leave this service, which must be loathsome to me, since I know the people whom I am to fight."

CLOUD: "Ah, Lieutenant! if the people of the two sections only knew one another better, our troubles would quickly terminate; but alas! they neither know nor understand one another; so there are many dark and trying days to come. If there was no other cause nor influence to force you back to your colors, your lady love would soon prompt you to return. Ladies admire brave men. You could not bear to hear the praises of others on every tongue, and still remain at home regarded as a shirk from duty and danger. The silent reproach from your Effie's eyes would be an order you would not attempt to disobey. Young men in the South who lag at home are ostracized by young ladies as vagabonds. It will come to this with you."

PLEASINGTON: "You are right. Effie is a proud, high-spirited girl, far above my plane of life in the social world, and is heart and soul with the Government in favor of the war to preserve the Union."

CLOUD: "My time with you, Lieutenant, is ended. Farewell."

PLEASINGTON: "Farewell, Mr. Cloud, and may health and safety attend you."

Thus parted these youthful warriors, but children of nature and the souls of sincerity. The highest standard of honor, and the most laudable nobility of purpose, pervaded and controlled their minds and their hearts. Of such material are the finest models of heroes molded. Little did these guileless sons of obscurity dream of the wild and trying scenes through which they were destined to pass, in their alloted parts in the wild drama of life.

About their meeting and its sequence thus far there is nothing particularly extraordinary. Thousands of cases might be reported that would not materially differ from this one in some features. The incidents on the battle-field and at the hospital that night and the next morning, were similar to ten thousand; and had that completed the history, the record would have no place in these pages. Smuggling letters for prisoners, and delivering them from the hand of one picket to that of his foeman in person, was not an unfrequent occurrence. Hence the sending and receiving of letters as detailed, was not a very remarkable circumstance: isolated, it would deserve no attention. But the winding vicissitudes, in their tortuous progression from cause to effect, invest these otherwise untenable positions with ramparts of importance that stand forth bristling in defiant impregnability. To indicate these features, would be to anticipate the startling surprises which they hold in reserve. They will, in due time, develop and demonstrate some masterful mysteries of Destiny in the affairs of mortal life on earth. And the meeting of these boy-foes had various ends to subserve.

Cloud had not been five minutes out of the presence of the wounded captain, when his letter passed into the hands of Uncle Jake.

Colored people were used in secret service, in the interest of the Federal army, to very great advantage; but, as a rule, when manipulated by Southern Unionists. The Union element that existed in some of the Southern States was often a powerful auxiliary to Federal commanders, and furnished them with most valuable information. Many Union men were in the employ and service of the Confederate Government; and in the chief departments at Richmond were some of them to be found.

Miss Van Lew, of Richmond, a character that does not properly belong in our plot—one, however, well known in National circles, by her real name, which therefore we do not disguise, and which we use merely to strengthen a position already assumed relative to secret-service mysteries—was a power worth more to the Union cause than some major-generals who graced, and probably sometimes disgraced, the rolls of the United States army during the war.

She was a lady of some considerable means. As she was a Southern lady, we cannot admire her as an ideal heroine—arrayed, as she was, against the people of her native land—as we

would be forced to admire her had she been a citizen of a Northern State. But, however, with her it was a case of freedom of conscience, that required nerve and indomitable will to support her in the perilous part she assumed in the BLOODY DRAMA, so truly grand and heroic as to outrival any other individual instance of feminine devotion to the cause of the Union to be anywhere found on record, because the hazard with which she was all the time imperiled was appalling. This at once placed the wondrous grandeur of her devotion beyond comparison with that of ladies in the Northern States.

Miss Van Lew had a residence in Richmond, a farm in the country below that city, and owned and employed slaves.

As a matter of course, she knew the Union men of Richmond, including those employed by, and in the service of, the Confederate Government.

She had influence brought to bear to secure the appointment of young Ross, a nephew of Frank Stearns, a rich Unionist of Richmond, to the position of an office in Libby Prison.

Young Ross was, ostensibly, a terror to Union prisoners, and cordially detested by them, while he was constantly and systematically permitting and aiding them to escape—a fact never known to those who had not escaped, many of whom sought him, to take his life when the end did come, and they were liberated.

Miss Van Lew, in the meantime, concealed and sent the escaped prisoners out of the Confederate lines. Besides her own home, she maintained at her own expense several other houses in Richmond at which escaped prisoners were concealed. In order to secure the safe conduction of such prisoners to these places of rendezvous, she constantly kept several bright negro men on duty in the vicinity of Libby to watch for escaped prisoners.

She had friends and accomplices in the Adjutant-General's and Engineers' Departments at Richmond, who furnished her with correct statistics of the army and plans of the defenses of Richmond, which she transmitted regularly to the Federal commander. This was safely accomplished by the assistance of a shoemaker, who inclosed the documents in the hollow soles of brogan shoes, invented for that purpose, and worn by negroes who came regularly from Miss Van Lew's farm to market in Richmond—two pair of shoes being provided for each individual; but he never wore the same pair back to the farm which he wore to the city. The shoes were exchanged —the ones worn back to the farm contained contraband information; the others were left behind to be thus prepared for the next trip.

These are facts that may be substantiated by the best authority in the nation, yet are no more real than others which we shall present, with the true names of characters disguised.

To Miss Van Lew, we think the National Government has manifested monstrous ingratitude in not rewarding her self-sacrificing devotion with the full restoration of her fortune, contributed to the cause of the Union, and in not granting her a life pension, instead of compelling her to continue laboring for the Government in order to earn a subsistence, abundantly due, without additional services.

Ross has been dead some time, and Miss Van Lew is publicly known in her true character, or we should not now name them. Their accomplices will not mention

CHAPTER VIII.

BEYOND THE OUTPOSTS.

" We wither from our youth, we gasp away—
  Sick—sick; unfound the boon, unslaked the thirst—
Through to the last, in verge of our decay,
  Some phantom lures, such as we sought at first—
But all too late—so are we doubly cursed.
  Love, fame, ambition, avarice—'tis the same—
Each idle, all ill, and none the worst—
  For all are meteors with a different name,
And Death the sable smoke where vanishes the flame."
                                    —BYRON.

THE immediate comrades of Garland Cloud were much surprised when an order was promulgated detaching him from his company for special but unindicated duty.

But Cloud knew well enough its nature, and the efforts he had quietly made to secure it. It was scouting beyond the Confederate outposts, around the pickets and into the lines of the enemy; any points that it might be practicable to reach wherever information could be obtained.

For many days at a time he was absent, and his company would not hear from him. When he did sometimes visit his comrades, they could gain from him no information relative to the scope of his duties, nor the adventures necessarily inseparable therefrom. Malignant fever decimated the ranks of his regiment until there absolutely were no really well men for guard duty. Then he visited his company often, always bringing the sick some delicacies, and usually on a captured horse. Sometimes, but rarely, he had a prisoner.

He came in one evening, late in October. The night was chilly and damp. Edgar Harman, one of the most haughty aristocrats in the company, and one who had been most notably unkind to Cloud, was detailed for guard duty. The man was actually too ill to do any duty, but there was no one in the company in better health to take his place among those subject to detail on that day. He staggered as he walked. Cloud watched him take his post, and walk the beat three or four times; he could bear it no longer, and he went over to the sick man.

CLOUD: "Harman, you are too sick for this duty; this night's service will kill you. I have been watching you, and thinking of the agony the sight I beheld would cause your father and sister, could they see you now. It really seemed to me that I could hear them entreating me to save you; and I must do it."

HARMAN: "Oh Cloud! you could certainly think of doing nothing for me, was this possible. I have treated you so shamefully in the past. There is no way by which you could save me. I am conscious that this night will kill me."

CLOUD: "I shall take your place. Call the officer of the guard, please. I am not considering the past. I am thinking of saving the life of a comrade."

HARMAN: "Generous fellow! now do you heap coals of fire on my head. I am unworthy to receive your kindness. Forgive me, Cloud, and to the end of life I shall be your true and devoted friend. It pains me to see you take my place. You appear to be worn out. But to reject your offer would be madness, little short of suicide."

The next day Edgar Harman was delirious. Cloud obtained permission, and remained with him forty-eight hours, until the fever was broken. After this he came in every other day with some refreshments for his sick comrade, until he was sufficiently convalesced to be sent home.

Some weeks later the beautiful and accomplished sister of Harman, the belle of her community and of the renowned school where she had recently graduated, wrote a letter to Garland Cloud, breathing in every line the finest sentiments of deep and unfeigned gratitude; as she and her family recognized themselves to be indebted to him for his kind and magnanimous treatment of her sick brother. She concluded by assuring him that, henceforth, between his family and hers there was no longer a social barrier. This letter awaited him at headquarters on his return from a ten days' expedition. This embarrassed and troubled him; yet he answered it with polite and guarded brevity, delicately assuring the young lady that all he did for her brother was simply done in obedience to the bidding of duty, due at all times to a comrade, and in acquiescence to the obvious demands of humanity. Other letters followed.

This aristocratic young lady wrote to the plebian soldier-boy, entreating him to regard the members of her family as friends who acknowledged his natural nobility of character, and admired his chivalrous bearing as a soldier,—qualities which they esteemed second to those of no one embraced in their own select social circle. With witching and irresistible suavity of style, and the most delicate modesty of diction, she conjured him to write to the family sometimes, and give a few sketches of the wild and perilous border-life he was leading, which she believed to be full of the most intensely thrilling romance.

For a long time he replied indifferently and briefly, excusing himself on the ground that he wanted the accomplishments of finished education necessary to enable him to write so as to entertain people of refinement. But this defense availed him nothing.

Few men, and more especially young soldiers whose vanity has been a little flattered, can be so niggardly and ungallant as bluntly and persistently to refuse a reasonable, or even an unreasonable, request to one among the most elevated and beautiful of women. This was precisely the predicament of young Cloud. Sometimes he would remember with bitterness the social line of the olden time; his own still lowly station in life; would reflect upon the uncharitable comments and heartless criticisms a long letter from him would provoke in that brilliant circle to which he was solicited to expose himself on paper; how he had obstinately refused his comrades and every one else the vaguest account of his service, or even trivial incidents connected with it; how unkindly many of his comrades felt, and how jealous they were on account of that service; and how it would expose him to ridicule and jeers and slurs as soon as others learned that he had recounted his adventures to a young lady of rank with whom it was well known that he was personally unacquainted; then he would resolve persistently to excuse himself until the subject should be abandoned by the witching enchantress.

When a young lady who is accustomed to receive homage from everybody, everywhere, under all circumstances, sets her heart on some special conquest and is, for the first time, in her triumphant reign, crossed in her purpose, she does not abandon it with alacrity, but becomes more intensely engrossed with its prosecution, provided this be to bring the rebellious heart of a man to the recognition of his allegiance to the sway of the imperial princess.

To Miss Harman, Cloud's perversity seemed wonderful. His humble station in life and the moderate nature of her request augmented the aggravation of his unreasonable conduct. Thus she viewed it, and this provoked her to redouble her efforts to bear off the palm of victory. She could rely on the chivalry of Virginia to meet her strategy with diffident courtesy, for a son of the Old Dominion—whether of the mountain or the vale—ever treats a lady with admirable gallantry. Upon this a lady may presume, although she be pressing the most unreasonable demands.

Had Cloud never yielded, the thread of his startling story might never have traced its meandering course over the earth.

After the lapse of nearly twenty-two years we have succeeded in procuring copies of a few of the more prominent letters of that correspondence of the dark and bloody days of wasting war. How we obtained these will be demonstrated in the due course of developments. But here is the place for the letters to appear. At last he thus wrote this earthly angel:

"ARMY OF NORTHERN VA., December, 1861.
"MISS CARPIE V. HARMAN.

"*Estimable Lady:*

"In reply to your interesting letter, I beg to assure you that it would afford me real pleasure to comply with your request, but for obstacles referred to in my last note, which still appear to me insurmountable. I know my course must appear rude. This I regret, but see no feasible way to remedy it. For reasons too tedious to detail, I could, under no considerations, think of complying with your request, except on condition that my communication should in no wise become public while I live, and the war continues. This, as a matter of course, would rob my narrative of its imaginary charms of anticipated fascination for you. For your family, means for the public. For either you or your family the only interest an account of my little services could have would be in their public discussion and criticism among your friends; and you may rest assured that in this you would be sadly disappointed.

"If it would be a source of pleasure to you and your friends, I should be under the stern necessity of not thus contributing to innocent diversion.

"Craving your pardon for my tardy response, and for my apparently obstinate and ungallant conduct in this connection,

"I am, very respectfully,
"GARLAND CLOUD."

Cloud deemed this the end of the discussion; yet the following reply was promptly received:

"GLENDALE, VA., December, 1861.
"MR. GARLAND CLOUD.

"*My Esteemed Friend:*

"Your much appreciated letter has been read with deep interest. In reply, I beg to say that if your objections rested on a substantial foundation, they would be unanswerable; but I assure you that in the main they are utterly imaginary and groundless.

"No one in this community dreams that I have written to or received a line from you—not even father or Edgar. This remains my secret. Now what of your fears that your denied communication would be paraded before the public? I am too selfish for that, should your generosity prompt you to confide the coveted boon to my care.

"I wrote in the name of the family, on the score of gratitude, because I reflected the family sentiment. I made my oft-repeated request in the family name because I deemed that would have more weight; and you have as repeatedly declined to entertain that strong petition. I dared not make the request in my own name alone, because I feared you would not waste the time and take the trouble merely to interest one little girl. I am, however, driven to the extremity of changing my tactics. I now make the request anew for myself alone, and make it to the gallantry of a soldier and the chivalry of a Virginian.

"Can these refuse to gratify the simple whim of a simpler girl? I have set my heart on obtaining this romance of the Border, and if you could realize how acutely continued disappointment pains me, you would not withhold the hoped-for narration.

"I now rest my petition before the highest tribunal to which I can carry it, and I entreat you to grant it, and pledge my earnest assurance that no eye but mine shall read one word, and that not one syllable of its contents shall escape the lips of your expectant friend   "CARRIE."

This letter was overwhelming. Cloud was driven from his position of defense, and surrendered as follows:

"ARMY OF NORTHERN VA., Christmas Day, 1861.
"MISS CARRIE V. HARMAN.

"*Esteemed Friend:*

"Your late letter was read with care and appreciation. Since you so much desire a communication relative to our well-controverted subject, which it appears you have won—

whether fairly or not, and which I have decided to attempt, with the compliments of the season.

"There is nothing strange nor mysterious about my assignment to the duties which I have partially fulfilled for the past few months, unless it be the silence I have strictly maintained up to this moment with every one except the officers to whom it was my duty to report, and the controlling hand of Destiny. This service was but a part of my allotted rôle; hence, naturally, I applied for, and was, therefore, as a matter of course, to it assigned.

"The prevalent notions that this service between the lines of the two armies, and often inside those of the enemy, is peculiarly dangerous and wonderfully exciting, is altogether erroneous. There are few posts of duty where the soldier should, under all circumstances, so rigidly shun the companionship of excitement, and there is no other post so securely exempt from danger as this in which I serve. Cool, cautious and prudent at all times, one may be comparatively safe from harm, except on some extraordinary occasions. Excited, reckless and rash, his liberty or his life is hourly in jeopardy. In five months I have not fired a shot nor had one fired at me, the popular stories that I have killed a number of men, whose horses and arms I have brought in, to the contrary, notwithstanding. To account for this is easy. I dare not shoot unless unexpectedly attacked, and forced to defend myself as a last desperate resort, because this would attract attention and draw around me additional dangers. I am always on the alert. The enemy is rarely ever looking for me where I might be found. When I challenge one to surrender, I am quite sure he is not near friends. He is off his guard, and certain to surrender before he recovers from his surprise. Nine times out of ten, perhaps, the man would not surrender, if he was expecting, or even in a locality where he was likely to meet, an enemy. In addition to other considerations I should regard it cold-blooded murder to waylay and shoot a straggling soldier not on duty, inside of his own lines, unprepared to meet an unexpected danger.

"The service in which I am engaged is thoroughly organized, and performed almost entirely by civilians, chiefly ladies and colored people inside of the enemy's lines. I am a very insignificant factor, expected to render the more dangerous duties that connect this important bureau with the regular service of the army; and I am by no means the only nor the most important soldier thus employed. There are scores of them along the front.

"There are regularly established and well defined signals employed both day and night, but understood by none not members of the secret-service society; and there are channels for transmitting information from point to point, so skillfully planned as to defy detection, but never so as to arouse suspicion.

"Some of these signals and methods of communication are very common-place, simple and meaningless to persons ignorant of their purport, and unacquainted with the arrangement with which they are connected.

"One blind of a certain window open; both open; both closed; the end of a red curtain hanging out of the window; the end of a blue curtain; the end of a yellow curtain, or the end of a white curtain—each has its special meaning, and tells as much miles away as a page of note-paper would contain. Two, three, or more of these tell a separate and different story, according to their arrangement. These are day-signals. Night-signals are various arrangements of lights burning in windows with both curtains up; both curtains down; one curtain down—each tells its simple or compound story. About forty different ways to conceal letters passing from house to house or between neighborhoods, so that the carriers do not know that they are bearers of communications, have been invented. The bearers are mostly little darkeys sent on some other trivial errand of a very different nature.

"I cannot define all these things, because obligations to duty will not permit.

"An ancient colored man is one of the most important personages connected with this service, and is, in some relation, an almost indispensable assistant in everything attempted of any special importance. Some of the most zealous and active members and agents of this organization are the fairest and the most accomplished ladies in the land. To them is due much credit, which circumstances, and the delicate and peculiar situation which they occupy, preclude them from enjoying; because was their position known, many would very quickly be in Northern prisons.

"But for this, some of them would not hesitate to use the revolver or the carbine. Each lady connected with this secret border-service is worth more to the army than ten soldiers in the field. These fair ladies are cool, shrewd, and heart and soul devoted to the cause. There is no hardship too great for them to endure without a murmur; and some have already made great sacrifices.

"Thousands and thousands of others all over the land, would do the same if they had the opportunity. God spare them such opportunities where the pall of destruction and death hovers and grows daily thicker and blacker. These ladies have fathers, husbands, brothers and sweethearts in the Confederate army or in Confederate graves; some of them wear the deep, sable emblems of mourning.

"Often I carry letters back and forth through the lines. From this fact, you may imagine that I am popular with the soldiers and their ladyloves. Expectation is on tip-toe, anxiously awaiting my return as the time approaches, has arrived, or is past, when what they jestingly term the underground mail is due from the army.

"Such are about the arrangement, the nature and the relation of parties to one another in this service.

"The first adventure in my experience worth relating was with a young captain of Federal cavalry. This young gallant persistently and assiduously endeavored to pay special attention to a young lady member of the secret-service league,—an organization not designed to provide pleasing pastime for gentlemen of his class. Naturally, therefore, it was not in the harmony of things for her to league with him. Indeed, this rather prepossessing, extra-stylish individual was actually obnoxious to the fair object of his whimsical adoration. While he was innocently indulging in dreams of Elysian rapture, and contemplating the blissful ecstasies of love, the unreciprocating, unappreciative little rebel lady was actually plotting his discomfiture and undoing: designing to rid herself at one fell and cruel stroke, effectually and permanently of his society. Perhaps too, she desired to test the efficient utility of her league in cases of emergency. In her opinion, so far as she was personally concerned in the person of the ill-starred captain, the emergency had arrived. She knew what evenings to expect him.

"I was duly posted and advised of the part she expected me to play. As soon as it was dark, on the appointed evening, I observed that none but safety signal-lights were burning.

"The parlor designed for the comic scene was brilliantly illuminated. The young lady was seated at the piano, playing with harmonious cadence the stirring notes, and singing with spellbinding melody—' Dixie.'

"The captain stood by her, turning the music, his countenance beaming with admiration and his heart blazing with enthusiastic delight too fierce to last. The scene was one well calculated to enthuse a classic painter with an ardent desire to catch the outlines, in order to reproduce the picture with some semblance of creation approaching the impressive reality.

"As stated, the young man in appearance was a fair Adonis. But at the present moment the tints of nature were heightened to the last gleam of perfection to which the fullness of earthly enjoyment could fire them. To his eye and enchanted mind, the young lady was an unrivaled, an unapproachable, Venus. Dressed in bright and most fascinating summer style, her long, wavy, black hair, wreathed with flowers, flowed over her shoulders in gentle undulations, as it was fanned by fragrant zephyrs laden with perfume—odors sipped from the balmy nectar of a soft summer evening; a large bunch of variegated rose-buds was pinned to her heaving bosom, almost directly over the strongly palpitating heart; her eyes flashed and sparkled with burning witchery. Never before had the captain found her so courteously civil, so studiously polite, so graciously kind and pleasingly condescending to him. Evidently the crisis was past, the prejudice was vanishing, and the prize was about to be won at last. Before him were all the silent yet eloquent and unmistakable tokens the blindly infatuated lover could wish—the heaving bosom, the tell-tale language of the love-lit eye.

"Ah! could he but have divined the secret depths of these charm-beguiling, so highly-prized tokens, his Cupid-soothing blood would have been instantaneously transformed to ice, and ceased to flow in its wonted currents through his veins.

"The bland and winning smiles were the fair petals of the delicate rose concealing a treacherous bunch of sharp and cruel thorns; the heaving bosom was the suppressed respiration of the fierce and crouching lioness about to launch upon her prey. The bright and sparkling eye was but the subtle and deadly gleam of the gazing viper, ready to thrust the venomous fangs into an unsuspecting victim. But for these facts, and these alone, it would have been gross sacrilege to break in upon this lovely scene, and awaken this dreamer from his love-lulled reverie.

"I stood in the open door an instant—perhaps two. Then in a clear, sharp voice I demanded the Captain's surrender to the Confederate Government. To this he offered no objection. He was not armed. One little instant had blighted all the brilliant glow of his cheek; an ashy hue now covered his features; he was the picture of despair. The lady uttered a subdued scream, then hurled at me a few well-feigned reproaches. Two hours later the Captain was turned over to old Col. J—— of, G— S—, much crest-fallen and dispirited. I told Col. J——, in the Captain's presence, that it was only after a desperate struggle that I made him yield, and to treat him as a gallant man. I made a mental reservation as to the true character of the struggle. The Captain used this clue to cover his shame, and created the impression that he fought desperately; broke his sword; emptied his pistols and threw them at my head before he surrendered. This story rapidly spread and grew as it went. It was to the interest of the young lady that it should remain uncontradicted, and the capture of her hapless tormentor be disconnected with her name and home.

"The next little affair included five officers who were disagreeably attentive to as many young ladies, members of the secret organization, or to their intimate friends.

"A special evening party was arranged for the benefit of these officers, to come off at the home of one of the young ladies, to be strictly private and entirely unknown to friends of the officers. At this the officers were elated, and zealously treasured the secret of their anticipated enjoyment until they met at the appointed time and place, to find all the young ladies assembled in the parlor, ready to extend a cordial greeting and an assuring welcome to their guests. They were entertained in an exceedingly agreeable manner with songs, music, games, conversation; in a word, by all the diverting and interesting means which the minds of the young ladies, so fertile in resources and imagination, could invent to make the hours glide softly, pleasingly, fascinatingly away.

"Midnight sounded from the old, deep-toned eight-day clock in the library.

"One minute later eleven of us, apparently unbidden guests, uncivilly, unceremoniously entered the parlor, without saluting even the ladies, and rudely introduced ourselves to their admirers, who were instantly marched rapidly away as prisoners, without time for complimentary adieus. Long before daylight they were turned over to Col. J——. Two other officers fared the same way afterward under similar circumstances.

"What stupid presumption in these people, who come with a sword in one hand and a torch in the other to slay and to burn, to imagine that their society could be agreeable to Southern ladies!

"Some persons are so uncharitable as to impute to this class of Federal officers insincere and dishonorable motives. I do not believe this, nor do many of the young ladies who are annoyed by such suitors believe it. Why not? Because many such volunteer officers are mere adventurers, without property, social standing or even enviable reputations at home, and certainly they would marry the beauty, wealth, and social station they could not gain where known. This weakness is confined almost exclusively to the volunteer service, and will cost many their liberty, some their lives.

" West Point officers, if not born gentlemen, are educated soldiers; and the first and most essential requisite of a soldier is, that he shall be a gentleman. Besides being contrary to the cardinal principles of etiquette, as recognized by gentlemen all over the world, to intrude upon the society of a lady, under any circumstances, without an introduction secured with the lady's consent—and then not without her permission, nor even with this if reluctantly accorded, or if the society is manifestly unwelcome or disagreeable to the lady—it is a breach of discipline sufficient to disgrace an officer, for him to straggle away from his command on such errands, and almost in the very presence of the enemy. For these reasons, regular officers will rarely expose themselves to such disastrous dangers.

"In September there were some odd little incidents down in front of Arlington Heights. Colonels E—— and J—— were both there—two kindred spirits, very like in appearance, dress, speech, even to the peculiar nasal twang and rather whining voice and profanity. I was out with them, part of their staffs and an escort, on an expedition of reconnoissance well up to the front.

"Suddenly our party was unpleasantly exposed to the fire of a number of sharp-shooters. As the peculiarly singing balls passed, humming their spiteful music round our ears, the spectacle our troop presented was grotesque and ridiculous, produced by the way each one manifested the effect the disagreeable position had on his nervous system. Some dismounted on the off sides of their steeds; some lay flat on the pommels of their saddles; some dodged their heads backwards; some to the right and others to the left; some turned deathly pale and trembled violently; and the faces of some others glowed with an unearthly radiance.

"My solemn vow made to my native and beloved hills, as I beheld them the last moment in the grey twilight of that memorable morning which you have not forgotten, when the emotion of a sister's love thrilled your soul, and the torrents from the fathomless wells of a sister's heart blinded your eyes and scalded your cheeks, was never to dodge, flinch or manifest one emotion

3

of fear;—this I have studied and practiced until it has apparently become a second nature. I am much supported by the abiding faith that if I am not destined to perish in this war, no deadly aim can lay me low, and that if destined to perish, no precaution can save me from the fatal missile directed by the finger of the Destroying Angel; for on the fields of strife and carnage, as well as everywhere else in the world, both the destroying and the guardian angels are present. For this reason, which is unknown to every one on earth, I am regarded as a brave, intrepid lad, who tosses in the game of life and death with contemptuous indifference. This is erroneous, because my natural instinct is as strong as that of my most timid comrade, as I stand on its margin, to shiver at the prospect of a plunge into the waters of the dark river.

"I watched my companions—either one of whom would have gone as far into the jaws of death and remained as long as I—a few moments, with a half unconscious smile on my lips, then slyly turned my eye on the two old veterans who were a few paces from the other members of their party, appearing, talking and swearing the same as before they left camp, paying far less attention to the flying bullets than they would have done to the same number of mad hornets.

"I heard my name mentioned. Col. E—— said:

"'Oh! he got tempered in the sharp-shoot's work up around the old Henry house on the 21st of July.'

"'Yes, and case-hardened outside of the lines since,' was Col. J——'s reply.

"Col. E—— then turned abruptly toward me, and said:

"'Cloud, why in the —— don't you dodge? You are just as 'fraid of these singers as I am, and they would hurt you worse than me, because you are tenderer.'

"'I want to dodge very bad, Colonel, but am afraid,' I answered.

"'That is a —— of an idea. Explain yourself, young man,' he said.

"'I am afraid that I might dodge in the way, and also that those fellows would see me, know they are striking close, and improve their aim,' I replied.

"'That will do, Cloud. Next witness come forward,' was his ejaculation.

"While writing of Col. E——, I must tell you about an incident that occurred between him and our Corporal E——, whom you know very well, the night I relieved your brother from guard duty.

"My post was next to the Colonel's quarters. Charles J—— was in front of them. Col. E—— had been away, and returned during the midnight watch. There was some hitch in the countersign; he could not pass the guard, and ordered the corporal called.

"'Corporal E—— appeared, but the matter was not mended.

"'To what company do you belong, corporal?' the Colonel inquired.

"'Captain J——'s,' was the reply.

"'Corporal,' hissed the Colonel, with merciless sarcasm, 'go and tell Captain J—— to send me a corporal who has got some sense;' and the old man waited until all was right.

"Then we rode on, and soon passed behind a skirt of timber to a high point in the road, where there was a carriage-house in the centre of a wagon-yard. From this point we could see a body of cavalry coming from the direction of Georgetown, evidently bent on our capture.

"In about a minute Col. E—— had two pieces of old stove pipe mounted on and lashed to the axles of two carts, and these rapidly rushed to the middle of the road; the whole party at the same time raised a vociferous cheer.

"The troopers hearing this, and seeing wheels with their dark and threatening-mouthed burdens pointing down the road, and men standing in position, as if waiting for the command to fire, turned and fled percipitately.

"Pretty soon a balloon cautiously rose above the tree-tops at no great distance from us, paused an instant, and then went suddenly down.

"We did not have business to detain us in that vicinity very much longer, and soon hastened back to the main body of our command.

"The night following these incidents, several regiments of as fine infantry as any in the army, were badly stampeded by a sudden alarm, which awoke the men, under the conviction that a division of Federal cavalry was in their midst.

"All this disturbance was caused by about twenty horses that had been tied to one side of the fence which surrounded a neighboring mansion, breaking the plank fence down, and running with it dragging after them into the grove where the infantry was sleeping. For a few moments the noise was terrific. Just then one hundred good troopers could have completely annihilated this fine brigade. In ten minutes, however, all was quiet again; and the men lay down to sleep with as little concern as though they had just been to roll-call.

"I have captured several couriers, officers and stragglers, in out-of-the-way places, usually where duty did not require their presence. Not one of them attempted to resist. Two or three times I have challenged a plucky chap, who turned his superb steed, and fled in admirable style; from this I fancy I have learned a valuable lesson—one that may sometime be of inestimable service to me. I have been in some pretty close places, by this cool fellow returning with a squad of troopers to hunt me. But my old colored friend is usually near, and sends them off on a wild-goose chase, that enables me to get to a place of safety.

"I have sleeping- and hiding-places, that would be as hard to find as the most cunning fox's den. The timbered districts, deep ravines, and long lines of fences, make it both easy to hide and comparatively safe to travel long distances, even in day-light, inside of the enemy's picket lines.

"Now you have this marvelous and romantic story, and feel disappointed. It is very much like anything else in this world, when we exchange the imaginary shadow for the reality: wonderful as obscure mysteries: contemptible nothings as familiar acquaintances.

"But permit me to call your attention to something more serious and unromantically real.

"In the early spring-time, before 'the purple lilacs blossom,' this service and these scenes will be no more. Do you want to know why? Yes. The North is collecting and training a powerful army. Often I am able to see vast legions of them drilling, and to hear the swelling strains of their music away in localities which the eye cannot survey.

"Ere long I must take my place in the ranks, and live or cease to live in the iron and leaden hurricane, rushing on to the cannon's blazing, bellowing, deadly mouth.

"In fancy I see, or seem to see, you shudder as you think of your only brother. It is well. The dark storm will burst in all its fury around his head amid shadows of the Death Angel's wing. Pray for him. Virginia, our mother, says, 'My sons, I demand this;' and we must obey.

"Should you by mischance hear that I had been permitted to render any service, such as erroneous judgment sometimes terms conspicuous, pray attribute it to its proper source. To Garland Cloud? No, indeed! but to the spirit inhabiting that poor tenement of mountain clay. It is the spirit's fire aroused that blazes and leaves on mankind the imprint of heroism and immortal renown. As the cold and inanimate locomotive is warmed to throbbing pulsation by its life-breathing steam, so the body of man becomes electrified by the spirit's subtle current, and under the spell of that potent influence performs prodigies of heroic valor which flesh and blood are as incapable of accomplishing as the engine would be of fulfilling its gigantic task without steam. It is this defiant spirit that fears no death, and renders the body insensible to pain until after reaction causes the spirit to subside back to the normal condition of nature, that makes heroes.

"I saw Beauregard and Jackson near Stone Bridge, on that July Sabbath, when their natural faculties were as dead as those of poor Bee and Bartow, while their spirits wielded the sway in triumphant grandeur. There was the grand in soul displayed in matchless majesty.

"But of all the towering monuments of living heroism and unpretentious, unselfish devotion that I have yet seen or ever expect to see, was the one by my side on sharp-shooting duty, through the long and trying hours of that fearful Sabbath. This was a delicate, pale-faced, frail little boy, apparently without strength sufficient to hold up a rifle at a steady aim, a member of another regiment, but thrown by my side in closing up after crossing some broken ground.

"His pale face glowed, from the instant he delivered his first round up to the moment when his last one was fired, as the crimson cheeks of a blushing girl. He loaded and fired with a rapidity and deliberation that was astonishing. Once his gun-barrel became so hot he could not handle it. He threw it down, walked ten paces, and picked up another from the side of a dead comrade. Twice his ammunition was gone; as often he supplied it from the boxes of dead men. At one time, when actually mixed up with the enemy, defending a battery, and they recoiled a little, he snatched two loaded navy pistols from the belt of a dead trooper; threw his gun-strap over his own head; stuck one pistol under his cartridge-box belt; took the other in his left hand; with his right hand drew the same dead trooper's sabre from its scabbard; discharged the pistol rapidly; threw it down; discharged the other; cast it aside; made some incredible strokes with the sabre that brought blood, and when the enemy were out of reach threw down his sabre and resumed his rifle.

"After this there was a momentary lull. I said to him, 'My brave friend, you expose yourself too much; they will kill you.' 'I am not afraid; God will take care of me,' was the modest and blushing reply.

"You want to know this lad? A son of some old and chivalric family of the highest order of aristocracy, you are fancying. You are mistaken as to the present. Of his ancestors I have learned nothing. He is a simple child of nature—of the mountains. His name is Jesse Flowers. His widowed mother and little sister live alone, perhaps almost friendless, in a little cabin on the southern steeps of Beaver Mountain, within one dozen miles of your father's mansion. Such is the partial pedigree of a living young hero, to equal anything you can find painted on canvas or the 'pictured page' of fairy tale—this masterful sublimity of spiritual heroism. Of such material are the great martial heroes made.

"With no officer near to encourage and inspire him; no eye gazing on in admiration for, him to seek to please; no approving voice to stimulate him to superhuman exertions ten times greater than his natural force could endure, the grand spirit of simple, fearless duty rose in this child of the mountain forest, and transformed him into a young giant, raging and reveling in the destroying tempest of battle, almost rivaling the imaged Hector of fabled Troy. The magic of his example led me on, or held me spell-bound throughout the wildest scenes of that bloody drama.

"You may sigh because you cannot emulate my fair companions in the secret service of the border in direct aid to our beautiful, our beloved, your own Virginia.

"But, my friend, you may rival—yes, far outstrip them. How? By organizing a little society of your own to provide for the destitute families of our mountain soldiers in their cheerless, desolate, want-threatened homes, which are scattered all around your beautiful valley. Levy contributions on our 'stay-at-home gentry' without mercy.

"By doing this you will inspire hundreds of soldiers with redoubled courage and determination. They would then rush onto the thundering battery with the consoling thought in their minds and the inaudible words on their lips:

"'If I fall, Carrie Harman, the angel of consolation will not allow my wife and babes to suffer.' Then the devoted breasts would be bared to the storm of death with cheerful, unmurmuring resignation.

"Yet, on the other hand, when the gloomy tidings come that the loved ones at home are suffering, these hardy mountaineers will say: 'We have nothing more to fight for: the rich are letting our babes starve; we will go and care for them or die in the attempt.'

"What a frightful demoralization this would soon create! By preventing in your section what must cause it, you will render finer and more meritorious service to the country than it is possible for two of our best companies to perform in the field. I know these poor men of the mountain, and tell you what would happen.

"You have earnestly protested that you desire an opportunity substantially to manifest the gratitude you claim to owe me.

"I entreat you, then, the first thing you do, to see that the mother and little sister of Jesse Flowers are not suffering. There is nothing else in your power to do that I would appreciate so much. The poor boy has such simple, implicit faith that God will not let his mother and 'sissie'

suffer, that I do hope he may not be disappointed. My friends on the border have sent him little presents. He believes God told them about him. I wish you could see him then. What sublime manifestations of gratitude!

"I tell you about this boy because I alone am his witness. At one time he had nine witnesses who were cheered on for an hour—some of them more—and encouraged by his cool intrepidity. You are wondering why I am his only witness now. Eight of the nine are dead. When the firing ceased and the smoke cleared away, we found them all, their fair young faces cold and rigid, resting on the bloody ground around the spot where that desperate hand-to-hand struggle had swayed back and forth so long over that fiercely contested battery.

"I want you to tell his old mother and little sister about him, in that graphic, impressive language that is so natural to you. They will be proud of him. Ah! yes; and a queen might well be proud of him. And some morning, when a dark shadow crosses that humble threshold, and in pitiless accents tells the poor widowed mother and the little orphan sister that little Jesse Flowers, the son and the brother, their hope and their all, has died nobly, right up at the cannon's mouth, it will then, after their wail of despair has subsided, and the settled melancholy of a hopeless resignation has imprinted its cruel seal upon their features, be a comfort to them to recall that 'the aristocratic but real lady, who was not a bit scornful, but was so kind, so gentle, so good, had praised him.'

"I must draw this letter, that has rambled so much, to a close.

"I have not sought to amuse, but to interest you. Yes, to interest you in the cause of our common country and of humanity; not only to interest, but also to enlist, your heart and your soul in these potent causes which at this time are one and inseparable. I have been bold and fearless in my appeals. But my religion now is to serve my country. I do not hesitate nor stand on ceremonies when I see an opportunity, no matter in what direction it may lead, to service.

"If worthy of your attention, I shall be much pleased at any time to hear from you, and to learn how far, if at all, I have succeeded in enlisting your sympathies and interest in the direction indicated.

"Your encomiums have encouraged me and caused me to resolve to strive harder, to render some service in the future more worthy the kind approbation of my friends and of my country. But, alas! my extreme youth and my obscurity are obstacles in my way, that appear insurmountable, and render the prospect of success desperately discouraging.

"Your humble friend,
"GARLAND CLOUD."

Such was the letter of the scout, the obscure mountain-boy, to the aristocratic belle. No dreams of love vexed that youthful mind. It is transcribed *verbatim* from a copy furnished by the lady herself, in her own hand, and copied from the original, which is in her possession. How much she has modified the phraseology we have no means of knowing. We have her assurance that the copy is a faithful one.

CHAPTER IX.

THE PICKET BIVOUAC.

" The fire smoldered low and dim,
The wind blew bleak and chill."

THIS is a subject of interest to troops in the field.

Upon the lonely sentinel, who is posted from the picket bivouac, often depends the safety of not only his immediate companions of the reserve, but of the whole army. His duties are stupendous, and his powers so despotic that his commanding general dare not trench upon them without conforming with prescribed rules. Such commander, although he may be intimately known to the sentry, dare not attempt to cross the picket-post without the countersign. Should he presume thus to attempt to pass the lines, it would be at the peril of his life. Military law confers upon the picket the absolute power to arrest and detain his commander, under such circumstances, or even to shoot him, should he disregard the sentry's authority and attempt to escape. Hence the importance of the duties of the picket are rarely properly estimated and duly appreciated by people outside of the circle of educated or experienced military men.

The soldier on picket duty stands on the altar of his country, whose fires incessantly burn, a sacrifice ready to be offered up at any moment. He must ignore self—remember duty. Personal danger and self-preservation must not be an influence to actuate him to abandon his post, or seek to save his life at the peril of his trust. Although he be surrounded by menacing foemen, with leveled muskets, drawn pistols, and flashing sabres, the picket-sentry must discharge his gun —sound the tocsin of alarm, to warn his comrades of approaching danger—in the very face of instantaneous death.

This is his duty. Of him no less is expected. Upon his faithful discharge of this obligation the army implicitly relies. Thus assured that they are safely protected against the dangers of a surprise, the commanders and soldiers sleep in confiding security.

Into the soldier's being is this wondrous duty, with the dependencies it shields, energetically inculcated from his first day of service, and constantly continued until he is graduated in the important routines of a private warrior.

Upon his superior authority as a picket-sentry, the young soldier early learns to pride himself. Of his supreme prerogative he becomes intensely jealous.

From the earliest historical, and even legendary ages, we have the grand pictures of individual heroism—standing out in bold and unrivaled relief—drawn from the sentry on duty, standing and perishing, without flinching or recoiling, at his post. Some few of their names have been immortalized in song and in portraits on History's "pictured page."

Of many others equally grand the world has never heard—not even their companions of the day knew more of their story than that they sent the sharp notes of warning back to the reserves to prepare for danger, and then died. Their names went on the lists of "missing" or "killed," on the muster-rolls, and thus passed away.

In our Civil War, many cases of grand individual heroism, on both sides, might have been recorded, portrayed and sung; yet few have been given to the world.

The most pathetic picture of this theme now extant, so far as we know, is to be found in the poem, written by a Confederate trooper, "All quiet along the Potomac to-night;" but no names are mentioned.

There has been a case recorded in the columns of the *Detroit Free Press*, over the *nom de plume* of M. Quad, of a Federal sergeant of the guard, in a fort in front of Petersburg, surprised and entered by the Confederates, before daylight, in the early months of 1865.

This soldier continued to fire after he had been repeatedly wounded; and to his coolness, intrepidity and courage, was the failure of the Confederates largely due.

No one of our characters, unfortunately, ever seized the crown of this matchless heroism in the destroying prosecution of war.

The armies of Northern Virginia and the Potomac picketed by brigades during the winter of 1861-2. From the brigade, detachments from each regiment were sent out a little distance from the bivouac of the brigade: the main body of the reserve picket. These detachments were established on roads and other approaches by which it would be practicable for the enemy to advance. From these detachments, companies were sent farther to the front; from these, small detachments were sent still farther to the front; and, from each of these, went out the individual sentries who were so stationed as to guard the front intrusted to the care of the brigade, with one unbroken chain of pickets.

The company detachments were the reserves of the individuals, upon which these were to fall back in case of emergency, or from which they were supported if this course was practicable. The company detachments fell back on, or were supported by their companies: these were the detachment reserves. The companies fell back on, or were supported by the regimental detachments. These were the reserves of the companies and were supported by, or fell back on the brigade. This, when all the detachments had rejoined it, was able to deliver battle on a scale sufficiently formidable to retard the advance of a powerful army for hours at a time.

But all, in a great measure, as was often demonstrated, largely depended on the vigilance and invincible courage of the individual picket.

If he was not on the alert, the enemy might quietly pass his post, capture or pass one after another of the reserves, penetrate, surprise and rout the main body of the army. Such was the fate of some large bodies of troops, several times during the war of the rebellion.

It was midnight in the early days of 1862. Garland Cloud lay by the smoldering fire of the reserve out-post, where his own company was on duty. He was reading. Every one else was asleep. Capt. J——, of his company, was making the rounds of the posts, but returned about this hour.

CAPT. J——: "What are you reading, Cloud, so earnestly this bitter night by that handful of coals?"

CLOUD: "The Cavalry Manual, sir. I need it sometimes. I often meet a fancy Yankee chap below Annendale, who makes his handsome bay turn on the hind feet in the twinkle of an eye, falls over to the off side, and flies away from there. I want to learn his tricks, and to catch him, too. I am going through the lines in a few minutes. I could not sleep, was lonesome, and had nothing else to read."

CAPT. J——: "You are a very foolish boy to expose yourself so much. You get no credit for it."

CLOUD: "I am not seeking credit. I am doing duty. I enlisted to destroy the enemy. Every man or horse the enemy loses tells. Our brigade has lost more men from fever since the 21st of July than it would have lost in the same time with every man actively exposed all the while as I have been. Just look at my ruddy health. I can kill any two of you at hardships."

CAPT. J——: "You may be right, but you are lucky. I hear horrible stories about your recklessness on the 21st of July, and down at the front since."

CLOUD: "I never have exposed, never shall expose, myself more than the demands of duty require. It would be suicide."

CAPT. J——: "You may, at all events, get more glory than all of us. If you were a little older, you would soon have a better commission than I have. For this you are working so hard; this accounts for your studying tactics by a dim fire on a bitter winter night; you intend to get promoted from the ranks."

CLOUD: "I am trying only to do my duty. I am obscure, and without influence, experience or capacity. Any service, then, that I may be assigned to must be on the score of merit, and not of friendship."

CAPT. J——: "You have the most powerful friends and the strongest influence in the army—are personally acquainted with generals, while the rest of us are almost afraid to approach our Colonel. I feel sometimes that it is a judgment sent on us for thinking ourselves a little better than you when we left home. I have long been ashamed of this, and wanted to beg your pardon."

CLOUD: "All these things of the past were the outcome of class education and social usage, and hence were but natural with you. I tried to treat their indication with indifference. War, as you all have found, is a great leveler, with no respect for social conditions nor previous rank, but rather rewards men according to their actions, their merit, and their virtue. I have long since proved to you all, that I cherish no animosity in memory of the past. I have nothing against any of you, Captain, to forgive, and trust that I have no reason to seek pardon for anything from you or from any of the boys."

CAPT. J——: "You are a generous boy, Cloud."

The Captain then grasped Cloud's hand, and pressed it violently.

For a moment the two proud and haughty boys stood speechless, their grand blue eyes filling with tears which the fierce wintry blast, beating chillingly on their cheeks, was ready to congeal should they flow. They heeded not the pinching, stinging cold. Their bodies were warmed by the fiery glow of souls replete with the thrilling emotions of a grand and courageous devotion to the cause and the land they loved so well.

At length Cloud broke the silence: "Oh, Captain; this is a priceless assurance to me!"

CAPT. J——: "From the bottom of my heart I thank you, Cloud. I have long desired this interview, but my heart failed me. I feared you

felt a rankling bitterness in your heart for me because of some hasty words at some time spoken before I knew you. Some strange presentiment often tells me that some day the sun will go down shrouded in the smoke of battle, amid which one of us is weltering in blood, cold and dead. I cannot bear to think of going with your ill-will unabated, for I shall be the stricken one: you are a child of destiny."

CLOUD: "Nonsense. You have the blues, Captain. I must leave you. Good-night."

CAPT. J——: "Good-night. Be cautious."

Five minutes later Garland Cloud had disappeared in the darkness, and was traversing a dense woodland wilderness.

CHAPTER X.

SILAS WORTHINGTON.

"Roll on, vain days! full reckless may ye flow,
Since time hath reft me of all my soul enjoyed."
—BYRON.

"HALT! hold up your hands; dismount; surrender, or you are a dead man in an instant."

This was the startling, cheerless salutation which pierced the still and frosty air in the grey twilight of the January morning after the night referred to in the preceding chapter, addressed to Col. Silas Worthington, Quarter-master United States Army, and fell with quite an unwelcome cadence on the old gentleman's ear. There was at the moment, as the situation then appeared to him, no other alternative but to acquiesce, and submit to the pressure of circumstances, which he did, and surrendered, though reluctantly, yet with an air of cheerfulness worthy of admiration.

Col. Worthington was a wealthy New-Yorker, though a native Virginian and Southern sympathizer. He was a bachelor merchant. His property and business were so situated and conditioned that the war caught him with his interests all hopelessly tied up in New York City. His strong and well-known Southern sympathies rendered his affairs desperate, subjected him to danger of military imprisonment, and jeopardized his property to the liability of confiscation; and, in order to avert these menacing dangers, it was imperatively necessary that he should do something to appease the wrath before its concentrated fury should explode on his head—something counteracting; that he should act, and act vigorously and immediately.

However, under the peculiar circumstances which enthralled him, there was but one action that could avail him: this was to enter the army; therefore he tendered his services in the capacity of quarter-master.

His extraordinary business capacity, consummate commercial experience, powerful financial influence, and, above all, his great wealth, admirably qualified him for that department—made him a thoroughly desirable man; and his services were without hesitation accepted.

He was on duty with the Army of the Potomac. On the morning in question he received an order at his quarters on Arlington Heights, about two o'clock, to report immediately to some general up at the advance infantry post, then some distance to the front.

In the darkness, among the numerous military roads,—all of which constant and extensive use had formed into much the same state of appearance when viewed even in daylight,—he missed his way, and rode a number of miles in a direction that was every moment widening the distance between himself and his objective point. Having discovered this and obtained proper directions, he was hastening over a cross-country by-road to gain his destination, when he was so suddenly and rudely halted and made prisoner.

His pistol, the only weapon which he carried, was unbuckled from his waist; the belt rebuckled and hung over the horn of his saddle, in obedience to the order of his ruthless captor; then, in compliance with a request made by the same uncouth individual, he led his superb black horse forward.

"Your rank and command?" was the next demand made by his captor.

This information given, the prisoner desired to know to whom he had surrendered.

"You have surrendered," was the reply, "to Garland Cloud, of the Confederate scouts, sir. I regret to be under the painful necessity of discommoding you; but there are many unpleasant experiences connected with war, and unfortunately for you this morning, you have met with one of

them. You appear to be cold. Take to that path, and walk as rapidly as you please until you get warm. I will take charge of the horse."

Instantly Cloud was in the saddle with the agility of a trained trooper, and the poor, dignified old Colonel was going along the blind pathway ahead of him at a rather unmilitary double-quick. For some time they thus hastened on, not a word being uttered. At length the pathway was no longer visible; they were in a dense thicket, where it would have been impossible to see a man at any great distance—not ten paces at many points. Cloud then informed his prisoner that he could halt. Bitter cold as was the morning, which had covered Cloud's slight moustache with icicles that completely hid his mouth, the Colonel was perspiring profusely.

CLOUD: "Now, Colonel Worthington, I will tell you something of the situation, and what I am going to do. We must remain here probably all day. Moving, we are liable to be fired at by the guns of either army. You might, in that event, get hurt,—what I want to avoid while you are in my care. You may light a small fire if you wish, there in the hollow of the rock-cliff, as you will get cold after awhile. It is necessary, for the reasons stated, that I shall leave you alone much of the time, although I shall hardly be out of sight of you more than two or three minutes at any one time; then other eyes will be upon you. I must watch some manœuvres from the brow of this hill. I will caution you against the mad peril of an attempt to escape. If you move ten paces from that rock, you will be shot without being halted. Our scouts are all around you. I will have word passed that in case you do not move you are not to be molested."

COL. W——: "You need have no apprehension. I am not disposed to take any of the chances named, although I should almost as soon be killed as remain a prisoner. My loyalty is mistrusted. Now the authorities will claim that I have deserted to the enemy. They will want no better pretext to confiscate my property and to court-martial me whenever I am exchanged."

The old man actually sobbed, while his cheeks were copiously suffused with tears.

CLOUD: "Were you not a citizen of New York?"

THE TROOPER AND THE SCOUT.

"HOLD, CLOUD, HOLD! DON'T FIRE! IN HEAVEN'S NAME HOLD!" —See page 42.

Col. W——: "Yes; but I am a native of Virginia, and believe the South is in the right. I have two brothers in your army. I am regarded as a traitor, although I have not claimed citizenship nor held pecuniary interests in Virginia since 1835. I am in the United States service. I had two alternatives: this or a casemate cell in a fort to choose between, and I have taken this, which I regarded as a semi-civil service, in which I could feel that I was a non-combatant."

Cloud: "As a citizen of New York, you owed her allegiance as clearly as I owed mine to Virginia."

Col. W—— : "So I have tried to persuade myself. Yet I am sure we are wrong in many respects. I know you well, now, Garland Cloud."

Cloud: "I guess you are mistaken."

Col. W——: "I refer to your kindness to Lawrence Pleasington."

Cloud: "How do you know anything about me in that relation? Who is Pleasington? Where is he now?"

Col. W——: "I know these facts fully from him. He is one of the finest young men in the army, a graduate of West Point, and the best horseman in our service. I know him in the best society in New York, where I have often met him, and where I heard all about your kindness to him, in ten days after he was wounded. He has been back on duty since some time in November. He is scouting almost constantly up around and in front of our outposts, somewhere near here. He picks up a good many of your boys, and gets into some tight places himself by riding into ambuscades: but so far, his self-possession and skillful horsemanship have enabled him to escape."

Cloud: "How about his Effie love, Colonel?"

Col. W——: "An heiress to immense wealth, and justly termed the belle, if not the queen of the belles; certainly one among the rarest of them in the circles in which she moves; and she is as modest and good as she is rich and beautiful. She favored Pleasington on account of his handsome figure, his intelligence, and above all, his purity of character and life. He is poor. For this reason, her relatives bitterly oppose him; but she does not care for their objections. He has been promoted since he returned to the army, and is a general favorite. He has assured me that he would not raise his hand against you after he had recognized you, such is the magnitude of his appreciation of his debt of gratitude."

Cloud: "I trust we may never meet in mortal combat. How about the horse, Colonel? Is he fast? How would he stand fire? And the pistol; is it loaded and reliable?"

Col. W——: "There are no faster horses in the army, and an old cavalryman has thoroughly trained him to stand artillery fire and all other frightful sounds; the pistol is one of the finest and best made, and contains fresh loads."

Cloud: "Well, Colonel, I will relieve you of the care of these articles. You will have enough to do to keep from freezing. Make yourself as comfortable as you can under the circumstances. Just as soon as there is no danger of getting you mixed up in a skirmish we will move out from here."

Without waiting for a reply, he rode away, leaving his hopeless prisoner alone, with as much reliance that he would not attempt to escape as though he was guarded by two sentinels.

Cloud's motive at this time was safety for himself; to reconnoiter; to seek a way out for prisoner and horse if possible, but more especially to avoid personal capture. His prisoner was an unexpected contingency, and cause for solicitous embarrassment at this hour and in this particular locality. When capturing him he over-estimated the military rank of his victim, or the latter might have been permitted to pass unmolested. But after leaving the prisoner in custody of the rocks and the forest-trees, an enexpected circumstance suddenly frustrated all his calculations and changed the features of affairs.

CHAPTER XI.

WHY THEY DID NOT FIGHT.

"We have met and we have parted,
And we may never meet again."

Cloud rode to the brow of the hill, whence the surrounding country was visible miles away. South two hundred yards distant, and in plain view, there was a cavalryman on vedette duty;

two hundred yards beyond him there was a squadron—the reserve vedettes.

Upon finding the enemy in force thus uncomfortably near, Cloud turned and rode slowly north, keeping well in the edge of the thicket in a narrow cattle trail.

The cold seemed more intensified as dark and threatening clouds closed over the horizon, and hung low, like a suspended pall, and the bleak north-east wind increased in velocity from a stiff, whistling and disagreeable blast to the whooping current of a sweeping gale.

Cloud had rode barely two hundred yards when an abrupt turn in the pathway opening disclosed a magnificent horse less than ten paces in front, and his rider, who had dismounted to pass a tall fence obstructing his passage south, was cautiously filling up the gap which he had made and passed. When Cloud discovered him, he was stooping to raise the last rail. A crisis was at hand. Nothing could prevent it. Leveling his carbine, Cloud quietly and mildly said:

"Surrender instantly. Make one aggressive move, and you are a dead man."

What was his amazement to see the rail, which the trooper in the meantime had raised straight up, laid quietly in its place instead of being dropped in panicky confusion; instead of turning deadly pale and trembling like an aspen-leaf in the wind, the deep crimson of defiance mounted to his foeman's cheek, and the force of spiritual heroism pervaded his frame with a strength, a presence of mind, and a will truly superhuman. Cloud recognized at a glance the agile horseman whose feats he had witnessed when leaving a demand to surrender unsatisfied on other occasions. But now flight was impossible, resistance out of the question. Cloud was half disposed to conclude that the man was deaf, and had failed to observe his imminent peril. Yet this hallucination was quickly dispelled. Cloud was amazed at the coolness thus far displayed; but he was paralyzed when he saw his adversary, at one wild bound, spring into the saddle, and his long sabre, with a dazzling gleam, flash from its sheath.

After months of daring, always presuming on the panic created by surprise at the critical moment as a sure preventive for the necessity of fighting, Cloud had at last met his man; he must now surrender, die, or in one instant send a fatal bullet into his foe. He realized the great impropriety and danger of firing a shot. But what was to be done? He had no sabre. In one instant the naked blade which gleamed before his eyes would cleave him from the saddle. Already the able and daring trooper was gathering the reins, bending forward and poising himself to send the spurs into the fiery charger. There was not half the danger in a whole squadron which Cloud's fire might attract, compared to that which he now faced. His resolution was quickly taken, and the carbine ranged for the mortal aim with a coolness and determination equal to the bearing manifested by his antagonist. Now for the first time the trooper's eye was fixed in one instantaneous gaze on the face of the scout. He turned pale as a ghost. His sabre was lowered; his hold on the reins slackened; the spurs did not pierce the sensitive flanks of the noble steed to goad him on to the fearless, maddening plunge; and the trooper hoarsely stammered:

"Hold, Cloud, hold! Don't fire! In Heaven's name, hold!"

What could have so suddenly changed the rash determination of a foeman so cool and so intrepid? Was it terror at the prospect of certain and instantaneous death—with which the slight advantage at that moment in his opponent's favor appeared to threaten him—that had caused the color to fade from his courageous cheek? No, indeed; fear was in no wise an agent that had any part in exercising the influence by which he was actuated at this supreme moment. What then was it? It was that rare and radiant gem now and then found in the combination of human nature —*Gratitude*.

"Very well, then, surrender," was Cloud's cold retort.

"No, Mr. Cloud," was the reply, "I will neither surrender nor fight you. Shoot me you can. But you are too brave, too noble to do that. I do not fear it. I will make a truce with you for a few moments, and then pass in peace. You do not seem to recognize me. I am Pleasington, whose life you saved at Manassas."

CLOUD: "But this, Major Pleasington, this is a different affair. You are not in the same condition you were then. My position is a serious one. It is my duty to capture or kill you. You are an open enemy on my native soil. Were we on yours I might deem it reasonable to pass you."

The Major appeared to be greatly distressed; almost desperate.

MAJ. P——: "But your magnanimity will not allow you to refuse me a truce that is honorable to you."

CLOUD: "The only honorable truce I can make with you would be in regard to your surrender."

MAJ. P.——: "Then let us make one to consider the terms; if we cannot agree, we can part in peace."

CLOUD: "But we can discuss this without a truce; I have not needed and do not need one. I do not propose to stand here parleying until some of your forces come up, nor am I so simple as to permit you to ride down yonder and turn that squadron out after me. That is a ruse of strategy, Major—a very fine one—but I cannot allow it. I entertain more personal kindness for you than for all the other men under your flag combined; but were you my brother I should be obliged to do my duty, however painful it might be to me."

The Major bit his lip with feelings of mingled rage and despair; then said slowly and with emphasis:

"Mr. Cloud, on the honor of an officer and a gentleman, none of our forces will pass this path. I am supreme commander, for this day, of the posts of nearly one mile of front here. No troops under my orders shall molest you unless you first openly attack them.

"I have repeatedly vowed to my intimate friends that you might cut me to mince-meat and I would not raise my hand to harm you; and they commended my sentiments of gratitude to a generous enemy. Now, do you believe me capable of resorting to a base and cowardly trick to get you into my power? No sir; that is beneath me. Had any other man in the world except little Flowers—God bless him—been in your place, one or both of us would now be dead or desperately wounded. I want to talk quietly and civilly with you for a short time."

CLOUD: "All right, then I accord your wish. Our mutual parole of honor is the basis. We will dismount and lead to the east, a hundred yards or so into this wilderness, where scouting parties will not disturb us."

Cloud lowered his gun, and, suiting his action to his words, he dismounted and led the way.

Arrived at a point of perfect seclusion, he stopped; set his gun down; tied the horse; unstrapped the blanket from behind the saddle, and spread it on the ground. The Major then went through the same motions, which, when completed, opened the way to mock formalities. Cloud advanced two paces to meet him—hand extended, as he said:

"Maj. Lawrence Pleasington, as a soldier of the State of Virginia and of the Confederate States, I meet you amicably under an informal truce, and hope you are well."

MAJ. P.: "Mr. Cloud, as a soldier of the United States army I meet you on the same basis, and cordially return your greeting and salutations."

In another minute they were seated on the same blanket, talking with the easy informality of two comrades. Of the two, the Major displayed the most unreserved freedom.

MAJ. P.: "Well, friend Cloud—for friend true and tried you have proved to me—through your kindness and the doctor's good and careful attention, I was soon out of danger and sent on to prison, and thence, before long, home. I was better treated throughout than most of our people, and all owing to the recommendation of the doctor—your good friend sent with me. Please thank him for me.

"I found mother and Effie in ecstasies to see me back alive and well. Your name is often praised by them. Should ill-fortune ever make it your lot to be a prisoner of war in the Northern States, write to mother, and you will want for nothing that money can supply. Mother and Effie will provide for you."

CLOUD: "I will do what you request when I can. I am grateful for such kind sentiments from your good friends. I trust neither of us may need friendship as a prisoner; yet there is no telling what a day may bring forth in these regions."

MAJ. P.: "That is very true.—As I live, you have got poor Col. Worthington's horse and equipments. Where in the world did you secure them?"

CLOUD: "From a no less important personage than the gallant Colonel himself, astride of his charger."

MAJ. P.: "Oh, please do not make sport of him! The old man would not hurt a flea. Where is he? I sent a courier to him last night with an order from Gen. R——, of some importance."

CLOUD: "He got lost in trying to obey that order, and fell into bad hands. He is now in a place of safety."

MAJ. P.: "If not hopelessly beyond your control, let me take his place as a prisoner, and release him. He will never harm you. It will ruin him, and probably blast all my hopes in life, if he goes to a Southern prison."

CLOUD: "It is not in my power to grant your wish. Is it possible that you would go to prison instead of a man at heart a traitor to your cause? He is a commissioned officer in your army. I am unable to understand how his property could be confiscated, unless he is first convicted of treason. If being captured away from their posts constitutes treason, a good many of your officers are traitors. But this is none of my business. The Colonel told me some such story about his danger."

MAJ. P.: "Yes, I will go to prison for him. He has been my best friend in this world. I owe him everything; even my appointment to West Point was obtained through his influence. I owe him directly my other features of education; my social position—even my acquaintance with Effie."

"Effie's aunt by marriage has been striving for years to make a match between one of her daughters and the Colonel's gold. But for this fact, I am sure that her family would long since have broken the friendship between Effie and I, which they bitterly oppose.

"This lady also wants Effie's gold married to a dissipated nephew of hers. Before the com-

mencement of the war, and after the Colonel gave up his mercantile pursuits, they had made no progress in the direction of entangling him in Cupid's snares; but now, when he visits New York, he is idle, and feels blue.

"They make it exceedingly pleasant for him at the home of the young lady, and consequently he spends many hours there, and has grown much fonder of her society than he was in former years. In the army he has much time dragging on his hands. Hence he cheerfully maintains quite a voluminous correspondence with the young lady; and I think, unless this calamity with which he is now threatened spoils it all, she will secure him.

"Now, you may appreciate how very important to me it might be hereafter if I can save him."

CLOUD: "My sympathies, Major, are certainly with you. Should I be able to have the Colonel liberated, you may have the credit that he was released on your account."

MAJ. P.: "Oh, a thousand thanks! May I hope?"

CLOUD: "I can promise you nothing. Everything depends on circumstances; and what their nature may be I dare not attempt to conjecture."

MAJ. P.: "I feel assured that if you can, you will help me; so I will not press the question."

CLOUD: "It would be unnecessary. If I am able to release the Colonel and take you in his stead, at day-break to-morrow, I will find a way to advise you in time. It seems like a poor trade to give a colonel for a major even; but I suppose the difference in the mischievous propensities is enough in the Colonel's favor to make up for your lack in rank. We will know by to-morrow what happens."

MAJ. P.: "I do hope it may work all right."

CLOUD: "I want to warn you of something, Major. There have been a good many houses wantonly burned, and other outrages committed by your people, lately, in this vicinity. The avengers are abroad. You are about alone a good deal. If you cross their path, they will feel sure you are a prowler, and may shoot you without warning."

MAJ. P.: "These things are a disgrace to our

uniform. General McClellan deprecates and does all he can to suppress them.

"I can now understand why my letters went. I can also see how and why so many of our straggling, pleasure-seeking, bandbox-drawing-room volunteer officers are missing so frequently. These things are no longer mysterious wonders, with you and your comrades in our lines, with greater freedom than our own men, without a pass, could possibly enjoy."

CLOUD: "Oh! we know the country. We have no regular time to come nor certain route to travel; we turn up when least expected, and almost always surprise somebody. You are never safe without a strong escort, after you get from under the protecting shelter of the guns of Arlington Heights."

MAJ. P.: "I shall never doubt this, after the evidence of its truth which I have this day witnessed."

CLOUD: "Now, Major, my engagements are of a nature so pressing, that I am under the necessity of terminating this interview. I trust you will, so far as you can, protect the defenceless and the helpless from insult and injury; and, in the meantime, I shall bear in mind the fact that you are Col. Worthington's friend.

MAJ. P.: "I am sorry you are going so soon. Rest assured, I shall do everything in my power to suppress lawless, uncivilized warfare against women and children.

"Without either a tacit or an implied assurance from you, I shall hope, just a little, for my friend Col. Worthington."

CLOUD: "You return, Major, the way we came. I part with you here. Remember the parole for the day. Farewell."

MAJ. P.: "The parole is as sacred as my life. Rely upon it.

"I trust soon to owe you another debt, on the score of my friend Col. Worthington. Farewell."

Thus met, and thus parted, on this bitter winter morning, two brave, tender and sympathetic hearts, that would never quail before a mortal danger.

CHAPTER XII.

COSMOPOLITAN ARISTOCRACY.

"Of its own beauty is the mind diseased;
And fevers unto false creation. Where,
Where are the forms the sculptor's soul hath seized?
In him alone. Can nature show so fair? Where,
Are the charms and virtues which we dare,
Conceive in boyhood, and pursue as men!
The unreached Paradise of our despair,
Which o'er informs the pencil and the pen,
And o'erpowers the page, where they would bloom
again!"
—BYRON.

READER, if you have grown tired, hungry and cold on the battle-field and among the outposts of the great armies, let us leave them in the chilling, pelting storms of rigorous mid-winter, and pass to the gay and charming circles which throng the brilliant saloons at this season, in the superb realms of aristocratic New York.

Aristocratic New York of 1861 must not be confounded with aristocratic New York of 1883. The gigantic strides of nearly one-quarter of this progressive nineteenth century, have told on the then comparatively circumscribed, yet rarely select, domain of the olden time—have actually annihilated it. The places where it then flourished in its enviable, unapproachable pride and grandeur are illuminated with the witchery of its splendors no more. The swelling notes of joyous mirth with which its then resplendent halls resounded are silent and still. As to these once charming circles, oblivion has spread her sable mantle over the mansions, the streets, and the avenues, once so bright and splendid. Scenes of loveliness gone with, and like the days that are dead—to return nevermore!

To-day, squalid wretchedness prowls, or vice and shame carouse in their midnight revelries, where twenty-two years ago the belles smiled, and the high-life queens of beauty held their sway.

A wave of time has swept over the little kingdoms which were then subject to the swaying sceptres wielded by those fair and haughty hands; submerging some deep down, deep beneath its ruins and its wrecks; bearing others out to where their individuality and the dominating superiority of their sterling characteristics and unsullied virtues have become blended with, and hopelessly lost in, the chaotic confusion produced by the new order of things, in broader and more ex-, tended realms.

In plain English, this class in 1861 *was aristocratic.* Of the validity of its claim to this title, none even dared presume to question, but at once conceded that it was genuine. It was acknowledged at that day, and still reverentially esteemed as authentic testimony of tradition. This was the aristocracy of the good old days of *ante-bellum* times — the pure, deep, clear, blue-blooded article, which had been handed down from generation to generation as a legacy from the centuries gone, and slumbering with the dead ages of the past; or had been acquired by years of long and patient toil.

There was nothing spurious about this ideal aristocracy. No members of this chivalric patrician community had sprung up by the aid of the low-pressure force of army contracts, or by the sudden appreciation of an inflated currency, or from questionable speculation. The days of colossal hot-bed fortunes had not then appeared. Aristocracy, minus every essential requisite save money, was as yet unknown. At that time, fortunes had not been coined as if by a stroke of the Enchanter's wand.

At that now ancient period, aristocratic New York was not pressing up near 100th street. All that section where now stand princely mansions, were desolate, woe-begone-appearing old fields, far out in the country. Central Park,—that most charming oasis of to-day,—was then a rude, unsightly, uninviting rural landscape, covered, to a large extent, by squatters and their browsing goats. It was a park; but its present grandeur was then not even a theme for the indulgence of the wildest and the most extravagant dreams.

Grand Central Depot, the Elevated Railways, the Brooklyn Bridge, and the Hudson River Tunnel,—realities now,—would then have been subjects so apparently impossible, as to render their consideration preposterous.

But, however, while the progressive men of to-day pause for a moment, in their hurried journey of life, to bestow a passing thought upon the men of twenty-five years ago, and to smile at their simplicity, let them not forget to contemplate the wonders which await the men of twenty-five years hence. Then all present barriers to wider spreading will have been outstripped and overcome. New York will still be looming up and moving onward—the world's wonder—a modern Babylon.

However, we are on our way, and about to enter aristocratic New York of twenty-two years ago. The dazzling scenes of to-day are still behind the mystic curtain.

The little domain we are rapidly approaching is bounded by no long catalogue of streets, and contains but a few blocks of mansions.

Modern belle of society, queen of beauty, pray stifle that glow of contempt mounting to your beautiful cheek; do not permit that disdainful smile to wreathe your pretty lips at the association of that unpretentious region with the name of aristocracy; because within its now unhallowed precincts were you born, and there you passed your tender years. Deign to bestow upon the blighting stains which have marred its once bright and untarnished escutcheons, one sigh of regret; and for the sake of some of its beautiful queens, who as martyrs, were sacrificed on the ruthless altars of a degenerate age, bequeath one tear of commiseration.

The social circles which we are about to enter are composed of elements as gay, as brilliant, as pure, and as good as any in the same walks of life to be found anywhere in this world. The mask, with the bitter remorses which it obscures, yet cannot all conceal, is rarely worn.

Still, however, the good people in this model state of amiable harmony and exemplary friendship, have their petty jealousies to cherish, their little piques and spites to avenge, and their ambitions to gratify.

The match-scheming mammas, looking out for gold to which to wed their daughters—yes, alas! they are there. Then the character of those whom they plot to entrap has to be irreproachable: this and ample gold constitute the acme of eligibility. It is unnecessary that they should be young, or handsome, or lovable, or the objects of their dear daughters' choice—those conventional husbands—and usually the fair victims submit meekly to their fate.

At the period when we are about to look in upon the gay scenes being enacted on this exclusively select stage, the faintest breezes of that air, laden with the blighting contagion of social pestilence, are just beginning to pervade the blissful structure, and stealthily to fan the cheek enshrined by beauty's sheen. As yet its dangerous presence is unrecognized. So like exhalations from the purest nectarine, are the odors of its agony poisonous perfumes, that unsuspecting innocence recoils not from the soothing subtlity of its opiatic influence. Thus, little by little, its malignant seeds securely germinate in pure and guileless hearts. These ultimately awake from the allurements of this fatal fascination to a sad consciousness that they are hopelessly enthralled in the direful meshes of immedicable destruction. Now, without the semblance of disguise, the treacherous tempest bursts with savage, cruel fury upon the defenseless heads of its victims. Those baneful seeds, from which spring the wild, deleterious, all-blasting social Upas, are to be nurtured into dark luxuriance by copious fertilizing with deep mulches of confusion, peculation, and demoralization, deluged with rivers of blood.

Such is the unblemished purity and spotless repute, and such the threatening epidemic which menaces that social sphere of wondrous perfection, challenging the admiration of all times and countries. Here are the yet sparkling, untarnished gems of virtue, directly bequeathed as a heritage to this generation by the illustrious planters of LIBERTY'S TREE.

Here, now and then, are yet to be seen, a few noble, living relics, that have come down from those glorious, transplendent days of the by-gone time, tottering, vanishing mementoes of the REVOLUTION.

Now they behold the dark days of civil strife rending the fraternal bonds of that country which they have loved so well,—the pride and glory of their youth, the consolation of their declining years,—and see, with their age-dimmed eyes, seeds of corruption taking root in that society for which they have labored so many years with precept and by example, that it might retain its time-honored standing of exaltation,

on the waning verge of decay, as they, ripe with fullness of years, and loaded with the honors of a well-spent life, with sorrow-broken hearts sink into the tomb.

We go back to them, to that haven where the noble ships in which they made their voyage of life proudly and triumphantly, rode the rough and tumultuous waves of Time, to seek an anchorage for the tempest-tossed, helpless crafts of another age.

We have promised a picture of human nature, drawn from all colors, shades, and phases of actual, real life of the present time. We find that the base, the great sub-strata—from which nearly all the most striking characters of human nature at the present day have sprung, and upon which they now rest,—is but treacherous quick-sand, the seething dregs of our Civil War—a sad and lamentable heritage.

This being unquestionably true we are, per force, under the inevitable necessity of taking its glaring, deep-crimson colors of commingling fire and blood for a back-ground. But we desire slightly to modify it, if possible, by throwing upon it a shade of contrasting reflection from the brightly shining radiance of the pure, the beautiful and the good. Then, when all the little, almost innocent, social slips, and the great crimes, in all their multifarious forms, that shame and degrade the human race of our own time, are spread upon it, little, if anything more, will be required to render this picture consummately thrilling.

The few who yet with trials and dangers to the last weather, the gale or float on the *débris* of their wrecks to a safe and friendly shore, will merit earnest applause and rich rewards. Some, who go down with the seething torrents may be objects for a passing sigh of pity.

We pause and hesitate to enter that brilliant realm where beauty and purity reign, because it is a Paradise like that of old to our ancient parents, which we, too, are doomed to leave!

But, however, it is worth the trouble; let us see it. There we shall meet our Major Pleasington's own Effie, and Colonel Worthington's friends, in their own princely homes. Yes; and, besides these, we shall become acquainted with other actors, who will, at times, rush upon the stage, and act their parts—some wildly and fiercely —in our drama.

It is a painful task—a duty, which makes the heart sick and the mind sad to present some of these actors, in the whirling, giddy tranformation scenes through which they must be hurled.

CHAPTER XIII.

THE MOUNTJOYS.

"They were meek and they were modest,
  They were handsome and they were tall,
  Their hair was black, and they wore it curly,
  And oh! their sweet blue eyes withal."
  —SENTIMENTAL SONG.

THE above lines describe the four Misses Mountjoy with due, impartial appropriateness.

The Mountjoy mansion, situated in the centre of the little domain styled in the preceding chapter as "Aristocratic New York of 1861," was famous in its day.

Norman Mountjoy was a wealthy, an enterprising, and a prosperous wholesale merchant, the head of an old house. His father and grandfather before him had been merchants. The business had grown up to be something of stupendous magnitude, upon a foundation more than a century old.

Early in life Mr. Mountjoy married Helen Noel,—a majestic young queen of beauty,—from a proud and imperious old family. She was a bright social ornament, and while profusely liberal in the appointment of her household, she could not, in her earlier matrimonial years, be deemed extravagant beyond what her husband's means and their social position warranted—nay, almost demanded. He idolized his lovely young wife. Even her most trivial whims and foibles were gratified with spontaneous alacrity. Whatever Helen wanted was her devoted husband's greatest pleasure to grant. He often said: "If it affords Mrs. Mountjoy as much pleasure to spend money as it affords me to make it, we are a consummately happy couple."

In every relation of life, social and commercial, Norman Mountjoy was the quintescence, the very soul, of honor. It was a common watchword in his business sphere concerning any commercial transaction: "If Mr. Mountjoy says so, it is all right: his opinion is as good as law."

Mountjoy House had been a grand old surburban mansion of the olden time. It stood in the centre of a broad tract of ground, artistically laid out into most beautiful flower-plats and shrubbery arcades, intersected ever and anon by handsome gravel walks, fringed with evergreen, trimmed and arranged with the most scrupulously delicate taste. Around and above all loomed up and spread out their paternal, protecting arms, the grand old shade-trees, some of them sentinels of departed centuries, monumental children of a virgin forest.

The house itself was large and roomy, with grand old porticoes resting on hugh pillars; broad, high hall, parlors, drawing-rooms, library, dining-hall, and chambers of dimensions to rival those of baronial palaces of the dead, the legendary, and the historical ages. This princely old mansion was furnished in most exquisite style, well becoming the state of a merchant prince, and in harmonious accord with the tastes and the wishes of his refined and adorable wife.

Aristocratic New York, as we now behold it, in, as it were, a dream or vision, had steadily encroached upon and sprung up around Mountjoy House, depriving it of its rustic environments, without, however, robbing it of its own peculiar rural distinctiveness and traditional exclusiveness —privileges that its modern neighbors could not enjoy—enviable luxuries, denied to metropolitan denizens, save the rarely exceptionable few.

Such were the parents, such the home, and such the surroundings in which, under the fostering shelter and benign influence of its guardian walls, had sprung up, budded and bloomed into sweet and perfect womanhood, like incarnation nymphs created by the old Romancers in their scenes where appear the fairy enchantresses, four matchless young ladies, to rival any who ever graced the gilded saloons, amid the splendors of Oriental palaces. They were tall, stately, and dignified; and in every delineation their robust model figures presented to the admiring eye the most pleasing proportions and symmetrical harmony of form that the most infatuated dreamer of beauty could picture; in every lineament of their charming features was clearly and unmistakably discernible the imprint of all the graces combined; and in their large, dreamy, deep blue eyes, which seemed always speaking in a silent yet pathetic language, sparkled that brilliant gem of a rare and radiant virtue. To these wondrous and divine charms of nature were added all that refined art and cultured associations could bestow, to render these young queens of fashion and of beauty delicately polite, meekly graceful, gently dignified and modestly adorable.

Many good, old-fashioned, unassuming old people, often said of the four sisters: "Why, they are just as near alike as four black-eyed peas."

However, while in appearance and conversation the resemblance was so striking that a person not well acquainted with them, was liable to mistake any one of them, for some other of the four, yet still, in some characteristics, they were not, by a wide difference, as closely alike one other as the peas.

Cassandra, the oldest, was a trifle the most haughty and impatient. Beatrice, the next in years, was like her sister, in a milder degree, with the slightest tendency in some matters to be fickle. Rosalind, the third sister, was predisposed to be intensely romantic. Evalina, the youngest, was patience and resignation personified. These were the four fair daughters of fortune. They never imagined a want that was not gratified, if not even anticipated; and they had never known a sorrow. Could their voyage on through life ever glide with the same unruffled serenity, they would fulfill the highest earthly destiny to which it is possible for human beings to attain, crowned with consummate honors. But should the wild tempest of disaster hurl their light craft swiftly and furiously upon the cruel breakers, and leave it there stranded, a hopeless wreck, how would these frail and delicately tender green-house flowers brook the merciless storms that would beat with relentless violence on their defenceless heads. These children of fortune had never dreamed of misfortune; they scarcely knew the true definition of the term, and were certainly

4

not nurtured to bear its stings with unmurmuring fortitude; to indomitable self-reliance, such as the stern exigencies of some terrible, soul-testing calamity demand, they were utter strangers. To contemplate the pitiless grasp of misfortune seizing the self-willed and self-reliant, is terrible; but when the helpless children of fortune are the hapless victims, it is appalling.

CHAPTER XIV.

EFFIE EDELSTEIN.

"Blue were her eyes as the fairy flax,—
Her cheeks, like the dawn of day,
And her bosom white as the hawthorn buds,
That ope in the month of May."
—LONGFELLOW.

This, friends, is Lawrence Pleasington's Effie love. Do you, in the secret recesses of your hearts, blame him for idolizing, even worshiping, this little earthly angel? If you do, we do not. Every one who knew her loved her. With her, wherever she went, there went a halo of sunshine in her smile, an echo of love in the cadence of her voice. In her were combined all the charms, all the graces, and all the virtues of her fair cousins introduced in the preceding chapter, without one of the slight imperfections, that it was mildly hinted that the three eldest possessed. In addition to all this, she was mistress of all the self-reliance and courage necessary to sustain her in any possible emergency.

Is this concise description satisfactory? If it is not, there is no language in this world to do the subject justice.

Her father was a descendant in direct line from a noble German family,—his immediate ancestors having come down through the rude, pioneer experiences of the old Dutch colony from its earliest days. Her mother was Norman Mountjoy's only sister, who died when Effie was a little child.

Her father was a prosperous merchant, and the intimate friend of Silas Worthington. He, too, died after a protracted and lingering illness, when Effie was ten years old, leaving her, his only child, an immense fortune for that age of the world.

Silas Worthington was appointed administrator, and little Effie was left to the care of Mrs. Kate Eber, her father's sister, between whom and Lawrence Pleasington's mother there had been a life-long and intimate friendship.

The will, under the sagacious supervision of Mr. Worthington, was drawn up by one of the ablest and most skillful lawyers, with admirable tact and wonderful ingenuity, so that it was impossible for any portion of her fortune to be touched, except a moderate annual stipend set apart for her support and education, until she was twenty-one years of age.

Lawrence Pleasington was the protégé of Mr. Worthington. This fact, connected with his relation to Effie, and the friendship existing between her aunt and his mother will account for the intimate, perchance more tender and endearing, ties between these two young persons.

Effie loved her cousins, and spent much time with them. Between her and Evalina, there was an extraordinary affinity, devoted attachment. Of the same age, with the same tastes, and the same opinions in all things, on all subjects—even to Effie's strong preferences for Lawrence Pleasington's society and friendship—there is no rule by which the depth of love, springing from their pure and innocent hearts, can be measured. Nothing could ever shake the foundation of its steadfast affection—a consecrated shrine, where the incense of love ever glows, forever rekindled by the sparks of a sublime friendship, an endless and an eternal devotion.

CHAPTER XV.

MAUD PLEASINGTON.

" The sorrows that bow down my head
Are silent as the midnight gloom."
—From KITTIE WELLS.

This is Lawrence Pleasington's widowed mother. She is from a good old family—but now, the last of her race.

Her husband, a self-made man, from Virginia, married her when they were both young. He prospered as a merchant, and became the bosom friend of Silas Worthington.

Around the young couple sprang up, in the course of fifteen years of prosperous and happy matrimonial life, a family of seven children—Lawrence, the baby.

Then came dark days of reverse, trial, and death. The mercantile interest was consumed by fire the same night after the insurance had collapsed at noon. Through an oversight, caused by illness in his family, which had for several days kept him absent from his office, the policy had not been renewed.

In the brief space of ten days, the malignant fever laid six of his children beneath the sod; and on the fourteenth day the broken-hearted father followed his little children across the dark river; and left behind—oh, cruel fate!—his poverty-stricken, grief-smitten widow and orphan babe on this desolate, friendless shore.

Oh, God! what would have become of them, in their dismal, hopeless despair, but for one noble heart, one true friend, Silas Worthington, constituted by Heaven their guardian?

Assisted and encouraged by their foster protector, they lived; and Time, the great healer of the broken, bleeding heart, and the love of her sweet little bright-eyed boy, soothed the widow's woes. She saw her son, a handsome young officer—her pride.

CHAPTER XVI.

ARNOLD NOEL.

" In virtue's ways he never took delight;
But he loved wine and carnal company."
—BYRON.

This is the young scapegrace, dissipated nephew of Mrs. Helen Mountjoy, whom that lady is resolved shall possess that rare and priceless jewel, Effie Edelstein, and her wealth.

His father is a prominent merchant, in a neighboring city; and his family, which is large, ranks first-class. One brother, although a very young man, is already an officer in the United States navy; and one sister is married to a first-class New York merchant.

Young Arnold, from a small boy, has been the black-sheep of the flock; yet, notwithstanding this fact, he is his father's favorite child. The old man, however, often tells him, with tears in his eyes, that he will come to some bad end, and bring him in sorrow to the grave, in his last declining age. But, to the youngster, these are idle, meaningless words, and are unheeded.

At the period of life where we now find him, aged fifteen years, he is in New York, at school, under the care of his aunt and sister; never knows his lessons, and is always in scrapes, both in and out of school. Sometimes, indeed, it is only on account of his well-known family that the police do not take charge of him. For less cause, many poor lads are every day arrested.

On one point he appears sane; that is, getting possession of the Edelstein fortune. The money to gratify his vicious appetites and indulge his indolent propensities, is the dream of his life. He has been educated to regard it his prize. For this reason, he practices an artfully studied decorum whenever he is in Miss Effie's presence; and tries to please her. She, on her part, is too refined, and too good and tender-hearted, willfully to wound any one's feelings.

CHAPTER XVII.

SOME FREQUENTERS OF MOUNTJOY HOUSE.

" Thine eyes, like the stars that are gleaming,
  Have entered the depths of my soul;
And my heart has grown wild with its dreaming,
  And with feelings I cannot control."
                            —SENTIMENTAL SONG.

LIEUT. ORLANDO OGLETHROP.

THIS was a class-mate and is the bosom-friend of Lawrence Pleasington. He was an obscure, New York mountain-boy, who found his way to West Point through the influence of a member of Congress from his district, who met the lad during the canvass, and took a fancy to him.

He spent some weeks in New York with Lawrence. Met Mr. Worthington, who became his warm and admiring friend; and through him the young man was introduced to the Mountjoys.

Despite the fact of his plebian origin, Miss Evalina likes him. He worships her, but has the good sense and prudence not to let the fact be known. He is always welcomed at Mountjoy House, and always calls whenever he visits the city.

SAMUEL VAN ALLEN

is a wealthy, prominent married New York gentleman. He is a friend and favorite of Mr. Mountjoy. He stands well as a business man, and is a prominent pillar of one of the leading churches. This gentleman is extremely fond of the society of ladies.

FELIX MORTIMER

is another city gentleman, wealthy, influential and married. He is also a special friend of Mr. Mountjoy, and much esteemed at his house. He is the business partner of Mr. Van Allen, and the President of a prominent bank.

IRA ATKINSON

is a wealthy bachelor, and a great favorite. He is a merchant, a member of the first house in its line in the city. Although old enough to be her father, he is designed by Mrs. Mountjoy to be the husband of one of her fair young daughters.

ADAM STRINGFELLOW

is also a bachelor, with an ample hoard of gold. He is the business partner of Mr. Atkinson; and Mrs. Mountjoy desires that he shall be united in matrimony with another one of her daughters. While this man and his partner are thus prized by Mrs. Mountjoy, her husband, for purely commercial considerations, lightly esteems them.

CHRISTOPHER SINGLETON

is a young gentleman, possessed of more handsome features and fascinating manners than money. He has a fancy for Cassandra the designed fiancée of Colonel Worthington; but the Colonel's wealth and the mother's aversion are against him. These are the most brilliant lights that often grace the grand old parlors. Besides these there are many others of prominence, but not as actors in this drama.

We do not deem it important to define our characters more elaborately in this connection, as their predominating propensities will be fully demonstrated as their parts develop. The careers of some of these characters, just introduced, would be ample foundations for complete and independent stories; while their parts in this book are comparatively limited.

CHAPTER XVIII.

THE SENSATION AT MOUNTJOY HOUSE.

"On with the dance,—
No sleep till morn, when youth and beauty meet,
To chase the glowing hours, with flying feet."
　　　　　　　　　　—BYRON.

At last we are in the fairy dream-land of gay and festive New York, and on our way to the Mountjoy sensation of the season.

As our friends are there presented to us, we shall not be under the necessity of speaking aside in an embarrassing undertone, to explain just who each particular one is, as this duty has been, already, fully performed on the journey from the front from beyond Arlington Heights.

Mercy! Just look! What transparent brilliancy! See how the grand old mansion is illuminated! What wonderful taste has been displayed in arranging the lights! How indescribably tempered is the mellowness of their enchanting shades! How captivatingly ravishing to the eye the charm of their fascinating reflections in tints of orange and of gold! Behold the witching groups upon which they shine!—fair women, noble and brave men—assembled chivalry and beauty—all upon which the eye delights to feast. How elegantly, how superbly, they are dressed! Everything perfect decorum, in harmonious accord with the latest and most approved styles and fashions of the day. Nothing, not the smallest possible item, in any respect, whether with reference to the appointments of the magnificent saloons, or the personal decorations and appearance of the polished and selectly chosen guests, has been omitted that could by any sort of peradventure tend to render the event, if not matchless, certainly unsurpassable.

Let us plunge into the crowd, and mingle with the festive and the gay, and see and hear what we may.

Can it be possible that the widely contrasting scene, amid canvas and smoke, which we left last evening, is in the same country, composed of the same people, even the very same families, as this which is now before us, under the bewildered gaze of our open eyes? Surely not; yet it must be.

Just think of it!—those menacing armies face to face; the infernal machines of war, being every hour, day and night rushed forward to perfection—the agents of death merely slumbering,—waiting for the igniting spark to arouse them from their lethargic inertness to throbbing pulsations of vigorous life. Then will they madly bound in their wild and pitiless career of destructive carnage, turning in one hour all these festive wreaths which we now behold in wondering admiration to sable badges of saddest mourning; those fair and radiant cheeks all aglow at hearing the praises of their own loveliness to the pallor of death,—and these rose-tinted lips to the whiteness of despair; the same as was witnessed in Belgium's proud capitol, one festive night forty odd years ago.

Our thoughts instinctively turn from these bright and blissful scenes to those dark and melancholy ones, with emotions of horror; and the contemplation of the painful and sad transition, conjures up a thrill of inexpressible sadness.

Well, our object, however, in visiting the grand fête to-night, is to meet those actors who have assumed the responsibility of filling rôles, performing each a part in this drama of life; and here to learn, as far as we can, how they are mapping out their parts, and what relation, if any, these parts are going to bear to one another; and to detect, if we can, what influence they are likely to exercise on the actors themselves, and in what manner that influence will affect them. With other parties, and other themes, at the festival, we have no business; and we must refrain from meddling with them.

We must remember, also, that we are merely tolerated spectators, and not privileged participants; therefore, let us take a commanding seat in a central position, and observe the gay and festive scenes as they are enacted around us.

Ah! this will do—magnificent! What exquisite music! Splendid! There is Lady Mountjoy and Mr. Mortimer taking that seat near us. Look! listen! they are in animated conversation.

MORTIMER: "How charming Effie is in that waltz! Look at Arnold—but is he not in his glory? How graceful he is!"

LADY M——: "Yes; Effie is rarely so radiant

as she is to-night. She makes Arnold dignified. For several days before he is to meet her, he is a different boy. If he could only see more of her, her influence would soon cure all his wild, boyish impulses. I regret that they are so young."

MORTIMER: "Ah, my dear lady, you are right about that. Many things of which we do not now dream are likely to happen, to thwart your plans relative to this young couple before they arrive at an age for your wishes to be rewarded by a realization of their consummation. Frankly, Madam, the young man's wild freaks are among the most dangerous. It will be impossible to prevent the knowledge of his conduct from reaching Miss Edelstein's ears; it is familiar in all business circles where his name is known. Pardon my plain language. You desired to consult with me on this subject. I must, therefore, state rude, unvarnished facts, that you may see clearly with what you have to cope.

"And then next, and but slightly less in importance, comes Lawrence Pleasington, who is almost daily performing some feat of daring that forces all to sound his praises, and predict that he will win immortal laurels. This, with his unquestionably handsome face, his unimpeachable, virtuous, and temperate life, together with the potent friendship of Col. Worthington, are obstacles sufficient to defy the combined counteracting influences of this city, brought to bear upon any young lady favorably impressed by this young officer. How, then, with Effie Edelstein, who was thus impressed before he went forward to mingle with danger and death?"

LADY M——: "This is provokingly true. Do you know that the most embarrassing feature of the combined difficulties with me is Col. Worthington's strangely mysterious fancy and friendship for that young man? You are aware of our relations with the Colonel, and his sensitive, impulsive nature. A slight toward young Pleasington would be a personal insult to Silas Worthington.

"I dare not assume the risk of incurring his displeasure: hence I am forced in this respect to act a part, continually, that I detest—that of dissembling; but unless I wear a mask, I must fail, and I to fail am resolved—never—no, sir—never!

"No matter what it costs me, Effie Edelstein shall be Arnold Noel's bride. As to young Pleasington, the fickle decrees of Fate will yet doom him a sacrifice on his country's altar—a sad but glorious lot."

MORTIMER: "I admire your courage. It is idle to have an object in life unless we follow it to success. However, under all the circumstances, there seems to me but little more to do except watch and wait for Time to render whatever assistance she is pleased to bestow.

"Pleasington now is fortune's favorite. Sometimes she smiles long upon a man, preserving him through all perils; then suddenly forsakes him."

LADY M——: "Yes; and she will forsake him in the end, because his blind infatuations will lead him to tempt her too far. He seeks, ever seeks, to soar far beyond his natural sphere. His aspiration in the direction of winning Effie is a presumptuous effort to ascend from the earth to the stars. This will eventually prove his bane. It is this that tempts him on to those desperate feats of daring that are making him famous, and that may yet wreathe his brow with immortal laurels, should his star not set forever, in the smoke and din and thunder of battle. This is the fate I predict will be his.

"I cannot say I wish him harm. I only desire him to remain in his own proper latitude, and not interfere with my plans. Then I could applaud his heroically acquired honors with as much genuine and enthusiastic zeal as any one in the land. But to think of him circumventing the long-cherished and dearest anticipations of my heart—this is what makes me furious—transforms me from his friend, yes, even patroness, if necessary, to the most bitter, vindictive, relentless mortal enemy.

"Why is it that those obscure vagrant lads that some misguided impulse causes men to pick up as they would genuine ash-kittens, and send them to West Point, outstrip all our well-bred lads in every respect—have better morals, are handsomer, and meet with greater favor and admiration in society? Then how provoking to think that because they are graduate officers in the United States army, a false etiquette compels the best society to open its doors unto them. There are seven of them on the floor now, that, but for this fact, could not put one foot inside of my yard. One thing redeems their obnoxiousness to some extent—they are polished and gentlemanly in their manners and deportment.

"Young Oglethrop, a regular mountain ignoramus by birth and breeding, who occasionally calls here, is a shining ornament in any society, and liked by everybody; and, by the way, I understand he is equally as daring and venturesome as young Pleasington. It makes me wild to reflect upon these facts. I am unable to comprehend them."

MORTIMER: "Those lads are genuine children of Nature. They are robust, well developed, and strangers to the degenerate traits of our city boys. These simple aids—indomitable force of virtue and self-reliant will—have produced the greatest men in every sphere of life, in all countries and ages of the world, sprung from the most obscure and humble ranks.

"Our wealthy city children, both boys and girls, lack this force. They are never educated to rely upon themselves. And those who from time to time are deprived of their supporting force, and compelled to fall back on themselves,—a shadow catches them,—find their hopes are placed on broken reeds.

"They are utterly unqualified and unable to help themselves; and they soon sink into oblivion, where they are quickly forgotten;—as their wealth and social position, so pass away their names from the remembrance of their former friends."

LADY M——: "Do you know that I am so horribly oppressed with the bare thought of what these terrible times may bring to any of us, that I dare not think? I am forced—driven to seek excitement. I often shudder at my extravagances. We have an abundance, and a present income to warrant a large expenditure; but it appears to me necessary constantly to increase it. I cannot curtail, nor can I be content to remain stationary; so I shut my eyes as a rule, and try not to see the approach of cloud or storm, and to anticipate only continued prosperity and sunshine throughout my voyage of life.

"Oh! but for these match-making vexations and disappointments, I should have always remained in tranquil serenity and blissful happiness! But they have become the passionate, all controlling objects of my life: such they will remain."

MORTIMER: "My dear Madam, you have the 'blues,' the worst case I have ever witnessed. Come, let us join in the dance, and think on more cheerful prospects."

LADY M——: "Thank you. How glad I am to mingle in that intoxicating whirl, and drown all thoughts of the subjects, upon which we have been dwelling."

Now, what think you? Has she not shown at least the main bent of her purpose, and that she is in course of preparation to prove equal to any emergency, and not to scruple about the nature of the intrigue, so that it facilitates the progress toward the end which she seeks to attain?

But now enters Mountjoy and Van Allen coming to the same seat.

MOUNTJOY: "I tell you, Van, the times are terrible. Such festivities as these, considering the state of public affairs, are too gay and discordant; but ladies are ladies, you know, and want everything cheerful and bright around them; and perhaps it may be as well in the end."

VAN A——: "Yes, Norman, I fear black days are coming? The horizon of the future is overcast with a portentous gloom threatening dreadful storms. I tremble at the coming fate awaiting many of our staunchest mercantile barks."

MOUNTJOY: "I am unable to prevent the same horrible dread from entering my mind; constantly it haunts me.

"We lost large sums in the South. True, we have made most of it up; but the value of money is depreciating—expenses are on the increase.

"The Southern people will have privateers slaughtering our helpless merchantmen on the seas. Should they strike for several times vessels bearing large invoices to the same house, at its own risk, this would soon stagger the best of us.

"I want to haul in sail. It is absolutely the duty of us all to curtail and prepare for the worst; but I cannot do this without mortifying my family. They do not know of my forebodings which by the merest chance may not be well founded. I conclude, therefore, in consideration of this hope, clutching as it were at the drifting straw, to take the chances of their being caught in the worst fury of the storm, and subjected to the sudden shock which would engulf them with the crashing wreck, rather than torture them for months, perhaps years, with anticipated ruin."

VAN A——: "Ah, Norman! that is a great trial—I think, however, your course is the wisest you could have taken.

"Your family forces have their social battles to fight, and cannot afford to wait until the country has finished hers; so I think it proper for you to furnish all the means they require. After victory crowns their efforts, then you will have peace and tranquillity—a priceless boon."

"MOUNTJOY: "Would to God that boon was mine now.

"I detest this social match-making, although it is the legacy of ages in our family—inculcated into our minds almost as a religious ritual of our education. For this reason, I do not meddle with it.

"These girls of ours are not proper mates for old men. And young Noel, would he not be a companion for Effie? You know he is unworthy to be her footman; but he is Helen's idol. She is blind, and cannot see his faults.

"I would not give the little fingers of such young men as Pleasington and Oglethrop for a whole troop like Arnold; yet they are obnoxious to Helen. I let her have her way in these matters, and never cross her."

VAN A——: "Effie will never be Arnold's victim. She is too smart, and too much influenced by Col. Worthington."

MOUNTJOY: "I try to hope she will not, and could perfectly rely upon this presumption but for Helen's indomitable persistence."

VAN A——: "There comes Oglethrop, just from the front. He is coming right here. Look! They have all spied him, and are coming forward to meet him."

MOUNTJOY: "You are right; that is him. Look what a noble brow and majestic mien—a soldier of fortune."

CHORUS OF VOICES: "How do you do—how are you, Lieut. Oglethrop? Do sit down and tell us about the army and our friends?"

LIEUT O——: "The army is snowed in, and very quiet now. When I left the front, last evening, your friends were well, and commissioned me to present their compliments and kindest remembrances to all."

LADY MOUNTJOY: "Did you see Col. Worthington?"

LIEUT. O——: "Yes, madam, and a pitiful plight he was in, too; his one-thousand dollar horse and fine pistol gone, and he himself half frozen from lying out all night in the wilderness, in that terrible snow-storm. I do not think he will soon smile again. They treat him shamefully at head-quarters; call him Falstaff, and insist that he should have brought off the horse."

ALL: "Oh, shocking! What in the world. Do tell us?"

Lieut. Oglethrop here details the mishap and capture of Col. Worthington as the same have already been detailed in a previous chapter.

He also describes the meeting of Cloud and Pleasington after the former left Col. Worthington alone in the wilderness, so far as the latter has divulged the particulars of that affair to his friends.

The Lieutenant entertains decided opinions as to the mental reservations of his young friend and brother officer, and strongly intimates that a mystery thus remains unsolved.

He then continues:

"Three from my squadron came upon Cloud in a position where flight was impossible. They were sure of his capture. He rushed upon them like a demented fury. This must have paralyzed them with surprise for an instant; yet they emptied their carbines and revolvers at him. How many shots he fired they are unable to tell. The affair did not last one minute; yet it was long enough for two of them to be shot out of their saddles, seriously wounded, and the other knocked or dragged out before he had time to draw his sabre after discharging his fire-arms.

"In the shortest possible time, this poor fellow, half senseless, yielded his arms; then under the influence of his own sabre, drawn in one hand, and a presented revolver in the other, he unbuckled the arms from his wounded comrades, and hung them on poor Col. Worthington's saddle; tied the three horses in a string, bridles and tails together, and mounted the first.

"Up to this time Cloud had appeared a raging demon; now in the mildest, most sympathetic voice, he expressed his regret that he was unable to extend to them the offices of humanity which their hapless condition demanded; informed them that the one able to walk could find assistance just over the hill, at Maj. Pleasington's bivouac; asked them to tell the Major they had attacked him, and to send a white flag after the wounded man, and in the twinkling of an eye disappeared with his prisoner and booty; this is the last reliable information about him.

"The bullets fired by our boys rattled all round the Colonel.

"This so unstrung him that he dared not move all day. His fire went out. He feared to rekindle it. With the darkness it commenced snowing, and then he could not re-light it. Fortunately he was protected from the wind and sheltered from the snow by an overhanging rocky cliff. He kept from freezing by standing up and stamping all night.

"At daybreak he moved out, and soon fell in with a party of our cavalry. He was returned to his quarters very much crest-fallen and dejected.

"I think our boys attacking Cloud saved the Colonel from imprisonment. Pleasington says he would have been released. But I dispute it, on the ground that Cloud and party are not in the habit of releasing prisoners who are not wounded; and this assertion is verified by the action he took with regard to our unwounded boy."

LADY M——: "Oh, that is shocking! Why don't some of you put that desperado Cloud out of the way?"

LIEUT. O——: "Simply, madam, because it is catching before hanging. He lives inside of our lines more than half the time; is constantly capturing our stragglers, many of whom are volunteer officers, absent from their posts, seeking to make love to rebel ladies. The instance just related is the only time any of our forces have been able to lay eyes on him, except as prisoners;

and this also is the first occasion on which he has fired a shot at any of our troops; he never bushwhacks, and even as an enemy he is brave, kind-hearted, and magnanimous."

LADY M——: "I do not consider his treatment of Col. Worthington magnanimous; it would shame brigands and savages."

LIEUT. O——: "The Colonel merely met an ill-starred chance of war, and is exceedingly fortunate that he is not now in prison."

LADY M——: "How is it that Maj. Pleasington's horse and arms were not taken from him. the same as were the Colonel's?"

LIEUT. O——: "That is a hard question. Pleasington is as game and daring as Cloud. My theory is that he was surprised at great disadvantage, but would not yield; and that, as it was to Cloud's interest and safety to avoid creating the alarm which firing would cause, they agreed to a mutual truce. Certain it is that the advantage, f there was anything of the kind, was not with Pleasington. In the Colonel's case he surrendered at discretion.

"This is all the news I have. Please let the festivities proceed."

Ah! how gracefully that new comer dances! Well! we will look on, until that seat is retaken. Here come Mr. Singleton and Miss Cassandra to appropriate it now.

SINGLETON: "Miss Cassa, are you determined always to remain indifferent to me, and receive my protestations with coldness? When will you deign to consider my miserable lot, and bestow on your devoted adorer one word, one look, even one thought, as an emblematic token of distant hope?"

MISS C——: "I have considered kindly and earnestly all you have ever said to me on this serious subject, and decided with dispassionate unselfishness. What my sentiments and feelings have been, or might have been, are of no consequence now. Circumstances over which I exercise no degree of control, render it utterly impossible for any relations ever to exist between us, more tender and sacred than those of simple friendship. I have been, and am still, willing to continue your friend. More than this I can never be. If you desire to retain my friendship, if it is worth retaining, you will henceforth refrain from remotely broaching this subject which to me is one fraught with inexpressible pain. They are waiting for us."

This young gentleman can detect no consoling ambiguity in that answer, upon which he may found a forlorn hope. But here comes Mr. Atkinson and Miss Beatrice to the favorite seat.

Mr. A——: "Have you, Miss Beatrice, reconsidered the question relative to fixing the date for our nuptials? Can you name no more definite period than 'after the war,' as you promised to do at our last interview?"

Miss B——: "Oh, yes; but I have not changed my resolution, Mr. Atkinson. These are not proper times to think of marriages. If the war is long, it is better we remain single; if short, why then, the time will the sooner become definite."

Mr. A——: "I acquiesce in your decision the more readily because I at first agreed to that arrangement, and hence could not consistently insist that it be changed unless entirely agreeable to you. Now we will discuss it no more; and I will anxiously watch the signs of the times, and wait."

Miss B——: "Matrimony is a lady's day of slavery: the longer she defers assuming the responsibility of this solemn obligation the longer she is free. But here comes Mr. Stringfellow and Rosalind for this seat; it is our turn to dance, and they are waiting for us."

Stringfellow.: "Well, Miss Rosa, what has been the final decision relative to the happy event of celebrating the double ceremony in which it is our blissful anticipation to participate?"

Miss R.: "After the close of the war, Mr. Stringfellow, just as soon as peace is fully assured. Don't you think that is rushing things with a vengeance? I contended for a grace of one season, so we could enjoy, untrammeled, the gay and festive celebrations of peace; but Beatrice would not hear to it; and mother supported her — which decided the matter."

"Stringfellow: "I was selfish enough to hope the time would have been more definitely

fixed, and not, at what now appears in all probability, so distant a period."

Miss R——: "And you then wished to hasten matters more? Why, Mr. Stringfellow, I am amazed at the idea! It is too bad that I did not know this sooner. But the information now comes too late. The decree is recorded and stands irrevocable. But they are waiting for us; and here comes Evalina with her gallant cavalier for this seat."

Lieut. Ogletunop: "Miss Eva, everything here to-night is bewitching and fascinating. It is like a transformation scene of the Celestials suddenly emerging from the wide waste of grim terrors, compared with the scenes in my daily life and experience, sometimes in the tented, but oftener in the untented, field. Thus not unfrequently alone at night, riding along from one picket to another in impenetrable darkness, through a dreary wilderness, with no sound disturbing the awful silence, save the doleful, lugubrious notes of the owl,—that solitary, discordant, desolate, echo-conjuring bird of dismal gloom."

Miss M——: "It must be terrible. I sympathize with you, and often think about the dreadful dangers you face. I hear sometimes, through Effie, Col. Worthington, or the newspapers, how you and Maj. Pleasington court appalling dangers and tempt fate. I fear some heart-rending news will come some day to your friends,—reflections which make me shudder."

Lieut. O——: "Thanks, Miss Eva, for the compliment conferred, by bestowing so much as a passing thought on a poor soldier-boy doomed to rely upon his sword as his only sure and constant friend. It is, therefore, the more comforting and priceless consolation to know from your own lips,—which I am sure the voice of flattery never tarnishes,—that, even in your walks of life, my poor services to my distracted country are appreciated, and that my safety sometimes engrosses the mind of one so fair and socially elevated as yourself."

Miss E——: "You are mistaken in supposing that your sword is your only constant friend. You have many true friends here this evening, who regard you as the equal of any one in the land; and who possess the good sense to know that a few dollars do not measure the merit, value and social position of men in these dark and trying times."

LIEUT. O——: "Oh Miss Eva, you overwhelm me with compliments that I am unable to acknowledge appropriately. If it would at all interest you, I will send you once or twice a month a journal embodying an account of the most striking occurrences that come under my observation. I offer this in recognition of my deep and unutterable appreciation of your kind expressions, but for which I should not think of daring so much presumption. As a matter of course, I should not expect you to acknowledge their receipt."

MISS E——: "Oh, Lieutenant, a thousand thanks for this flattering consideration, which I eagerly accept! I shall look forward to the coming letters with anticipations of real pleasure, knowing they will prove genuine treasures replete with rare and thrilling interest. Please inclose, and direct them to Effie. I will promptly return my acknowledgment of the receipt of each highly-prized compliment."

LIEUT. O——: "I trust their nature, when you receive them, may not prove a sad disappointment. By the way, Mr. Noel appears to be progressing in favor with Miss Effie."

MISS E——: "Seems to be is all. Everybody, except poor wild Arnold and mother, knows that, heart and soul, Effie is devoted to Lawrence Pleasington. But here comes the truant and Effie to change places with us; our set is waiting for us now."

ARNOLD: "Miss Effie, are we not going to be better friends now, and see each other oftener than formerly?"

EFFIE: "Arnold Noel, I think from your conduct, without further reference or one particular as to detail, which is fully known to me, that you are determined we shall be much worse friends, and that very soon."

ARNOLD: "But I am reforming, Miss Effie. I see the errors of my wild ways—mere boyish folly, you know—a weakness to which most boys are subject."

EFFIE: "Since when has this freak of reforma-

tion influenced you? Since you began to prepare for this occasion, as you have before prepared for others. You are a disgrace to your family, and to every one who stoops to recognize you. But for the veneration which I have for your aunt, I would not speak to you. I am glad you have given me this opportunity. I pity you, and would do anything in my power to save you, if I could, by reasonable sacrifices, exercise some degree of influence over you. I do not wish to incur your aunt's displeasure, nor do I desire to wound her feelings; but seriously, regardless of consequences, unless you continue in an uninterrupted course of reformation, I shall never again address you. Prove the sincerity of your professions of reformation, and then talk to me of friendship."

ARNOLD: "Oh, Miss Effie, I will enlist in the navy to-morrow morning, and be on the sea to-morrow night, in order to get away from my evil associations, and to blot out the stain with which they have blighted my name. After that would you again be my friend?"

EFFIE: "I will be your friend whenever you have proved yourself worthy of my friendship, no matter how or where you reform; and my daily prayers shall accompany you wherever you go. Until then farewell. The company is preparing to break up, so our interview must end."

Now, indulgent readers, you have seen some of the actors who are to perform complex parts in this drama. They are now leaving the stage; the curtain is slowly descending to obscure the beautiful scenery among which they have moved —perfect in its loveliness as the fairy-tales the poets tell, of mythical lands beyond unknown seas.

But after many days they will reappear. The curtain—enveloper of the mystic and the mysterious,—again rising, will reveal upon the stage these same interesting characters, who must further disclose additional lines in Nature's wondrous book. Each is the architect, the author, the embellisher of his or her own peculiar page. As he or she makes it, so will we faithfully render it.

If we find that the pure and exquisitely perfect colors they first used are becoming soiled and dim, and that the magnificent back-ground that promised so much for the future tracings of the beautiful and the good, has become soiled and polluted, we shall try to remember the primæval splendors and unmeasured bliss enjoyed by the fallen angels, and the once unapproachable earthly happiness of the heaven-favored inheritors of that blessed Paradise which they forfeited and lost.

But these are forfeitures—the doom of the Eternal, beyond the everlasting pale of redemption. So are the destinies of our beautiful and pure, after they have once descended from their Paradise—illuminated by the undimmed brilliancy of radiant virtue and suffered that matchless earthly crown—glittering with priceless gems of honor, which decked their brows—a wreath of hallowed glory, a legacy from the immortelles—to be rudely torn from its wonted resting-place. Then, after the despoiler places in its stead his own ignoble brand, there is no hope for perfect restoration to that lofty eminence from which they have fallen. But consumed continually by devouring flames of despair; lacerated constantly by the scourge of remorse; and, forever groaning under the stings inflicted by an all-subduing but unavailing regret, in sorrow and in shame, all the days of their lives must they unceasingly eat from that evil tree which they themselves planted, the fruit of bitterness and ashes.

However, there is still safety and hope for thousands and thousands who have not so far forfeited their priceless heritage. To these can the lessons which one by one our tale unfolds, become subject matter for consideration of grave and serious import.

We are slowly, but steadily and surely, unrolling a chart of the voyage of life: striving to leave no dangerous reefs nor treacherous points unindicated by clear and securely anchored buoys or head-land beacon-lights, as signals to warn the mariner of his danger.

A close observer will quickly divine, as we progress, where and how the bark of any one of our voyagers, either unwarily or willfully, first touches the treacherous reefs or the dangerous rocks, and how it is still further drawn on and away from the course of duty, to which it may return no more.

Be patient: the voyage is long; its vicissitudes and dangers are multitudinous.

Do not look with contempt upon the bright features of our characters while they are, measurably all, yet beautiful and good, because you are satisfied that some of them are destined for shipwreck. While they are pure and honorable, they are admirable and worthy. Were none of them fated to perish, or rather too weak to resist the toils of the destroyer; and were there no others in the world liable to become victims to a like dreadful doom, the necessity for lessons of warning against such impending and menacing dangers, which boldly, almost defiantly, threaten on all sides, would not exist.

To cause the thoughtless traveler to pause and consider these dangers, as he gazes on the wrecks that strew the way on every hand, in time to escape a similar fate, is the object of these labors—to incite in the good and the pure a purpose and a resolve to retain their jewels—to show them how priceless are those little gems which so many lightly value and trifle with while they have them, and of which they so bitterly bewail the loss when they are theirs no more.

Take one last lingering look at this scene of beauty and purity blended in such lovely harmony, to retain an impression of its exquisite splendors, in order to contrast them properly with those that are to follow as its successors. If they are less bright, less pleasing to the eye, and less appealing to the heart, we can do no more than lament the shadows and the gloom that have surrounded them, where we should prefer the sunlight of beauty and purity to shine forevermore.

Those of our characters who may, perchance, long weather the gale and breast the billows to a haven of safety—nay, should but *one* arrive, pardon us if we laud that glorious achievement—will well deserve a wreath of laurel and immortelles. Those who may go down beneath the waves in the fathomless depths of the sea, for them permit us to weep, shed tears of contrition all we can bestow; for we know, oh, how truly, the nameless woes their bitter cups will have contained!

We deal with the problem in its carnal bearings: the thralldom of spiritual penalties is the minister's theme. Our mission henceforth is to contrast the fruits of good and evil in this life. We design this as a solitary, grim, and ghostly sentinel, to warn mariners of their dangers on the sea of sin; to denounce the wiles of the destroyer and the wages of his victims, as practiced and realized in this world. We make this sentinel cry aloud, as it were, until hoarse from excessive shouting, in a voice of thunder tones, to resound above the wild roar of the surrounding tempest, echo and re-echo, and go on reverberating and moaning "Danger! danger! Ruin! ruin! ruin!" down through the centuries.

CHAPTER XIX.

THE MOUNTAIN CABIN.

"Can tyrants but by tyrants conquered be,
  And freedom find no champion and no child :
Such as Columbia saw arise when she
  Sprung forth a Pallas armed and undefiled ?
Or must such minds be nourished in the wild,
  Deep in unpruned forests, 'mid the roar
Of cataracts, where nursing nature smiled
  On infant Washington."
              —BYRON.

" Full many a gem of brightest ray serene,
  The dark unfathomed caves of Ocean bear ;
Full many a flower is born to blush unseen,
  And waste its fragrance on the desert air."
            —THOS. GRAY.

THE true romance, or drama of life, is life itself; in which mingle alike the prince on his throne, and the outcast beggar-lad crouching hungry and cold on an unfriendly stoop, with no other place to lay his little head. Both are sometimes necessary characters to present a real life-scene. There are, indeed, few lives either so humble or so obscure that cannot at some period furnish one little chapter of thrilling romance, making an intensely interesting character in one act of a drama, if the episode could only be reproduced exactly as it occurred at the time.

Romance is by no means always fiction. Its highest types that have ever been produced in the world, had for their foundation stern, stubborn realities, true as the pure gospel. "Often there is the glowing light of genius, the boundless treasures of feeling, and the most sublime lessons of morality in the obscure walks and lowly lives of the humblest peasant, the solitary wagoner, or the lonely shepherd."

For these simple, yet powerful and irrefutable reasons, the stern and sometimes pitiless lessons of this drama will often be found with the most intensified and thrilling romance entwined about them.

It is often simply incredible how the lives of different persons, apparently without either common bond or mutual sympathy between them, are influenced and controlled by one another; —how an idle word, spoken without the slightest motive at the moment it was uttered; how the most trivial act, performed under the influence of spontaneous impulse; and how a casual, purely accidental meeting with a stranger, changes the whole bent and current of lives. How mysteriously strange and incomprehensibly true are the means by which actors who have never known, or even heard of, one another, are drawn together; and without any mutual compact or concert of purpose, prosecute in perfect harmony each a requisite part tending to produce one final and accordant result, which they did not design nor desire. Are not many such incidents often romantic?

Now we are away in the wild, bleak, desolate mountains—a gap in a branch of the Blue Ridge chain, which we gazed upon at a distance of thirty miles, one bright May morning, from the point where the actors in our first scene were gathering.

The forests are nude and dreary. "There is not a flower on all the hills," and the earth is draped in a deep mantle of driven snow. The little brooklets, which rippled so transparently and murmured so sweetly then, are solidly bound in the icy embrace of winter's fettering chain.

Never at any time is this rude, wild region—always replete with rugged Nature's fantastic and weird scenes—so inhospitably uninviting as on a day like this. Blinding clouds of fine snow are driven before the sweeping blasts of the howling wind. Not a track of the prowling beasts of prey which inhabit these neighboring mountain fastnesses, is anywhere to be seen: they do not venture out from their lairs.

The primogenitive peasants stay closely beside

the broad log-fire in their one-story, one-roomed primitive, half-camp, half-cabin huts. From time immemorial have their ancestors thus lived—it would be sacrilege to depart from the custom.

In every respect their lives are blameless. They are temperate in all things; believe the Bible, and fear God. Their churches are the same as were God's first temples—situated, even until this present day, in a dense grove of stately oaks, maples and hickories, buried deep in an untained virgin forest, often more than a mile from any human habitation. Under the friendly branches of those grand old trees the rude benches—made from saplings of chestnut-wood split open, and the splinters smoothed off by a hand-ax—are arranged. Their earthly wants are few. In their frugal dwelling-places luxuries are unknown; yet incredible degrees of comfort are there found.

Any one who has passed through these wild regions, and called for a bite to eat at one of these humble abodes, expecting a rough crust of corn-bread, will readily recall the sensation of agreeable surprise experienced at finding a really excellent, palatable and varied meal.

These simple children of the mountain forest are healthy as their herds of swine which roam the wilds, and almost as hardy. They are robust, well-developed and athletic. The girls have cheeks decked with the hues of the full-blown rose, and are extremely modest and bashful.

These people reap the promised reward of pure, temperate, virtuous, well-spent lives with large interest. As a rule, they live to ages ranging from eighty to ninety years; and many of them see the frosts and hear the wailing winds of a hundred winters, before they go to their long and peaceful slumbers, with their consciences clear and the implicit, confiding faith of a little child, to sleep the sleep of the innocent in their narrow cells on the cloud-capped summit of their native mountain.

Before the shrill, harsh notes of the trumpet of war disturbed the even tenor of their humble and peaceful lives, pure, devoted emotional love, and true genuine happiness, such as may rarely be found in mansions of wealth, reigned supreme in the home-circles of these obscure and simple mountaineers.

But with the war, wails of distress were heard from out these mountain coves, where formerly only songs of gladness had resounded.

Decendants from Revolutionary veterans, adorers of Virginia, their mother—these zealous sons of Liberty, as soon as the foot of a foeman was heard tramping on their native soil, rushed to the front, old and young, almost to a man, leaving their section depopulated of able-bodied male inhabitants. So universally was this true that many families were left without a male member; and scarcely any had one between the ages of sixteen and fifty years.

It is easier to imagine than to describe the privations and sufferings to which many such families are exposed in this cold and cruel weather.

We are at a cabin—or rather climbing over snow-drifts, and emerging from a deep and rugged ravine, toward it—to secure shelter until the weather becomes more favorable. The cabin outside has much the same appearance as those of the better-to-do classes all through this section. There is a chicken-coop; a little out-building called a "smoke-house;" because in this the meat used by the family is kept, and smoked to bacon; a corn-crib; a milk-house, just below the bold mountain-spring; a pig-pen and a stable; a pony and a cow in the stable; and a few cattle and sheep on the lee-side, seeking some shelter from the cold and pitiless wind. There is a fine orchard of various fruit-trees, and a handsome little vineyard clustering round the cabin.

While we are yet quite a distance away, we see a sleigh drive rapidly up to the gate, a young girl descend from it, and go lightly tripping into the cabin, while the sleigh turns and dashes rapidly back in the direction from whence it came.

We soon tap at the door, which is opened by a meek, sweet-faced lady not past the middle-age, and strangely beautiful, despite the clearly defined traces of care which are deeply imprinted on her features. With an air of refinement and a dignity of manner which unmistakably indicate a degree of high-breeding that causes us a thrill of astonishment, she welcomes and presents us a seat in front of a cozy fire of hickory. She seats herself at one corner-place of the hearth. The young girl just mentioned is warming her pretty little self at the other corner.

There is no other human being visible about the tidy little premises, which present a comfortable, home-like appearance, and are scrupulously clean, neat, and tastefully arranged. The occupants are mother and daughter.

MOTHER: "Rosalia, why, in mercy's name, did you come home on a day like this? I was not expecting you."

ROSALIA: "Mother, I could not think of staying away from you another hour, and the weather growing worse; on your account they were anxious to send me before the roads and country are entirely impassable."

MOTHER: "You are a good dear child, Rosalia, to brave such a snow-storm to come home to mother. True, darling, the roads may all be blocked and impassable by to-morrow."

ROSALIA: "Oh, mother! I must tell you about yesterday. We went away up nearly to the Mountain Meadows, to Captain K——'s funeral. He was killed last week in a skirmish somewhere out West, and they sent him home to his poor wife and children, to be buried. He was cousin to the Clouds. How my heart bled for his wife and children! Their grief was wild and pitiful.

"The church was crowded until there was no standing-room, and people built fires outside.

"Col. Cloud, Garland's father, was there with his arm in a sling, from the wound which we heard he received. His daughters, Virgie and Hattie, were there. They never saw me before; but, broken-hearted as they were from grief for their dead cousin, they came straight to me, kissed me, and said they were going away to Beaver Mountain to see us just as soon as the weather would permit. The old Colonel came up to me, and held my hand long and firmly pressed in his, while two great tear-drops stood in his large hazel eyes, as he gazed on me in silence, as though he was reading every line in my features, and some stifled emotion struggled in his breast, until at last he said: 'Little girl, you are a stranger to me, but your brother's name I know as that of the bravest lad in the army of Northern Virginia. I am glad to meet the sister of such a noble soldier-boy, and I want to know his

mother. I intend to call and see you and her as I return to the army, which will be in a very few days.'"

Just at this point in Rosalia's narration, there is a gentle tap on the little cabin door. The mother hastens to respond. On opening the door, there stands the beautiful figure of a majestic young lady, enveloped in rich furs. Her cheeks glow, her sparkling eyes flash with the fire of resolution. She is a fairy-dream image of beauty. On beholding her, the mother and daughter utter each a sharp little scream.

We are stupified with amazement, and begin to wonder if we are mingling in or beholding a scene where the angels congregate. We have been in sight and inside of the cabin only a very few moments. Even now we begin to feel that it is not impossible to meet any other new wonder, and that such awaiting to burst in upon us, here in this magical domain of the unknown, should not be regarded as at all strange.

Instantly the two fair hostesses recover from their momentary surprise, and, trembling apparently with the secret dread that this strange visit forbodes something terrible to themselves—is an angelic comfortress come with the evil tidings which might be brought,—and with white lips they both simultaneously but whisperingly exclaim:

"Oh, Miss Harman! what terrible occurrence has brought or caught you in these wild regions, so far from your valley home in a storm like this? Do come quickly to the fire. You must be nearly frozen."

MISS HARMAN: "I crave your pardon for having frightened you, ladies. Calm your fears. Duty brings me here. I bring no evil tidings. I am seeking Mrs. Flowers and her daughter, Rosalia. Are you not these ladies? You seem to know me, though I do not know you."

MRS. FLOWERS: "Oh, yes, Miss Harman, we know you, and are the ladies you seek. But what, permit me to wonder, can bring you here, twelve miles through such terrible weather to seek us?"

MISS H——: "The terrible weather, madam, and the knowledge that you were two lone, feeble women, away in this desolate mountain, perhaps sick, helpless, and destitute. while your brave little son is exposing his health and life, away yonder, near the banks of the Potomac, in this weather, defending old Virginia and me.

"I have received a mandate that I cannot, dare not disobey, to look after his mother and sister, and see that they do not suffer while he is away. I could not rest nor sleep peacefully until I performed the duty of seeing you, so that you could write him the comforting words of assurance to cheer his brave heart, that mother and little sister had friends sent to them by that God whom he believes so confidingly will provide for them.

"I am organizing *A Soldiers' Family Relief Society*, having for its object the care of soldiers' families in all the mountain districts surrounding our valley, and expect to have the coöperation of every lady in my section. Thus can we idle, worthless girls find employment and serve our country. The same voice that sent me to you commanded me to perform the other duty of organizing the society named. In this service nothing but sickness excuses from duty. Inclemency of the weather and lighter matters we must not pause to consider.

"But, separate and independent of the Society and its labors, I have taken it upon myself as a pleasing individual duty to call on you and see to your comfort and welfare. For this purpose, in the name of Jesse Flowers, the bravest of the brave soldier-boys am I here to day; and proud am I to have this honor, and to know his mother and sister, with whom I hope to become intimately acquainted, and that we may be the best of friends."

Mrs. F——: "Oh, Miss Harman! your kindness dumbfounds me. I cannot understand how you know so much about, and why you take so great an interest in, Jesse, and praise his bravery. We are hearing much about him, but it all comes from strangers, and not from himself or his comrades. He wrote that he fought very hard, and a great many were killed near him at Manassas; and that was all. Now the country is beginning to sound his praises. There must be some mistake about it."

Miss H——: "Not the slightest, madam. I assure you it is true."

Mrs. F——: "So far as I know, the boy has but one true, devoted friend in the whole army, outside of his simple, kind-hearted, neighbor boys. Garland Cloud is that friend; and we hear he is the boldest boy from these mountains. Are you acquainted with the Clouds?"

Miss H——: "No, madam; I have never met one of them. Col. Cloud has already distinguished himself, and been promoted three times for gallant and meritorious services. The mountain people are winning many laurels."

Mrs. F——: "With reference to your kind Christian mission here to us, Miss Harman, by the goodness of God, we are in a condition to need no assistance for a long time. Our little crop was excellent. We have received considerable money from Jesse — all his wages, and some assistance from unknown sources, that we are unable to understand, about which you shall know."

"But your driver will soon freeze. I will show him where he can put your horses under a shelter; and tell the poor fellow to come in to the fire, as I must detain you some little time before you set out to return."

Miss H——: "Thank you, madam. You are very kind. I am disposed to remain an hour or two, as there are many things about which I desire to talk with you."

[Mrs. Flowers passes out of the room.]

Rosalia.: "Excuse me, Miss Carrie, but mother did not tell you how we knew you so quickly. We have seen you often at camp-meetings, and also where they were organizing companies to go to the war."

Miss H——: "Yes, Rosa, I remember you and your mother now, but never knew who you were, nor where you lived."

Rosalia: "Miss Carrie, here is a little old wine, made from our grapes. It will do you good after your long ride in the storm."

Miss H——: "Ah, Rosa, this is equal to the finest champagne. Did you and your mother make it?"

Rosalia.: "Yes, Miss Carrie, we made it. We prepare a great many things from our grapes and fruit, that enable us to subsist; and we like them."

Miss H——: "You have not always lived here, or at least you have been away at school, have you not?"

ROSALIA: "We have lived in this cabin since before I was a child less than a year old. Jesse and I have been to no school never a single day in our lives. Mother taught us all we know. She graduated when she was a girl; has been a lady in her day, with all the wealth that heart could wish.

"She saved a great many valuable books, which have been her only companions in many a sad and lonely hour while Jesse and I were growing up, and since, when we are sometimes away from her. She has taught us, from the time we first began to speak, French, German, Italian and Spanish, until now each language is as familiar to us as the English. She also taught us to trust in God, and to believe that in His own good time He would remove the shadows and clouds from our pathway; and that some day, in the far future, we would walk in the bright sunshine of life, and fill useful positions in the world. Thus have we grown up and lived to what you see and know of us now. However, we have been quite as happy and comfortable as the majority of our poor neighbors. These people are very good and kind to us.

"Mother has taught their children, and crocheted fancy work for the girls. They have paid her in work, honey, flour and many other things that helped her along. The old hunters frequently send us some choice pieces of the game they kill. Mother now has a piece of bear baking and some venison cooking.

"Those kind-hearted old men often come to hear Jesse's letters and the paper read, and take a meal with us. Mother occasionally writes something for a Richmond paper, and they have sent her a daily ever since the commencement of the war."

Miss H——: "Rosalia, have I been dreaming, or listening to a veritable romance of mountain life? To think of the hidden treasures, pictures of real, pure, natural life buried here in the remote recesses of these grand old mountains—

things for which we poor, school-crushed girls of the valley pine and ransack the libraries to find in vain—being, all these years unknown to us, within two hours' ride of our doors!

"But concerning your mother before she came here—how was her life then, Rosa? I am all impatience to hear that part of the story. What brought your mother from the midst of fashion and wealth, to these wild and dreary shadowed mountains?"

ROSALIA: "Here comes mother, Miss Carrie. She will tell you."

Miss H——: "Mrs. Flowers, Rosa has been relating to me something of your experience in the mountains, and that you came here from the world of fashion and affluence. If agreeable, how delighted I should be to hear something about that romantic transition!"

MRS. F——: "Not a word of that until dinner is over; then I will recount it to you, although it carries me back to memories fraught with inexpressible pain.

"Uncle Jack, take this seat, and warm—poor fellow, I know your hands and feet are nearly frozen.

"Now, Miss Harman, I am going to give you a regular rough-and-ready mountain dinner, including some spoils from the chase, just to show you that we are in no immediate danger of suffering for the necessaries of life. And while I am preparing the rude repast, I wish to complete my statement, explaining why we do not now require assistance, in order that you may understand fully that we are not actuated by a false pride when telling you that we need no aid, because I realize that the day may come when we will sadly require it."

Miss H——: "I am proud to have the honor, Mrs. Flowers, of dining with a realistic living heroine; for this, I am sure you are,—that ideal type of the heroine which I was persuaded had never existed in the world, was a mere mythical creation coined in the fertile brain of visionary authors. And I am inexpressibly pleased to find you in a condition to need no help now; and hope and trust you may so remain. I shall listen with deep interest to what you say in explanation relative to this cheerful feature

SCENE IN THE MOUNTAIN CABIN.

"'I BAPTIZE YOU WITH MY TEARS, AND CHRISTEN YOU,' THE ANGEL OF THE MOUNTAIN.'"—See page 70.

of your present condition, from now until dinner is over; and will not disturb you until your narrative is completed."

Mrs. F——: "Well, in the first place, Miss Harman, Jesse has been supplied with an overcoat, blanket, boots, underclothing—in fact, everything he needed, through the instrumentality of Garland Cloud. This enables Jesse to send us all his pay. Then again we have received several small anonymous sums—nearly two hundred dollars in all,—within the last four months, which fact has caused me no little anxiety, as I was entirely unable to conjecture the source whence it came, or for what reason it was sent."

"Moreover, to cap the climax of my bewildering astonishment, last week these two letters and the articles referred to in them reached us. Read them, please, and see if you can advance a theory that will solve this strange mystery, which to me is so truly incomprehensible. Read them aloud, please, that I may hear them one time in a new voice."

"'New York, Dec. 25, 1861.

"'Mrs. Gertrude Flowers,
"'Beaver Mountain, Va.
"'Madam:

"'As a token of my gratitude and appreciation for the kindness of your son Jesse in aiding to save the life of a wounded United States officer at the battle of Manassas,—a very near and *very dear* friend of mine,—I beg that you will deign to accept from an unknown Northern girl, the articles inclosed in the package to be found in the accompanying box, marked with your name—they are for you. The one with Rosalia's name is for your daughter.

"'I trust the articles may reach you in safety, and be serviceable to you in these deplorable times; and that your good son may be spared to you. I am, madam, with sincere, heart-felt gratitude, "'Very respectfully,
"'Effie Edelstein.'"

—

"'Washington, D. C., Dec. 25, 1861.
"'Mrs. Gertrude Flowers.
"'Madam:

"'Inclosed are five hundred dollars in sterling bills, for yourself and daughter, sent in acknowl-

edgment of my gratitude for the kindness of your son, in aiding to save my dearest friend's life at the battle of Manassas,
"'Respectfully,
"'Silas Worthington.'"

Miss H——: "What has Jesse written you in relation to this matter?"

Mrs. F——: "Never a word. We have written to him about it since these letters were received. He answered that he aided in caring for the wounded nearly all night after the battle at Stone Bridge."

Miss H——: "Did he mention any other persons by whom he was assisted in that work?"

Mrs. F——: "Oh, yes!—Garland Cloud."

Miss H——: "Then I can probably solve this mystery. Doctor Chamberlain, when he was at home, told us about a Lieut. Pleasington, of the Northern army, who was brought off the field to him in a very critical condition by young Cloud and a companion; and that he had never before witnessed such intense gratitude as this young officer had manifested to those young men while they were with him, and in relation to them after they were gone. The doctor took a great fancy to this young foeman, and interested himself in having him paroled and sent home. The parties sending you these tokens of gratitude are, undoubtedly friends of that young man; perhaps the young lady is more than a friend. However, be this as it may, here is unmistakable evidence of a gratitude far beyond anything I have ever heard or read."

Mrs. F——: "That is, in all probability, the true explanation, and all that I shall doubtless ever obtain. Jesse has thought this incident too unimportant even to mention it. But look what wonderful results that little seed of kindness, cast out by hazard upon the wild waste of human appreciation—from which so little gratitude ever springs—by striking a moist, rich spot in the arid sterile desert, has produced for his lonely, humble little home. Such results the poor, poor boy could not have attained by the sweat of his brow and the labor of his hands in two long and tedious years."

Miss H——: "Now, Mrs. Flowers, please do

for favor to tell me how you have become proficient in the making of these nice butters, jellies, preserves, wines and other things. We are ignorant of the secrets of this fine art, much as we have studied and practiced it."

Mrs. F——: "I learned it from my husband, my father, and from original formulas in old French books which I have. Mr. or Gen. Flowers, my father-in-law, was a great utilizer of fruits and grapes, and was a perfect master of the art.

"He sprung from a noble French family, served under La Fayette in the Revolutionary War, and was a general in the war of 1812-14. After we were married, his son and I, we spent considerable time with the old gentleman. Although he was very old and feeble, he prided himself upon personally superintending the productions of his orchards and vineyards; and took special pains to initiate me in the secrets of the art, which he said might some day be serviceable to me, should the dark wing of misfortune spread its unfriendly shadow over my head. He spoke thus in a serious tone, and always with visible emotion. Prophetic words! But dear, devoted old man, he had passed serenely over the deep waters of the dark river—he did not stay to endure the torture of seeing them fulfilled. Miss Harman, you will excuse my weakness—the tears will come."

Miss H——: "Weep, my poor sister, weep! Those are sacred drops—the tears of gratitude and devotion. Better, far better, for other unfeeling, unthinking hearts, were their eyes oftener dimmed by the same moisture. My unworthy heart bleeds for you. It seems that I have gained the experience and knowledge of an age in the one little hour that it has been my good fortune to be under your roof.

"I fear the task will be too great, the sacrifice more than you ought to make, to complete your narrative, which I perceive is bitterly painful."

Mrs. F——: "No, Miss Harman I will complete it. It may contain a lesson worth even your consideration. I am stronger now. I will not break down. Dinner is over, and if you are ready to listen, I will proceed."

Miss H——: "I am very, very anxious to hear it. I shall listen with deep interest and sympathy."

Mrs. F——: "I have already sufficiently detailed the history of my father-in-law. I will but add that he had accumulated quite a fortune; that he had an only son, and no other blood kinsman in America. This son, Jesse, was a graduate of West Point, and also has been trained by a large old New York firm for a merchant.

"On the breaking out of the Mexican War he joined the army, and filled an important office with bravery and distinction throughout the entire conflict.

"I was left an orphan when two years old; the yellow fever carried away my parents in one day. I was their only child, and an heiress to an immense estate in Louisiana. I was raised and educated with great care by my grandfather, who died when I was still young. He left me another fortune.

"After this I went to New Orleans to live with the family of a dear friend of grandfather's. I met Col. Flowers there, on his way home from Mexico. It was a case of mutual love at first sight, resulting, young as I was, in a speedy marriage.

"For two years we divided our time about equally between my Southern estates, where we spent the winter, and his father's Northern home, where we passed the summer. At the end of this time the old gentleman died.

"Then we sold both estates, and made our home in New York, where he entered the wholesale trade with two old merchants, or rather men who had spent their days in that business, although they were not then very old. Their names were Ira Atkinson, and Adam Stringfellow, and that of the firm, Atkinson, Flowers & Co. With the trade and experience these two men already possessed, added to the large amount of money which Col. Flowers carried into the firm, the business soon grew to prodigious proportions, unsurpassed by any other house in the same line.

"The second year we were in New York my health failed, and we decided that it was best I should go to the Sulphur Springs, just beyond Elk Mountain.

"On our journey by rail, I became greatly

exhausted; but we proceeded at once in a carriage. When we arrived at this very cabin, I could go no farther. Col. Flowers called at the cabin. I was taken in without one moment's hesitation—in fact the place was virtually abandoned to us; although the good man, Milton Land, and Emma, his wife, remained to wait on us. She cared for little Jesse, and nursed me like a mother. I never can forget that angelic face bending over me, nor her tender, sympathetic voice, which then sounded sweeter and more melodious to my ear than the most rapturous music I had ever heard.

"The tenth morning I was much better. I thought then the water from that grand old spring surpassed the most delicate nectars in the world; and that the soft, ripe peaches and cream brought forth from out that stone spring house, excelled all the dainties I had ever tasted.

"That evening I was able to continue the journey.

"Those people would neither accept one cent of compensation nor receive any sort of present from our hands; and they actually manifested strong indignation when we endeavored to insist. The Colonel took their address; and we parted with the young couple, who were then only a short time married.

"In about four months my health was perfectly restored, and we were back at home in New York. I then sent Mr. and Mrs. Land some presents, and wrote them such a letter that they could not refuse to accept them. From that time I wrote to the good little woman every month. I called her the *Angel of the mountain* and she was worthy of the name.

"Col. Flowers was happy, and so was I; more on his account, however, than from any special fondness I cherished for the grand and brilliant life which I was leading in the city; because there was in it and its intoxicating whirls, for me at least, not one scintilla of true enjoyment, except that found in the quietude of my own home.

"I can never forget one queen of fashion, Mrs. Mountjoy, who called on me at times, and appeared very fond of me. Her beauty was wonderful, and her pride and her ambition

knew no bounds. In society her will was law, her rule despotic.

"One fine morning in July, Saturday, Col. Flowers and I went to the Sea Beach. His spirits were buoyant. He was happiness and contentment personified. He loved the sea—and from a child had sported at will on its billows. This morning there was a fine breeze, and his heart was set on having a sail. As the sea had always made me sick in very calm weather, whenever I had been on it, even my going with him was not mentioned.

"When he was ready, there chanced to be no acquaintance near by for him to invite as a companion, and he set out alone, gay and joyous as ever the impulsive Frenchman enters upon any amusement or pleasure which he intensely relishes.

"I watched him from my window at the hotel, and we exchanged signals by waving our white handkerchiefs as the little boat sped on its way before the fair and stiffening breeze, until it appeared a mere solitary speck on the wide waste of waters with which it was surrounded.

"My babe, little Rose, attracted my attention for a moment. Quickly my longing eyes turned back to rest again upon their fond object, but in vain: it was nowhere to be seen. Like a pall of despair, the mist of spray had woven a thick and purple curtain, that fell across the surface of the deep, between me and the solitary figure upon that grand yet cruel ocean, which I eagerly strained my eyes to see once more.

"It was as though I was lost in darkness, gazing on and on into the *shadows*, striving to catch one guiding star of light—a light that will bless my pathway, leading me to safety—a light that I see not, that will not break across my dreary way. And like a child, I cry out, frightened, and knowing not what I fear.

"The little phosphorescent waves glowed against that dark, hazy back-ground of spray with a brilliancy, lovelier than any jewel that ever gleamed on a monarch's brow.

"Never can I forget the sensation of loneliness which in that moment crept over, and oppressed me. Great drops of cold perspiration stood upon my brow. My blood seemed to be curdling in its veins. But once since have I experienced an ordeal like this: that was the morning when Jesse disappeared round the curve of the road up yonder, on his way to the army; then I felt the same sensation of hopeless loneliness.

"For hours I gazed out on that watery solitude. Oh, those terrible hours! In them I lived ages of mortal, agonizing anguish.

"Gradually the sky away out at sea became overcast and lowering. Within twenty minutes after I first noticed this, a white squall was sweeping over the face of the placid deep, and lashing its tranquil waters into wild and boisterous waves. These came with deafening roars, breaking upon the beach; each cruel sound striking my wretched heart as the pitiless vibrations of the death bell, tolling out the sad dirges of some departed spirit.

"When the storm had spent its fury, and the sun appeared again on high, bright and joyous as if there were no woes in the world, and no hearts to break, the boat was found on the beach, not more than two hundred yards from the point from which it had sailed in the morning. And one hour later—oh, cruel fate! pitiless destiny!—the body of my poor husband was found a mile away, white and cold, in the icy embrace of death.

"I was a lonely widow, without, as far as I knew, one near relative of either my husband's or my own in the world.

"I was delirious with grief. I cannot recall anything distinctly, until the next day I awoke to consciousness, in bed, in my own room. Mrs. Mountjoy was by my side nearly all the time until a late hour that night; and came home with me from the funeral the next day, remaining then also until late.

"On Tuesday, the day after the funeral, I received numerous calls and tokens of condolence. On Wednesday morning it was formally announced that Atkinson, Flowers & Co. had suspended; that the late Mr. Flowers, as it had transpired, had been engaged in extensive speculations without the knowledge of the other members of his firm, which was found to be hopelessly involved. And with this announce-

ment was coupled insinuations too contemptible to utter.

"The next condolence I received was a visit from an officer, accompanied by Mr. Stringfellow, to seize the house and property.

"I was coldly informed by Mr. Stringfellow that I would be a beggar in the streets, and that I must vacate the premises within the space of thirty days. A man was left in charge of the property. They then deprived me of many rights, and a legal allowance that I did not know I was entitled to receive; but I was too wretched and helpless to seek counsel.

"At once my former flattering friends abandoned me; not one of them came to my aid: did not even deign to recognize me on the street when I went out a few days after; the servants were insolent; and some poor persons to whom I had been kind and liberal, treated me with marked disrespect.

"One day Mrs. Mountjoy's carriage passed me on the street. Messrs. Atkinson and Stringfellow occupied seats with her in it, and were as jovial, and apparently as happy, as possible.—They compromised at twenty-five cents on the dollar.

"My greatest terror was where to go and what to do, and about my sweet, innocent little babes, all unconscious of that hopeless despair and grief wrenching the heart-strings of their poor, helpless, friendless mother. My tender darlings! what would become of them? These were the questions always and ever ringing in my ears, and driving me mad, because they were truly unanswerable.

"I realized that I must descend to a low and humble sphere of life. But how? What could I do? I was as helpless as a little child, and more ignorant of the world below the high sphere where I had always breathed the air of boundless independence.

"I went out into the quarters of the city occupied by the middle classes, but gained little information and met no encouragement.

"The next day I went into the laboring-man's and the tenement quarters. Oh, God! what sickening, soul-moving scenes there met my eyes—what sounds grated with harsh and discordant cries upon my ears! Before I would have gone into that region of misery, my babes might have famished with hunger on my breast; and then I should have waited with unmoved composure for the summons of the grim messenger.

"As I was hastening to leave this domain of wretchedness, disgusted, faint and despairing, I came suddenly to a neat dress-making establishment on the ground-floor. Impulsively I rushed in and asked for the lady in charge. A kind, polite, pale and delicate woman stepped forward, and greeted me. I drew her aside, and told her briefly my situation, and implored her to grant me some advice. She informed me that her duties were such that it would be impossible for her to do so then, but that she would take my address, and call on me with pleasure that evening.

"As I went slowly and sadly back to what had only a few days before been my peaceful and happy home, I would have rejoiced to know that my babes were dead. But when I returned to them, their rosy cheeks, their bright eyes, and their innocent childish laugh fanned to a glowing flame a mother's love. I then and there vowed, with one hand on the head of each little innocent, that night, in concert with the woman who had promised to aid me, to devise some plan to save them, and follow it through weal ·or woe, or until it had left me in the grave.

"The little woman was prompt. She said in substance:

"'City life and intrigues are virtually unknown to you. You have learned more from the bitterness of one little week than in all the years of your life. May God spare you from knowing more from anything nearer the actual experience, than what I shall relate to you to-night.

"'In poverty, abject dependence on your own exertions, your beauty will put every hour of your weary, anxious young life into an unmitigated torment, from which there is neither escape nor redemption.

"'I was left a widow when about your age, and suddenly reduced from comfort and plenty to poverty and want. I was what the world terms passably fair, but did not approach within many degrees of your beauty.

"'I sought employment of prominent firms who employed lady help. In three instances in one day I was shown into the private office, and informed that I could have work, but times were dull and wages low; and then in each case, those dignified gentlemen (?) told me that if I chose to do so, I could have plenty of money and the luxuries of a lady's home. Two or three others were too busy; but if I would call that night at their residences they had no doubt but that satisfactory terms could be arranged.

"'I had a terrible experience, and have gone to bed many a time hungry and cold. Thank God I had no children, or I do not know what would have become of me: there is nothing in this world so strong as a mother's love. I preserved my soul, and, by constant hard work, am now able to keep comfortable.

"'The stories of some of those poor women in my shop, the continual ordeals through which they are now passing, would make your heart ache.

"Beauty is the greatest misfortune a poor woman, forced into the midst of the city's turmoil, can inherit.

"'Now for my advice. Fly, by all means fly, from this modern Babylon. Do not stop to look back. The farther into the country, and the deeper and more remote the seclusion, the better for you. Sell whatever you cannot conveniently carry. Act, act. Do not waste one needless day. If you know any one in such a locality as I have mentioned, so much the better. But if you would save yourself and babes, fly from the impending doom of inevitable destruction.'

"Fly! fly! was ringing in my ears all through that night. Before the dawn of day I had completed a letter to 'The Angel of the Mountain.'

"Eight days—eight ages of suspense—would elapse before I could hope to see an answer. But there was much to be done. It was a terrible experience, selling my little surplus trinkets at one-tenth their value.

"I had some diamonds and pearls that had been my mother's. These I prized more than all my former wealth. I thought I could not part with them. But I found it impossible to realize sufficient money to satisfy half the probable demand and keep them. I gazed first at them, then at my little babes. To my eyes, they were jewels far brighter and more precious than all the soulless gems in the world. I turned from them again to those dear mementoes of my angelic mother, and bathed them in tears of an affectionate but eternal farewell.

"Fifteen days after the date of my letter, I was installed in this cabin, as you now see me; and Milton Land was on his way to Illinois with 'The Angel of the Mountain.'

"Ever since then I have maintained an irregular correspondence with her. Up to the commencement of the war they were prospering. The last letter she wrote informed me that Milton had joined the Northern army.

"Since my arrival here, you know the story.

"All the years which I have passed here, full of trials, privations and hardships as most of them have been, have not seemed longer, nor one thousandth part as terrible, as the same number of trying, woeful days which I spent in New York, writhing in the living death-throes of cruel wretchedness.

"Here I have found friends, true, devoted, unselfish friends, with rough exteriors and unpolished speech, but oh! what hearts—so noble, so tender, so pure!"

Miss H——: "Oh, Mrs. Flowers! my unfortunate sister, thrice tried in the ordeal of the fiery crucible and come forth the emblem of truth and purity, permit me, my poor friend, in the name of all that is pure and womanly, to embrace you; and to baptize you with my tears, which sympathy with your pathetic sorrows cannot but bring to my eyes; and to christen you, henceforth, 'The Angel of the Mountain!'

"And you, too, little Rosa, precious flower of your mountain-dale, pure as yonder drifted snow so deeply bleached in the northern wind. Dear little girl, let me press you to my heart and call you my own, my little sister. From this day I am your sister and your mother's sister-friend, and as such shall you find my devotion and my love; and you will be often, often my companions in my own circle and I in yours.

"My dear mother has been long sleeping in the silent church-yard; a sister's love and a sister's kiss I have never known.

"I have looked forward to the conclusion of my years at college with longing fondness, as a happy period of re-union with my only brother, to whom I was almost a stranger.

"Just as this dream was about to be finally realized, this cruel war severed us more widely and hopelessly than before, as it parted you and your heroic little Jesse, and so many other loving hearts all over this unhappy land.

"But for the unselfish devotion of a noble child of the mountains, I would have no brother to-day. And quite a just resentment of his unthoughtful, haughty unkindness shown to this mountain-boy, on various occasions, would have caused almost every one to remain aloof. But not so with this noble comrade. When my poor brother had been abandoned by his own class, intimate associates, to his fate, this man, from whom he could hope for nothing, came forward with the tenderness of a brother, to his rescue. That act leveled for ever all barriers between our family and the mountain people. Since its knowledge reached me, I have longed to know more of them, and to manifest in some substantial manner my gratitude. The work in which I am engaged afforded the opportunity I so much desired. Eagerly I embraced it. Already, even before the harvest, I am reaping a rich reward; the blessings of the dying defenders, whose days of battle are over, and the prayers of the loved ones they leave mourning, yet not bereft of human consolation, follow me, and aid me in my mission. Now, in this moment of hallowed associations and sacred remembrances, I solemnly vow to devote my life, be its years many or few, be its days passed in the sunshine of peace or in the shadows of sorrow, to those noble hearts who have given their all for the sake of the cause I honor and the land I love."

Again must the curtain go down to obscure this scene of devotion, faith, purity and love. After the clash of arms has ceased to echo, and the smoke of battle has been dispelled, and the withered violet once more opens its blue eyes to the spring-time sun, we will see again "The Angel of the Mountain."

————

CHAPTER XX.

UNCLE JAKE AND THE FAIRIES.

"For I am getting old and feeble, I'll never work no
more—
I'll ne'er hoe the corn fields o'er again;
Yet bright angels they'll watch o'er me as I lay me
down to sleep.
In my little old log-cabin, in the lane."
—LOG CABIN.

UNCLE JAKE, whose ebon face we have met
before, was a veritable old Virginia log-cabin
darkey. He had been a character in his little
day. He could draw more and better music out
of his old banjo than any other person on the
Virginia banks of the Potomac. And sing—
"Land alive," as the old colored aunties used to
say, the most stoical went into raptures if they
once heard Uncle Jake's sonorous voice when it
was just a trifle oiled with old peach-and-honey,
and he had fully unbent himself and come down
to his work; his instrument vibrating with one
incessant roll of varied, gently rolling and bursting swells of harmonious melody, with his vocal accompaniments flowing in stirring strains, a
deep, full current of his most wondrous incan-
tations.

"The Little Old Log-Cabin" was his special
favorite; and he was at the *acme* of his glory
when he held an admiring crowd applauding with
zeal, or spell-bound with his magical rendering
of this most pathetic song of the olden time.

With the young lady members of the secret
information society and underground communication service, described in the chapter "Beyond
the Outposts," Uncle Jake, besides being an
unrivaled favorite in consequence of the musical
treats which he had always furnished them
since their earliest remembrance, and of his many
other mirth-provoking accomplishments was,
because of his unswerving fidelity to the friends
of his tender years, his mature manhood, and his
declining age, in their dark hour of trial and of
danger, in very many other respects utterly
indispensable.

On account of the many strange and mysterious
signals adopted between neighboring houses—
often extending in one unbroken circle to several

settlements or neighborhoods and on up into
even Alexandria itself; because of the mystic signs
among themselves when they were assembled;
and furthermore, in consequence of the peculiar
masquerade balls given as a concession, to all
ostensible appearance, to some Federal officers
who were invited, and always attended,—Uncle
Jake styled these young ladies "the Fairies."

These balls, in reality, were simply ruses skillfully planned by the young ladies to hold all important business meetings, and see some of
their relatives and friends from the Confederate
army. These appeared at the balls in ladies costumes, without arousing the suspicions of the
Northern troops in the vicinity.

To similar organizations in some form, perhaps differing very widely from this particular
one, yet objectively the same, in every part of
the border districts of the Southern States, may
justly be attributed the reasons why it was so
nearly impossible for the National troops to
attempt any move without their opponents being
immediately apprised of the fact and of its
nature. On the other hand, it clearly explains
the reason why the Confederate commanders
could keep their movements concealed from
their opponents behind a cloud of impenetrable
mystery.

Whenever there was a programme for a ball
arranged on the afternoon preceding the designated evening, hours before the time appointed for the Federal officers to appear the
young ladies, accompanied by any contraband
male friends who were to participate in the
festivities, decked in their strange feminine dis-
guises, and heavily veiled, assembled with Uncle
Jake at the designated place of rendezvous.

The only Federal officers invited on these
occasions were West-Pointers of undoubted
repute as gentlemanly disciplinarians and warriors, prosecuting their inhuman profession on
strictly civilized principles. They were in no
danger whatever of becoming victims to snares
similar to those in which we have already seen
some of their volunteer brother officers en-
trapped. So delicately deferential were these
officers toward the peculiar and sensitive position of those with whom they were to enjoy the

diverting pleasures of an evening, that, rather than take the chances of their obnoxious uniforms marring in any degree the pleasures of the hour, they always appeared in full evening costumes. They were, therefore, when masked, difficult to distinguish from the non-combatants of the community, a few of whom were sometimes present, acting an indifferent part in the festival phase of the performance.

Owing to a large portion of their duties being the patrolling of the country, and the capturing of all prowlers or improper absentees from their command, whether they were officers or enlisted men of the Northern army, two of our friends had become quite extensive favorites, as enemies, among the citizens. Those officers did their work so vigorously and effectively that the citizens were relieved from innumerable annoyances and losses. To stragglers, they soon became a greater terror than the rebel scouts, because even the shelter of the guns on Arlington Heights was not a protection to which they could fly with defiant impunity from pressing danger of capture, and find secure immunity from arrest, as they often could easily do if menaced by hostile pursuers. Those indefatigable officers and their followers did not fear the frowning battlements of Arlington. They were no less familiar personages than Maj. Lawrence Pleasington, and Lieut. Orlando Oglethrop. They were, as a matter of course, always invited, and, unless their duties rendered it absolutely impossible, were present as participants in these unique and mystical festivities.

At this time, about a fortnight since, we saw Maj. Pleasington and his antagonist, Cloud, meet and part, and heard Oglethrop, amid the enchantments of Mountjoy House, depicting the woes of poor Col. Worthington in the wintry midnight and the snow of the wilderness-solitude, there is a masquerade-ball on the eve of transpiring at an old Virginia mansion, not more than a dozen rods from where Pleasington and Cloud last parted. It is the same mansion where Cloud captured the madly-infatuated officer who was so blindly in love with the young lady of the house.

This young lady was betrothed to the young master of Uncle Jake's home; hence the old man regarded her with an affection approaching his reverence for her affianced husband, a dashing, daring cavalry officer in the Confederate service, who had had several severe encounters with Pleasington and Oglethrop and their men, on disputed belts of ground up at the dead-line points, between the two extreme out-posts; in these several men had gone down on both sides.

After the young ladies, their companions, and Uncle Jake had assembled, the masks, together with all restraints, were thrown off. They united usually in the dining-hall, or some other private room. Whatever business they had to transact was quickly dispatched. Then the intervening hours before the masqueraders were expected to appear, were passed in pleasures of their own devising.

Uncle Jake, with his banjo, was called into requisition. First he played and sang some wild and uproarious plantation songs. These were followed by strains more plaintive and wild; this again with music of melting pathos and sorrowful melancholy. His acting was simply grand; unsurpassed not even by Booth's Richelieu nor Jefferson's Rip Van Winkle. From uncontrollable, hysterical laughter he transformed his audience to tears of tenderest compassion. Then he seemed happy; and would regale them with stories and mimic representations, sometimes of imaginary, but oftener of real, scenes which he had witnessed. The more he was plied with interrogatives, and the more they savored of sarcasm and skepticism, the better was the old man pleased.

On this particular evening and at this specified place, where we will doubtless be spectators for a time, there are present two Confederate officers, and but eight of the ten ladies, listed in the programme, the missing ones having resigned their places in favor of the two officers to whom we have just referred. Uncle Jake has just closed his musical and vocal prelude, set his banjo down, and heaved a deep-drawn sigh, his large white eyes rolling in their sockets from the features of one to another of his patrons, with profound and searching scrutiny.

Evidently, the result is satisfactory in the high-

UNCLE JAKE AND THE FAIRIES.

"HIS INSTRUMENT VIBRATING WITH ONE INCESSANT ROLL OF VARIED, GENTLY-ROLLING AND BURSTING SWELLS OF HARMONIOUS MELODY."—See page 71.

est degree. Complacently the old man folds his arms and awaits an indication as to what scene he is desired next to present. For a few moments the silence of the tomb pervades the apartment. The last song rendered was a memorial ballad to Napoleon Bonaparte, a few closing lines of which ran thus:

"No more she'll behold him, at Cloud in great splendor;
No more he'll appear, like the noble Alexander.
Louisa may mourn for her husband departed,
Like a dove that's forlorn, or one that's broken-hearted.
She may sit down and think of the battles he has been in,
As she sighs for his bones on the rock of Saint Helen."

The mournful air and sadly tremulous cadences of Uncle Jake's voice, together with the affecting tenderness and touching sentiments breathed throughout this lengthy ballad, have made a general and deep impression.

But the silence is, however, at length broken.

FIRST OFFICER: "Well, Jake, old imp of darkness, what is the news down here in this mystic region, where Cupid, the Yank patrols, and the rebel scouts hold alternately such high carnivals, and get mingled together sometimes in such unpleasant and heterogeneous confusion? Now, out with the truth, old man. We can learn nothing up in the command. The scouts, when we get to see one, once in a little age, are mum as the Egyptian mummies. And these pretty little coquettes, the sweet innocents, they are as ignorant as Comanche papooses on the plains. Come, now, you know all about it."

UNCLE JAKE: "Fore de Lawd, mas' Clem, dis chile bin done brok he nec purty ni 'bout forty lebbun times trian to cotch dat crittur, de nuse; but golly, he de wilest colt ebber I tri to get de bridel on too, cepten my name done an eny mo Ante Jake. Bress ore sole hunny dis ole niggur mo in de dark dan all ob ye togedur. Ders mo tawken on de fingurs and wid hankchurs an all sots fol da rol da, an no body nebber seed an he all Chuctow to ole Jake shure as de Lawd libs."

SECOND OFFICER: "How about those two Yanks, Pleasington and Oglethrop, who patrol around here, and that scout Cloud? Do you know them, Jake?"

UNCLE JAKE: "Lausy mussy; dat I do. Dey iz de two bess Yanks 'roun' dese diggins. Dey keeps de thebbun tras' clend outin and iz peerlite to ebbery body, an doan kum cortin de gals whoze sheetharts deyz trian ter kill. An uze axin me bout dat ung Cloud. Heze zactly like de Iershmun's fle. When uze doan got yor fingur onto he, den he been skip outin da', kerflumix."

FIRST OFFICER.: "But Cloud is doing nothing but flirt with the girls, Jake, is he? He has quit catching Yankees lately."

UNCLE JAKE: Darze whar uze fuled. He nebbur gwine inside a house ceptin to cotch a Yank. Heze too sharp for dat—too frade gotten traped. An las nite he cotch a offacur dats bin boddurin ung missus dis long time. Peers dat chap allurs nowed when de patrols gwine sum udder way, kase dey nebbur cotch him. Now las nite he war dar, Missus, plain de piana. Ant Hana war roun 'bout de parlur. Jake war in de kichun, an dis ni jiste what she cum back dar tellin me, an de ole gal war puty ni whit as a shete. 'Jake' she sed, 'all at onct Missus, stop plain an say Hist—de rebbuls—hide 'hind de piana, Majur. Den bout a minit mo ung Cloud war in de parlur, tawken crose to missus; kusin her harbburin Yanks, an she nien it jist like a little lade, when Cloud finde de Majur, an order him out, an tell Missus he gwine to member dat and settle wid her anudder time, an porh Missus 'gun crian, an Cloud he hurry off wid de Majur, an I jist lafe at Hana."

SECOND OFFICER: "The Yanks want to catch Cloud. Some fine day he will find that you have sold him. He is a big fool to trust you as he does. I would not."

UNCLE JAKE: "Heze bettur juge humon natur dan u, dat aur de splanin queshum ob all dis."

MISS CORNELIA: [Coming excitedly to the door] "Hist! Pleasington and Oglethrop are in the front parlor and their patrols out in the lane. Be quiet. There is no danger. They are here to meet Cloud under a truce, and expect him directly."

FIRST OFFICER: "Ah! Jim, let us eavesdrop them from the back parlor. Now learn we can some of these mysteries."

CLOUD: [Entering front parlor] "Maj. Pleasington, I am here in response to your note requesting an interview."

MAJ. P——: "Yes, Mr. Cloud. But first allow

me to introduce Lieut. Oglethrop, who was anxious to see you."

CLOUD: "Ah Lieutenant, I have heard of you. The chances are rather more than even that we may meet a little more unpleasantly one of these days. I suppose you want to be able to recognize me, in that event—is it not so?"

LIEUT.—— O: "If you are going to handle me proportionately as roughly as you handled my three men that day, I would like to shun rather than meet you."

CLOUD: "Well Major, your business?"

MAJ. P.: "Maj. Eugene Lovelace, a staff officer, started from Alexandria, late last evening, for a ride in the direction of Annendale, as he frequently starts, and failed to return. Somehow a report has reached head-quarters to-day that he was shot, or rather that one of your scouts told some colored people that he had shot an officer about dusk last night on that road, and that his horse ran away into the woods with him. Gen. M—— has requested me to try and discover the particulars, and also learn, as near as possible, the locality."

CLOUD: "Present my compliments to Gen. M——, with the information that Maj. Lovelace is now on his way to Richmond, and was sound and well this morning; and that he was captured miles from the road which you have just named."

MAJ. P——: "Did you capture him, Mr. Cloud, and if so, the particulars if you please, that I may render them in my report?"

CLOUD: "These are delicate points Major, which generosity to the unfortunate captive force me to decline to furnish. For particulars, you will certainly be under the necessity of waiting until the Major has an opportunity of supplying them himself. I have not reported the circumstances to my own commanders; decidedly, then, I cannot entertain the idea of furnishing them to you."

MAJ. P——: "I see my mistake and withdraw the question. Now tell me about little Flowers. How is he?"

CLOUD: "Well, and in high spirits. He has just heard from home. His family has lately received a handsome sum of money from a friend of yours, whom I will not name. Also

his mother and sister and mine have received magnificent presents of cloaks, dress-goods, etc., with the sweetest little letters, full of gratitude to the sons and brothers who saved the life of the writer's *nearest* and *dearest* friend, at the battle of Stone Bridge. This friend, very delicately, mark you, Major, *is not named*. But we boys happen to know that it is to Maj. Lawrence Pleasington, and to no other person, that reference is made. And to those letters was the superscription of the sweetest little name—the most precious little name. Effie Edelstein—that *Edelstein*, Major, don't it translate *precious stone or jewel?*

"There, now, Major, don't blush so. I told you this merely to dispel any shades of doubt which might creep or be forced into your mind about her fidelity and devotion. Better tell her, Major, that this proof is overwhelming; and that if she undertakes to reward all the Confederates who may, or would save your life under similar circumstances, she is likely to be very poor at the close of the war. That is all."

LIEUT. O——: "There, now, Pleasington, is proof that all the social strategy of New York can never prevail on that girl to discard you in favor of any man living, while you are above the sod.

"Mr. Cloud, that is worth a small mint to him. He has the blues fearfully, sometimes, because of the powerful influence working against him while he is down here in the cold winter, near at any time to the valley and shadow of death. But I heard Uncle Jake's banjo and voice as we come up the lane. Would you not like to her him, Mr. Could?"

CLOUD: "Yes, one song. I have not time for any more."

LIEUT. O——: "I will go to the door, ring the bell, and send for him."

He suits the action to the words, and Miss Earl responds.

MISS CORNELIA: "What do you wish, Lieutenant?"

LIEUT. O——: "Uncle Jake, with his banjo, Miss Earl, if you please."

She hastens away and Jake enters the parlor.

UNCLE JAKE: "Ebnin to uze, gentilmans. Ize kum ter see wut uze want wid dis ole niggur."

PLEASINGTON and OGLETHROP: "A song: 'Log Cabin,' Jake."

CLOUD: "And this, then, is the old reprobate who is all the time giving you people information to get us scouts captured. It is a good thing I am under a truce, and Jake under the protection of his friends, or he would very soon be on his way to Richmond."

MAJ. P——: "Oh, our people have great confidence in Jake, and trust him any where he chooses to go; but as to his information, I am beginning to set but little value upon it, as we have never yet captured a man on it. I think you can deceive Jake easier than our troops."

CLOUD: "His will is better than his information. You don't want to get out of hailing distance of your friends here, old man. Do you understand? But the song—'Log Cabin.'"

UNCLE JAKE: "Yes, massa. Ize berry furd."

Jake immediately launches forth in his song; and the first verse is rendered with thrilling impressiveness until he strikes the lines:

"But now ebbery ding iz changed, de darkies am all
gone—
He nebbur h'are dem boin in the fields again—
An Ibe nuffln left me now but dat little dog ob mine,
In my little ole log cabin in de lane.
Not many months ago aroun' my cabin door,
De darkies were happe den I no,
Dey sang an dance all nite as I play my ole banjo,
But, alas! dey kan nebber do so any mo—
Oh! my chimne's tumbling down, de stars am peepin
al' roun',
An de time's soon comin' when I must go,
But brito angels dey will lede me to dat far-off happe
lan',
Whar Ize to mete old Massa an' Missus once mo'."

Then the old man rose to sublime and matchless grandeur. His frame swayed and heaved with powerful emotion; his eyes rolled; turned heavenward; then closed, while the twitching pupils were steadily raised by the great sluices of big tear-drops which poured from them in torrents. His voice rose and fell in tremulous waves, from the wildest notes of woeful distress, in the first dread moments of its birth down to the low, faint, pitiful moans of despair after the last flickering-ray of hope has vanished. And his instrumental performance—it mocks the power of words; a description of it is impossible. In every respect and particular, it harmonized in strict ac-

cordance with the gestures, the emotions, and the tones of the voice, of its skillfully artistic master. He would disengage one hand; point away in the direction of the fields; his cabin; the graveyard, or heaven. While in this position, the instrument would turn bottom upwards, as if by some magical influence which it was beyond the cunning of spectators ever to detect. Thus it would remain for a moment, and then turn back in the same mysterious way, while the unbroken current of the music continued to flow in the same rapturous strains, without missing the proper measure of time by so much as the thousandth part of a second, or failing in even one note to breathe in pure, articulate perfection.

The three auditors had risen, and were standing with folded arms and pale faces, the hot tears streaming down their cheeks, when the echoes died away in the grand old mansion, where, in days that are dead, often, often had resounded the voice of Washington. Here were three soldiers weeping over a negro song, rendered by a simple old darkey of the by-gone time; men whose eyes would flash defiant fire in the face of mortal danger.

You might smile with disdainful incredulity, until you had once heard the performance as we have; then you, too, with hearts thrilled by the mournful melody, would find your lips quivering and your eyes dim.

A silent pressure of the hands among the soldiers, and Uncle Jake said the farewells; the former left the house, mounted their horses, separated, and rode rapidly away without uttering a word.

———

Some well-known historical illustrations, more romantic still than the scenes portrayed of the regular characters in this plot, might frequently be advanced, with the real names of the parties, without the least disrespect to propriety. One case in point is too prominent and too good to be ignored. It constitutes such overwhelming testimony in support of features of this work which might be viewed with skepticism that we cannot resist the temptation to produce it undisguised.

Oakland, Maryland, 2,800 feet above the sea-level, is on the Baltimore and Ohio Railroad. Before this railroad was built, that sequestered spot was buried deep in a primeval forest which stretched its prodigious length far along the border line between Maryland and Virginia. This spot, Oakland, was a famous and charming mountain resort before the war. It then consisted of the few cabins, cottages, a church and an express office about a well-ordered house, called the Glades Hotel.

A Virginia family by the name of Dailey came to Oakland the year before the war, to spend the summer. The head of the family was a genuine specimen of the rural Virginia gentleman of that by-gone time—courteous, jovial, hospitable to a fault; the mother, a queenly lady and amiable housewife, devoted to her son and two daughters, was envied by many tourists.

The day came that made a sensation for the mountain-crowning Oakland: the hotel was to change hands; there was to be a sale by auction. At the appointed hour Mr. Dailey sauntered in merely to gratify curiosity. When he was seated with his family at the dinner-table, he gave his wife a great shock by saying, "Ma, I've bought the hotel over yonder!" The difficulty of "keeping a hotel" was probably not as profoundly impressed on the understanding of Mr. Dailey at that time as it is now generally appreciated. However, he bravely undertook the task, and succeeded admirably in giving satisfaction to all whom he entertained.

His family negroes were brought to supply the hotel with its requisite corps of servants. In almost all bodies of plantation or family slaves in the South, and more especially in Virginia, there was one noted character. This was Uncle Jake, at the Fairchild homestead. In Mr. Dailey's numerous family of colored people this important personage was Aunt Cynthy, a tall yellow woman. She had been the foster nurse of Mars Jim, a young man then in his teens.

Naturally, therefore, Aunt Cynthy was installed as the presiding genius of the kitchen—the queen of the culinary department of the hotel; and she ruled with a despotism that often caused the troop of colored waiters to rush with suspicious precipitation from her domain back into the dining-room when any of them had delivered her an unwelcome order. But this was on her bad days only, some two or three of which occasionally came together. Then the mistress deemed it most wise to absent herself from the kitchen, when she confessed herself in mortal terror of her own indulged slave. At these times it was recognized that no one but Mars Jim, her idol, could do anything with Aunt Cynthy. This old woman would make a strong character in a story of real life, with its plot located chiefly at Oakland.

But the central figure of this family picture, and the admirable heroine of romantic vicissitudes, was the oldest daughter, Miss Mary Dailey. To a lithe, elastic, beautifully symmetrical figure, slightly under the medium size, a bright face full of animation, deep blue eyes, and light brown locks, slightly curling, she added a brilliant charm of ready wit. She was always good-natured, and manifested a generous impulse of heart that made her an unrivaled favorite at Oakland.

When the war came, with its scenes of horror and tales of woe, it was by the aid of those exceptional qualities that she was enabled to play well a very difficult rôle in those times of trouble, danger and distress. Her family and herself were ardently heart and soul, in all their sympathies and affiliations with the South, while the location of Mr. Dailey's property and its surroundings constantly exposed it and his near and dear ones to the "two unequal fires" of the blue boys and the grey. There is little room to doubt but that, by her tact and personal popularity Mary Dailey, young as she was, did much to save her family and neighbors from the loss and suffering which would have become their lot as the inevitable consequences of their well-known, notorious and undissembled Southern proclivities.

We have before us now a clipping from an ancient newspaper, published before the war, aptly illustrating the ready-wit of this fairy enchantress. This article went the rounds of the press at that time. Miss Dailey was then in her teens, and a school-girl. President Buchanan was on his way to Wheeling, and stopped for some usual delay at Oakland Station, where many persons were presented to him, each of whom he asked from what State he or she hailed. At last the turn of little Mary Dailey came to be presented to the Chief Magistrate of the first Republic in the world. Then he said to her, "And what State are you from, Miss?" "From the same State as your Excellency,—the state of single blessedness," she quickly replied. Thus early were visible indications of a boundless fertility of the sentimental demonstrated.

Much the same state of affairs prevailed in the circle of which Mary Dailey was the leading spirit, as that at which we have glanced, where Uncle Jake was the sublime genius. The object of each compact was identically the same—that of serving the South; and they were both indirectly and, in some respects, directly connected—Miss Dailey's league, and that with which Jake labored. In the former, Cynthy, in many respects, performed much the same functions as Jake in the latter. With Miss Dailey were associated other ladies, under much the same conditions as those which governed the 'Fairies" of Uncle Jake. Her rendezvous was a great central point with which many other secret-service leagues of the Virginia border maintained regular and systematic communication. The location was admirably suited for this purpose, owing to its secure approaches, utterly unknown to strangers, and which, therefore, could not be guarded to prevent contraband communications from passing.

The strategy practiced by Miss Dailey was almost too grand to be creditable. She made personal sacrifices which are admirable as anything to be found on the pages of fairy tale. We much regret that consistency denies her a number of chapters in this book and a prominent place in its plot. Her strongest point was gained by winning the admiration of her foemen—an art in which she was a most skillful adept. This she accomplished in many ways and by divers means. One of these, an early, simple but potent experiment, has been since related by the lady herself.

"The new wing of the hotel, before its completion, was taken by the Union forces, in possession of the road and encamped at this point for temporary barracks and a hospital. Some sick and wounded Union soldiers were brought in one day. I looked across from my window into the opposite rooms, where the poor fellows had been laid on blankets—a few on mattresses. My heart melted at the sight of the suffering enemy. I braved even the terrible Cynthy,—who was none too favorably inclined toward the *Yanks*,—so great was my compassion, and insisted upon making a large caldron of chicken-broth for them. When this was done I carried a smoking bowlful in each hand to the window. One young fellow, pale and famished, took the savory mess, and put it eagerly to his lips. 'Hold on Bob! may be that stuff's poisoned!' sang out a comrade on the floor beside him. The sick man hesitated for one moment, as he gazed eagerly at me, while my blue eyes, frank as day, on this occasion at least, doubtless flashed their indignant protest; he said: 'Oh, for shame! I'll trust that girl's face for my life. Here's thank'ee to you, miss!' and down went the soup."

In the fiercely varying vicissitudes of the war on this often-disputed borderland—the railroad to-day in possession of the Government, to-night torn up thirty or forty miles by Stonewall Jackson's brigade, the *personnel* of the social circle not unfrequently became strangely mixed, sometimes distressingly embarrassing at the hotel. Both the secret and the suspected sympathizers with and aiders and abettors of the rebels dined side by side with the Union officers in command of the post and district. They even smoked pipes of seeming peace together on the veranda of the hotel, and sang sentimental ballads to the witching accompaniment of Miss Mary on the parlor piano. Strange companionship!

Gen. Kelley was in command most of the time. While his head-quarters were at the Glades Hotel, young James Dailey and a boon companion of his conceived the bold and daring project of crossing the lines to join the Confederate army. Both familiar with the all but impenetrable trails in the woods of the border they accordingly laid their plans. A few trusty friends were in the plot. This proved successful, although Gen. Kelley personally headed a pursuing party, after the alarm was given the next day.

Sometime later, General Crook was associated with Gen. Kelley in the command of forces assigned to the protection of the Baltimore and Ohio road. To this circumstance he owed his acquaintance with and subsequent relations to the Dailey family at Oakland. But at the time the incident which we are about to relate occurred, the official head-quarters, however, were located at a hotel in Cumberland, Maryland, a most charming and beautifully picturesque town on the road, half way between Piedmont and Oakland.

One night in this lovely city, nestling so admirably in its oval-shaped valley among innumerable hills, a party of cavalry wearing the blue uniform of the United States, entered the city. From all appearances, they were troopers returning from a scouting expedition with important dispatches. After having taken the strange precaution to capture their own pickets, they galloped straight to the General's head-quarters. Such was the urgent nature of their important business that they pressed without ceremony to the bedrooms of Gens. Crook and Kelley, where these toil-worn warriors slept the sleep of the innocent in fancied security. The leader of this audacious party was a man of not many words. "Get up and put on your clothes," was his rude greeting to each of the generals in turn, who were dazed by being startled out of a profound slumber by this ruthless summons.

The party was a band of Confederates in disguise, among whom were Jim Dailey and his companion. They had come to turn the joke of pursuing them on Gen. Kelley, to the reality of accompanying them on a reckless ride for the dead time. In ten minutes, at the muzzles of revolvers, the two generals made their toilets, and were mounted at the door of their hotel. Thus surrounded by their volunteer body-guard, they were led out of the dark, silent and slumbering city, and hurried off to Richmond.

But the magnanimity of these Federal generals to those unhappy Southerners, whose lives and property lay at the mercy of both friend and foe, on this critical line of sectional demarcation, secured the intercession of the most powerful influence at the Confederate Capitol to clamor for their release. This was early brought about, and they were soon reinstated to their former command.

This was not, however, the last time that Gen. Crook was destined to be captured by a member of the Dailey family, nor the one of the most serious importance to himself.

Sometime later he was wounded, and borne to the Mountain Hotel. Mary Dailey, the little rebel maiden, became his volunteer nurse. No sentiment pervaded or swayed the courageous soul of this sweet child of "Nature and of Dixie" but the impulse of charitable pity for her suffering foeman, and a zealous desire to overwhelm him with a debt of deep gratitude that would incline him to deal yet more leniently with her suffering people. Thus, with a singleness of unselfish purposes, she labored, all unconscious that her eyes were steadily and surely entering the depths of his soul, and the gentle touch of her delicate hand causing him to tremble, as she daily ministered beside his couch of pain. Little did she dream that she was vanquishing the great and gallant soldier; he was captured by the sister as well as by the brother.

It is an old story, and soon told. He then planned to capture her for aye. The sequence of these conditions follows in due progression: an altar, a ring, a little wife—Miss Mary Dailey, the Confederate heroine of border warfare, is the bride of General Crook, the Union cavalier: antethetically mixed—conquered conquerer was he!

CHAPTER XXI.

THE MASQUERADING SEQUENCE.

"Sleep, soldier, sleep, though many regret thee,
Who stand round thy cold bier to-day;
Soon, soon shall the fondest forget thee,
And thy name will from earth pass away,
But there is one that shall still pay thee duty,
Of tears for the true and the brave,
As when first in the bloom of her beauty,
She wept o'er the soldier's grave."
—SELECTIONS OF WAR SONGS.

WHEN the two Federal officers and the rebel scout had disappeared, the young people with Uncle Jake, reassembled in the same room, where the appearance of those untimely visitors had temporarily disturbed them in their diversions.

When order was again restored, they spent much of the remaining time in animated discussion of the strange developments which they had witnessed between the two Federals, the Confederate and Uncle Jake. The two Confederate officers of the party were open in their denunciations of Uncle Jake as a spy and informer against the interest of the Confederate people; the remarks of the Federal officers were conclusive on this point. There could be, according to the opinion of the former, no doubt as to Cloud's mistrust in the old darkey, or that he deceived and misled the old man, in order to escape the snares which he was satisfied Jake aided constantly in laying for him.

To the young ladies, who fully understood Jake's relations with themselves and Cloud, and thoroughly comprehended the part which these individuals played before the Federal officers, this obstinate conclusion of their army companions is extremely amusing. They know that to the Northern army, Uncle Jake's mask is impenetrable, because there is not a shade of suspicion concerning his loyalty to the cause of the Stars and Stripes. With Uncle Jake, this suspicion is a grave and serious matter; and more especially is this true, owing to the fact that one of these officers is his young master.

As to Cloud, he has advanced greatly in the estimation of his two comrades, while they regard the two Federal officers in an exceedingly favorable light.

The masqueraders arrive promptly, and appear to be highly satisfied and delighted with the entertainment, which glides smoothly through the hours, until the time arrives for the interesting festivities to close.

The gay participants have departed, and once more the old mansion assumes its quiet tranquillity, and appears as though deserted. Of all the assembled guests of the early evening, but one lingers on the threshold, taking a more special interest and solicitude in the ceremonies of bidding Miss Cornelia good-night than had any other one of her friends—one who has been a very particular favorite partner among the Federal officers, who have been each other's rivals all the evening as to which could first secure this admirable—to them—young lady for the next set. This individual was Jake's young master.

MISS CORNELIA: "Oh, Clem, this is terrible thus to meet and part with you in my own home. How cruel is this war to true and loving hearts!"

CLEM: "Yes, darling, it is indeed bitter beyond anything I have ever before experienced; and my nature revolts against it. But like everything else in this troublesome world, it must end."

MISS C——: "End—yes, Clem, that is the word. But for us, what may not this end mean? This is a question which I struggle against, that many of its answers may find no lodgment in my mind, yet how vain the effort! How many, many chances there are against us! Think of the numberless unknown dangers through which you must pass almost daily. I wish you would not take such fearful risks as this to see me. Even young Cloud, although he is almost entirely in the lines of the enemy, could not be induced to take a risk like yours."

CLEM: "I suppose he is right. He is a cool-headed boy. But, darling, I must leave you. After I reach home and change this dress, I shall have no time to waste if I would pass through the enemy's lines before day-light. So I must bid you good-night."

MISS C——: "Good-night, Clem. I wonder when I shall see you again. Take care of yourself, for my sake."

CLEM: "One last kiss, darling. There now; I am gone."

MISS C——: [Solus.] "I will look through the gloom at the white figure receding, and hearken to the sound of his horse's hoofs, as they grow fainter on the frozen ground. From my chamber window will I watch and listen, until I hear him leave home in his true garb of grey, and with his armor on. How weird and ghost-like he appears! Oh that I could shake off these misgivings, and experience another moment of strength-assuring confidence.

There, now, I see a light in his room. How quickly he has completed the transformation. Out goes the light. In a moment, now, I will again hear the clatter of his horse's feet, as he rides across the field for the wood which is such a friendly cover. There! I hear his foot-steps as he goes down into the stable-yard. Mercy! how the least noise is wafted to-night on the still and icy air! The cold is intense. He will surely almost freeze to death riding for two hours through it, so soon after leaving the warm hall below, heated from the excitements of the ball-room. Oh, Heaven shield him!

"There are three instantaneous shots at the gate! Here comes his horse, like a flash of lightning. Oh, my God! the saddle is empty— he is shot! he is shot! There goes a light to the gate. It is Uncle Jake and Hannah. Oh, pitiless fate! It is he! It is he! He is dead! dead!

"What pitiful and heart-rending screams poor Jake and Hannah are uttering! His poor sister! poor Leonora! poor Leonora!—there she goes. Oh, God! she falls beside his prostrate form. Listen to her agonizing cries. What is she saying?—'My brother! oh, my brother! look at me! speak to me! It is your sister—your sister Leonora! Oh, Jake, he is dead!' She is swooning. My poor heart is breaking; but I must alarm the house and run to him. Poor Clem, your breath is scarcely cold on my cheek, and are you dead! Oh cruelest of all fates!"

LEONORA: "Oh, Cornelia! Cornelia! they have killed, murdered my poor brother! They never halted him, nor demanded him to surrender. They were concealed behind the open gate. The blaze of the guns has scorched his coat. Poor Clem! Look at him! Oh, Cornelia! I have no brother now! Clem and Tim both killed so soon in this war. What shall I do?"

CORNELIA: "Oh, Leonora; and he but a few moments ago lightly bade me good-night! I was watching restlessly out from my window, oppressed with some secret dread, saw the murderous blaze, and then the riderless horse come dashing up the lane! Oh, poor Clem, how little you then dreamed that we were parting forever; and that I, broken-hearted, should so soon be weeping over your dear form all inanimate and cold!"

The next evening, there is an open, new-made grave in the little old church-yard on the hill-side. Down at the mansion a plain black coffin is being borne from the parlor to the hearse. In the lane, in front, a long funeral procession has formed. Behind the hearse follows the family carriage, in which Cornelia Earl, as one of the principal mourners, has a seat. Next in order is Uncle Jake and Aunt Hannah, with bowed and uncovered heads, on foot. Then there are a few neighboring carriages, such as the position of the two armies would permit to attend. After these follow Maj. Pleasington and Lieut. Oglethrop, at the head of a squadron of dragoons, on foot, with heads uncovered and drawn and inverted sabres. Behind these the troopers follow, in regularly formed fours, their horses, one man leading eight.

At the grave the hymn "Nearer, my God, to Thee," is sung impressively, chiefly by the soldiers. Then the beautiful and solemn burial-service of the Episcopal Church is read; and the mortal remains of Capt. Clem Fairchild are lowered to their last long resting-place. As the frozen earth begins to rattle with horrible, hollow sound upon the planks, the wild and pitiful bursts of grief and cries of lamentation from Leonora, Cornelia, Uncle Jake, and Aunt Hannah rend the bitter frosty air. Fainting, the three women are soon borne away from the grave; and, alone, Uncle Jake's mournful wails continue.

The grave is filled, and the native mourners depart. Then just as the last red glow of the setting sun is fading on the distant mountain-tops, the squadron is formed, in obedience to the clear, ringing voice of Maj. Pleasington, which causes some of the retiring citizens, to whom the meaning of this manœuvre is unknown, to pause, and look back in amazement. Directly, the same sharp, musical voice floats out on the wintry air, "Ready! Aim! Fire!" There is a bright, blazing flash; a volley rolls over the grave; its echoes go reverberating back against the hills and re-echoing across the neighboring plains. It is the burial salute—the last and the highest token of honor that the soldier in the field can bestow on his dead comrade—thrice precious when bestowed by a brave and generous enemy.

So ended the masquerade-balls among the

out-posts. So for a time we leave Uncle Jake and his Fairies in sadness and despair. May He who is the consoler of the broken hearted—"the rock and sure foundation" in the hours of need, watch over them now—watch over all to whom shall come, with the smoke of battle and the cannon's thunder, a crown that is worn only beyond the stars—a glory that is found in the Shadow of Death.

CHAPTER XXII.

THE PLAINS OF MANASSAS AGAIN.

"Flows there a tear of pity for the dead,
Wide scattered o'er the ensanguined plain?
Come here! bathe thousands who are lowly laid."
—MISCELLANEOUS.

THE great change of base has been made. The Confederate winter-quarters at Centreville and Union Mills have been broken up, and present the appearance of deserted and ruined cities. No more the roll of the drum, sounding the tat-too and the revelie, is heard. The slow and measured tread of the sentinel is silent and still. The bray of the mule and the neigh of the war-steed no longer disturb the solitude of the ghostly night. Desolation wields her sway indisputed and supreme.

Even the owl—the lugubrious chanter of the dreary forest and dismal night—has taken wing and flown away from this woe-begone, famine-haunted region.

Our early friends of the out-post scenes are scattered; their old haunts know them no more.

Arlington Heights and the vicinity of Alexandria no longer resound with the clamorous commotion of the "Grand Army of the Potomac." Long since it has disembarked on the historical shore of Virginia, at Yorktown.

Garland Cloud is once more in the ranks of his company. He has broiled oysters, and slept in the trenches at Yorktown many a rainy night. He has charged up to the very trench, filled with water, that surrounded a fort, at the battle of Williamsburg, on the retreat from Yorktown, where his comrades in the brigade fell like autumn leaves.

Then his Captain, J——, whom we met in

6

company with Cloud, one stormy winter night, at the "Picket Bivouac," was killed.

His former Colonel—now Brig.-Gen. E——, was terribly wounded.

He has passed through the fiery ordeal of Seven Pines, that scourged his command so terribly. He has rode on the tempest of battle through Cold Harbor, White Oak Swamp, and Malvern Hill unharmed.

Little Mac, as Gen. McClellan—a master military genius and strategist—was facetiously called by the "Boys in Blue," has lost his head beneath the relentless stroke of the political guillotine.

We challenge the world to produce a more masterful military achievement than McClellan's retreat from before Richmond, through the Chickahominy swamp—regarded by Confederate engineers as being impossible at that time—with a defeated and dispirited army, almost surrounded by a victorious and an exultant enemy.

Pleasington and Oglethrop have met the shocks of the impetuous, indomitable Ashby, and heard the thunder of Jackson's cannon again and again in the valley of Virginia.

"The Army of the Potomac" has once more changed its position, and returned to its former encampment.

"The famous warrior on horseback" has been assigned to its command, and passed in triumph over and by the camps and the ruins of the once bristling parapets and frowning battlements that shed a halo of terror about, and clothed in mystic grandeur the name of Manassas.

Gen. Lee has broken up his camp in front of Richmond, and advanced with two invincible legions beyond the Rapidan, to meet his new antagonist in the open field.

His strong right arm—the immortal Jackson—has swept the enemy from the path at Cedar Mountain, where Pleasington and Oglethrop were blended in the perplexing scene, and forced him to take shelter beyond the Rappahannock.

The houses at Culpepper Court House have trembled to their foundations from the shocks of the terrible artillery duel across the Rappahannock.

This was opened by Gen. Lee as a stroke of grand and subtle strategy—a ruse that served his turn admirably, and deceived the enemy beyond the expectations of the most sanguine officers.

Just as the shadows of evening veil the antagonists from each other's view, the "Boys in Grey" observe batteries quietly moving into position all along the line occupied by the advance troops of Gen. Lee, whose main body rests between the Court House and the railroad bridge, across the track and below for some distance, and above to a little county bridge, called Waterloo, where Jackson is posted.

Pope's army lines the opposite hills, facing Lee and Jackson, in formidable array, and in easy range of light field-batteries.

Before day-light the next morning Lee's advance troops eat their frugal meal,—for breakfast it could not be termed,—and are in line of battle in the bottom down near the river.

Jackson is no longer at Waterloo Bridge; but other troops are in the positions held by him the evening before.

Just as the first grey light streaks the eastern horizon, a cannon fires on Gen. Lee's left, and sends a shell screaming down toward Pope's left; this is answered by a cannon on Lee's right, which sends a shell hissing up in the direction of Pope's right.

Instantaneously one blinding sheet of flame bursts from Lee's entire front; the ground trembles from the concussion of batteries as if convulsed by an earthquake; the thick curtains of fog which line the hills and hang low down the banks of the river like a funeral pall, are suddenly transformed from veils of sable mourning to transparent hues of the rainbow, to outrival the gayest scenery that ever graced a mortal stage, to hold in rapturous admiration, spell-bound and applauding multitudes.

Quickly the opposite hills are wrapped in rivaling flames of awful grandeur; and now high above the flashes from exploding shells, lend new terror, if not fearful beauty, to the brilliant scene.

Gen. E—— has crossed the river above. Heavy rains cause its waters suddenly to rise; and it goes sweeping between the two armies like a mad and an irresistible mountain torrent.

Gen. E—— is cut off and menaced with destruction. He is ordered to hold his position, and at the same time asked if he could hold it, and how long. His answer is characteristic of the man.

"Tell Gen. J——," he says, with grim and sarcastic asperity, "that I cannot hold my position at all; but that by——I can stand here, be cut to pieces, and die." But he almost miraculously extricates his command from a position of wondrous peril.

The fact that he is already across the river, that there are momentary indications that a column is about to attempt a passage at Waterloo Bridge, and that Lee is in line of battle all along the bank of the river, makes it clear to the mind of the Federal commander that the frightful artillery fire has been opened and is maintained with such fury, in order to prepare the way for and cover an anticipated crossing of Lee's army. Such is true.

As a matter of course, Pope taxes his skill to its utmost capacity, and devotes all his energy in making preparations to defeat this audacious presumption. How insane he must imagine Lee to suppose him capable of such rash madness!

Between the two embattled hosts the dreadful artillery duel is maintained until late in the day.

How different is Lee's plan to cross the river, from the ostensible one demonstrated to the perception of Gen. Pope.

While the artillery duel is progressing, Gen. Jackson debouches to the left, under cover of a dense forest, and marches up the river above its fork, where either branch is fordable.

In the meantime, the restless, dashing Stewart crosses the river, rides with audacity into the camp of Gen. Pope, and plunders his headquarters.

Dailey, Pleasington and Oglethrop are forced to meet the shocks, and strive to sustain themselves against the furious onslaughts of this redoubtable warrior, "The gay cavalier of Dixie."

While these side-scenes are progressing, Jackson is making his famous flank movement, having for its objective point Manassas Junction, far in the rear of the Federal army, which he speedily reaches and captures without meeting serious opposition.

When these tidings reach Pope, chagrin and consternation are no adequate terms to express his emotions. The lady of the house where he had his head-quarters told the story thus:

"Gen. Pope and his staff officers had just seated themselves at the dinner-table when the dispatch was handed the General. He read it, struck the table violently with his fist, and exclaimed, 'By——, I am whipped again!' They left their dinner untouched, mounted their horses, rode away, and I saw them no more."

The other corps of Lee's army follow in Jackson's foot-steps by rapid forced marches.

Jackson is in critical peril. Nothing but his wonderful genius and the blunders of his adversary save him from utter destruction.

He is menaced on all sides, while the great mountains separate him from his friends and from Thoroughfare Gap—the only available passage subject to seizure by the enemy.

This may be held by ten thousand troops against Lee's combined legions, until Jackson's annihilation is complete. But Jackson fights and manœuvres as few others could fight and manœuvre in cases of desperate emergency.

All day long, on August 29th, 1862, as the corps of Longstreet approach Thoroughfare Gap, the men can hear the ceaseless roar of Jackson's cannon rolling up in battle thunder far away beyond the blue smoke-capped mountains.

Longstreet finds Thoroughfare Gap in possession of the Federal army, and is thus forced to halt late in the afternoon and all night in inactive suspense. He makes feints, and does whatever else seems possible during the night; but the situation appears desperate—almost hopeless.

However, to the inexpressible amazement of every one in Longstreet's command, daybreak reveals the astonishing fact that the road is open; that the Federal troops have abandoned that impregnable stronghold during the night, and thus lost an opportunity to strike Lee a mortal blow.

Early in the morning of August 30th, therefore, Longstreet is able to reach the field of conflict, and take up positions to support and relieve his sorely-pressed countrymen of Jackson's corps.

Now we are once more on the ensanguined plains—the bloody stage of that July Sabbath. The ground is the same; but the antagonists have changed positions, and their forces are more formidable. Instead of raw troops, their ranks on either side are filled with trained, disciplined, war-inured veterans.

This day throughout there is much desperate and bloody, but rather desultory, fighting at various points along the line. There are only partial, indecisive engagements; but the suspense of anxious expectation and foreboding uncertainty is something fearful to the contemplation of every thoughtful mind.

With darkness, however, the firing ceases and the silence of night falls over the field. The sky is overcast, and the weather is oppressively hot.

The Confederates sleep on their arms in battle array. A large portion of the Federals pass the night on their feet, changing and marching into positions.

The last day of August dawns with the elements still overspread with gloom. The sun refuses to shine. The atmosphere is close and stifling, and full of dust, drifting like lazily-creeping masses of thick fog.

Not a breeze of air ruffles the delicate texture of the aspen-leaf. Strong men gasp for breath in the early morning while passively inactive. A breathless suspense pervades the Confederate lines. The humblest mountaineer feels that this is a day destined to be recorded, and to pass down through the ages as historical; and all are haunted by the dark shadow of the Death Angel's wing as it hovers silently over the heated and breathless plains.

The early hours of the day pass over a stillness not unlike the solemnity of an audience at a funeral; not even a picket shot is heard. But, at length, however, dense clouds of dust begin to rise in front of the Confederate positions. This is ominous. The storm is about to burst forth in appalling fury. The Federal army is advancing—moments are ages—eternity!

Jackson is along the railroad, behind the embankments and in the cuts, and will receive the shock of the blue waves. Longstreet is on Jackson's right in the open field, and will assume the offensive.

Now a cannon fires! In another moment the air is black with the smoke from exploding shells!

The bloody drama is opened, and unfolding on the stage! What an evening to this last waning summer-day!

The blue waves break against Jackson's thundering breakers with terrific violence, only to be hurled back shivered and broken. Goaded to desperation, again and again they rush madly upon the murderous embattlements, but to meet the same disastrous reception.

Under cover of the fearful hurricane of iron hail, the serried columns of Longstreet roll forward. Pickett's division—the Old Guard of the army of Northern Virginia—moves in columns down a slightly inclining plane to a ravine on the edge of a corn-field, which gently inclines upward. Here the knapsacks and blankets are deposited, and a line of battle is formed. Pickett is well to the left of Longstreet's corps, the main body of which has almost level, and but slightly timbered ground to traverse.

Pickett moves by quick-step through the corn-field. Shell, scrapnel, grape-shot shriek, scream, whistle, tear indiscriminately through the deep green corn and the surging mass of humanity.

At the upper edge of the corn-field there is a beautiful grove of timber. Through this Pickett moves at the same steady step.

Emerging from the cover of the trees, what a spectacle greets the eye! One vast sea of blue spreads across the plains—line behind line! Bright armor and uniforms reflect a dazzling sheen, and brighter guns of polished brass gleam amid the bristling lines of bayonets. Lazily the Star Spangled Banner droops from hundreds of color-staffs, unruffled by so much as a gentle breeze, until it appears as though the vast plains are decked in the gay and splendid regalia appropriate only for the celebration of Independence Day.

The front line of the Federal army stands in stoic immobility, as if prepared to pass review.

Over to the right of Pickett, in the open plains, other divisions of Longstreet's corps are rolling forward toward the blue sea in admirable order, in the face of an iron and leaden tempest of menacing death.

Pickett debouches from the woods into the open plain to great disadvantage, with his position so much obliqued as to render it imperatively necessary to change front in short musket-range of the enemy's line of battle.

As he comes into the open ground the enemy's infantry sends withering volleys to greet the Confederate onslaught; and, while changing front, every known missile of death employed on the battle-field is crashing or tearing through his ranks.

In his front are a large house and yard, surrounded by a picket-fence, which his line of battle strikes in making the swing to face the enemy. This breaks his line, and throws a number of companies into disorder. But they pass to the right and left, and when beyond the yard-fence they close up the breach in the line, which is now squarely in front of the Federal position.

All this time he moves with shouldered arms at quick-step, firing not a shot.

Thus he continues to advance on a compact line of battle, in the perfect order of a dress parade; for such is the appearance each regiment in the Federal front presents.

In Pickett's advance a gentle declivity slopes down from the Federal position. Between the serried sections of infantry lines, at regular intervals, are brass cannon. Thus a twenty-eight-gun battery is posted in front of Pickett; and he designs to capture those thundering scourges.

This battery is manned by United States regulars. Their guns were presented to them by the ladies of some Eastern towns, cities, and perhaps States. The recipients and custodians of these beautiful gifts had sworn to die by, but to yield them never.

Onward Pickett still moves in the face of flaming death, while the wild huzzas of Longstreet's assaulting legions—now coming into close quarters—rise above the deafening roar of cannon, and the unbroken and appalling roll of musketry. And yet on Pickett's left, all along Jackson's lines, there are tumult and carnage raging madly over which demons might gloat to surfeited satiety.

Now Pickett is within one hundred paces of the line which yet presents an unbroken front of seeming invincibility. Canister, grape—double charges, and rifle-balls decimate his ranks. Behind him the ground is thickly strewn with grey uniforms, bleeding, helpless, lifeless! Officers and privates go down by hundreds! Men drop forward on their faces so fast that their commanders conclude they are falling to escape the murderous storm of iron and lead, before which it appears impossible for anything mortal to live one moment; and they actually take a number by the collar to force them to their feet, only to find that they will rise never more.

Onward the survivors move, closing up the frightful gaps which at every step rend their ranks.

Longstreet,—the Ney of the Southern army—a regular "bull-dog of war,"—dashes back the blue waves before the impetuosity of his sweeping surge.

Jackson comes out from his cover and precipitates his legions violently upon the shattered ranks of his discomfited assailants; and as if by magic at this moment the guns of Pickett leave the position of shoulder-arms. They blaze, crackle, echo and reverberate, mingling their deathly, discordant notes with the uproarious tumult of battle.

There is no halting. Forward the melting ranks move with unchanged steps, loading and firing with a rapidity and deadly aim that quickly mows frightful swaths through the late beautiful line that stood arrayed against them in such imposing martial grandeur.

Now they are right among the battery's thundering guns. The flames must singe their very hair.

The supporting line sinks to the earth, or the men are swept away,—metaphorically lifted from their feet and hurled back upon their reserves. Flesh and blood are unequal to the overwhelming shock.

The guns are passed. Some gunners, in order to escape being bayoneted, fall down under the carriages, as if dead; but not one abandons his post.

There is a wild yell. A reserve column is rushing forward to re-take the battery. Pickett receives the shock, and checks the assault, while his support hastens at double-quick over the blood-slippery ground.

The gunners rise up from under the carriages,

and give the grey line a reception of grape. In a moment they are either killed, wounded, or again fall down under the carriages; but they keep their oath; not one abandons his post nor surrenders to the enemy until too badly disabled to perform further duty; and their beautiful brass guns are dearly bought trophies to the enemy.

The Washington Artillery, of New Orleans, comes up at a sweeping gallop, and forms between the captured guns, even turning a number of them on their late friends and protectors.

Speedily, now, the Federal positions are all carried, and their lines hopelessly broken.

To complete the horrors of their trying distress, the relentless squadrons of Stewart charge with pitiless fury upon the rear of the broken and flying infantry.

The benignity of the Creator, however, had prepared for the discomfited Federals almost as miraculous protection and deliverance as were vouchsafed the flying Israelites to shield them from the menacing dangers impending at the hands of the pursuing Egyptians; at all events, they served the Union hosts the same purpose, and perhaps saved them from annihilation.

Bull Run, swollen by recent rains, interposes as a barrier to prevent a general and overwhelming onslaught all along the Confederate line. Darkness in mercy spread her sable mantle over the harrowing scene, soon after the general repulse of the Federal army, to render effective pursuit impossible.

Thus the Union army is spared additional horror of confusion and dismay, inseparable from a vigorous and continued pursuit.

The carnage was frightful. The wounded can be estimated only, in comparison as to numbers, with army corps.

The sun goes down on a scene horrible and pitiful beyond description.

Under two broken gun-carriages, in the battery above referred to, about ten feet apart, are Garland Cloud and Edgar Harman. Cloud under one, with a bullet hole through the body; Harman under the other, with a broken ankle.

HARMAN: "Who was that called my name?"

CLOUD: "It is I, Garland. Are you much hurt, Lieutenant?"

LIEUT. H——: "My ankle is broken. What has happened to you, Garland?"

CLOUD: "I have a hole through my body. Can't tell any more. That is what they call serious. A bad night before us! It is getting dark fast, and may soon rain. But there are thousands suffering around us, many doubtless far worse than we."

LIEUT. H——: "Yes, Garland, and many must die for want of attention. It is terrible. I think half our boys fell in taking this battery; and God only knows how many of them since. I shudder at the thought of it."

CLOUD: "It will be a woeful day in your valley and its neighboring mountains when the news of this day's work reaches there, as well as in every section of every State, North and South. But yonder are two figures some distance apart, peering into the faces of the dead, assisting the wounded, and giving them water. They are moving this way right over the ground where we charged. There! The nearer one is Maj. Flowers. Ho, there, Maj. Flowers! Come here, please."

MAJ. F——: "Why, Garland, I was hunting you. I saw your captain, after we made the last charge, and he told me you had fallen. I would have been here much sooner, but as I came along over there in the edge of that skirt of timber, where Jackson's right charged, I found Maj. Pleasington and his friend Lieut. Oglethrop both badly wounded. I stopped to care for them, enemies that they are. They were both visibly affected when I told them you had fallen, and that I was on my way to seek you. Pleasington said he had been remarking to his companion that he wondered if you would find them. I have promised to return that way and let them know your condition. Are you badly hurt?"

CLOUD: "An ugly shot hole through the body —one of those wounds whose severity time alone can determine. I tore up a silk handkerchief, which I pulled from the pocket of this poor artillery officer here by my side, and plugged up the holes soon after I was hit, so that I have not bled much; and I am now suffering but little pain. You are very kind to come to my relief so promptly, Major."

MAJ. F——: "Oh, Garland, my friend! I wish you would call me Jesse, as you did in the olden time. Don't talk to me about kindness, when directly or indirectly I owe you near everything I hold. Don't let a petty rank come between us."

CLOUD: "I love you none the less, but esteem you all the more. But who was that just behind you, Major?"

MAJ. F——: "I could not recognize him; he was behind me, intently seeking some one."

CLOUD: "It is—it is, father. Listen how pitifully he is calling Garland. He seeks me, poor old man. Major, please tell him—call out here is Garland."

MAJ. F——: "Here is Garland Cloud, if you are seeking him."

COL. CLOUD: "Oh, Garland, my boy, how thankful I am to find you able to speak to me! I was about to despair and to begin to mourn you for dead. Your comrades lie thick as the autumn leaves between here and the woods; nearly all are dead. I saw your captain, but he could tell me nothing more than that he thought you fell between the woods and battery. You are shot through the body. Bear it like a soldier— and a Cloud. While there is life, there is hope. I will soon have you away from here. This is a sad meeting for the first time since you left home.

"I was disappointed in not being able to see you during nor just after the seven days' battle at Richmond. Early in the morning of the day on which I was going over to visit you, Gen. Jackson started on this campaign. I have commanded a brigade since the battle of Port Republic, which has kept me busy. But who is this, Garland, standing here by you?"

CLOUD: "Maj. Jesse Flowers, father; a true friend of mine."

COL. CLOUD: "Maj. Flowers, I am proud to meet the bravest lad in Gen. Lee's army. I congratulate you on your rapid and well-merited promotion."

MAJ. F——: "I am equally delighted to meet you, Col. Cloud. My promotion has been a sad affair—over the graves of my dear and superior officers. How thankful I am to you for calling to see mother and sissie, and for the kind visit of your daughters to them. It was a kindness they highly prized."

Col. Cloud: "Yes, I was determined to see them. I shall ever remember them with kindest feelings of friendship. From your home I went directly to visit 'The Angel of Consolation,'—Miss Carrie Harman—and spent the night at her father's house. In her I saw devotion and self-denial for the cause of humanity and the suffering poor that have never been surpassed in this world. Many a poor fellow have I seen die since with her name on his lips. 'I die, but Miss Harman, the Angel of Consolation, will care for my little children.' I would rather be that girl than the Queen of England."

Cloud: "Father, there is Miss Carrie's brother, with a broken ankle, by that next carriage. Both of you go speak to him; he is my friend."

Col. Cloud: "Lieut. Harman, I am happy to know the brother of such a sister, and I retract nothing that I have said. I regret to meet you in this plight; but I will soon have you cared for."

Maj. F——: "I am pleased to know you, Lieut. Harman, and can assure you that I heartily join Col. Cloud in his sentiments of regret, and sincerely trust that you may save your foot."

Lieut. H——: "Col. Cloud and Maj. Flowers, I am truly thankful to have the honor of your acquaintance, and am most grateful for the sentiments of kindness and sympathy you express for my misfortune."

Col. Cloud: "Now, boys, I will go and obtain means to have you removed. Be patient. I will be as quick as the darkness and circumstances will permit."

Cloud: "One moment, father. There are two Federal officers with whom I am well acquainted, lying badly wounded up yonder to the left, in the woods. If it should be a last favor which I am about to ask, please obtain their parole, and have them sent into their own lines. Maj. Flowers will explain everything to your satisfaction as you go along."

Col. Cloud: "All right, my boy; I am proud to find in you a spirit of such commendable charity." And he then departed, and sought the

two Federal officers, Pleasington and Oglethrop.

Col. Cloud: "Well, boys, you are in a pretty rough fix, here in the hands of enemies too poor to take proper care of their own unfortunates."

Lieut. Oglethrop [Startled from a doze]: "Oh, Pleasington, is that the long, grey-whiskered Colonel or his ghost, on the same black horse, peering at us there through the gloom, and speaking to us in a tender and kind voice?"

Col. Cloud: "It is not his ghost. Don't be alarmed boys; I am come to you on a mission of mercy and kindness."

Maj. Pleasington: Do I dream, or do I hear of mercy and kindness from a Southern voice, not that of Garland Cloud nor Jesse Flowers?"

Col. Cloud: "You do not dream. I am Garland Cloud's father. You are indebted to him for this visit. He lies wounded over yonder, near that white house, and asked me to look after you. Maj. Flowers had told him you were wounded."

Pleasington: "Merciful Heavens! You Garland Cloud's father; and we have been trying so hard all last spring and this summer to capture or kill you; and now you are come to offer us kindness."

Col. Cloud: "You are powerless and harmless now—proper objects to receive the kindest offices of humanity: I hear of you as gentlemen and soldiers waging civilized warfare. As such I respect you. It is those cowardly people who burn and pillage, and wantonly make war on the helpless, defenceless non-combatants, that arouse my anger."

Lieut. Oglethrop: "How magnanimous in you not to kill me, when you had disarmed me at Port Republic. I did not expect to find an infantry officer so expert with the sword, and such a good horseman."

Col. Cloud: "My father was in the dragoons, in the war of 1812. From a boy he trained me to ride, and use the sword. I carry the same one that went with him through that war. Your escape, after I had captured you, was sufficiently daring to atone for the mortification of being disarmed."

Maj. Pleasington: "I paid dearly for my audacity in charging you at Cedar Mountain, and again to-day, when I thought your men were in hopeless disorder."

Col. Cloud: "Boys, time presses. I have come to say to you that you will be paroled early in the morning, and sent into your own lines, so that you may go where Effie and Evalina can nurse you, which will be more agreeable to you than the care you would receive at the hands of our rude, uncouth nurses. I have no time to stay and hear your thanks. Duty tears me away from the couch of my perhaps mortally wounded son. I cannot tarry longer with you. Farewell."

CHAPTER XXIII.

THE ANGEL OF CONSOLATION.

" Be kind to thy sister—not many may know
The depths of pure sisterly love—
The wealth of the ocean lies fathoms below
The surface that sparkles above."
—From BE KIND TO LOVED ONES.

By some means Col. Cloud sent a dispatch to Carrie Harman, giving a list of the killed and wounded in the Mountain companies of his brigade, who were from the vicinity of her home. This reached her two days in advance of the Richmond papers, containing an account of the battle of August 31st, 1862, on the "Plains of Manassas." As the company to which her brother and Garland Cloud belonged, was not in his brigade, no reference was made to it or them. The list of killed among the sturdy mountaineers was frightful.

At once she entered upon the sad and trying task of breaking the news to bereaved families, and of offering them such sympathy as it was within the province of human power to bestow. But these were cases for which consolation was no soothing balm: it was an antidote too mild to meet the requirements of the deep and desperate malady to which it must in vain be applied.

These mountaineers love with the wild, fierce devotion of Nature, in all the grandeur and potency of its unsullied purity; and their grief is equally unmeasurable, whenever terrible affliction suddenly overtakes them.

Miss Harman, mounted on a spirited, fleet-footed horse, her long black hair flowing over her shoulders, and a broad-brimmed, home-made straw hat on her head, hastened from cabin to cabin, with the reckless impetuosity of a trooper riding for life. Faster and faster, all that day she urged the noble animal onward through the yet burning heat of a September sun, until her sad and pathetic mission was fulfilled.

On the night preceding the fourth day—the day on which she would finish this trying labor—as she approaches the old homestead, which is wrapped in the golden hues of the radiant setting sun, and stands out in bold relief on the rising ground in the centre of a mountain-encompassed valley—one of those rarely-beautiful spots of earth that admits of no comparison, because there is nothing in this world with which to compare it, save alone another valley, which lies somewhere, like itself, nestling within the encircling bases of the Eternal Mountains—she gazes on the grand old semi-baronial mansion, and contrasts it with the rude huts within whose walls her heart, so tender and sympathetic, has been so many times wrung by the sorrow and despair of the inmates at the tidings her lips have brought. She wonders why there is such disproportionate inequality in the conditions of the human family, and why men war against one another with such savage inhumanity, creating such pangs of bitter sorrow in a world filled with so much natural beauty, that it should hold nothing but happiness and peace; and she shudders with an indefinable dread of reaching the house.

It is time that news should have arrived from her brother's company. Has it come? What will it be? Will a silent, unsympathetic mail-messenger coldly bring to her the same sad story which she has been imparting to other anxious and loving hearts? Thus musing, she mounts the steps where her father is seated.

Carrie: "Oh, father! Is there any news from Edgar?"

H——: "No, darling, not one word. His division is terribly cut up; but no names are given."

Carrie: "This suspense is agonizing. Why cannot we know the worst, like these poor people in the mountain? There is no reason why Col. Cloud, who many of our foppish officers sneeringly term a hoosier ignoramus, should have a long report of the casualties in his command here three days in advance of our own class of officers."

H——: "That is true, Carrie. But Col. Cloud is an extraordinary man, and a worker of almost inexhaustible energy."

CARRIE : " What made him extraordinary ? Not education and numberless advantages enjoyed by men in our sphere."

H——: "Nature, Carrie. The natural always excels the artificial; Nature's handiwork is perfect. Cloud is a model of her workmanship, and merits a rank socially equal with any class in our country."

CARRIE : " We are agreed on that point. I am weary. Good-night, father."

H——: "Good-night, Carrie; I hope you may sleep well."

She retires to her chamber, and there her pentup thoughts find utterance.

CARRIE : [Solus.] "Merciful Heaven! If father only knew the tempest of conflicting emotions that sweep through my breast and rack my brain, he would not imagine that balmy slumbers and tranquil repose will be my comforting companions to-night. Nothing but broken, unrefreshing sleep and hideous dreams, with their spectral, ghostlike shadows, will haunt and startle me this night through.

"Those poor women wringing their hands in despair; their little children clinging in terror around them; their mingled shrieks, wails, moans, and sobs, are pictures that will be flitting before my vision, and sounds of frightful discord that will be distracting my ear whenever weary Nature asserts her sway, and lulls me into the shadowy realms of dream-land.

"My poor, dear, only brother, where are you to-night? Is your spirit hovering near me, to witness my restless anxiety and grief when the dread news—war's accursing legacy—comes? Heaven shield and preserve him, I pray. And Jesse Flowers,—the boy hero, the little major,— where is he? Oh, my God! spare me the ordeal of bearing to the 'Angels of the Mountain' a bitter, cruel cup of woe. And Garland Cloud,— the mountain scout and tempter of fate—I

wonder if his faith in the protecting arm of the guardian angel that shall ward off danger until the destined dark hour comes, is well founded, and has still preserved him. Surely some superhuman power shields his gallant, noble father.

"How strange that the magical influence of that recently obscure and unknown boy should control me, and stimulate me to such wonderful degrees of exertion, and nerve me to endure such incredible fatigue! Why do I crave his praise and esteem? It is because he saved my brother, and is brave and chivalrous. But he seems never to appreciate my labors but for their own sake and that of the cause in which they are rendered. Yet why should he? Are not all his heart, soul, and life devoted to that cause? Apart from it and its relations his thoughts never stray."

The next autumn eve Miss Harman dismounts in front of her home, much wondering why the grand old portico is deserted, and her father nowhere to be seen.

Her labors, in their present sorrowful form, are finished; the last scene of mourning in her jurisdiction, so far as she knows, has been visited.

She walks wearily up the gravel path and the broad stone steps, and enters the spacious hall. There she utters a little scream, and exclaims: "Oh, Edgar! Edgar! my dear brother, is it you, and wounded ?"

EDGAR: "Yes, sissie, it is I. But don't be alarmed. It is only in my ankle. I have come home, my sister, to be comforted by 'The Angel of Consolation.'"

CARRIE: "Oh, Edgar! thank God that it is no worse. But pray do not begin making light of your poor sister so soon. Where did you get that sacrilegious appellation ?"

EDGAR: "Pardon; but not so hastily, my little sister. God forbid that I should make light of you. There is no one else in this world that I am prouder of than you, and the noble mission of mercy in which you are engaged.

"And in relation to that blessed name which I have just called you, if you had heard it fall from the same lips, under the same circumstances as it did when it first greeted my ears, you would not style it sacrilegious.

"Lying on the field of battle, perfectly helpless, in the deep gloom of the last fading rays of twilight, surrounded by the shrieks of the wounded and the groans of the dying, Col. Cloud and Maj. Flowers, who were seeking and helping the wounded, met for the first time in their lives, not ten paces from me. Col. Cloud had not uttered a dozen sentences, including the remarks of introductory formality, before I was startled to hear the markedly emphatic words: 'Carrie Harman, the Angel of Consolation. Many a poor fellow have I seen die, with her name on his lips, consoled by the thought that she will not let the little children suffer. I would rather be that girl than the Queen of England.' In a few moments I was, although a stranger to both made known to them. The Colonel affirmed that he would not retract a word, and that the brother of such a girl should be cared for. Long before day my wound was properly dressed, and I was in an ambulance, in a special train, on my way home. But for that man, I would not be here to-night, nor for many a day to come."

CARRIE: "Thank God, I begin to reap my rewards. The secret prophecy that first induced me to engage in this cause, is being fulfilled; and here is my dear brother, one of its first fruits, saved once more. What a debt of gratitude the Clouds are heaping up against our family!"

MR. H——: "Yes, my children, greater than we can ever cancel, even were Garland and Edgar to exchange sisters."

EDGAR: "Poor Garland, the Confederacy is his bride; and I fear that, as far as he is concerned, she will soon be, if she is not now, a widow. The poor boy is desperately, if not mortally wounded. He was within ten feet of me. I heard the surgeon tell his father that he would have to be moved on a litter; and then they conversed in a low tone for a few moments. The Colonel came, and took leave of me, and returned to Garland. I could not hear what they said until as the Colonel was turning away to mount his horse, to rejoin his command, I heard Garland say, 'May God bless and preserve your father!'

"As the brave old man rode past me he was sobbing audibly, as if his poor heart would break. What a trial for a father thus to leave a son, and resume the stern, rough duties of an active commander!

"As the ambulance rolled away, Garland sang out, 'A race now, Lieutenant, who will be the first back to duty.'

"Oh, my God! how my heart bled thus to leave the poor boy!"

CARRIE: "What do you think became of him after you left?"

EDGAR: "His father had made provision for his care; but I am not able to say what they were. Circumstances were not favorable for making any desirable arrangements. But what is the matter with you, sissie? You are as pale as a ghost."

CARRIE: "I was thinking of that poor father's struggle, and the bitter pangs it must have cost him to leave his son; and that but for that same father's kindness, you would have been left in the same condition; and I blush with shame to say it, but I was thinking of your aristocratic unkindness to that poor boy in the early months of the war."

EDGAR: "Yes; and I thank God that it is unknown to his father. Poor Garland will carry the secret pangs which those cruel, private wrongs caused him to suffer, concealed from the world in his generous heart, to the grave. I am cured of my aristocratic follies. But my being at home now, you can attribute to Col. Cloud's esteem for 'The Angel of Consolation.'"

CHAPTER XXIV.

THE FIELD OF GETTYSBURG.

"But soft! our step's o'er a brave young nation's tomb:
An Empire's dust lies sepulchred here:
Oh, come, do not molest this defenceless urn:—
'Tis Dixie's grave—far more than Waterloo."
                                        VARIOUS.

SUMMER, 1863—that interesting season when "May showers" bequeath "June flowers,"—comes to witness gigantic developments on the American continent.

"The Armies of the Potomac" and "Northern Virginia" occupy much the same positions assumed directly after the battle of Chancellorsville; Hooker and Lee in command.

Hooker failed at Chancellorsville to demonstrate a prowess of strategic skill and military genius requisite to enable him successfully to cope with Lee in playing desperate games on the great chess-board of life and death. At Chancellorsville he was most sadly checkmated.

Since Chancellorsville, Lee has been intensely studying their chess-board, watching his antagonist, and planning for him a surprising game.

However, Hooker is no contemptible rival: thus Gen. Lee esteems him.

To say that Gen. Joseph Hooker was not a match for Gen. Robert E. Lee, is no disparagement to the former.

Early in June, Lee decides to move. It is a grand conception. Few great captains whose illustrious names grace the pages of history, save perhaps alone Napoleon I., would hazard its possible consequences.

But with Lee, continued inactivity might prove a greater disaster than even the failure of the move itself was likely to entail.

It requires an iron will thus to decide to make, and an indomitable courage to attempt, this move; yet Lee seems not to hesitate.

Numerous feints, cavalry expeditions and other exciting ruses are employed to divert the attention of the enemy from the real move contemplated.

Numerically, Lee's army is much inferior to that of Hooker's. It is the only barrier between Hooker's army and Richmond.

According to military tactics and established precedents in the scientific schools where arts of war are taught, for Lee to oblique either to the right or to the left, is to expose not only his flank to disastrous attacks, but his line of communication—the road to the Confederate Capitol—to seizure by the enemy.

That he would dare this perilous venture, must appear to the mind of Gen. Hooker too absurd for serious attention, if not, indeed, for any consideration whatever.

But be this as it may, history tells the story. Lee makes the move under cover of clouds of cavalry. When Hooker awakens to a realization of the situation, Lee is no longer in his camp: the road to Richmond is open; but Washington is menaced.

Lee has suddenly broken up his camp, boldly passed from the front of his adversary, turned his right flank—thus securing advantage of position baffling Hooker's powers of remedy, and forcing him to hasten to the defense of Washington. This he accomplishes with admirable success.

He is checkmated beyond the bounds of consistency or reason, yet he does all there is for him to do in the direction of counteracting the impending consequences of having allowed himself to be out-generaled. From this point to Gettysburg Lee moves triumphantly.

On the inhabitants of Gettysburg the bright sunshine of the morning of July 1st, 1863, casts but a gleam of ominous and portentous gloom. They know legions of foemen are at their doors. This is a beautiful place and a sublime locality.

The region about Gettysburg is composed of picturesque hill, wavy green forest, undulating plain, and craggy, precipitous ravine, interspersed ever and anon with bright, clear, silvery brooklets and rills, chiming their rippling murmurs of melody, as they glide along, gladdening their grass- and flower-bordered margins, grouped in such proportions as to make a picture of matchless loveliness. Set in a frame circlet of great blue mountains, it is colored in all the varied hues which conspicuous thrift and intelligent husbandry can bestow.

All Nature is startled by the wild shouts of foemen, the terrific roll of musketry, and the reverberating peals of thundering cannon.

To the good, quiet, peaceable citizens of this hapless region, who have only read of those warlike machines, the tragic drama,—which has selected for its stage their orchards bending under burdens of fruit, their gardens decked with delicious viands and rare flowers, and their fields crowned with golden harvests of ripening grain,—is not utterly divested of all the terrors associated in the minds of the human family with the dread annihilation of the Day of Judgment.

Early in the day the gallant Gen. Reynolds, of the Federal army, falls. Nearly all day long there is obstinate and steady fighting.

The First and the Eleventh Corps of the Federal army sustain the brunt of the shocks of this day. The van of Lee's army, led by Gen. Heth, of Hill's corps, is first and early on the field:

Providentially, as it seems, Gen. Wadsworth, of the Federal army, marching from the village of Emmitsburg, hears the familiar sound of battle thunder, hastens at double-quick through Gettysburg, and strikes the advancing Confederate column barely in time to seize and occupy a range of hills that overlooks the place from the north-west, in the direction of Chambersburg.

Just about this time the brave Reynolds is killed while making a personal reconnoissance. Here, prostrated on his face, with a ball through his neck, he baptizes the soil which gave him birth, with his life-blood.

Gen. Doubleday assumes command; but is forced by the sheer pressure of numbers to fall back precipitately to Seminary Hill, a little west of the village.

The Eleventh Corps arrives, and Gen. Howard assumes command. Thus encouraged by reënforcements, the Federal troops arrest the tide of disaster about to overwhelm them. But about one o'clock, P. M. they are furiously assailed by Ewell's corps, directed to the field, while marching from York, by hearing the thunder of battle.

Thus outflanked and outnumbered, utterly disheartened, the Eleventh Corps wavers, breaks, and flees in helpless rout. The First Corps is forced to follow or be annihilated. The Federal hospitals and wounded are thus left in the possession of the Confederates. Nearly half the Federal troops engaged are dead, wounded or prisoners.

The situation appears desperate, hopeless, amazing and incomprehensible! The Confederates merely occupy the grand amphitheatre of hills north and west: they do not advance.

Is it Fate that stays their forward movement—the mysterious, mighty, invisible hand—the hand of Him who presides "over the destinies of nations!" Thus it seems: there is no opposition to prevent their advance.

The broken lines of the Federals take possession of Cemetery and Culp's Hills, both of which might be occupied by the Confederates; but they seem content with the results of the day. Round Top, another formidable eminence, remains in possession of the Federal army.

The shadows close over the defenders of their soil and their fire-sides, discomfited and dispirited, as the light of day fades, and darkness, in benignant mercy, spreads her thick mantle over the earth, suspending for a time the savage strife and fiendish carnage on this ensanguined field.

The Union army passes the night in bringing up and posting reënforcements, collecting stragglers from the rout, and strengthening its positions, while the Confederates rest in apathetical inactivity.

The Federals have positions to strengthen, already rendered formidable by Nature. They hold the keys of Gettysburg, considered as a battle-ground.

Cemetery Hill, south of the town, is a commanding position; Culp's Hill almost as important; while Round Top is invaluable. All of these are not in the hands of the Confederates, because the "God of battles" willed that they should halt, and not occupy these points whence would issue the turning tide of battle and the palm of victory.

In the meantime, Gen. Hancock comes upon the field. With the experienced eye of a trained soldier and skillful commander, he recognizes and approves the great advantages of position in favor of the Federal army. Gen. Mead, who has succeeded Gen. Hooker as Commander-in-Chief of the Army of the Potomac, selects Gen. Hancock for this momentous duty. Undoubtedly he knows and properly appreciates his man: certainly he does not mistake his abilities.

Proof of this obtains in the fact that Mead defers to Hancock's judgment as to the most promising battle-ground, and abandons that selected by himself in person in favor of the one recommended by his abler lieutenant.

With favorable opportunities, Hancock would have been the peer of Lee as a commander.

As a gentleman and true soldier, he is the equal of any man of any age or country.

During the night, the main body of the Federal army arrives in the vicinity of Gettysburg, and Gen. Mead comes to the front.

Such is the situation upon which dawns the second day of July. It passes in comparative quiet, with only an occasional picket shot, until about the middle of the afternoon.

At this hour Longstreet hurls his legions with the impetuosity of an avalanche, and with all its destructive force, upon Sickles; and makes the memorable charge through the peach-orchard, near the little brick house. Sickles is beaten back in great confusion, and sustains frightful loss, a part of which is his own leg.

In this struggle the Confederates make a desperate effort to reach and possess Round Top, which Gen. Sykes barely prevents them from accomplishing. This failure is a terrible disaster to the Confederates. Before they can withdraw across the plain, they are furiously assailed by Gen. Hancock with a large force. Their loss is fearful. Longstreet encounters his match in "bull-dog" tenacity in the open field.

Near the foot of Round Top, Kilpatrick, with his cavalry, charges Hood, to prevent the capture of the Federal ammunition train which lies back in the direction of Chambersburg. Ewell carries some strong positions and portions of the Federal works well up Culp's Hill.

While these scenes are developing, Stewart and the Federal cavalry, twelve miles away, at Hanover, measure the prowess of their arms in wielding flashing blades of polished steel. Thus Stewart is held engaged, and prevented from obtaining the information that the Army of the Potomac is arriving on "The Field of Gettysburg,"—information that would be of inestimable value to Gen. Lee.

The second day ends in a deeper gloom for the Federal army than the first, and the third and last day dawns.

Indescribable is the suspense of the hour. Deep anxiety, but fixed and immovable resolution, are clearly and unmistakably depicted on every feature alike of the raw reserves and the war-worn, grim-visaged veterans.

The world looks on in wonder, and shudders at the thought of the appalling spectacle that the sun of this day is destined to go down upon. Everywhere it seems to be realized that this day is to decide all.

The preparations on both sides are prodigious. From the commanders-in-chief down to the humblest private in the ranks, all appear to understand and appreciate the stupendous magnitude of the stakes for which they are about to play in this desperate game.

The Northern troops are marshalled in the cause of preserving the Union. But at the present moment they are stimulated by that same formidable incentive which has before actuated the Confederates, and most powerfully aided them to their success,—that of repelling the all-devastating demon of war from ravaging and laying waste their own beautiful land. This now is in their favor, and weighs against their invaders. And, moreover, the supernatural genius and legionary name of "Stonewall" Jackson is no longer against them.

The daring Southmen have their very existence, as they now believe, at stake. They rebelled against the asserted authority of the National Government. In this they assumed desperate chances: the alternative of becoming abject provincial slaves, with all the possible and attendant penalties of treason.

This morning their bright little Star of Empire shines brilliantly in the zenith of its glory. Thus poised, it trembles and flickers amid the contending tempests of battle which hurl their fury against it with desperate resolution, to precipitate it from its enviable pinnacle down into the abyss of everlasting darkness and oblivion, there to remain eternally extinct.

On this fated field they are entangled in the toils of a mortal mistake: that of neglecting to seize the vital positions the first day; worse yet is to be their error: that of assaulting these all but impregnable ramparts, now strengthened by thirty-six hours of labor, the work of an army inspired by desperation and the startling promptings that instinctively admonish its performers of the dreadful necessity of self-preservation.

Moreover, Gen. Lee's lieutenants hesitate; do not promptly obey his orders, or suggest a different plan of battle at one point, at least, on the line where the action should be progressing in compliance with the original plan and orders.

Accustomed to rely on Jackson to act up to the requirements of emergencies developed by sudden and unpropitious circumstances, he seems to have overlooked this important feature when issuing the orders of this his first great battle since the one in which his able associate fell. However, had his commands been promptly obeyed, and had all his subordinates fulfilled the expectations of their chief, this would not excuse the crowning mistake of Gen. Robert E. Lee's brilliant military career—that of assaulting the craggy steeps on the field of Gettysburg.

It is presumable, however, that he was ignorant of the fact that "The Army of the Potomac" was on the field, and that he relied upon the irresistible momentum of his hitherto invincible legions to overwhelm the weaker and dispirited troops in his front; then to beat the others, coming to their relief, in detail. But this was not Gen. Lee in his true character. Perchance the finger of Destiny, hitherto propitious, was guiding him in paths of destruction.

The sequel of "The Field of Gettysburg" is indicated by the words, fraught with melancholy, Hancock! Pickett! Cemetery Hill!—or thus it proves to the Confederacy.

With other features of this scene we shall, therefore, refrain to deal.

Now the earth trembles from the incessant shocks of hundreds of cannon. From one end to the other of the far extended lines an unbroken sheet of flame blazes with the continuous uniformity of evenly regulated blast-furnaces; and the roll of musketry is as steady and unfluctuating as the beat of angry waves on a rockbound coast; intermingling with these are the maddening shouts of charging hosts; and the air is filled with the shadows of the departing spirits of the dying.

Cemetery Hill thunders defiance. There the soldierly bearing, the intrepid spirit, the indomitable will, and the heroic courage of Hancock are unmistakably perceptible.

These restore order; these inspire confidence. His genius is everywhere conspicuous. In the outlines and construction of his defenses; in the

disposition of his batteries and troops its indications stand out in terribly telling grandeur.

Cemetery Hill is a frowning battlement, a seething, fiery volcano, belching forth its hissing lava in volumes and torrents of deathly destruction. It is the awful prize which the Confederates purpose to seize. Thus they hope to overwhelm the Federal army, and in this they reckon not without foundation, provided, however, that they can storm and hold the dreadful Hill. When an easy prey they would not, attempted not, to grasp it. Now, when a forlorn impracticability, upon which depends the fate of a nation—the grandest stake ever ventured on one single issue of rashness—they are ready to rush up its appalling steeps.

Look yonder now! There is the "Old Guard" in battle array! Pickett looks across the plain and up the hill to the summit. What madness! What a journey to contemplate! But such is his lot.

The end is near. This is the supreme throw for the grand prize in this desperate game.

There they go—the legions of Pickett! How grandly they move! What splendid order in the face of that tornado of canister and grape! How steadily their grey waves roll across that plain of death! They step quickly at shouldered arms!

The regiments are well filled. See how far the colors are apart! Look what long lines the division makes! An army in itself—ten, twelve thousand muskets—there must be more. They are about to charge Cemetery Hill; they are about to try and break the enemy's line. Devoted Virginians! What a noble sacrifice! Up the Hill they go! Look how rapidly the regimental colors are drawing nearer one another!

Now they are concealed in the blaze and smoke. There bursts the men's wild huzza. They are storming the heights; the guns are silenced. The Virginians are on the Hill. Is there any force left to hold it?

They are attacked by the reserves. It is lost. The wild vociferous cheers of the triumphing Federals are heard above the roar of the battle's storm; they are rolling on down the slope.

Pickett's division is annihilated. "The Field of Gettysburg" is lost. The Confederacy has received her death blow. Her star has set in the darkness of eternal night.

This tells the story. Pickett's failure on Cemetery Hill decides the battle of Gettysburg, and seals the doom of the Confederacy.

The history of this field is indelibly written in letters of tears and of blood. The mournful wails of a nation will rise above it, and ascend to Heaven, crying pitifully against the blighting curse of civil war—the blood of brothers by brothers shed—ten thousand times that of Abel again and again multiplied.

Every house, the friendly shade of every tree, grove, orchard, is an improvised hospital. For miles around, the country is transformed into one vast appalling, ghastly burying-ground.

Pickett's division melted away in the white heat of the battle flame, and perished on the field.

The great Confederate waves which were hurled with such terrific impetuosity upon the opposing breakers, at other points along the line, were shattered, broken and rolled sullenly back as the baffled billows of the angry deep recede from the headland boulder upon which their fury has been spent in vain.

The Confederates were foiled, and forced to retire, leaving the flower of their army on the field; but they were not routed.

Their adversaries received serious mementoes of the shock—so great that had the results extended no farther than the mere abstract issues of the conflict, the advantages gained could not be termed a decisive triumph.

Yet, nevertheless, the palm of victory was theirs; the ultimate fruits of the day were conclusive, and probably saved the Union.

The shattered fragments of Lee's army fall back; re-form; face the enemy, and prepare to receive the onslaught of their vanquishers with cool desperation, such as sectional pride and individual heroism alone can inspire.

Thousands of Southerners from the advanced lines, that made the desperate charges, are cut off from the main body of their comrades and captured when the swiftly turning tide breaks against them. Let us look for a moment at a group of these discouraged warriors under guard in an open field, and hear what two of them have to say.

GEN. CLOUD: "Why, Garland boy, how do you happen to be here? When I last parted with you on the field of Manassas I never expected to see you again. The doctor said you could not live twenty-four hours. This is a fatal field to us—a sad day for the South and poor, dear, old Virginia. Half my command remains on the field. I feel as though I will never be able to smile again."

CLOUD: "A spent ball knocked me senseless, on top of that fatal Cemetery Hill yonder, just as we took it, and when consciousness returned I was a prisoner. Oh, father, the 'Old Guard of the Army of Northern Virginia' has made its last charge, captured its last battery; you will never more behold Pickett's division, unless you could be permitted to go over on that infernal hill and see it buried. I do not believe that a thousand men returned; and they are nearly all dead, those who were left behind. But how were you captured?"

GEN. CLOUD: "When they were beating us back, in the last final struggle, my horse was killed under me. My right foot hung in the stirrup. The poor nigger, my constant companion on every field from Romney to this, fell on my leg; and before I was able to extricate myself I was a prisoner."

CLOUD: "Since you are a prisoner, father, I am exceedingly thankful that we are together. Amid all our misfortunes, do you not regard this circumstance as being fortunate?"

GEN. CLOUD: "Only for this night. They will separate us."

CLOUD: "I am aware that they would separate us. It is for this one night, and this only, that I am thankful on the score of our being together. I fully understand that this is the last night we are to pass together before the war closes. It may be the last one on this side of eternity. But is it not enough to be thankful for, that we are permitted to pass one night together in this long, dark, cruel, trying-war, and that the first one of our captivity? Often in this cheerless world, the highest ecstasies of a life-time have been crowded into the brief space of one night."

GEN. CLOUD: "Yes, Garland, but nothing ecstatic can live one moment amid scenes like these, unless it be the departing spirits of the poor fellows now dying around us, if their dim eyes, as they emerge from their suffering tenements, can behold the open gates of Heaven. You are too young, my boy—your mind and spirit too elastic and buoyant, properly to estimate and duly appreciate the gravity of the situation at this bitter moment, either of ourselves personally, or of the South."

CLOUD: "Pardon me father; but you are laboring under an erroneous impression. I see utter ruin and hopeless slavery, as conquered subjects, for the South and her poor people, who have loved her, if not wisely, oh how truly well! For ourselves, I see ahead of us months—dreary, tedious months, in the gloom of a Northern prison, and perhaps a miserable death as traitors. But yonder comes Maj. Pleasington straight to us. We will resume our conversation after he leaves us."

MAJ. PLEASINGTON: "How are you, General and Garland? I have been riding among your wounded. I hoped not to find you there. I was riding by up the road, and recognized the General. Regret to find you prisoners, but since I do find you captives, I am glad you are in no worse plight. You will not long remain in custody. The little Colonel, Josse Flowers, where is he? Is he safe?"

GEN. CLOUD: "We are both reasonably well, save some bruises. Accept our thanks, Major, for this visit, and your kind expressions. Col. Flowers was unhurt a few moments before my horse fell. He has been in my brigade since the battle of South Mountain. He has not been absent from duty since he entered the army, and has never received a scratch. I believe he is safe."

CLOUD: "How about Oglethrop, Major?"

MAJ. P——: "Oh! the poor lad was wounded in Kilpatrick's charge on Hood—an ugly flesh wound in the arm. I guess he is at home before this time. How did you come out with your wound, Garland, received at Manassas?"

CLOUD: "I was a long time at death's door, concealed in an upper room of a house about six miles from the battle-field, near the Sudley Ford road. In about two months I was removed to a remote point in the mountain, where I remained until January, when I was able to set out to seek my command, which I found in North Carolina. This is my first important battle since. How did you and Oglethrop fare?"

MAJ. P——: "We both reached our homes very soon. We were well nursed, and recovered by Christmas.

"Oglethrop came down to the city for the holidays before rejoining his regiment. We rejoined our command about the middle of January. Oglethrop was very happy. He was engaged to Evalina, with the consent of her parents. Mr. Mountjoy was prepossessed with the matrimonial candidate; and the most favorable yet purely fortuitous circumstance that could possibly occur, transpired to aid him in overcoming the opposition of the mother.

"Col. Worthington returned home in season for Christmas festivities, and consummated an engagement with Miss Cassandra. This circumstance and Col. Worthington's interest in the cause of Oglethrop, overcame Mrs. Mountjoy's opposition, and she consented to give him her youngest daughter for a wife.

"Immediately after the permanent establishment of peace, if all the parties are then living, there will be a grand quadruple wedding at the Mountjoy mansion.

"Mrs. Mountjoy is, however, still uncompromising in her opposition to a match between Effie and I, and unshaken in her determination that Arnold Noel shall win Effie. He is in the navy, and out at sea. Garland, do you ever hear anything about Uncle Jake and his young mistress, and his dead young master's sweetheart?"

CLOUD: "I went down there before setting out for my command. Both mansions and Uncle Jake's cabin are in ashes. Leonora Fairchild, Cornelia Earl, and Uncle Jake are in Richmond, where they have devoted their lives to nursing their sick and wounded countrymen."

MAJ. P——: "Well, gentlemen, I will hasten to arrange for your parole. Expect me early to-morrow. Good-night."

Maj. Pleasington rides away.

GEN. CLOUD: "Garland, that is one grateful, magnanimous, noble young man. Do you believe he can get us paroled?"

CLOUD: "Certainly I do. There is no doubt about it."

GEN. CLOUD: "Well, then we are very fortunate indeed."

CLOUD: "But let us consider the subject in the light that we would have considered it had he not found us. Let us see what we can obtain from this little night, either pleasant or useful, while we are together. It is ours now. Let us profit by the privileges of these hours, and. employ them in arranging plans connected with our dark future.

"As soldiers, we have done our duty. Should we live to see the gloomy end, that now appears inevitable, our poor, desolate, mourning country will demand much of us, in aiding to bind up and soothe the desperate wounds which we have helped to inflict upon her. For my part, I do not intend to hesitate about entering upon those duties nor flinch from their performance, no matter what personal unpleasantness they require me to endure. The opportunities of this night we shall never see again."

GEN. CLOUD: "Your sentiments and force of reasoning amaze me. I have unjustly estimated your first remarks. But in what way would you employ the night?"

CLOUD: "You would trust me either with your liberty or your life, would you not, father?"

GEN. CLOUD: "Unhesitatingly; but what a question!"

CLOUD. "You do not wish to go to prison, nor do you want to remain inactive, trammeled by the sacred obligations of a parole, while the remnant of your comrades continue the hopeless struggle to obtain better terms when the end does come. Rather than accept either alternative, you would not hesitate to lead the charge over again, in a forlorn attempt to take and hold that cruel hill of death."

GEN. CLOUD: "Certainly I would not. But what can you mean?"

CLOUD: "Lay your head nearer to mine; I must tell you softly and cautiously."

GEN. CLOUD: "Now, my boy, I am ready to listen to you."

CLOUD: "Father, I mean to eat my breakfast, if they have any to give me, and if they have not, to fast with the Confederates to-morrow morning in their lines. Are you with me?"

GEN. CLOUD: "What reckless madness, Garland. It is simply an impossibility. We are closely guarded in the very centre-rear of the Federal army. We cannot pass the guards, who immediately surround us. Even were we beyond these, there are numerous others to stop us before we could reach the out-posts; and there we would find a compact skirmish-line almost as solid as a line of battle, probably within less than two hundred paces of a similar body of our troops. I have heard many wild stories about your daredevil recklessness beyond the advance-lines and on the battle-field which I did not believe; but now I have overwhelming testimony of their truthfulness. I have often wondered why you were not promoted. It is now clearly explained. The authorities dare not trust your rashness. You would not hesitate, I plainly perceive, to attack a division with a single company, if you had the command of so many men. I am pained to find this true."

CLOUD: "Well, father, I much regret to leave you here. This day I charged that fiery hill. It was in obedience to orders from my commanding officer. Worse than ever before my poor country now demands and requires my services. In attempting to place myself in a position to render them, I am not less performing a duty than when I responded to that fatal order, and moved into the flaming mouth of that life-destroying volcano, belching forth in torrents its showering missiles of murder. I go, father, and without an order, save the promptings of my conscience, which are now with me more potent than my dear father's rebuke.

"In all that I have done, for which I am termed rashly wild, it has been of my country, and not of myself, that I thought. For my country's sake I have been cautious and prudent. Never once have I been more rash and reckless than circumstances justified, as the results have always proved.

"Father, you have been a steadily rising officer, from a lieutenant to a brigadier-general. You have been constantly occupied with important duties which daily devolved upon you, in connection with your command. With sword in hand, you have led your men again and again into the jaws of death, and cheered and encouraged them to stand before the storming avalanche of overwhelming numbers at Antietam and Fredericksburg. But of the minutiæ, the smaller details, on the out-posts, you are profoundly ignorant, save in theory. I know all your theoretical problems: they are on the end of my tongue every word of them at will."

"By a flickering camp-fire, often in the deep solitude of a wilderness, all alone in the wintry-midnight, I studied infantry and cavalry tactics and army regulations until I committed every word to memory. In camp, on the march, and on the battle-field have I witnessed their practical utility. But to the solitary scout and the lonely picket, beyond the lines, and on the farthest outpost, they are utterly worthless in cases of extreme emergency. There the man soon learns that he must rely on himself, and be governed by circumstances. It is there that the close, industrious observer learns the moral of human nature, under the pressure of exhausting labor, and exposure to sudden, unexpected startling dangers.

The Federal troops are exhausted from fatigue. They know that our army is beaten, and that they are in no danger of being surprised by a night attack. They will sleep; the night will be dark. Many a time have I placed myself in greater peril and more treacherous pitfalls than this, when they were on the alert far more than they will be to-night; and I am going to escape from here."

GEN. CLOUD: "I will accompany you, if my leg will permit."

CLOUD: "Oh, I do not propose to walk. I have quite often mounted myself where the horses were scarcer and far harder to obtain than they will be to-night."

GEN. CLOUD: "Well, Garland, you are more and more a mystery to me. What time do you propose starting?"

CLOUD: "Some time about one o'clock. Now, father, you are going with me. You are in my sphere of service. You must trust me implicitly. We will take no chances of being fired on, at least not until the last moment, at the extreme danger line. If we are captured before reaching that point, why, we can be no worse off than we are now. So let us drop this subject.

"I know you are weary and want to sleep, and that my boyish nonsense will not interest you; but at all events, my father, I want to talk to you all this night, every minute that circumstances will admit."

GEN. CLOUD: "Let us talk my boy; I am more than willing. You more than interest, you astonish, me. I begin to hope that I have unjustly estimated you."

CLOUD: "That is mainly the tenor of my subject.

"By apparently providential circumstances, the road to render my country valuable services around and beyond our pickets, was laid open before me. I presented the question to the proper officer, who regarded it as sufficiently feasible to assign me to duty on that line.

"The circumstances just referred to transpired partially as a direct result of my befriending young Pleasington when he lay wounded at Manassas. Out of that simple act, many other circumstances beneficial both to the service and to individuals, have sprung—things already familiar to you.

"One night I took upon myself Edgar Harman's guard duty, when I believe his death would have resulted from his performing it. Personal gratitude to that young patrician did not prompt me. Between us there was no individual love. But he was my brother soldier. Duty to my country and to the cause of humanity prompted me to relieve him. Out of this little act directly, and befriending Pleasington indirectly, have sprung 'The Soldiers' Family Relief Society' and 'The Angel of Consolation.'"

GEN. CLOUD: "Why, Garland, are you connected with that puzzling mystery? Do tell me all you know about it."

CLOUD: "On conditions that you never divulge your knowledge until the war is ended."

GEN. CLOUD: "Certainly, boy; I will hold it sacred."

CLOUD: "The Harmans were grateful for my act. Miss Carrie overstepped the boundary line of class formality, and wrote me a letter, breathing beautiful sentiments of gratitude and pledges of the undying friendship of her family to our family. Courtesy compelled me to reply, which I did briefly and indifferently.

"About this time the wildest stories relative to my services as a scout were circulated. Miss Harman wrote to me most entreating letters, urging me to send an account sometimes, giving her family the true particulars of my most thrilling adventures. I most obstinately set my face against this; and I fear my blunt replies were almost uncivil; but she persisted.

"I read a good many distressing letters from the poor families of mountain soldiers. One cold, sleety night in December, lying in a bed of leaves, under a rock-cliff down beyond our out-post, I could not sleep. I had no fire. So I was forced to think. Under such circumstances a man thinks of a great many very absurd things, some of which are often unreasonable because they are never attempted. This night I conceived the bold and grand idea of enlisting Carrie Harman in the cause of the suffering families of our mountain comrades. The next day I wrote to her that in reply to her late letter I regretted I could not comply with her request, unless upon her solemn promise not to divulge the contents of my narratives while I lived and the war continued; and that, as matter of course, under such restrictions, she would not wish my interdicted statements.

"To my astonishment, she quickly replied that she was too selfish to have shared them with the public; and hence my conditions harmonized with her inclinations.

"I immediately wrote her about thirty pages of cap, detailing particulars of the out-post service that I have never unfolded to any other person; and in this same letter was the plan for organizing 'The Relief Society,' which I fearlessly asserted would be to me substantial manifestation of her gratitude for my kindness to her brother, and the only proof of it I would ever expect, or even accept. With the results you are sufficiently familiar.

"Regularly she sends me detailed reports of her good labors; and I send her accounts of my evil work. I wanted to tell you, father, while I could, because no one in this world dreams that a single line has ever passed between Miss Harman and I.

"This original proposition of mine to her, you would have branded as unpardonable and presumptuous folly. Like it, father, has been all my dare-devil, reckless rashness—with an object in each separate act, directly to benefit our cause.

"So of this to-night, and of all I accomplish until the Confederacy is dead.

"Then I shall mourn over her grave, as I have mourned, do and shall mourn every day of her existence, over the cause that created her, and go on laboring to assist in benefiting and in promoting the interests of the tillers of the soil—the poor of my native and dearly beloved but fated Sunny South. To her I have devoted, I do devote, I will ever devote—my life."

GEN. CLOUD: "God bless you, my boy You are a hero. Now I understand Miss Harman's scarlet face whenever your name was mentioned; this secret explains it.

"But beware of falling in love with her. Remember the traditional curse that for over five hundred years has rested upon all the male members of our family who have become involved in love affairs with ladies in high life or of noble birth. One of our ancestors pronounced that curse in a dungeon, where for over forty years he had been confined because he loved a noble lady who also loved him. It is said that no less than ten of our race have since, for the same cause, suffered either imprisonment or assassination; and that in every instance their affections were reciprocated by the ladies; and within my father's memory, his uncle proved his love for a beautiful and aristocratic lady with his life.

"Miss Harman is an earthly angel. Unquestionably, either on account of gratitude or esteem, or both, you exercise a wonderful influence over her. But remember that all in her sphere are not like her—angels."

'CLOUD: "I have for Miss Harman a divine adoration, similar to that I cherish for the sister of charity who nursed me so devotedly when I was wounded, back from the margin of the grave; but nothing more.

"Father, I must tell you that I am continually haunted by something like a presentiment that I am doomed to a long life, with all its days full of the most cruel wretchedness and the most bitter sorrow. Since the very first hour when I learned that war was inevitable, has this conviction oppressed me with its ever darkening shadow. It was in the howl of my dogs when I left home. It seemed to me that the little brutes felt it and pitied me. I hear it murmured in the sighing voice of the pine-tree, and in the notes of the little brooklets as they go singing along on their way to the sea. When I was convalescing in my solitary rambles in the grand old woods, I could hear it in the lugubrious reverberations of the mountain's echo. Thus all Nature speaks to me in the same cheerless, prophetic strain. Concerning my getting killed or dying from wounds, I never give myself the least concern, so thoroughly am I persuaded that I will be reserved for some other and perhaps sadder fate.

"But here are present things demanding our immediate attention — realities, not visionary shadows. Our hour has come. How dark it has grown, and how still! See down there against the horizon the dark figures of our two nearest guards asleep on post. Poor wretches! Human nature, with them, has been taxed beyond its capacities of endurance. Quickly now—not a word, father, but follow me, and do everywhere just what I tell you. There, now, we are nicely outside of our guard line. Here is a musket; I will take it. Lie down in that tall grass in the fence corner, while I stand guard here, and take some observations."

Suiting the action to the word, he soon meets his desired opportunity.

"Halt! Who comes there?"

A horseman approaches his post.

HORSEMAN: "Friend, with the countersign."

CLOUD: "Dismount, advance and give the countersign." . . . .

"All right. Go ahead."

The horseman rides away, and Cloud says:

"Now, father, we will go along this road for the present."

GEN. CLOUD: "Where in the world did you get the countersign, Garland?"

CLOUD: "Why, from that courier. Where else do you suppose I could get it? That is why I played sentinel."

GEN. CLOUD: "Well, that rivals all the audacious coolness I have ever before witnessed."

CLOUD: "That is the way I have captured many an unsuspecting fellow. Under more favorable circumstances this one would have shared the same fate.

"But soft! There is a house all aglow with light, and full of bustling life; and here, just ahead, are several horses at the fence, more than fifty yards from the house. Look! There are officers supping at the table. These are their horses fully caparisoned, with even their overcoats and arms on the saddles. How fortunate! Not a living soul nearer than the house, and no sentinel visible there. What superb animals and equipments—cavalry officers, colonels and above. Choose quickly and mount. Ah! you take the jet black. I will take this one; it appears a dark bay. How strongly the lights reflect out here. It is grey twilight here; but they can't see, looking in this direction.

"Button up the blue over the grey carefully. Now a ride for liberty. Slowly until we are out of hearing of that house. Now, faster and faster like the wild horse of Tartary. Why, they do not appear to have any camp guards out. I want to bear for our extreme left. I think this is about the direction. We seem to be leaving the camps behind. Slack up. I hear a horseman coming toward us.

"Can you tell us how far it is to the out-post, and what command holds it up this road?"

HORSEMAN: "About two hundred yards. The Pennsylvania reserves hold it."

CLOUD: "We are right after all. Thank you. Good night."

"Now, father, the crisis is at hand. We must be cool, and ride slowly. If the sentinel wishes to detain us until the officer of the guard comes, mount quick as a flash of lightning, lean forward and to the side from the guard, and make the horse fly past him. Here is the main body sleeping on their arms, on both sides of the road. Yonder is a sentinel, walking a beat in the road.

SENTINEL: "Halt! Who comes there?"

CLOUD: "Friends, with the countersign."

SENTINEL: "Dismount one, advance, and give the countersign."

"All right. Come ahead."

CLOUD: "Is there a sentinel beyond you?"

SENTINEL: "If there is, he is a rebel one. They had a vedette up on the hill about two hundred yards from here at dark. There is no infantry in front of us."

CLOUD: "Well, we are glad to find you on the alert. We are making a tour of inspection of our posts, and at the same time reconnoitering to ascertain whether or not the enemy is falling back. We will go up the road until we find the vedette, and you must not shoot us as we return."

SENTINEL: "It is nearly time for my relief, but I will post him."

CLOUD: "Come General, let us surprise a rebel vedette.

"Now, father, if we can reach our lines thus easily, we are fortunate. My greatest apprehension is that our vedettes have orders to fire without halting; but perhaps not on only one or two. I think we have rode nearly a mile since leaving the Federal posts."

GEN. CLOUD: "It is some distance. I believe our troops are retreating under cover of the darkness. Well, my boy, there seems to be method in your recklessness, if you conduct all your operations as systematically as you have conducted this one, and far less danger than I imagined. Ignorance is not a word sufficiently strong to express my lack of knowledge in the rôles that you play."

CLOUD: "I am thankful that you are undeceived, father. It causes me a thrill of gratification to hear you speak some words of approbation. But yonder is the solitary horseman. The end is near now——"

VEDETTE: "Halt! Who comes there?"

CLOUD: "Two Confederates, who have escaped from the enemy, without the countersign."

VEDETTE: "Dismount, and advance—one."

CLOUD: "How fortunate father. I will advance. To whose command, vedette, do you belong?"

VEDETTE: "Gen. J——'s Virginia brigade. To what command do you belong?"

CLOUD: "Gen. J—— knows us well. Send us to him at once. I am Cloud, the scout of 1861-2, and that is Gen. Cloud, of Jackson's old corps."

VEDETTE: "Advance, General. Yes, that is Gen. Cloud. I recognize you in the dark, General. I remember you since Antietam and South Mountain, where I saw you so often in such wondrous peril. The officer of the post is coming. Ah! here he is now. Lieutenant, here are Gen. Cloud and his son, who have just escaped from the enemy and wish to be conducted to Gen. J——."

LIEUTENANT: "All right, gentlemen: follow me."

CLOUD: "Now, my General, I am ready to recognize your rank and respect your authority; we are in your sphere."

GEN. CLOUD: "I thank God for it. I breathe easier again. What will your friend Pleasington think of this?"

CLOUD: "Oh! Pleasington will not be in the least surprised. He has known of me being in other tight places and then very soon out of them. He will be glad of it, more than sorry, only he will feel disappointed that he failed to realize the pleasure of extending to us the kindness which he anticipated, and which I am certainly well assured he so much desired to bestow. But I see the long, grizzly beard of the old, uncouth General, who is writing by a wax taper, out yonder in the gloom. How weird and unearthly is his appearance! Let us enter, and present ourselves; all is over and we are safe."

CHAPTER XXV.

GENERAL W. E. J——.

" The brightest flower of her own Southland's bloom,
    Her shroud the sea-foam, woven without a stain,
The coral ocean depths her silent tomb,
    And his own heart's grave, for he never smiled
        again."
                                    —M. A. BILLINGS.

GEN. J——, who was referred to as Col. J——, in the chapter "Beyond the Out-posts," and whom we beheld writing by a dim waxen taper, in the sombre foliage of a Pennsylvania forest, in the immediate vicinity of the fatal "Field of Gettysburg," the same night of its most mournful, soul-stirring scene, was a native Virginian—a true son of the South-western blue-grass yeomanry.

In his tender years he was elected to a cadet-ship at West Point, where he graduated with high honors.

From the military school he passed to the United States army with a clear record, blemished by no dishonorable mark. He was amiable, witty, fascinating: hence a general favorite among his comrades and in society, wherever duty led him.

In the Mexican War he rendered meritorious service, and displayed conspicuous gallantry on the field of battle, and also rendered valuable aid in many Indian campaigns on the Plains and in Texas.

But back amid the enchanting dells of his native blue hills there was a luring charm to draw his thoughts and soul from the stern duties of a soldier; an object capable of awakening emotions the most elevating and ennobling that ever wield the sway over the heart and control the life of man—a pure woman! true love!

Miss D—— was the fair object of his gallant adoration. She was of the fair flowers of that far-famed beauty-producing, blue-grass region, one of the very fairest.

To this lovable young lady Captain J—— offered a soldier's worthy hand, and sued in return for hers of spotless beauty. He loved her; she loved him—a beautiful mutuality. With them the course of true love ever ran smoothly.

She accepted his offer of marriage, and yielded to him her heart, and plighted vows.

Capt. J—— then returned to his post of duty in Texas, where he was stationed some years after the Mexican War, with a joyous heart and a hopeful future.

Time rolled by some seasons. Capt. J—— returned again to claim his long-time affianced bride.

After the nuptial ceremonies were consummated, the ovations from friends had subsided, and his furlough was almost spent, Capt. J—— set out with his beautiful wife for his distant post, with dream-land, day-dreamland anticipations.

His journey was by way of the Crescent City, the beautiful metropolis of the South, which he reached in safety. Between him and his destination rolled the blue, the sweeping, the treacherous surge of the Gulf of Mexico, above its hidden treasures and its buried hopes.

But what were these to Capt. J—— and his bride? Little recked these young and confiding hearts of the terrors of the deep or its wide waste of waters. The ecstacies of love stifled the rising thought of storm perils and dangers on the sea. They had, this happy couple, just embarked on the voyage of life. What was a little span of water in their path? What had it been to him? No barrier to stay his eager journeys to the land of his birth, the home of his love. To them it would be but a pleasing sail, a delightful voyage.

Thus, little fearing, they embarked on a Gulf Outside-line steamer, passed the mouth of the noble "Father of Waters," crossed the bar, and sped onward to break "the blue crystal of the seas."

When the voyage was nearly half accomplished a white squall suddenly struck the staunch ship. A white squall on the Gulf of Mexico is the mariner's terror. It is something terrible to contemplate, appalling to experience.

It comes suddenly, without a moment's warning; and did it give warning, the situation would not thereby be rendered less fearful. It is the raging tempest's breath doubled, twisted and concentrated.

The pent-up force of the tempest and the hurricane bursts into a devastating whirlwind that twists vast craters down deep into the bosom of the sea. When this strikes a vessel, she is doomed.

Thus was the ship which carried Capt. J—— and his bride, with their hopes suddenly foundered, and forced to be abandoned with demoralizing precipitation.

All the lady passengers were placed in the largest and the staunchest boat; and among these, was Capt. J——'s bride.

This boat capsized, and every soul on board sank to rise no more.

The men were saved in the other boats.

What a lamentable voyage, and what a bridal tour for Capt. J——! What a sorrow had replaced the joyous hope in his heart, to be borne in sadness, back to his cheerless duties!

From that day Capt. J—— was a sadly changed man. His life became soured and embittered; he was ever after morose and taciturn, caring neither for himself nor for the world.

In course of time he abandoned the army and returned to his agricultural estate, where he lived in quiet seclusion, a silent mourner.

Thus he remained with his sleepless sorrow and his broken heart hid away from the eyes of the heedless, unsympathetic world, until the tumult and the commotion of the gathering civil storm of 1861 aroused him from his lethargic slumbers.

His first love, the lifeless and voiceless idol of his young life, once the inspiration of his soul, carried his vitalizing characteristics down with her into the bosom of the deep; and left his nature inert, indifferent, cold and inanimate, with seemingly nothing on earth able to revivify him into activity.

But he had another cherished idol, a natal love, a love that he had never been called upon while in the peaceful remoteness of civil life, to be jealous of its sanctity; something none had attempted to violate. This was OLD VIRGINIA.

Her call reanimated him once more. He quickly responded, and espoused her cause; took to himself another bride.

He hastened to the field of strife with a company of cavalry, the first from his section of the State.

In the old army, Capt. J—— outranked J. E. B. Stewart. For some personal reasons of a strictly private nature, the most vindictive animosity existed between these men, dating back to the days of their associated service in the old army. This hostility time did not abate.

With this hatred still rankling in their hearts, Fate decreed that they should be associated directly together in the service of the ill-starred cause of the Confederacy. Stewart started as a Colonel; J——, as captain under him and in the same regiment. Throughout their careers their grades of rank remained in about the same proportion as they ascended in the scale of promotions.

To-night we find this veritable night-hawk, Gen. J——, with his brigade in position, to hover as a protecting cloud on the rear flank of his crippled and dispirited countrymen, as their vanquished hosts sullenly and slowly drag their shattered columns on their long, painful, sad retreat through a hostile land, in the face of the victorious legions of the enemy, who were expected to be relentless pursuers.

Note his greeting to the unexpected arrival of his friends.

GEN. J——: "Well! Are there not enough dead men in this ghastly region to satiate the Infernal, without sending out ghosts into the dread shades of this doomsday night, to frighten to death those who escaped the thrusts of the pale horseman's blade? Why, Gen. Cloud, I heard to-night that you were killed, and I thought Garland's bones were purifying for the resurrection morn on the plains of Manassas."

GEN. CLOUD: "It was only my horse that was killed. He fell on my leg, and I was captured before I could extricate myself. I suppose my comrades think that I was killed. Garland was knocked senseless on Cemetery Hill, and captured. When I was turned into the herd of prisoners, he was almost the first man I met. This work is all his. I was, I am now truly ashamed to admit, opposed to it, until I found my suasive powers and rebukes were alike unavailing.

GEN. J——: "Had I known you was a prisoner General, and Garland with you, I would have bet my horse that you were both in our lines before daybreak in the morning. It is charging those infernal, fiery mouthed batteries that beats the boy, where he cannot employ his light-fingered strategy and startling little ruses. I am glad you are both safe and with me for to-morrow, when I expect to see some tight work. General, you can do the praying, I can do the swearing, and Garland the scouting for the brigade to-morrow. May be we can get through."

Cloud: "It is a pity you swear so, General. But for that, you and father would make the best match harness-team in our army."

Gen. J——: "Yes, Garl; and by —— if the old General had his old brigade here with me, like it was at South Mountain and Antietam, we would make a team the Yanks would get—— sick of driving before to-morrow night."

"Those maiden battles of ours, as brigade commanders, General, were the ones where we rendered our most brilliant services."

Gen. Cloud: "Ah! But then our star shone brighter than now."

Gen. J——: "Than now? I am unable to find it anywhere in the canopy of cerulean blue to-night. It went out, my dear friend, to-day, when Pickett's division failed on that now blood-christened Hill, and left us and our cause in the midnight darkness of despair."

"From this day forward I shall shut my eyes to the consequences that are surely coming on, and fight everywhere and under all circumstances with the reckless indifference as to myself that a pirate under the black flag displays when he finds himself at last face to face with the inevitable, and stands at bay, selling his life at a price worthy a far better cause.

"Early in life the cruel waves of an angry sea robbed me of happiness and hope forever. In my declining years, so long embittered with a cureless sorrow, I espoused this young but, as I find too late, fickle creature, 'The Southern Confederacy,' which I have this day beheld hopelessly engulfed in the blood of her truest and bravest defenders. Oh, my friends, I feel to-night some acute pangs of that relentless anguish of 'the long ago!' But let us try to sleep a little."

Cloud: "Yes, General; for to-morrow I start on a career, be it long or short, with the one ever changeless watch-word, 'Remember Gettysburg.'"

Gen. Cloud: "That is a memento that will haunt us all to the grave."

Gen. J——: "Now Lieutenant, watch them closely, observe your instructions to the letter, and post me promptly whenever there is occasion for it."

Cloud: "Can I accompany him, General, entirely independent."

Gen. J——: "Yes, Lieutenant, he acts as he likes with you or not."

Gen. Cloud: "I think I will serve under you to-day, boy."

Cloud: "No, father; this is no proper service for a general."

Gen. J——: "He is right; stay with me Gen. Cloud."

The Lieutenant and Garland Cloud ride away; and the two old generals lay down on their blankets and sleep until morning, when they awake and continue their conversation.

Gen. Cloud: Did you sleep General? I did quite soundly."

Gen. J——: "Oh, yes; I was completely exhausted. I wish that boy of yours was trained in the cavalry manual."

Gen. Cloud: "He tells me he has memorized every word of both it and the army regulations. I know him to be an expert rider."

Gen. J——: "I am pleased to learn this. He is a good scout, a fine judge of human nature, and thoroughly understands the great advantages afforded against men in a moment of temporary excitement or confusion by the loss of their presence of mind.

"How feeble is the vigor of the pursuit to what I expected; the enemy must be badly crippled. It is nearly night. Yonder comes the Lieutenant. It has not been long since the relief started to him."

Gen. Cloud: "I do not see anything of Garland in the party."

Gen. J——: "Oh, we may not see him for a week to come."

"Well, Lieutenant, I perceive you have captured some prisoners and horses."

LIEUTENANT: "Yes, General, but this is partly your young infantryman's work. He can shame the best of us on horseback.

"He got among detached parties of a Dutch squadron, and actually destroyed them. They could not ride, nor shoot, nor use the sabre; and their clumsy horses could not run. The horse he rides is well trained, and goes like a flash. He wounded some, or else they were disabled in falling off their horses. He soon had the horse loaded with the ammunition of sixteen-shooters, and has fired about five hundred times to-day. He did not mind tackling a half dozen Dutchmen at a time. But this afternoon the Dutch were relieved. He soon began to be cautious, and did not attempt to provoke their fire, nor to run on to a half dozen detached in a party; he sent me word that they were the best regulars in the Federal army, then next to us."

GEN. J——: "That will do, Lieutenant. Feed your men on horses.

"This dispatch, Gen. Cloud, is a peremptory order from Gen. Stewart to burn this wagon train, which is worth more to the army than my commission. If I do not obey the order, he will court-martial me. If I obey it, and he learns that I might have saved the train, he will then reprimand me for not exercising discretionary judgment. What would you do under similar circumstances?"

GEN. CLOUD: "I would obey the order when satisfied that it was impossible to save this valuable property, which is not, from every present indication, yet the situation."

GEN. J——: "Yes, and—— me if I don't take that course."

GEN. CLOUD: "Well, General, I shall take this opportunity to rejoin my command, as I may not soon have another. So I bid you adieu for the present."

GEN. J——: "Good fortune to you, Gen. Cloud. Farewell."

Some time after the Confederate army had crossed the Potomac and encamped in Virginia, Garland Cloud reported to Gen. J——.

CLOUD: "Well, Gen. J——, had you booked me as lost this time?"

GEN. J——: "No, Garl, I shall never do that until the sod is growing green over your grave. The old General is uneasy about you, as you were not accounted for when the last of our rear guard crossed the river; but I sent him word that you would turn up yet all right. You must have a large credit now on your Gettysburg account. I see the fine horse has a flesh wound on the rump."

CLOUD: "Yes, General, father seems to regard this service as being more dangerous than charging batteries, but I do not thus consider it. I have caused them all the annoyance that I could. The horse, brave, fine fellow, got that scratch from long range.'

GEN. J——: "Now Garl, I wish you would take charge of that squadron, and put it through every evolution of the drill and sabre exercise.

* * * * * * *

"That will do. You understand that as well as some of my oldest and most efficient officers. Let me see some of those grand feats of horsemanship the boys have been telling me about.

* * * * * * *

"Well, Garl, there are few men in any service can outride you."

CLOUD: "Now, General, I will turn the horse and trappings over to you, and go and see the wreck of my command!"

GEN. J——: "Ah! wreck it is, too. I understand that on the retreat, Gen. Lee, when passing a small body of troops, asked Gen. Longstreet whose battalion that was; and that he shed tears when answered, 'That, General, is Pickett's division.' I will keep the horse for you until you are sent on the scout again."

CLOUD: "That will be most kind. Good-by, General."

GEN. J——: "Good-by, Garland. Our watchwords are the same. Some time in the gloomy midnight or on the field of battle we will meet again."

CHAPTER XXVI.

THE TRANSFER, AND PART OF ITS SEQUEL.

" Who loves raves—'tis youth's frenzy—but the cure
  Is bitterer still ; as charm by charm unwinds
Which robed our idols, and we see too sure
  Nor worth, nor beauty dwells, from out the mind's
Ideal shape of such ; yet still it binds
  That fatal spell, and still it draws us on,
Reaping the whirlwind from the oft sown winds ;
  The stubborn heart, its alchemy begun,
Seems ever near the prize—wealthiest when most
  undone."
                    —BYRON.

CLOUD: "Capt. Harman, I have just been relieved from my guard-post, and ordered to report to you. What does this mean?"

CAPT. HARMAN: "How are you, Capt. Cloud? Let me congratulate you."

CLOUD: "Captain, don't make sport of a poor ragged soldier."

CAPT. H——: "There is no sport. Here is your commission in the cavalry of the regular army, and an order to report at once to Gen. J——. We are sorry to lose you; but I have long been expecting this, and have been surprised at its delay."

CLOUD: "Well, it is a surprise to me of which I did not even dream."

Soon after he is greeted by his general.

GEN. J——: "Well, Capt. Cloud, I am pleased to find you prompt. I want you to take the Gettysburg horse and accoutrements, and proceed without delay to S——, in the South-west, where you will find a squadron of rich men's sons— a regular mob. Take charge of them, and drill them thoroughly, at the same time leaving no clause of the most rigid discipline unenforced. They will hate you, but never mind that.

"I expected to accompany you, but I am forced to remain here now to answer a charge for not burning a wagon train, instead of bringing it out of Pennsylvania. I may be able to join you within two months. I want you to commence with that squadron what I mean to enforce in every company in that department. Make a model squadron. The material is the very best in the world."

CAPT. CLOUD: "I shall comply with your wishes, General, to the very best of my ability."

GEN. J——: "I am satisfied that you will not disappoint my expectations. You are a young man of the mountains, and are destined to see desperate service in them, for which the credit will be small; but it is a service of the most grave importance to the South.

"In loving the cause which we serve, you are I think, Capt. Cloud, the only young man I know who loves her with the blind desperate devotion similar to mine; that would treasure her memory, long years after she is dead, with the same constant fidelity as when she was young, beautiful and strong, promising to stand proudly forth among the nations of the earth crowned with a diadem of unsurpassable glory. But now, my dear boy, she is maimed, sick and emaciated; yet still she is that same late beautiful and lovable form. Let us stand by and defend her lowly couch of death; and force from her ruthless despoilers their reluctant consent to her decent burial and funeral obsequies worthy the lofty nobility of her tender years.

"Think of her poverty-stricken orphans. It is for them that we fight, from this day forward, to secure for them a peace under the old flag that will enable them to scrape up the fragments from among the *débris* of ruins, and with these lay a foundation upon which their posterity, as they are able to procure materials, may build a new structure, that will, in time, render their existence tolerable.

"I am regarded as being heartless and unfeeling. It is false. I am miserable. My pangs of cruel, unabating agony have made me reckless and rendered me indifferent to myself—and myself only. The world cannot look down into my heart and read the secret emotions there concealed. Because I am rough outside, because I enforce discipline with unfeeling severity, and because I am wicked, I am deemed a hater of the human race. I admit that I hate corruption, and the political abominations that have deluged the country with blood; but the true, the pure, and the good I reverence and adore.

"Your father detailed to me your sentiments expressed to him, the night you came to me near Gettysburg. This is why I am talking to you with so much freedom. Although you are so young, there is harmony between our spirits. I want you to know me, since we are to work together, perhaps die together,—not that either, Cloud, for you will be there when I am no more.

"I love the poor toil-worn agriculturist, and deplore the ruin that has overwhelmed and will yet overwhelm him. When this war is over, the South cannot be represented by anything in this world, so truly well as by Byron's picture of modern Greece. What a spectacle! The black curse of demoralization will run riot over the land. The rich will be poor and helpless; the poor will be discontented and desperate.

"We need not regret the war nor its results: it was an inevitable destiny. Come it must at some time. Better now, before the country grew more prosperous and powerful. We poor worms had better bear its wasting storms of desolating destruction, than for them to be reserved for generations unborn.

"What will it matter to us a hundred years hence? Long before that period of time will have elapsed, the country will be recovered from the material effects of the war, but of the moral effect—never. The high standard of morality and honor and integrity for which this country was once so characteristically famous, will go glimmering with the things that were, and be replaced by deceit, treachery, fraud, and every imaginary kind of intriguing chicanery. These will be practiced by persons of both sexes once possessed of irreproachable reputations. They will resort to these degrading devices of low cunning in order to gain existence, sustain precarious social positions, or support fast and intemperate living—habits contracted in the flush times of the fickle bubbles of war—by their wits, rather than take their true and proper stations in life, and support themselves by respectable and honest labor.

"All these things are the legitimate offsprings of war, and are felt, to some extent, by every nation connected with it directly, although the soil upon which the actual conflict is waged may be in a remote region of the globe. History teaches this. With the army of occupation, in Mexico, I witnessed it.

"Never has any country on the earth suffered from this blighting curse worse than this country must suffer after this war is over, because there are so many people to be affected by it; and then there is no hamlet so remote, no hovel so humble as entirely to escape this thrice damnable influence, neither North nor South.

"Garland, remain firm, I entreat you, in your faith and resolutions to be the devoted friend of the tillers of the soil; for upon them rests the country's only hope.

"Remember my words. Think of them, and compare with them the signs of the times, as you may some day, away yonder on the other side of this bloody curtain of smoke and flame, see and experience them. Then you will, I hope, bestow a thought of kindness on the spot, wherever it may be, that is the lonely, friendless grave of your friend, poor, uncouth, eccentric old Bill J——."

CAPT. C——: "Oh, alas! my poor General!"

GEN. J——: "Ah, Garland! I see you pity me, and deplore the cause for which I am suffering so bitterly—the sad and cruel fate in store for my poor country. This from your young, tender and yet pure and innocent heart, is a real comfort to me. I am little pitied and less loved in this cold world, but it may be my own fault. But how could I help it? My heart was buried beneath the wild waves of the Gulf of Mexico, with my lost Rose. I was unable to dissemble, and act a part I could not feel; and hence I became estranged from society and the world, and have thus, I suppose, forfeited all claim to the consideration and sympathy of mankind.

"This is enough. Your tears to me are more preciously eloquent than all the words your tongue could speak. Until we meet again in the South-west, farewell."

CAPT. C——: "Farewell, my General and my friend. While I live, I shall remember your sad words."

GEN. J——: "God bless you, Capt. Cloud, my dear young friend."

Now we find Garland Cloud on the parade-ground, in front of his squadron, addressing the soldiers.

CAPT. CLOUD: "Officers, soldiers, young gentlemen: I have been ordered here by the Confederate Government to take command of you, drill, discipline, and prepare you for active service; and to do this rapidly and thoroughly. This means unpleasantness for you, but I have no discretion.

"I am pained to find you utter strangers to the simplest rudiments of what you must begin to experience this day.

"From the order which will be promulgated, there will be no deviation on my part, under any state of circumstances; but in every instance will its provisions be enforced, and the penalties for their infraction promptly inflicted."

The scene changes to Cloud's head-quarters.

FIRST CITIZEN: "Capt. Cloud, my friend and I are fathers of two of the young officers under your command, on a visit to them. The complaints are loud against your severity, so much so that we have been induced to bear to you a remonstrance signed by every member of your command."

CAPT. CLOUD: "To me remonstrances are in vain. I am simply obeying orders—a duty which good soldiers perform blindly—simply what these young men have sworn to obey."

SECOND CITIZEN: "Then you will not modify your stringency?"

CAPT. C——: "By no means and in no wise, gentlemen."

FIRST CITIZEN: "Well, Captain, this is discouraging for the boys."

Cloud is again before his squadron.

CAPT. C——: "Officers and soldiers: your mutinous remonstrance has been read with surprise. It is the authority and dignity of the Government, and not mine, that you assail. From this moment, every one, without exception, connected with similar insubordination, will be transferred to Gen. Lee's infantry.

"Kid-glove, band-box soldiers are handsome to look at on reviews and grand parades, where there are lady spectators; but they are soon spoiled in the dust, mud and hard knocks of an active campaign.

"It is a concession from the Government that you are not in the infantry. Your horses are mustered into the service, and just as much under the control of the Government as you are

yourselves. It is my duty to see that they are properly treated.

"You are gentlemen. A true soldier must be a gentleman. Once separate the duty of a soldier toward his immediate commander from your ideas of the school-boy's resentment, and your chief trouble will be over. I am held as strictly accountable to my superiors as you are to me. The day will come, and before long, when you will recognize your present folly."

The scene changes to the parlor of the home of one of Cloud's officers.

FIRST YOUNG LADY: "Capt. S——, how handsomely your squadron marched through town this evening. How was it that not one left his place, or scarcely turned his head to greet his friends, while all the other companies were nearly broken up and scattered over town?"

CAPT. S——: "That tyrant, Capt. Cloud, would not allow it; nor could one of us leave camp to come in to-night, without his permission; and we must be in our places by sunrise."

SECOND YOUNG LADY: "He doesn't seem unkind. I think when his sun-bronzed face was flushed, as his tall form appeared—when he rode forward on that handsome deep bay horse, in response to the request of the Colonel that he thank the ladies, in the name of the regiment, for the flag which they presented—that he was the picture of good-nature and kindness; but at other times he appeared very sad."

LIEUT. M——: "I should think he would be sad, since he has not one friend in the squadron, and never speaks to any one; nor is he ever spoken to except when the stern compulsions of duty render it unavoidable."

MISS M——: "Why, brother Joe, you ought to be ashamed. Where did he go to-night?"

LIEUT. M——: "He stayed in camp, and let all the other officers come to town; and all the men, too, he granted a leave of absence, fifty at a time, for two hours—but I pity those who fail to return within the specified time, or get drunk. I guess he knew nobody would invite him; and had he been so much favored as to receive an invitation, I am certain that he would have declined. He commands the regiment to-night."

MISS M——: "Brother Joe, could you have

ry

heard the compliments lavished upon you all, and upon his laconic, yet beautifully appropriate little acknowledgment speech, and the ludicrous remarks made about the disgraceful comparison which the other companies made with your two, you would feel flattered. To whom is all this due? How did the men get their handsome new uniforms, cavalry saddles, sabres, revolvers, carbines, etc.? Why are the accoutrements so bright and the horses so sleek? Why can the men ride so well and march so finely? Then, finally, why do the other companies lack all these things? Answer these questions creditably, so that the answers will support your position taken against your commander."

Lieut. M——: "I am forced to admit, sissie, that this is all his work, and necessary, were we ever going to the front. But the Colonel told us again this evening, that the speech of this Captain, in which he intimated that the time when we would need discipline was near, was mere bombast; that we were organized to guard the public works in this section, and that we will do this until the war is over."

Miss M——: "Hum! What does Col. S—— know about war? But I hear cousin Carrie coming down stairs. I wish she could have arrived in time to witness all this controverted military display to-day. She will take my side."

Servant Girl: "Here is a note for Capt. S——."

Lieut. M——: "What is it, S——? You are pale as a ghost."

Capt. S——: "Read for yourself, Lieutenant."

Miss M——: "Why brother, you are as pale as Capt. S——."

Lieut. M——: "Read it, sissie, for the information of all."

Miss M——[Reading]:

"'Head-quarters, Cavalry Camp,
"'Sept. 8, 1863.

"'Capt. S——will inform all the officers of the first squadron who are in town that we march at five A. M. to-morrow, sharp, with light baggage. The remaining companies of the regiment will follow as soon as they are in a condition to take the field.

"'Our destination is lower East Tennessee, to meet Burnside. I state this fact, in order to give you warning to take appropriate leave of your friends, because it will be many a weary day before you see them again.

"' Respectfully,
"'Garland Cloud,
"'Capt. C. S. A.'

"There now, you see the kind of home-guards you are.

"Cousin Carrie, I wanted you to help me in defending this poor captain, whom they hate on account of his rigid discipline, because they said they would never need it.

"But why, coz, you are as pale as anybody else."

Miss Carrie Harman: "Let me see that note, please, coz. Why, that, is my best friend, who saved dear Edgar's life. Was Edgar here, he would challenge you all to mortal combat. This young gentleman is one of the bravest of the brave, with a heart as tender as a schoolgirl's; and his father is a general who has distinguished himself on all the bloodiest fields, everywhere that Jackson's old corps has fought."

Capt. S——: "Well, Lieutenant, since he is Miss Carrie's friend, and has all the ladies here enlisted in his defense, we will have to apologize and seek his friendship.—This business breaks up our ball arrangements rather sadly."

Lieut. M——: "Yes, we retract; for who dare offend 'The Angel of Consolation.'"

Now the scene is a running battle ground.

Gen. J——: "Captain, who commands these men here?"

Capt. S——: "I do, sir, this company."

Gen. J——: "Who are those ahead here, where that heavy firing is?"

Capt. S——: "Look here, stranger, what of your business is this? I have my orders to take up a position on the next hill yonder, and have not time to waste answering questions. You had better get out of here about as fast as you can."

Gen. J——: "I am Brig.-Gen. J——, commanding this department, and have just arrived on this field to find our forces, as far as I can see, in panicky disorder and flight. I am unable to learn anything."

Capt. S——: "Beg pardon, General. You are a stranger to me. Capt. Cloud is up there, with the other company of his squadron, and some two or three hundred stragglers from other commands rallied by him and his officers. He says that unless we hold the enemy in check, in this rough country, until dark, our little army will be destroyed."

Gen. J——: "Thank you, Captain. Obey your orders now."

The General rode forward and joined Cloud.

Capt. Cloud: "Well, my General, I am very glad to see you, but regret that you should find things so desperate as they are. For God's sake gallop to the rear and collect all the stragglers, the artillery and everything possible for defense, on the bluffs beyond the creek. They are flanking me. I must fall back to the next hill in a few minutes. The men are discouraged, and have no confidence in the General, who has been running for more than a hundred miles, and much of the time far more precipitately than necessary.

"My boys are better than veterans, because they do not know when they are whipped. They are all my friends now."

Gen. J——: "My anticipations are more than realized. The scout can command and inspire others to action. My staff are rallying stragglers at the point indicated. I will hasten back. Don't let them capture your fine, brave fellows; and send me word occasionally at what time you will probably be obliged to fall back to that point, and I will send you word how the out-look is for defense."

Capt. C——: "They can never drive me to the creek to-day."

Gen. J——: "Well, then, by to-morrow I shall be organized. I shall try to see you to-night."

They parted, but met again that night.

Capt. C——: "Well, General, things will appear better in the morning than they did to-day!"

Gen. J——: "Oh, yes, Captain. Everyone will be in his place, and I shall have some veteran regiments here before day-light. I hope we can soon turn the joke on the blue-coats."

Capt. C——: "I was pleased to hear the court acquitted you."

Gen. J——: "Yes; and I plead guilty to the specification of disrespect to my commanding officer, and told the court, in his presence, that if I had ever shown him any respect, I begged his pardon."

The scene changes to the bivouac of Cloud's officers.

Capt. S——: "Well, Lieutenant, Capt. Cloud is a trump."

Lieut. M——: "Yes, I cannot see how he escapes death. He does not seem to think of danger for himself, but is very careful about exposing the men."

Generals J—— and Cloud meet.

Gen. J——: "Ha! there, Gen. Cloud, whence did you hail?"

Gen. C——: "How are you, Gen. J——? I did not expect to meet you. I left the army the day after the battle of Spottsylvania Court-house, and came out here to testify before a court-martial to-day. I am waiting for the train to come along, to return to my post. How do you happen to be here?"

Gen. J——: "I have been up to M—— on business, and have just arrived on the west-bound train, returning to my command, which has, since Longstreet evacuated East Tennessee, been slowly verging toward the East."

Gen. C——: "Come, General, and sit down with me in the waiting-room, and tell me about my boy, and your rough-and-tumble fall and winter campaigns in the Tennessee mountains. I have heard of your terrible sufferings, both from hunger and cold."

Gen. J——: "I guess I will do that, General, and then sleep until morning, instead of riding to my command to-night, as I intended doing. We may not soon meet again, Cloud. It is a long time since Gettysburg, yet this is the first time we have met in all those days.

"We are of the true old revolutionary stock of yeomanry, Cloud, sympathetic, kindred spirits, who understand, and can appreciate each other. Your boy is the same: sturdy, watchful, active, cool, self-reliant, and reliable,—acquitting himself at all times and under all circumstances with the same comparative degree of credit that he acquitted himself in the army of Northern Virginia.

"On my arrival here I found the situation all but hopeless; no discipline; more like a mob than an army. By the first of November I had discipline, and the men were fairly drilled.

"On the 4th day of November, I set out to surprise Burnside's cavalry, nearly one hundred miles from my camp, at R——, down on the Holstein River, near Clinch Mountain. I marched day and night, until the morning of the 6th, at daybreak. Then I surprised and captured a large part of the command, with valuable trains, stores, and treasure, and returned in safety with all the booty and prisoners.

"To give you an idea of the commanders I found here: The colonel of a regiment of mounted infantry had never joined me until after the fighting was over that day. I sent him an order to escort the captured trains, and press forward all night with the utmost vigor, while I followed with prisoners, horses, and my command. Before day this home-guard hero got tired and sleepy, and went into camp. This blocked the road, and delayed the column about an hour, before I could work my way to him. He had never met me. Wanted to know what I had to do with it. I was flatly told that he captured the train, and would do as he —— pleased with it. I put him under arrest, and never let up until he was cashiered.

"The first day out I put Capt. Garland under arrest half a day, on account of a gun going off in his command; but it was for effect in the command more than anything else, although he answered me rather curtly when I rode up and asked him about it.

"On the morning of January 1st, 1864, with the mercury below zero, we set out and marched day and night for forty-eight hours; and fought all day at the end of the march, when the enemy surrendered. I had more men frozen to death than were killed in the fight.

"Sometime after this, I surprised and captured a regiment of infantry, near Cumberland Gap.

"During all this time we had no tents or other shelters, and no cooking utensils; for forty days we never saw our baggage, nor a clean shirt; and we subsisted for seven days at one time on a little parched corn. Our bread, when we had any, was unsifted corn-meal, made up on an oilcloth and baked before the fire on a chip, or a flat rock.

"Capt. Garland's and other scouting parties severely damaged the enemy in no small way. He was sent against some large bands of bushwhackers, and saw some rough times, but destroyed them in the end. They captured him once, and had the rope ready to hang him; but finally let him go on some mutual truce, with apparently all the advantage in their favor. I think they were influenced by the threat that every cabin would be burnt, and all the women and children carried off to a fort, in retaliation for any harm inflicted on him.

"Another time he rode into a regiment of Federal cavalry alone, when reconnoitering in a dense fog; but the quick and well-trained horse wheeled and brought him out of the danger before a move was made to prevent it.

"On another occasion, when reconnoitering on foot, he was captured; but escaped by jumping from the wagon in which he was being transported and guarded with some infantry prisoners to the rear, through a rough country, on a dark night, and was in his saddle again at daybreak.

"He has served as a member of a court-martial; and I sent him to take command of the lamehorse camp, where a large number of men imagined they had found a bomb-proof for the war; but he soon broke it up. I never saw a hardier soldier."

Gen. C——: "You have suffered fearfully, General. With us, we are coming to the final stage, and the last scene. We will never be north of Richmond again. That is the universal feeling among both officers and men. We had 87,000 muskets at the first of the Wilderness. Every day the number decreases, and we enroll no more recruits."

Gen. J——: "Yes, Cloud, the end cannot be far now.

"How is the little hero, Col. Flowers?"

Gen. C——: "Safe and well. There is hardly more than a corporal's guard of his original regiment left. I hear my train coming to part us, General."

Gen. J——: "Ah, Cloud, to part us! that is the word! Yes, to part us! but till when? Echo must answer!"

Gen. C——: "We cannot tell. God bless you, my friend. Farewell."

Gen. J——: "I part with you sadly, Cloud. I feel some strange sensation, which I suppose they term a presentiment, that one of us is under the wing of the Death Angel. I hope that it is not you. Farewell."

The campaigns referred to in the foregoing conversation have been much under-estimated by the historian. Upon them and their results most important issues depended; great interests were involved in their decision.

Early in September, 1863, important events were transpiring in East Tennessee. Chattanooga was the great objective and strategic point — the Federals the defenders, the Confederates the aggressors. With the latter the gods of war long seemed disposed to be most propitious.

But early in the fall campaign a most disastrous reversal of the fortunes of war became the heritage of the Confederates, that then greatly marred and ultimately dissipated all their dearly bought yet vital advantages.

This great and irreparable misfortune was the loss of Knoxville, the key of upper East Tennessee, which severed direct communication between Generals Lee and Bragg, and deprived the Confederates of a large—and one of the most bountiful—supply districts in the Southern States; with its wheat crop but recently harvested, and its abundant and maturing corn crop still in the fields, its cattle and swine in the pasture and the forest.

If this was all but hopelessly ruinous to the Confederates, it was incomparably valuable to the Federal army, and became at once the source of vitality to man and beast in the Union camp.

For these potent reasons, it at once became the purpose of the Confederates to drive the Union troops out of the district; that of the latter to hold the desirable country at any sacrifice.

This foreshadowed desperate struggles, trying hardships, and excruciating sufferings.

The country is broken, mountainous, and interspersed with rapid rivers, rising in the mountains and rapidly decending to the valleys.

Gen. Burnside commanded a powerful and well-equipped army with which to hold the disputed territory. Opposed to this formidable host was little better than a rabble—a mob—a few thousand ragged, poorly-armed, poorly-fed, and undisciplined troops.

Hence the Federal army took up a triumphant line of march for South-western Virginia, meeting little more opposition from its feeble adversaries than is usually met in the skillful resistance of a well-disciplined picket force.

This march continued uninterruptedly until the Confederates were driven out of Tennessee, and the Federal army had entered the fruitful blue-grass region of South-western Virginia.

Here Gen. J—— comes upon the scene once more, and the Federal commander finds himself not only check-mated but also out-manœuvred, and forced to retreat without accepting the challenge to combat.

Gen. J—— soon brought order and discipline into requisition and practice, and restored confidence in the ranks of his little army.

In less than two months he surprised, routed and captured a large part of Burnside's cavalry, with the camp equipments, trains, stores and treasure of great value.

In the meantime, Lieut.-Gen. Longstreet was detached, with a strong army corps from the Confederate army, in front of Chattanooga, and advanced by rapid forced marches upon Knoxville and the rear of Burnside, who was thus forced to fall back precipitately, and take refuge behind the defenses of Knoxville, where was his depot of supplies. Gen. J—— followed in his footsteps.

In a short time Knoxville was a beleaguered city, Burnside's army suffering the pangs of a siege beneath the gathering pall of despair; for starvation or unconditional capitulation daily grew to be inevitable alternatives as the meagre stores of provisions steadily diminished.

Gen. Bragg's disastrous repulse at Missionary

Ridge constituted the foundation of hope for the besieged. Relief may be sent from Chattanooga; but could it arrive in time?

The situation was familiar to Gen. Longstreet. If he could capture Knoxville and its defenders, he might then turn on the column marching to their relief, and rout or annihilate it; while should it come upon his rear, he would have no alternative but to raise the siege and retreat in the direction of Virginia. This would expose his column to an attack in the flank, and its retreat to be cut off by a column of the Federal army marching from Cumberland Gap, also, designed to aid in the relief of the imperiled army of Burnside. Gen. Sherman was detached from the Federal army at Chattanooga, with a grand corps, for the deliverance of his distressed comrades at Knoxville.

Gen. J—— had completed the cordon of investment which consummated Burnside's environment, while Maj.-Gen. Ransom, with a fine division from the army of Northern Virginia, was advancing to support and assist Longstreet.

The situation was critical. The suffering suspense of Gen. Burnside's army became intense, and daily grew more painfully hopeless.

On the 28th of November the beleagured army was reduced to desperate straits. But a few rations of bran and the mules and horses remained as a supply for subsistence. To add to the distress and discomfiture of the besieged Longstreet kept up a terrific bombardment both day and night, to which, however, Burnside replied with spirit and serious effect.

Up to this date the weather had been extremely mild. But on this night, winter set in vigorously; and Longstreet's preparations to attempt to take Knoxville by storm were complete.

His bombardment was vigorous and appallingly redoubled at this time

The winter wind blew a sweeping gale, that roared and howled and thundered in the mountains, the hills, the ravines, and the forests with which Knoxville is surrounded, and almost lifted sentinels, pioneers and gunners off their feet. Apparently, it had defiantly risen to outrival the deafening terrors of the antagonists' cannon, beneath whose pealing shocks the ground trem-

8

bled for miles around, and whose reverberations clashed and crashed and groaned as they met and mingled with the wailing moans of the tempest's icy breath.

Screaming shells filled the air. These terrible projectiles exploded continuously, lighting up the scowling elements in one incessant blaze, while portions of shells and their charges of missiles came hissing down among the troops on duty and those vainly seeking to sleep in their bivouacs. It was thus rendered truly a night of grim terrors!

Long before day-light Longstreet's columns of assault were moving on the flaming batteries, and against breast-works, battlements and parapets, with deep trenches and ditches in front, guided by the reflection of light streaming from rifles and cannon—Gen. McLaws commanded the assaulting troops.

The objective point was Temperance Hill, upon which stood the frowning battlements of a formidable fortress—the key of Knoxville.

With the famishing Federals, it is a supreme moment. They know the columns of their friends are hastening to their succor; and, nerved by desperation and the all but forlorn hope of relief, they nobly man the works, stand to their guns, and bravely vow to die or hold the fort.

Above the roar of the wind and the thunder of cannon rose the clear notes of the song from lips pale with cold and quivering with emotion—"Hold the Fort, for I am coming."

Telegraph wires had been stretched by the Federal troops on the outer edges of their trenches, in order that they might trip the advancing Confederates and precipitate them head foremost into the ditches.

As they approached the works, a withering fire of musketry greeted them. The advance line—or rather the first men of the disordered mass—for lines and columns there were none—was precipitated into the ditch. Their yelling friends came rushing madly forward to meet the same fate, falling, with fixed bayonets, upon those who had fallen before them. The sappers and miners of the pioneer corps, with axes and scaling-ladders, were inextricably blended in the disorder and confusion, and proved a detriment, rather than a benefit to the assault. Men behind could know nothing of the situation in front. On they rushed to helpless destruction.

Want of harmony and concert of purpose or actual misunderstanding, if not disobedience of orders, seemed to prevail among the Confederate commanders. Longstreet claimed that his orders were disobeyed; but this pretext often serves the turn of commanders as an excuse for their failure.

While Longstreet was the Ney of the Confederate army, as a lieutenant to an able commander, as a detached and independent commander, forced to rely on his own skill and strategy, he was a monumental failure to rival poor Banks or Burnside.

To add to the horrors of the sanguinary scene, the Federal troops behind the breastworks and in the fort hurled a shower of hand grenades on to the struggling mass of Confederates in the trenches and ditches, while grape-shot and minnie-balls literally swept the face of the ground upon which the Southern troops stood.

The result of the assault remained not long in suspense.

The capture of the threatened fort would quickly seal the doom of the beleaguered army; but the storming column was ill-starred.

Again and again the baffled Confederates made the vain attempt to carry the works by storm only to be met anew by discomfiture and overwhelmed by fresh disaster.

By noon the forlorn assault was abandoned, and a truce established, in order to care for the wounded and bury the dead.

The Confederate loss was appalling. The dead were in tiers and heaps in and around the trenches, mingled with and often under whom were helpless wounded men in great numbers.

Thus terminated the plan to take the city by storm.

Now came the alternative of reducing the garrison to submission by starvation. To insure this result, but a very few days would be required.

But before these critical days, that contained so much suspended destiny for the combatants, should come and go, the advancing columns would arrive to succor the distressed and famishing Federals.

Nothing remained for the Confederates but to retard the advance of these columns until hunger, cold and despair forced Burnside to surrender or to raise the siege and retreat.

Longstreet determined to hazard the former chance.

The column, advancing from Cumberland Gap, was met and driven back by Gen. J——, while Sherman was greatly annoyed at finding the direct route impracticable and a swollen river to cross. Opposition frowned on its banks. Bridges and ferries were destroyed. The prospect of rescuing his friends became desperate.

But the stakes for which he played were too high for an ambitious and rising commander to yield resignedly, and to withdraw from the desperate game with placid indifference; and he persevered.

After much fatiguing effort, he succeeded in surmounting many formidable and opposing barriers, and effected a crossing of the river.

But, was he not too late? He would most undoubtedly be obliged to pass over ground stubbornly contested inch by inch, before Burnside would be relieved. If he could only apprise him that the river had been passed, and relief, if tardy, was sure. But could such tidings pass the close and vigilant cordon of investment, which would be more than usually alert? Nothing was more certain than that the Federal commander would attempt to send a messenger through Longstreet's lines into Knoxville. And unusual watchfulness was maintained, with the hope of intercepting any one who might make the attempt.

However, a shrewd and daring officer in Sherman's command undertook the perilous duty; not only undertook, but also accomplished it most successfully.

Upon the arrival of this welcome messenger, Burnside suspended negotiations, in order to consider terms of surrender, and assumed a defiant attitude.

This decided the fate of the siege. It was raised by Longstreet during the night, and he began a retreat but little more promising than Burnside's predicament had been for so many days.

Yet, however, he succeeded in extricating his army and saving his train and munitions throughout a harassing retreat.

Gen. J—— prevented the Cumberland Gap column from attacking Longstreet's flank, hovering with his intrepid cavalry, for many days, between the two antagonists, and often fighting desperately.

For many days and nights his command passed the day in battle array and the night in the saddle, with no rations but a little corn, which the men rarely had fire to parch; and, in addition, the weather was very cold.

Thus Longstreet's campaign failed, and left the Federal army in indisputed possession of the long contested and vitally important territory, with a line of direct communication between Virginia and the South-west.

This was a deadly wound to the Confederacy, and assured the practicability of Gen. Sherman's march to the sea and the dismemberment of the Southern Empire.

Burnside pursued Longstreet and encamped at Bean's Station, a beautiful watering place some miles from where the Confederate commander had halted, at the pretty town of Rodgersville, resolved to retreat no farther.

After a few days, Longstreet, with true bull-dog tenacity,—his predominating characteristic, which rendered him invincible when simply executing an order under Gen. Lee,—turned upon his adversary and assaulted his position with the sudden impetuosity of an irresistible avalanche.

It is a clear, still, sharp December morning as Longstreet's grey columns, like undulating waves, roll steadily and grandly down the charming valleys and over the picturesque hillocks, which intersperse the intervening miles that separate the contending armies.

Soon the thrilling notes of the rifle ring through the calm and frosty air, as the advancing Confederates rush upon and sweep from their path the Federal pickets, to startle the Union troops, cracking jokes and cooking breakfast in tranquil serenity around their camp-fires.

Unsuspecting disturbance from the now foiled and crippled Confederates, the Federal troops are but little prepared for this abrupt summons to battle.

Close upon the heels of the hard-pressed and rapidly driven pickets are the yelling enthused Confederates. The thundering of the hoofs and the roar of the wheels of the artillery trains roll away from the frozen road in ominous tumult and reverberate, echo and re-echo away back amid mountain crags and ravines and over the Federal camp.

Intense excitement is prevailing in the Union camp, but it is unmixed with symptoms of panic or even disorder. As batteries gallop into position and regiments swing into line of battle at double-quick step, Longstreet's grey lines debouch into the open valley in front of Burnside's position, which they move upon with unfaltering steps, apparently contemptuous of the tornado of shot and shell which sweep and rend the face of the ground over which they rush.

Such are moments in which the hearts of men, with all their hopes and inspirations, seem to soar upward to the stars of heaven, whether, alas! the souls of many follow swift and soon.

Burnside is everywhere hurled back from the field and driven until darkness in mercy spreads her sable mantle, to close the sanguinary conflict and murderous carnage.

Gen. J—— is master of Burnside's rich supply train.

Longstreet procrastinates a whole day.

The second morning, long before daylight, however, he advances in solid phalanx, with his whole force upon Burnside's new position, sanguine that dawn of day will witness it overwhelmed by an irresistible onslaught, only to find the works and camp evacuated. Burnside withdrew during the night, retreating in the direction of Knoxville.

Longstreet has few fruits of his victory.

He has lost the opportunity of achieving a grand triumph, and retires inactively into winter quarters.

Gen. J——, in the meantime, prosecutes an active cavalry campaign throughout the winter, inflicting much damage on the enemy, but at the cost of extreme hardships and great suffering from exposure to cold and hunger, numbers of his men freezing to death in their saddles.

Garland Cloud was one of the dashing horsemen who accompanied his cool, sagacious, and skillful commander in these perilous mountain expeditions, and whose confidence the young mountaineer possessed in a degree due only to educated and experienced officers. For this reason many important and dangerous duties fell to the lot of young Cloud, by the directions of his brave and devoted commander.

History tells not the story of this chivalrous general of the Old Dominion, who merited eulogies to rival those lavished upon more conspicuous but never more deserving leaders.

With a small force he destroyed more than twice his number in the Federal ranks, captured hundreds of thousands of dollars' worth in stores within the space of six months, with a loss of less than one hundred men, from all causes, in his own ranks. Few others, in either army, could claim such results in a winter campaign amid the mountains; yet he received no adequate credit at the time, nor has justice since been rendered to his name.

History has told the story of Longstreet's change of base from his East Tennessee winter quarters to the field of the wilderness, a tale, therefore, unnecessary for us to repeat.

CHAPTER XXVII.

THE MIDNIGHT MEETING, AND SEQUEL.

"'Tis night when meditation bids us feel
    We once have lov'd, though love is at an end;
The heart lone mourner of its baffled zeal,
    Though friendless now still dreams it has a friend."
                        —BYRON.

THE early summer days of 1864 did not find the army of Northern Virginia checkmating the army of the Potomac, as the previous year had witnessed it doing.

Now the early June flowers find that once proud and invincible army still dragging its shattered, bleeding columns along the despairing retreat from the disastrous ' Field of Gettysburg " up to the very gates of the Confederate Capitol.

And, O God! what a retreat! A whole year from Gettysburg to Richmond! What a sterile track lies in its wake! Fredericksburg, the Wilderness, Spottsylvania Court-house, each and all

the ghastly tomb of army corps! Now comes the appalling slaughter-pens of Cold Harbor.

All the available troops are drawn from every quarter of the South to the defense of Richmond. The chivalrous Breckenridge leaves the valley of Virginia, and hastens to the support of Gen. Lee, which leaves the road open to Lynchburg and Danville, in rear of Lee and Richmond. The temptation is too great to resist.

Maj.-Gen. Hunter, with a fine army, is dispatched from Harper's Ferry and Winchester, to seize this favorable opportunity to cut off Gen. Lee's comunications with the South. He moves unopposed by rapid forced marches up the valley turnpike. The situation is appalling. In two days more he will pass Staunton. Gen. Lee is powerless.

He can throw no force adequate to cope with this army, in its pathway, short of Lynchburg; nor is there time for this move to avert the threatened danger.

Gen. Lee detaches Gen. E—— with a corps to save Lynchburg and to protect his rear. It is found that Hunter has a day's march the advantage, and will reach Lynchburg first unless his progress can be arrested for one day. But there are no troops in the land that can be thrown in his path in sufficient force in time to arrest his march for an hour.

The eyes of the South and the Confederate army now turn to Gen. J—— in the South-west. He may throw one-tenth of Hunter's numbers in his path, composed of raw militia, dismounted cavalry, and a few decimated regiments of infantry.

The plan is conceived, the order issued, and Gen. J—— proceeds by rail to Staunton barely in time to meet Hunter's advance one day's march down the pike. What a forlorn prospect! But it is the last hope for the South and Lee.

Gen. Lee knows and appreciates his man.

Gen. J—— is the right man in the right place; and he has lieutenants upon whom he can depend in such crises as great emergencies sometimes develop.

There is little time for preparation, less necessity for special and systematic disposition to meet the enemy, because there is no certainty which road he will choose.

The alert vigilance of Gen. J—— assures him the knowledge of his adversary's movements far enough in advance to intercept his march, no matter on which road; and he assumes an intermediate position, and waits.

It is Saturday evening, the 4th day of June; midsummer heat prevails. But Gen. J——'s bivouac is in a dense grove of timber: hence it is shady, cool, enjoyable as a peaceful scene.

But the anticipations of the morrow,—these mar the refreshing enjoyment of the cooling mountain zephyrs which sigh and chant their plaintive melody amid the tender leaflets of the forest; sad and anxious suspense pervades the camp.

The momentous duty which had devolved on the little band is a theme for solemn reflection. Officers and men, as a rule, appear meditative and restless.

But in the little camp there are two officers who seem to have flung forgetfulness around them, and to be indifferent as to themselves. Seated on the grass, against the trunk of a tree, they are intently interested in a closely contested game of chess, when the shadows of evening close over them to suspend their pleasing diversion. They are practiced players, too, in the game of life and death. One of them is Maj. Brewer, once an officer in the old army of the United States, a member of an old chivalrous Maryland family, and a special favorite of Gen. J——; the other is Garland Cloud.

Maj. Brewer: "Put up the chess-men, Capt. Cloud, until after the battle, as it is too dark to play. To-morrow we must doubtless try our skill in a far more serious game."

Capt. C——: "Yes, and get checkmated, too, with the odds so much against us. But whither goes that deep drawn sigh?"

Maj. B——: "Back to my Maryland's shore, and the old judge, my dear father, whom I shall never see again."

Capt. C——: "Well, we cannot divine to-day what is in the store-house of Fate for to-morrow. 'Sufficient unto the day——' you know; so let us try to sleep the sleep of the innocent, and dream of the days of happy childhood that we shall never see again."

Cloud walks away for a few moments.

Maj. B—— [Solus]: "Poor, impetuous, philosophical, destiny-confiding Cloud, would that I could share your contempt for the dangers of the battle-storm."

A courier rides up to the bivouac after they are asleep.

Courier: "Gentlemen, Maj. B—— and Capt. C——, Gen. J—— desires to see you at once at his head-quarters."

Capt. C——: "Some desperate enterprise for us, Major."

Maj. B——: "This is what I have anticipated for several days."

They mount and are soon before their General.

Capt. C——: "Oh, my General! this is the weird midnight taper of Gettysburg again, amid the spectral shadows of a sombre forest's silent gloom. Is it the dark shade of the Death Angel's wing hovering over our little band?"

Gen. J——: "Yes, Garland, to-morrow he will swoop down upon us. But this is that midnight meeting which I told you would come, when we parted last, in the lower valley, when you were setting out for the infantry camp. Just two weeks ago to-night I parted with your father among the shadows of the depot's flickering midnight-lamp. Day before yesterday he was in the hurricane of death at Cold Harbor; to-morrow it is my turn.

"Gentlemen, the situation is desperate. My orders are imperative without one provisional exception. Gen. Lee dispatches to stop Gen. Hunter's march one day at any cost. Three thousand seven hundred mixed troops, with one little battery, against thirty thousand with thirty pieces of heavy field ordnance. At last the day comes for us to prove the sincerity of our first love. To-morrow our waning country's altar demands some new sacrifices. Are you prepared to join with me to-night in a solemn pledge to devote ourselves to that tottering shrine?"

Capt. Cloud: "Always, now and forever."

Maj. Brewer: "The same are my sentiments, my resolve."

Gen. J——: "Byron truly sang our lot when he chanted:

'Vainly his incense burns, his victim bleeds:—
Poor child of doubt and death, whose hope is built on reeds.'

"The enemy have obliqued, and will advance up the Port Republic road. We must cross the river. It will take until some time in the forenoon to get all the forces to the river, across and in position to receive the enemy. This I shall attempt to do with my centre resting on the little village of P——, my left on the river bank, and my right on the woodlands.

"I wish you to cross the river without delay; advance through a grove about half a mile beyond P——, and there, on the edge of the field, post your seven hundred men to best advantage: Cloud on the right, covering the road. If you are prompt, you can be in position by daybreak; and you will not be idle many moments. Now hear my orders:

"Hold the enemy in check until I send you an order to fall back, which will be as soon as I am in position, provided you are then hard pressed. Let the enemy pass your post only over your bodies. Inspire all your men individually with this unyielding spirit. Fight in your position—die there if you must—but neither fight nor die retiring. I pity, but cannot help you. May God give you aid.

"Remember my parting words to you, Cloud, on another occasion, and apply them at this moment. Go! Good-night."

Capt. C——: "I remember them well. Good-night, my General."

Maj. B——: "I will remember my duty. Good-night, my General."

They rode rapidly away to obey this desperate order.

Gen. J——: "Ah! Capt. M——, those are two noble fellows to select for such certain doom. But they are the men for an emergency like this; to stand unmoved, after the last spark of the most forlorn hope is extinct, and they are left enveloped in the darkness of eternity."

Now Cloud and Brewer appear in the battle-storm.

Maj. B——: "Look out there, Captain, the cavalry is going to charge you again."

Capt. C——: "You will find out in a moment what kind of cavalry that is."

Maj. B——: "I see. They are unlimbering gun after gun, not more than five hundred yards from our line. What an ordeal! We must endure it, and cannot reply. Our two little guns will not last ten minutes. They intend to smoke out this hornets' nest."

Capt. C——: "Look Major! The prelude is over. The blue waves which are to engulph us are beginning to roll forward."

Maj. B——: "Come a little this way. I will meet you. The crisis is at hand, Captain. Let us sell our lives dearly. How do you feel? It seems to me that the ferryman of the dark river has me by the hand. Should you escape, tell my brother, the doctor, to let all the family know that I died, as our ancestors have often, worthy of the ancient name I bear."

Capt. C——: "I feel that our doom is sealed. We need have no scruples about exposing ourselves. Fortunately, the old fence ridge affords the men much protection; but we must remain on our feet. Let us walk along the line, and entreat every man to stand up to his duty to the death. Poor fellows, how nobly they have endured this torrent of iron hail for nearly three hours!"

The scene changes to the field-hospital of the Federal army.

Maj. Pleasington: "Why, Capt. Cloud, I have searched for you all over the field. One of your wounded officers told me that you were killed up yonder in the lane by a cannon-ball; that your sword was picked up, with a severed hand firmly clasping the hilt.—How are you, poor fellow?"

Capt. C——: "My sands of life are numbered, Major, and ebbing out. In an hour from now you may bury me up yonder beneath that battle-scarred willow-tree. I thought to-day, during the storm that raged around me, it would be a quiet resting-place. Take the things from my pockets, and send them in a little package to my mother. You know where, and you will find a way. Send with them a line, telling how I died, and how and where you buried me.

Thank God that you are here. Stay by me, if you can, to the end; it will not be long."

MAJ. P——: "Doctor, come here. Save this man, who has twice saved me. He is bleeding to death. Don't shake your head."

SURGEON-GENERAL: "All the doctors in Christendom can't save him, Major. He would die under an operation."

MAJ. P——: "Pray, then, tell me how long he can live without it?"

SURG.-GEN: "Less than an hour. He is sinking rapidly."

CAPT. C——: "You need not talk in an undertone, Doctor. Perform the operation. If I should die under it, Heaven will hold you blameless."

SURG.-GEN: "All right. I must do it myself. I have nobody to spare. Our own wounded are dying for want of attention."

CAPT. C——: "Thank you, Doctor. Now, Major, tell me about the battle."

MAJ. P——: "We were nearly whipped, but now we hold the field, and are camping on it to night. But why are you smiling?"

CAPT. C——: "Only because the object of our sacrifice is attained."

MAJ. P——: "Your gallant Gen. J—— lost his life leading a charge on our disordered line, which probably saved us from defeat. Some of his class-mates and associates in the old army, are burying him with the honors of war. Maj. Brewer, who fought with you, is mortally wounded. He wished me to bear you his greeting, if I found you alive, and to tell you that you had fairly won a colonel's stars to-day. I have promised to see him again. He says about six-sevenths of your mutual force remained on the field."

CAPT. C——: "Now, Major, I want to take one last look at this summer Sabbath's setting sun. There, now, I am ready to inhale the soothing chloroform. Let me hold your hand, Major, or rather you hold mine. I am going to sleep, but who will arouse me from slumber again? I hear a band playing the Dead March, and the drum's muffled roll. It is my General's cortége to his lonely grave. I feel the mystic volatile's subtilty creeping through my veins. Farewell, Major;

farewell, world; and my native land, farewell; for thee I ——"

Yes: Gen. J—— is dead, and buried with the honors of war, by generous foemen. He was respected for his gallantry on that fatal field; he was esteemed for his high type of chivalry and irreproachable character as a gentleman. His desperate mission is accomplished; he met the expectations of his chief with fidelity; obeyed his orders to the letter, and died like a soldier. The enemy's advance was stayed twenty-four hours. Thus Lynchburg was saved, and a vital wound warded off from the heart of the slowly dying Confederacy.

Poor Gen. J——! he no longer bears his great and silent sorrow over the earth; no more will he appear at the head of his squadrons on his white charger! Let us hope that he has at last reunited with his long lost bride.

Maj. Brewer died on the field of battle.

Upon this field were some pitiful scenes.

A number of old men and boys from the immediate vicinity of the battle-ground were engaged in the terrible conflict. The havoc among them was fearful.

Late in the evening, after the firing had ceased, and the shadows began to spread their mantle over the ghastly ground, old ladies, young ladies, and little children were on the field seeking their friends. Often, alas! their search was sadly rewarded. Then the wails of despair which rose, to drown the shrieks of the wounded, melted the stony hearts of veteran foemen to tender compassion.

There, was an aged mother bending over her son; *here*, was a wife, with her babe upon her breast, moaning piteously over her husband; *yonder*, a group of little children screaming round the rigid form of their father; a young girl wringing her hands in voiceless agony, as she crouched beside the lifeless form of her brother: and up on the hill-side, beneath the weeping-willow-tree, a faithful dog sat beside his dead master howling mournfully,—seemingly the only friend of the deceased!

CHAPTER XXVIII.

THE THREE VICTIMS OF RETALIATION.

"This is thy curse oh! man, thy hard decree!
That boundless Upas—that all blasting tree,
Whose roots are the Earth—whose leaves and branches be
The skies which rain their plagues on men like dew;
Disease, death, bondage—all the woes we see,—
And, worse, the woes we see not which throb through,
The immedicable soul, with heart-aches ever new."
—BYRON.

APRIL, 1865, found the Confederacy in the last throes of death. But, oh, how hard she struggled, how slowly she died!

Through to the last, her ragged, starving soldiers maintained their dignified and lofty bearing; displayed their intrepid courage and indomitable will; her officers retained "the pomp and circumstance" of authority, and exercised the prerogatives of a living and mighty empire. Even to the extreme of retaliation were their war attributes employed in the same degree as when their cause was most promising.

Away down in the wilds of North Carolina some Federal freebooters ruthlessly executed three Confederate officers, in the early days of April.

Two or three days later, a party of Federal officers fell into the hands of a hot-headed Confederate general, who was acting almost independently on the extreme out-posts, and hovering on the advance flank of the Union army.

In retaliation for his officers who had been executed, he resolved that three of his captives should die.

Concerning such matters there was little ceremony in border semi-guerilla warfare. Usually the victims were selected by lot, condemned and executed all in a few moments. Sometimes they were sent near or into the enemy's line, in order that they might be speedily found, to inspire the designed terror, or prevent a repetition of the occasion for which they were doomed.

These murders were most generally committed by independent commanders of small forces, without the sanction or the knowledge even of their superiors, to whom the facts were seldom or never officially reported.

By regular commanders in the field, these atrocities were committed rarely, and then only in extreme cases and under greatly aggravated circumstances.

We have occasion now to portray one of these pitiful scenes, conducted, however, with more than ordinary decency and humanity, if we may be permitted to associate these names with such diabolical brutality and savage murder.

The scene is at an out-post head-quarters in a rural farm-house.

CONFEDERATE OFFICER: Col. Cloud, there are three prisoners outside, under charge of my guard, sent you by Gen. R——, with this dispatch, which relates to them. Please relieve me of them, that I may rejoin my command immediately."

COL. C——: "Maj. H——, go with him, and receive them; then turn them over to the officer of the guard."

The officers retire with the prisoners.

"What can this all mean, sending prisoners to the out-post?" [*Reads.*]

"'HEAD-QUARTERS, DEPARTMENT OF——
"'April, 1865.

"'*Special Order No. 369:*

"'1st. Col. Garland Cloud, commanding the cavalry, will cause to be executed at daybreak of the 8th inst., just beyond his extreme out-post, in retaliation for the three officers of this command, executed on the 4th inst., the following named officers of the United States Army, selected by lot, this day; to wit:

"'LAWRENCE PLEASINGTON, Major U. S. Cavalry.

"'MILTON LAND, Captain Co. G——, Illinois "

"'FRANK STONE, 1st Lieut. Co. K——   "

"'2d. He will leave their bodies on the spot where they are executed, with a copy of this order attached to each body.

"'3d. Immediately after the execution he will withdraw his pickets, and resume the line of march indicated in Special Order No. 364.

"'By Command of BRIG.-GEN. R——

"'SAM. M. O'H——,

"'Maj. A. A. A. Gen.——'

"Oh, my God! that poor Pleasington should be one of them. Poor, miserable, unfortunate

THE THREE VICTIMS OF RETALIATION.

"DREADFUL TO CONTEMPLATE! THREE INNOCENT MEN PARTICIPATING IN THEIR OWN FUNERAL CEREMONIES."—See page 133.

man! Wretched man that I am to have this horrible order to execute. I would rather desert to the enemy than obey it."

The officer returns.

MAJ. H——: "Col. Cloud, one of the prisoners begs to see you. Oh, Colonel, it is pitiful, heart-rending to witness them!"

COL. C——: "Summons all the officers immediately, Major."

MAJ. H——: "They will all be here in a few moments."

Other officers enter.

COL. C——: "Gentlemen: There are three United States officers here under my charge. I am ordered to execute them at day-break. This is terrible. The war cannot last thirty days longer. Talk it over, and I will join you again in ten minutes."

Col. Cloud passes out, but soon reënters the room.

MAJ. H——: "Colonel, the unanimous opinion is that you would be justified, under the circumstances, and by the noble cause of humanity, in permitting them to escape to-night."

COL. C——: "Gentlemen: Our sentiments and our feelings are in accord, but our positions are not; the cruel order is to me, not to you. Who among you will volunteer to be officer of the guard, and assume the responsibility of accounting for those prisoners, merely relieving the officer now on duty and receiving your instructions from him? I observe you are all silent. This is conclusive as to what you would do were either one of you in my place. This is all I desired to learn. The order must be obeyed. You are dismissed, gentlemen."

The officers especially called go out.

"Major, have the guards trebled, and rigid instructions given to each man. Then bring me Lieut. Stone. Say to the other two that I shall see them one at a time, and render them every facility and assistance in my power, in preparing for their sad fate, and in communicating with their friends. I shall devote every moment of the night to them."

The officer goes out, and reënters with a prisoner and guards.

MAJ. H——: "Here is Lieut. Stone, Colonel, as directed."

COL. C——: "Take a seat for a moment, please.

"Now, Major, ride over to G——, and tell Col. T——'s chaplain that he must come here and spend the night in administering the Divine consolations of his heavenly mission. Explain to him."

The officer goes out, leaving prisoner and guards.

"Lieutenant, my poor fellow-man, what can I say to you or offer to do for you that will not appear hollow mockery?"

LIEUT. S——: "Oh, Colonel! My poor wife and little babes! It is of them that I am thinking! My last whisper will lisp their names; my last breath will go out a sigh for them. You are kind to send for a minister. The Major told me that you said I could write. I do not blame you, Colonel. I saw the three poor men for whom we must die going out to their death. We deprecated the inhuman act. How I felt for them. Now I know how they felt."

COL. C——: "Yes, Lieutenant, you can write all you wish. I will send everything you all desire, by a truce, into your lines, early in the morning. Just step into the next room. There is everything—candle, writing material, table, and all that you need for writing. When you finish your letter, you can go at once into another room and see the chaplain. You shall not be disturbed."

LIEUT. S——: "Thank you, Colonel. This is more than I expected."

COL. C——: "Corporal, go and tell the officer of the guard to send me Capt. Land; and also to tell Maj. Pleasington that I will send for him in about thirty minutes."

The guards go out with their prisoner, but soon reënter with another captive.

CAPT. LAND: "Oh! Col. Garland Cloud, cousin to my poor Emma, it is you, the little prattling boy who clung to my neck and wept so bitterly when we started for Illinois, that is to make her a widow, and her sweet innocent little babes—orphans! Oh, Garland! if she could only look upon your stern, pale face now, with her grand, sweet blue eyes, her blood would run into icy congealment. How often she has written to me: 'Milton, if you are captured, try to fall into cousin Garland's, or uncle Cloud's hands: they will treat you well, the kind, noble, good hearts!' I have complied with her request."

Col. C——: "Oh, alas! Milton, my poor cousin, that I should have lived to see this day. I would, under any other circumstance, put my own life into the breach to save you. I am in no way responsible for your present terrible fate, and I am powerless. I cannot help you further than to furnish you a minister, and to allow you time to make all dispositions, in writing, that you desire, which I will send into your lines by sun-rise in the morning. Nerve yourself. At day-break, my poor cousin, must this inhuman decree be executed. You have little time to waste in lamenting your fate to me. Pass through that door. You will find Lieut. Stone in the room waiting, and a table and writing material for you. Now, corporal, I am ready for Maj. Pleasington."

Capt. Land: "Oh, Garland! how can I break this cruel news to her?"

Guards depart with Capt. Land, but return with Maj. Pleasington.

Col. Cloud: "Oh, Maj. Pleasington, has it come to this? Is all the kindness and consideration we have bestowed upon each other to terminate thus? Why did you not let me die when I was at death's door with my lost arm? But for you, in another hour I would have quietly passed away; and now, with what a horrible reward I must repay you!"

Maj. P——: "Calm your emotion, Colonel. I am an educated soldier. This is a hazard of war, that has fallen to my lot. It is but just. It was no more nor less than a shameful murder, executing the three officers for whom we three victims must suffer. I will die like a soldier. I do not blame you, Colonel. I know you would be the last man in the world to put me into this jeopardy if you could help it. I understand your position. Since I am destined for this wretched doom, I am thankful that I have your sympathy to comfort me in my last sad hour, and your kindness to permit me to communicate with those

the very thought of whom wrings my miserable heart."

Col. C——: "In that room, Major, there are table and writing material. When you are through writing, there is a chaplain ready to commune and pray with you. My order does not specify the mode of execution: hence, I have determined to make it the regulation-file of soldiers; and they will fire from their saddles but one volley, at day-break to-morrow morning, just beyond our lines. There is one chance perhaps in ten thousand that all three may not be instantly dispatched. Were I in that situation and condition, I know what course I should pursue. Our pickets will retire immediately after this volley is fired; and in a few moments the bodies will be in the hands of your people. Now, go in and write your cruel letters."

Maj. P——: "I understand you. Thank you, Colonel."

Guards go out with Maj. Pleasington. The officer returns.

Col. C——: "Now, Maj. H——, cause the commandants of each battalion to draw lots, to determine which one shall furnish thirty-six men and three commissioned officers to execute this fearful order. This decided, command the officers to draw lots, to find which three must go; and then, again, the men must draw, in order to ascertain the thirty-six who must become the cruel files of fatal execution. All this completed, arm the men with Mississippi rifles; march them quietly into the dining-room; have them stack their arms, and then march them back to their bivouacs, and let them sleep. During the night the guns will be loaded. I am going to separate the poor victims, and send one out on each public road.

"Ask, also, Major, for about a dozen volunteer singers, to sing a hymn at the last closing sacred service, immediately after the conclusion of which the sad and mournful corteges will move off for the places of their bloody, murderous destinations."

It is the silent hour of three o'clock in the morning; the camp fires have flickered low or gone out; even the horses are asleep. The pine forest of North Carolina sighs and moans plaintively as its branches are gently fanned by the April-night wind. A spectral crescent moon swings low in the Eastern sky, casting its faint, slanting rays into the deep gloom of the dismal pine-woods, creating a weird and unearthly appearance. In the midst of all this there is a large, old frame dwelling, tenanted by two old bachelors. The parlor-room is unoccupied and bare save the thick meshes of spider-webs with which the large high ceiling is covered. In one end of this deserted, neglected, dirty, and cheerless abode there is to-night a small table, upon which burns a small feeble tallow-candle, whose slight radiance does not illuminate one-tenth part of the gloomy apartment. Fit stage and scenery for the dread, solemn, heart-rending scene so cruelly being enacted upon it!

Behind the table stands the ghostly figure of the man of God, clad in the official sacerdotal robes of the Episcopal Church. In front of him, their heads resting against the little table, their knees upon the dirty, moldy floor, are the kneeling, grief-smitten, heart-broken, earth-hopeless forms, of three officers of the United States army, engaged in supplicating the Throne of Mercy, the last refuge to which ever instinctively turn the truly miserable, and the utterly despairing hearts, when the helping or the saving friendly hand of earth is out of reach forevermore. Dreadful to contemplate!—three brave men, whose cheeks would not blanch beneath the impregnable battlement's angry frown of death, guilty of no crime, and in the full vigor of health and of manhood, participating in their own funereal ceremonies. They are about to receive the last Communion—the most blessed consolation the Church can bestow.

Behind this group, around which hovers a halo of such awe-inspiring shadows: the man of God and the Death Angel—the one barely visible, the terrible oppressive feeling that the other is equally near and real unmistakably perceptible—kneel about twenty grim-faced soldiers of the Southern army. Behind these, in the thick gloom, kneels the towering form of Col. Cloud, convulsed with emotion, and sobbing as if his heart would break. One by one he has already taken final leave of the unhappy men whose lamps of sweet and hope-dawning life he has been ordered to extinguish; he does not wish them to see his face again.

Slowly, in a mournful, tremulous voice, the man of God pronounces the lines of a closing dirge, " NEARER, MY GOD, TO THEE ;" and the soldiers with much difficulty, because of the choking emotions, which they cannot stifle, sing in cadences, slow, plaintive, and direful :—

> " Now, like a wanderer—
> Daylight all gone,
> Darkness comes over me—
> My rest a stone;
> Yet in my dreams I'll be
> Nearer, my God, to Thee—nearer to Thee."

Then the good man commends their souls to God, and one by one bids the wretched, hopeless men an affecting farewell, as they are led away and delivered up to the cruel ministers of death. Then for a few moments more he remains alone in silent solitary prayer. Now, with the spectral candle in his hand, he passes out of the terrible room, almost frightened at the hollow, lugubrious echoes of his own foot-steps, closes the door behind him, and listens on the portico, with folded arms, to the receding sounds of the horses' hoofs of the three merciless parties. Thus he continues standing, until almost simultaneously three volleys of musketry ring through the still, dewy air: then he exclaims : "*Lord Jesus Christ, receive their souls!*"

CHAPTER XXIX.

THE LAST SCENE OF THE TENTED FIELD.

> " Desperately his soldiers still fight on,
> Determined to die or yet be free,
> Unconscious of what their general's done
> Beneath that budding apple-tree.
> But, look! a courier is hastening on
> To still the cannon's deafening roar,
> While silently they stack their arms
> To fight on Virginia's soil no more."
> FROM LEE'S SURRENDER.

AFTER a halt of nine months in front of Petersburg, Gen. Lee again resumes his retreat from "The Field of Gettysburg," leaving behind him a wake of devastation and death rarely surpassed in history, seldom equalled.

From this ghastly burying-ground he moves away in the direction of the South-west, facing the red glow of the setting sun, with his back to a redder scene of blood, which deluged the earth in his last futile struggle to repel the onslaught which broke his puny lines and forced him to evacuate his long and well defended works.

Thus reduced to the mere skeleton of an army, ragged, bare-headed, bare-footed, and famishing, he takes up his line of march through an open country, after an overwhelming defeat, in the face of a victorious, well-clothed, well-fed, well-equipped enemy that nearly twenty times outnumber him. Matchless chieftain! devoted followers! thus to move after every ray of hope is vanished.

But in this there was method and policy. Well did Gen. Lee know that all was over; still he wished to escape the humiliation of surrendering at discretion the brave remnant of his once proud and mighty army. Well did he realize that this feeble band could inspire respect amid the victorious and exultant ranks of the enemy; that before its wasting yet serried phalanx the multitudinous hosts would pause and stand at bay.

But still, however, above all these considerations was that supreme incentive which swayed and convulsed his noble nature with intensified emotion: that of securing for his desolate and mourning country an honorable and a tolerable peace.

Inspired by these powerful and laudable motives, which shed about his name a ray of glory that reflects more lustre upon the grandeur of his fame than his most masterful feats of arms, he marches to gain the fastnesses of the great blue mountains, many miles away.

After some days of weary marching, at last, sometimes wrapped in gauzy veils of misty haze, the dim outlines of the great and cloud-kissed peaks are descried, seeming to beckon their distressed sons to hasten on to their protecting friends; for such these grand old mountains had oftentimes proved to the sons of Virginia and the South.

But these friendly guardians were, like the inviting refuge of the distant headland promontory to the perishing mariner, surrounded by engulfing waves. He sees safety in the dim distance; but, sadder than none, it is safety he may not reach. Thus was it with the imperiled band of Gen. Lee. At length it found itself emcompassed by the engulfing surge of blue waves; and thus it was forced to stand at bay.

The stage for the last scene was destined to render one of the most obscure county seats in the old Dominion forever famous—"The Appomattox" of endless historical renown.

This quaint old town contains a little dingy brick court-house, in a diminutive square, surrounded by a few shabby store and shop buildings,—thus does it appear in the early days of April, 1865, when Gen. Lee halts, plants his guns, and forms in battle array upon this sequestered spot, where the once proud and invincible army of Northern Virginia stacks its nine thousand muskets forever.

It is somewhat painful to take issue with the grave historian on one feature of this scene,—that of the famous apple-tree, under which Gens. Lee and Grant are reputed first to have met—and to assure the reader that this is an erroneous impression; that the two great captains never met under "that budding apple-tree." That story is pure fiction.

But Gen. Lee and some of his lieutenants meet under this gnarled apple-tree, just beginning to bud, and hold a short council of war, at which it is decided to surrender. This is on the morning of the 8th of April, 1865. From this spot starts the ever memorable flag of truce to the Federal army.

A little later the commanders of the two armies meet in an open field, converse less than ten minutes, and then ride back to their quarters. This is their first meeting.

About noon they meet again; this time in a room of Maj. McLane's house, definitely to terminate the tragedy in which they have been so long engaged.

The terms accorded to Gen. Lee in the articles of capitulation here consummated are magnanimous to a degree that reflects undying credit on Gen. Grant, and will ever glow on "the pictured page" of history, should the lustre of his military renown ever wane.

Nothing was more certain than that Gen. Lee could be forced to surrender, and in a short time, at discretion.

But behold the respect in which his triumphant foeman holds him! No disposition is manifested that a desire even is entertained to humiliate the vanquished chieftain of the South, nor to compromise his common soldiers by imposing the hard conditions of surrender that might be exacted and enforced.

When these honorable and favorable conditions were secured, what a weight of anxiety must have been lifted from Gen. Lee's agonized mind. For what haunting probabilities of the woe this supreme crisis might develop, must have oppressed him since the failure of Pickett on Cemetery Hill!

He knew that it was merely a question of time; that sooner or later he was doomed to be vanquished.

The day after the terms of surrender were signed, the disconsolate Confederates part with their rifles, lay aside their trusty companions, and bid farewell to their commander, whom they love so well.

At this moment, strong men weep like little children.

"You did your part well little band;
  Outnumbered, yet brave and true you stood,
Ever battling for the land
  Of the brave, the noble, and the good.
Farewell, Southern fallen braves;
  Wo thy loss most deeply feel;
We'll strew flowers o'er your graves;
  Yearly at your tombs we'll kneel."

The only object which the South had any hope to gain, that for which she has struggled since the fatal field of Gettysburg, is attained: *an honorable peace and protection.*

The Star of the Confederacy has set forever; the Star of the Union has risen re-illuminated to set NEVERMORE!

Three friends who have been continually together, in their laborious duties and painful dangers, from the first day at the Wilderness until this scene, which is their last, are seated once more by their bivouac fire, after returning from their farewell visit to Gen. Lee.

GEN. CLOUD: "Well boys, the end has come

at last; all our precious blood has been shed in vain."

COL. FLOWERS: "Yes, General; but man proposes and God disposes; and so let us try to be resigned, and to believe that it is all for the best."

MAJ. HARMAN: "I guess the Colonel has got the true philosophy on us this time General."

GEN. CLOUD: "Yes, it is better to accommodate ourselves to the circumstances than to allow them to accommodate themselves to us; which they would certainly do.

"I have been counting up, as we rode back from Gen. Lee's quarters, how many of our three original companies will stack their arms. There are but seven of them now present with guns, and four company officers—fourteen of us altogether, out of three hundred and sixty, who were mustered into the service at the commencement of the war; not less than three hundred of them are dead, and about forty of the remainder have been wounded."

COL. FLOWERS. "I wish Col. Garland was here to go home with us."

GEN. CLOUD: "Ah! poor boy! poor Garl. It will be many a weary day before ever he sees home. God only knows what will become of him. The Tennessee bushwhackers, against whom he operated, have sworn vengeance against him. He dares not return home; and he does not know where to go nor what to do until the reign of terror, which we are destined to have, is over. He writes to me that he has some idea of plunging into the North; but he has no money, and his arm is gone; so he cannot earn a subsistence at hard labor. That miserable Dutchman, Mueller, an inveterate enemy of his, is affiliating with those murderous desperadoes, and will inform them where he is, should he return home or to any point within a long distance of home. He is now somewhere on the coast of North Carolina. It was cruel to put him into active field service after he was so badly maimed. He has done much hard fighting since, and but little scouting duty. He appeared only in the light of simply obeying orders, and took no other interest in the services he rendered."

Maj. Harman: "None of us has met him since his promotion."

Gen. Cloud: "I have not since the night of Gettysburg."

Col. Flowers: "What can Mueller have against Col. Garland? He was a Confederate officer, and loud-mouthed for the war."

Gen. Cloud: "He was a coward. Somewhere in the Tennessee campaigns he was abandoning his post in the line, at a critical moment; and Garl rallied the men and re-posted them; caught Mueller by the collar, and at the same time, brandishing his sword, roughly rebuked him for his cowardice.

"During the same campaign he gave a lot of his men leave to go home; and Garl picked them up the first day out from camp, and returned them to their command.

"This greatly increased M——'s indignation, besides making enemies of all the men, who have sworn vengeance.

"Even now there are numerous political secret societies, known ostensibly as Red Strings, etc., but really Union Leagues, all over our country, having for their principles the division of all the landed property among themselves. All the deserters have already joined them. Many of the soldiers will join them. Demoralization, discord, and every species of confused anarchy will distract our country until we get some established government in the States; and with the railroads destroyed, and no mail service in operation, this will take a long time."

Col. Flowers: "It is sad to return home to find this state of affairs. I will have been absent four years in a few more days. Poor Garland, my best friend, how I pity him!"

Maj. Harman "And then to know that we cannot help him, nor even hear from him, renders his case still more deplorable."

Gen. Cloud: "It is another one of his war curses. From the very first he has averred that he would never see another happy day on the earth; and it now begins to appear as if he was right. Except his most devoted friend, poor Gen. J——, from all that I can learn, he was one of the saddest soldiers in the army. At Gettysburg he pictured to me his gloomy forebodings,

both for the country and for himself. I much fear his predictions are to be fulfilled."

Steadily the martial hosts vanish; directly they have all disappeared, leaving the hitherto unknown village to resume the monotonous tenor of its way; nothing save the ashes of their camp-fires remain to indicate that legions have lately thronged these sterile hills. THE WAR IS ENDED FOREVER!

CHAPTER XXX.

MOUNTJOY HOUSE IN THE STORM-CLOUD.

" The tree will wither long before it fall.
  The hull drives on though masts and sails be torn;
  The root-tree sinks, but moulders on the hall,
  In massy hoariness; the ruined wall,
  Stands when its wind-worn battlements are gone;
  The bars survive the captive they enthrall,
  The day drags through though storms shut out the
      sun."
                                            —Byron.

Norman Mountjoy: "My dear Helen, for months have I struggled to spare you the cruel stroke which it becomes my bitter and painful duty now to inflict, rather than suffer you to go on day after day as I have gone, hoping even against hope, until it smites you all at once with a thousand public-envenomed darts. I can no longer supply the means to support our princely extravagance. I am a ruined man, with inevitable bankruptcy and disgrace staring me in the face, if it continues one month longer.

"For many years our expenditures have been frightful; for months and months they have averaged $10,000 per month. The loss of our Southern trade, and the money there due us, and of the several valuable cargoes captured by the Southern privateers, have sadly impaired the capital of the firm—so much so that even in the business itself it has become necessary to retrench in every possible way. The plain, unvarnished truth is, that our excessive expenditures have absolutely absorbed every dollar of my capital that should have been left in the business. Truly, I am now in the firm on sufferance only. At a meeting to-day it was agreed that I might draw $10,000 per annum for my family expenses. Such are the lamentable facts and the true state of the circumstance to which we are under the unavoidable necessity of accommodating ourselves. I trust you will do this with that characteristic tact and skillfulness for which you are so famous."

MRS. MOUNTJOY: "Norman Mountjoy, do I dream, or am I listening to the sound of your real voice, and looking into your face with my open eyes? Do you tell me this worse than ghostly story, on the very even as it were of our daughter's nuptial ceremonies? How am I to get along? It will take more than your paltry year's allowance to supply the bridal robes, to say nothing of the presents, the party, and the supper.

"I know you can borrow money. You have plenty of friends who will either loan you the funds or indorse your note for a sum sufficient to consummate the dream of my life. I cannot think of relinquishing this, although I know that I am on a sinking ship, without realizing all that it implies. But we must by all means, at any hazard, buoy up and keep afloat until we get the girls into the haven, let come to us whatever may after this is done. The money to do this I must and will have."

MR. MOUNTJOY: "Helen, is it possible that I have never known you in all these years of our smoothly gliding journey of life? I have never yet denied your slightest wish nor your most extravagant demand. Unmurmuringly have I supplied them with a lavishingly open hand, until now I have nothing left but my unsullied and sacred honor, which, too, you eagerly demand.

"Yes, there are hundreds of men who would loan me any amount of money within the bounds of reason, unquestioned. Why? Simply because they consider my name gilt edge; they would not know my true condition. As a man of honor, it would be my bounden duty fully to inform any friend to whom I might apply, just how I am situated; then very few, if any one of them, would aid me. I shall not apply to any of them: hence there will be no cause for dissembling nor occasion for explanations."

MRS. MOUNTJOY: "Then you flatly refuse to assist me? Fie on your sentimental compunctions, when there is so much at stake.

"After the girls are married, we could procure the money among them to cancel the obligations contracted in assisting to complete their happiness and secure their independence for life; and even if we failed to do this, the end to be attained abundantly justifies the means that it appears necessary to employ in order to succeed.

"The failure to make the anticipated occasion one equal to expectation will be *prima facie* evidence to the world that we are under a mysterious cloud. This may blast the prospects of our children, and make us appear as the leading characters in a disgraceful scene of a consummate force."

MR. MOUNTJOY: "Helen, all these things have had my serious consideration.

"It is an infallible principle in the divine law of human nature that he who does wrong is admonished, before and during the act, by the dictates of conscience. It is often as criminal to conceal the truth as to steal. Where pecuniary interests are involved between man and man, he who deceives him who assumes the risk, by false representations or appearances, is a criminal. This law is clearly and unmistakably expounded, and is thus interpreted by all true and unbiased minds.

"For any loss or damage thereby entailed, morally, the responsibility is more terrible than would be that of the professional depredator who had taken a similar amount, or inflicted a like injury with violent hands. The breach of confidence in the former instance, added to the milder and more genteel yet by no means less dangerous system of theft and robbery, can but enhance the enormity of the crime far beyond that of the latter, who makes the rude, unceremonious despoiling of mankind a life business. Against him all the world is on guard: he is watched and suspected.

"It is, therefore, unpardonable dishonesty to contract any obligation, with a reasonable moral certainty that it can never be liquidated. No matter if not one word is uttered on the subject, the silence implies a tacit admission that all is right—yes, and more: it is, with the interest being put in jeopardy, a declaration; because of the abiding faith in the culprit's moral honesty that if all is not right, the indulgence would not be accepted. This is a predicament in which I will never place myself. I love my children, and suffer unmitigated torture to be under the necessity of causing them pain or disappointment. But, Helen, if I had twice as many loved ones, twice and thrice as dear to me as those I now have, I would not stoop to one mean or dishonest act, to keep them from the poor-house. I may yet fill *a pauper's grave*, but *I will die an* HONEST MAN. My remotest posterity shall never have cause to blush at the mention of my name. No mask on the earth will ever degrade my brow, nor deck it with the red glow of burning shame.

"Not one of our children, save alone Eva, has one iota of heart in her marriage, nor love for the husband to whom it will bind her. I have told Oglethrop that Eva will be without a dowry, and the brave, noble fellow said that it was her he wanted; he would make her comfortable and happy, and he will.

"Concerning the other parties, if money considerations influence them, I shall not pity their disappointment, nor will it render the girls more unhappy than they would otherwise have been. I will leave informing them to you."

Mrs. M——: "You don't imagine, I hope, that I am fool enough to do it. As to love in those matches, that is nonsense. The vulgar proverb that 'when poverty comes in at the front door, love flies out at the back window,' has in it more reality than romance.

"But, Norman Mountjoy, let me tell you, once for all, that your sentimental sermon has had no tendency to change my mind. My resolution is taken, my purpose firmly established. *The money I am going to have, without your aid.*"

M——: "It appears that you are applying the proverb in our own case with a vengeance. Let me warn you that I wash my hands of the transaction. If you raise any money, it must be with the positive understanding that I am in no way responsible. If I am driven to desperation, I shall publish this caution to the world.

"In calm prosperity, I have permitted you to guide the helm at pleasure. Now, in the crisis of the storm, at a day forever too late, I must assert my long lethargic yet proper authority. Since

you will abandon my steerage, I am resolved that you shall not wreck my honor with your own.

"Had I asserted my rightful authority at the proper time, this deep mortification and shameful rupture would not now exist. I have acted most indiscreetly, and must now pay for my folly a terrible penalty."

Mrs. M:—— "Have no fears; I will in no wise compromise you."

With the ferocity of the baffled lioness flashing in her grand eyes, the lustre of whose beauty still glows with undiminished loveliness, and her winning face, yet unblemished by the wrinkling strokes of time, livid with rage, she defiantly turns her back on her noble, long-indulgent husband, and proudly glides out of the room.

Poor Mountjoy; admirable, adorable relic of a race that is no more—of an age that is dead! He has received a mortal wound, piercing deeply into the fountain-source of his vitals—hopelessly incurable. He is truly a *broken-hearted man.*

At this late day, when overwhelmed with the dire burdens of other cruel misfortunes, he sees his queenly idol, at whose shrine he has bowed with a blindly confiding adoration for more than twenty years, divested of her divine robes of true and pure womanhood, standing before him in the nude enormity of her rebellious mutiny against the hallowed sacredness of plighted vows and conjugal devotion. The ideal diadem of other and brighter days, when she was his joy, his pride, and his hope, is displaced by the dark and deeply obscuring mask. Now she is unscrupulously avowing her resolution to go forth and practice the curse-breeding art of fraudulent deception.

Her heart, once so tender, so loving, and so pure that her guardian angel could have but adored her with the purity of a celestial devotion akin to that mutual spiritual love ever springing eternally in the breasts of the heavenly born hosts, she has cruelly, unfeelingly steeled against the loving, noble appeals of her distressed husband's sad and wretched heart.

She denies him the priceless boon of so much as one little word of comforting consolation—a balm which the broken, bleeding heart craves with sleepless fondness, even when there is no

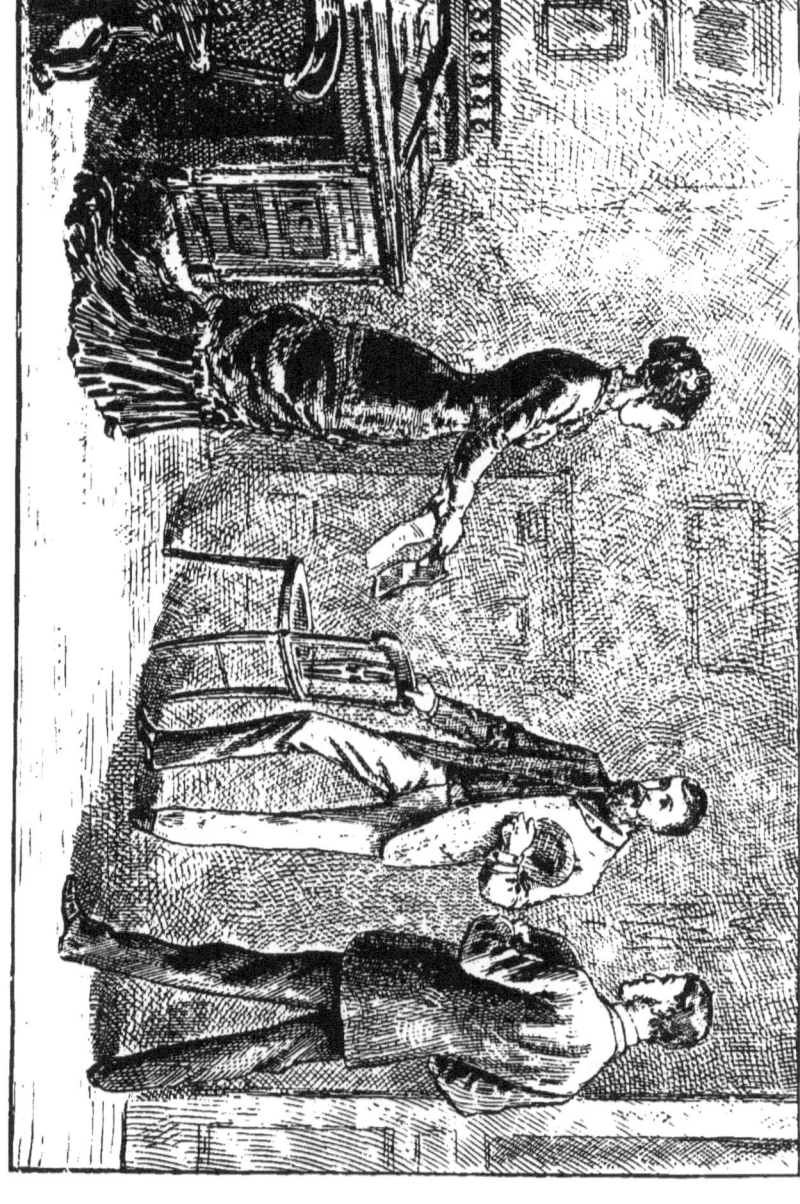

THE INTERCEPTED LETTERS.

"READ, VILLAINS! AND LEARN WHETHER OR NOT THERE IS PLEASURE IN MY VISIT."—See page 139.

source to which the anxious, weary eyes of the despairing watcher may turn, in anticipation of beholding that blessed form approaching, to administer the soothing antidote.

Such is a vain desire, doomed and fated to be realized—never in this world. Ten thousand times more bitter and cruel must be the pangs of disappointment experienced by him who possesses their source in the copious profusion of pearly richness, when he finds the sparkling wealth of its fountain closed and barred, coldly, unfeelingly against the craving thirst of his parched and lacerated soul. This inestimable treasure of Norman Mountjoy, he finds in the trying hour of his direful extremity, when he turns to it as a last source to seek that consolation which he sorely needs in this bitter moment of cruel misfortune, hopelessly, irretrievably sacrificed on the altar of a madly blind AMBITION!

Years ago, unknown to him, the Guardian Angel of this spell-bound dream of his life has been again and again forced to turn away from his fond charge, and weep. Worse and worse grew this frenzied madness, until at length his influence was utterly disregarded; he was under the inevitable necessity of reluctantly abandoning her to the fate of her choice, and of standing *alone* on his mountain top of nobility and honor.

A very few days after the unpleasant interview between this hitherto agreeable couple, who have at this time discovered that their spirits are widely severed, we find Helen Mountjoy alone in the superbly furnished private office of a wealthy down-town firm, apparently laboring under the almost uncontrollable emotion of some highly agitating excitement. Evidently, she is impatiently waiting for some momentarily expected party. Quite soon, however, is her anxious vigil rewarded. Samuel Van Allen and Felix Mortimer enter the apartment together, in a state of ill-disguised embarrassment; and both in the same breath greet her with the ejaculation:

"Why, my dear Mrs. Mountjoy, to what are we indebted for this quite unexpected but most agreeable surprise?"

With an air of freezing disdain and dignified haughtiness, she recoils a pace, hurling at first one

9

and then the other looks of proud and triumphant defiance; then re-advancing, a paper in each hand,—while the two men turn livid, then pale, and tremble violently,—she extends her hands, one to each, as she says in a thrilling tone:

"READ, VILLAINS; and learn whether or not there is pleasure in my visit!"

As each victim, in the presence of his relentless persecutor, opened the paper and beheld the well-known characters of his own hand-writing, embodied in a clandestine *billet-doux*, intended for other eyes than those that had read the dark mystery of its secret intrigue, he felt as though he would like to vanish through the floor.

Each letter was of the same purport, nearly the same words—one addressed to Beatrice, the other to Rosalind Mountjoy. They ran:—

"May 1st, 1865

"MISS BEATRICE MOUNTJOY:

"*My Heart's Adoration:*

"Every contemplated arrangement for our stolen meetings has been completed. Together, Mr. Mortimer and I, have rented and furnished a cosy little cottage in a romantic spot, just beyond the suburbs—a nice drive there and return—where we can go, with you and Rosalind, in a handsome carriage; enjoy each other's society for a while, and no one else in all the world need be any the wiser, as all of us will have equally potent motives for guarding our mysterious secret, both before and after your marriage.

"To-morrow, at two o'clock P. M., go veiled to —— Place, where you will find a carriage with black horses, standing closely to the north side of the statue: enter it, without a word: the driver will be posted. Don't fail.

"Your devoted slave,

"SAMUEL VAN. ALLEN."

MORTIMER: "Well, Madam, to say the least, we have all been guilty of an unpardonable indiscretion. Beyond any sort of doubt the young ladies have most imprudently encouraged us, in meeting all our advances more than half-way."

MRS. M——: "Miserable, detestable wretches! Married men—ingrates! life beneficiaries of Norman Mountjoy, your more than friend, who would have confided the care of his daughters, regarding you virtually in the light of a member of the family—to your honor, as though you were his own brothers. If this is the gratitude that you have feigned to feel—the coin in which you repay friendships, I pity those upon whom you would wreak vengeance.

"Should this become known, your lives are not worth a penny. And become known it will, unless you make ample atonement before the sun goes down to-morrow.

"One condition : never dare recognize nor communicate with my daughters again. Understand me : I shall never either meet or recognize you. Should you wish to communicate with me in relation to obtaining these evidences of your guilt, commission a third party. I scorn to speak another word to you, more than to inform you that early day after to-morrow you will find your abominable cases of base infidelity to your own pure wives, and fiendish perfidy to the confiding friendship of my sadly duped family, in the hands of attorneys, with changeless and unrelenting instructions."

Before either one could sufficiently compose himself to reply, she had passed out of the door into the street, entered her carriage, and was rolling rapidly away.

VAN A——: "Well, Felix, we are in a pretty pickle. See to what the anticipated sweets of stolen felicity have brought us. Ecstacies of bliss not only too fierce to last, but even too much forbidden ever to be realized! The sheen of beauty decking those temptingly fragrant roses, was guarded by sharp and merciless thorns, which still remain deeply and immovably punctured in our flesh."

MORTIMER: "Oh, and I see no available remedy! Our irretrievable ruin may be the ultimate penalty. For my part, I would pay fifty thousand dollars to be out of it. The amorous minxes! Never were men more tempted and encouraged. It is past my comprehension to understand how those letters fell into the old lady's hands. I should rather be at the mercy of any other woman in the city."

VAN A——: "It is of little consequence how she obtained those tell-tale papers : we know she

has them; and with us the vital question is to get them and ourselves out of her grasp. I will pay fifty thousand dollars; but I do not believe that she will accept it. She will squeeze us for our last drop of blood. I move that we go to Madam Vais-entre, and employ her to negotiate the matter for us. She is a match for Madam Mountjoy. We will authorize her not to exceed twenty-five thousand dollars, and if this is declined, to ascertain the final *ultimatum* demanded. What say you, Felix ?"

MORTIMER: "Agreed; let us go at once."

Madam Vais-entre is famous in the science of clairvoyance. She is wealthy; and among her aristocratic neighbors, she is reputed to be fairly entitled to a claim to respectability. Certainly there is nothing disreputable about her house nor her surroundings. The most respectable of both sex, openly and fearlessly call at her residence at any seasonable hour, day or night, to seek her services in divers ways. Hence, by degrees, she becomes the repository of many and varied secrets.

To her immediate neighbors the fact is not known; yet nevertheless, through her instrumentality some of the shadiest intrigues ever perpetrated in high life are negotiated. In this rôle she is utterly unknown, except in aristocratic society; and even there not extensively. She is far more cautious in selecting her clients than some families in the most exclusive circles are in discriminating as to the characters of young men permitted, and even solicited to call on the young lady members of such households.

To Mrs. Mountjoy, Madam Vais-entre is no stranger; hence she will neither be shocked nor surprised at finding this lady representing Van Allen and Mortimer, to negotiate terms with her, concerning the result of which she is far more anxious than they imagine her to be.

Norman and Evalina Mountjoy are alone together at home.

EVALINA: "My poor, dear papa: What terrible thing has happened ? What is the matter with you? What crushing, silent, unutterable sorrow is bowing down your head as though it was overburdened with the ponderous weight of years, and distracted with cruel anxiety and hopeless cares? Have you never another smile, another loving word, another caress, another kiss for your little Eva, who loves and pities you, oh, more than words can tell?

"Come, papa, let me put my arms round your neck once again, as I used to do in the good, bright days of yore—that dear old time of happy childhood, when cruel care had written no sorrow-wrinkles on your placid brow, and your face ever wore a sweet and tranquil smile. Oh, whither have they flown—those blessed days, with all their joys? Alas! cruel Custom's giddy splendors have robbed us of our serene and loving blissfulness. Let me kiss your lips as then, my poor papa, and soothe your aching brow with the gently loving caress of my hand. There, now, my papa, rest your weary head on my shoulder.

"I could not go away to-night into the festive throng, and leave you alone to the mercy of your consuming sorrow. I have staid at home to try and comfort you."

MOUNTJOY: "God bless you, my angelic Eva. I would not exchange the bliss of this blessed night, alone with my darling, for years of cruel, bitter, disappointing life. How thankful I am for this precious opportunity. You are my last and only hope in this heartless world. Poor Cassandra! poor Beatrice! poor Rosalind!—for them there is no happiness treasured up in the storehouse of Fate. You are each about to embark on the all-serious voyage of life: they, as the victims of cruel, plotting, match-making conventionality, with neither heart nor love as a soothing balm to ameliorate the bitterness of their social sacrifice; you, of your own free will and choice. You are a good, sensible girl, Eva; you have made a most admirable choice for your life companion. I am proud of it. It is now with you whether your lives are happy or miserable.

"Look into your loving father's care-worn face; picture it indelibly on the tablet of your memory; and hearken unto the words that he utters to you, while your eyes thus lingeringly gaze upon him; and let them be engraved on your heart as though seared with a rod of white heated iron.

"Eva, you can reduce Orlando Oglethrop to the pitiable extremity in which you now behold me, or you can render him ever bright and joyous, as you now recall knowing me in the olden time, which to me is dead forevermore.

"If you devote your days and your nights to the giddy whirl of social frivolities, and neglect your husband and your home; and if, in addition to this, you spend all the money he can make; run him into debt; and coldly, cruelly, unfeelingly lash him with your tongue because he cannot nourish your extravagance more bountifully, you will drive him to the wretchedness of despair. On the other hand, if you are a comforting helpmate to him; save all you can; cheer him with your smiles; firmly insist in the very outset of your journey of life, that plainer and cheaper appointments connected with all departments of your household than those he will be resolved to supply, is preferable to you; and that when brightened by the halo of cheerfulness which true and pure love will shed around them, they will be far more handsome than the most elegant luxuries would appear, in the chilly atmosphere of diffident formality that pervades the conjugal abodes of aristocratic coldness;—how happy, how thrice blessed is his lot!

"Take this latter course, my child; stand by and pursue it with unwavering constancy, and you will render him supremely happy. Even the bitter trials of misfortune would be alleviated by the soothing balm of such an exquisite antidote; for misfortune often pines for sympathy.

"There is no other road to happiness for you in this world; no foundation for the shade of a hope in the eternal. You must start poor. You do not know even the bare definition of the term *economy*. Alas! you have never witnessed its practical operation in any respect whatever. In applying it, your good sense must be your guide.

"Now, my Eva, let me take your hand in mine, as a binding token of fidelity, while I tell you the secret of my bitter woe. Nerve yourself, my poor daughter, in order that the revelation I am about to make may not shock you beyond your capacity for endurance. I have told Orlando, the brave, noble fellow!

"You are a poor, dowerless girl, not a millionaire's daughter, as the world imagines. You have witnessed your fortune melting away around you, in the gay and festive scenes through which you have been passing for the last few years. I am a poor man. My family is unprepared for the transition. My heart is broken.

"Do not mention this to your sisters, nor betray any emotion on account of it. Your mother desires to guard the matter as a profound secret from you all until after the wedding; but I could not bear the idea of withholding it from you. And this opportunity, and the tender manifestations of sympathy and love which you have so profusely lavished upon me to-night, have combined to influence my determination to undeceive you in regard to the treacherous cloud lowering so near, and ready to obscure the bright light which shines with such glorious brilliancy in your so much envied home, leaving you all in the ever rayless midnight of despair; as I am now.

"Do not grieve for the loss; you are young. The world, with a promising future, is before you. You will gradually but surely advance. You enjoy yet unsullied honor and spotless purity, worth more, ten thousand times, than untold millions of glittering gold, and all the false honors it could bestow.

"For myself I do not care. I could cheerfully descend to a more humble sphere of life, and there be happy. It is for my family that my heart bleeds. It would kill your poor mother should the storm that has been so long brewing suddenly burst with its furious violence upon her head.

"As a leading merchant, from my first day in that sphere until now, more than thirty years, I have never in any respect or degree swerved from the path of strict integrity and honor. I have nothing connected with my counting-house to look back upon with shame or regret. From this fact now springs my chief source of consolation.

"Oh, my daughter, how little the gay and festive social world knows of silent sorrows and secret struggles that much of the money which contributes to its enjoyment have cost its overworked commercial slaves, in the gloomy, cheerless precincts of the counting-house. Here, often the heart grows sick and the brain whirls, harassed with the vexations and disappointing problems ever occurring and recurring again. And at the same time, the incessant drain which the always increasing and pressing demands of the home circle make, as they steadily encroach upon the reserve forces, and undermine themselves, the vital safety of its pleasure-nourishing institutions, perpetually engulfing some poor, harrassed toiler in miserable ruin!

"The mental strain and nervous debility thus engendered saps the healthy current of the system, and soon drives the wretched victim, if not to crime or suicide, certainly into a premature grave. Note a business man with heavy dark circles under the eyes, his appetite failing, his conversation languid and forced, and his entire deportment abstracted and listless, and you will see a man upon whom the immedicable malady is surely preying. The gay world may meet him in that brilliant drawing room of his palatial home, and receive his sickly, meaningless smile, wholly unsuspecting that a cruel and merciless torment is steadily causing his vitality to ebb out. Many will gaze with envious eyes upon the gilded magnificence of his princely mansion, and the manifest fullness of joy in which his family revel, and exclaim, 'Fortunate, thrice happy man!'

"These are the stern and dreary truths that I desired to impress on your youthful mind, my Eva. Remember them; treasure them up in your tender heart, and so model your course of life as always to shield you and yours from the hopeless thraldom of the sure and inveterate curse which they infallibly entail.

"Eva, my dear child, keep the words I have uttered to you to-night fresh in your mind when the tongue now speaking them is silent and cold in the grave. I am warning you now, as it were, from the margin of the tomb. Ere long, in a few little weeks, or at most months, and you will see your father's troubled face and hear his trembling voice no more."

EVA: "My poor papa! Oh, cruelest of all fates! Papa, forgive me ere you leave me; and pray Heaven to pardon me for the part I have unconsciously taken in bringing upon your devoted head this terrible, more than cruel, wretchedness. I have never asserted it to any one but Effie, yet these extravagant follies have always been loathsome to me.

"This is why I selected Orlando: in order that I might escape from the endless slavery of social exactions such as ours, to the blissful quietude and sweet repose of the tranquil life Effie has always been picturing to me. Oh papa! it will break my heart, the thought that if we had all been as economical as Effie has been, you might now be well and happy. And she was worth more money than all four of us ever were, yet she never has spent more than half her allowance on herself, still everybody, everywhere she goes, loves her for her own sweet, simple self, more than any of us were ever loved.

"In her plain yet handsome and tastefully made dresses, she always appears more fascinating than any of us, in our costumes costing many times more than hers.

"Sometimes I have made a feeble attempt toward remonstrating with mamma, but in vain. She would tell me that I was intended to wash dishes and mend old clothes for some trash like Oglethrop; that I would then be able to economize to my heart's content. I suppose that her words were prophetic. Poor mamma! I do not know what will become of her, when the storm which you have pictured to me, overtakes her.

"Cassandra, Beatrice, and Rosalind will be protected; but they loathe the sheltering care to which they are going. I esteem Col. Worthington, but never could endure the presence of the other two, with all their influential wealth and exalted social station; but they will be kind to my sisters."

M——: "Yes; and they will care for your mother. There has always been the strongest mutual friendship between her and each of them. Usually, she drops any member of our social circle who fails in business, or in any other way passes under a cloud; but not so with them. When Atkinson, Flowers & Co. failed, sh. threw open her doors more widely and cordially than before; and she has since planned the union between them and her hapless daughters Instinctively, I have ever since felt an aversion toward them, but always try to persuade myself that it springs from the natural repugnance that

business men all cherish for those of their brethren who have dropped out of line by the wayside. I have never been able to regard their failure in a favorable light. More than ever now should I like to hope and believe that it was fair and honest; and that poor Mrs. Flowers was not victimized, with other creditors of the firm. But the truth is, they started too soon, and were at once strong.

"Worthington is the unblemished soul of honor, and would surely make Cassandra happy, if there was not so great a disparity between their ages; and if she loved him.

"As to forgiving you, my poor daughter, there is no cause to forgive. Neither Heaven nor I can deem you guilty. You are neither directly nor indirectly responsible for the disastrous consequences which have overwhelmed me.

"Your mother has conducted her social campaigns, under, and in strict conformity with the tactics of the school in which she was trained. But for the war and its blighting, ruinous influences and effects, we never would have known a financial want. This proves how unstable and uncertain in this world are the best grounded prospects and hopes."

EVA: "How thankful I am that you do not blame me, my dear papa. It would kill me to think that you blamed me. Papa, how cruel it is in mamma to be resolved to sacrifice poor little Effie to naughty cousin Arnold."

M——: "Yes, but her labors will be in vain. Worthington is against her, and no power in this world can change him. I think that is why she so readily consented to give you to Oglethrop,— she thought it would put Worthington under obligations to her, and ultimately to secure his coöperation and influence with Effie, in behalf of Noel, who is so bad that it makes me blush to think he is related to my family by kindred ties of blood —but still, however, your mother is blind to his most glaring faults, and mildly terms them natural, youthful foibles. I have no sort of fear that Arnold Noel will ever be any nearer related to Effie than he now is; and there is fixed between them a fathomless impassable gulf."

EVA: "Mamma is so desperately resolved, I much fear she will cause Effie great trouble before she ever determines to abandon her purpose."

M——: " That is of little moment, as long as it does not succeed. It were a thousand times better for Effie if these efforts drive her into the grave, rather than into a union with Arnold Noel."

Eva: " Oh, my dear papa, Effie loves you so fondly, your troubles would afflict her as cruelly as they do me. How sadly painful your distressing words are now—they will forever rankle in my breast!

" Papa, tell me pray, is there no way in this world to save you? Can Gilead supply you no balm of hope? Is there nothing that you can even imagine possible to attempt, that by the barest miracle could either bring you relief or temporarily alleviate the bitterness of your cruel lot? Whisper but the faintest breath of the comforting consolation of a shade, the most mythical form of hope. Oh, my poor papa! your own little Eva would give freely and joyfully her young life to save you. Speak to me, papa, of hope!"

M——: " It were cruel, my darling, to deceive you. There is no hope. I am beyond the reach of mortal skill and power; my case is hopelessly incurable."

Scene changes to the sitting-room of Mountjoy House, where Madam Vais-entre and Helen Mountjoy meet.

Madam Vais-entre: " Why, my dear Mrs. Mountjoy, I am so glad to see you. I meet you to-day as a peace-maker; and I desire to arrange with you the unfortunate unpleasantness between yourself, Van Allen and Mortimer."

Mrs. M——: " The villains! You can arrange nothing with me. I am resolved to bring them into court. What proposition have you to make, pray?"

Madam V——: " My authority is rather indefinite, being merely of a nature empowering me to open negotiations with a view to paving the way to an ultimate amicable, or at least peaceable and quiet, settlement. It would be a very shocking and a most damaging affair to get before the public, scandalous alike to all parties when once in the mouths of gossips.

" It would, therefore, be far better for the sake of your family, and in view of the interesting period so near at hand with your daughters, to punish those imprudent, disloyal Benedicts with heavy damages in money, as a partial balm to your much outraged feelings. I am persuaded that they would each pay a few thousand dollars to stifle the matter."

Mrs. M——: " A few thousand dollars? I would not even stoop to consider a direct offer of less than fifty thousand dollars from each of them ; and this I might indignantly refuse. Until you can talk more definitely, our interview is at an end. Good-day, Madam Vais-entre."

The clairvoyant departs, and soon joins Van Allen and Mortimer.

Madam V——: " Gentlemen, the case is desperate. If you wish it settled, authorize me to make a direct offer of one hundred thousand dollars, and place me in a position to close the offer the same moment it is made. She is furious, and will hardly talk about settling at all. Unless you have some very compromising letters from the young ladies, with which I can throw a damper on her aggressive rage, nothing can be done. I have no assurance that she will accept any offer that could be made."

Van A——: " We have not the scratch of a pen from them; and more than this, to our detriment, they have never acted, except on the one occasion, but with the most perfectly commendable decorum and modest propriety. We had better, therefore, I think, arrange a check, Mortimer, and authorize Madam V—— to settle the matter before sun-down to-day."

Mortimer: " Certainly, by all means, and without delay."

She departs with the check, and later, returns with the letters.

Madam V——: " Well, gentlemen, here are your dangerous letters. You have paid dearly for seeking forbidden fruit. But for my being prepared for her on the spur of the moment, the settlement would not now be made."

She then withdrew from the scene.

Van A——: " Oh, Mortimer, this folly is a terrible blow! Should any unusual stringency or business depression occur, the want of this sum of money will seriously cripple us; but, my God, I would rather part with the last dollar, and go to the bottom of the river, than allow this affair to be made public."

M——: "This is the way that I feel about it. It is a lesson that we will carry to our graves. It now appears clear to my mind that we both had much better sense than to have placed ourselves in a position where we were even liable to become subject to the dangers of such disastrous consequences as these which have overtaken us, and those worse calamities which we have escaped. It makes my blood run cold to think to what a desperate result this miserable indiscretion might have led.

" It now strikes me as being a little singular that they both should have insisted on our writing to them each a separate letter."

VAN A——: "Ah, Mortimer, had our blood run as cold then as it runs now, we would not be in this plight.—This is the experience of almost all men who, either through indiscretion or actual crime, get into trouble. Could they have seen as clearly and felt as sensibly while in fancied security they were weaving about themselves the meshes of the inextricable net, as they see after they awake to the realization of their situation, and find that they are hopelessly entangled in the toils of their own ingenious folly, they would stop and regain a place of safety before the last open spot is forever closed around them. But it is ever the same with all men who embark in any forbidden or improper enterprise or career, as it was in this lamentable instance with us. They become blindly infatuated with the delusive enchantments of their mad and ruinous folly. This blunts the naturally keen perceptions of the finer sensibilities, and stifles the mutinous admonitions of the ever infallibly true conscience. Then they are rational madmen, capable of perpetrating any unnatural excess, and awake to find ' The way of the transgressor is hard.' "

CHAPTER XXXI.

THE SPIRITS OF DEFIANCE AND MENACE.

" For a woman's heart when loving, loyal is past any proving;
And a woman's will is strong, never bent by Passion's blows;
And should any seek to harm her, fiery scorn is woman's armor;
And her pride is cold and frozen as eternal Arctic snows."
—M. A. BILLINGS.

MRS. MOUNTJOY: "Now, Arnold, I have arranged that you and Effie be left alone in the parlor for a time this evening, and I want you to make good use of the opportune moment thus afforded you, and win her hand. Don't be backward. She treats you very graciously, and appears to take a lively interest in the story of your cruises. This is the very best sign in the world. Put the question boldly and press it obstinately, and the chances are all in your favor that she will commit herself, and you will have won your fortune in one little evening. Go to her at once."

ARNOLD NOEL: "You can rest assured, my dearest aunt, that I shall do my very utmost to succeed; for this is the dearest and the all-absorbing dream of my life."

MRS. M——: "That is right, my boy; you are very sensible."

Noel left his aunt, and entered the parlor.

ARNOLD NOEL: "Well, Miss Effie, I have told you everything I can think of concerning the navy and the sea. But permit me now to say to you that there is a nearer, and to me dearer subject about which I wish to speak to you, for which I crave your earnest attention and most serious consideration. That is your own self, and my love for ——."

EFFIE: "Pursue that subject no further, Arnold Noel. My heart and my hand can never be yours —not even if you were a prince. I will hold no conversation on the subject. Our interview is at an end forever. Farewell."

She indignantly walks from the parlor.

NOEL [Solus]: "Well, that is the coolest I ever read of. I must seek in some other quarter for wealth, ease, and luxury. Hang it! To think of the good, jolly times I have lost for the sake of this scornful, unappreciative girl."

Her aunt enters the parlor.

Mrs. M——: "What, Arnold, alone so soon? How is this?"

Noel: "She left me forever, the instant I broached the subject."

Mrs. M——: "Keep up courage, boy. I will take her in hand and teach her some manners and common sense. A pest on that Dutch aunt of hers."

Noel: "Do anything you like and can. I am certainly a dead failure when she will not listen to my uttering a word."

She at once sought and found Effie.

Mrs. M——: "How is this, Effie, that you treat Arnold so badly?"

Effie: "I have not treated him badly, madam, my aunt. He had the presumption to insult me by attempting to make love to me. I left his company, which I was under no promise to remain in. This was my right. Pardon me, I do not desire to talk about it."

Mrs. M——: "Beware, miss, how you talk to me. You may repent it. Arnold is in every way your equal."

Effie: "I do not wish to wound your feelings, nor to have you wound mine. What does it signify if he is my superior in many things, which I doubt not he is—am I bound to throw myself at his feet? Never, a thousand times never. Understand me, my aunt, I am not your daughter. I do not recognize your right to make a match for me. I owe you nothing; am under no obligation to you, beyond the good-will and love of a niece; and this I have ever faithfully rendered you. We will now part this very instant; and I shall never again darken your door until you have utterly abandoned this question."

Mrs. M——: "Do not be so hasty, Effie. I did not mean to offend you. It will appear strange for you not to be at the wedding."

Effie: "You can easily frame a plausible excuse. Good-by." [Exit]

Mrs. M—— [Solus]: "I have met my match for once. Who could have thought that this quiet, modest girl would have said a word contrary to my wish? But I swear to bring her to terms, and to make her bitterly repent this audacious conduct."

Behold this unscrupulous woman, with her masterful bent of inclination to evil! Nothing is too outrageous for her to attempt if it but promises to consummate her wicked designs—to enslave purity, innocence and happiness in the thraldom of vice, of sin, and of wretchedness!

Poor Effie Edelstein! sweet child of Nature, fair flower of beauty and of goodness! Alas, that this shadowy phantom of plotting mischief should hover about, and ever seek to darken thy pathway, redolent with perfumes exhaled from springing blossoms of hope!

Oh, guardian angels, defend her now!

CHAPTER XXXII.

FROM THE SHORES OF THE DARK RIVER.

"While the purple lilacs blossom
We have, dearest, met again,
And the robin and the blue-bird
Greet us with their sweet refrain.
In the soft and gentle twilight,
Where we ofttimes, love, have met,
Won't you tell me, little darling,
That you dearly love me yet?"
SENTIMENTAL SONG.

Effie: "Lawrence, do I dream, or are we sitting here side by side as in the peaceful, happy days of yore? Yes, this is you. It cannot be a delusive spirit, such as I have met so many times in the shadowy realms of inconstant dream-land.

"Oh how good God has been to you, to shield you throughout this long and cruel war, when the grave was so often opened to receive you, and to snatch you out from the very jaws of death!"

Lawrence Pleasington: "Yes, my dear Effie, it is I; and I am very happy and thankful that we are once more safely together, and my days of danger and separation from you are over.

"The last ordeal through which I passed was the worst of all, a thousand times more terrible than all the balance of the war together—that rayless night of death! Oh, the unutterably nameless horrors! there in the dire, cheerless midnight of that dreary pine wilderness, making ready for death amid the stern formalities of preparation for my execution, which I knew were going on around me. The thoughts of you and of mother that tortured my agonized soul!—every moment I died a thousand deaths!"

EFFIE: "Oh, Lawrence! how good we ought ever to be, as an acknowledgment of our grateful thankfulness to heaven for your miraculous deliverance in the last final moment of that horrible night. Surely an angel guarded you. I have often wondered whether or not Garland Cloud took any part in sparing your life—whether, indeed, it was in his power to have done so. That he would have saved you if he could, I do not doubt."

LAWRENCE: "I, too, have studied much about this. It was only possible, in two ways: to load the guns with blank cartridges, or to instruct the soldiers to fire over my head. This last I feel confident he would not have ordered. I believe he would have thus loaded the guns, provided it was known to no person but himself. This possibility I am, as a matter of course, unable to determine. I cannot say whether or not I heard bullets. I experienced a sensation such as no other occasion in this world could produce. The clear, sharp voice of the officer: 'Ready!' the click of the locks, 'aim! fire!' ran through my frame like a current of electricity. The blinding flash and simultaneous report, like the shock of a sudden thunder-clap, blinded and deafened me, and there was a roaring in my head. I was weak. I must have nearly or quite lost consciousness. I rather indistinctly remember deciding in my mind that I was killed. See to what extremes the imagination will lead. Had I been subject to heart disease, I should undoubtedly have died.

"When I reached head-quarters, two hours later, I found my letters and other little trinkets already there."

EFFIE: "Well, thank God! however it may have been, you are safe now; so let us talk on more pleasing subjects than that shocking experience through which you have passed."

LAWRENCE: "Well, of what shall it be? If I undertake to talk about you and our anticipated relations, you might serve me as you did my persistent rival. I will try to dream the time away until Christmas—that to me happiest of all the joyous days of my life. I wish it was to-morrow,

that Time might not have so much space in which to play her fickle freaks."

EFFIE: "Well, it cannot be otherwise. The time will soon pass away. We can see each other whenever we wish, thanks to Col. Worthington for securing you a position in the bank. Aunt Helen would annoy me, but she shall not have the opportunity. I am not going near her again until there is no danger of her broaching her distasteful subject. We will be happy, and the time will glide smoothly and serenely for us, between the pleasant moments in which we shall enjoy each other's society."

LAWRENCE: "Yes, my darling, it will not be like the tedious, gloomy days of separation of the past four dark and cheerless years.— *We will be happy?*"

CHAPTER XXXIII.

THE QUADRUPLE HYMENEAL CONSUMMATION.

" Few—none—find what they love or could have lov'd :
   Though accident, blind contact and the strong
Necessity of loving, have removed
   Antipathies, but to recur ere long,
Envenomed with irrevocable wrong;
   And circumstance, that unspiritual God
And miscreator, makes and helps along
   Our coming evils, with a cruel crutch-like rod,—
Whose touch turns hope to dust—the dust we all have
   trod "   —BYRON.

THE preparations and the appointments for the occasion of the wedding at Mountjoy House far outstripped, in magnificence and splendor, the most extravagant dreams entertained at an earlier day by its ambitious, scheming mistress—the mother of the four young ladies destined to bestow their hands, with their vows of plighted troth, if not their hearts, to the four men with whom they are to be formally bound for life.

We have beheld her wringing her poor husband's heart with relentless, unpitying cruelty; and then again extorting the money to supply the demands of this sumptuous festival from the two would-be false and traitorous friends of her family, with the audacious coolness of a consummate actress scientifically versed in all the dark mysteries of the delicate art of black-mailing.— We saw her displaying throughout the progress of the affair the most unwavering firmness and disdainful indignation — proud, haughty, injured, tender-hearted, delicate creature!

As Milton pictured the scornful and lofty bearing of fallen Satan, on some occasions in the horrible realms of the Infernal, so appears this most wonderful woman—still the more wonderful when better known—while the gorgeous preparations were in progress, and when they were completed. And as on the last evening, near the hour of the ceremonies, she is receiving her guests, she beams with radiant smiles; her natural imperiousness shows no indication of having descended from the heights of its unrivaled prestige in the brilliant past, when she was the envied, matchless young queen of fashion, society, and beauty. Now, as then, she seems the perfect picture—the veritable quintessence of earthly happiness. So completely is she mistress of her faculties, and of the mysterious art of dissembling, that it would baffle the most astute effort of the skillful analytical reader of human nature to detect in her face, her actions, or her voice the faintest trace of that secret devouring flame of cruel and undying torment ever raging in her breast, permitting her no peace by day and incessantly haunting her dreams by night.

Still, however, with untiring perseverance and an indomitable will, well worthy the grandest cause in this world, has she pursued, still is pursuing, and ever purposes to pursue, her ambitious schemes, until the last design is perfected and accomplished. She will not hesitate as to the means employed. She will grasp and use them with unscrupulous indifference of the bitter affliction and the cruel despair she forces other and unsuspectingly innocent hearts to endure. For three of her own beautiful and most amiable daughters she has conceived and modeled destinies of life bitterly disappointing to them, dooming their days of earthly existence to elegant yet still pitiful wretchedness.

She has broken her husband's once fondly doting heart. To what infamy she has descended in the dubious transactions with Van Allen and Mortimer, conjecture may never divine; and where she will stop in her desperate endeavors to blast the happiness and the fondly cherished hopes of Lawrence Pleasington and Effie Edelstein, we involuntarily shudder to contemplate.

This is the woman, envied, adored, worshiped, to whom the most exclusive in the grand metropolis would deem the permission to pay personal homage a highly honored privilege. Thus she is viewed by the hosts of the social eclat thronging around her on the evening referred to, as bidden guests to the marriage feast. So it is with many, ah, many, in this world, who conceal beneath a smiling countenance, a false and deceptive heart!

In their private boudoir, are closeted the three eldest daughters—the legitimate victims of a mother's cruel intrigue.

CASSANDRA: "Well, girls, you appear charming in your witching bridal robes. Are you in reality as brilliant as you seem? For me, I feel as if about to participate in the solemnities of a funeral. From my heart I wish this was, instead of my wedding robe, my burial shroud."

BEATRICE: "I cry 'Amen,' Cassandra. We are a fated trio. Alas, for the result of our ill-starred lives! I have always clung to the delusion that this would never be."

ROSALIND: "Ah, my unhappy sisters, how truly your feelings and sentiments harmonize with my own.—To think of Eva,—how I would envy her going to the altar as she goes, with heart and hand bestowed together, if it would better our lots! She will fulfill her destiny with credit and honor, the sweet child of Fortune, upon whom Destiny and all the Graces have been pleased to smile with kindest benignity."

CASSANDRA: "Poor, suffering father! I can never cease to reproach him because he did not assert his rightful prerogative as master of his own house, and save us; for I know he has never approved of mamma's course. She is the most heartless woman in the world."

BEATRICE: "Her equal never lived; and still none know her. All the world regards her as a model wife and mother.—As a modeler of misery, she is a success."

The scene changes to Mountjoy's chamber. He and Evalina are together.

EVA: "My poor papa! I have come to see you, and to ask your blessing, before I go to the church. You do not know how it grieves me that you are not able to go."

MOUNTJOY: "I would like to see you married, my child, but I am glad that I am unable to see my other daughters wedded to misery. No good will ever result from their marriages. Where is Effie? I want to see her, and ask her to stay with me a few days. I shall be very lonely when you are gone. "

EVA: "Effie and mamma have quarreled concerning Arnold, and she will not be here. I am very sorry about it."

MOUNTJOY: "Poor Effie! God alone knows the bitter trials which she may be doomed to experience."

EVA: "Papa, Orlando and I are decided to remain with you, and afford you all the comfort we can, in lieu of a bridal tour. I wanted to do this, both to save the expense and to be near you, to minister to your wants; and he consented willingly to both features of my proposition. We will stay with you as long as you need our services."

MOUNTJOY: "May God bless you, my loving and dearly beloved daughter, as fervently and as truly as I do now ; and may he prosper and shield you in all the vicissitudes of your journey of life, from all harm with which its many dangers may threaten you."

EVA: "Thank you, my dear papa! Kiss me now, and put your arms around me once more, while I fold mine lovingly about your neck. Now then, if you were well, and no longer a victim of sickness and sorrow, I should be happy. God bless and comfort you, my papa. Orlando and I will steal away from the festive throng, and come to you a while, after we return from the church."

MOUNTJOY: "That is enough, my daughter. You may keep them waiting for you. Good-by until you return."

Here alone, confined to his room, languishes the rapidly sinking, neglected husband, who for twenty-five years has supplied his wife with all the elegant luxuries that money could buy or heart desire.

Now, since their stormy interview, she rarely ever speaks to him; and when she does speak, it is with unkindness.

This true and noble man is dying by slow, cruel, torturing degrees, the hopelessly incurable victim of a broken heart, caused alone by his heartless wife's unfeeling conduct.

The congratulations, the supper, the party, the presents, and the final leave-takings were much the same as those so often and so graphically portrayed by master artists, engaged in producing pictures of the bright and smiling side of life. We do not attempt this. Our materials are disappointments, heart-aches, and tears.

CHAPTER XXXIV.

THE DARK CONSPIRACY.

" Black was the mind that coolly could have planned,
Such cruel deeds for a desperate hand."
—ANONYMOUS.

HELEN MOUNTJOY, Atkinson and Stringfellow are closeted together.

MRS. MOUNTJOY : " Now, my good sons, what I wanted to see you about, is concerning the engagement between that contemptible sharper, Pleasington, and Effie—the head-strong little simpleton. I could freely burn that traitor, Cloud, for not letting him die, or for not finishing his meddlesome career in that bungling execution. Such trash is fit only for gibbets of retaliation. If the fool had hung him, I would not now have all this trouble. I have sworn that Effie Edelstein shall be Arnold Noel's bride, and I mean to keep my oath. This unpromising engagement must be broken. I must have your assistance about it; that is all."

ATKINSON : " Why certainly, dear mother, anything that I can do to aid you, will be most cheerfully performed. I do not, as a matter of course, know your plan, nor in what way I might promote its success."

STRINGFELLOW : " That is exactly my ticket, my mother. But just at this moment, for the life of me, I am unable to see in what way either of us can further your project.

" Now, there is Silas Worthington, who is in the very position to render you all the service you require in this enterprise, to complete its sure and speedy success; and his relations to you are the same as our own."

Mrs. M——: "Yes, the ingrate! he is under obligations to me. It was solely my object to secure this claim on his services for this very purpose,—in order that they would be ready at my command whenever the present crisis might come,—that I consented, at his request, to give Eva to Oglethrop—about the same ash-cat stripe as Pleasington. Now, he actually laughs at me, as he imagines, in a good natured way; and tells me, with the most complacent nonchalance, that whatever influence he can command, if any, would be thrown in the scale against me. He means it, too. I know the man. All New York cannot turn him. He never gave me any grounds, is in no way pledged to assist me. I merely expected it on general principles. I think if he was not an utter stranger to the sense of the imperative demands of personal gratitude and the reciprocity of its obligations, he could not have for one moment hesitated about the decision that my appeal to him should have received.

"I find, from this instance, as well as from many others, that one can never implicitly rely on one's friends to repay, mutually, favors past. But this case is simply outrageous and entirely unpardonable."

Atkinson: "Unfortunately, the fact that Worthington does not hold Arnold in very high esteem, is the chief point in his opposition,—you know he is Effie's guardian. In business circles down-town, I am sorry to say Arnold is regarded as a very wild and somewhat dissipated young man."

Stringfellow: "Yes, mother, this is true; and the opinion, I regret, is but too well grounded. Arnold is much slyer since he came back from the navy than he was before; still the fact is patent that he has not in the least improved."

Mrs. M——: "Well, this has nothing to do with my purpose. Effie would influence him to abandon all his youthful follies. Very soon he would be redeemed.

"Now for my plan and its execution, about which there must be the least possible delay:—

"*By some means, Lawrence Pleasington must be put out of the way, and so effectually as to stand as an obstacle to my plan no more. Do you understand?*"

Atkinson: "Oh, horrors—commit murder or something little or no better! What! Do you imagine us capable of this atrocity? Never, never! We cannot be parties to this crime."

Mrs. M——: "There is no need to commit murder, nor any other crime of a more scarlet hue than such as that in which the hands of both have already been deeply imbued. Why, my amiable, virtuous, honest sons, I wonder that the angels do not come and carry you away bodily from this wicked world!

"What, pray let me most earnestly ask you, has washed from your sensitive consciences the ignominious stain of the cool, deliberate, systematic, unfeeling, pitiless and cruel robbery of Gertrude Flowers and her two little orphan children? This without granting or leaving them even the pittance legally theirs, had the failure of Atkinson, Flowers & Co. been legitimately honest; to say nothing of the other creditors, paid at a shamefully low percentage of a compromise scale, with their own money, after using it a year without interest.

"Ah, well may you start, and sink back in your seats in despair! I pity you, and want you to pity me. I have not mistaken my men. You will assist me without another manifestation of reluctance."

Atkinson: "It was you, madam, my mother, who first suggested that disreputable affair, or we should never have dreamed of it."

Mrs. M——: "Silence! You were apt and eager scholars, poor whining second Adams, and without the manly firmness to reject an improper suggestion from a woman. Understand me. I did that to get you in my power, which I am thankful that up to this moment you have never given me occasion to use against you, as I then feared you might, in relation to other matters. I hold that power over your heads, fully conscious of the terror that it awakens in your hearts. From this moment do my bidding unmurmuringly, and all will glide smoothly and serenely for you; and you will find me as docile and as amiable as a pet lamb. But cross my wish with but the slightest indication of defiance to my will, and you will arouse a savagely furious lioness to the desperation of the most cruel and unmerciful heartlessness.

"I shall immediately confer with Madam Vaisentre, and learn from her the most desirable course to be pursued, and the most approved, available and practicable means to be employed in following it up to a successful issue. If she does not at once know, she has ample facilities for ascertaining so quietly that no one in the daylight world will ever have the remotest inkling of what is transpiring while in process of development, nor how it was brought about after it becomes public property. Caution is not an adequate term fully to express fully the prudent care I shall exercise in covering up our steps as we move along, and in making doubly sure that no suspicious fingers point in our direction.

"Now, thus far the question is settled. In due time I shall apprise you of the parts you are to play, and as to how and when they are to be performed. The expense and all the trouble as to details shall have my attention. Good-night."

ATKINSON: "Well, Adam, we are in a pretty dilemma. That woman is desperate. See how true is the proverb of retribution. Ours has been so tardy that we had almost forgotten that we owed it. Now it is about to explode with all its long pent-up reserve forces, and compel us to pay the terrible penalty, with its many long years of ever-compounding interest. What the aggregated sum total may be ere we see the end, my blood runs cold at the bare and but casual contemplation. Poor, innocent Gertrude Flowers! the widow's woes and the orphans' tears we have caused you and yours—alas! their magnitude and their cruel pangs may be immeasurably terrible! Oh, Adam! why did we do that dark and horrid deed, whose legitimate offspring are now demanding at our hand the black perpetration of perhaps still more deeply dyed and infamous crimes against yet other innocent and unoffending hearts, doomed to endure torturing agonies that are untold?"

STRINGFELLOW: "Ah, Ira! regrets are unavailing now. Nothing in this world can recall those cruel wrongs. There is neither atonement nor redemption for us here, nor hereafter.

"If Gertrude Flowers, or either of her children, or all three, are living, and I knew their whereabouts, I would return my part of her stolen fortune with interest. It should not be left to heirs with Madam Mountjoy's blood in their veins.

"In our family relations, also, we are doomed to wretchedness. Our young wives do not and never will love us; and the chances are that they will find younger men more congenial to their tastes, and love them clandestinely. There are a thousand means by which our ills may be augmented and again multiplied."

ATKINSON: "You are uttering uncomfortable truths, Adam. I wish we knew the fate of Mrs. Flowers, or, rather, the present abiding-place of her and her children, or any one of them now living, and I should readily join you in making such restitution as is in our power. If we could but do this, I should then defy Madam Mountjoy, and flatly refuse to take any part in a criminal or even unfairly purposed act. Let us put the matter in able legal hands, and instruct that every possible effort be made to find Mrs. Flowers or one of her children."

STRINGFELLOW: "All right, Ira, we will do this to-morrow, and find in the meantime some pretext to procrastinate with the Madam. I am thoroughly horror-stricken at the idea of participating in the cruel outrage which she now designs to commit on poor Pleasington, whose little finger is truly worth more than young Noel's ignoble heart. Satan would blush at the thought of this vile atrocity."

CHAPTER XXXV.

THE BLIGHTING WAVE OF NAMELESS WOE.

"Oh, Love! no habitant of earth thou art
  An unseen Seraph, we believe in thee,
A faith whose martyrs are the broken heart,
  But never hath seen, nor e'er shall see
The naked eye thy form, as it should be:
  The mind hath made thee as it peopled heaven,
Even with its own desired phantasy,
  And to a thought such shape and image giv'n
As haunts the unquenched soul, parch'd, wearied, wrung
    and riven."   —BYRON.

LAWRENCE PLEASINGTON and a bank-teller are together at the home of the former.

BANK CLERK: "Let us go up to your room, Lawrence, before we go out. I want to write a note and brush my hair."

LAWRENCE PLEASINGTON: "All right, Tim, I too

want to brush my boots. Glad you named it; I was about to forget it."

They go at once up to Lawrence's room.

BANK CLERK: "Lawrence, I am very warm and thirsty. Have you some water in the room?"

LAWRENCE: "No; but I will go for some ice-water. Make yourself at home. I shall not be many minutes."

* * * * * *

BANK CLERK: "Ah! that is indeed refreshing.—By the way, that Effie of yours eclipses all our belles. You are most fortunate in possessing such a rare jewel."

LAWRENCE: "I do not yet possess her, Tim; and I have always heard that there is '*many a slip between the cup and lip.*'"

Scene changes to the president's room in the bank, next day.

CHIEF OF POLICE: "Have you no suspicion as to any one who might have participated in the robbery? Have you noticed no suspicious looking parties around the bank lately?"

PRESIDENT: "Nothing whatever unusual. We have actually no clue, and no sort of grounds upon which we can base a suspicion against any one."

CHIEF: "Well, then, it is clear to my mind that some one connected with the bank is in the party. It is not the work of an utter stranger, but of a person intimately acquainted with the building, and with the inside of the bank, even to the inmost chamber of the vaults. Here, sir, is the starting-point upon which work must immediately begin, if you wish to ferret out the crime and capture the guilty parties, and, perhaps, recover some of your money."

PRESIDENT: "All right, sir, that is what we want. Spare neither effort nor expense that promises to reward you with success. By all means take the most prompt and vigorous measures, with every one connected with the institution, from myself down to the humblest messenger-boy."

CHIEF: "It will be necessary to search the dwelling or room of every one employed in the bank."

PRESIDENT: "Stop at nothing, I tell you, man;

and do not hesitate to begin your unpleasant work."

The officer goes out with the president, but returns alone soon.

CHIEF: "Is your name Lawrence Pleasington, young man?"

LAWRENCE: "Yes, sir, that is my name."

CHIEF: "I want you to take a little walk with me, and to assist me somewhat in seeking a clue to the robbery."

LAWRENCE: "All right, sir, I am entirely at your service."

They go out, and proceed to the police station, and meet the president.

CHIEF: "This is the culprit, Mr. President.—Now, Pleasington, you understand the situation. You know, without my telling you, that you are at police head-quarters, a prisoner, charged with the crime of robbing the bank, your employers—ungrateful man. The proof against you is overwhelming. We have found much of the missing money concealed in your own bed-room. The very best thing for you to do now, is to make a clean breast of it, and thus put us on the tracks of your accomplices, and the way to recover the balance of the stolen money. It will go much lighter with you if you thus assist us. Heaven itself cannot save you."

LAWRENCE: "I am the victim of some vile and villainous plot. I know no more about the robbery than an unborn babe. Heaven alone may bear me witness that I speak the truth; but I am innocent."

PRESIDENT: "Come now, Pleasington, this acting will avail you nothing. I should rather have lost all the missing money than to have believed this of you. But of your guilt there cannot be the semblance of a shadow of doubt. It is as clear and positive as the noonday sun. I am utterly dumbfounded. I cannot perceive what could have ever possessed you—you with a record so enviable and a future brighter with promise and fuller of hope than that enjoyed by any other young man in the land, no matter what his family name, influence and wealth might bestow upon him. To think that you would stake all these, and lose them in this infamous game—an act immeasurably degrading, for which there can be no excuse, and connected with which there cannot be one single mitigating circumstance! Col. Worthington will be here to-night. This will break his heart."

LAWRENCE: "If I was on the gallows, and had but barely time to utter three words before the trap would spring, they would come in clarion tones: *I am innocent.*

"My bright future is what has caused this deadly venomous blow to be wreaked upon me with such mad fury. I can see, from the light in which the case has been presented to my mind, that I am doomed to the most miserable and wretched fate to which flesh and blood is ever consigned without the shadow of a chance to escape from its hideous consequences. I see the ruins of all past and the wrecks of future hopes commingling in one wild mass impelled by chaotic velocity, whirling downward into the fathomless gulf of black and ignominious oblivion. I am powerless. Do unto me as you may, at the end I will be the same unchanged and unchangeable victim of inexplicable circumstances, and shall be unable to make any other answer but that already declared unto you. I realize that for this world, all is as effectually over with me as if I was guilty. And to the hard and cruel decree I can but bow my head in mute despair."

CHIEF OF POLICE: "Sergeant, put him in the sweat-box until the morning. See that no one speaks to him, and allow nothing passed to him. Some of this starch must be gotten out of him.

"Now, President, that is decidedly the best acting I ever met in my long and varied experience; but I think he will weaken."

PRESIDENT: "I can assure you that it troubles and puzzles me beyond measure. Worthington is our only hope to induce him to reveal those who were his accomplices. So until morning, as far as I am able to judge, there remains nothing further to be done."

CHIEF: "Nothing, sir. You may now go home. I shall leave no stone unturned to find a clew to lead me to the discovery of the other parties. Some trifle or uncovered foot-print may unexpectedly betray them."

The next morning Silas Worthington calls on poor Pleasington.

WORTHINGTON: "Oh, Lawrence,—alas! thou wretched boy, you have opened the flood-gates of misery! Your poor mother now lies stark and cold in the icy embrace of death—the victim of a broken heart; and a more horrible receptacle than the grave is gaping to receive you. I had intended to talk severely serious to you; but now you are draining your cup of woe to its bitter dregs, I will spare you the mortification of listening to my reproachful words."

LAWRENCE: "Oh, my God! I can bear anything now.—Spirit of my angelic mother, hover over thy poor despairing son; and for the sake of the worthy name he bears, attest unto the world that he is innocent, and the victim of some dark and mysterious machination.—Col. Worthington, I know your opinion. I am powerless to change it. Speak! Nothing can now add to my present torture."

WORTHINGTON: "Well, Lawrence, I have obtained a guarantee, that, on condition you reveal the whole affair to me, with the names of all the parties connected with it, you shall be immediately and unconditionally released. I think this best; for I tell you frankly that nothing else can save you from a long term of years in State prison."

LAWRENCE: "I thank you for your kind intercession; but if I had a thousand lives doomed to endless imprisonment, and divulging one iota relative to the robbery, or as to how the money got into my room, would redeem them all, I could not divulge one word, because I know nothing. On this point, it is idle to talk to me, because I cannot do what is desired: give information that I do not possess."

WORTHINGTON: "Reflect upon this after I am gone, when you are alone. If you want me, let it be known, and I will come."

LAWRENCE: "I shall never want you again, unless something in some way transpires to cause you to change your opinion. Until then I must bid you a last farewell."

They parted, and Worthington joined the president of the bank.

PRESIDENT: "Well, Colonel, what was the result of your interview?"

WORTHINGTON: "Just the same as yours. You

might subject him to the most cruel, slow torture, and he would never change his position. He has taken his stand and will go to the grave unyielding.

PRESIDENT: "Well, it is a sadly deplorable case."

Worthington soon called on poor broken-hearted Effie.

WORTHINGTON: "Well, Effie, my poor child, the chilling winds of ill-favored Fate are beating furiously down upon us. I pity you. I know the cruel blow has crushed you without mercy."

EFFIE: "It is more terrible than the day of doom. But tell me truly, is Lawrence guilty?"

WORTHINGTON: "Alas! it is impossible for him to be innocent. All the proof and the circumstances are against him so strongly as to leave him not the benefit of a single doubt. Yet still he obstinately denies it, and maintains that he is innocent."

EFFIE: "Then my resolution is taken. I desire to make my will, to remain sealed while I live; then I am going at once into the deepest seclusion of a convent, there to pass my remaining days—a broken-hearted, hope-bereft woman."

WORTHINGTON: "Effie, that is madness. I implore you do not throw away your brightly promising young life so rashly!"

EFFIE: "All words are idle. The sun of my life has gone down! The world shall not mock me to my face. If Lawrence is false and base, who in this world can I trust and esteem as noble and true? That fair young brow, the gem-like emblem of honest purity; that ever temperate and exemplary life, so nobly brave and faithful to his suffering, bleeding country on whose altar his youthful blood flowed so freely, now degraded and blackened with the indelible stain of the basest ignominy! After this, what is there in the world for me to trust? He was my ideal of manly purity and excellence. Before my mind no other can ever rise to the same exalted eminence upon which I beheld him stand.

"My friend, be good to me now, and accord my wish without delay; because this night I am resolved to pass to my living tomb, whence I shall never emerge again, until I am borne out to the silent church-yard. This is the consecration of my plighted vows, the proof of my abiding constancy, and the test of my fidelity and undying devotion."

Late this same evening, in the deepening gloom of his lonely prison-cell, there came to poor Lawrence Pleasington a letter, which ran as follows:

"June —, 1865.

"MAJ. LAWRENCE PLEASINGTON.

"*My lost Friend:*

"When we said good-night, so gay and cheerful, the last time, how little we dreamed that it was for evermore!

"Oh, Lawrence, that we have lived to see the light of this day, so bitterly fraught with hopeless disappointment and irremediable wretchedness! What shall I—what can I say to you?

"A blinding flash of lightning and deafening peal of thunder from a serenely cloudless sky, could not have so shocked and surprised me as did the cruel tidings of the terrible fate that had overtaken you—a fate a thousand times more dreadful than the most horrible death—the death-knell of all our hopes,—the direful force that has cruelly severed our hopes forever.

"I know what unutterable agonies you are suffering, and pity you from the depths of my soul. Beyond this point I cannot go—am powerless to help you.

"The dark mystery which has overwhelmed you is between you and your God, where I fear it must remain.

"You are in prison, as you may be doomed to remain for many long and weary years. I also am going to a convent prison. This is the strongest proof I can afford you of my faithful adherance to my plighted vows and constant devotion to yourself. This may prove an empty source of consolation; but it is, under the existing circumstances, all that I can render you. While your life is dark and cheerless, embittered with the gall of despair, you shall know that I am not bright and joyous amid the giddy and maddening whirl of the fickle, flattering and false social world. I will not accept its smiles nor give it mine.

"I should call and see you, but think it better for us both that I remain away, as I am going into the convent to-night."

"Words fail me. I cannot express what I feel. Bear your trying afflictions, your cruel hardships and hopeless fate with Christian fortitude and resignation. At best, our days would have been transient and comparatively few, and, perhaps, far less blissful than we anticipated. Be that as it might have been, we now know that to us the realization of that happy day-dream anticipation is over, blighted,—forever gone.

"Let us live for the hereafter, and strive to meet again in the great and ever-enduring Unknown. God help and bless you.

"Until we have passed over the dark river— FAREWELL.

"Your sympathetic friend,

"EFFIE EDELSTEIN."

Two days later, in the retirement of her exile and within the pure and sacred precincts of the convent of the Blessed Cross of Mercy, the heart-stricken, world-weary Effie received the following answer to her letter:

"County Prison, June —, 1865.
"MISS EFFIE EDELSTEIN.

"*My lost Love:*

"The last and only consolation I shall ever know in this world, reached me last evening in your tenderly kind and delicately comforting letter, for which I thank you a thousand times more than pen can write or tongue could tell.

"You do not unfeelingly reproach me. The tenor of your letter satisfies me that you at least hope I am innocent.

"Circumstances that are utterly dumbfounding and unanswerable are against me. All the world will be forced to believe me guilty. But, my lost Effie, before God, in the name of our pure and ever constant love, and in the name of my angelic mother, I solemnly declare to you, in the sad and bitter cadence of an *eternal farewell*,—the veritable breathing of my dying words to you, my unhappy darling—that of this crime I am as innocent as the angels in Heaven. That I cannot prove it, is my more than cruel misfortune, not my fault. With the world it is just the same as if I was guilty, but not with my conscience, my God, and my poor Effie, who is taking upon herself a cross of self-denial almost as burden-

10

some and as physically severe as that which I shall be forced to bear. I should have wished this otherwise, and that you might yet be happy, if that was possible. But now I know it is too late to entreat you to pursue a different course. You have already taken the step, from which all the world could not induce you to recede. You know your heart and feelings, which have determined you to banish yourself from the world. I pity you, my darling. But for your sake, the blow would not be altogether so terribly crushing as it now is.

"Yes, my Effie, my life shall be ever pure and blameless. I will live for you and Heaven, where I hope we may meet again. Always remember and pray for me. My thoughts will cling to you until their force is stilled in death.—FAREWELL.

"Your unhappy friend,

"LAWRENCE PLEASINGTON."

Thus parted these two devoted, young, and loving hearts. How could Heaven permit them to become the victims of this hard and cruel fate? Was it the doom of retribution pronounced against the third and fourth generations, that they had inherited; which had been handed down to them as a legacy from wicked forefathers, whose criminal bones had been sleeping beneath the snows of two hundred winters, far away beyond the Atlantic's blue and sleepless tide? The mysterious echoes of ages, wafted from those distant shores, must answer.

Against poor Pleasington the most speedy, vigorous, and unrelenting prosecution was waged, until he was, in due form of law, pronounced guilty.

Poor, brave, noble young man, what a demoniacal echo that one terrible word made in the grim and breathless silence of the dreary old Court-room and its adjacent corridors, as it fell in stern and pitiless tone from the lips of the jury's foreman! The handsome young soldier, care-worn, haggard and pale from the terrible ordeal through which he has lately passed, stands forth before the bar of the Court, to hear the sealing notes of his doom.

He had spurred his charger up to the muzzles of Jackson's guns at Stone Bridge; of Col. Cloud's in the valley of Virginia and on the plains of Manassas; and of Hood's on the field of Gettysburg. He had passed through the *rayless night of death* in the North Carolina pine-woods, and faced her grim visage at other points a thousand times; had served his country long and well, where he could proudly and defiantly look danger in the face; but how different now the nature of the menace with which he is imperiled! Alone, and friendless, and helpless, with the very weapons of truth and justice—the only defense and succor that could have availed him—perverted and turned against him. Such is the gloomy picture which he now beholds.

At Stone Bridge, alone, among enemies, with his life in the most imminent peril, he had beheld the youthful face of Garland Cloud bending anxiously over him, and heard the kind tones of his sympathetic voice speaking words of comfort and cheer; and again, under similar circumstances, he had received at the hands of Col. Cloud on the plains of Manassas, identically the same treatment. Even on the night when the stern preparations for his execution were going on around him, every possible kindness and the most unmistakable manifestations of sympathy had been his. Now, in the trying crisis of the present moment, surrounded by his own people, for whom he had fought and bled, he quietly turns his eyes from face to face, seeking the slightest indications of sympathy—but, alas! poor boy, in vain.

In each sternly set face, he could clearly read the revelation, that every heart in all that throng, then crowding the room almost to suffocation, was desperately steeled against him. In silence, he then listens to the long lecture of the Judge, and hears his sentence—the last day the extreme penalty of the law would permit—being pronounced against him.

He is rushed with precipitancy away to the State prison, where the harshly-grating massive door closes behind him, shutting out the sunlight of hope—FOREVER.

CHAPTER XXXVI.

THE SERIOUSLY MISTAKEN IDENTITY.

"Roll on, noble rivers, in grandeur and pride;
Waft the stores of my country from every side.
Bring a full share of wealth o'er the wide-spreading sea;
Though comfort and hope, they be strangers to me."
—MISCELLANEOUS.

WE last met Garland Cloud amid the pitiful and trying scene of preparation for the execution of "The three victims of retaliation," in the spectral night-shadows of the North Carolina lowland piny woods.

About the same time, we heard a conversation between his father, Gen. Cloud, and some brother officers, by their last night's bivouac fire at Appomattox, from which we learned that Garland dared not return home.

This was true. The daring young horseman was thoroughly acquainted with the desperate state of affairs in his native section, and knew too well the character of the men who had sworn vengeance against him, to place himself, unarmed, in a position where they could get him in their power.

Immediately, then, after Gen. Joseph E. Johnston's surrender, Garland Cloud fled for life; intending to seek a safe asylum where he would be unknown, in a Northern State, until his native land could afford him a more promising and congenial dwelling-place.

The first day he set foot on the soil of the State which he had selected, still dressed in the uniform of a Confederate colonel, he was arrested by the civil authorities, who claimed that he was a local desperado who had been committing depredations in the country, throughout the war, and against whom there were a number of indictments standing ready on the docket, in order to make quick disposition of him whenever he might be captured.

In vain did Cloud protest that they were mistaken. His captors would permit no explanation, but told him bluntly that his ruse, under the disguise of a rebel colonel, would not avail him; that his time had come. Court was then in session.

He passed the night, heavily shackled, in the iron cage of the county jail.

Early the next morning he was placed in the dock for trial.

JUDGE: "Sam Greg, are you ready for trial?"

CLOUD: "Your Honor, I am not. I am not the man; which fact I can prove by officers and soldiers—citizens of your county—if you will lay this matter over a few days until they reach home. I demand this in the name of equity and justice."

JUDGE: "If that is the only ground for delay, the trial will proceed. We are not disposed to grant any time for your clan to come and break open the jail, and release you. There are plenty of good citizens who will swear that you are the right man. If you are what you claim—a traitor and rebel—you deserve the penitentiary, or rather the halter; therefore we cannot go far astray in condemning you. The garb you wear would shame an honest man."

CLOUD: "There are no indictments against me for treason, sir; and I deny your right to refuse me a fair trial, by putting my liberty in jeopardy without first giving me the time and opportunity to prove that I am not the man named in the indictments."

JUDGE: "Silence. Proceed with the trial. Have you any counsel, Greg?"

CLOUD: "I am not Greg. I defy you to try me as him. I have no counsel, and will not submit to this outrage."

JUDGE: "We appoint you to defend him, Mr. R.——."

The jury is soon impanelled. Three Dutchmen swear most positively that he was the ring-leader of the gang that had robbed their houses and stolen their horses. One after another the jurymen convict him on three indictments, without so much as even leaving their seats.

Without a moment's delay he is brought to the bar of the Court for sentence, and in a sarcastically solemn tone the Judge says: "Sam Greg, if you have aught to say why sentence shall not be pronounced against you, in accordance with the verdicts of the jury rendered against you, say it now, or ever after hold your peace."

CLOUD: "I have. You have denied me fair and impartial justice, manifesting your unblushing partiality by asserting that if innocent of the alleged charges, I was a halter-deserving rebel. You have transformed a Court of justice into a stage for a scene of ribald mockery—a Star-Chamber Inquisition. And now you mock me with your cold formality, when not even a voice from Heaven could stay your predetermined sentence, nor abate its diabolical severity.

"I protest against it, but to no more purpose than a feeble swimmer, riding the tempest-flying wave, might sue for safety. I hurl back your accusations as basely infamous, damnably unjust, barbarously, inhumanly cruel; stigmatizing my life with an odious curse that will warp with its obloquy, attaint with its poison, and freeze with its Arctic congealment the genial currents of the soul, transforming its lightest burden into the unmerciful torments of a raging hell, that will eternally prey upon the riven fragments of the heart, blotting out forever the last gleam of hope.

"May all the distress, affliction, sorrow and suffering that you thus cause to pursue and curse my after-life, re-act with undying severity upon you and your posterity forever. Bear witness, Oh, ye eternal heavens! that I receive and must suffer an unjust penalty, and avenge my innocence."

JUDGE: "Were your words appropriate, and employed in a worthy cause, they might move me to compassion. The Court sentences you to the fullest extent of the law—thirty years in the Penitentiary at Bay City, and regrets the want of power to make the term one hundred years."

On board the train, bound toward his prison home, Cloud hears his name, and feels, simultaneously, his shackled hand firmly pressed in the strong grasp of two powerful hands. Turning his sad eyes, he almost involuntarily, half to himself, half to the man he beholds by his side, exclaims, "Lieut. Stone!"

LIEUT. STONE: "Col. Cloud!"

For a moment the two men gaze at each other in silence, while the wells of their hearts are in commotion, and sending up to the eyes great pearly drops of briny tears. The sheriff and his guard *posse* look at the two men, and then at one another, with astounded wonderment, because they know Lieut. Stone to be one among the first and most influential citizens of their county. At length Stone asks, and Cloud briefly explains, the cause of his present and most uncomfortable predicament and future hopelessness.

LIEUT. S——: "Col. Cloud, I have not yet reached home. It has now been three years since I have seen my wife and babies. I was waiting here for the down train, and recognized you through the window. But for you, my loved ones would never see me more. None can ever call you to account for the action now; and I tell you that you purposely spared my life. The volley fired at me was nothing but blank cartridges. I owe you a debt that I can never cancel; and this is an unexpected and deplorable opportunity for me to manifest the sincerity of my gratitude to you, and to make one instalment of its payment. I will never settle quietly down at home, nor for one day cease nor abate my efforts, until you are a free man."

CLOUD: "I thank God that they did not harm you. Thank Him all your days, for shielding and delivering you from that terrible danger. On that score I have no claim upon you. Let us not talk about the bitter ordeal of that ghostly night. It was the most cruelly trying experience of my life, to which even the gloom of the present rayless prospect cannot be compared.

"For charity's sake, and in the name and cause of humanity, if you desire to do something that will remove this unjust, remorseless and cruel burden, beneath whose crushing weight I am doomed, alas! to groan unpitied for so many dreary years, I shall be most thankful to you, and patiently await the result, never doubting that it will arrive.

"But I implore you to suppress my true name. In the name of that Heaven that spared your life, I entreat you, do not permit my name to become connected with this apparent infamy, that might be magnified and misconstrued as it flies over the world."

LIEUT. S——: "I shall be more speedy than you dream.—Upon the honor of a soldier, your name shall be guarded *with the silence of the grave.*"

CHAPTER XXXVII.

THE BANEFUL SUPERNATURAL AND ITS VANQUISHING ANTIDOTE.

"Oh that the desert were my dwelling place,
  With one fair Spirit for my minister,
That I might all forget the uman race,
  And hating no one, love but only her!
Ye Elements!—in whose ennobling stir
  I feel myself exalted—can ye not
Accord me such a being? Do I err
  In deeming, such inhabit, many a spot,
Though with them to converse can rarely be our
    lot?"   —BYRON.

TWO MONTHS after we left Garland Cloud talking to Lieut. Stone on the train, in shackles, he is seated in the parlor of an aunt of his, in one of the most war-wasted districts of the Old Dominion, two hundred miles from his father's home. He has been there now for three days. He is pale, care-worn, emaciated, melancholy.

There is a military government in the State, which has stopped Brownslow's high-handed game of kidnapping, and fully suppressed the roving bands of free-booters, but which cannot control the rifle of the secret assassin. This fact young Cloud understands, and knows that, therefore, he dares not return home, nor even write a letter.

As we now behold him, he has a fair suit of clothing on his back, and one-half dollar in his pocket.

It is night. All the members of the family have retired except Fannie, a bright little fairy-like maiden of less than twenty summers. She is sitting in silence, gazing most intently into the gloomy face of her cousin, but at length speaks.

FANNIE: "Now, cousin Garland, you promised to tell me to-night why you are so melancholy; and I am all impatience to know what heavy sorrow or malady is oppressing you so cruelly that the woeful image of your face causes tears —involuntary, spontaneous tears—to come into my eyes."

CLOUD: "Why, my sweet coz, in my tender youth I was wedded to misfortune. My bride was the then young and beautiful Confederacy, whose deep crimson-dyed grave, where I beheld her ghastly remains buried, to moulder down to oblivion's darkest shade, left me a bankrupt in spirit—an orphan of the heart. The companions of my youth are all quietly, peacefully sleeping on distant battle-fields. Why was I left for a sadder fate? Why did the dread missile of death seek only my enfeebled arm? Oh that it had in mercy shattered my body and stilled my proud heart while it yet beat buoyant with youth and hope, leaving a spotless name with the 'unnumbered dead.! Then I would not now be nameless forevermore.'

"You conjure me to look at the bright side. How can I, all being but darkness? To-morrow I leave you and all brightness, for many, many weary days."

FANNIE: "Alas! what a deep-cast gloom overshadows you. But pray stay with us. Do not go forth, weak, feeble, despondent. Tarry until invigorating strength and reviving spirits return once more. I will sing for you; cheer you with fantastic pictures of fairy-land romance; build air-castles in some imaginary vale of Vaucluse, where the zephyrs are laden with fragrant perfume dispelled by orange-blossoms, and odoriferous with the magnolia's exhalations.—But, pray, whither are you going?"

CLOUD: "To this dream-land you would picture, did it exist. I don't know, coz; the situation is not clear to me. But it is so late that we must say good-night."

FANNIE: "Good-night, cousin Garland. May your sleep be refreshing and your dreams far brighter than your thoughts."

CLOUD: "Good-night, little coz; sweet slumbers and blissful dreams to you.

"Nature's own, joyous, happy child—she is gone. Her fairy foot-falls are receding; now they die away in the distant hall, and I am alone, as I must ever be; guiltless, yet still a pardoned wretch. Alas! the deep thralldom of that hapless curse! My heart sickens, my brain reels at its contemplation. I would have died ere it expired; but what have I gained by my release from it? A hopeless, life-long misery, anguish, sorrow, despair—and what? Or soon, or late—death."

Garland Cloud sits in the rocking-chair, head bowed down upon his breast, under the mystic influence of some strangely potent spell, half

sleep, half trance. Evidently the same which creeps upon mortal flesh, when a vision from the Unknown comes to the immortal spirit inhabiting the frail, weak body of mortal man. And that such visions do come, both from the celestial and infernal worlds, either in mild and less perceptible, or strong and more overpowering currents of spiritual electricity, who of rational intelligence can doubt, and at the same time accept the doctrine of that still small voice of ever admonitory warning, speaking to the soul of danger and of death? And that other doctrine of the alluring, beguiling, menacing, threatening wiles of Satan, tempting man to sin—sometimes in a mild and almost imperceptible guise of seeming modesty and abashed timidity; then again in his hideous form, almost perceptible to the naked eye, and speaking in a voice almost audible to the natural ear?—Thus he appears and speaks to-night to Garland Cloud, whose conscience has begun already to transform him into a moral coward.

A combined force of strangely ordered circumstances has conspired to induce him to assume the mask. This brave, frank, generous, noble spirit, that had quailed before no mortal danger; valued and esteemed by friends as an ideal self-educated youthful officer; and respected by enemies who knew him, for his magnanimous humanity, has hesitated, wavered, recoiled before a moral social duty: the duty of announcing openly, frankly, and fearlessly to his friends and to the world, if necessary, just what had befallen him, and how it had occurred. Instead of this he took refuge behind the miserable subterfuge of concealment—that shuffling make-shift of curse-breeding falsehood—the most prolific source of social hope- and happiness-destroying damnation that ever lays hold of weak, irresolute humanity with its heavy and merciless hand. After its fiendish grasp is once securely fixed, no earthly power can ever force it to relax.

At first this dark subterfuge is presented with graceful seemliness. Its obliging convenience is usually gratefully accepted, owing to the momentary annoyance or embarrassment that is distressing or threatening the hapless victim. This small error is lonely behind its great veil of concealment and sternly demands company; and sooner or later is satisfied, until at length that bosom becomes a groaning, living, earthly hell. This is of a nature so horrible that, could all such victims at the same time utter their doleful shrieks and wails of stifled agonies, with the shrillness that the heart would send them forth to pierce the startled air, nothing ever has occurred since the flood, and never may occur again, until the awful grandeur of the Day of Judgment bursts upon the earth, that would create such soul-moving lamentations.

It is this that drives the proud, hard-pressed merchant into the inextricable entanglements of the interminable labyrinths of prevarication, ultimate crime and disgrace,—surely crime, whenever he contracts obligations under the cloak of misrepresentations or concealment as to the precariousness of his affairs, when he knows facts, that if known to his creditor, the accommodation would be withheld. Morally, there is no difference between the concealment and the false representation and little between either and downright robbery.

It is this concealment of some indiscretion or other disreputable episode in the lives of people, and the perpetual dread that they will become known, that renders such lives more intolerable than the publication of their concealed chapters could possibly make them. It is the murderer's sleepless terror and flight, when naught but the accusing conscience pursues.

We deal with this question only in the relations that it bears to his life and its temporal weal or woe. This is a feature of visible, tangible, to many of but too truly well-known, real existence, needing the light of no revelation to make it clear; and it defies skepticism.

It is, beyond any question, the immortality of man at which the Infernal powers aim; but in the mortal relations this direful influence works at the same time untold ills. To combat this, is our bounden duty and special province; while the other belongs to the ordained man of God.

APPARITION OF SATAN: "Mortal of sin and sorrow, list and dream! Thy shame shall follow thee, magnified, to credible guilt. With this for their weapons, thy envious, unsated enemies shall marshal against and pursue thee with secret obloquy, assailing thee in high or low places; shall undo thy prospects and turn thy hopes to dust, driving thee to pangs and extremities to which the present is thy unreached Paradise. Thou shall not escape, save by defying thy fast-breeding ills in a courageous flight from an intolerable existence. Be wise: or suffer, and drag untold numbers down with thee to wretchedness."

CLOUD: "Have I slept! What terrible visions have haunted me, more vividly real than if under the noonday's sun! Misery, ruin, and all the inconceivable woes, real or imaginary, in the hard decree of earth-born affliction! It will be thus. And is there no escape? No, none! And what can be worse than the eternal dread of this—but the reality. Oh, horrors! To-morrow I will say adieu to this hospitable roof, walk away, and quietly end it all in the placid water above the dam of the forge. What misery this would cause poor Fannie and the family! But perchance they will never know it. To-morrow night I know not what may be."

Early the next morning Cloud met his little cousin, when the following conversation took place:

FANNIE: "I am provoked, cousin Garland, that they did not call me in time to breakfast with you. I have just finished my breakfast."

"CLOUD: "I was waiting for you. I have bid aunty and the boys farewell, and now, little coz, comes the last pang: I must say good-by to you."

FANNIE: "But you cannot shake me off so lightly. I shall wander down the lane and over the bridge with you. I have much to say to you before farewell. Now, why that look of disappointment? Don't you want my company, or do you dread my lecture, or whatever you term it?"

CLOUD: "Neither. Would I could ever have such company and counsel."

FANNIE: "Cousin Garland, this despondency shames your nature and name, that never flinched or recoiled before mortal hardship, privation, or danger.

"Look now, on your distressed, poverty-stricken, ruined country, the same land that you buckled on your armor and drew your sword so many times to defend, now defenseless and helpless. See the desolate homes, the bleak and solitary chimneys standing as grim monuments of war-wasting destruction, and your fallen comrades' widows and orphans, all appealing to you, in mutely silent yet solemn eloquence, to be yourself again; to be brave as of yore, and lend your aid to heal their ghastly wounds.

"The energy and brain power that could work the rustic mountain-boy from the ranks to the command of a thousand brave men, can do something in the peaceful battles of life, when the cry for help is so stern and pressing.

"You say that had you been five years older you would now be famous; and that you would rather have Jackson's name than a thousand years of life. Jackson was never so truly glorious amid the wildest shouts of his victorious legions as I would be now were I a man, and that man you, in the struggle to redeem my war-blighted country from the thralldom of misery hovering over its blue hills, once so verdant, and its magic vales, once so fruitful, like the grim visaged Destroying Angel. Oh! I had such horrid dreams about you last night, that I could not bear to see you leave without speaking to you of all these things.

"Now I am going to take your hand in both of mine; and while I thus hold it, I want you to promise me, in the name of a true soldier's sacred honor, that you will take care of yourself, and do everything in your power for poor Virginia, your disconsolate mother."

CLOUD: "Little coz, for your sake, and in memory of this moment, I will strive to do my duty."

FANNIE: "Now I must return to the house. I am glad you came to see us. When shall I ever see that anxious, sorrow-stricken face again?

"Now, cousin Garland, seal your promise with the kiss of a cousin's pure love. My poor cousin, farewell. May God bless you."

CLOUD: "Little coz, I cannot say when we may ever meet again. God bless your pure little soul. Farewell."

"Alas! how her retiring footsteps widen the space between us. Now she disappears over the brow of the hill.

"Nevermore shall my tear-dimmed eyes behold that graceful form, nor my ears listen to the harmonious cadence of her enchanting voice. Too good for earth. She has saved me from a watery shroud. Adieu.

"Without money and without friends; with an odium darker than the demon's curse to pursue me, which I must strive to keep silent as the tomb; but with the secret dread of its muffled approach ever haunting, threatening to crush and contemn me—an invisible spectral ghost hovering about, shadowing and ever darkening life's pathway—I go forth an exile from the home of my boyhood days, maimed and enfeebled and oppressed with the gloomy shades of Futurity's dim picture, a wanderer on the devious, cheerless road of life. Visions of youth's dream, farewell!

"Ever ringing in my ears must be the vibrating and endless echo of that one admonitory word, *Duty! duty! duty!*

Oh that I may never disobey it, nor its stern charge forget!"

> "Once more upon Life's ocean, yet once more;
> May the waves bound beneath me as a steed
> That knows his rider.—Welcome to their roar,
> Swift be their guidance whereso'er it lead,
> Though the strained mast should quiver as a reed;
> And the rent canvas fluttering strew the gale—
> Still must I on, for I am as a weed,
> Flung from the rock on Ocean's foam to sail
> Where'er the surge may sweep, the tempest's
> breath prevail."

CHAPTER XXXVIII.

THE CHANGING WIND AND TIDE.

> "In the desert a fountain is springing—
> In the wide waste there is a lone tree—
> In the solitude a bird is singing,
> That speaks to my spirit of thee."
> —BYRON.

THE fifth day after Garland Cloud parted with his cousin Fannie, he is at the railroad depot of an important Virginia grain-shipping town, one hundred miles from the residence of his aunt; a distance which he had traversed on foot.

This is a section of the State where he is a stranger, a county in which he believes there is not one person who knows him—the reason that induced him to wend his way in that direction. He has just reached the place, and is both tired and hungry.

In ten minutes after his arrival a passenger train steams up to the depot. There is quite a large crowd on the platform, hurrying to and fro. Cloud rises from the box upon which he was seated, and slowly, and indifferently, and aimlessly saunters down the platform, and mingles with the throng. As yet he has spoken to no one, nor has any one spoken to him.

Just now he meets with an incident as unexpectedly as if it had been a tangible spirit in the broad light of day; an incident such as often wholly revolutionizes the lives of people, and such, too, as are occurring somewhere every day— events that cool, dispassionate, non-enthusiastic persons, as well as the far more numerous rabble— which might with probably greater propriety be styled "the happy-go-lucky" class—regard as being entirely fortuitous, purely accidental.

But these, we, with due deference to the opinions of others, are compelled to esteem, viewing them in the light which is reflected upon them from our stand-point, as clearly unquestionable and irrefutably established cases of the ever-mysterious, all-unseen, all-controlling, all-dispensing hand of Destiny—that Destiny which shapes, builds up and overturns our affairs both great and small, despite our most carefully planned, cautiously prosecuted and vigorously executed counteracting opposition.

Cloud feels a hand clasp his arm, and hears a voice pronounce his name from behind him. Turning round, his eyes meet those of a well-known and familiar war friend; a man who has known him under all circumstances, in all positions where he had acted in dark and bloody scenes; a member of an old and prominent commercial firm, composed of three brothers, domiciled in a large town less than a hundred miles away—a man in whose store-house he had his head-quarters, and whose brother had been his adjutant when he was operating against the bands of mountain desperadoes—a man at whose table he had taken many a repast, and in whose residence he had occupied a room for a long time,

when wounded and unable to endure the privations of the field. This friend says:

"Why, Cloud, whence came you? We heard that Kirk's band hung you at the close of the war. I am glad to find you above the sod, old boy—the last man in the world that I expected to meet here, but the very one I want, if your leisure serves you."

Cloud: "Well, Mr. Daño, how happy I am to meet you. I assure you it is a most agreeable surprise. I was captured at the close of the war, and have been free now only a few days. I cannot go home for fear of those blood-thirsty villains. I have just arrived here, and am so overburdened with serving leisure that I am actually embarrassed to know how to dispose of it. What can I do for a friend, true and tried when I was wounded and in distress?"

Daño: "We want to buy some surplus grain that is away back in the mountains, twenty or thirty miles from here. I came down on this train to see whether or not I could arrange with a merchant, or some one else, to undertake it; and you are the first man to whom I have spoken, and will be the only one to whom I shall speak, if I can agree with you to do the business. We will furnish the money, and allow you five per cent., provided you find enough to make it an object; otherwise, we will recompense you for your time. What say you?"

Cloud: "It is a bargain. I will do my best for you."

Daño: "What luck! If we are quick, I can return on the up train, now nearly due."

To Garland Cloud this simple incident was a foundation of adamantine solidity and most wondrous magnitude. Upon this sprang up one of the most extraordinary, yet vicissitudinally checkered careers that ever fell to the lot of mortal man in the purely civil walks of life, situated as he was then, and driven as he must be afterward, by adverse winds of envious opposition, and waste-sweeping hurricanes of fell, merciless disaster, upon Fortune's dismal rocks of dreary and cheerless desolation.

The work which he undertook for his friend, then clutched with the desperation that the drowning man grasps the drifting straw, proved far more important than either he or even his friend had anticipated. This was undertaken with a hope that it might be the temporary means of warding off the menacing ghost of abject want, humiliating vagrancy, and gnawing hunger. All of these he had acutely felt preying upon him most savagely during the past four days, on the lonely, war-desolated highway. Without a single meal at a table, and with a bed at night on the grass beneath the friendly foliage of a forest tree, he made the journey: because he had no money to pay for either, and was yet too proud to seek lodging or meals without it. His solitary fifty-cent piece fed him four days and ferried him over two rivers. But this new employment soon filled his pockets with money.

The wants of the country were dreadful, and the pitiable condition of the people often heart-rending to behold. Very many times, poor, weak women and delicate little children came on foot twenty miles, packing their little burdens of grain, in order to obtain a trifle of much-needed money. Those who had a horse left, brought their stock on its back; and others yet still more fortunate, loaded wagons.

All these little and larger, steadily pouring, and ever increasing streams, rapidly, rapidly filled up cars. At the high prices which grains then commanded, every four cars counted one hundred dollars for Garland Cloud; and occasionally that number were filled and shipped in one day.

The merchants were grasping and merciless in their barter dealings with the poor, helpless farmers, entirely in the power of those blind mercenaries; who could not perceive the mad folly they were perpetrating when "killing the goose in order to secure the golden egg." They did this when refusing to receive anything but cash or grain for staple articles, and when selling other goods, at from two to five hundred per cent. profit, in payment for farm products, for which they would not allow more than two-thirds actual cash value.

Cloud witnessed these things day after day, with deep chagrin, rankling mortification, and bitter indignation.

At length, poor women who had come twenty, sometimes even fifty miles, to procure a little coffee, cotton yarn, or other staple in exchange for

articles of produce such as appeared in the merchants' proscribed list, began to go to Cloud with tears in their eyes, and to implore him most piteously to buy their eggs, their chickens, their cheese, butter, or whatever it was, at any price, in order to enable them to obtain the articles for which they came so far, and with such painful inconvenience.

He now had hundreds of dollars idle, which every day was steadily increasing in amount. This decided him to yield to their solicitations. He bought some of their produce, and made trial shipments to old comrades, who, poor and dependent like himself, had embarked in the commission trade at points of commercial interest. These were men whom he believed would exert themselves, be prompt, and make honest returns. He wrote them, fully detailing the situation of the poor farmers, and the circumstances under which he had been driven to make the experimental purchases and shipments.

The results were of the most gratifying nature, and aroused in the young cavalryman the long lethargic and wellnigh extinct embers of his fiery genius.

Wheat harvest is passed, a magnificently bountiful one; and the golden grain will soon be ready for market.

It is midnight of an August Saturday when Cloud finishes loading his last car, receives his bill of lading, sees the cars that he has ready coupled on to the freight train, drops his letter in the post-box, and starts across a meadow and orchard to his room, nearly a quarter of a mile distant.

On the way he seats his weary frame under the boughs of a grand old walnut-tree, to think quietly for awhile, where nothing will disturb his reflections.

Thus seated, he in fancy sees the pale ghastly features of his lamented friend and beloved General, as they appeared one night in the valley of Virginia; and hears his sorrowful and plaintive voice, as he heard it then, when he was entreated by his now long-mourned commander to devote his life to the interest of the poor toil-worn agriculturists of his desolate yet ever sunny South. And beside this spectral shadow of a vanished friend, hand in hand, stands the angelic form of little Fannie, radiant with the glowing splendor of her grand soul, as she stood before him on that but lately flown July morning, pleading with him in behalf of the same sad cause; enthusiastically contrasting the glories of peaceful heroism and devotion, with Jackson's undying military renown.

Up to this moment he has done, perhaps, all that he could do, yet the labor has been performed without special effort or extra exertion. Now the spectral forms which imagination places before the closed eyes, speak, or seem to speak, together:

"Your time is at hand. Act! Act! Act!"

From this seat Garland Cloud arises under the strongly intensified conviction that to him his duty has been revealed, and its pathway clearly demonstrated. With his hand upon his heart, he raises his tear-dimmed eyes to Heaven's clear and starry vaulted dome—night's mystical and canopied wonder—and swears, there beneath the sombre shadow of the low spreading thick foliage of that old walnut-tree, in the solemn silence of this summer midnight, by the ghostly shades of his battle-slumbering comrades, to devote his life, through weal or woe, to promoting the interest and encouraging the prosperity of the husbandmen of their Southern-land—the land they loved so fondly, and died for so bravely, often amid the victorious shouts of their legions, with their yet defiant "Bonnie Blue Flag" flaunting in the breeze, as the last sands of their devoted lives were ebbing out—unembittered by the humiliating spectacle reserved for their survivors, of witnessing it trailing in the dust.

But for one sadly lamentable circumstance, here is a rare and enviable character well worthy of emulation. But, alas! that terrible circumstance—overcasting with a gloom deeper and blacker than the most rayless midnight that ever oppressed the earth with its impenetrable darkness, all that he is or ever may be; covering with a stain that all the Atlantic's flood of blue and crystal tides could never wash away, a fast-set ebondye that all the Polar snows might never bleach to its wonted whiteness—that deadly fatal concealment. Its spectral ghost haunts him as he walks, slowly walks, on to his room. How deeply he regrets it—yet all too late. The terrible step has been taken with unthinking indiscretion, and can be recalled nevermore, but must remain forever the same in the eternal past. It is a deeply planted and most securely rooted seed; ever flourishing in dark luxuriance that defies alike the summer's drouths and winter's frosts; always heavily laden with, and still prolifically yielding its bitter fruits, from which the wretched planter is doomed to eat, in sadness and woe, all the days of his weary life.

Oh! as our mind lingers upon this wretched mortal's silent and heart-rending agonies, and his pitiful struggles to bear up beneath a crushing thralldom, while striving to respond with unmurmuring, unswerving faithfulness to the stern behest of imperious Duty's unpitying voice, what emotions thrill our being! Now, as from this picture,—which is of necessity hidden from the eyes of the world in which its victim moves, where it might not enlist the slightest breath of pitying sympathy, was its reality known,—we turn to the bright and hope-buoyant young lives all over this land who are doomed to kindred fates,—tears, unworthy yet bitter, blinding tears of pity well up from the deep, almost sterile cavities of our heart. Our cold benumbed, weary fingers clutch the pen yet tighter; and we resolve anew that our midnight lamp shall never be extinguished until our task is done, and our perchance unimpressible, yet conscientiously earnest, voice of warning has gone forth on the swift wings of the pure winds, telling all men whither they are tending.

Poor Cloud! he is past the hour when pity's tear or misery's voice can soothe the bitterness of his woe or warn his wayward foot from the brink of the slippery precipice where he once stood hesitating whether or not to assume the mask of concealment. When he decided to accept its services, this was the mad leap over the giddy crag and down into the fathomless depths of the yawning abyss of never-ending despair, from whence he may rise no more. Hence, for him we have no tears to waste, no word to stir the wells of other hearts to overflow in sympathy, because all pity would be bestowed in vain.

But we draw the dark outlines of the grim and spectral shadows that have extinguished his lamps of hope, and enveloped his fair young life with a gloomy darkness that no prosperity, no power, no love can ever permanently and wholly re-illuminate, with the desire that they may cause sympathy and excite alarm for those who have not quite taken the irretrievable step that sooner or later leads to ruin. Thus we hope to arouse vigilance and action before it is too late; to put forth determined and properly directed efforts to save those tempted likewise—something far more feasible and practicable, and of graver import to this great country than all the missionary work beneath the cerulean dome of heaven!

Cloud's usefulness to the agriculturist may often and for long periods appear unimpaired. But what is life to him, and what is he? He is but the ghostly spectre of vanished hope; his life doomed to be but a cruel dream, with its every destined sweet deeply impregnated with the tincture of poison's gall. Yet still must he be sufficiently endowed and uncomplainingly nerved—

" In strength to bear what time cannot abate.
And feed on bitter fruits without accusing Fate."

The breakfast of the Sabbath morning finds him with his resolution taken and the plans connected with it matured.

Now, in the peaceful pursuits of life, does the trained genius of the scout and the commander, the strong point characteristically in his nature, begin to manifest the potency of its usefulness: decision, coolness, action, simultaneously blended.

Five minutes' time suffices for him to arrange with the railroad agent and his brother to care for his interests for ten days.

When the sun goes down he is two hundred miles on his way to the East. Monday night he sleeps in New York.

He finds Silas Worthington early Tuesday morning. The old Colonel receives him cordially, and listens with interest to his concisely detailed plans. When he has finished, he is quietly informed that he will be immediately placed on a footing to buy all the goods he desires or may desire. In addition to this, the Colonel gives him an important agency.

He returns by Philadelphia, Baltimore, and Richmond. In each of these commercial centres he establishes most important connections: among others, the buying of grains for mills, on commission, for cash; they furnishing the money.

He arranges for the shipment of every species of produce; and to draw to a liberal extent on bills of lading against all shipments whenever he desires to do so.

In New York he buys an immense stock of goods for the market to which they are intended to go.

Learning from New York merchants the prices at which similar goods would be offered in agricultural districts not located in the Southern States, he has a large number of posters printed, naming prices at which he will sell many leading articles: "Strictly for cash; no bartering under any circumstances whatever." Then follows the bold and startling announcement that, "For every description of produce, a fair market value will be paid in cash."

Thus situated, he returns. The same day he arrives he leases an immense store and warehouse down at the railroad track, for a merely nominal rent. Before noon he has some carpenters and a gang of freedmen at work putting the premises in good order. By the time the goods arrive, everything is ready.

He at once employs the most experienced salesmen. For himself he fits up an office between the store and the ware-house. In this ware-house all produce is received and weighed, and the owner furnished with a ticket by which the settlement is made in the office. But before the produce is bought it is sampled in the ware-house; and the owner passes with his samples into the office, where Cloud buys his stock. Then, after the settlement, and the man has received his money, he is cordially solicited to call again whenever he has anything to sell; and passes from the office out into the store. But Cloud never once intimates to a man that he wishes to sell him goods; yet, notwithstanding, he always sells more than he could have sold had he attempted to buy the produce for part trade and with far less trouble.

In the brief space of two months, the business

is so large that it astonishes even himself: it enslaves him. Wagons arrive from a distance of one hundred miles on either side of the railroad. Everything Cloud touches turns to gold. By the New Year's season, he is the most prosperous man within a radius of one hundred miles around him; and is far surpassing the business of any one else.

He reduces the price of goods to a fair and legitimate standard, and opens up channels to receive everything the farmer can produce, at liberally remunerative figures. He certainly fairly redeems his pledges fully a thousand times more extensively than he had any reason or grounds to anticipate. Still he goes on increasing.

For eighteen hours every day, he labors incessantly. He is in bed no more than four hours, from one to five o'clock A. M.

Just now he finds, as it were, an oblivion of blissful forgetfulness, without time to think of the past, and feels:

"Yet though a dreary strain, to this I cling,
    So that it wean me from the weary dream
Of selfish grief or gladness—so it fling
    Forgetfulness around me, it shall seem
To me, though to none else, a not ungrateful theme."

CHAPTER XXXIX.

THE CHAMBER OF DEATH.

"There is not a flower on all the hills; the frost is on
    the pane;
I cannot live to see the snow-drops come again.
    *   *   *   *   *   *   *   *   *   *
O sweet and strange it seems to me, that ere this day
    is done;
The voice that now is speaking may be beyond the sun—
Forever and forever with those just souls and true—
And what is life, that we should moan? why make we
    such ado?
    *   *   *   *   *   *   *   *   *   *
On the chancell'd casement, and upon that grave of
    mine,
In the early, early morning, the summer sun will
    shine."   —TENNYSON.

AFTER the bustling excitement of preparation is over—the jubilee of the wedding celebration has died away, the *débris* been removed, and the old mansion has assumed an air of pensive quiet, in ominous sympathy with its unhappy master,— Norman Mountjoy rallies again sufficiently to

attend to business in a purely mechanical method, acquired from long years of perpetual habit. But the heart of the poor man is no more in his work: it is broken, and its fragments are buried in the sepulchre of the past. Literally, his soul has gone from him.

He knows that the wife of his bosom has grown heartless and unscrupulous. That she has stooped to employ some basely ignoble means in order to command sufficient money to prepare the brilliant and princely wedding of her daughters, he is most positively assured; as to its nature, he as a matter of course cannot conjecture.

His wife, the adored idol of his early manhood and of his life's summer, has been almost entirely estranged from him ever since their unpleasant interview relative to funds for this identical purpose.

The fate of poor Pleasington, and the blighted life of hapless Effie also weigh with bitter severity upon his mind. He feels satisfied that Pleasington is not only innocent, but that he was the victim of some demoniacal machination, and that Mrs. Mountjoy is its cause and instigator. Two days after Effie's retirement within the seclusion of the convent, Madam Mountjoy calls at that institution to see Miss Edelstein; but this young heart-stricken mourner obstinately refuses to grant her admittance.

The misgivings of Effie in relation to the cause that wrought Lawrence's destruction, and so cruelly blighted her own fair young life once so full of blissful dreams, are the same as those of her poor, slowly-dying uncle.

After Madam Mountjoy's return from this visit, she is like a demented creature, a very lioness in human form; and appears the picture of despair— a prey to that unrelenting demon: remorse of conscience. This spirit, in her case, has been aroused from the callousness of lethargic inertness, only when she finds that the spoils of her more than savage atrocity are securely beyond her grasp, and safe from the reach and power of her fiendish influence. She ceases to make calls or to receive visits.

Two months later, Arnold Noel, her nephew of such truly kindred congeniality of nature and propensity, is arrested for an aggravated case of burglary in his own city, and is held in thirty thousand dollars bail, which his father furnishes, the young culprit jumps, and the old gentleman has to pay.

This effectually terminates all the damnable designs of his wicked aunt in relation to him, as far as he is now concerned. But, alas! it does not atone for the ruin which they have already entailed upon others, nor relieve them from the odium, nor the active operation of the cruel, impending thralldom beneath which they groan.

As to Norman Mountjoy, he is preparing for the end with all the diligence and dispatch of which his feeble and ever-declining strength admits, because he knows that it is near.

Oglethrop and Eva are his source of consolation and cheer—true, faithful, constant. For them he wrestles with the grim, unpitying Angel; of them he thinks. For their sakes he plans and labors; rouses himself, by superhuman efforts, to endure the painfully trying ordeal of going to and from business; and laboring in it, day after day, in order to arrange for the future of these two tenderly devoted children. He desires to instruct his son-in-law in the firm principles and sterling truths requisite to direct and control a young man, that he may achieve certain and stable success, and establish a well-merited reputation as a merchant of undeviating integrity—the unblemished soul of honor. This he had himself ever been, and as such he will sink into the grave. Early in the cold and bleak December of 1865, these labors are all consummated to his satisfaction.

Christmas-day he is no longer able to leave his room. From this day, he sinks rapidly. On New Year's eve it is evident that the end is near with the poor, patient sufferer, who, rational and in the full possession of his faculties, never utters a groan.

Oglethrop and Eva keep a solemn watch-meeting—a sad yet beautiful picture of devotion and resignation, here in this chamber of death—the two young and tender-hearted children watching beside the couch of a dying father, in the last hours of the dying year.

With a great effort he partially raises himself higher upon the pillows and speaks:

"Eva, get Tennyson's poems, please, my dar-ling, and read me the second part of 'The May Queen.'

"Now, my children, remember this, and its beautiful gospel sentiments, breathed in every line. Yes, I too, shall be 'often, often near you' if I can. I know you will come sometimes to see my grave.

"One thing: bury me neatly; plain, but not extravagantly. This is an injunction; do not, I entreat you, disregard it. Be kind to your mother; she is mad with despair—the victim of circumstances which peculiar social influences and errors have heaped upon her. God help her!

"Well, my children, I am keeping the watch-meeting with you, a double watch-meeting.

"Last year, my Eva, we were at the church, watching and praying for peace for our poor country during the New Year. Thank God we have lived to see it. Now I am watching and waiting for that peace that will last for evermore, 'where the wicked cease from troubling, and the weary are at rest.'

"Live my children, I beg of you, live true, natural lives. In your private, social and other relations in and with the world, act fully up to what you appear. Do not dissemble and deceive; for your own hearts would give your actions the lie, and the conscience forever render your lives miserable by its perpetual accusations.

"There is rarely very little, if any, present pleasure or benefit in acting and living falsely—in appearing to the world in the light of day, a far different creature from what in God's and your own sight you are viewed. And its certain and unavoidable penalties are terrible.

"I have, in my active career as a merchant, a husband, and a father, but one feature in my life to look back at with regret; and that is not one of commission, but of omission. It eclipses and darkens my whole life with the rayless blackness of despair. It is comprised in my neglect of duty to my family, in omitting to govern my own household with wise and prudent economy. Now I am paying the penalty: sinking into the grave the pitiable victim of a broken heart. But I thank God that it is this, and not dishonor.

"I could have taken my station in a lower sphere of life, and been resigned; but your poor mother could not. She did not realize, could not realize the situation, nor what she was doing.

"This disappointment crushed all hope out of my being. I have been lingering in slow and fearful torture; but now the pangs of going are much alleviated, since I can leave you, my poor children, with a brightly promising future opened up for you. Take care of it. Guard it with religious zeal; and never permit yourselves to be allured from the path of truth, honor, right, and you will fulfill your destiny most nobly, by leading pure lives illuminated with the brilliancy of exemplary usefulness.

"Remember my words, because they are the offsprings of a bitter experience—and still more: they are uttered from between the threshold of Time and the portal of the great Unknown.

"Should my summons come suddenly, before your sisters come again, tell them I love and pity them in my last moments; and that I left with you my blessing and my farewell.

"And little Effie, the wounded dove—poor, broken heart! I will not have to wait but a little while for her to come—convey to her in tender words, gentle tokens of my sympathy and my love; and that my consolation is, that when for her cross she receives a crown, we shall meet again. Tell her that for her this was my last farewell.

"And now, my little children, I am weary and sleepy. I go to sleep, but you must call me as the New Year is coming in, for I would hear the knell of the departing year, as you must hear mine."

It is the immortal, the spirit of poor Mountjoy, that has rallied the prostrate form, animated the pallid cheek, unloosened the tongue from the paralytical chords of death, that enables him to speak. This creates in the breasts of his sorrow-stricken children the delusive hope that he has taken a sudden turn for the better.

He sleeps as tranquil as a little babe—the beautiful sleep of the innocent, with a sweet smile on his lips.

The gas is turned low, and renders the appearance of the apartment semi-spectral. Perhaps, with the dim shadows reflected by the low-burning lights, is mingled, too, the awe-inspiring hues of shade created by the solemn influence of the presence of the Death Angel.

Without, the merciless northern blast of winter's chill and cruel wind wails a mournful requiem.

Steadily the unerring, ever-moving hand on the dial of Time glides smoothly along, meting out, one by one, its measure of little seconds from the great reservoir of inexhaustible Eternity; unheeding the mortal agonies that are wreaked upon the children of Earth, while these items of infinitesimal ages are multiplying one short hour.

At last, the old clock on the mantel, that has measured so many painfully weary and sleepless hours for the poor sufferer within the past year, marks ten minutes to midnight. Then Eva goes cautiously up to the bed-side, and falteringly, yet softly and tenderly, says: "Father, the hour is come for the bells to toll."

Slowly he opens his grand, sad, dim eyes, and turns them from first one object to another around the room; finally they rest upon his children—fixed in a steadfast gaze of fondest tenderness.

Now, like a thunder clap, the first sharp notes from the brazen throats of a myriad of bells are borne and wafted by the cold and bitter wind, and break upon the startled ear of night—the death summons of a year.

Poor, world-weary, sinking sufferer! He hears; for he smiles, and makes a perceptible effort to fold his arms more tightly across his breast. As the pealing chorus swells and reverberates, his eyes gradually close; the flush on the cheek, that rose with the smile, fades as its traces vanish; and the face assumes a marble placidity. There is no labored breathing—not a struggle within that poor, pain-racked breast.

Poor children! they think, "how easy papa has gone to sleep;" and he has, too, gone quietly to sleep—the sleep that hath no dreams.

As the last knell of the bells is tolled and dying away, and while the departing year, with its stores of joy and sorrow, pleasure and pain, festivity and death, is fast disappearing on the completed revolution of the wheel of Time, the suffering soul is free, and winging its way to its long and merited abode.

Norman Mountjoy is dead! Poor, world-weary, heart-broken, noble, pure, true man!

Alas that he should pay a penalty so terrible for an omission of duty so apparently trivial in its nature. Sad to reflect, that it was so shamefully abused by a cruel hearted, a basely unappreciative wife. Wretched woman! when she beheld the matured fruit which she had planted from the seeds of indiscretion, nurtured so lavishly from ambition's copious fountain for so many years, rather than submit to the humiliation of partaking of its bitter substance, she did not scruple to stab him to the heart with a yet more unmerciful and venomous thrust than the dagger which found Duncan's breast, directed thither by the wicked whisper of a woman.

But brave man, admirable mind, constant, faithful heart! To stand firm for the true and the right, and behold all his hopes vanish, the last prospect in life destroyed, and even experience life itself steadily, day by day, ebbing out, rather than stain the fair and brightly shining name with dishonor—rare and beautifully exemplary manhood! The last of his name in his race and line, he leaves to the great world a noble example of virtue, and an appalling warning against ill-order and neglect in the little world of home.

CHAPTER XL.

THE ANGELS OF THE MOUNTAIN.

"His queen, the garden queen his rose,
Unbent by winds, unchilled by snows,
Far from the winters of the West
By every breeze and season blest."—BYRON.

WE last saw Gertrude and Rosalia Flowers in their own mountain cabin, the evening when, long years ago, they related to Carrie Harman the story of their lives and wrongs, and were by her christened "The Angels of the Mountain."

We were, when taking leave of them, promised that after the gloomy shadow of the warcloud had been dispelled, we might be permitted to meet them once more in the sacred retirement of their remote seclusion. But we are doomed to sad disappointment. We have tarried too long in our wanderings. The mountain roses have been plucked and borne away; the strong eagles of the valley have swooped down upon the timid doves,

and carried them away from their own cozy mountain cote.

Little Rosa has bloomed to perfect and most beautiful womanhood. Their Jesse returned to them in safety.

The admiration and sympathy of Carrie Harman for these two adopted children of the mountain, would neither permit their pathetic story nor themselves to remain buried amid the obscurity of their simple neighbors, in the deep remoteness of their lonely solitude. She visited them, and induced others to visit them, and actually, as it were, forced them to go to the valley. They were both admired and esteemed by every one with whom they became acquainted

Upon both Carrie Harman's father and brother, they produced a vital impression, which resulted in a rather novel double wedding during the holidays of the Christmas of 1865, and a grand festival at the Harman mansion. We now find the guests there assembled, to enjoy the liberal profusion of this happy occasion. But we are not specially interested in the present relations of the happy couples, and will not for the moment disturb them.

But, after the guests have all partaken of the supper, let us hear what one of the most honored, yet still a volunteer waiter at the table, and Miss Carrie, who are seated alone at a small side-table, to enjoy a quiet supper, have to say.

CARRIE: "Well, General, it is a comfort to sit down. I know you must be wearied. I should be vexed at you for forcing yourself into this menial position that young people should fulfill, were it not that I have both the pleasure and the honor of supping with you."

GEN. CLOUD: "I could not resist the temptation to assist the "Angel of Consolation" in her burdensome duties as mistress of ceremonies on this happy occasion; and the pleasure of this quiet moment with her would more than compensate for the labors which I have performed, were they a hundred times as great."

CARRIE: "Thank you for that compliment, which I prize, coming as it does from one who detests flattery.

"But, by the way General, do you not regard this as a novel affair?"

GEN. C——: "It wants only one thing to have rendered it indeed unique—that is you, and Jesse, the heroic little Colonel; and I am rather surprised and somewhat disappointed that you two are left out."

CARRIE: "How unkindly ungenerous and uncharitable it is of you to say this, General, when neither of us ever for one moment even dreamed of such a thing. Col. Flowers is to be to me as a brother; I to him as a sister: this is settled.

"To use a vulgarism, I do not know one young lady 'who would not accept him at the drop of a hat.' I for one, was the opportunity afforded me, but for the fact that there are reasons unknown to any one but myself, that keep me free from matrimonial entanglements. One cannot always vouch for the freedom of one's heart, but I am resolved to be free in person, at least, until my vow is fulfilled.

"Our young men are so badly demoralized by the war that, as to the most of them, a girl cannot promise herself much when marrying any one of them."

GEN. C——: "That last remark is a sad and lamentable truth, and I often cannot refrain from shuddering when I contemplate the dissipation and the degeneracy that I witness spread broadcast everywhere I go; and still it increases every day."

CARRIE: "Oh, it is horrible! I deplore it; and I much fear that this will prove a greater calamity to the country than all the blighting effects of the war itself.

"The dear, dead faces were radiant with honor, and noble as the pictures of true manliness—their sad memory is a comfort. But an unworthy man is continually augmenting his own depravity, and leaving behind him, as he journeys over the earth, its indelible stains, which contaminate and mar with venomous poison many other lives.

"When did you last hear from Col. Garland, General?"

GEN. C——: "Not since the surrender; nor have I the remotest idea where the poor boy is. This is enough to warp, sour and embitter his life for all time. I do not think that he would be in much danger at home, certainly there could be no sort of risk in his writing; but this he does

not know. I feel quite certain that if he did, he would write. I do not suffer much uneasiness about him; yet still I would like to know where he is and what he is doing."

CARRIE: "How cruel that this ghost of the war should still haunt him. Our gratitude to you and him can never be repaid.

"How does his lady-love bear his silent absence? Does she remain faithful and true, under this severely trying test?"

GEN. C——: "Fortunately there are no such tender relations between him and any young lady. He has no lady-love to sigh for him."

CARRIE: "How singular! and his life the veritable spirit of romance. Did he correspond with no young lady during all those dreary years of home- and social-severing strife?"

GEN. C——: "All the romance about him was intense and earnest; and I am compelled to admit that, though apparently desperate and madly reckless, it was cool and deliberate action.

"In regard to your question, it is direct and pointed; and a true, non-evasive answer forces me to reveal a sacred secret, confided to me under peculiar circumstances:

"On the field of Gettysburg, I reprimanded him for his rash and reckless exploits, which I have since much regretted.

"In self-defense he, among many other things, detailed to me the particulars and results of a correspondence between himself and a young lady, together with the motives which actuated him to engage in it at the outset, and the desires that prompted him to continue it.

"Pardon me, Miss Harman, if I say too much, when I inform you that it is you who could give me ten times more information about the nature and the reality of this correspondence than he gave me. You have forced me to say to you what no one could have done. To all the world besides, my lips are sealed.'

CARRIE: "Well, General, there is nothing in that correspondence to cause either of us to blush. Of it and its results I am piously proud. There is in all his cautiously guarded pages naught but careful reserve. Not one sentence, phrase, or even word meant as coming to clothe a personal sentiment from him to me, for myself alone, that would console or soothe the weary longings in the heart of a sentimental, sighing maiden. Gen. Cloud, I tell you they would chill an icicle.

"His beautiful sentiments, flowing with the currents of all his profuse compliments, that might have flattered a Venus, were in the name of the mountain boys and the country. *That was all.*"

At this stage of their conversation a messenger comes in to say that their presence is specially desired in the parlor. Supper being finished, they hasten to respond.

In the parlor every one is on the tip-toe of expectation, awaiting in breathless suspense for the announcement of some strange and startling mystery connected with Mrs. Gertrude Flowers.

On the afternoon train a gentleman arrived from the East, and registered at the principal railway-town hotel, a number of miles from the Harman mansion.

After taking some refreshment, he made special inquiries of the landlord concerning Mrs. Flowers, of Little Beaver Mountain; and, as a matter of course, learned her connection with the festive occasion at the Harman homestead. Without delay he procured a conveyance, and ordered the driver to speed post-haste, in order to arrive there before the gay scene should close; which was done, much to his gratification. This was an eminent New York lawyer, and a member of the firm employed by Ira Atkinson and Adam Stringfellow several months previous, to find Mrs. Flowers and to restore to her her rightful heritage, with interest, after its long years of purloined service had aided them to amass colossal fortunes.

For a long time the efforts of the attorneys were discouragingly futile.

At length, however, late in December, Silas Worthington's eye chanced to fall on their advertisement. His well disciplined business mind at once recalled the circumstance of the Christmas presents of himself and Effie Edelstein, sent to the poor mountain widow in acknowledgment of the care and kindness bestowed by her son on Lawrence Pleasington; and he recalled also the address, and at once informed the attorneys

Upon this information the gentleman referred to, set out personally to investigate whether or not the clue thus obtained would lead to the result they sought to accomplish.

After a few moments' consultation with the senior Harman and Jesse Flowers, the interview was arranged between the attorney and Mrs. Harman, to take place immediately in the private parlor, in the presence of the most intimate friends of the two families, as they were before the wedding, but now merged into one.

In response to the interrogatives of the legal man, Mrs. Harman stated concisely the same points which she so fully and graphically detailed in the chapter, "The Mountain Cabin"; which satisfied him that she was the veritable Gertrude Flowers whom he sought; and resulted in his declaring her to be the legitimate heiress of "an immense fortune, which he was prepared to transfer to her."

CHAPTER XLI.

THE ANGEL AND THE FIEND WRESTLE WITH THE GRIM MESSENGER.

"I can't forget the day she died,
    She placed her hand upon my head,
And softly whispered, 'keep my child'
    And then they told me she was dead."
                              —OLD SONG.

SUCH were the lines, which, in her delirium from a fiercely wasting fever, the pale, patient-faced Sisters of Charity, as they anxiously watched beside her lowly cot, often heard Effie Edelstein repeating, in the middle days of January, 1866. Thus her mind traveled back in its wildly incoherent wanderings to that affecting scene in her tender childhood of the death and the parting with her mother; and that other still more recent and bitterly cruel experience of persecution from which she sought refuge in her present asylum for a little while, there to wait for that more secure and enduring protection that always comes as a grateful boon to the pure in heart who can find no repose nor peace in life—"the merciful quietude of the cold and silent grave."

The diagnosis of the physicians determined her case to be one of pulmonary consumption, suddenly developed from the deep-rooted seeds of a violent cold; but, poor Effie, how little they knew of the mysterious truth

Let those who desire to know the veritable origin and the actual nature of her malady read Washington Irving's most beautiful and pathetically tender essay, "The Broken Heart." There this case is pictured in its true and appropriate colors, so vividly natural that we dare not attempt a description of it, because to do so would be but to produce something so nearly modeled after this masterpiece from that matchless pen, as to incur the risk of an apparently well-grounded charge of that most detestable of all non-legally punishable crimes—*plagiarism.*

Effie was ill—confined to her bed—when she heard of her dear uncle's death.

From this day, it was but painfully evident to her sympathetic sisters—among whom there were many hearts which had bled like her own—that her days were few. They were satisfied, before the end of the first month of the new year, that, wrapped in her shroud of spotless white, rivaling the bleached and snowy ermine that in its purity mantled the earth, Effie Edelstein, whose heart and life had been ever pure and spotless as that snow, would be borne out from the friendly shelter of the consecrated walls and bars which form a saintly prison where the weary soul may find peace and security alike from persecution's darts and passion's flames, to the endless repose of the silent church-yard.

Her earthly wealth was bequeathed to Orlando and Eva.

The same night on which tidings of Effie's prospective death reached her, Helen Mountjoy took poison. She lingered for ten days, was often rational, and talked freely to Orlando and Eva.

Remorse of conscience was preying upon her with unpitying severity every breath she drew, on to that which was her last; when she died, as she had long lived, in miserable wretchedness.

CHAPTER XLII.

CONFIDING THE DARK SECRET.

"A man cannot possess anything better than a good Woman, nor anything worse than a bad one."
—SIMONIDES.

THE year 1866 was well advanced when there came to Garland Cloud a letter from Orlando Oglethrop, proposing to form a firm, to be composed of himself, Cloud, Jesse Flowers, and Edgar Harman, to be domiciled in New York, for the purpose of prosecuting a direct Southern trade with such Southern branches or connections as might be deemed desirable and expedient.

After consulting Flowers and Harman, Cloud proceeded to New York with their powers of attorney, to consummate the arrangement. This he entered into with alacrity, because it opened up to him for the benefit of the Southern people a far more extended field in which to labor.

The arrangement was completed, business to open September 1st, 1867. It was stipulated that Cloud should master the cotton trade, the art of grading and classing. In order to do this, he at once arranged to spend part of the season of 1866-67 in a prominent New York office, and at the same time to have his home interests properly protected.

This plan was suggested by Silas Worthington, who had become Cloud's warmest and most admiring friend.

The time for starting a business such as contemplated, was most propitious. Rarely, if ever, was there a firm organized with brighter or more hope-inspiring promises than those which cheered the four young men who were preparing to embark in the enterprise just indicated.

While in New York, Cloud met and became most intimate with Major Eugene Lovelace, the staff officer whom he captured in the winter of 1861-2, in the parlor of the Fairchilds, where he was so happily entertained by Miss Leonora.

After he has been in New York some two months, he is seated one night in a private parlor alone with Oglethrop, where they had met pursuant to an appointment.

CLOUD: Well, Lieutenant, it is of poor Pleasington and his woes, and of nothing else, that we are to talk to-night. Poor fellow! How I pity him!"

OGLETHROP: "Yes, Colonel, for that we have met. I have promised to tell you something about which it makes my blood run cold to think. I may do wrong, but I rely on your word of honor that in case it can be turned to no account in poor Lawrence's behalf, you will never think of it very intensely in the presence of any one, and breathe it under no circumstances."

CLOUD: "I swear that it shall be as securely locked in my breast as if it was eternally buried in the grave."

OGLETHROP: "Oh, my God! alas that it is my mother-in-law of whom I must speak—a name that should be sacred and hallowed. What a memory to associate with the dead!

"She commenced to make her confession to Eva and I, about midnight of the second night after she drank the poison. She was perfectly rational, and suffered the agonies of torment while recounting the terrible deeds.

"She stated that her first erroneous step was inducing Atkinson and Stringfellow to rob Mrs. Flowers.

"Previous to this she had conceived the idea of a union between these two men and her two daughters. Her object was, while augmenting their store of wealth, thus to place them in her power, in order to insure their compliance with any wish she might choose to intimate to them. This part of her plot was all that she designed it to be.

"The next was to procure money to furnish the princely wedding of her daughters, after she learned her husband's distressingly straitened circumstances.

"She skillfully arranged to place her two daughters in the society, and under the ostensible protection of Van Allen and Mortimer, having previously instructed the poor girls how unseemly to conduct themselves, with utmost *abandon* of propriety.

"The girls acted their parts to perfection. They agreed to clandestine meetings, and stipulated that they must be at some out-of-town cottage, which their intended victims could rent and furnish indefinitely; and that as soon as completed, they must each write a letter to each girl, fully describing the locality, the time, the place, and mode of their first meeting.

"The letters were not tardy in coming, and went, as a matter of course, into the mother's hands, who used them so adroitly as to obtain all the money she wanted.

"After the wedding, her schemings wanted then only the union of Arnold Noel and poor Effie to make them all a success fully equal to her cruel heart's desire; and she was not slow in her mind and actions to conceive and put to work such machinations as she deemed would insure the result which she sought to attain.

"But, fiendish horrors! this involved putting Lawrence out of the way.

"She drew, or rather drove, Atkinson and Stringfellow into this plot; but found so many readily available facilities, that it was not necessary to bring into it her biddable sons-in-law. I am truly glad that this stain is not upon them, since they have doubtless made restitution to Mrs. Flowers; which fact goes far toward proving that but for their mother-in-law's influence, they might never have been guilty of that ignominious crime.

"It seems, from the tenor of her narration, that the most confidential teller in the bank in which Lawrence was employed, the night watchman and two policemen on the beats most nearly adjacent to the bank, were easily bought into the scheme, with a large sum of money—the balance of that so adroitly extorted from Van Allen and Mortimer.

"The plan was this: On leaving the bank in the evening, the teller was to take quite a large sum of money with him—having previously arranged with Lawrence to call for him at his home, to go out together for the evening.

"Once in the home of Lawrence, then there was nothing more to do than to frame some pretext to get into his room, and find an opportunity there to conceal the money, where it would be found as irrefutable evidence of Lawrence's guilt.

"During the night, while one of the policemen watched, the other was to slip into the bank the back way and tie the watchman hard and fast in the director's private room; and the watchman was to tell the story that masked men tied him, among whom there was one who knew the combination, opened the safe, took the money, and then locked the safe again. Lawrence knew the combination.

"The next day, when search was instituted in the houses and rooms of bank employés, because of this fact being stated that one of the robbers knew the combination. the money, or rather about one-fourth the amount missing, was found in poor Lawrence's room, which speedily doomed him to his present gloomy and hopeless fate.

"It seems that the safe was not touched in the night, that story being merely a part of the plan to fix the evidence of guilt upon Lawrence with greater certainty.

"It was not, perhaps, the design of the plotters to take any more money from the bank than the amount to be left in Lawrence's room: but the opportunity was too good and the temptation too great. There can be no doubt but that the teller appropriated the balance.

"This made it go much harder with Lawrence, as the bank officers and the authorities believed that he knew who had the balance of the missing money, and might give them information that would lead to its recovery."

CLOUD: "The demon's subtlety! Were the angels from Heaven to come down and testify to poor Pleasington's innocence, no court nor governor would believe them. This woman's confession, had it been legally taken, would have no sort of weight, without some evidence of the guilt of the actual criminals; and this we cannot well get. Her testimony that she had employed those parties to commit the crime, but that she did not see it committed, and hence could not have known who did commit it, would amount to nothing, not even if we had it in shape, without corroboration; and there can be no corroboration but testimony sufficiently overwhelming to convict the guilty parties; and that is not within the reach of mortal man."

OGLETHROP: "Then you really think we can do nothing for him."

CLOUD: "That is worth no more to Lawrence Pleasington than a dream would be, except to convince two or three of us that he is innocent; and that amounts to nothing while all the balance of the world will believe him guilty. No, Lieut. Oglethrop, it would be cruel to attempt to do anything for him with not the ghost of a show to succeed. Against the terrible array of evidence on record against him we have absolutely nothing to offer that is either pertinent or plausible a dying woman's confession made to two of her own family, and those two persons Pleasington's devoted friends.

"So far as I am concerned, I do not doubt but this is just how the infernal plot was concocted and executed, in order to blast Pleasington's fair fame and life; but no governor would accept it as a basis upon which he would consent to issue a pardon."

OGLETHROP: "Poor Lawrence! then he must continue to drag out the weary days of long and tedious years in the dread hopeless gloom of that dreary, cheerless prison.

"To think of the misery and ruin that misguided woman has caused and wrought! Her husband and Effie in their graves—Effie in a living, almost the real tomb—and Lawrence's life a thousand times worse than the grave.

"Mrs. Flowers and her little children—the silent sorrow and lonely suffering she caused them to endure, no tongue may ever tell nor pen record, except that terrible account of the Recording Angel.

"Add to all this, then, the humiliation and anguish she meted out to her own daughters, and few parallels can be found in any age or life, hardly excepting 'Bloody Lady Macbeth.'"

CHAPTER XLIII.

THE INTRIGUE.

" Vice is a monster of so frightful mien,
As to be hated, needs but to be seen;
But, seen too oft, familiar with her face,
We first endure, then pity, then embrace."
                                    —POPE.

LOVELACE: "Now, Col. Cloud, I want to tell you that I owe you an undying debt of gratitude, because you did not divulge when and how you captured me; and that you thus saved me from disgrace.

"In consideration of this fact, I have a plan for you, to give you for a paramour one of the handsomest and finest society ladies in this city —a genuine, romantic, free-love affair, which requires no money, and in which you run no risks in any respect whatever. It is one of those peculiar cases where the lady wants a lover who is unknown in society, and not a permanent resident in the city.

"It comes about in this way: Madam Vais-entre is a party wealthy and aristocratic, a kind of fortune-teller, one whom the first people visit without scruple, to consult on any subject. In this special line of which I am now speaking, she is known to but very few. I am known to her to an extent that she has confided in me, to select for the lady named a discreet and suitable companion. The lady has applied to her to find her such a person. As a matter of course, I do not and cannot know who the lady is, because she belongs to the class of society in which I move, and is some one whom I am liable to meet in a fashionable gathering of the bon ton, any evening during the season. She knows that by some means the Madam finds gentlemen well vouched for, but that is all.

"I thought of you the moment she mentioned the subject to me, and promised to carry you up this evening. Neither Madam nor the lady must know your true identity, nor will you know the lady's. She will never call any one's name, in either society or business circles, with whom she is acquainted; nor must you breathe the name of any one of that class with whom you may be acquainted, for fear it might be, perchance, some of her own family.

"You will meet the lady in the Madam's private parlor. If you fancy each other, you will there arrange a subsequent meeting at some other point indicated by the lady, but a place of the highest respectability, where neither gentleman nor lady would blush to be seen, either going to or coming from, at any hour of day or night. Upon this you may most implicitly rely. That you might some time become a resident of the city and a member of society, is something for which I am not responsible. Just now you are about as far from being either as any gentleman I know. You will go?"

CLOUD: "Well, Major, it is a bad sort of an affair to get mixed up in. Still, I have some curiosity to see what this lady resembles. In that there cannot be much harm."

LOVELACE: "Ah! my friend, wait until you know the ways of the world in city life, and you will soon get bravely over your rural squeamishness about such matters. Why, my dear sir, those of prominence who are not mixed up in some affair of this nature, form the exceptions. I do not attempt to defend, but, to the contrary, deplore the degenerate unhealthiness of social moral restraint, that tolerates and fosters and renders such conduct but mildly unpopular in some circles of society."

Pursuant to appointment they are in the presence of Madam Vais-entre, in her house.

LOVELACE: "Madam Vais-entre, my friend Scud, of whom I spoke to you last evening."

MADAM VAIS-ENTRE: "Ah, I am glad to know you. Walk right in."

LOVELACE: "You will find me in the billiard-room on the next corner, Colonel, when you leave here. Good-night, Madam."

He departs, and the Madam, with Cloud, enters her private parlor.

MADAM V——: "Col. Scud, Mrs. Lovewell."

MRS. LOVEWELL: "I am pleased to make your acquaintance, Colonel, and trust that we may be good friends."

CLOUD: "Thanks, madam, and accept similar sentiments. I know of no reason why we should be enemies."

MADAM V——: "I will leave the Colonel in your care now, Mrs. Lovewell."

She withdraws from the room.

MRS. L——: "Well, Colonel, you understand my desire for cultivating your friendship to be the sole object of my seeking your acquaintance, I presume?"

CLOUD: "Perfectly, madam, but imagine that with my appearance that desire vanished."

MRS. L——: "Just to the contrary. Are you disposed to meet my views—or rather to meet me again for a more definite interview?"

CLOUD: "Certainly."

MRS. L——: "Well, then, go to-morrow at half-past four in the afternoon, to the street and number indicated by this card. I have rented the house, which is elegantly furnished, and have it in charge of servants. Ring the bell, and hand the card to the servant, who will then admit you. If I am not there, you will not have to wait many minutes. Now, I must reluctantly bid you good-evening, as we are not expected to have a protracted interview here; and then it is time that I should be home."

CLOUD. "All right. You can rely on seeing me."

The next day Cloud is in the counting-room of Silas Worthington, with this gentleman.

COL. WORTHINGTON: "Look here now, Cloud, you have been promising to dine with me at home, for a long time, but you never fulfil your promise. This is a dark, stormy day, and there is nothing doing. I am going to dine at home to-day, at three o'clock; and then I am going to a directors' meeting. Come to the office, half-past two, sharp; go up in the carriage and dine with me; then, if you want to go down town again, I will send the coachman with you; if not, you can remain and entertain the Madam, who is all curiosity to see the Rebel Scout, as we all call you. As I have told her that you had promised to dine with us, she has been expecting you.

"Poor woman, I am such a slave to business that she, in consequence, passes many lonely evenings; but the requirements of trade demand my time."

CLOUD: "I think I can go to-day as well as any other time. Yes, Colonel, I will go to-day.

I shall not want to be down town again. I will be on hand promptly."

WORTHINGTON: "All right; I shall depend on it. I will write the Madam a note informing her that she can expect you with me, without doubt, to dinner this afternoon."

CLOUD: "Then I will go directly to my head-quarters and make my arrangements accordingly."

Promptly, Col. Worthington and Garland Cloud arrived at the superb residence of the former, and entered the parlor. Even here the old gentleman could not refrain from talking on his favorite theme—"the new South and her commercial future." Of all others, this was the one subject that most interested young Cloud. He tried to persuade himself that for this one cause—the interest and prosperity of the decimated South—he lived; and that besides this he had no object in life. For these reasons, with eager avidity, he grasped the opportunity at all times and under all circumstances, to listen to the sage and experience-matured counsels and precepts which his old friend was ever so ready to inculcate and impress into and upon his susceptible mind.

Last evening we saw Cloud with a Mrs. Lovewell, and heard him make an engagement to meet her at half-past four this evening. In consequence of this he feels a little nervous lest he may be detained at the Colonel's table and after dinner, so long as to be unable to keep his engagement promptly.

After the two men have been engaged in animated conversation some minutes, a rustling of silks behind admonishes them that Mrs. Worthington is entering the room, and that the formalities of an introduction must be performed.

The tall, athletic form of Cloud rises and turns with true military gracefulness to face his hostess; and the first glance of his eye discovers standing before him in queenly majesty a form as athletic, almost as tall, and far more graceful than his own, and a beautiful face glowing with tints of resplendent crimson, but which, as soon as he is fully faced about and has fixed his piercing eye upon her, turns ashy pale; and she trembles violently.

Col. Scud and Mrs. Lovewell stand face to face.

This is a dilemma, a crisis—perhaps a fainting

scene. Never had Cloud experienced a danger for which he would not have gladly exchanged the embarrassing position of the present moment. Yet, as he has often been in those desperate games when his life was at stake, he fully realizes the situation, and that something must be done to avert a ruinous catastrophe. His characteristic coolness and self-control do not forsake him. But stepping forward with the most nonchalant *sang-froid*, he extends his hand, and says, in a re-assuring tone:

"My dear madam, I am delighted to make your acquaintance; and can assure you that I am a very quiet, inoffensive person, not at all the man-devouring character of war repute as you may have pictured me. So calm your fears: I am a notorious coward when I have to face a lady."

MRS. WORTHINGTON: "Pardon my weakness, Colonel. I was like some who are suddenly brought face to face with a being that they have learned to regard as terrible. The moment you faced me, I thought of the flashing sabre about which I have heard the soldiers talk, and was about to utter a womanish scream. I would not make a very brave soldier. I am glad to make your acquaintance, and extend to you a cordial welcome."

COL. WORTHINGTON: "You need never laugh at me again for surrendering to Col. Cloud so meekly, my dear, since his mere presence has so much disconcerted you."

MRS. W——: "No, dear, you shall never hear that from me again."

By this time the erratic young wife is composed, and enters into the conversation with an apparently hearty relish.

The dinner, the small talk, etc., etc., are perhaps similar to the majority of such affairs, uninteresting often to those who are actively participating in them.

Immediately after dinner Col. Worthington takes his leave to attend the meeting of directors of a stock company, leaving Cloud in the care of his wife.

After the Colonel is gone, the two culpables look at each other for some moments in painful suspense, as though they both dread to speak; but Cloud breaks the silence.

CLOUD: "My God! Do I dream, or do I see with my open eyes?—Mrs. Worthington, in Heaven's name, are you mad?"

MRS. W——: "Oh! Col. Cloud, this is a judgment sent on me in time to save me. Have pity on me, and do not betray me. I have as yet been false to my husband in my heart only. As a matter of course our anticipated meetings are at an end, and never again will I be guilty of such a thing. It is my fault; do not reproach yourself. What a blessing that you came to dine here to-day.

"Col. Worthington is an angel, but so deeply immersed in business that he neglects me, or I fancy he does neglect me.

"Several of my lady acquaintance have told me about having lovers; and this Madam Vais-entre assured me that this was quite fashionable among married ladies of the first families, and that it was my only remedy.

"Just to think that the amiable and discreet stranger, as ignorant as a babe, of New York and its society, whom this wicked woman selected for me, should be my husband's esteemed friend! What an escape we have both had!

"This has made a Christian of me, at least on that subject, no matter how lonely and slighted I may feel.

"In your estimation, I am sunk low and deep in the seething gulf of infamous connubial infidelity."

CLOUD: "Have no fears, madam. I shall never expose you. Always remember this day and your vow. Farewell."

Garland Cloud leaves the threshold of his friend's door, fully resolved that no solicitation shall ever induce him to darken it again. He feels that another weight is added to his already crushing burden of woe. How can he ever face that friend again? Ever he must feel and imagine, when in his presence, that the conscience-stricken wife has made a complete confession to her husband, making the affair serve to exonerate herself as far as possible, lest by some other means he might learn it, and so colored as to cause her to appear in a very unfavorable light.

On the other hand, this misguided woman ever trembles at the approach of her husband; fearing that by some chance, he has during the day become acquainted with her secret.

Thus, day after day, these two persons suffer a penalty for their indiscretion that no words can measure,—" that of silent unutterable dread, and the shadowy images that are ever and anon conjured up as its concomitant horrors."

Once more, the inexorable mask fastens itself on Cloud with still greater security, and serves to cover a second act, or contemplated one, which on his part is equally as bad.

Had the affair progressed, it is doubtful whether, as long as he did not know that the woman was related to friends of his, he would have suffered much compunction of conscience relative thereto. He might never have taken the trouble to reflect, that although then unknown to any member of her family, he was liable to make the acquaintance of those most intimately related to her; and at any time to meet them with her under circumstances calculated to render the situation extremely embarrassing.

CHAPTER XLIV.

THE DAY-DREAM OF A GLOOMY LIFE.

" The mosses of thy fountain still are sprinkled,
By thine Elysian water drops; and the face
Of thy cave-guarded spring, by time unwrinkled
Peeps forth, the meek eyed genius of the place."
—BYRON.

THE prosperity of Cloud's Virginia business is undiminished during his sojourn in New York. He returns home after an absence of five months, thoroughly satisfied that he is sufficiently initiated in the cotton trade speedily to become an adept in the business.

He enters upon his routine labors as though he had returned from a short business trip.

During his absence from the town, Judge Harman, the father of Edgar and Carrie, settles there in order to prosecute a manufacturing business in which he becomes largely interested. His residence is some five hundred yards from the town, at " the cave spring."

Edgar and his Rose, with her brother Jesse, remain for the time being at the old mansion, many miles distant.

Before Cloud's return, a brother merchant, who hates him most intensely, and who is also a zealous church member of the same persuasion as the Harmans, has become intimate with the family, and smitten by the charms of Miss Carrie. He immediately learns, however, how deeply and firmly rooted their friendship is for Cloud.

On arriving at home, Cloud is surprised to find this man, if possible, a more enthusiastic friend of his than the Judge himself.

As a matter of course, he cannot avoid an early visit to the father of Edgar Harman and the mother of Jesse Flowers.

Miss Carrie is absent on a visit to the same relatives with whom she was that night staying, when the young officers under Cloud were expressing the vindictive feelings which they cherished for him.

The Judge and his good lady much desire that Cloud shall take a room in their large house, and his meals at their table; but this he will not consent to do.

During the temporary absence of the Judge from the parlor, Mrs. Harman makes it a point to express regrets that Miss Carrie is absent; and to say that she trusts Cloud will not be sparing with his visits on her account when she is at home.

Carrie Harman returns home on the last day of April. The next day there is a May-day Sunday-school picnic and dinner in the grove near her father's house. Cloud is a member of the active committee; so is Miss Carrie.

The weather is unusually warm for the season. Cloud is at the cave spring bright and early. He has just received pine-apples and other delicacies by express from Richmond, and is donating toward the dinner. These he is putting into the capacious stone spring-house, in order that they may be cool by dinner-time.

Up to this moment Cloud and Miss Harman have never met.

As Cloud comes out of the spring-house door, which is some six feet from the mouth of the cave, whence issues the limpid, crystal spring, half concealed by the shadow of the cave, close to the side, quite even with the mouth, with hair half disheveled, half curled in nature's wavy ringlets, in nymph-like beauty to rival Numa's fairy-fabled Egeria, his eyes behold a witching image—the graceful form of Carrie Harman, of whom he has dreamed so many dreary years, amid so many varying scenes.

At one enthusiastic bound, both her velvet hands clasp his solitary hand, as in accents of thrilling pathos she says: "Oh, Col. Cloud! savior of my dear brother, inspirer of all that has been grand and noble in my life, am I at last permitted to thank you in person for your patriotic kindness and unselfish devotion to poor Edgar?"

CLOUD: "I am enraptured with pleasure to meet you in this romantic spot. I thought you were Egeria, haunting this pretty cave. For the past you have paid me a thousand times over again. I am your debtor. And for the ecstasy of this moment, standing as I am, almost in the mouth of a fairy-land cave with "The Angel of Consolation," no words are adequate to the occasion; nor yet to express to you my gratitude for your angelic care of the children of the mountain."

CARRIE: "Ah, Colonel, upon these points I see that we can never agree; so, therefore, we will leave them in the past, with its other stories and images of dark and saddening scenes. It is enough that we are to labor together to-day in a charming entertainment. under the auspices of a cause so glorious—a most lovable scene of blissful peace, in harmonious accord with our obscurely visaged conception of what should be the happy rest of eternity. You must take no exceptions to the rudely informal mode of my greeting. We have been too long friends now to stand on ceremonies as to the simple form of an introduction."

CLOUD: "You are right, Miss Carrie on all these points. I would not exchange this greeting for a hundred introductions; and I deeply thank you for having thus accorded me the inexpressible pleasure this meeting affords, beyond what there could have been in one occurring at any other place, and under different circumstances.

"I am delighted with my good fortune in having the honor of laboring with you to-day in this good cause."

CARRIE: "We are exceedingly fortunate in having secured your services, together with your liberal donation; for both of which I sincerely thank you, and at the same time assure you that both will be duly appreciated by the school and the community.

"Colonel, I hope to be successful in inducing you to take an active interest in our Sabbath-school, and in the building of our new church."

CLOUD: "Certainly; I will do anything I can. I am a friend to the good causes of every nature, although I lay no claims to goodness myself.

"I must return to the village now. I will join you promptly at the hour designated for the committee to meet."

CARRIE: "I must then introduce you to the young ladies. The ladies here think you are a hermit, or exceedingly selfish. They say you avoid introductions, and never have made a call. They all have an idea that you are an old-time friend of our family. I told some of them that your father claims you are far more afraid of a lady than of a cannon."

CLOUD: "If they say anything about to-day, hereafter, tell them that I am not afraid of "Angels of Consolation.""

CARRIE: "Oh, now, Colonel, that is an unkind injunction, one I cannot obey; because some of them are genuine little angels, and well qualified to console the most forlorn heart."

CLOUD: "I do not yet know them in that light. Let them engrave this fact in bold relief by acts that will entitle them to this claim, and I will then recognize it."

The picnic and the dinner are a grand success. Throughout the day Garland Cloud and Carrie Harman are inseparable. Whenever they are not actually at work, and passing from one part of the grounds to another amid the beautiful cedars and pines, she is on his arm, as though they had been intimate friends from childhood. In the opinion of spectators they are the happiest couple at the picnic. But most of the people present do not regard this fact as being an indication of anything beyond the delight of two old friends on their first day of meeting after a separation of more than six years.

To one person this appearance of a warmly attached intimacy between the young couple is bitterly mortifying, and fills him with implacable chagrin. This individual is Walton Paulona, the merchant who is so much attached to the Harman family, so deeply fascinated by the charms of Miss Carrie, and who has suddenly discovered that he is a firm friend to Garland Cloud.

Time rolls on into June. Cloud has subscribed one-fifth part of the sum to build the new church; and through his New York friends he has supplied the Sunday-school with a handsome and extensive library. He is also a teacher in the school and a regular attendant at church.

To and from both these places Miss Harman is always his companion. He never attempts to escort, and never makes a call on any other young lady. To visit her, he will not neglect his business; but many are the notes that pass back and forth between them through the week.

At length Cloud recognizes a fact that has existed for nearly six years, despite his efforts to persuade himself that it has not: that Carrie Harman is the dream of his life, and the custodian of his mortal fate, for weal or woe.

He at once resolves that the reality of this question shall not continue poised in doubtful or uncertain suspense. He therefore makes an appointment to call upon her on a certain evening during the week. The elders are discreetly absent; thus he finds himself quietly alone in the parlor with the one woman who ever kindled within his breast the faintest spark of love. His heart beats wildly in this supreme moment that is to decide his fate; far more wildly than if he was riding into the jaws of death. Yet he is cool, and every outward indication of emotion is absent from his apparently serene face. He does not hesitate nor delay, but boldly approaches the subject.

CLOUD: "I requested this interview, Miss Carrie, for the sole and express purpose of speaking to you on a most delicate subject, that may be very disagreeable, and at the same time very unexpected and surprising to you. However, be this as it may, I must speak, regardless of the consequences; and I crave that you will deign to listen with all the patient indulgence and forbearance that your generous, tender heart can accord.

"Our acquaintance and friendship were germinated, have been cultivated and developed from the moment that you penned me the first note breathing naught, dreaming naught, but a loving sister's gratitude, up to the moment you met me, in nymph-like witching imagery at the mouth of the cave. It has been one unbroken series of incomprehensibly strange realities, more marvelous than fairy-tale romance.

"As they progressed, my interest in them became more and more intensified. I persuaded myself, or fancied I persuaded myself, that the foundation of this ever-growing interest was my devotion to the cause in which we were mutually engaged. Strange mutuality!—I creating, and you soothing, mortal woes.

"When the lapse of time forced me to admit a deep sentiment of personal admiration and esteem, it was that of the nature of pure reverence, such as I cherish for the Sisters of Mercy. Beyond this, I strove to stay my wildest dreams from straying.

"When the war was ended, I deemed our relations severed. I had not presumed to write you so much as a friendly letter up to the moment of our meeting on that bright May morning.

"Instantly then, some strange spell, as if it were the magical touch of the enchanter's wand, possessed and thrilled my being. Steadily and persistently has it grown on me, despite my vain struggles to overcome its tendency. I have tried to persuade myself to vow that I would see you no more, only to find myself resolving to see you again.

"I was sensibly conscious of my folly. I dreaded the inevitable wreck of hope to which I was madly flying; but realized that I was powerless to resist the force that impelled me onward, or to escape its impending consequences.

"I have been a soldier. I am now a man of business. Neither position has given me a social polish. I detest flattery at all times and under all circumstances. In any enterprise I am impatience personified: cannot brook suspense: must rush on to results.

"Miss Carrie, I cherish for you the most intensified love: I am not to blame. I have struggled against, it tried to persuade myself that I was merely laboring under the spell of some wild hallucination; but all in vain.

"I dare not let the situation remain in suspense. If this sentiment can be reciprocated, I must know it; if it be hopeless, I must know it.

"I cannot expect your love to flow, if at all, with the same fierce spontaneity as my own. But if the subject be not repugnant, and if there be merely a disposition to cultivate it, then I am content.

"You are the only lady for whom I have ever experienced this tender and endearing sentiment. A decision I crave and await. No matter what its nature, it still will be a mercy."

CARRIE: "This, Col. Cloud, is an announcement that takes me entirely by surprise, and finds me altogether unprepared to cope with it. I deemed your heart impregnable, and have never, therefore, permitted myself to dream of making upon it an impression. True, I have long esteemed you as an ideal type of bravely chivalric manhood, and prized you as a friend—yes, a brother. But had the secret longings of my heart sought to dream of more tender and delicate sentiments, the icy coldness of your letters would have chilled the little spark to extinction long before it had reached the point of ignition to claim a recognition even as a spark. How then could it ever have produced a pure, fervent flame of love?

"Now, like an overwhelming tornado, you announce your love. I can hardly believe my ears but that they are deceiving me.

"This is a very serious question, Col. Cloud, that demands calm reflection and mature consideration. I will so consider it, and also counsel with you. Then in due time, I will express to you frankly and fully my decision."

CLOUD: "I shall then, Miss Carrie, regard the future of this affair as being not utterly hopeless, and thus feeling, bid you good-night."

CARRIE: "Good-night."

He leaves her alone to muse and soliloquize as follows:

"Well, just what I could not dare expect; and had I dared hope, what, above all things else, I most desired: that this man should love me. My sorrowful day-dream of so many years, sorrowful because apparently hopeless, is realized. The envied, prosperous man, the brave and untiring friend of humanity, regarded as cold and indif-

ferent to everything earthly save the cause in which he is engaged, wherein seems to be all his heart and soul in concentric combination—to love with quick and fierce impetuosity! Can I believe it? The great wild fish that I feared no art could ever catch—to think that he has been entangled in Cupid's meshes while I was trying to devise some skillful plan to capture him. I am fortunate.

"Oh, he fancies that his love is wild, fierce, and heart-consuming, and that mine must yet be ignited; does not even exist in low, smoldering embers. How little these cold, matter-of-fact-hearted creatures know us poor, emotional girls!

"His love is cold as an Arctic berg, compared with the raging volcano that is consuming my wildly throbbing breast, and must be suppressed. I must dissemble; must consider; must hesitate; must not, for formality's sake, reveal my pure, womanly emotions, while these indifferent men may declare theirs at pleasure. And they may, while we are employing time to consider what we had already, before appealed to, fully decided, 'be drawn away,' as they are pleased to term it, after some other pretty face, and against this we have no security, not even when their vows have been sacredly sealed! Inconstant, treacherous, heart-breaking men!

"The churl! to declare his love and say good-night both in the same breath; thinking I was too bashfully timid to look him in the face. What stupidity! The idiot! I could listen to his discordant strain until it died into an echo, and then sigh to hear more, did it discourse only of love."

As to Cloud, for him the sun seems to shine brighter and the birds to sing sweeter than ever sun had shone or birds sung at any other period of life, since the mellow summer sunshine of his own native blue mountains gleamed for him in careless days of dreamy happy childhood—those mountains that the last of seven years is now swiftly passing over since his eye beheld them, with their majestic summits kissing the clouds.

He now realizes, or rather acknowledges to himself, that it was through all the luring dream of Carrie Harman that prompted him to conceal from the world the unhappy nature of that wondrous peril from which Lieut. Stone delivered him; when, of all other persons in the world, she was the one who would have sympathized most deeply with him.

Now he feels that there is no longer a question about the realization of his dream; and that soon he will possess the priceless reward of his far-reaching prudence.

Ecstacies of bliss are sweets sublime when they are not too fierce to last!

CHAPTER XLV.

THE LONG-CHERISHED REVENGE.

"Hate and envy, with visage black,
And the serpent, Slander, are on thy track;
Falsehood and guilt, remorse and pride,
Doubt and despair, in thy pathway glide;
Never had warrior greater need:
Pause, and gird all thy armor on."
—BATTLE OF LIFE.

FRANZ MUELLER: "Well, Smith, you have been to the camp of Cloud, our hated enemy, and find him a prosperous and highly esteemed merchant, away out there where he is unknown, so I understand?"

SMITH BROOKS: "Even so; and he is so popular and powerful that I dared not breathe one word against him. The moment I mentioned his name to any one, even a negro, that individual went into raptures about Cloud, extolling him to the skies. He has too good a footing there for us to reach him."

MUELLER: "And you hinted to no one a word about his convictship at Bay City, and left him in his glory undisturbed, after we have so long and diligently sought to find his hiding-place?"

BROOKS: "No. I tell you, man, it would have been madness. But I made a discovery which may result in our being able to uncover and reach his vulnerable point.

"Just to think of it! Judge Harman's daughter, the belle, you know, of the adjoining county before they moved away, is thought to be engaged to him, or in a fair way to become so.

"The Judge believes in Cloud, perhaps because he appears to be a rising man. But you know the Judge is a stickler for honor, and much prides himself on his proverbially renowned ancestry. Might not this be employed as a means, and be so skillfully brought to bear against Cloud, as to discomfit and ruin him?"

MUELLER: "Let us see: Your brother wrote you from Tennessee that the mule-trader who staid all night with him, was one of the guards who carried Cloud to the penitentiary, and that it was positively the same man who had charge of the execution of the three Federal officers in the early days of April, 1865."

BROOKS: "Then there can be no doubt but that Cloud escaped from the prison; because my brother wrote as you have said. How could Cloud be at liberty? You know my brother suggested that we keep a lookout for him, as he was smart enough to escape, and would most likely do it."

MUELLER: "Yes, we have him now at last. You write a letter, anonymously, to Judge Harman, merely stating that there is a terrible dark and mysterious secret to the community where he now is, against Cloud, and refer to me for particulars and facts, and I will picture him. The Judge knows me personally. Send this letter to your brother to mail. Did Cloud see you?"

BROOKS: "Certainly. He showed me a polite contempt—a more stinging sarcasm than an openly abusive insult. His face glowed and his brow was haughty and defiant as when, on the dark charger, he was leading his blood-thirsty squadrons in a furious charge on a mass of flying, scattered infantry."

MUELLER: "The merciless villain. And I suppose like he looked when he had me by the collar, and was brandishing his then bloody sword over my head; or as he looked when he was taking your leaves of absence from you all, and placing you under guard, to be returned to your regiment. Every dog has his day, and ours is coming now. How sweet to contemplate the realization of our too long-deferred but now swiftly fierce revenge."

Thus is it ever with the meaner mind. Garland Cloud had risen by his own exertions, aided by his brilliant genius, from the ranks to his position above these men. They, possessing neither minds lofty enough to appreciate his merit, nor souls unselfish enough to rejoice in his success, in their petty malice not content with throwing obstacles in his pathway in revenge for fancied injuries received at his hands, sought to pull him from the heights to which by slow and laborious ascent he had climbed. They fancied by dishonoring him and dimming the lustre of his bright name, their own tarnished titles would gain lustre from the fallen brightness; as others beside them are striving every day to mount to the stairs of their ambition upon the ruin and lifeless bodies of those, they, in their eager struggle, cast beneath their feet.

But Revenge,—twin sister of Hate, more powerful than princes, stronger than the boasted strength of Israel's prophet, deceived by a woman's false-hearted smiles, more potent than all the creeds of ancient pagan or modern Christian, blacker than the waters of the dark river when Charon, in its gloomy midnight rows his craft, —had entered into the hearts of these men, and impelled them to plan and create the cruel downfall and the merciless destruction of Garland Cloud.

CHAPTER XLVI.

WORK-A-DAY SKETCHES OF BUSINESS LIFE.

"But the youthful form grows wasted and weak,
And sunken and wan is the rounded cheek:
The brow is furrowed, but not with years:
The eye is dimmed with its secret tears:
And streaked with white is the raven hair:
These are the tokens of the conflict there."
—BATTLE OF LIFE.

GARLAND CLOUD is in his office. The railroad agent enters.

LORENZI: "Can you give me a memorandum, Colonel, of the cars you are loading, as I want to make up my way-bill?"

CLOUD: "Certainly, Mr. Agent. Be seated. I will go into the ware-house for it at once, and return directly."

He goes out, and soon a gentleman enters.

DAÑO: "Why, how are you, Mr. Agent? Where is Col. Cloud?"

LORENZI: "Why this is the gentleman for whom he bought so much grain when he first came here. He has just stepped out into the ware-house for a moment. Be seated. Glad to see you, sir."

DAÑO: "Yes sir, he served our interests faithfully. I understand he prospers."

L——: "He is the best send the farmers of this section ever had. He works incessantly almost day and night. He is sober and charitable, but no allurement can tempt him from business. The young people are piqued because they can never get him to a party. I am sure there are weeks that he never undresses at night nor sleeps in a bed."

DAÑO: "He was the same way in the army, from the time I first knew him a private soldier until the war closed. He would lay by a fire nearly all night, studying tactics and army regulations, which he could retain, master, and put into execution so thoroughly as to stand on a par with old graduated officers. But here he comes."

CLOUD: 'Here is your memorandum, Mr. Agent. Why Mr. Daño, what wind blew you hither? Some good one I hope. How are you?"

DAÑO: "I am quite well, thank you. I came down to see you relative to an arrangement to control the wheat crop of this section and upper, middle and East Tennessee in the interest of some large exporters and extensive mills. Can you go into it, and arrange your affairs to be absent from your business here three or four weeks right away?"

CLOUD: "Certainly, provided it pays. The agent's brother Charles is my confidential man, an excellent and a good one, too."

DAÑO: "Come up, then, Saturday night and remain over Sunday."

CLOUD: "Very well. We will then have time plenty to talk over the matter and arrange the details."

DAÑO: "Then good afternoon. I shall depend upon you."

CLOUD: "If I am able to get there, you will see me. Good-day, sir."

He departs and Charles Lorenzi enters.

CHAS. LORENZI: "Ha! Colonel, I just saw Miss Carrie at the depot, seeing her cousins off on the train; and when Mr. Dano spoke to her and told her that his business here was with you, you should have seen how she blushed and blushed. I tell you she loves you, sure as we live."

CLOUD: "It is a pity that you are not a girl. You think of nothing but girls and love. I find your Miss Bettie's name all over the blotters and in sundry other places. The drawing-room claims these frail sentimentalities: this is no place for them.

"I want you to put on your soberest steady cap, for I am going away on to-morrow's afternoon train, to be absent some weeks."

CHAS. L——: "All right sir. Everything is shipped, I will go to supper."

He goes out, and Charley, the colored porter, comes in.

CLOUD: "How now, Charley, Satan's sleep imp? Are you ready to begin to load those cars? It must be done before we sleep."

CHARLEY: "Yah, sah, all redde, sah. I dis cum in specting may be ye wants me to take note ober to Miss Carrie. Seed her dis eben. She look at me mite strate, like she spects note. Golly, I jis likes to take notes to dat lade."

CLOUD: "No boy, not to-night. Car are too scarce and demurrage too sure to waste time with Cupid's whims. Weightier things are on my mind now."

CHARLEY: "Bery well den, Ize dis goen to shub dem niggers."

Charley goes out, and Judge Harman and Paulona enter.

JUDGE HARMAN: "Always at work, Colonel. How are you this evening?"

CLOUD: "Yes, gentlemen, you know the penalty of 'the sweat of the brow.' I am striving to fulfill the sentence to the best of my ability, but think that just now, in fulfilling it, I am serving the farmers and the railroads more than any one else; which I suppose may be also a duty."

PAULONA: "I called, Colonel, to see if I could buy some drafts."

CLOUD: "All you want. I need piles of currency. It is quite difficult just now to get cars to move stuff, but that does not diminish the demand for money."

JUDGE H——: "You seem to be the Exchange Bank here, Colonel.

"It was very kind in you to advance the entire amount of your large subscription to the Church Building Fund, and the committee thanks you. By the way, you failed to attend the meeting today."

CLOUD: "In the exchange business, the advanvantage is mostly in my favor. As to the subscription, it had to be paid some time; you needed the money, and so I thought it best to wipe out my part of it. At the hour of your committee-meeting, my friend Dano was here, which kept me away."

JUDGE H——: "I regret that you did not call while my nieces were here. They were anxious to see you, because so many of their relatives and friends served under you, and on account of the stories they have heard those soldiers tell about you."

CLOUD: "I am sorry that I did not have time to call. Well, gentlemen, call again. I am always glad to see you. Good-night."

They leave Cloud alone to continue his work.

CHARLEY [coming singing]: "'Twill cause you all to shed a tear, o'er the grave of my sweet Kittie Wells."

CLOUD: "Charley, those lines

'Sometimes I wish that I was dead,
And laid beside her in the tomb—
The sorrows that bow down my head',
Are silent as the midnight gloom.'

have always impressed me most seriously."

CHARLEY: "Golly, I, don't wonder at dat, kase you seze mo' ob de mid-nites dan any odder man in dese diggens. Oh, Lorde! dis nigger ize tired an' sleepe, fur shure."

CLOUD: "Give me two or three licks of 'the break-down,' and then to your pallet."

Charley dances furiously for several minutes.

CHARLEY: "Golly, boss, dat makes me swete."

Later in the night the room is dark; a noise wakes Cloud.

CLOUD: "Charles! Oh, Charles!"

CHARLEY: "Sah."

CLOUD: "What is that noise, boy?"

CHARLEY: "Somebody rolcn' bacco outen de war-house. Ize been waked up by it, but waze frade to call you."

CLOUD: "No gun, no pistol, and no anything. Where is the axe?"

CHARLEY: "De axe down in de war-house, Wherze you gwine, boss? Les get outen de bake door. It'll hurt our feet to jup out de up-stair winder. Golly, dayze up dare too. Ah, Ize getten behind de desk. Don't go in de war-house, boss."

CLOUD: "Come out of there, coward. It is nothing but hogs rooting the big scales about on the outside platform, and raising up and letting one edge fall. You big fool, to think I would jump from a window. I went up there to try to look out at the front window, and finding it nailed up, was why I hurried down-stairs."

CHAPTER XLVII.

THE BITTER FRUIT OF RETRIBUTION.

"He who ascends the mountain top shall find
 The loftiest peaks most wrapt in clouds and snow;
He who surpasses or subdues mankind,
 Must look down on the hate of those below.
Though high *above* the sun of glory glow,
 And far *beneath*, the earth and ocean spread,
Round him are icy rocks, and loudly blow
Contending tempests on his naked head,
And thus reward the toils which to those summits led"
—BYRON.

NOTHING in this world of woe is so sure and inevitable as retribution in some shape, either mental, physical or social, one if not all, for mis-deeds. Violating either the laws of nature, the laws of the social circle in which we move, or the laws of the land, constitute the grand errors and crimes of mortal life.

It is such misdeeds and their retribution that produce nearly all the woe and wretchedness that afflict, with a scourge-like curse, so many fami-lies; and so cruelly disturb the peace and well-being of society all over this busy and prosper-ous world.

Retribution may, and often does, come tardily; but then it is apt to come at a time and in a shape not expected, and hence strikes heavily.

Not unfrequently, a towering ambition to rise in the gradation scale in some sphere where promotions and honors are to be sought and attained, or to achieve success in the ordinary battles of life, prove to be the means of drawing down upon mankind consequences almost as direful and as terrible as the retribution entailed as a direct legacy, which misdeeds bequeath. Hence all are, if neither misdeeds nor mistakes, certainly misfortunes; especially when they cre-ate such detrimental results.

If they do not thus prove, it is never because there are not people to create and help forward such ill-breeding consequences; people too, who are in the same walks of life from which the aspirant has emerged, and who were his warmest friends before he started on the ascent up the slippery steep in his desperate struggle to reach the pinnacle of Fame, or the height of earthly Glory.

This is an innate proneness inseparable from human nature, and the legitimate offspring of jealousy and envy. To a majority of this class of people, the discomfiture or the fall of their rising fellow-being, is a source of secret, if not of ex-pressed, gratification; although the aspirations at which he aimed were moderate, certainly by no means inordinate, yet sufficiently elevating above the plane from which he has risen or is striving to rise, to alienate from him both the sympathy and friendship, as well as the affection, of those whom he has left or seeks to leave below.

That he aspires to benefit or is actually benefit-ing them, often makes not the slightest differ-ence; for if they have not struck, nor even aided and abetted the striking of the fatal blow, they will feel a sense of consolation springing from the conscious certainty that it has been struck, and effectually.

It matters not how kindly and even consider-ably condescending he may be toward them, they are sure to deem him overbearing and proud, and certain to consider him as continually scornfully snubbing or ridiculing them. This latter remark may apply more forcibly to the middle walks of life and downward, than to the classes above the intermediate line.

From a very close scrutiny of Garland Cloud's career, we perceive in him, deeply rooted, this ambition. Perhaps this is his in an extremely inordinate degree, coupled with a tireless, ceaseless, almost sleepless perseverance, supported by an indomitable will guided by a calmly nerved hand. These attributes are usually supported by masterful self-control, and directed by the dictates of a cool judgment, ever impelling its possessor, obstinately driving him, often slowly, yet still steadily and patiently, onward over one obstacle after another, inch after inch, in the direction of the objects which he.set out to attain; and which, once seeing, he ever keeps in view, never faltering, nor hesitating, nor turning back in that discouraging and dangerous course.

From the very outset, Cloud seems to have fairly realized the situation and the nature of the obstacles which he must surmount, and to have determined to do this alone and unaided. In this his extreme youth appears to have been the most retarding obstacle.

It would seem, from the fact that he cut loose from both kindred and neighbors when embarking in the fatal ship of the "Lost Cause," that he then knew enough about the weakness of human nature to withhold him from making the attempt to rise among them or to allow them to aid him in so doing, when he declined to permit them to elevate him several rounds up the ladder, and announced, "I will rise from the ranks or die in the ranks."

Dreading the ridicule that failure always attaches to those who attempt the seemingly unreasonable, we never find him confiding to any one the nature of his aspirations, nor seeking recognition for any dreamy claim to merit which he may have cherished, and which he doubtless did cherish.

Twenty-eight months in the ranks of an infantry regiment did not seem much like fighting out of the ranks any other way than into the grave; yet at last we saw him suddenly rise.

From the picket bivouac and the out-post service of 1861 up to the last interview with her, that Carrie Harman, although for so many years but the spectral shadow of a most forlorn and to Cloud's mind, clearly ill-fated hope, was the inspiring genius of many, if not all of his acts, is too obvious to admit a discussion; and to the

influence of this hapless spell we can safely attribute his greatest misfortune: concealing the sequence of "the mistaken identity."

His present relations with her, and position and prospects in the commercial world, are such as to provoke the envy of those who have been his most appreciative friends for two years, in the region of his domicile. These were people, who, had she not appeared on the scene, and her society been so thoroughly monopolized by him, would never have been inclined to harbor one spark of envy or one unkind feeling against him; but who are now, for all these reasons combined, nevertheless, in a state of mind to be prepared not seriously to regret his downfall.

As to Mueller and his accomplices, their original grounds of hatred, upon which they based the oath of vengeance, would never have been manifested against any other officer on account of a similar discharge of duty, except alone Garland Cloud, their hitherto own humble neighbor.

Several persons are together in Paulona's office.

PAULONA: "Well, Judge, Mueller's letter in reply to yours is rough on Col. Cloud. A terrible shock to the community, if it be true."

JUDGE HARMAN: "Yes; but I believe it a base concoction of falsehood."

PAULONA: "So do I; yet still I think it too grave to be disregarded. I deem it your duty to all parties to write to the warden of the penitentiary at Bay City, and ascertain the truth or the falsehood of this grave charge. Furthermore, I would suggest that Charles Lorenzi write to the Colonel, and give him, in the meantime, a chance either to explain or refute this accusation.

"We should not condemn an innocent man, nor can the community afford to permit an impostor to sail about among its citizens under the colors of a gentleman. Where is the Colonel now, Charles?"

CHARLES LORENZI: "His address is K——. Judge, I think Paulona is right about this, and that I should write fully by this mail."

JUDGE HARMAN: "Perhaps so; then we will both write, as suggested."

They separate. The same evening the Judge is at home and unusually serious.

CARRIE: "Why are you so morose this evening, dear father? Are you unwell, or what has happened?"

JUDGE II——: "I have always, in every possible way, encouraged your friendship for Col. Cloud; but read this terrible letter, Carrie, my child, and find, if it be true, how sadly we are both disappointed in our estimation of the real character of this seemingly admirable man. Should it prove true that he is false and unworthy, I can never again fix in my mind an ideal of true and perfect manhood—hardly trust any one."

CARRIE: "It is false, my father. It is but the cowardly stab of an enemy, through the whispering medium of vile slander—the Satanic subterfuge of calumnious obloquy, designed to blast the hopes and the life of a man on whom Fortune deigns to smile.

"Would a base and degraded man pursue the high, the useful, and the noble calling in which he is so helplessly yet devotedly enslaved? I say no, a thousand times no. Not because he is an esteemed friend, but because it is his meed of merit that I would accord were he an utter stranger."

JUDGE II——: "Well, fond girl, I would, were I in your place, not write to him again until the matter is cleared up. Good night."

He retires and leaves her alone in the parlor.

CARRIE [Solus]: "Palsied be the hand that penned, accursed be the brain that conceived, this all blighting slander, more fell and destructive than the contagious breath of the pestilence. It is already sapping my vitality. I feel the venomous fangs buried in my young and affectionate heart, the poison coursing through my veins. Would that I had given him my true heart's answer, and gone with him immediately to the altar, before there was a chance for the grim shadow of this horrid ghost to estrange him from me. Oh that I could see and reassure him this night!"

Some days later the Judge, Charles Lorenzi and Paulona are again in the latter's office.

JUDGE II——: "Well, gentlemen, here is a conclusive telegram from the warden, branding the charge against Col. Cloud as a base falsehood, just as I told you. I am ashamed that I did not 12

burn the anonymous letter, and never breathe its nature, instead of writing to that most execrable Dutchman."

PAULONA: "That is indeed gratifying."

CHARLES LORENZI: "That is the best news I have heard since the war."

The railroad agent now enters the office.

LORENZI: "Mr. Paulona, here is an express package from Col. Cloud for you."

PAULONA: "A special power of attorney. Here is a conundrum."

Charley now comes hurriedly in with a letter.

CHARLEY: "Massah Charles, herze a letter from de boss man, sure."

Charles Lorenzi reads the letter, turns ghastly pale, and trembles like an aspen-leaf before the mad breath of the tempest; then he reads it aloud:

"K——, Tenn., August 4th, 1867.

"'MR. CHAS. LORENZI:

"Dear Sir:

"'The contents of your letter startled and shocked me more than a clap of thunder from a clear sky, and as much as the terrors of Doom's-day itself could have done. A credited slander is as blighting to my prospects, hopes, and future of this life as any truth could be, however damnable. So true is this, that it renders the ill unbearable.

"'Ere this scrawl is read by you, the hand that pens it, and the heart that never recoiled before a mortal danger, will be cold and still in the icy embrace of death, beneath the rippling bosom of the waters of the Tennessee.

"A long and hopeless farewell.

"Your desperate friend,
"GARLAND CLOUD."

ALL: "Oh, horrors! what have we caused?"

CHARLEY: "Oh Lorde! Oh Lorde! Wo-a-day! De onle frend ob dis pore chile ded. Misable me! Oh Lorde! whatze gwine ter become ob me now?"

Charley rushes out into the street and past the depot, where, while still lamenting as if his poor true and faithful heart will break, he suddenly meets Miss Harman, who accosts him:

"Charley, in Heaven's name, what has happened to you?"

Charley: "Oh, alack, missus! my ondliest frend ded—drowned—poor nigger got nuffen left him now."

Carrie: "Who is dead? Speak, boy!"

Charley: Oh, missus! dis am an ebel hour—a sorry day! My ondliest friend, Col. Cloud, ded missus; de life an' lite of dis town done fade away an' done gone out, an' ebery ding will be ded again. God help us, missus!"

Carrie: "Oh, my God! I must go home. Oh, alas, thou cruelest of all fates, thou heart-severing death! Envious Heaven, to permit me such delusive dreams! Cruel, heartless man, thus to destroy them! Break, my surging heart, poor bankrupt of wild, inconstant anticipations! Hope, doff thy joyous plumage, cease thy airy flights, and fold thy reckless wings on the baneful Upas' all-blighting branch, and seek solace from its deadly, agony-breathing nectar.

"What more of life remains for me to live? I am but one more victim of the broken heart, doomed to pine away my weary existence in unpitied silence!

"Poor Effie Edlestein! now I know the bitter depths of thy nameless woe!"

Miss Harman goes into mourning, and withdraws from society.

Miserable Cloud! Could he have known the constant intensity of this woman's devotion, and realized the cruel wound which his desperate stab would inflict in her pure and tender heart, surely he would never have so unfeelingly blighted her fair young life.

But, poor wretch, how could he know this? He had passed less than one dozen Sabbaths in her society, and one other evening—that on which he declared his love. It was on this evening only, that any tender relations between themselves had ever been mentioned. At all other times their conversation had been confined exclusively to the labors in which they had been engaged and the scenes through which they had passed in the by-gone time; or to projects for the alleviation of suffering humanity in the future. This was all.

Between them, the social gulf of the olden-time had been broad, deep, and impassable; hence it could have been only with misgivings that Cloud finally introduced the delicate subject. When he said good-night to her that evening, how little he then dreamed that it was for evermore!

How often, in this world, do people lightly say good-night, walk down a street a block, and turn the corner, expecting to return in an hour, next day, or the next week, when that absence is doomed to be for long and dreary years, or for an endless eternity. Some sudden accident or recounter consigns them instantly either to prison or the tomb, or causes a flight little better or more comforting to contemplate than death or a felon's cell.

Look how admirably Cloud's dark secret was guarded; so well, that could he have known the result of the inquiry sent to the prison, its dangers would have been totally destroyed and the haunting shadows of its ghostly spectre forever dispelled.

Still, how appalling to contemplate the dispensations of that wondrous Hand, that orders and directs the little, apparently irrelevant and insignificant points that overturn and destroy all the skillfully planned and carefully constructed strength of whatever they may be so small a part, or to which they may be, even howsoever remotely related. It seems to be a moral impossibility to escape their consequences.

Such things are of a nature to render the ground taken by the superstitious tenable, if not sufficient to confirm their faith in the doctrine, that, intimately connected with them is an invisible, supernatural hand. Certain it is, that there exists some fate, against the influence of which the arts of man to design and his powers to execute counteracting forces, are ever unavailing. *That grand coward—conscience—flies from imaginary dangers.*

The reported suicide of Cloud created a profound sensation in the community where was his adopted home. As is always the case under similar circumstances, the latent propensities of people with whom he had been maintaining active business relations, were promptly manifested.

Let a business man very suddenly and unexpectedly pass under a seriously damaging cloud, or into the grave, and at once many of those with whom he has been dealing for years with harmonious smoothness, discover flaws in his transactions.

Train loads of grain are in transit on Cloud's account. Connected with these transactions are drafts, checks and sundry other considerations unaccomplished, to the amount of many thousands of dollars; and agents are actively engaged at many points receiving and loading more. At home, there is a large stock of assorted goods, and some purchase bills unpaid.

Drafts and checks are protested; accounts and shipments are attached, and lawsuits instituted between merchants, and by banks against the merchants.

The grain accounts of numerous farmers in the vicinity of his store, for whom he made shipments on their own credit, to pay which as a last act he sent currency, are bought up at twenty-five cents on the dollar.

All summed up, there are wide-spread confusion, disaster, sorrow and suffering, to which must be added many no better than criminal acts, connected with this sad affair. These sprang as direct and legitimate fruits from one and the same seed,—a seed of unwise indiscretion, deliberately and willfully planted by Garland Cloud himself, in culpable disobedience to the dictates of his own better judgment, against which his conscience arose in stubborn rebellion.

From the bitter fruits of this seed he had almost incessantly eaten ever after. That ill-breeding germ matured in the affair of his hapless imprisonment at Bay City, was planted in his resolve to bury the sad story of that painful experience in the silence of oblivion; was matured to deadly perfection, by his persistent effort to fulfill the condition of that fatal resolution. He not only suffered the penalty himself, but entailed, directly or indirectly, on untold numbers of other human beings, the bitter consequences of MORAL COWARDICE.

CHAPTER XLVIII.

SOME OTHER HEART-ACHES.

" Love, by harsh evidence,
   Thrown from its eminence,
Even God's providence
   Seeming estranged.
     *   *   *   *
Owning her weakness,
   Her evil behavior,
And leaving with meekness,
   Her sins to her Saviour."
      —THE BRIDGE OF SIGHS.

BEATRICE ATKINSON: "Well, sister Cassandra, and how are you progressing with your free-love affair? And what of your lover? What does he look like, and how do you fancy him?"

CASSANDRA WORTHINGTON: "I most miraculously escaped the affair, by the identical man, the very next day after I met him at Madam Vaisentre's, coming to dinner with the Colonel. This man was a Southerner, and the Colonel was perhaps the only man in the city who would have invited him to dinner: he is so nearly an utter stranger here.

"What a strange fatality that he should be one among the Colonel's most esteemed friends; and that he should come here, of all times, on that particular day, to dinner! I tell you, girls, I felt as though I was sinking through the floor when I recognized him; but he came very promptly to my relief in a way to prevent a scene. That affair so thoroughly frightened me, that I abandoned all idea of having a lover, and resolved to be henceforth a resigned, true, and faithful wife."

ROSALIND STRINGFELLOW: "Oh, Cassa, that was Heaven's own blessing!

"If any two women were ever in a living, earthly torment, Beatrice and I are the ones. I do not see how we are to endure it much longer. How I envy you! Your lot is perfect bliss, compared to ours.

"The men are unkind; we despise them, and would escape and turn back from our wicked career if we could. They know who we are and where we live. They are what might be termed elegant sports. They defy us to abandon them, and coolly tell us that the penalty will be full exposure. We therefore fear them as we would Satan, with his chains and firebrand in hand.

"But alas, was this all and the worst of our ills, our lives would be a paradise to what they are now, with the dread realities of their torture day after day bearing down with ever augmenting affliction.

"Some sharks possess our secret, and day by day they bleed us afresh for hush-money. The amounts of their demands have grown to such frightful magnitude that it would soon break a bank to meet them. We can no longer obtain the money from our husbands. We have just pawned our diamonds, in order to raise the funds necessary to keep them silent for a time; but it is only deferring the evil hour, which must come at last with redoubled severity.

"I tell you, Cassa, there is neither help nor hope for us poor miserable wretches, except in flight or suicide. In flight, there cannot be much, if any, hope; and we already have enough to answer for in the hereafter, without deeper dyeing our stained souls with the unpardonable sin of self-destruction.

"Then again, on the other hand, exposure, and being denounced and driven from home and protection, by righteously indignant husbands, is frightful to contemplate, and would be truly intolerable. What can we do? Oh, Cassa! we are mad!"

BEATRICE: "Yes, Cassa, Rosa has told you of our lamentable, pitiable and utterly helpless condition.

"Thank God that you are still safe and pure, and thus both capable and worthy to give some wholesome and much needed advice to your unhappy, unworthy, and sinful sisters. Oh, Cassa! help us, because you are the only one in this world to whom we can confide the dark secrets of our dreadful trials; and at the same time pray strive to forgive us.

"You know our mutual trials, when we three together drained the cup of woe to its last bitter dregs—that cruel cup that poisoned the pure and healthful current of our young lives, and crushed out from our hearts every vestige of earthly hope. Oh, Cassa! remember those bitter trials over which we have together wept so many times, while we were yet as pure and as innocent

as the angels in heaven—and we might have so remained, as Eva has, had we, like her, been permitted—and do not, I implore you, do not judge us too harshly !"

CASSANDRA: "Oh, my poor sisters, how I pity you! I can judge you only as I must judge myself. That I am not as you are now, is owing to no prudence nor goodness of my own. I can forgive you, as I hope to be forgiven, and as I know God will forgive you if you will at once turn and flee from the near and certain destruction that so nearly enthrals you as to preclude almost the possibility of escape; yet still there remains to you barely time to be saved.

"My poor miserable sisters, you have now nothing left you in this world, where you have never known true happiness. Your only hope is beyond the sun, in the great Eternal. Turn, I implore you, turn before it be too late, and flee to that one source of consolation and safety that remains your only solace and shelter. Now is the time—this day. Delay but for to-morrow, and you are lost, and hopelessly.

"Never pay another penny; never see those accursed lovers again ; and never let your husbands see you more.

"Take the money you have, and fly, fly ; not as though it was for life alone, but for still far more —your souls.

"Seek the deep seclusion of a convent. Confide to the Mother Superior the nature of your relentless pursuers, from whom you seek protection; confess your sins, and she will take you in and afford you comfort. There you can repent, and learn to minister unto suffering humanity, and thus perform a most beautiful mission of mercy.

"This is open to, and invites you as a last refuge the only flight in which you can even hope for present safety and ultimate repose. This is indeed gloomy and cheerless ; but what is anything else which you could attempt? You have already abandoned your husbands, and are fleeing from the dread consequences of that act as much for their honor as for your own safety.

"Your mysterious disappearance will create a sensation, and overwhelm your husbands with grief and anxiety. But to what does all that amount, compared with the disgraceful humiliation of exposure, and all its direful and inconceivable consequences, among which the grave probabilities of suicide are too terrible for contemplation. You cannot afford to delay and to hesitate in deciding which course you will take: the one gently leading to tolerable security, or the one rushing on with wild and furious impetuosity to swift and surely inevitable destruction."

BEATRICE: "Oh, Cassa! my blessed, thrice blessed sister, ministress of mercy, grace and hope, angelic deliverer of my body and of my soul from present torment and from an unending hell!—put your arm around my degraded neck, kiss once more my shame-polluted cheek, and bless me, for I am saved. Your counsels have triumphantly prevailed. I am resolved on immediate flight to the Elysian repose of that tranquil refuge to which you have directed my wayward, stumbling footsteps from this crime-benighted pathway. There, no matter how gloomy be its sombre-shadowed walls, nor how bitterly mortifying to the flesh its restraining discipline, I shall find a kindly benignant, earthly refuge.

ROSALIND: " And I also, Cassa, my sister, to us Heaven's ordained medium, to pronounce to our despairing hope-exiled souls the dulcet words electrified by the ever glorious and revivifying current of consolation, that as they soothingly permeate down, deep down into the empty, hollow, hungry caverns of our wretched hearts echo and re-echo again and again in stirring, comforting tones, the thrilling reverberation of PEACE! PEACE! Oh, thou only hope-inspiring word, Peace, blessed Peace, to thee I flee! Oh, my sister, let me press you to my heaving bosom once more, and kiss your cheek while you bless me!"

CASSANDRA: "Not my lips on your cheeks nor brows, nor yours on mine, my sisters, poor penitent children of our angelic father; but it shall be LIPS TO LIPS and HEARTS TO HEARTS!

"May God bless and comfort you with His loving grace and holy spirit, my miserable sisters; and may He grant you for guardian angels, to watch over and to shield you from every danger and from all harm, the tenderly loving spirits of our error-unsullied father and saintly martyred Effie—should her spirit fly its sacred prison while you remain in yours.

" For myself, my earth-banished sisters, while I live and am able to move, I will visit you once every week, and minister unto you in every way within my power."

" I alone of all the world must be the custodian of your secret, and know the place of your living tomb. This, I hope, will afford you some consolation.

" As we suffered together in our tender but hope-wasting years, and were each to the other, by turns, our only comfort and consolation, let us now still remain constant, true and faithful to one another throughout the remainder of our weary, dreary, cheerless journey of life.

"As my countenance, visits, fidelity, undying love and endless devotion to you may cheer, comfort and strengthen you in your new lives; so may your patience, your resignation, your faith, your hope, teach, help, guide and enlighten me to understand, to appreciate, to fulfill my duty toward you, the world, myself, and my God.

"Now, my heart-broken and sin-stricken sisters, here with you, in unworthiness as deeply dyed as you, I most solemnly vow, from this day henceforth, to devote my life and to exert my energies in the cause of weak and suffering humanity here in this great and wicked city, and see if I cannot accomplish some good; to atone, in some degree, for the wayward and frivolous follies of the past; and, in due time, perhaps, connect my labors directly with yours.

" I shall be devoted, faithful, and loving to my husband. This change in my life, and the cause in which I shall engage, will meet his warmest approbation, receive his most zealous support, and render him supremely happy—something, undutiful woman that I have been, I have never yet once studied nor striven to accomplish.

"There, now, my weeping sisters, your tears and mine have together mingled, as we have on the necks of one another wept. These blessed tears are washing away your dark impurities and mine. This is a scene to make angels rejoice —not alone one, but three sinners together repenting.

"Life with us has been one grand failure. Let us therefore make death one grand and glorious success. As redeemed Magdalens, then, we can in purity soar away to a blessed welcome, where father will be waiting for us to come—

> "'To lie within the light of God, as I lie upon your breast—
> Where the wicked cease from troubling, and the weary are at rest.'"

Grand, noble shades of a departed father I see them triumphing over the vile weeds of dark luxuriance, from the evil seeds sown by a wicked mother in their young and tender hearts, the natural abodes of purity and of love.

But for the want and absence of good seed there to germinate and be nurtured, the evil ones quickly sprang up in that genially salubrious soil, and flourished in undisputed mastery until the multiplicities of their production were struggling to force out some germs from their overburdened and encumbered soil to seek a lodgment in other tender, pure and innocent hearts. Yet suddenly, as if by some magical breath, the one long, lowly smoldering and apparently but utterly extinct spark of a father's purity is fanned into a raging flame, that instantly scorches and consumes them, root and branch, expelling their venomous dross, cleansing and purifying the poor, polluted, aching hearts.

Beauty of beauties, the wondrously sublime picture of a crime-burdened and despair-engulfed human wretch firmly and apparently irretrievably held in the suction of the whirlpool's fathomless quick-sands, where every feeble effort toward extrication tends to sink the victim only deeper and more hopelessly in that dread social Serbonian bog, rising up, as if by one grand, herculean effort, from the clinging mire to the solid suface of the eternally rock-bound shore; fleeing for safety and for life to the eulogistic fountain of tears to wash away the dark, deep stains from the impure heart, that purity may shine in undimmed splendor, and illuminate with transcendent, empyreal brilliancy that regenerate and redeemed soul FOR EVERMORE!

CHAPTER XLIX.

THE WOES OF THE FORSAKEN HUSBANDS.

"The mills of the gods grind slowly,
But they grind exceeding fine."

THE mansions of Ira Atkinson and Adam Stringfellow are adjacent, both having been built at the same time, with the dividing wall forming a part of each building. They are elegant, and contain to repletion all that heart could wish to render life both comfortable and happy, save alone that one often shadowy and delusive element that is purely spiritual—an attribute that is inseparable from, and that will blend with naught but purity; a most beautiful thought that is always "softly bodied forth;" an adorable sentiment; an ecstatic emotion; a high and holy passion—love. The utter absence of this home-brightening essential in the luxuriously appointed households of Atkinson and Stringfellow, and in its stead, on the part of the wives, absolutely cold-hearted indifference, bordering even on loathing and hatred, render them anything but the abodes of happiness.

The masters of these homes, having already steeped their hands, long years before, in the indelible, deep, double dye of most atrocious crime, are, as a natural consequence, suspicious of and mistrust everybody with whom they come in contact, no matter what the nature of the relation nor who the parties.

They are each sufficiently old to be the father of his young wife. It is, the world over, a constitutional weakness in old men to be jealous of young and beautiful wives, whether their grounds be real or imaginary; and this veritable ghost of the imagination not infrequently drives the woman whom it causes to be unjustly charged with infidelity and unjustly persecuted. to make a foundation for it, true and real.

Unfortunately, in these instances, the foundation for jealousy was not a spectral shadow, but a sadly true reality.

The two men are at all times prepared to receive from their wives nearly any style of announcement; so, therefore, when they return home on the evening of the day on which we saw in the last chapter their two wives with their sister arranging to abandon their husbands and their princely homes, and seek an asylum within the cheerless precincts of a convent, the husbands are but little astonished, and but slightly mortified to find, from under the hands of their faithless wives, notes, each of which alike ran as follows:

———"Park, New York, May, 1867.

"My Husband:

"That I have never loved, can never love you, you are consciously sensible. On this point I have never deceived you. I have never acknowledged nor professed to love you.

"You know the sad history and true nature of our formal courtship, and little better than mock marriage, entailing on me, as far as my heart was concerned, the odious bondage of a legalized and a church-sanctioned prostitution, which to me is too fraught with pain to be needlessly recounted.

"I know that my presence and the thoughts which it ever is conjuring up in your mind, tend but to augment your unhappiness, and perpetually to render my existence more intolerable.

"For all these reasons combined, I have this day resolved to leave your roof, to part with you, and to turn my back on the hollow mockeries and the cruel delusions of the social world forever; and shall therefore, without further explanation, say ' Farewell.'

"Beatrice."

Atkinson: "Well, Adam, the end has come at last."

. Stringfellow: "Yes, Ira; it indeed seems to me that our cups of woe should now be full to overflowing.

"Surely this will satisfy Gertrude Flowers' relentless Avenger. Oh, what a surfeit of bitter fruit that curse-breeding crime has forced us to eat! It seems that the restitution did not suffice as an ample atonement, but that the miseries of our doom are endless. Perhaps it is better that the women, unfaithful creatures, are gone. But, poor wretches, I wonder what will become of them."

A———: "Why, they will go somewhere with their lovers. They have absorbed nearly half of our fortune in the past few months. It was truly frightful; and had we not shut down on it a month ago, it would never have stopped until we were beggars.

"It now appears that they have been all the while preparing for this step, and deliberately and systematically working to get possession of our last dollar before they left us.

"I am unable to understand where the money went. Our households have been economically administered, and I do not believe either one of our wives has bought an article for her wardrobe during the past three months. Blockhead dotards that we were not to divine all this, instead, like simpletons, mistaking their well dissembled graciousness for loving devotion, and hoping to buy off their last vestige of antipathy, our money flowed like water."

Some five days after the disappearance of their wives, these two men begin to receive at their business office from leading retail houses, bills for enormous amounts, all sold on the written orders of the wives, which accompany them as vouchers. This establishes the validity of the bills, and clearly fixes upon the husbands the liability for their payment.

All the new accounts had been opened after the husbands had been compelled to curtail the supply of money, for which the ever increasing demands called. This was, therefore, with the wives, one more desperate expedient to hold at bay those most voracious of all cormorants, *the blackmailers*, by giving them, in lieu of money, an extravagantly increased amount in goods, until, finally tiring of this, they demanded money again. And so great was the terror of those wretched women, that, in order to raise it, they pawned their diamonds.

Just now, with the advent of these uncomfortable bills, the woes of Atkinson and Stringfellow commence with a vengeance that is both merciless and unrelenting. They are prepared to submit to the loss of their faithless wives with uncomplaining resignation; but when it comes to beholding the bulk of their remaining fortunes following them, the crisis is at a climax. The old men's spirits are completely broken; they suddenly lapse into a morbid state of waning apathy as to their ordinary affairs of life. Burdened with self-reproach and the weight of years, and afflicted with the corroding cares of disappointment, they become the melancholy victims of the often slow, but relentlessly sure remorse of conscience.

CHAPTER L.

JOSEPHA DEL-CAMPANO.

" In that tale I find,
The furrows of long thought and dried up tears,
Which ebbing, leave a sterile track behind,
O'er which all heavily the journeying years,
Plod the last sands of life, where not a flower appears."
—BYRON.

THE young woman bearing the name at the head of this chapter was a beauty belonging to the middle-class of society, in 1867. Of her family antecedents and her own, suffice it to say that they are unexceptionably good. Her education was above the average for her class, and her manners were polished and attractive.

It was her misfortune to be introduced to Arnold Noel, after he fled from the impending consequences of crime committed in his native city, leaving his father to pay his bail.

This young scapegrace at once became desperately enamored of Josepha Del-Campano, and courted her with apparently enthusiastic sincerity. She fully reciprocated his passion.

The speedy result was that three or four of the young lady's intimate friends one day accompanied her on a little excursion into a neighboring State, where there was a quiet wedding.

The young couple then returned, to reside at the home of the bride.

For some time this young imp of Satan, Noel, was devoted and very attentive to his fondly-trusting wife, and supplied all the money requisite for her comfort; although she was all the time deceived as to what profession he followed and how he obtained his money.

He was connected with a band of thieves—the only genial calling or natural element for him.

At length he began to tire of the young woman. He absented himself for days together. Rapidly his true character began to develop. He often came home bearing unmistakable indications of dissipation.

The tears and the remonstrances of Josepha made no more impression on him than the wind blowing on the bald head of a granite-capped mountain.

One day he invited her to take a ride. He stopped in front of a house and conducted her into the parlor. There he introduced her to a man who he informed her would now be her lover, as he was going to leave her; and at the same time coolly stated to her that he had been no more than a lover, as their marriage was simply but a mock one, the pretending Justice of the Peace who performed the sham ceremony being one of his own accommodating associates. And thus without further ceremony he left her.

She feigned satisfaction, and thus was permitted to return home, in order to pack a trunk, which enabled her to delude and escape from the ruthless villain to whose fiendish care she had been consigned.

Deceived, disgraced, forever blighted, she grew hopelessly despondent for a time, and then rallied to a temper of rash desperation.

She arraigned Man under the charge of being the deliberate and willful perpetrator of her ruin, and she swore a desperate revenge on mankind.

She well knew the power of the spell that her fatal beauty might wield over the pliable hearts of men. And she madly, furiously, recklessly entered upon a career of horrible crime.

Thus are many of the most wicked and dangerous women goaded to desperation, deceived, lured, driven from paths of purity and the throne of honor, by the base treachery of mankind. Again, after they have made one misstep, the hard decrees of that society which yet bestows its greeting smiles upon their destroyers, preclude their return—they are outcast waifs forever.

CHAPTER LI.

THREE IN LIEU OF FOUR.

"And this is life: men come and go
And heed me not,
Forgetting all, I quiet rest,
By all forgot."
—M. A. BILLINGS.

THE failure of Garland Cloud to fulfill his part of the compact does not retard the New York enterprise with which his name was to have been most prominently associated. No delay is occasioned on account of his terribly caused absence from the post of duty which he had pledged himself to assume. There are some expressions of disappointment and regret; his name and signature are stricken from the articles of copartnership; the firm is promptly organized under the style of Oglethrop, Harman & Co., and commences business at the time originally specified, as though Garland Cloud had never been expected to be a member. Out of pure charity his name is not only expunged from all association which it bore with the firm, but it is not referred to in conversation. Thus it is that the man who would have been the moving spirit in the enterprise is rapidly forgotten.

Such is human nature, and a wisely ordered essential in its composition, that for the bereavement and the affliction entailed by death there is a mysteriously soothing antidote—Time; which, as a general rule, heals the wounds inflicted in the hearts of sorrowing friends, and even near and dear relatives, more speedily and effectually than any remedy relieves those sorrows caused by some quite comparatively trivial and temporal misfortune.

Wounds inflicted by death usually heal. But it is the broken heart severed by the dart of disappointed, baffled, or hopeless love that is incurable, for which sometimes there is no remedy. Such is a malady that the great healer, Time, often fails to cure or abate.

It is not, therefore, in the harmony of things for the death of Garland Cloud—no matter however horrible its nature is esteemed by his friends, —to interfere materially with their life-plans, nor long to retard their prosecution.

This seems to be a wisely ordered dispensation of Providence—that when any important person in any sphere of public life or duty is suddenly cut off by the relentless hand of the Destroying Angel, however indispensable his services may seem, there is always some one ready to supply his place; so that usually there is little or no detriment suffered by the interest involved under the care and direction of the dead, before he was swiftly deprived of life.

Such doctrine, however, fails to hold good in the case of more tender and endearing ties of life, where the loss of its fondest and most cherished object breaks the doting heart and leaves it to pine in silent and ceaseless sorrow, with no attainable relief but death, with its blissful quietude and endless repose.

To Garland Cloud, in the main at least, was due the foundation of the New York enterprise. But when he failed to appear to fill his place as the building architect, there were others to take the position he would have occupied; and the structure rose in stately magnificence, and perhaps as surely and rapidly as though he had remained as its creative and directing genius.

The combined capital of the firm is such as to give it an immediate and a high rating; and nothing in human shape may be more nearly perfect than the beautiful and unblemished character of its young, sober, energetic, intelligent and promising members. Every one at all familiar with it, predicts for this firm an enviably prosperous career. Perhaps it is fortunate that the shadow of Garland Cloud's blighting curse is destined never to cross the threshold of the door leading to the prospective counting-room of his admiring and confiding friends.

Had he remained, they might have become innocent victims, and been thus forced to partake with him, at least to a certain extent, of the bitter fruits of the indiscretions of his misguided and erroneous mistakes and misdeeds,

———

CHAPTER LII.

THE WOUNDED AND FORLORN DOVE.

*

" She is far from the land where her young hero sleeps!
And lovers are round her sighing;
But coldly she turns from their gaze and weeps,
For her heart in his grave is lying."
—MOORE.

CARRIE HARMAN is inconsolable. So long styled the angel of consolation herself; yet still for her there is no such being.

Little dreamed Garland Cloud of the cruel stab he would inflict in a true, devoted, loving heart whose pulsations vibrated for him alone, and thrilled at the sound of his name. He believed that she disliked him as cordially as he devotedly loved her. For this reason he deemed that his mad act would cause her no pang, otherwise than one of regret that she had ever known him.

How often, alas, misunderstanding or misconstruing each other severs the ties of love! This celestial passion is prone to be over-jealous, strongly inclined to skepticism whenever a guarded reserve essays to conceal the true emotions of the heart, to stifle the fondest sentiments and most ardent longings of the soul—that of declaring or confessing an unspoken love. Alas, that it should thus sometimes be rendered voiceless for evermore!

How frequently men love women almost to insane desperation, and construe the artful strategy of the fair enchantresses as cold and repulsive indifference, when in reality their smothered flame of affection contains more pent up devotion than ever convulsed the heart of an inconstant man. Deep motive sometimes prompts this baffling dissimulation: to prove the sincerity of the man who overwhelms the doubting girl with bewildering declarations of love; to rend the chain that binds her to less desirable entanglements in the subtle meshes of Cupid's luring snare, or to await the pending issue of more promising expectations. Most often, in all probability, the latter cause exercises the swaying influence by which the lady is actuated. It matters little, however, with the man, which motive controls the woman:

he is certain to conclude that she neither appreciates his passionate sentiment nor cares for him. Thus are many buds of love blasted ere they blossom; some hearts broken and left to pine with the blight of irretrievable woe.

To Carrie Harman, Charles Lorenzi and Walter Paulona are unbearable. Why this is so she, perhaps, could not explain. It is in all probability an instinctive aversion.

Poor Carrie! very soon after receiving the tidings that so cruelly wounded her, she leaves her father's roof and returns to the scenes of her childhood's home, and of her labors in dark and trying days of the near past—days to others no more dark and trying than these present are to her. Amid the bright faces of her former little protégés of the mountain, beaming with Nature's true smiles, she finds the one grain of comfort she is conscious of experiencing anywhere, under any circumstances, in any relation of life.

Numbers of young gentlemen seek to comfort her, but in vain. For more than two years she continues to mourn.

She hears from Gen. Cloud the story of the ancient curse of his family, and also of his warning to Garland on " the field of Gettysburg."

In Garland's farewell letter to his father he wrote: " I wish I could bequeath to Jesse Flowers all my vanished prospects and hopes."

Evidently the " prospects" were measurably, at least, of a commercial nature. But the "hopes"—ah! the hopes—to what or to whom did they relate? Beyond any question to Carrie Harman. To what other being could they relate? What other creature of earth, bearing the imprint of angelic beauty and heavenly grace, could cause the fountain of hope to spring in that arid sorrow-parched breast? To Garland Cloud, Carrie Harman was all the world. Without her, life was disrobed of its every charm.

For these reasons, what could be more natural, after he was obliged to regard her but as a vanished dream, to desire that she should become the life-jewel of Jesse Flowers? This young man was Cloud's dearest male friend. A better and truer young man could rarely, if ever, be found beneath a saintly sphere.

Because Garland Cloud thus esteemed and admired him, and desired that he should become the custodian, the protector and the comforter of poor, disconsolate Carrie, she, doubtless, was materially impressed with the conviction that duty to the memory of her vanished idol sternly required her to make that sacrifice on the shrine of love, should it ever be demanded. Thus influenced, she had nothing to do but wait, as she ministered to her fond charges through many mournful days.

Perhaps this emphatic declaration of Cloud, made on the dread confines of the "Nevermore," created a deep impression on the mind of Jesse Flowers. Certainly there was nothing more natural than for Carrie Harman to make a vulnerable impression on his heart, especially since there remained no visible barrier between him and her, to preclude him from entering and pressing the suit of love.

We may be permitted to imagine that Jesse contemplated this enterprise with misgivings. Well did he know the lofty esteem cherished by Carrie for him; yet he could but remember that it was simply the solicitous regard of a sister, and nothing more. Under these circumstances, we cannot deem it very wonderful that he permitted the months to go by and multiply, years before he ventured to speak of love.

Besides, the memory of Garland Cloud, as it was associated with Carrie Harman, doubtless inspired Jesse with a certain sense of awe: the terrible end of the absent adorer of the Angel of Consolation was sufficiently painful to deter this modest young gentleman from hurriedly seeking to occupy the void in the aching heart of the fair and silent mourner.

In the fall of 1869, Jesse Flowers visits his old mountain home. While in the dreamy dells of his childhood years, he, modestly doubting, sues for Miss Harman's hand. Whatsoever be the nature of the influence that decides her, it results in her consenting to return with him to New York—*his bride.*

CHAPTER LIII.

BUSINESS AND SOCIAL FLASHES.

" Commerce, friendship, love, all blend—
Weal or woe—all social ties but tend,
To bow at her shrine, and howsoe'er bold,
Yield to that winning goddess—Gold."
—ANON.

BUSINESS, society, love, and war are inseparably connected with and irretrievably subject to the influence and the power of money. Hence it is that business, which is ever esteemed and designed to be the greatest of all money-producing factors, is one grand social lever and creator. Business makes or mars society, in this latter-day acceptation of the term, according to the extent of its prosperity or the magnitude of its reverses.

The scale of social rank is, as a rule, measured and graded by the amount of money its members can lavish on all the appointments and equipages that make up the perfect rôle of brilliant and matchless display. As the full tide of prosperity rolls up its hoards of wealth, so is the social position of the fortunate advanced; while, as the ebb tide takes them away, so is the social status of the unfortunate diminished.

Let it be but known that a man is prospering rapidly, or that he has become a millionaire,—though the nature of his business is not such as the most scrupulous approve, and though many of the transactions from which he derives his wealth are of questionable repute,—still both he and his family receive the smiles of society, and their friendship is sought with eagerness, and assiduously cultivated.

But, on the other hand, if he has made heavy losses, is losing, is in a failing condition, or has already failed, all the world instinctively experiences a thrill of aversion for him and his.

The firm of Oglethrop, Harman & Co. prospers wonderfully. Business pours into it from all over the South, in one perpetual and ever-increasing stream.

Oglethrop's wife is so well known and prized as to be regarded a general favorite in society. Rosalia Harman, *née* Flowers, and Carrie Flowers, *née* Harman, formerly esteemed Angels of the

Mountain and of Consolation, are both soon her constant friends.

They, as a general rule, are for some time placed in the rather ostracized Southern element of society; and are, therefore, quite exclusive; and manifest the most serene indifference.

Cassandra Worthington, who is almost fanatically immersed in the cause and works of philanthropy, is also, as a matter of course, their friend. Together these four women become enlisted in the same cause, and work largely in direct concert with the Sisters of Charity—*Beatrice* and *Rosalind.*

The four ladies make a new departure as to themselves and their homes. They wear no jewelry, no extravagant nor superfluous apparel, nor do they administer their households but with the most modestly simple yet still comfortable economy. This enables them to contribute continually and liberally to the wants of suffering humanity, that they know personally to be both worthy and deserving of assistance.

Mrs. Worthington previously set the example in this direction by selling her handsome diamonds, with the cordial approbation of her husband, who values and appreciates people not by what they wear in the way of clothing or ornaments, and devotes their proceeds to the cause in which she has already engaged herself.

After this change in the course of his wife's life, Silas Worthington is a new man. Instead of leaving the uncongenial society of his wife, as it had been in the past, to attend a business meeting, or to meet a friend on business on an evening after dinner, he remains at home, or goes out with her; and both seem personified devotion and happiness combined.

In time, Rosalia Harman and Carrie Flowers became known and appreciated for themselves, everywhere in the compass of that social sphere where Cassandra Worthington and Evalina Oglethrop move.

The members of the firm of Oglethrop, Harman & Co., and their estimable and beautiful wives, are now basking in the salubrious and congenial smiles of fortune. With them the current of life has ever been more than comparatively smooth and cheerful for the times in which they lived. No great and terrible personal misfortunes have ever fallen to the lot of any one of them, except the heart-aches experienced by Carrie Harman for Garland Cloud and his sad end; and these, it seems, have yielded to the treatment of that great and mystic heart-healer—Time. There were no convents in the land where she dwelt, and she went to the mountain, and was healed.

The trials and the wrongs of the Flowers children had passed the climax of their bitterness during the tender years of the poor fatherless little ones; and the experience through which they passed after they arrived at the years of accountability, had tended to beautify their lives and to prepare them to shine in the paths of usefulness and honor.

The Harmans had lost much property by the war, but, nevertheless, do they now appear to advantage.

Oglethrop, and his jewel of a wife, have met no crosses.

Exempt from unmerciful disaster, and far removed from and shielded against the baneful influence and too often potent sway of temptation, these six young people should glide smoothly over life's ocean in peaceful serenity and blissful happiness; and this they will do, provided they do not draw the penalties of indiscretion, nor the retribution of crime upon themselves.

Had Effie Edelstein been a dowerless girl, Lawrence Pleasington's hopes and happiness would never have been shattered on her account. Seeking to win her as an heiress was neither an indiscretion nor a crime; but entailed a terrible misfortune.

Had Garland Cloud resisted the temptation to conceal something that properly and justly was no disgrace, he would be, with his former friends, useful, prosperous, and esteemed.

It is those who bear the relentless scourge of misfortune courageously, and pass through the fiery crucible of temptation unscorched, who are *truly beautiful.*

CHAPTER LIV.

THE LONELY MYSTERIOUS TRAVELER.

"In my youth's summer, I did sing of one,
The wandering outlaw of his own dark mind :—
Again I seize the theme but then begun,
And bear it with me as the wind
Bears the cloud onward."   —BYRON.

IN the winter of 1869–70, there is on a rail-road survey in the Louisiana lowlands a well dressed, peculiarly mysterious stranger; all alone, with the light field paraphernalia of a civil engineer, he is passing quietly along at the rate of twenty miles per day, on foot.

As to his business and himself, he is obstinately reticent wherever he takes refreshments at noon or lodges at night. At other times of the day he rarely ever speaks to any one, although he passes near numbers of people, sometimes right among hundreds of cotton-pickers, and through the main streets of large towns.

Just now there is considerable excitement about the building of the anticipated road, which has been long deferred; hence, therefore, many are the conjectures, and rumors are rife as to the object of this solitary individual; and the tidings of his coming travel before him.

The most current conclusion is that he is locating depots on the sly, and spying out the most desirable property, in the interest either of the company or of speculators, who will send secret agents to buy it quietly.

It is evident from the bronzed appearance of his face, that he has long been exposed to the vertical rays of a Southern summer's sun.

When within about forty miles of the terminus of the road, a Friday's noon finds him near the beautifully appearing mansion of an extensive cotton planter, nestling in a handsome grove on a high, gravelly knoll.

Being hungry, and seeing no other house ahead of him nearer his line of travel than this one, he turns aside to seek his dinner there, just as he has turned every day for the past week at other points, to other houses on his pathway.

Arriving at the gate he shouts loudly: "Halloo! "

Instantly the blustering old gentleman makes his appearance on the portico, and sings out, "Halloo yourself."

TRAVELER: "Can a tired, hungry man get dinner here, sir ? "

PLANTER: "Certainly; walk right in, sir. Be seated just a moment, while I go and have you a plate prepared, as we are now dining. All ready, sir, come in."

A young lady of the family has surrendered her place at the table, in order to make room for the new comer promptly. She is a beautiful, blooming, blushing, Southern rose; and her name is Manonia.

She takes a sly peep at the stranger through the aperture of a door slightly ajar, as he sits at the table. Then she glides into the parlor, seats herself at the piano, and plays the dreamy air of a Southern sentimental song, "The Broken Spell," singing one verse and the chorus with the thrilling pathos of a music-nurtured child of sunny Italy.

"Years I may spend still in pleasure,
But memory will cling to me yet,
There are feelings that words cannot measure,
There are tones that I cannot forget.

Vain are the vows we have plighted :
Would that we never had met ;
Love's a flower that blooms to be blighted,
And a star that rose but to set."

The dulcet notes of her voice echo through and die away in the large high rooms and halls, faintly but sweetly penetrating to the distant and closed dining-room.

She then rises from the instrument, takes up a peacock's-tail feather duster, and dusts the furniture as she soliloquizes:

"The same face of the stranger of whom I have so often dreamed, and awoke weeping. Yes, the same, plain as daylight.

"Well, from my stolen peep, I cannot see that there is any cause connected with him to weep over How very ridiculous! But that is just like dreams. In order to interpret, one must transpose them, and draw an inference opposed to what they appear to mean.

"But they are coming from dinner, and I must dust from here."

PLANTER: "And how do you manage to make a living, stranger, with but one hand?"

TRAVELER: "Oh, in various ways, sir. I can do all the head work of building a railroad. I am a merchant, and a thorough master of everything connected with commerce in the commission, or the general wholesale and retail business, and of the keeping of all the books of either line named. Could subsist as a book-keeper, was that the only show to live."

PLANTER: "Oh, then I can give you a handsome job. I have started my son in a large business at the town five miles from here, and I am exceedingly anxious to procure the services of a practical business man and book-keeper, to stay with, and train him for at least a year. What would you undertake the work for, by the year?"

TRAVELER: "About twelve thousand dollars, I I suppose, if I would undertake it at all, which would not do now."

PLANTER: "I reckon you don't lose much sleep about making a living. Oh, I remember now. You must be the man I heard of at town last evening. Are you not going over the survey of this railroad?"

TRAVELER: "Yes, sir; but in the most informal, careless manner."

PLANTER: "Oh, I understand it all now. Can you tell me anything concerning the road or its prospects?"

TRAVELER: "Absolutely nothing, sir. The company now negotiating for it will quickly build if they get it; but there seems to be interminable delays and all kinds of obstacles to prevent any successful issue of the enterprise."

PLANTER: "How long would it take you to teach a man to keep books, and would you teach a class, provided such terms as you might yourself propose were complied with?"

TRAVELER: "I could give a man a practical start and copious examples for his future guidance, in a month. I have never thought about attempting to teach, and at present I have not the time."

PLANTER: "I will pay you one hundred dollars, board and send you to town and back here every day, if you will teach my son; and I am sure you can get a good, large class. Will you stop long enough to ascertain?"

TRAVELER: "Impossible. I am on my way to take the contract to build a long and difficult bridge on the railroad beyond the river. I can leave you my address and will take yours; you can see your friends and write to me the result. I will then, if your letter warrants it, write and tell you if I have time to return and fulfill your engagement before the work on the bridge is ready for me to commence on it. Here is my address on this envelope. I must now be off. What is my bill?"

PLANTER: "Nube Garland. All right, Mr. Garland, thanks. I shall write to you very soon. Your bill is to call again should you ever pass this way. Say no more to me about pay. I wish you would stop over a few days; but since you will not, here is my address on this envelope."

GARLAND: "Eldred Donné. Thanks to you, Mr. Donné. I am exceedingly grateful to you for your generously proffered and hospitably extended kindness, and much regret my inability to comply with your wishes. Farewell."

DONNÉ: "Farewell, my friend. Much success to you."

Just as this man is passing out of the gate, he hears the old gentleman call his name, and turning, says: "Yes, sir; what do you wish?"

DONNÉ: "See here, Mr. Garland, this is Friday noon. You cannot reach your destination before Sunday noon, if you should travel on that day. Your road is both muddy and swampy. Stop over until Monday. To-morrow I can find out just what can be done. Monday, bright and early, I will start you behind a fast team that will land you at your destination before night, and that will bring you back the next day if you can return. Anyway, you will only lose a day and at the same time you will escape a slavish walk. From here on, there is not very much to be seen, and you cannot follow the survey half the distance, there is so much water in the swamps, and even on the bottom-lands, just now."

GARLAND: "That appears a fair and liberal proposition; but I would do you an injustice to accept it, because there is scarcely the shadow of a chance that I will ever return."

DONNÉ: "I will not feel harshly toward you if you do not, and still make you the offer with the distinct understanding that you are not to return."

GARLAND: "All right then, sir, I will remain. But look at those fine squirrels in that hickory tree. Have you a gun?"

DONNÉ: "Yes sir; but I never shoot, and you cannot."

GARLAND: "Give me the gun and I will soon show you."

DONNÉ: "Well, I never saw such shooting: four without missing; that is a fine mess."

GARLAND: "Then I will stop."

The ultimate result is the formation of a class, and its being taught by Nube Garland.

During the first two weeks, the old gentleman, who is an incessant talker, tells his guest all his own history, during the evenings between supper and the old planter's invariable nine o'clock hour for retiring.

He married at the early age of eighteen, and very soon thereafter inherited and amassed a handsome property in one of the old cotton States.

He indorsed largely for friends. The old bankrupt law went into operation, and they, to a man, took the benefit of it. He would not take such benefit; but instead, paid the obligations to the last dollar, and this reduced him to chill and pinching penury.

He is a powerful, muscular man; and he made it a point, after paying the last dollar—which he, did by raising two crops on rented land, and by driving hogs from Tennessee—to whip every man whose debts he had paid.

This resulted in thirty odd true bills of indictment being found against him at one sitting of the grand jury.

Finding it too hot, on account of this state of legal jeopardy, to be comfortable or safe, he migrated between two suns, to the "cany regions" of Texas; and, after there making a few crops, he then moved to Louisiana and settled in the woods on the spot where his house now stands.

He had one negro man, himself, and one boy large enough to work when he started his new home. With this small force he opened the land, and raised sufficient surplus cotton the first year to buy another land.

From this period his prosperity was rapid to a degree that the war found him the owner of hundreds of slaves, an immense plantation, and the most extensive store to be met anywhere in that section.

At the close of the war his slaves were gone; but he had several cotton crops on hand that yielded a very handsome fortune in gold.

He had then four living children, and he made each one of them independent by placing one-fourth of his war cotton as a dowry to each child.

The old gentleman himself then goes to work on the plantation, leading a gang of freedmen; continuing the year round, right along, one year after another.

He is a man of boundless ambition, and has, withal, a passion that is simply terrible when it is once thoroughly aroused. In his day he has been a carnate devil, and as wicked as the arch fiend could wish him. But he is ever, to some extent, restrained by the gentle influence of his meekly patient, angelically devoted wife.

Through her influence he finally professed religion and joined the church sometime previous to the war.

He is given to fits of despondency whenever the drouth or the cotton-worm is cutting short his crop; then he leaves his religion at home, goes to town and drinks too much. On these occasions he is specially ugly and disagreeable.

He has two sublime qualities, drunk or sober: the story of distress and want of the poor always moves him to compassionate kindness and liberal charity; and he is the soul of honor.

This man lives for his children. And at this period, two of them, the eldest, a son, the youngest, a daughter, have caused him much trouble by marrying contrary to his will; the son to his own cousin; the daughter to a young man who was raised, as the saying goes, "with a silver spoon in his mouth," but who is left, at the close of the war, "as poor as a church mouse," ignorant of all kinds of business and unused to work, having never in his precious life soiled his dainty hands with any class of labor, but kept them ever encased in delicate kids. In a word, he needs everything else in the world except a wife. He was too young to go to the war.

The other two children are single; the son, who is the merchant, and the daughter, who is at home—the exquisitely charming Manonia. This son is christened Eldred, for his father.

The third Sunday that the stranger has been there, the son comes home on a visit, when the following conversation occurs:

DONNÉ, Sr.: "Well, son, and how runs the business?"

DONNÉ, Jr.: "Tamely, father; too much credit. Everything is forever going out, and nothing coming in.

"That man Garland, who is teaching me book-keeping, says that nothing short of a mint of money can keep such a craft afloat, and that we have not got yet; still, he don't know it. But where is he?"

DONNÉ, Sr.: "Oh! out somewhere. He is a deep mystery to me. He courts not, but rather shuns our society. Is as polite and respectful as a dancing-master, which shows that his breeding has been refined. He will talk to me with fascinating eloquence about war, business, and railroads; but he has no word for women folks.— Does he know it all about books and business?"

DONNÉ, Jr.: "He does; and he is teaching me far more than he agreed to do. If I only knew all he knows, I could succeed.

"He is not sociable, and never converses with one of us on any subject outside of our lessons; and in this he is seriously earnest, and as solemn as a preacher.

"Manonia, were I here with him every evening, as you are, I would find out his history, which is, beyond question, a most romantic love story."

MANONIA: "Why, Eldred, the man has now been here more than two weeks, and in all that time he has never yet once deigned so much as to speak to me. He actually seems half-frightened whenever ma speaks to him at the table.

"Father has twice asked him about love experience, and he rather impatiently replied each time, 'Yes; I have been there;' and then he adroitly changed the subject. How can I break such Arctic ice?"

"He sits here alone, writing, or with his head resting on his hand, as if deeply immersed in thought, until midnight, and even later. Father goes early to bed, and I go to the dining-room. I am sure that were I to remain, he would instantly leave the parlor."

DONNÉ, Jr.: "He would show both your presence and your questions more respect than he does father's. Virginians are famous for chivalry and gallantry toward the fair sex. He is young, clearly manifests that he is temperate, and therefore, no matter what his sorrows or his disappointments may have been in the past, the romantic is perhaps slumbering in his soul, yet is not extinct. But there is his footstep in the hall. Speak of —— and his —— you know, will appear. So we will drop this subject."

MANONIA: "Yes; I think we had better discuss it no more, never."

CHAPTER LV.

UNFOLDING THE MYSTERY.

"He, who, grown aged in this world of woe,
  In deeds, not years, piercing the depths of life,
So that no wonder waits him; nor below,
  Can love or sorrow, fame, ambition, strife,
  Cut to the heart again with the keen knife."
                              —BYRON.

ON Monday night following the Sunday on which the conversation that terminated at the closing of the last chapter ensued, the man Garland occupies his customary seat at a table in the centre of Eldred Donné's grand parlor, with a lamp on the table, his back to the fire-place, in which there flickers a low, smoldering fire that reflects scarcely any light, between the hours of nine o'clock and midnight, writing as rapidly as the hand can drive the pen.

The house is as still as death, so that the ticking of the old eight-day clock in the dining-room sounds like the measured beat of a forge-hammer in perpetual motion. The night is oppressively dark, and a cold sleet-storm is moaning and howling outside.

The one lamp in the middle of the large old parlor is so dim, and lights the room so imperfeebly, that weird shadows are reflected on all sides; and the ancestral portraits with which the walls are profusely adorned, look down upon the strange man, or seem to look, so like veritable ghosts, that it makes him shudder to raise his eyes to look at them.

He is occupied writing examples and instructions for his class, and with the corroding canker of his own dark thoughts; which, evidently, are much of the time far away from the page of manuscript that is steadily and rapidly growing beneath his hand, and the room in which he is seated. Certainly, he has no heart there.

At least such is the conclusion of Manonia, who has stolen noiselessly into the parlor, and taken a seat in a darkly shadowed corner of the hearth with her knitting, after watching him more than two hours. She can observe him and knit at the same time. To her mind, she is witnessing a solitary performance of a highly wrought dramatic act; and so she is.

Sometimes he sings in a low, plaintively sad refrain the same lines over and over again, at intervals of some minutes, without checking the ceaseless scratch, scratch of the pen:

> "I have sailed 'neath alien skies;
> I have trod the desert path;
> I have seen the storm arise,
> Like a giant in his wrath;
> Every danger I have known,
> That a reckless life can feel,
> Yet her presence is not flown,
> 'And her bright smiles haunt me still.'"

At length he throws down the pen rather impatiently, and rests his forehead on the velvet-cushioned edge of the table for several minutes, breathing laboriously as if dozing; then, suddenly rousing up with a start, he soliloquizes aloud:

"Thou fairy image of blighted hopes, Angel of Consolation! Why haunt my solitary wretchedness, since we are severed for evermore?"

At this point he suddenly discovers the presence of Manonia, and, nonplussed with confusion, he ejaculates with stammering embarrassment:

"Oh! a thousand—oh!—pardon—Miss, I was not aware—my mind was straggling—I forgot—was quite unconscious of your presence at the

moment—must have been absorbed or dreaming and aroused up muttering. Don't be alarmed."

MANONIA: "No harm, sir. I should beg your pardon for being here; but the fire was out in the dining-room, and I came quietly in here, hoping not to disturb you."

GARLAND: "You owe no apologies for being in your own parlor, where you properly reign supreme its mistress. It is I that owe you apologies and penalties for having usurped its use. Treat my presence hereafter as though you were alone. Never quit your realm again because I am sitting here, either writing or thinking. Usually I am quiet. I will no more think aloud when you are here."

MANONIA: "Use the parlor as though you were at home. We are far down 'South in Dixie,' yet still we strive to show civil strangers who come among us, always the most cheerful hospitality that we can; and to extend to them our blunt, old-fashioned style of welcome."

GARLAND: "Stranger! civility! home!—what deep meaning these words impart! I have been so long among the rude and semi-civilized that I must be more strange than I am stranger, and strangely uncivil. I am informed that contact with madmen has made men mad.

"When I came under the shadow of this friendly roof, thirty months had then elapsed since I had uttered a word to a lady or womankind; hence it is no wonder that I am uncouth, and have lost my wonted politeness.

"Better days and brighter thoughts have been my lot.

"But pardon me, I am beyond the boundary of my proper sphere. These are things of no import. I will not allude to them, nor will I thus intrude upon your attention again any other subject."

MANONIA: "I pity you, sir; and am persuaded that it is a question replete with grave import to which you allude. My curiosity to know more of it is intensely excited; it must be romantic, and fraught with deeply thrilling interest. Please, sir, would you very much object to recounting it for me?"

GARLAND: "It has never been breathed to mortal ears; and I have always intended that it never should escape my lips. At this moment, such is still the state of my inclination. I can assure you that in it there is not one iota of interest for you; and it would be painful to me to relate.

"But before explicitly answering your question, tell me, please, did I speak intelligibly loud just now?"

MANONIA: "You did, sir, as clearly and as distinctly audible as you do even now. That little sentence is what has most tended to arouse my curiosity!"

GARLAND: "Then you have a clue that is the key to my story, but for which nothing in this world could induce me to narrate it, because in doing so the pity which you now generously cherish for me will vanish, to give place to a sentiment of contemptible abhorrence. At all events, however, I will not confide it to you, only on the express condition that you give me your most sacred promise not so much as to hint it to any one until after I am gone."

MANONIA: "I most solemnly promise not to divulge it even after you are gone, should you so prefer; and I further promise that my feelings of pity shall not abate because of the story being an unpleasant one to yourself.

"I am now all impatience to hear a real life-picture romance. I have always heard that truth is often stranger than fiction."

GARLAND: "Very well, then, if this story must ever be told, there is rarely a more appropriately fitting time for its disclosure than to-night, when the war and wails of the elements are distressing nature—in strikingly sympathetic accord with the war of the narrator's life with the tempest-lashed waves of Time, and the storm of emotion that will surge in his breast while the slumbering mystery is unfolding from its long and silent sleep.

"Nerve yourself, Miss Donné, to hear some shocking recitals; if as shocking to you as they are painful to me, I much fear that your anticipated pleasure may but prove a mocking disappointment.

"As you know, from the tenor of my inadvertant disclosure a few moments ago, there is a lady connected with it; and you are aware that without a lady the story would be wholly di-

vested of every semblance of the romantic. I tell you that it would not exist.

"You have heard me telling your father about my war engendered enemies and my business career since the war. The relation the lady in question bore, both to the machinations of those bitter, unscrupulous, unprincipled enemies and my future mercantile plans and prospects at that time, is what sent me aimlessly adrift on the great and boisterous ocean of life, to be driven and buffeted as a weed by its waves; and doomed me to the hard and pitiable fate of being an orphan of the heart for evermore.

"Those enemies realized that this was my only vulnerable point, and assailed it with fiendish vengeance. I loved this adorable young lady with zealous devotion, and I believe now, that she reciprocated my passionate fondness.

"My enemies perverted truth, and concocted the most damnable and black conspiracy ever conceived by a Satanic mind—far more terrible than the swiftly dispatching dagger of the assassin, because it inflicted a cureless wound of lingering and horrible torture.

"Had I not loved this girl, or had she alone, among all the others whose friendship and esteem had vanished, stood firm and confidingly unshaken in her faith, I would have defied the whole crew, and shown for their malicious attack a disdainful contempt.

"But, alas! the curse of vanished centuries was upon me.

"My faithful confidential clerk and a Christian merchant wrote me a joint letter, bearing the despairing intelligence of the thoroughly complete revulsion of public sentiment unanimously against me.

"This pictured, the hopeless estrangement from me of the friendship of the young lady's family, which declared was so vindictively bitter that the old gentleman who was by many years my oldest friend in that section of country, and perhaps the most devoted, personally, that I had in the world, would not so much as condescend to write to me on the subject; but that he had suggested that my own confidential man was in duty bound to write me, and the merchant had from a charitable impulse, voluntarily joined him.

"They informed me, in the concluding paragraph of their letter, that while they were disposed to build a more liberal construction out of the affair for me, than any other person in the community, still the circumstances were of such a nature as to preclude the possibility of their ever again recognizing me.

"They therefore advised me to have my affairs settled by an attorney; and for the sake of my own feelings, never to return again to where naught but the grave of my hopes would be found.

"Nothing—not one faint gleam of the semblance of hope—remained for me on the face of the earth after I had read that heart-rending letter.

"This drove me almost mad. For me, the world had come to a sudden end. Promptly, overcome by despair, I resolved to seek the only refuge left me: the friendly shelter of the rippling, peaceful river.

"I made a power of attorney to the merchant just referred to, authorizing him to have my business wound up, and my earthly affairs settled; and with this I sent a large sum of money by express to pay off any unsettled balance due my patrons, together with other definitely explicit instructions, and wrote a few, hasty farewell letters.

"When all was accomplished, I remembered that I had a balance of some five hundred dollars in the hands of a firm in the city, which had escaped my mind while making up my documents. I went and drew it; but there was some delay, so that the train passed before I could get it ready; and I left it at the express office to go the next day. Then I returned to my hotel, and packed and labeled my trunk for shipment.

"At this time, the sun was nearly down. I then at once set out to wend my way to some lonely spot on the river below the city, to seek a watery grave.

"Just as twilight was beginning to drape the earth and the water with her shadowy mantle, while I was in a dim pathway in a dense forest, rapidly approaching the river bank, some children who lived a little way down the river, overtook me.

"A bright, talkative little girl of the party wanted to know if I was going to their house; and when informed that I was not, she promptly told me that I was lost, as there was no road beyond their house—nothing but wild, precipitous crags and cliffs.

"She then told me a story about a man, who, she said, had drowned himself in the big, deep bend of the river just ahead of us, and that the Devil had carried his soul away to the bad place, because the preacher said that whoever kills himself is doomed to torment.

"The words of this guileless child knelled on my wretched heart, and I faltered and wavered; then softly told the child that I was taking a walk, and must turn and hasten back to the city, or darkness would overtake me.

"Up to the moment that I had met these innocent children, I had only thought of escaping from the intolerable miseries of this life, and not of those to which I would be flying in the dark Unknown. Since they aroused my mind to a reflective realization of the horrible step I was taking, it appeared a thousand times more appalling and terrible than all the multiplied and combined ills of earth, whether real or imaginary, could possibly be; and my resolution was to fly, fly—where, I knew not, cared not, if it was but away from all places, all scenes, and all people, where and to whom I had ever been known.

"I hastened back to the city, to my room, and snatched up my shawl; then to the express office, and withdrew the money package before mentioned; then to a dark alley, where I wrapped myself in my shawl, pulled my hat down over my eyes, and then hurried to the depot, arriving barely in time to board a South-bound train, from the dark side opposite the depot.

"I paid my fare to a junction about one hundred miles distant; crouched down in a dark corner, and was not again disturbed. Arrived at the junction, I bought a through ticket to the farthest possible Southern point, and continued the journey uninterruptedly.

"Very soon thereafter I found myself in a yellow-fever-plague-stricken city; where it was almost impossible to bury the victims of that scourging epidemic, so terribly rapid and frightfully numerous were the cases of mortality. I deemed this cause more worthy of my life than the river, and plunged into it to aid the suffering in every way in my power; and exposed myself day and night with reckless indifference for more than two months, without feeling at any time at all physically indisposed.

"From that point onward you have heard my story : the voyages to Mexico and South America; the hide trade, and the railroad-building in which I have been engaged up to the day of my arrival here.

"From the moment I entered the car, the first night of my flight, up to this night, not one familiar object or face has ever greeted my eye, and all who ever knew me deem me the victim of suicide. Ere now I have been long since forgotten.

"Oh that all the people and memories of the past were only as dead to me as I am to them. Heaven alone knows my vainly silent struggles to consign these sadly bitter memories to sombre oblivion and never-awakening forgetfulness! But go where I will, do what I may, the ghostly shadows of the past haunt me still, haunt me ever.

"This is the substance of my story, the source of my sorrows. If the details on any special point are not sufficiently explicit to satisfy your curiosity, you are at liberty at some future time, opportunity serving you, to question me.

"The clock has just tolled the hour of one; now is the time that ghosts are abroad, and that we should not be here."

MANONIA : "Mercy, how late it is! How thankful I am for the courtesy you have accorded me in narrating this story, that so closely borders on the terrible and the tragic. It has aroused in my nature a deep and sympathetic interest.

"I trust that our strange acquaintance may not prove unpleasant to you during the remainder of your sojourn with us, and so I must say good-night. Oh, Mr. Garland, I am so sorry for you ! "

GARLAND : "Good-night. May my story not disturb your dreams."

Left alone, he continues to soliloquize as follows:

"Guileless innocence ! winning witchery ! fairy enchantress ! Unschooled in coquettish arts—a novice in the icy formalities of the cold-hearted duplicity of the giddy social world, Nature's own child of the open heart's best, ever true and pure impulse ! Deep black eyes, more to be dreaded than the frowning battlements of Gibraltar, and more irresistible ! Directed against a defenceless heart, it could but become their helpless prey.

"But my heart, had I one, would be unmoved alike by the emotions of hope or the tremors of dread. Poor, lone wreck of the past! wretched, sick, riven! Hopes may spring and perish in thy fountainless desert without provoking one pang of disappointment or one sigh of regret.

"Until the last few hours arrived with their strange events, I have been obstinately resolved to avoid this simple child of Nature. But why deny her amusement, if such there be for her in my narrative? Surely it would be most disagreeable in me to withhold this innocent diversion when I can accord her whatever pleasure she may derive from it, knowing who and what she is, without forgetting who and what I am. The gulf separating our spheres is as impassable as that dividing heaven and earth. Hers, purity, innocence, and truth; mine, deceit, concealment and falsehood—even to my very name. I would start at its merely true echo as at the blast of the Archangel's trumpet. I made my life, without valid cause, a false nature, that has since been transformed into an endless curse.

"Her impressions can be naught but the passing thought of the moment, mine but the cold indifference of my frozen existence. Away hence with these insane musings."

This poor remorse-scourged, conscience-stricken wretch bows his head, overcome by the subtle influence of the stupefying spell that suddenly thrills his being as the ethereal form of an evil spirit approaches him, and speaks to the helpless, half-dreaming ear:

"Hesitating, ambling hypocrite. It is not in thy anatomy to serve Heaven's exacting King; still with my brand of falsehood decking thy brow, thou seekest to rebel against allegiance to my power.

"A flickering spark of respect for the Nazarene hath twice, through His agencies, stayed thy murderous hand, raised to destroy thyself. Thou wast forewarned of the affliction thou wouldst cause others, and the bitter wretchedness of thy own lot, didst thou continue to live.

"If thy loyalty must be retained by strategy, thy restless ambition and false position suffice. Go forth and prosper. Thy identity is oblivion. This fair daughter of Grace will love thee, will be thy foundation and spring to wealth. It wert well for thee to secure the peaceful sweets of life, and cease to roam aimlessly over the earth. Her eyes shalt soften thy stubborn heart, her charms tame thy stern will, so obdurately steeled against their alluring spell. Softly, unconsciously, but steadily and surely, will they find their way into thy being. Thou desireth peace, honor, purity—they bide thy pleasure.

"When thy star is in its ascendency and the sun of glory is shining brilliantly around thee, we will meet again. If then found obdurate and vacillating, disdaining to obey the dictates of thy ambition, pride wilt rouse thee to action.

"This child of Heaven wilt tame thy fierce nature, but only to store greater reserves of wrath against thee: for unto all others, with continued disobedience to my will, shalt be added the curse of her wrongs.

"Serve me truly and faithfully, and all shalt be well with thee on the earth. Seek to rebel against, and attempt to fly from my service, and the bitter fruits of the past have been but the diluted essence of those thou shalt ever pluck, inflicting miserable torture, as the inevitable consequences of disobedience. Be wise, and escape them. Until then, adieu!"

GARLAND: "Thank Heaven, it is but a dream! The horrid nightmare conjured into shadowy visions by the vivid recollections of the by-gone time, ever fresh and present memories, as undying as their wounds in my heart are cureless, provoked but to bleed afresh, by recalling and repicturing their sadly woeful scenes.

"Vain and idle dreams! Your colors of more bitter afflictions have no terrors for me, your flattering illusions of happiness no charms. Between me and this fair Southland flower there is not, never can be, affinity. Rather than make one advance in the direction even of attempting to gain her

most indifferent esteem; yes, rather than so much as consider it seriously, I would suffer my remaining arm to be severed from my battle-scarred body.

"Cruel delusions of the sad past! I have not forgotten thy bitterly deceptive, heart-wringing pangs, that I should permit anything on earth, however alluring, to tempt me into betraying innocent purity, with the hope-blasting phantom of a spectral and shadowy love, was such vile baseness within the bounds of possibility.

"No; a thousand times no! Neither this most beautiful creature, nor any other fair daughter of earth shall ever behold me in any light sufficiently amiable to enlist even so much as a mere passing sentiment of cordial friendship.

"This is my resolution despite the dreams of day or the nightmare visions of darkness.

What! I the blighter of womanly happiness, to gratify the selfish cravings of an empty heart, famishing for unattainable peace? NEVER! NEVER!! NEVER!!!

CHAPTER LVI.

THE IMPRUDENT WOOING.

" When she had spoken, I turned to go away,
But the sweet little creature, she bid me to stay;
She said that she was lonely—her heart it would break—
Her voice—'twas so lovely, her hand I did take."
—SWEET EVELINA.

THE days come and go, while Garland's engagement hastens to its close.

Each night, one after the other, finds him at his usual post and occupation, with patient Manonia always at hers, in the corner with the traditional knitting.

In her opinion he is rudely taciturn and morose, but in replying to her questions, to which he always replies with polished politeness and truly refined courtesy. But still, this fact notwithstanding, she experiences an embarrassing delicacy in asking questions or introducing conversations, when the man is incessantly at work, as he always is until long after that hour when stern propriety forces her to bid him good-night. She deems him icy indifference; unemotional selfishness, and utterly devoid of appreciation.

During the last week of his sojourn, as then contemplated, he is invited to the wedding of one couple and to the festival of another couple. It is so arranged, that in each instance it is necessary for him to accompany Manonia. And such is the position in which he is placed, that no man not an utter stranger to chivalrous gallantry, can decline without incurring the stigma of being a morose boor.

The wedding is five miles from the Donné plantation.

Time: early candle-light.

The supper is over, and at about ten o'clock the guests begin to disperse.

When Garland and Manonia are ready to take their leave, it is ascertained that the horse which he rode has slipped the halter, and quietly departed home without a rider.

This necessitates Garland, or rather he accepts it as the inevitable, to walk back in front of Manonia's horse, a feat which he performs so swiftly and so very cheerfully that the young lady cannot restrain herself from expressing enthusiastic applause.

The evening after the wedding, Manonia is at the store when Garland is ready to set out for the plantation. As a matter of course, they ride out together.

The next evening, Garland and Manonia are returning to the plantation from the festival just about sunset. When some two miles from their destination, Garland's leg, a little above the knee strikes a snag that tears his pantaloons down to the hem at the bottom.

This circumstance so embarrasses him as to provoke Manonia to tease him on account of, as she styles it, such an insignificant trifle; too ridiculous to be confused by, since he could not have avoided this unexpected accident.

On the evening following the festival, and the last but one that Garland ever expects to spend at the Donné homestead, he returns from the store to the plantation again with Manonia. The last two miles of the ride is through a frightful storm of wind, and in deluging torrents of cold pelting rain.

After supper, Garland excuses himself to the old planter, and proceeds at once to his writing, which he designs to finish that night. From the moment that he takes up the pen until half-past nine o'clock, he utters a single word to no one; nor does the customary voice of Manonia greet his ear, who he imagines has retired in consequence of the drenching she has received. At the hour mentioned, his work is completed, and he throws down the pen, exclaiming:

"Thank God this loathsome, monotonous task is done."

MANONIA: "And you have finished your labors, have you, Mr. Garland?"

GARLAND: Oh, yes; at last, Miss Donné, they are completed. They have been very irksome and excessively slavish, because I have performed the manual part of them in just one-third of the time they justly demanded.

MANONIA: "Oh, yes, sir, you have worked hard and constantly. I have often wondered how you could endure it so long and incessantly."

GARLAND: "Ah, Miss Donné, this has become a second nature with me, to work unremittingly whenever I have the opportunity. But this experience of teaching I shall never repeat again I have had enough of it to last me all my days.

"What a fearful night without! How piteously, lonely, and plaintively sad is the moaning and the groaning of the wind. It is on a night such as this that I always think of the poor tempest-driven crews, far, far at sea."

MANONIA: "Such nights are fearful on land; on the sea they must be indescribably terrible. I shudder to think of a ship full of people at the mercy of an angry sea."

GARLAND: "The buffeting waves of Time on the sea of life, when the winds are adverse and boisterous, are yet still worse; for I have experienced both to an ample degree, and am, therefore, able to arrive at a fairly correct conclusion. With the wild raging of a tempest-lashed ocean is, in my mind, closely allied the idea of a life tossed hither and thither over the earth, by the all-impelling heavings of the cruel waves of unmerciful disaster. From the one I am ever unable wholly to dissever the idea of the other; I deem the affinity of both as being to each other so inseparably connected."

MANONIA: "This much reminds me of that other wild night on which you told me the sadly impressible story of the great trial and bitter disappointment of your life.   ·

"Your sojourn with us now draws speedily to a close. One evening more, and we will no longer see you sitting there at that table, writing as if for dear life; nor hear the sound of your voice again, softly humming some sad refrain.

"One week hence, and we will not engage so much as one mere passing thought of yours. Alas! what a pity that in this short life, we make agreeable acquaintances, only to part with them soon and forever."

GARLAND: "Yes, Miss Donné, my duties close here to-morrow. I must hasten to others. But when and wherever I go, I shall bear with me grateful and pleasing memories of the kind hospitality so generously extended to me beneath this friendly roof, that will live many days—yes, years hence.

"Parting with friends, old or new, when we feel assured that it is to meet again nevermore, is painfully sad. With regretful reluctance have I parted from acquaintances of an hour, years ago, and shall forget them entirely—never. Hence you perceive from this circumstance how impossible it will be for me to forget this kind family.

"But, by the way, last evening you said that to-night you would volunteer me some sound advice."

MANONIA: "So I did promise, and am ready to perform. I advise you to go back at once and seek the girl whom you loved so much, or some other one; marry, and settle down. Briefly and pointedly, this is my advice."

GARLAND: "Such counsel is more easily proffered than followed. As to my lady-love of yore, she is as dead to me as though she was all this time peacefully sleeping in the gloomy churchyard. We are severed forever.

"True it is that I might seek, and, after long and patient years of cultivated acquaintance, engage the affections of a lady suited to my fancy, before I had told my story, but certainly not after. And if not related until after securing esteem, then that favorable sentiment would quickly vanish.

"I have neither the inclination, the patience nor the time requisite to undertake and pursue so delicate an enterprise; and, furthermore, I do not intend ever again to recount my painful story. Thus you see how utterly impossible it would be for me to follow your advice; for which I am, nevertheless, gratefully thankful to you."

MANONIA: "All this is purely imaginary; would rarely prove to be a true reality. My advice is good, sound, and practicable."

GARLAND: "I readily grant you all but the practicability.

"I shall never return to that region which was the location of my sad scenes of the past; hence, in order to follow your advice it would be necessary for me to sue for the hand of some fair stranger.

"Years are likely to dawn and wane, as the ceaseless gliding-wheel of Time unerringly makes its never-varying revolutions, before I am again as much acquainted with another young lady as I am now with yourself.

"Just imagine, merely for the sake of argument, that you were yourself placed in that unenviable predicament: then recall my dark chapter, as detailed to you, and you can but vaguely appreciate the position of the hapless fair one whom you have advised me to victimize."

MANONIA: "I am not in her place, and hence am unprepared either to make or imagine an answer for her."

GARLAND: "Then imagine yourself in her place, and we will continue the argument."

MANONIA: "No, sir; that is a position in life that I cannot occupy by imagination, but must be solicited to fill it."

GARLAND: "Well, then, I will, in order to humor the current of the argument, and to drive you from an erroneous position on untenable ground, solicit you to occupy her position, and to answer for her. That is sufficiently pointed."

MANONIA: "The question would have to assume a more earnestly serious form, on your part, before I entertain it."

GARLAND: "With the same seriousness, then, if you please, as your own sentiment could possibly be, relative to the same question."

MANONIA: "Then, in that case, I will assume the argument."

GARLAND: "Well, then, Miss Donné, could you, under all the circumstances, after a fair degree of acquaintance, so much as barely entertain the idea of becoming my wife?"

MANONIA: "I could, without hesitation, provided you promise never to take me far away from father and mother."

GARLAND: "But you can't mean it. You say this merely to sustain your argument in support of a false doctrine."

MANONIA: "I mean it in good, quiet earnestness, if your question means the same."

GARLAND: "Your heart and hand, and the seal of the first kiss of love!"

MANONIA: "Yes."

GARLAND: "Why, Miss Donné, you must be rashly dreaming! Consider well what you are doing, before plunging into the darkness—a step of which you will surely repent, and a vow from which you would, after due deliberation, plead for a release. You should know a husband long and well."

MANONIA: "Marriage is a lottery of life. I know you about as well as it is possible for a single girl to know a man. Those whom I have long known and esteemed as being ideal models of perfection, have proven sad failures as husbands, and rendered miserable the lives of the poor, confiding girls who thus rashly intrusted their happiness to their keeping."

GARLAND: "But, my dear young lady, reflect a little. I am both nameless and heartless, well calculated to render a fair, a hopeful life such as yours, miserable with the most cruel pangs of bitter disappointment. I am not an object worthy of a pure and priceless affection, such as yours would be; nor am I able to reward it with that reciprocally deep, true, and unblemished devotion which it would demand and expect, and for which the unquenched thirst of a pure and loving heart would ever pine in vain.

"That day, when it would have been possible for me to scatter some roses among the keen thorns of life, to cheer and gladden its dreary, trial-beset, sorrow-incumbered pathway for some true, affectionate, pure and good woman, has gone by. You would but waste your young affections and lavish your heavenly concentrated love on the spectral phantom of a most bitterly cruel delusion.

"I should, with all the debilitated force of the shattered fragments of my once strongly impetuous and bravely ennobled spirit, strive to render your life happy, and to reward your devotional sacrifice, made for a wretched man, with that blissful comfort for which all hearts sigh with longing fondness—but, alas, only in vain! Earthly happiness and I are hopelessly estranged; with me it will nevermore dwell. And the ghostly shadows of the past that haunt me forever, would darken and distress your life, for they are contagious blighters of all hope-springing consolation.

"Again, there is another serious question for our consideration. This union could be thought of only as an affair of the future. Should I embrace it, and was it once again to rekindle in my heart one flickering spark of long-extinguished hope, during the long absence before the probational time would elapse, while the little bird was singing in my partially re-animated heart its delusive song of hope, in the lonely railroad camp, you would slowly but surely repent of this rashly precipitate act. My heart's softened incrustation would once more be subjected to the torturing cauterization of the searing iron, and receive in its crushed and mangled mass one more wound to bear with me in still, cold, unmurmuring, bloodless silence. Imagine, reflect on all this. as it must transpire."

MANONIA: "There is no necessity for you to go on the railroad again. You have an opportunity to engage in business here. You can go, and arrange your railroad affairs and return in three or four days. For more or longer absence there is no need.

"Then we can often see each other during the season of probation which we may deem appropriate to adopt. In the meantime, I shall strive to dispel your fears, and prove to your satisfaction that I am not only a most violent detester of, but also an utter stranger to, fickle inconstancy.

"My first love was blasted on the bloody battle-field. For that true and devoted one, I have

MANONIA.

"POOR MANONIA AWAKES WITH A START, WEEPING AS THOUGH HER TENDER HEART WOULD BREAK."—See page 201.

now mourned longer than you have mourned for your lost idol. I never expect you to love me as you once loved her, nor can I love again as I did once. On this point there should be between us a mutually consonant sympathy.

"I see in you a noble manliness going to destruction, and merely because you see proper to estrange yourself from the social world. You can yet be saved and won back to life and hope, and I can render you cheerful and happy."

GARLAND: "Then you shall be my divine genius, come weal or come woe! I am going to take you at your word. By the stage to-morrow night I will go, and cancel my railroad engagements, and return at once, to await the time when I shall consummate one with you, my volunteer guardian angel! Now then, that fair hand and sacred seal."

MANONIA: "There, my word is pledged. Now while you still hold my hand, promise me on the sacred honor of a gentleman that you will return and faithfully fulfil this life- and hope-depending engagement with me."

GARLAND: "I certainly will. Though false to myself and all the world besides I will strive to be true and faithful to you."

MANONIA: "That suffices. Now pray excuse me. Good-night."

GARLAND: "Good-night, fair angel of the South, good-night.

"Heaven defend you, poor confiding child of Nature's own sweet innocence! You are betrayed, deceived, and have bartered away your pure life's happiness for a shadowy skeleton of ill-fated, hope-wasting delusion, the treacherous offspring of mere mythical dreams. Madly have you plunged from the giddy summit of the precipice, down, deep down the yawning abyss into the fathomless gulf of unending despair. I lured you not. I desired not, do not desire, this very strange complication.

"Oh ye shadowy powers, controlling my ill-starred destiny, bear me witness, that, in order to have it not thus, I would part with my remaining arm! It would be more honorable, yes, ten thousand times more honorable to break this vow, that should be sacred, than consummate it, and thus make and help along the burning shame to which it tends, and the untold ills to which it must inevitably lead.

"Doubtless but few men are worthy the hand she throws away on a nameless wretch. Who could love angels, must fondly love her. But what is, whatever can be my love but the poisonous breath of pestilential, hope-blighting destruction? Ah! the bitter ashen-cored fruit of the Dead-sea shore; tempting perhaps to the eye, but full of and laden with contagious bane, that will sap and dry up the healthful current of her peaceful, confiding soul. Alas! alas! What have I done? What must I do? What can I do?"

The night before the one on which Garland is to return from his trip, to cancel his railroad engagements, poor Manonia, whose day-dreams are replete with ecstatic anticipations of future bliss, sleeps peacefully on her couch of spotless white—though less white and pure than her own guileless life and innocent heart. As she thus sleeps in dreams, an Angel of Mercy appears by her bedside and speaks to her:

"Gentle child of earth, lend thy pure spirit's ear to a voice of warning in mercy sent unto thee. Beware of the stranger whom thou hast most imprudently enshrined in thy innocent heart; and escape while yet there is time, ere thou awake, as thou must and shalt, from thy dream of bliss to find it but a dreadful woe, that wilt sorely grieve thee, and for which thou shalt weep most bitterly. He desireth to let thee go free."

Poor Manonia awakes with a start, weeping as though her tender heart would break.

MANONIA: "What horrid dreams! How for my love I have wept, and saw my future life full of misery. I wonder if he will come back to-morrow, or will he never return? Away, idle dreams and despicable doubts! He will come: all will be well· I will be happy.

"Though angels and men revile, still will I trust him with an unshaken, steadfast and abiding faith —as true and constant as the rocks that all the ocean's fury cannot shake, as firmly abiding as the everlasting hills!"

————

CHAPTER LVII.

THE WANDERER'S PRIZE IN THE LOTTERY OF LIFE.

"Oh beauty! fatal beauty, that could lure,
    The sons of Heaven from their blissful sphere,
To earth, sin, flood—the wrath of God t'endure—
    Who turn'd not from that doom, when warn'd from
    here.
        *   *   *   *   *   *
Beauty is but a vain and doubtful good,
    A shining gloss that fadeth suddenly;
A flower that dies when first it 'gins to bud,
    A brittle glass that's broken presently."
                            —SHAKSPEARE.

NUBE GARLAND, as he is known to the Donné family, returns promptly, and in strict compliance with his solemn vow made to the strangely infatuated Manonia.

We say that he returns. Yes, he returns, fully resolved to undo the part thus far wrought toward the consummation of a seriously complicated mischief and an inestimable wrong.

In his own mind, he is fully prepared to tear himself rudely away from her, in the event that he is unsuccessful in prevailing on the young lady to put the affair in the great and promiscuous category of idle jests.

While he is a man, agreeable to his own story as related to Manonia, who has been guilty of a terrible indiscretion which clearly demonstrates a very lowly ebbed moral courage, that consigns him to pass his days under the dark shadows of the cloud of a life-long and unavailing regret, he is not hopelessly dead to the keen sensibilities of the finer and more ennobling impulses of a nature constitutionally exalted and true. He knows, feels and appreciates to the fullest and most terrible extent, the all-crushing weight of the burden of his own curse, which he deems will but prove the sure and inevitable despoiler of the peace and joy of Manonia's pure and faith-abounding life. For himself, he realizes a deep sense of the unmistakable consciousness that nothing earthly can ever impart so much as the most transient and fleeting ecstasies of true and substantial happiness; and that, therefore, it will be both a moral and a physical impossibility for him to bestow on any one aught but wretched misery.

This sad fate he most earnestly desires that Manonia shall escape; and he shudders at the gloomy contemplation of the stern ghost of her ever-approaching yet never-ending, afflicting disappointments, that is certain to haunt both himself and her. To avoid this, furthermore augments his anxiety to disentangle her, and free himself from the meshes of Cupid's ingeniously designed net; which it is almost beyond the latitude of doubt, was set by the young lady herself, either unwittingly or willfully.

As to Manonia, she is too pure, too innocent and good; too deeply imbued with the confiding, joyous, rapturous quintescence of nature, in the primeval beauty of its unsullied endowment even to heed the admonitory dreams of suspicion, although whispered in dulcet strains by an angel of light. How, then, may she be expected to doubt with her open eyes, especially when that doubting must run contrary to the fondest yearnings of her tender heart?

Descended on her mother's side directly from the good, olden-time primitive Quakers of North Carolina, and on her father's side from a clear-blooded Scotch-Irish line,—to which many traditional superstitions inherent with both nations from which it sprung still cling with tenacious obstinacy; from the peculiar religious tenets of the one side, and the strangely superstitious faith of the other,—she imbibed the idea—firmly, immovably fixed is it in her mind as an infallible doctrine—that in the lottery of life, for each man and each woman there is a mate—a connubial mate—styled "the right one"; and that if they will but patiently bide the time, one will at last appear; the two will finally meet and recognize each other; and some circumstance, however trifling it may be in appearance, will, notwithstanding the absurdity of the confidence, ultimately lead on to the destined result of their union.

Garland struggles persistently for a time, but struggles in vain, to persuade the young lady that it is impossible for him to regard the affair in any other light but that of a mere jest—a simple, pastime flirtation on her part; or that it will be necessary for him to make an Eastern business trip before engaging in permanent co-partnership with her brother.

She believes that he is her fate-ordained life-companion, and resolves to hold him firmly to the responsible post of liability to which he committed himself. He is truly compromised, and finds himself, at last, without one single expedient of an honorable character, by which it may be at all possible to extricate himself from that position.

And, as if to multiply his already distressing embarrassment, he begins most sensibly to experience unmistakable indications of the certainty that he is rapidly passing under the supreme influence of the all-controlling power of her magnetic spell, which with him fast becomes irresistible.

Less and less strongly grows his resolution to tear himself violently away from the luring fascination and witchery of her sway. At first he hesitates, then, after a second protracted interview, he wavers; and, finally, in three or four days, he abandons the idea of flight altogether, and unconditionally surrenders, with a fairly firm resolution to devote his life to the fair woman who declares that she is going to save him; to deliver him from the burdensome oppression of remorse beneath which he groans; to redeem him from the perdition of despair in which he is plunged; and to win him back again to the blissful felicity of peace, hope and love. What beautiful philanthropy! How divinely charitable! Generous, guileless, matchless, but misguided Manonia!

We are told by the highest authority ever recorded on earth, that beauty of the daughters of the most wicked and perverse men in the worst age of the world, attracted the sons of God—as it would seem, under a liberal construction of the testimony—from even, perhaps, their stations in glory, or unquestionably from what was much the same; birth-right heritages to such stations, could the allusion have been to men, not angels. Can it then be a theme of wonder that an earth-born child of Heaven, endowed with all the perfectness of Beauty's charms and Grace's smiles ever inherited by flesh and blood, should win such a sin-stricken son of Earth from his benighted, rayless sphere so far beneath her own?

Had it been within the harmony of possibilities for seeds of falsehood to produce and bring to perfection pure fruits of truth; had Garland stood forth under true colors, with nothing concealed beneath the thick veil of his then impenetrable mask of dark deception; and had it been compatible with the hard decree of his irradicable taint of wrong for him to escape its stern penalties, he would have been saved indeed. And not only saved, but he would also have been a substantial blessing to the people in the section of his adopted home, as well as to Manonia herself, whom he would then have been able to render permanently and supremely happy.

When the time for celebrating the nuptials is at first deferred to Manonia's decision, she names Christmas of that year; but when she perceives that Garland is restless, and desires to make a business trip, and wait until the new year before he concludes the co-partnership with her brother, she then determines that they shall be legally and solemnly united immediately; and they are on the first of March, accordingly, married. *Strange match! Unique incidents! Mysterious destiny!*

Let us pause a moment and reflect. Look how slender, how frail, and how improbable were the threads of circumstances that led to this unpropitious union.

Garland, so far as that section of country was concerned, was passing through it merely as an aimless wanderer; prospecting over the survey of a contemplated railroad, with an object to ascertain the most desirable points for taking contracts to build bridges. There was no certainty, scarcely any probability, that he would ever see the work under progress, as building the road then stood, as it long had done, in apparently hopeless abeyance.

For two miles before he reached the Donné plantation, he had been looking for a place to dine; and before turning aside to this house, he stood on a high hill and looked two miles ahead, to see if there was not some other promising habitation nearer to his line of travel than the one in view.

Had either object of his seeking just named, obtained, his foot never would have crossed the threshold, his form never darkened the door of the Donné mansion, whence his shadow can nevermore be dispelled.

When he said farewell, and was passing out through the portal of the gate, had no hailing voice arrested his footstep, he was then gone forever.

On the night of his first conversation with Manonia, had not his soliloquy been an audible exclamation, he would have passed from the parlor without speaking to her; and she would then never have heard his wild and startling story, that so deeply stirred her sympathy and awakened in her heart so warm an interest in the mysterious narrator who had suffered so much keen and terrible affliction.

But still, however, we have yet seen that neither of these delicately slender threads was rent asunder; and that they led to an almost incredible result.

Some time following the wedding, the fact transpires that after the first week of Garland's sojourn at Donné's, the entire family decided that this would be a desirable result; and that the young lady had not only been abundantly encouraged, but she had been also strongly urged to pursue the altogether extraordinarily strange course which she did, in this singular affair of love- and match-making.

Throughout the entire current of the negotiations, she certainly acted her part well, if not wisely—and that her action was extremely indiscreet, no reasonable person will hesitate to admit.

Garland was, however, as will be demonstrated in future chapters of this "drama of life," a man of a peculiar type and composition, and prepossessing above the average degree of that quality inherent with mankind, as well as being endowed with a singular power of fascination that was mysteriously attractive to the few persons with whom he was on terms of moderate intimacy. So clearly defined and fully recognized was this fact, as to dissipate to a large extent the well merited censure, or the ground for it, that Manonia's culpability appears to deserve; except as to the

precipitation of her course without first ascertaining, from well authenticated and undoubted sources, who this man was, and what was the true nature of his character. This omission was the fatally weak point in her conduct.

But for the false nature of his masked life, although, in all his days, the very worst act of his had been recounted to her before he dreamed of so much as enlisting her indifferent esteem, the mask concealed no crimes. The worst feature of his life not revealed to her was his assumed name. Still we say, all these things notwithstanding, had he only confessed all to her, he would yet have been not wholly unworthy of her love.

This he failed to do, and hence but justly incurred the worst imaginable penalties of earthly damnation that could possibly be inflicted by the sleepless and unpitying ministers of retribution, who, though often tardy about putting their scourges of justice into operation, are nevertheless infallible, and will, or soon or late, make a terrible visitation with lashes of most unmerciful chastisement.

From this point on to the scene in which he appears on the stage in this drama for the last time, Garland is one of the strongest, one of the most wonderful and astonishing real characters on the shady side of life's mysteries that we have ever met, or of whom we have even read in books of unquestionable authenticity, yet not half so well vouched for as his story shall be.

Our pages of charity for him and his, ended when he married that beautiful, pure and innocent woman, while still wearing the mask of falsehood; and therefore we shall be henceforth unsparing, and connect him directly with events that will fully and most authentically corroborate all the startling vicissitudes of his strangely checkered career faithfully and truly presented by us. All that is beautiful and noble shall stand out in bold relief, in company with the reprehensible, the ignoble, the dark and the criminal.

Immediately after the wedding, the co-partnership between Garland and young Donné is consummated.

Up to and until some time after this event, Garland is ignorant of the true condition of the business in which he has launched. When at length, after long and tedious work, he has the accounts adjusted and the books in a shape to strike a balance, he finds that an immense stock of goods has been purchased for one-third cash, and much more than half of this sold on a credit, to whom, he, as a matter of course, does not know; and the entire amount of the purchase balances remains unpaid, to which has been added sundry orders.

The cotton crop is more than half out of the country. After closely interrogating his partner and chief clerk, he ascertains that two-thirds of the sales on credit have been made to irresponsible freedmen, and a ride of two days reveals the startling fact that most of them have already made way with their crop and its proceeds. He now informs his partner, his father-in-law, and his wife that the firm is insolvent; and at the same time announces to Manonia his determination at once to withdraw.

The old gentleman is nearly frantic, the son in despair, and Manonia deeply distressed on their account.

Finally, all three combined, prevail upon Garland to remain in the firm, to take the helm, and to make a desperate effort to save the sinking craft.

This necessitates an immediate trip to New York and New Orleans. Garland undertakes this trip with more reluctance than he would have experienced in making ready for a battle; but he goes.

Before starting he sets the most vigorous collecting machinery to work.

His trip proves a successful one, and he returns promptly, notwithstanding the prophecy of many knowing ones to the contrary.

The firm does a good season's business, and collects a large per cent. of bad and doubtful debts.

They build a handsome residence, and Garland and his bride occupy it.

Never did a man work harder than wretched Garland works all day and until midnight, at which hour he leaves the office, to join his wife. At five o'clock in the morning he is dressed and at work at a desk in the parlor, until breakfast. Except the hours of dining and on Sundays, this is the extent of the time he spends in the society of his wife.

He reduces the price of goods fully twenty-five per cent., and establishes a reliable local cotton market; and is, therefore, soon the most popular man in the country with the planting interest, and highly esteemed in the metropolitan markets of the Union.

It was necessary for him to make four business trips each year.

The unpleasantness connected with, and owing to his peculiar position under an assumed name in the world, inseparable from those business journeys and the incessant work at home, arouse in Garland a desire to abandon the business, which is, in the fall of his second season, in excellent condition.

His wife's brother-in-law has a fine and well-stocked plantation which he desires to trade for Garland's business interest, and Garland is eager to secure the opportunity thus offered for him to escape from the commercial conflict to the peaceful retirement of a planter's life.

The plantation is in an out-of-the-way, semi-civilized community, some fifteen miles from the town. For this reason, Manonia entreats him, with tears streaming down her cheeks, not to make the transfer; and to her prayers he yields.

This same season the corn crop proves a failure. The immense fall and winter stock of goods for the firm from New York is caught in the river by low water, and delayed about three months— a damaging misfortune.

In the meantime, the price of cotton declines so fearfully that it is evident the firm will be forced to carry over large balances, as well as to advance corn to make the next crop.

In view of these facts, Garland proceeds, early in February, to the West, to buy and ship the corn. He finds the Ohio and Mississippi rivers frozen tightly above Cairo. At Cincinnati, St. Louis, and Evansville he tries in vain to secure tonnage for the first opening of navigation.

At last he buys a steamboat and two barges, at Cairo; and he here waits for the ice to break up. Nearly a month, however, elapses before the vessels are finally loaded in Indiana.

The steamer runs aground, and there remains for nearly two weeks. On the way down, also, one of the barges strikes a snag, which results in its loss with its cargo.

After the steamer and other barge are unloaded, they are sold in New Orleans for nearly their original cost.

Garland borrows a large sum of money in New Orleans, where he is esteemed one among the first business men in the State, and one of the best judges of cotton to be found outside of the city, and would be styled an expert even here.

He also establishes a branch house in a rich planting section, in order to work off the goods carried over from the past season. In every possible way, he makes the most desperate efforts this season; and in August, it is the most promising one since the close of the war.

In this month he goes to market, and buys a very large stock of goods.

On his return home, he finds the worms eating the cotton. The crop is cut short, and the price declines to an extent sufficient to demoralize the planters.

As if to consummate the climax of misfortunes, the small-pox breaks out in the country, transforming the plantations into pest hospitals, and suspending business for about two months.

The result is that Garland's firm cannot pay bills at maturity, and he determines to go into liquidation. To this the father-in-law and partner strongly object.

The final issue is a sale to the father-in-law for his paper, on sufficient time to allow the firm to recover, which paper the firm indorses to its creditors; and as this paper is strengthened by the support of the old gentleman's valuable planting property, the arrangement is accepted by the creditors. The assets of the firm more than double the liabilities, were they only available.

As to the father-in-law and partner, the sale is a sham—a mere makeshift to gain time; but with Garland, it is *bona-fide*, binding, and final.

It was covenanted that Garland and partner are to run the business for the old gentleman, as salaried men; and not long after, Garland is sent to New Orleans to make business arrangements for the season for his successor. After three weeks' assiduous effort, he finds it morally impossible to borrow a dollar for the new firm, or to

buy goods on the usually favorable terms that he had always obtained them.

While in New Orleans, Garland's best and most admiring friend—one of the oldest and most successful cotton factors in the city—strongly advises him to go immediately to the "Future City," then about beginning to make an effort toward becoming a cotton market, and there engage in the cotton commission trade, where he would find an ample field to employ his fine talents and extraordinary capacity.

On his return he at once announces his resolution to follow the advice of this New Orleans friend.

To Manonia's protestations and entreaties his ear is deaf, and against her tears his heart is steeled. The only concession she can obtain, is his promise that she may visit her parents as often and remain with them as long as she pleases. Thus virtually dies the last sickly sprig of her fast withering happiness, and chimes the last cruel knell to her hopes.

Now, for the first time, she beholds the seeds of indiscretion which she has so haplessly sown, begin to germinate. Poor child! she will see their plants spring up and flourish most luxuriantly with their copious nurturing from the fountain of her sad tears, until the day when she must eat their matured and bitter fruits, in dry-eyed and silent sorrow.

Without any delay, Garland proceeds to the Future City, and perfects all preliminary arrangements for commencing business on July 1st, 1873.

The day on which he returns to his Louisiana home for his wife, the vast store-houses of his father-in-law are one mass of smoldering ruins; they have been burned the previous night. Thus closely upon the heels of each other, follow misfortune and disaster.

In his visits to cities where were scores of men who had once known him intimately under his true name, this man Garland had, up to the day of his location in the "Future City" never been recognized, although he had often met some of them in a casual and informal manner.

Time had changed him wonderfully. Care and anguish had sprinkled his hair with grey, and his beard had become heavy; and furthermore, his identity was, too, obscured by an artificial arm that was so perfect an imitation of the natural that many persons with whom he transacted business did not know that his arm was like his life—*false.*

He is able to locate as many as twenty men engaged in active business, in the "Future City," who knew him under his real name, at the time he enters the list as a merchant in that rising metropolis of the Mississippi valley.

One among the number had been an officer in the same brigade with him for nearly a year, up to the time when he lost his arm. Near his new domicile reside two own cousins from one branch of his family, and an aunt from the other branch.

Surely it requires a desperate nerve to sustain a man thus circumstanced and situated; yet still, however this may be, he arrives here, and opens his house on the appointed day, apparently with indifferent fearlessness.

CHAPTER LVIII.

A RAILWAY INCIDENT.

" In him the painter labor'd with his skill
To hide deceit and give the harmless shew,
An humble gait, calm look, eyes waiting still,
A brow unbent, that seem'd to welcome woe;
Cheeks neither red nor pale, but mingled so
That blushing red no guilty instance gave,
Nor ashy pale the fear that false hearts have."

—SHAKSPEARE.

IN a palace-car bound from Washington to New York, and fast approaching Philadelphia, between the years of 1870 and 1873, one day, there is a little group composed of Edgar Harman, Jesse Flowers and their wives.

A few seats in front of them, and on the opposite side of the car, a man with a bronzed yet fair face and full auburn beard, wearing a broad-brimmed Southern hat, half concealing his features, occupies a seat, and seems to be traveling alone.

At length, after closely scrutinizing him for some time, Edgar Harman speaks to Mrs. Flowers as follows: " Sissie, I believe that is Col. Cloud's ghost, sitting over yonder. What do you think of him?"

CARRIE: "I have been watching him some time, and do not deem him a ghost at all, but think that there sits Col. Cloud himself, alive and in good health. What think you, Jesse?"

FLOWERS: "I really think that is him."

ROSALIA: "Go and speak to him, Edgar, and make sure."

Harman steps over to the man, and returns in a moment shaking his head.

EDGAR "We are mistaken. I asked him if he was not a Virginian, when he rattled off: 'Pardonnez moi, monsieur, je ne comprend pas ce que vous dit,'—and he has two good hands, which is conclusive, could I have understood his jargon."

ROSALIA: "Oh! then he is a Frenchman, and said: 'Pardon me, sir, I do not understand what you say.'"

FLOWERS: "It is certainly a very striking resemblance."

CARRIE: "There he goes; he stops at Philadelphia. Yes, you are right, Edgar; we are mistaken. He carries his valise in the same hand that would be missing was he Col. Cloud."

The firm of Oglethrop, Harman & Co., in New York, continues to prosper, to grow in popularity and influence as the years glide by; and its members continue exempt from all family, all social, all business crosses and misfortunes.

The wives of these gentlemen, together with Cassandra and her two erratic sisters of the convent, continue their good works of charity and mercy.

With all the parties, gentlemen and ladies, except the two social exiles, everything glides as smoothly, as merrily as marriage bells; and even these two unfortunates are by far more happy than they had ever been during the days of their married wretchedness. Further than this it is not within the limits of our province to deal with the bright and the happy phases of human life. These brief and potent sketches suffice to draw most impressively the lines and shades of contrast between them and their gloomy opposites, which it is our painful lot nightly to portray; and they furthermore serve amply to demonstrate the sweet rewards for walking in Duty's paths, and for heeding Honor's voice.

CHAPTER LIX.

THE COURTESAN'S REVENGE.

" Misshapen Time, cope's mate of ugly Night,
   Swift, subtle post-carrier of grizzly Care;
Eater of youth, false slave to false delight,
   Base watch of woes, sin's pack-horse, virtue's snare,
O Time, thou tutor to both good and bad,
   Teach me to curse him that thou taught'st this ill!
At his own shadow let the thief run mad,
   Himself, himself seek every hour to kill."
                     —SHAKSPEARE.

IT will be remembered that Josepha Del-Campano, the pitiable victim of Arnold Noel, who betrayed her under the nefarious delusion of a sham marriage, and then abandoned her, swore a desperate vengeance against the treacherous race of mankind, and plunged into a reckless career of crime. She did this in order the better to secure opportunities to accomplish her hate-envenomed design, as well as to fly that atmosphere of purity which she had once breathed.

In pursuance of this resolution, she adopts the life of a courtesan. She is conscious that she is a model picture of perfection, both in physique and form, besides being the mistress of a rare and most attractively fascinating beauty.

She plots to turn the giddy heads of men occupying the first social positions and abounding in wealth, by luring them under the honor-destroying sway of her enchanting spell, that she may then at pleasure wring alike their purses and their hearts, and gloat over the writhing throes of their torture to the fullest satiety.

In this, alas for the weakness of mankind and their susceptibility to the witching charms of beauty, though it be reeking in the sulphurous odors of the deepest damnation of the blackest social hell, she schemes not in vain.

We cannot pursue her wild career throughout its many vicissitudes, both because of the want of space and of its inappropriateness. We drag her execrable shadow of a woman once true and pure but vilely betrayed, on the stage at all, because this is necessary, in order to present in these perpetually-shifting and ever-varying scenes, in their legitimate colors, some of the poisonous fruits of Arnold Noel's evil deeds, springing as natural consequences, in strict accordance with the laws of the "philosophy of cause and effect."

It must suffice to say in passing, that in the earlier days of her sinful life, she destroyed the peace and happiness of more than one family, and drove more than one victim to suicide.

Later she dupes a man of such prominence as to be esteemed worthy the name of "Magnate," to install her in a mansion in her own right and title, with palatial appointments. Here the dignitaries of Justice meet to feast, drink, and issue restraining mandamuses of injunction at their midnight sessions in this wicked paramour's vice-gilded saloon. She induces a beneficiary of the "Magnate" to waylay and shoot him like a dog. This case is too notorious and well known to require comment.

But the story of her crowning ecstasy of revenge yet remains to be told. Its foundation and development were due to a circumstance which transpired while she was yet the reigning evil genius of the "Magnate."

Arnold Noel was living with a notorious shoplifter as his wife. This fact Josepha learned. Then she engaged a beautiful and artful soiled dove to fascinate Arnold. In the meantime, she sought and secured the acquaintance of his paramour, the shop-lifter, and ingratiated herself into her favor by buying her stolen goods at fancy prices.

In her scheme to have Arnold lured by the crafty wiles of a new siren she was not disappointed. This accomplished, she is not long in causing indubitable evidence of the fact to be presented to the open eyes of Tilla, the shoplifter. That green-eyed monster—Jealousy—at once seizes her, and drives her to desperate madness. But she is largely under the influence of Josepha, who counsels moderation. This prevails the more readily, owing to the strong out-pourings of sympathy manifested with subtle tact by her patroness. This assures her, and induces her to admit Josepha into her confidence. By this means, the relentless woman learns Arnold's habits and haunts, together with his true name and the residence of his father's family. In the meantime, Arnold's new infatuation is also in her confidence.

A wealthy guest of a prominent hotel is "spotted" through the instrumentality of Josepha. It is ascertained that a large treasure of valuables is carelessly left about his room on bureau and tables.

Between the two rival women Arnold is reduced to most desperate straits for money. Each threatens to forsake him unless her wants are supplied. The tempting bait of the wealthy hotel guest is offered to him. Eagerly he takes it.

Josepha, as a matter of course, has not been idle. She knows when the robbery is to be committed. Due precautions are taken that the thief shall not leave the hotel, and that the evidence of his guilt shall be complete and overwhelming. And thus it proves.

Arnold Noel is arrested in the hotel, with the stolen property in his possession.

He is speedily "railroaded" through the courts to conviction, and sentenced to the extreme penalty of the law.

Now, Josepha arranges the programme for a scene. The two rival women are induced to be at the grating of the condemned Arnold's cell, at the same hour. Just after the war of words between themselves has subsided, and they have mutually united now to torture the disconsolate Arnold with reproaches, Josepha appears before the grated door, and gazes in triumph at the cowering destroyer of her youthful purity and its dream of love. The fury of the enraged lioness gleams in her eyes, her face is radiant with fiendish delight, as she says with withering sarcasm and cold-hearted mockery:

"Well, I hope you are enjoying yourself. Thank God,—if I may be permitted to pollute that sacred name with my sin-cursed lips—contagion caught from your vile and deceptive kiss, the dread blight of innocent purity—you are at last wedded to a twenty years' bride you may not leave to the ruthless caprices of another lover, as you once essayed to leave me. Base deceiver! Long have I waited for this moment. Blessed day that dawned to light my way to its raptures! In swarms, I perceive your singed moths gather around you now. Deluded wretches! Not soon

14

again will your treacherous flame of love—accursed ingrate!—glow to allure confiding virtue to destruction. May my curse and its ever multiplying evils be your curse, and that of your house and name! While I live, it shall pursue and afflict you and yours with a pitiless vengeance that shall not abate."

ARNOLD: "Have a little pity for my father's innocent family, if not for me."

JOSEPHA: "Pity! pity! Ha! ha! Yes, such as you had for me and my father's innocent family will I have for you and yours. Remember me! Mark my words! I was your victim then: you the plausible despoiler. You are my victim now: I am your heartless persecutor. Know, Arnold Noel, and bear with you the consolation that your present undoing is my handiwork, and that I shall plan and leave for you a heritage of endless woe."

Josepha brought into play secret influences to induce Arnold's father to take Tilla into the bosom of his family, as an estimable and innocent girl, the lawful wife of his son. As soon as she had there won sympathy, and become a favorite with the family and its friends, she is exposed in her true character. Then, as a matter of course, they are horrified at the thought that they have entertained a vile miscreant in the guise of an injured angel.

Arnold escapes, but is soon arrested, and returned to his doom, through the connivance of Josepha.

In time he is released by the Executive of the State. In a very few months he is returned to his old quarters, for the same term of years as those to which he was first doomed. He is the victim of unanswerable circumstances, innocent of the crime for which he is condemned. Josepha deems his penalty a partial retribution for her own cruel wrongs.

During the early months of this second imprisonment, his father, mother and two of his sisters die, "the pitiable victims of broken heart."

Josepha's vow is fulfilled: "Even as thou hast meted out unto me shame and ruin, so have I meted it out to thee again, *measure for measure!*"

CHAPTER LX.

IN THE FUTURE CITY.

"In my school days when I had lost one shaft,
I shot his fellow of the self-same flight
The self-same way, with more advised watch,
To find the other forth; and, by advent'ring both,
I oft found both. I urge this childhood proof,
Because what follows is pure innocence.
I owe you much: and, like a wilful youth,
That which I owe is lost: but if you please
To shoot another arrow that self-same way
Which you did shoot the first, I do not doubt
As I shall watch the aim; or to find both
Or bring your latter hazard back again,
And thankfully rest debtor for the first."
—SHAKSPEARE.

GARLAND, HOPE & Co. is Nube Garland's firm, that opens a house, July 1st, 1872, in the "Future City," as Cotton and General Southern Commission Merchants.

In addition to Garland, the firm contains three excellent young men from the South, one of whom is to be largely backed by his father and some relatives of means. As to the other two, it is expected that a large volume of business will be controlled through the influence of their relatives and friends, especially in the States of Alabama and Mississippi.

As stated in a previous chapter, between the time of Garland's preliminary visit to the "Future City," and his landing there for the purpose of permanently locating, the stores of his Louisiana successor are burned.

He finds this event has seriously changed the aspect of affairs relative to his new enterprise. As soon as it is known among the creditors in the "Future City," they at once feel a presentiment that they are never to get back all their money.

In making his preliminary visit, Garland counted on the friendship, the countenance, and the assistance of these same creditors, as the very ground-work upon which he then calculated to build a commercial structure. He did not expect to borrow money from them, nor to have their indorsement of his paper. But he designed to fill his Southern orders by their aid, and thus more than compensate them for the loss of his former trade and the deferred payment of the balances due to them by his late firm in the South, while benefiting his new firm. He hoped and believed this would awaken among these men a sincere interest in his success, and induce them, whenever it was practicable, to speak a good word for his house.

During that first visit, he called on and consulted no other parties in relation to his project; and with two or three insignificant exceptions, the nature of the encouragement he received was all that he could possibly have desired, far more flattering than he anticipated.

When he finds the stores of his father-in-law in ashes, he has himself strong misgivings concerning the firm being able to cancel their debts, even if the partial insurance is paid promptly and in full. For he knows that as soon as the business fails as a supply depot, seven-tenths of the customers never will pay a dollar; and that they are within the pale of Homestead-protection so securely as to defy compulsory collection.

On his arrival in the "Future City," therefore, he finds among the creditors, with few and rare exceptions, a marked and repulsive coldness. He frankly tells them he fears that he will have to pay part of the money by his own personal exertions. This does not seem to turn the current any more in his favor.

The idea that he has a large sum of money from the assets of his old firm, drawn out before the sale to his successor, becomes current, and is thoroughly believed to be true among the creditors in question.

Some of these creditors are peculiarly vindictive. We can hardly reconcile their manifestations of this spirit with consistency. We might with propriety name them, but this is unnecessary. We may indicate a few of them by names appropriate to their proneness.

These creditors influenced other parties; and still others were drawn on their side, from motives and for reasons that will duly appear, although their names will not.

Bright names, such as soar high above petty malice, speak never but kindly of disagreeable competitors, and disdain to be uncharitable to the unfortunate, are hallowed lights that shine with rarely approachable refulgence among the dark shadows of the envious, dissembling, malicious crew. They are most beautiful and radiant diamonds of the purest water, that will stand the wear of time, cut all that falsehood and injustice can hurl against them, and yet remain undimmed. Hence it is with a thrill of pleasure that we image in the sleepless majesty of the mind such strong and matchless characters of perfect moral manhood. What an appalling contrast the bright tints of the clear, brilliant and shining lights reflect, when they penetrate and shed a beaming ray upon the gloomy back-ground in the odious picture of the dark side of life.

In this relation, we propose to present a true and well-authenticated picture throughout, not in defense of Nube Garland, nor to make his unworthiness appear more monstrous, but to demonstrate yet other shades of human life requisite to consummate its portrait. We shall follow in the wake of occurrences just as they have transpired and may be thoroughly substantiated in the commercial centre where located.

The opposition this man Garland meets is designed to preclude him from the possibility of perfecting arrangements that will enable him to do anything in the direction of conducting a regular business, or even starting it on a legitimate and practicable basis.

One creditor of his old firm, who might appropriately be termed "Duplicity," professes much solicitude for Garland's success, and specially desires to assist him in making financial arrangements.

The assistance rendered is in the shape of introducing him to the proper bank officers after they are privately admonished to have nothing to do with him. Some of the other creditors act a more honorable part—that of secret work without the guise of professed friendship. It is needless to name them.

One modest, quiet creditor deserves to be styled the "True Friend." While the prospect of his losing his large claim is no less disagreeable to him than to the other and smaller creditors, still he has sufficiently investigated the affair to be satisfied that it is not fraudulent. Hence, being a true, just man, he will not stoop to condemn and persecute an unfortunate debtor overtaken by disasters that have sprung from unavoidable causes.

Garland soon finds that the doors of all prominent and desirable banks are closed against him; and that, alone and unaided, he must combat the powerful and aggressive influence of his vindictive creditors at home and abroad. Nothing could well appear more hopeless and forlorn than his now discouraging prospects for success in his efforts barely to start a business.

In talking the matter over with the "True Friend," that wise, able, and successful merchant frankly informs Garland that his enterprise is a fated impossibility.

Nevertheless, whatever may be Garland's convictions—is he capable of experiencing such—he does not meekly accept the inevitable.

This obstinate effort and indomitable perseverance of his demonstrates a singularly peculiar freak of fortune, partaking strongly of the nature of a mysterious dispensation from the guiding power of a strangely ordered destiny.

Similarly situated, under the same force of circumstances, nine hundred and ninety-nine men out of every thousand, although in full enjoyment of untarnished virtue and true moral courage, would have abandoned an enterprise so wholly devoid of prospect, or hope, or probability of success. Why, then, the man Garland clings to it so tenaciously is, at this time, when the story of his antecedents is unknown, a mystery to every one acquainted with him and his efforts; now, with all the details before us, it seems incredible. Was it misguided moral courage, erroneous ingenuity, or what was it? We are unable to answer.

This strange and mysterious individual has apparently no future in life worth a struggle. Liable as he is, as indorser for the paper of his unfortunate Louisiana successor, with the bitter vindictiveness of the holders of this paper combined against him, there seems little to encourage him to start a business as it were, in the very jaws of a menacing danger threatening him with the most merciless and crushing destruction. And, then again, he furthermore has the ghost of his false position ever at his heels. Less serious things drive men who are well established, not only out of business, but to self-destruction.

Almost every day he meets parties whom he recognizes, but none of them seem to remember him.

As a rule he avoids talking about the past, but when he does speak of it, with the one exception of his name, he confines himself to truth, even to the county of his nativity, the regiments in which he served, and the rank of himself in that service from first to last.

After finding the true state of affairs and realizing the precariousness of the difficulties in which they involve him, he is very cautious how he moves, and extremely quiet in all his operations. However, the business community, to its surprise, soon learns that he has an account with a small new bank, and is doing a large amount of business from Texas all the way to Georgia—far more than many old-established houses, amounting frequently to thousands of dollars in one day with Memphis alone.

When the panic strikes him, his prospects are flattering indeed. For a new and not strong house, he has a large amount of exchange remitted from Memphis, drawn by the best bank there, on New York, to come back dishonored—the Memphis bank having failed while the bills were in transit as remittance. Besides this, two or three Memphis firms owing him large amounts fail, and others are in consequence of the financial lock-up, unable to meet their bills promptly for purchases in transit at the commencement of the panic.

Just now it appears that Garland is effectually crushed. The expectations of assistance from the friends of his partners totally fail. Not a dollar nor business worth a dollar, ever reaches the firm.

But dark as all seems, Garland does not despair. In a very short time the Memphis bank arranges to start again and he is able to get the paper of the bank discounted.

Before the banks resume currency payment, there is a distressing demand for cash to pay cotton-pickers in the South. Garland's keen and ever alert acumen perceives that this circumstance constitutes the strategical point of the cotton campaign, and the foundation for the future of the trade in the "Future City."

His little bank does not belong to the Clearing House Association, and never stops paying currency. He therefore draws all the money he can obtain, and sends three good men to the most promising cotton districts, with instructions to secure consignments with the least possible spot cash advances, to take orders for goods of any class against the cotton up to a full advance, or to promise the balance of a full advance in currency, by express, on the arrival of the cotton in his market.

The result of this adventure is immediate and surprisingly large shipments of cotton, that daily increase. And as this novel genius makes a new departure in the commission business by proposing to buy goods for his shippers free of commission, his orders for goods are nearly as large as those of any wholesale grocery house in the Southern trade. This feature creates for him the uncompromising enmity of one grocery firm doing an immense Southern business.

Up to the season when Garland's house enters the field, this city has never been a cotton market, and there is only one legitimate cotton commission house here, S —— & Co., the pioneer house of the trade in this city,—a firm whose members are always and under all circumstances warm and earnest friends to Garland, and who will not permit agents to talk against him nor to his detriment. Both members of this firm ever encourage him. They understand and appreciate how vastly he will aid them to establish a market in their city, and to draw a large volume of shipments to it—a result for which they have labored many years in the face of the antediluvian jeers and discouragements from the very men whose interests should have prompted them to encourage and assist this commercial life-inspiring enterprise.

This firm does not despise Garland's unquestionable talents and undoubtedly fine knowledge of, and thorough experience in, this important business, nor hesitate to pattern after him where tangible success is crowning his every effort. This house is strong, and at once adopts the plan of sending out men with money, and thus to meet success in a degree commensurate with the greater magnitude of their resources that Garland has realized.

Several other firms this season launch out in the cotton business. All are soon inspired to make the same effort. Within sixty days this city is a cotton market; a fixed fact.

In the meantime, F—— & Co., pork-packers, F—— & B——, flour merchants, and W—— & K——, wholesale grocers, extend extraordinary facilities to Garland, and are friends, if not to him personally, certainly to his enterprise. It is also about this time that George M——, then in the fancy-goods trade, and J. W. P. —— president of the Cotton Compress Co., become friends with and begin to take a lively interest in Garland.

Up to this period in his metropolitan career, he is a grand, courageous, and admirable character—a model worthy of emulation in every respect, save alone his false position, but for which we now see him on the high road to a pinnacle of unparalleled success, influence, power, and usefulness, in comparison with the circumstances under which he started, and the nature of the line of business in which he is engaged.

But, alas! the long treasured and ever accumulating retribution of that atoneless curse still remains unspent. Can any mortal skill, ingenuity, exertion, will or power, or all combined, redeem and spare him from its ultimate consequences? Or will these masterful struggles to escape, only tend to delude and to lead him into the entanglements of its treacherous snare?

This should be an interesting and an instructive study: whether it be possible for a man wholly to escape in this world the real palpable penalty, either in a greater or a less degree, that his false or criminal acts merit and demand.

Here is a man with the talent, the skill, the strategy, the nerve, the daring requisite to accomplish anything human in a strife with events controlled and directed only by human dispensation. But what will all these avail him in a conflict with the silent and mystical powers of an unknown and invisible destiny? We are driven to the unwavering conclusion that he is helpless, blind, and cannot escape.

What a lamentable thralldom for a man to be involved in—a man capable of rendering to the future prosperity of the city such extensively valuable commercial services in promoting an enterprise upon which depends, in an inestimable degree, the approaching, or at least the feasible, greatness of the city; an enterprise to which he is as zealously devoted as any man engaged in it who is free and untrammeled from the detrimental embarrassment of perpetually existing under the sombre gloom of a menacing cloud!

How can and why will an unworthy man devote, as it were, his very life in a laudable struggle to advance the interest of a community, actuated entirely by worthy motives? It is impossible for this man to reap a benefit from his assiduous labors that will not, and immediately, advance the general welfare of the community ten times as much as that to be realized for himself. Every step he makes in the direction of extending the infant trade at this period of its delicate existence, is planting a seed that will spring up and bear permanent and increasing fruit. This will continue to enhance the prosperity of commerce for all time, no matter what may be his fate as an individual actor.

A most trivial but potent incident transpires early in the season under consideration, that makes an uncompromising enemy for Garland of a strong, new cotton house. This firm seems to entertain the idea that all the business from one section is its own by an inalienable right; and thus it develops.

Garland has an agent passing through that section one day, on a mail-train that stops at a depot for a freight to come up. This agent steps off, and hands a card to each of a few planters who are standing on the platform, but has no time to talk. This results in one of the leading planters dividing a forty bale shipment, the next day, equally between the two houses. The day on which the cotton arrives, Garland's competitor, who is young in the business, and at this time utterly ignorant of the classification and grade valuation of cotton to that fine degree of technical nicety requisite to afford him absolute security against being "picked up" by a sharp broker, makes a very large sale, in which the twenty bales referred to are included. There is some extra delay about delivering the cotton, and more about getting the sales made up and remitted, while, in the meantime, the market becomes active, buoyant and advancing. Neither one of the parties knows of the shipment to the other. Garland is ignorant of the circumstances under which the shipment has been made to his house, as well as of the fact that the shipper is a customer of his competitor.

Garland is a classer of cotton equal to any in any market, and thoroughly skilled in both the New Orleans and New York methods of conducting a cotton commission business under the most approved, the most practical, and most scientific rules.

One of the first principles is, rigidly to class every bale in a list, and thus ascertain its exact average value before offering it for sale; the next is to mail to each shipper a notification of the number of bales he has in the list, the same day it is sold; and next to make up and forward the sales promptly.

Garland sells the twenty bales about a week after he receives them, on an advanced and excited market; so that they net over twelve dollars per bale more than the twenty sold by his competitor. This brings him a large per cent. of business from that section; and his competitor believes it is the result of sinister unfairness, while, in reality, Garland is himself ignorant of the cause. Circumstances very nearly similar to the one just related, made for Garland a number of other, but less important enemies.

It is a little remarkable that his emphatic injunction to all his soliciting representatives is, never to say a word, and that he never writes a line detrimental to any other house; nor seeks, by any unfair means, to take business away from any one, up to the point in his career now under consideration.

As to poor Manonia, she is literally buried alive in a hotel, and quite ill—almost past hope. Garland returns to her from his office at midnight, and leaves her at six o'clock in the morning. But personally, he is as kind to her as any man in the world could be, never giving her an angry word; and she loves him with all the passionate devotedness of her ardent Southern nature.

Just as soon as she is able to travel, she sets out to pay her first visit to her parents, leaving Garland subject to the baneful influence of his own dark mind.

Before leaving, she consummates an act of beautiful charity, that is productive of much good fruit. This act is accomplished through the medium of the following conversation:

MANONIA: "My dear, have you ever noticed the boy, little Frank, who takes the meal-tickets at the dining-room door?"

GARLAND: "Yes, casually, in passing. What of him?"

MANONIA: "He is a very bright, sweet child; and he has been very kind to me, and cheered me during many an hour that would have hung monotonous and dreary on my hands. He has a widowed mother, and they are very destitute. I want you to do something for him for my sake."

GARLAND: "Certainly. How much shall I give him?"

MANONIA: "Oh! I don't mean that. I want you to take him into your office, and pay him whatever he is worth."

GARLAND: "I would rather pension him off than be bothered with him. Those hotel boys learn nothing but badness, and he would prove an intolerable nuisance in the office."

MANONIA: "Now, don't say that, please, about him, for he is an exception. He begged me to ask you. His father was once a wealthy cotton merchant; but left his wife and boy beggars, owing to people having swindled him during a long illness before he died. The poor little fellow wants to learn the business. Take him, please. It might be the means of making a useful man of him, and of saving him from drifting down with the muddy tide in the maelstrom of the scum and dregs of life. If he gives you the least annoyance, blame me, but don't scold him."

GARLAND: "All right, then; I will give him a fair trial."

MANONIA: "How good you are! How pleased he will be."

The second month, Garland pays this boy Frank G. P.——, fifty dollars, solely on the score of merit. From that time, his destiny is established, and he steadily rises. He is a mimicking genius, that never has to be told or shown how to do anything the second time, in order to understand it perfectly.

His mother, a delicate little woman, he very soon transfers from the garret and squalid poverty to plenty and comfort.

At the present day, there are few men as well recompensed for their services as is this young man.

CHAPTER LXI.

THE MUTUAL AND SECRET INQUISITORIAL LEAGUE.

"Yet I must think less wildly;—I have thought
Too long and darkly, till my brain became
In its own eddy boiling and o'erwrought;
A whirling gulf of phantasy and flame;
And thus untaught in youth my heart to tame,
My springs of life were passion. 'Tis too late!"
—BYRON.

EARLY in the winter of 1873-4, associated with six other merchants, Garland is a member of a society or league of seven, organized to ascertain the moral habits principally of men in their own employ, and those with whom they are most intimately related in business. After this paramount object is attained, they gather any other subordinate information that either the fancy or the whims of any two of the members may prompt them to demand. Especially is it stipulated that any member on duty seeking information of any specific nature shall report to the meetings any other striking information that may casually chance to come under his observation.

The members of this novel commercial association are all older men than Garland, and all but he are well established and substantial merchants of the most rigid moral school. Some of them are deemed a little eccentric.

One of them with whom Garland is intimate, one evening suggested the utility of a compact of this nature to Garland and two others, in the private office of one of their number. The plan is at once agreed upon, and three other parties then named who would be acceptable as members. These last mentioned merchants are consulted, and the next night the league is organized.

Every member is sworn to observe a super-

Masonic secrecy as to the existence of the organization, its objects, its workings; and never to expose to the public any information gathered by its numbers that might prove damaging in the slightest degree, unless the interests of some one of their members imperatively demand it. In case of any member being referred to by the party whom such knowledge would affect, he may then impart it without specially indicating the source whence it is derived, as he would in strict confidence give any other commercial information. They are not to seek information for the benefit of any other parties than the members themselves.

Any member guilty of disreputable commercial conduct is to be expelled.

No new members are ever to be admitted.

One member is to be on duty every night, so that the turn of each will occur but once a week.

The duties of this member, when no special nor extraordinary instructions are imposed upon him, are to shadow drinking, gambling and other disreputable resorts, and there watch for the employés, etc., of himself and brother members. While thus engaged, it is but a natural presumption that the member on duty will find other people than those for whom he is looking, occasionally straying in devious paths. Such instances as those, if of notable importance, it is expected he will report at the meeting held the week in which the information comes into his possession.

It is agreed that immediately after the adjournment of each meeting, every member shall call to account such of his people as have come under the ban of the inquisition's proscribed list, and privately inform them separately the exact nature of the damaging discoveries, give them all one chance; but at the same time duly notify them that a repetition will not be excused.

The members of this strange fraternity determine to test the secret workings of family grocery-stores, in localities where the laboring poor reside and deal. To this end, they make up a little purse, purchase a diminutive pair of post-office scales, and place these, together with a part of the fund, each night, in the hands of the member on duty, with instructions to send some colored person or small poor child to buy some articles sold by weight from a few different stores doing a fairly large trade, and to weigh them promptly, at the same time carefully noting the purported weight of the seller and the weight by the delicate scales opposite each item, observing to keep each store's list distinctly separate from the others. The plan is to accumulate a combined result, including one hundred stores scattered all over the city, from which they design to make an average.

Howsoever trivial and insignificant this enterprise may appear at the first casual and hasty inspection and consideration, it is simply wonderful—almost incredible—what a vast and strangely varied amount of important information a similar organization may accumulate, in the brief space of but one week, in any city of ten thousand inhabitants, or in any manufacturing establishment employing one thousand people.

We allow this chapter to cover the space of some pages, not only because one of our wayward characters is directly connected with its subject-matter, but also because it reflects a shade of a peculiar hue that does not obtain in the composition of the colors furnished by our regular characters, without which a true life-picture would be falsely incomplete; and furthermore, because they are of a nature, at least to a large extent, that may not easily be obtained by other means, the immunity of the transgressors from detection and exposure being comparatively well assured.

This is a process that will unmask one species of unblushing crime, that of the bold and audacious theft and robbery that exceeds all other methods of criminally obtaining possession of property, for which the perpetrators are rarely or never legally punished, and seldom, if ever, personally rebuked by the organs of the public. These the transgressors usually disarm by lavishly liberal patronage; and by being charitable and loudly profuse in their donations to the church, they most easily dispel from themselves all suspicion of their outrageous and basely glaring dishonesty.

What is more atrocious and criminal than, day by day throughout the year, again and again, systematically to steal a portion of the scanty, meagre, hard-earned subsistence from the toil-worn, poverty-stricken, drudgery-enslaved man and his emaciated children in the pinching wretchedness of the squalid garret? Why should this loathsome depredator, who flourishes and revels in luxury, honored and esteemed in every community in the large towns and in the great cities, not be held as accountable, and punished with a proportionately severe penalty, as the hungry urchin who steals a loaf of bread?

The time for the first meeting arrives, to find every member of this organization promptly on hand and ready to report.

PRESIDENT: "Gentlemen, we have met in pursuance to the resolutions adopted at our preliminary meeting, and for the purpose then indicated. The secretary will read the reports of the members for the week, which will be disposed of as the meeting may deem proper."

SECRETARY: "Now, gentlemen, give me your attention, if you please, and I will proceed to read the reports as they have been submitted for your information :

"'January 4th, 1874.

"'To PRESIDENT M. S. I. LEAGUE:

"'I have the honor to report that I found Mr. Low's book-keeper playing faro and losing money. He was also drinking freely, and presented a general appearance of recklessness.

"'Mr. Still's cashier and Mr. Waterman's invoice clerk were two-parts drunk, and making the rounds of saloons and other disorderly houses, and, at the same time, conducting themselves in a manner quite ungentlemanly.

"'Mr. Thorn's collection clerk and Mr. Mundy's stockman were dancing and treating in a saloon on C—— avenue.

"'Two of Mr. Garland's account-sales clerks and two of my salesmen were full of beer, and drinking at the rate of about a glass every five minutes.

"'I observed a number of leading bank men and merchants, and the employés of like institutions and houses gambling, drinking to excess, or in company of questionable repute. And, I am pained to have to report that I saw a number of couples from good, respectable society, going in the direction of and coming from places of doubtlessly bad character.

" ' I was horrified to see a dear friend of mine with the wife of another acquaintance of mine, enter a well known resort near N—— and O—— streets; then a few minutes later his wife with another man glided into the same place; and, soon after, his daughter followed with a bank cashier who has a wife and grown-up children.

" ' I am exceedingly thankful that our regulations do not require us to report the names of people outside of our own business relations.

" ' Respectfully submitted,

" ' TIMOTHY FAIR.' "

As the other reports are of much the same tenor and purport we exclude them, except the consolidated reports on the one hundred stores, which result as follows:

Out of the entire number, seventeen gave full weight on every item, and eighty-three short weight, ranging from twenty to forty per cent., and averaging twenty-seven per cent., including the weight of the heavy paper in which the small parcels are wrapped.

There is a panic among the employés of the seven houses represented in this secret league, and their names very soon cease to figure in the weekly reports.

This brief reference to a deplorable and serious subject but vaguely reflects a faint ray of light on the shady side of life, under the mantle of which a sadly large per cent. from the middle and upper ranks of society might, at any time, be found lurking.

There is but one feature of it all, however, with which the laws of the land and the authorities constituted under them may successfully cope: this systematic, commercial pilfering from the confiding public, thus easily duped. Open, loud exposure of, and vigorously severe punishment inflicted on some of that cormorantic crew might have a most salutary influence over them all; though with none of the others will emblazoned scandal operate either as a remedial or a mitigating influence.

Each particular feature is a distinctly and well-defined type of social pestilence that baffles the skill of all moral and social physicians, and defies their antidotes—maladies that exposure rather tends to aggravate than to abate—but that the fear of public notoriety will often check, sometimes cure.

Society, collectively, controls, or rather might control, the only infallible remedy in existence, or the one that might under any earthly possibility exist.

A few discreet and honorable members of society in any community may, in a very short time, discover the members of that society who are leading lives such as should ever render them unworthy the esteem of the circle in which they move, or even tending in that direction. This accomplished, then quietly inform the wayward ones of the true nature of the situation; and that the alternative is to mend these erratic propensities or suffer the consequences of exposure—the pain of banishment from the pure atmosphere of their forfeited sphere down to the level of that plane to which they properly belong by reason of having adopted the abominations there practiced. This might save more, both as a preventive and as a remedy, than all the "Temperance Crusades," "Police Courts," "Workhouses," and "Reformatories" in the world, combined and multiplied over again, have ever saved or ever will save.

The time for society to effect the reformation of its viciously predisposed members, is before they have lost their caste and standing; and alone by the gently soothing balm of its own quiet and charming influence may this result be attained; but never, or at most, extremely rare will be the exceptional cases, through the interposition of the customary mediums of coercive agencies, which rather tend to make and help along than to cure their malignant disorders.

These are stubborn, irrefutable facts that the sooner the philanthropist recognizes in their true light, the better by far it will be for the nobly grand cause in which he is engaged, and in which it is a lamentable misfortune that a mistaken zeal should often lead him astray.

The proverb: "The school of experience is a hard one," contains often "more truth than poetry." A thousand-fold more forcible is its application when the subject-matter of its lesson thus inculcated is contained only in the dark chapters of the book of "Human Nature." But good people, in order to learn this ignoble lesson truly, that knowledge must be drained, with the cruel dregs, from the melancholy depths of the most bitter experience.

One of the principles of this organization of seven is that its members shall be true to one another; and that one member may impart to another at any time, either in or out of the regular meetings, any information of whatever nature, whether obtained on or off duty, that personally concerns only himself, and does not in any way relate to other members, nor to the chief objects for which they all are together combined.

It is a startling observation—the almost incredible rapidity with which the information collected by this league accumulated, and what a strangely curious volume of the dark mysteries of life grew weekly within the lids of the minutes of its meetings.

The index clues that point toward the catastrophe to which great institutions and houses are rushing with swift impetuosity, are there recorded; and within this hidden volume lay concealed from the light of day the leading outline of the dark mysteries of "the great Whisky Ring," in substance about the same as that which ultimately exploded the seductive spell of its potent sway.

One day, on the Cotton Exchange, Mr. Low, the president of this league, in conversation with the commercial reporter of a leading daily, makes a trifling, incidental allusion to that question, that the reporter grasps as being a pertinent clue that may lead to a "big find"; and which, as he reasons, may be most assiduously followed up under the specious guise of collecting statistics without arousing any suspicion, and which ultimately conducts him safely to the realization of the laudable object which he sets out to attain: "the disastrous undoing of that grand, national, spoiling combination."

Through the members of the league, Garland from time to time learns something of the muddy seethings of the subtle under-current which his adroit energy and far-reaching enterprise, is provoking to form against him. This, from the turbulent restlessness of its impatient nature, it is easily perceptible, will rise some day in mad fury to sweep him from a position that is daily growing so enviable that will speedily become securely impregnable and placidly defy the most formidable forces that may possibly assail him here, seeking to banish him effectually from the last vestige of a commercial existence.

Outside the circle of his brother members of the league, he never intimates to any one that the nature of the unequal struggle in which he will soon be forced to engage is at all known to him, the "True Friend" alone excepted. They rarely meet, and then, as a rule, in a way that is impracticable to discuss a subject so mysteriously sinister as is this. This estimable gentleman admits that all Garland's misgivings are well-founded, but at the same time, he declares most emphatically that he is wholly unable to divine the motives that prompt men of means, influence and high standing in business circles, to stoop to the attempt even, to crush a weak and comparatively friendless man. He deems that all should appreciate Garland's struggles as an humble actor in their lower ranks, in the grand battle to gain the control of a leading Southern industry and the trade that is inseparable from it, in which the city is now engaged and which will but tend to promote the common interest of the whole in a degree far greater than may by any means ever benefit their anticipated victim.

Sometimes people are too much blinded by jealous prejudice to perceive clearly their own interest, and are willing even to sacrifice this, to a certain extent at least, in order to gratify their malice. In the instance of this spirit, as manifested toward Garland, however, the aversion and spite must have been generated and influenced by the promptings of strongly actuating instinct, that vaguely intimated his dark and mysterious character. This appears logically reasonable, because there is some divining ken in the intellectual faculties of mankind, which often seems to understand that there are hidden sins in the hearts of other people, although there be no way by which this feeling might be explained.

CHAPTER LXII.

THE WILDLY FLUCTUATING VICISSITUDES.

"There is thy gold; worse poison to men's souls,
Doing more murders in this loathsome world,
Than these poor compounds thou may'st not sell.
* * * * * * *
Poor wretch! dark ambition and deep pride,
And cold disdain, for the buffeting tide,
Which thou would'st stem or sink in the vain
Attempt, were the compounds of thy deadly bane.
Could'st thou have brooked the ills of fate;
Or had'st thou been true, or mend'd ere too late,
And with a modest station been content,
Thou might'st not had greater faults to repent.
But thou must soar and fight for loft'or sway,
And be all or nothing, in one little day."
—SHAKSPEARE.

As THE weeks come and go, Garland, with a daily increasing business, finds his perplexities and difficulties constantly augmenting.

The money market is bare and perfectly stringent.

Owing to his acute knowledge of the value of cotton, and firmness against the principle of making concessions, he cannot always sell when he wishes to do so; in fact, the buyers meet his views, only when they are forced to take his cotton to complete their orders.

His demands for money are very soon in excess of the ability of his little bank to supply. Here is a dilemma. He has 'tried in vain to place his account with other banks during the flush times and the dullest season of the year before the panic. Of what use will it be to make the attempt now, when the banks are all taxed to their utmost capacity to supply the sorely pressing demands of their own customers?

However, he does nevertheless try; and not only does he try, but he actually succeeds in negotiating arrangements with three of the best banks in the city, in one day.

He has a deep plan to do business under the same privilege as is in vogue in New Orleans; viz. to borrow money on his bills of lading, giving at the same time to the bank an order on the transportation company to deliver the cotton on its arrival to some certain ware-houses, and an order on these to deliver their receipts to the bank when they receive the cotton.

In New Orleans, the cotton factor who wishes to borrow money on cotton before it arrives, takes the bills of lading for the number of bales that he desires to hypothecate, as collateral security for each loan the bank grants him, and indorses his order on them to deliver the cotton that they represent to the ware-house with which he designs to store it. Then he makes out an order on the ware-house to deliver the cotton described by marks in the face of the bills of lading to the order of his bank, and attaches all to his note for discount. The bank then sends the order and the bills of lading by its own collector or runner to the ware-house; the ware-house man accepts the order and retains the bills of lading.

The bank has its security, the *best in the world—a genuine ware-house receipt* for cotton; the factor gets his money; all parties are mutually satisfied with the transaction, as well as being equally benefited by it. In the "Future City" the ware-houses issue a separate receipt for every bale of cotton under serial numbers, beginning at number one, with the first bale received in the month of September, and terminating with the last one received in August—a system that first originated in the tobacco ware-house, and was then applied to cotton bales instead of tobacco hogsheads, because at first all the cotton was stored in tobacco ware-houses. Garland regards the system as being a nuisance, and tries to have it abolished.

So far as the transactions with the banks are concerned, they might, however, be effected under the "Future City" system, with the same facility as under that in vogue in the Crescent City; and to secure that end Garland makes his arrangements.

Then, for almost the only time during his business career, he breathes freer for a brief space of days; and he tries to flatter himself that the worst is over.

By some unaccountable fatality, however, there is a strong influence in the Board of each bank against him on the bill of lading arrangement; and in just three days after it is made, he is informed that he can have all the money he wants on the spot ware-house receipts accompanied by certificates of insurance, but on no other terms, against cotton security.

He is at last cornered. He has agents out in all directions in the cotton belt, who have made numerous arrangements under which parties are shipping cotton; and they are daily making still further arrangements with new shippers.

He has no resources with which to tide over the time between the drafts coming in for payment and the arrival of the cotton. And as if further to aggravate the embarrassing situation, the railroad becomes blocked with more cotton than it has facilities to move, so that it does not arrive promptly, while the drafts are not delayed.

It is the twentieth of the month. On the first day of the next month he will have city bills to pay, ranging from between twenty and thirty thousand dollars, and cotton drafts to meet for perhaps a greater amount; and, in all probability, before a bale of cotton arrives.

In the meantime, the instalment notes of his Louisiana successor become due; several of the insurance companies succumb to the pressure of the panic; the firm of his father-in-law collects no money from the planters, and the creditors are menacing Garland.

It is difficult to conceive a more hopeless and helpless predicament in which a man may be placed right in the active stages of a prosperous and rapidly growing business, than that which now distresses wayward Garland.

Up to this time, his record as a merchant will most favorably stand the test of comparison with the business men of this age, many of whom make most disgraceful failures that do not pay their creditors five per cent., under less plausible pretenses than he has had for suspending, both in Louisiana and also in the "Future City." But now the time has arrived when that alternative seems to be inevitable—the last and only course that harmonizes with honor.

There are few persons who know this strange man, who would hesitate to doubt that he would rather go to his last long sleep at the bottom of the noble Mississippi, than to abandon his ill-fated project, created under the stimulating intoxication of an ambitious delusion. But he nevertheless resolves to abandon his doomed craft. On Saturday night he leaves the office determined

to suspend on Monday. It is a bitter, gloomy contemplation.

He had once heard from an old cotton merchant, in his narratives of the ups and downs of the trade, and the rise and fall of houses in it, during a period of half a century, some strange stories about the many expedients to which sinking houses resorted to keep afloat until the crisis of the storm was safely passed.

Early on Sunday he meets and has an interview with a man who has been employed in the banks, and who also knows that Garland is embarrassed for the want of actively available facilities to meet cotton drafts, owing to his inability to obtain money until the cotton arrives. This man tells him of numerous instances of merchants who he knew to have been detected doing business on spurious collaterals, without experiencing any trouble other than being obliged to make their accounts good. These he says the bank officers well know would be made good, no matter what else was permitted to suffer.

He then finally suggests to Garland the feasibility of such a plan of operations, as a sure means of relief, and offers, for quite a reasonable consideration, to assist him in bringing it to perfection.

He suggests that Garland have blank warehouse receipts filled up with the dates, numbers and marks of those he is receiving, in order that they will be exact duplicates of genuine receipts, and turn them over to him, and he will have them signed so skillfully that the signature will without difficulty or suspicion, pass with any of the banks. He says he can make a set of duplicates for each bank, should Garland desire or need so many.

This is a great temptation, but Garland rejects it with contemptuous disdain. In parting, the man tells him that should he decide to change his mind at any time, his services are obtainable.

By Sunday's mails Garland receives the most bitterly reproachful letters from his father-in-law and brother-in-law, for having abandoned them, with the debts of the old firm unpaid, which are now threatening them with immediate and irretrievable ruin. Besides these, he also receives one from Manonia, breathing the most tender sentiments of love and devotion for himself, but, at the same time pathetically appealing to him to make one herculean effort to relieve the distress of her father, and save him from the cruel disaster that is about to overwhelm him. Garland is in a gloomy plight to afford consolation and relief to the afflicted and the suffering.

Immediately after supper this same Sabbath evening, he goes to his office; locks the outer and inner doors; makes a fire; turns the gas jet at his desk low; and passes the solitary hours between slowly pacing to and fro, and sitting with his head reclining on his desk, thinking, dreaming, sighing.

There is a war of fiercely conflicting emotions raging in this hope-void, woe-begone breast; and he soliloquizes:

Oh God, oh Heaven! names of refuge, sources of consolation to me baned and barred! Alas that thitherward I may not turn for counsel and comfort! False wretch! Base, damnable deceiver! Too late, too late! I cannot recall those wayward steps, nor again retrace them.

"Far above me, up, up precipitous and impassable steeps, is that broad and beauteous plain of honor, whence I descended, and from which I am an exile and a stranger! Below, down, deep down lies the yawning abyss—the fathomless gulf of perdition.

"To advance but another step is to make the dread and desperate plunge. Here I am on barren wastes and icy crags, amid the tempest's fury that must sweep me from this untenable sphere. Then, as for myself, I am lost, lost!

"But can I save any others without engulfing still some with me? Poor Manonia! but for her, I would care nothing for my own fate. Under no state of circumstances that rests within the pale of posibilities can I save her. I must go a veritable beggar onto the street—an object of scorn and contempt, to brook the jeers and insults of my gloating enemies. The doom of her father and brother is sealed. What then can I any longer be to her? Would it not be better to save them for her, and that she should lose me forever, than that all should be lost? If she but know that shadowy and false nature of my existence, my loss, for myself, would not cost her a pang.

"But how can it be within my power to save them. Surely they must sink with me.

"Oh that I could deprive my enemies of their rejoicings over my fall! What would I do to foil them? What would I hesitate to do? Nothing that Shakspeare makes Juliet conjure Friar Lawrence bid her do, rather than yield to the consequences of the dangers that menanced her.

"But why are they my enemies? Merely because it is the will of Fate. I have purposely provoked no one. I am and have been laboring for the interest of this city. For that reason, if for no other, I am entitled to a far greater degree of favorable consideration and kindlier encouragement than I have received from the masses of those acquainted with the true nature of my undertakings.

"I have offered the banks unquestionably safe security, in the best shape it was possible for me to present it under the circumstances, and demand money, to which, by the nature and importance of my business, I am clearly entitled, but which I am unable to obtain.

"Would it, then, if the banks are sufficiently unwary to permit it, be a great wrong to obtain this same money from them for identically the same purpose, without any security? I do not believe it would.

"But to what terrible consequences may not this lead? To what can it lead that is more to be dreaded than the disasters that are now about to crush me? Why, nothing; no, nothing. Not even the dungeon's gloom nor its clanking chains of bitter slavery.

"This scheme to use duplicate ware-house receipts appears to promise—what? Are there not sinister features in that? Would it not be forgery? Could it be safe for one day? I distrust it. It is but an infamous plot to entrap me. I would be immediately arrested the first day. I will not touch it.

"But then, what would being arrested amount to with me? I might as well go to prison for combatting to sustain a worthy cause by unfair means—to contravene unjust persecution, as to go on the street a vagrant for abandoning it. Can the end justify the means?

"Insignificant as it would generally be esteemed, my failure, just now, would be a calamity to the cotton interest here.

"But I must consult a lawyer. I will write at once. I will tide over to-morrow some way, and trust to Fate."

Garland at once turns up the gas jet, and writes:

"Hon. Simon Retainer.
        "City.

        'Dear Sir:
        "Enclosed find — amount, your customary fee for a legal opinion, which I wish carefully considered for a friend of mine, delivered personally to me by your messenger, before m. to-morrow, on the following point, to wit:

"Suppose a merchant, in active business, without making any statement relative to the genuineness of the paper, should use with a bank as collateral security against loans, duplicates of genuine ware-house receipts, for goods which he actually held; with no intention to defraud the bank, but with a fixed determination to pay the money at maturity; and using the money strictly in his business, without squandering or in any way attempting to conceal or put it beyond the reach of the law in the operations of its process: and should the bank, before the money was due, discover the worthless character of the collaterals, and arrest the party, who would then declare his ability and willingness to redeem his pledge; and was he able to demonstrate that such was a true state of the situation—would he, under the strict letter of the law, be subject to criminal penalties?

        "Yours truly,
                "Nube Garland."

            ⎯⎯⎯⎯

This letter is addressed, and the writer walks by the post-office, and deposits it in the night-box.

He then goes to his hotel, and retires to sleep —the disquiet sleep of the wretched, who know not peaceful repose.

Monday morning, he finds that two hundred bales of cotton have arrived since Saturday evening, which make ten thousand dollars that will be available that day; and there are bills of lading for four hundred bales, in the mails. Early in the day, he sells three hundred bales. That will unlock seven or eight thousand dollars more within the next three days.

Before ten o'clock, he receives the following:

"Dear Sir:
        "In reply to your question, I have to say that it is a well-established principle of law that to constitute a crime, in cases like that supposed by you, the intention to cheat and defraud must exist in the mind at the time the act is performed.

"As a matter of course, the state of the mind can be arrived at or established only by inference drawn from the acts of the party at the time and after the transaction is made. In such cases, the natural presumption generally is that the bent of the mind at the time was criminal.

"But in a case with all the points and circumstances just as you have proposed them, the law and decisions would not, in my opinion, sustain a criminal conviction.

        "Yours truly,
                "Simon Retainer, Atty.
"N. Garland, Esq."

This is the opinion of an eminent practitioner, who has served many years on the bench.

Thirty minutes after reading this letter, Garland is closeted with the same man who had advised him to resort to that means for relief, and opens the interview:

Garland: "Now, Mr. Expedient, I want to say here to you that I mistrust your sincerity, and believe that you come to me as a miserable decoy, in the interest of my enemies, who thus hope to trap me. I have, however, determined to test your sincerity. If you are acting, and propose to act in good faith, copy and subscribe to this paper, in your own handwriting, as a pledge."

Expedient: "Certainly I will; but I suppose you will allow me to retain a copy, or give me a counter-paper?"

Garland: "No, sir; I will do neither; nor anything but pay you the price per thousand named by yourself."

EXPEDIENT: "Very well, then; I will at once accept your terms. When shall I expect something to do?"

GARLAND: "To-night—if it can be arranged so soon."

A few minutes later, Garland is in a printing establishment, having the blanks run off. Before supper, four clerks have filled up twelve hundred of them, and they are in the hands of Expedient for manipulation.

At nine o'clock the next morning they are returned with the signature so well executed that an expert would be staggered to decide, in a comparison, wherein there is any difference between it and the genuine one.

Garland and Expedient are alone in a private room.

GARLAND: "You have done all you promised; and now here is your money. I want you now to understand me, and to appreciate your position. You are in my power. I shall at all times keep myself in a shape to take up this paper without delay. Do not, then, I warn you in advance, delude yourself with the imagination that I am at your mercy; nor make the fatal mistake of attempting to use me in any way through the influence of this connection between us; because if you do, let me tell you it will be woe unto yourself.

"I have taken the precaution in this matter to make ample preparation to guard myself against all such possible contingencies. I shall use you the same way, whenever occasion requires, for the same consideration; and you will not delay nor demand extra remuneration.

"I know you now to be a very dangerous man; but be true to your villainy with me, and I will never harm you, not even though I am in trouble, so long as I am well assured that you did not cause its origin."

EXPEDIENT: "You need have no fears. There was no danger of my ever betraying you, any way; now you are doubly safe. I now understand why you demanded that tell-tale document."

GARLAND: "You are correct in your surmises. I know human nature sufficiently well to be assured that any man who will propose what you did, and do what you have done, will not hesitate to levy blackmail or to sell his secret, as long as there is no danger of putting his own neck into the halter; but while you cannot do either without becoming the chief defendant yourself, you are harmless. To be more explicit, I can at all times, and under all circumstances defy you.

"My purpose is not to harm the banks, but merely to obtain money to which I am entitled, or which the nature and importance of my business should entitle me to receive; and I want immunity from all such annoyance as you might cause, and I have got it. That is all."

At twelve o'clock on this same day, Garland has to his credit in four banks sixty thousand dollars, on the faith of those twelve hundred worthless bits of paper. These represent a value of more than eighty thousand dollars. They are accepted by the banks without hesitation or question, and money loaned thereon, which he has sought in vain to obtain on the faith of legitimate value—and value which he would now be most happy to place under the control of the banks, in lieu of the detestable trash which he does deposit.

Here, now, at last, is the matured fruit of a little evil seed sown nine years before, in, comparatively speaking, almost an innocent way—a seed the production of which Garland struggled to destroy, but which the irrevocable decree of destiny had rendered irradicably fixed; secure against every ingenuity of man; able to defy every means that he might attempt to employ for its extirpation, as long as he did not assail it with unalloyed truth, and show in reality the nude deformity of the deceptive artifice by which it was at first planted and germinated. Thus the weed grew unchecked ever after, blossomed and produced fruit each time a little nearer matured. First the assumption of a false name; next the marrying of Manonia under that name; and now, finally, the perpetration of a great commercial crime.

This is a matter in its exact similarity to such prodigious numbers of cases in this country—a very inconsiderable per cent. of which never come to the light of day—that is fraught with such stupendous importance to society and its peaceful prosperity, looming up in a horrible form of hideous monstrosity and gigantic magnitude so fiendishly diabolical and so appallingly burdened with overwhelming curses, that we dare not lightly pass it by, nor wholly ignore its execrable destructiveness.

Taking a merely casual view of the case, hastily, as people of this fast country and age are prone to consider such, it is apt to receive an unmerited verdict, and the gravity of its import be too charitably estimated.

This is now a case that furnishes a commercial lesson of such momentous proportions that its value is not at all likely to be duly appreciated— a damnable thralldom of hope-wasting, life-blighting destruction, in which untold and unknown thousands of good and useful men are perpetually enchained; and who are every day of their false and dungeon-haunted lives, imperiling the brilliant prospects, the cherished dreams, the priceless name of promising and happy families.

Take Garland's case, as it developed, and it will awaken palliating sympathy in the breast of the average man, and receive from him a sentiment of charitable forbearance, to which it really seems that he is, at least partially, entitled.

He is engaged in a grand and laudable enterprise, which he has striven to prosecute with honorable fidelity, with unflagging energy, indomitable will, unyielding fortitude and courageous tenacity, in the face of crushing difficulties and hopeless discouragement, that are truly admirable. His distress has not sprung from any present misconduct on his part. And as to his motives, they are, unquestionably, unimpeachable. He does not dream, to all perceptible appearances, of defrauding the banks.

If he does design to defraud, he will raise a quarter of a million of money, take a short business trip, and fail to return. If his object is not fraud, he will be far more sure to redeem that dangerous paper at the maturity of his notes than were all his transactions based on genuine documents; because there could then be no danger of incurring criminal penalties.

His business is wonderfully important to the commercial prosperity of his adopted city. So, taking a liberal view of the case, as it appears hedged around by its strangely peculiar circumstances, we are almost persuaded to concede that the end justifies the means.

But, alas! when we endeavor to apply the inexorable and unbending rules of honest truth and majestic right to test the fabrication of this structure, it crumbles to dust. It will not bear an analytical scrutiny, because, no matter how beneficial the result might prove to the community or to the cause of humanity—even though it emancipate the pauper and the indigent toiler, and elevate them to independent affluence—it cannot stand, founded on deception and constructed by falsehood, from means unfairly obtained. Could it be possible for it to become the means of turning to the metropolis all the cotton in the land, or of saving the whole city from being plunged into annihilating ruin, not even both of these powerful results would justify nor excuse a course that truly, at all times, and under every state of circumstances or shade of color of a pretext, must remain unpardonable.

This man had flattering promises and bright business prospects to tempt him, besides other personal considerations. Extravagant dissipation leads many merchants into the snare of adopting this infamous expedient in some shape or other, in order to buoy up and keep afloat their sinking ships, without any reasonable prospect or definable plan for the future. Thus they drift as if by hazard, with no hope of ever extricating themselves, from the whirlpool of entanglement into which they are rushed by the fierce billows; although it is rarely the case that any one of them either designs or desires to defraud the banks or delude the private parties whom he victimizes. They make one forbidden shuffling shift, and it works well. Then it was so convenient in a case of extreme and pressing emergency, that it becomes but a natural result for it to be applied as a remedy to the next case of difficult embarrassment. And with men who find it necessary to seek relief through the medium of this expedient, trouble that imperatively demands it, is ever occurring and recurring.

In a little time the first transaction appears, demanding attention; soon the next follows, and other and new ones intermingle in the meantime, so that every day the doomed wretches become deeper and deeper involved, until finally they find themselves most helplessly and hopelessly shackled, loaded down with the galling chains and the ruinous consequences of their misdeeds; and discover also, that the plea of their honest intentions is both untenable and unavailing. Now they become reckless and extravagant if they were not already so; and if they were, which almost always is the case, they become yet more desperately rash.

To all these general rules, Garland was a remarkable exception. He worked harder than before, maintained his constitutional habits of temperance, and an almost miserly personal economy. His life merged into one concentral purpose, to which everything else with him was subordinate: to steer that ponderous, unwieldly overburdened craft of commerce into the haven for which he had launched her—to become the *first* and leading power in the cotton trade.

This opening he had discovered, but never dared dream of striving to fill, because he knew from the commencement that with him it must be one ceaseless struggle for bare existence in the humble ranks of commerce; and even this was very doubtful. But immediately on finding himself able to control an unlimited amount of money, he began to dream and to plan.

He effects an early settlement with the creditors of his Louisiana successor, and obtains possession of all that paper. He then writes in answer to their reproachful letters: "I have taken up all your notes. which may possibly prove to be an act of selling myself into slavery; and should it thus become, remember, I conjure you, when the echo of my clanking chains is wafted to you on the wings of the wind, that your unkind, unjust and cruel letters forged some of their unmerciful links." This done, he leaves that matter where, years before, he left his own name—with the things of the past.

After this, he fits out his ship, and sets sail on a wild voyage leading through the most dangerously treacherous reefs and breakers and rocks, subject and trusting to the guidance of breeze or gale or storm, without life-preserver, boat, rudder or anchor, fully resolved with her to float or with her to sink. Reckless, peril-beset captain!

15

His partners, his crew, and all those who are tempted by her imposing stateliness, her apparent staunchness, and the rapid speed she promises to hazard something in her cargo, are in blissful ignorance of her true condition, and the dangers that menace her and them.

Business flows to Garland's firm like water, in one perpetual and ever-swelling stream.

How promising the beautiful craft, had her timbers been substantial and the structure supported only by the truth! But, alas! the quicksands are beneath, and her structure is held together by falsehood's brittle cement.

Garland's firm will be dissolved by limitation, September, 1874. In the latter end of the active cotton-shipping season, an old gentleman who has heard of Garland's fine talents and thorough education in the cotton trade, through a prominent New Orleans house; and of his rapid rise in the face of such serious difficulties; and his flattering prospects for the future, through a prominent New York firm, comes on to the "Future City," and remains quietly around there for some weeks. Then he makes Garland's acquaintance, and proposes a co-partnership of five years with Garland, for his son, with three hundred thousand dollars in cash. Garland, after a week's consideration and inquiries, accepts the offer for Sept. 1st, 1874.

The old gentleman is exceedingly anxious that, in the *interim*, Garland shall so manage his business as to lay a grand foundation for the new firm. The holding of a large line of cotton, and making a sale of a champion list, at a season of the year when it will attract general attention, is suggested. And if possible, the engaging of a large amount of business for the next season is desirable. By making preliminary advances against the growing crop, this is practicable; and he is urgent to know the utmost that may be done.

Garland informs him that he thinks he can carry five thousand bales of cotton into August, and advance one hundred thousand dollars on the growing crop; but that he will be obliged to borrow the money, to be paid the first of September.

Then a lawyer is engaged, and the articles and contract of co-partnership are signed and sealed. It is conditioned that Garland shall do what he has asserted he can do. And he is to lay out on the tables a list of all the cotton samples that his sample-room will hold, which he estimates will amount to three thousand bales; and also to have this list photographed, and then handsomely lithographed on the back of cards and circulars, to be sent all over the cotton belt accessible to the "Future City" trade. This list of cotton is to be sold in the last week of August, and an M— *Republican*, with the commercial report of the sale marked, mailed to every man to whom the lithograph of it had been sent.

Furthermore, Garland is to buy and elegantly furnish a residence in the most desirable and healthful section of the city; and in it furnish his new partner and wife a home, as long as mutually agreeable to all parties.

His partner is to bear half the expenses and losses that may be incurred in connection with the commercial feature of this compact.

The old gentleman is to deposit a forfeit of one hundred thousand dollars in Government bonds, as a guarantee that his part will be faithfully performed, provided that Garland fulfills his promise as stipulated.

In all the morning papers of the first of September the notices of the dissolution of the old, and the formation of the new firm are to appear, as the first intimation to be made public. Until then no one is to be apprised of the revolution to take place in this firm.

The house is bought under the hammer for about one-half of its value: a grand old mansion with large and beautiful grounds. The whole, inside and out, is beautifully painted and frescoed, the grounds beautified, and an iron fence placed in front. Then the house is superbly furnished throughout.

This is the nature and character of the residence to which Manonia returns from her once happy childhood's home. She says it is too grand and too stylish for her. But she tries to be happy and cheerful, to reward Garland for the relief that he afforded her father and brother.

On the first day of June, Garland is carrying a fearful load, amounting to more than six hundred thousand dollars, mostly represented by thousands of bales of cotton, and more than one million pounds of hog product. He actually owes the banks about a half a million of money, and might just as easily owe them a full million. Both outside banks and numerous private parties press him to accept loans. He does withdraw one loan from a bank, and transfers it to a private firm, as a matter of accommodation. The reason that he owes no more money, is simply because he cannot employ it. He has all that he can use, including the one hundred thousand dollars which he obligated himself to advance to aid in the cultivation of the growing cotton crop. This he is and has been advancing at the rate of twenty-five thousand dollars per month.

He now holds in his own safe the genuine receipts for more than five thousand bales of cotton, while the banks hold perhaps nearly ten thousand spurious ones, purporting to represent this same cotton.

The cotton list, amounting to between twenty-five hundred and three thousand bales, is laid out; and a beautiful photograph made of the room. This is now handsomely lithographed on the back of circulars and cards, which are mailed to the cotton districts of the South, whence there is a probability that cotton may be influenced to the "Future City."

The grand Fourth of July procession in celebration of the completion of the great bridge, together with Independence Day, takes up its march, with Garland's firm represented by a strong wagon loaded with bales of cotton just as they leave the plantation press. This wagon is drawn by powerful mules. A framed photograph of the large cotton list is suspended from the ends of each bale of cotton. Above them, on either side of the wagon, is a strip of muslin, containing in large black letters the name of Garland's firm, and this prophetic inscription: "The Future City a rising market. Good for 250,000 bales. Crop of 1874-5." This is all; there is no regalia, no decorations; nothing about this wagon that does not portray the lofty aspirations and far-reaching purposes of Nube Garland.

Strange scenes, unique occupations for the prince of criminals, at least of that city at that time, to appear engaged in! Yet they are, nevertheless, recorded realities divested of every iota of the romancer's dreamings.

About this time, Garland contracts for about one hundred thousand dollars' worth of bagging for cotton. He also conceives the idea of having a controlling influence in or of owning a ware-house for the storing and compressing of cotton. His chief motive is to have for his own receipts of cotton ample facilities unencumbered by the merchandise of other large receivers; and for which, according to his reasoning, the capacities of the only legitimate compress ware-house will prove inadequate, and hence occasion much vexatious delay in delivering to the buyers. Furthermore, he believes that cotton press-stock is destined to be, and immediately, the best property in the city.

He proceeds at once in search of a suitable site for the building, and to the negotiation for two or three blocks of vacant property. This attracts attention. "Any ware-house that can control Garland's business will prosper," is freely admitted and asserted, even by parties unfriendly to him.

One wealthy estate owns the most desirable property. Quickly a representative of this estate, and four other parties connected with the largest iron works, prominent banks, etc., from the most conservative class, wait on Garland, and propose a stock company of six persons. This meets Garland's views; is just what he would have desired, had he imagined it a thing possible to obtain. Hence he is the originator of the scheme that created, as well as the christener of "The Factors' and Brokers' Cotton Compress Co.," to-day a wealthy and prosperous corporation.

Through the father of his prospective partner and connections of his in the commercial world, Garland is admitted into a ring formed to make a corner in pork for September. Garland is to buy quietly from time to time all the September contracts that he can, in one hundred thousand pound lots, buyer's option, prior to the last day of August; and at the same time to purchase all the spot stock that he can find, and store it. It is easy for him to do this without in any way creating suspicion, as he uses one hundred thousand pounds of meat sometimes in one week, and is always buying ahead and storing stock. It is generally understood that he expects to use three times as much meat in the Southern trade after the first of September as he is using at present.

It is calculated that he may, in all probability, buy, in spot stock and contracts, five million pounds by the close of August, necessitating a cash outlay of about fifty thousand dollars. And he buys about half a million pounds per week, on the average basis of eleven cents.

His future partner's side buy five million pounds, buyer's option contracts, for September, on a basis of ten cents. On this, and all that Garland may buy, they are equally to divide the results. Owing to the nature and extent of the combination, there can be no doubt but a large and active advance will ensue. This, on ten million pounds of stock, points to a moderately modest fortune.

Such is Garland's position and prospects when he enters upon the second half of July, within forty-five days of the grand haven in which there will be absolute safety beyond the reach of storms, far from the rock-bound coasts upon which the sweeping surge has so long and so often threatened to hurl him. Once safely arrived, he can then complacently defy all earthly power that might either threaten or assail him in his impregnable security.

The task appears already achieved. There is no more money to be borrowed. The cotton list is to be sold; some twenty thousand dollars more to be advanced to the cotton States, and his contract will be accomplished.

Then he will be enabled in one day to remove from existence all the dangerous paper with which he has so long kept afloat, and which has enabled him to pass by and over the dread breakers, where otherwise there could have been no escape from the threatened and sure ruin of a hopeless and irreparable wreck.

The first day of September he expects will install him in a position of influence, prestige and power in the business world that may insure the realization of the wildest dreams, and gratify the aspirations of the most towering ambition.

With an active capital amounting to hundreds of thousands of dollars, bank facilities for a million more, and the unlimited commercial credit which his new firm is likely to enjoy as soon as it is introduced to the public in the line in which it is designed to be engaged, there is, comparatively speaking, no limit to the results that may be possible to attain.

The twenty-ninth of July is the day appointed to organize the Cotton Compress Co.

Apparently, the dangers are all passed. The nature of Garland's transactions has neither been suspected nor questioned. All the banks understand that their notes are to be canceled in the early days of September. It does not seem possible that anything may transpire to disturb the serenity of the waters during the remainder of the voyage.

As the Indiaman, for months lazily traversing the placid waters of sleeping tropical seas, sees at length the dim outline of the welcome homeward shores looming up against the distant blue horizon—far across the gold-tinted crystals of the deep as they ripple in the mellow rays of the midsummer setting sun, only to find those waters on the morrow lashed by the Tornado's unsparing whip, driving her helplessly—whither her captain knows not, to a fate, be it what it may, from which he is powerless to stay her: so does Garland perceive the dark and angry cloud suddenly and unexpectedly rolling up, shutting out the lights which gleam so brilliantly in his hope-beaming sky—a hope built on sand and fashioned of reeds —and quickly feels the howling blast of the tempest's breath.

Contrary to every commercial calculation and probability, the cotton market, which earlier in the season promised to be buoyant and advancing in August and September, suddenly breaks down—grows panicky; then becomes so completely demoralized that September contracts are selling at a figure that justifies the street estimates that the cotton held by Garland's firm will, should the market become no lower, which the signs of the times indicate that it may do, lose at least one hundred thousand dollars.

Naturally, the banks are alarmed, and will either call for their money, or demand a margin equivalent to the shrinkage in the value of the cotton. The situation is far too serious and urgent to be ignored. Something must be done, and quickly.

The "True Friend" calls on Garland, and tells him frankly that he must unload; that there is no other alternative or salvation for him. The same course is unanimously urged upon him by his brother members of THE LEAGUE, in meeting for deliberation. He is forced to admit the stern necessity of adopting this advice.

In the meantime, meat is tending upward, and he has bought contracts within a few days for a million pounds, which stand open, on the words of honor and faith of mutual memorandums, that the margins shall be deposited and the contracts delivered on the fifth day of August.

Numerous parties, both in this country and Europe, have been negotiating for the large list of extra fine and fancy cottons held by Garland's house. He feels that, under his contract, the cotton must go to one party, in one unbroken lot. The decline will justify him in selling before the stipulated time.

But the delivery and caring for the one hundred thousand dollars advanced to the South, is the grand difficulty; yet it is a problem of easy solution with a man of Garland's fertility in creating resources. As he holds the genuine receipts for every bale of that list of cotton, he may easily deliver it. Then it is but necessary for him to procure sufficient fraudulent meat receipts to take up one hundred thousand dollars of the loans obtained on the spurious cotton receipts—a transaction most agreeable with the banks—and then apply the proceeds of the large list in canceling others of the same obligations. In this wise, the relief may be quickly found.

Accordingly, without any delay, most favorable arrangements are made for moving the cotton; the transaction is published; the papers are mailed to the South as agreed. In the meantime, forty thousand dollars of cotton paper is taken up with meat paper, and all the necessary arrangements made for the exchange of the requisite amount.

Thus it seems that another impending crisis is passed, one more threatening danger averted; and that, despite adverse winds and untoward circumstances, Garland will yet safely land.

What a fearful and horrible existence! What will power it must require to sustain a man under such circumstances, even though he has no other cares to harass his mind! How, then, it is possible for Garland, burdened as he is with the management of a large and actively working business, embracing enormous and complicated enterprises, to pass through this ordeal, month after month, without manifesting any symptoms of anxiety, is a deep mystery. Every breath he drew was bated by the intensified emotion of that feeling of suspense experienced by soldiers when advancing on a position where they think the enemy lies in ambush, and whence they are in momentary expectation of a withering volley—a thrilling sensation never yet truly portrayed.

CHAPTER LXIII.

WRECKED ON THE STRAND OF TIME!

"Oh unexpected stroke, worse than death!"
* * * * * * *
—MILTON.

"What am I? Nothing: but not so art thou,
Soul of my thought, with whom I traverse earth,
Invisible, but gazing, as I glow,
Mixed with thy spirit, blended with thy birth,
And feeling still with thee in my crushed feelings'
dearth."
—BYRON.

JUST as soon as the announcement of the big cotton transaction is made public, it becomes a topic of interest on the street and in the Exchanges, of mingled admiration, jealousy, envy and hatred. Almost all classes are agreed in the opinion that Garland will be "cornered" in the delivery of the cotton, and find himself unable to transfer the ware-house receipts for so large a lot, representing so much money, from the banks to the buyer. It is necessary for the buyer to have the receipts before he can procure a bill of lading. This he must have in order to negotiate the draft, enabling him to pay for the property. This buyer is himself one, who, as a competitor, will not sympathize with Garland, should he become embarrassed in the delivery of the goods.

From all quarters the progress of the affair is watched with impatient suspense. It is understood that the buyer will demand in the first instalment, receipts to cover an amount of one hundred thousand dollars.

On the morning of July 28th, Garland is duly notified that at half-past two o'clock, P.M., the receipts must be ready.

He is fully apprised of the character of the talk on the streets, and the predictions that are freely expressed. He therefore, because of his dangerous position, experiences an increased feeling of apprehension for the result; but he has permitted himself to be drawn into an ambuscade under an enfilading fire, and no longer is able to exercise discretion, further than to take the chances of running the gauntlet. He cannot with propriety recede from the transaction; for that is now impossible.

He, however, grasps the idea that he may, without any breach of good faith and in strict conformity with commercial integrity, assume a position that will provoke the buyer to repudiate the transaction. There are no rules of the Exchange relative to the method of delivering and receiving payment for cotton. The seller may use his discretion. Therefore, Garland notifies the buyer that, upon the surrender of the warehouse receipts, he must have the money in currency—a demand he believes simply impossible for the buyer to meet. He knows that there is no difficulty about delivering the cotton receipts; but he is, moreover, sensible of the danger it involves. But at the appointed hour, this opinion notwithstanding, the currency is ready.

Now, Garland resolves to distribute the money that same evening among his banks, and take up so many receipts that no wild stories may disturb the bank officers. By the time the balance of the cotton is ready to deliver, he will, with the money he will then receive, be able to redeem the last of the spurious cotton receipts.

But so much time is consumed in counting the money and the receipts, that the banks are all closed; and it is only by chance that he deposits the money in the vault of the bank nearest to his office that night.

In going home that evening, as on all other evenings, he will pass the door of one of his other banks, just before reaching the street-car.

The sun is setting; the atmosphere is stifling and oppressively hot. As he is about to pass the bank, the book-keeper, who is standing in the door, informs him that the cashier desires to see him a moment in the office.

Arriving at the office, he is ushered into the private apartment, where he finds not only the cashier, but also the president, an attorney and the cashier of another of his banks. Horrors! they know his secret—the long-caged mystery has at last escaped.

The buyer had proclaimed that he had a large number of the receipts for which he paid cash, and was, from the ready facility with which they had been delivered to him without the participation of a bank, somewhat suspicious that there was either some mysterious power behind the scenes, or some concealed fraud. As neither bank had delivered a receipt nor received a dollar of the money, they were not slow to believe the same.

The officers of the two banks met together, compared figures, and sent to the ware-house, where they obtained the startling information that the entire stock of cotton held for all parties, minus that large list then ordered out, was considerably less than the number of receipts which they held for Garland's house alone.

When confronted with these facts, he does not hesitate one moment, but states the situation just as it exists; tells them what he has done and can do; and that by the first day of September, the last dollar will be paid, provided his business is allowed to remain undisturbed by the deleterious influence of that unpromising discovery; that he will pay a large amount the next day, and then steadily reduce the balances until the debt is canceled. Further, if they deem a harsher course more wise and expedient, they will then have to take their chances amid the heterogeneous mass of *débris* from the wrecks of ruin that must inevitably ensue.

During the progress of this scene, on the very threshold, as it were, of a dungeon's grim and checkered grate, there is not the slightest visible demonstration of emotion nor discomposure displayed by Garland.

And his proposition is accepted almost without hesitation or doubt as to its fulfillment. With its acceptance there is vouchsafed to him a most solemn pledge that, provided he does not fail to redeem his proffered word of honor—all upon which the banks now have to rely—the knowledge of his disreputable slips shall never pass beyond the breasts of those who are present. The meeting breaks up, and Garland goes on home as though it had been no more than an ordinary and regular business affair—that is, so far as is indicated by appearances.

It would seem that he is Fortune's favorite in passing critical and dangerous crises.

He owes these two banks two hundred thousand dollars, for which they hold no valid security; and besides this, he owes a hundred thousand dollars that must be paid the first of August, four days hence.

The next morning he meets his appointment promptly at nine o'clock; assists to organize the Cotton Compress Co.; is elected a director, and pays his first assessment as a stockholder just as if nothing at all unusual had transpired the previous evening.

Then, before noon, he makes good his promise to the two banks, by paying them the amounts stipulated for that day.

Before the close of this day, however, the horizon grows dark with an overspreading cloud of portentous gloom.

The cashier of the other bank present at the time that Garland's uncomfortable negotiation transpired, broke his pledge, and informed the vice-president and a leading director of his bank of the whole situation, and what had been promised. The vice-president utterly disregarded the pledge of his cashier; and without consulting or notifying the other bank, he began a vigorous course of aggression, and held before Garland's eyes almost hourly the menacing image of a felon's cell in the county prison.

At noon, on the first day of August, he informs this banker that at the opening of bank hours on the next day the last dollar will be paid. Notwithstanding this promise, and the fact that in four days his bank has been paid ninety of the one hundred and twenty thousand dollars due it by Garland's firm, after five o'clock, P. M., of this same day that vice-president, who is a member of a large pork-packing firm, comes to Garland's office with an invoice made out from Garland's to his firm for a half a million pounds of pork. He leaves it to Garland's option to receipt the same and transfer the property, or to go to prison that night. The amount of balance that his bank will thus gain for one night is only about ten thousand dollars.

Garland meets all his obligations maturing on the first of the month, and pays the other bank a large amount besides. But all these things combined drive him to such desperate straits that he borrows fifty thousand dollars on the faith of some of the redeemed worthless paper.

On the next morning he pays the pressing bank the last dollar.

Before noon, the vice-president has disclosed the secret to the proper parties, for it to be quickly and fully advertised.

This is Saturday. When Garland leaves his office for home, the other bank wants only sixteen thousand dollars of being paid in full, and that he expects to pay on Monday. Thus, in the space of five days, he provided for three hundred thousand dollars; and he still owes a quarter of a million of money.

On Sunday, Garland's accustomed places in church and Sabbath-school are vacant. He suffers the stifled agonies of torment within the charming seclusion of his own beautiful home—charms and beauties that, with their enchantments and pleasures, for him are at an end.

For hours he is alone in the grand double parlors with the doors closed, curtains drawn low, and the blinds turned down—Manonia and the other persons thinking he is out.

The darkened apartments and the solemnity of their solitude are in strict harmony with the thoughts and the emotions of this wretched man, as he writhes unmasked beneath the scourging lash of retribution.

From one end of the room, the stern features of Lee and Jackson, in half life-size on their war steeds, in the scene of their last meeting, look reproachfully down upon him through the misty gloom; while on either side are an exquisite Beatrice and a matchless Madonna—the one, in her consummate beauty, seeming to gaze with fixed and scornful rebuke; the other, with saintly pity

As he returns the gaze of first one and then another, as his eye glances from face to face of these his favorite paintings, he instinctively experiences a sensation that inspires a strongly superstitious belief that in this moment, amid this voiceless scene, he is receiving a presentiment that the time is near when they must part. That this is now perhaps the scene which must be his last upon that stage.

Now, pausing suddenly, he exclaims in a voice husky with emotion, "I swear, until I am free from these cursed chains of ignominious slavery, never again to enter this palatial precinct fraught with such vivid perceptions of airy images conjuring up haunting fancies from the shadowy realms of the supernatural, unknown and mystic worlds.

"Oh, untarnished names of my brave chieftains, that I was only sleeping that innocent, tranquil, and reposing slumber with you! Farewell! Since I am unworthy to meet the inanimate semblance of your honest eyes, I must leave you. Farewell, my Beatrice! I have no claims upon you! But, my Madonna! can you not teach me how and where to find a balm to soothe my cureless wounds? Oh, thou image of the saintly mother of the true and the good, farewell! My other little treasures, farewell, too! We shall meet when I am unshackled; and then I will live with you in sadness, or else we are parting forevermore!"

Now this miserable man stands for a moment in the door, while some unavailing, unatoning tears course their way down his care-stricken face as he gazes back into the parlors. Slowly he turns away, and closes the door behind him.

After bathing his face and eyes, he joins Manonia, poor woman, who little dreams of the terrible nature of that volcano smoldering beneath the brittle, treacherous crust upon which the false idol that she so indiscreetly enshrined in her pure heart, is standing. He has never breathed one word to her of that fearful ordeal through which he has been and is still passing, nor to his partners, nor any other person than those who were present at that torturing interview of a few evenings before.

His sleep and its visions this Sabbath night are

no more pleasing than his solitary experience had been during the evening in the parlors.

Could words depict the sufferings of this miserable man during six days and seven nights, in colors sufficiently vivid to render them distinct to the understanding, so that they might be properly estimated in a clear light—in the forcible nature of their true reality—they would be sufficient by themselves, to say nothing of those springing from the same source for months previous to this period, and which must, as a matter of course, continue to flow unabated—to deter any rational man from incurring the risk of becoming subject to similar disastrous consequences, for which untold gold, nor honors, nor power could ever compensate. That deep midnight of the mind, where all its ministers are but the grim-visaged geniuses of despair—could it be possible to picture it to the world as it is, it would drive many who are hovering about its ragged edges away, so far and so effectually, that they would never make the fearful plunge into its uninviting and inhospitable realms, as they are now blindly ready to do—to rue their rashly mad act only when too late, when regrets will be unavailing.

Long before bank hours on Monday morning, Garland is apprised that scores of persons know his condition; and that the tidings thereof are rapidly spreading. He learns from the manager of a commercial agency, in person, that his office is already in possession of the damaging information.

That other creditors will learn this fatal truth, is now beyond doubt; but Garland believes that he can make a showing that will insure an amicable adjustment. Laboring under this impression, he sets about writing letters, and doing other things preparatory to the temporary modifications of his plans.

At two o'clock, P. M., he draws eight thousand dollars in currency from one bank, and from there directs his steps to another bank to draw a like amount; thence to pay the balance due the bank where he was first confronted with the tangible ghost of his crimes.

This bank acted with him in strict conformity and good faith—true to the pledge made by its officers on that night. He had paid the money due it

so rapidly, simply because he had been driven to similar measures with the other bank so much sooner than stipulated—not owing to any annoyance from its officers.

The first package of eight thousand dollars is a very large bundle, the bills all being of small denominations. A few blocks away from his office the package bursts, and he runs into a bank to obtain larger bills. This is not convenient, and therefore he accepts the cashier's check for the amount, payable to the order of his firm. This occasions considerable delay.

When he arrives at the other bank its currency has been sent to the Safe Deposit Company, so that after some detention, he obtains only five thousand dollars — several minutes after three o'clock.

Before he is a block away from this bank, he is informed that the little bank with which he first commenced to do business has discovered the true situation, since he left his office, and has in this short time placed the case in the hands of the Police Department; and that the officers are already out to arrest him and every one connected with his office.

He now at this late hour hastens home to apprise poor Manonia of the blow that is about to crush her hopes. She swoons under its weight, and lies insensible for some time.

He tells her of the other trouble through which he has been passing, and assures her that he had expected to arrange this present one in an hour. He gives her the cashier's check and five thousand dollars currency, and tells her to deliver them in his absence to no one but officers of the law. Now he seats himself on the portico to await the officers; and he has not many minutes to wait.

In leaving the house he tells Manonia that he may return in time for supper. She does not know that he is under arrest, as he went down stairs and met the officers at the front-door. A few moments later he is at the County prison, where he finds his partners and nearly every one of his employés under arrest.

No terms, arrangement, nor even propositions, will be considered other than paying the complaining bank in full, immediately. Garland obstinately refuses to do anything without his other creditors being present as participants; but states if they are promptly summoned he will make a statement, and propose something for the mutual security of all. He unhesitatingly admits that the paper held by the bank is worthless, and asserts that he alone is to blame..

His request to have his other creditors summoned is treated with contemptuous indignity, and he is ordered to a dungeon. During the night his house is ransacked, and it is the opinion of some neighbors who are with Manonia that she will not live until morning.

Now early the next day the arrested parties, all except Garland, are released. He writes a card to his creditors, in which he asserts that, if released at once and permitted to remain at liberty even under the most rigid police surveillance, no one will lose a dollar. But the authorities ridicule the idea, and the pressing bank demands its money in full. This conceded, the officers of that bank care not what course the other creditors pursue.

On the next night, the principal creditors meet at the prison, and Garland states from memory the condition of the business in which he has been engaged.

The next morning, August the 6th, the papers contain columns relative to this affair. One leading journal says of him:

"He is rather handsome, prepossessing, and is master of most engaging manners and conversational powers. He was a bold and daring officer in the rebel army, where he lost his arm. With all his sins, he has done more than any other man toward establishing a cotton market here and influencing cotton to it. His business talents, qualifications, and experience are extraordinary, and not often excelled. His entire business, embracing gigantic and most complicated transactions, he has at his fingers' ends."

The creditors are not able to agree among themselves. This results in the matter going at once into bankruptcy.

A certain element among the creditors, or some of them, believes that there is a very large sum of money buried somewhere, that may be unearthed.

Manonia has no money. The creditors seize the house and furniture; hence she is forced to vacate, and return to her father's home. Her wardrobe is plain, cheap and scanty. Garland's is not worth fifty dollars, and hardly cost more when new. In that quarter, at least, no money has been squandered.

As to Garland, he remains in confinement, month after month, while his assets are constantly melting away under the control of inexperienced hands.

By the fifteenth of September, his joint pork operations would have realized a clear gain of over half a million of money.

All of this stock that passed into the hands of the creditors, they sold at once, before the large advance was established. The contract with the parties concerning the large list of cotton was not carried out by the creditors, and hence the other side was absolved from performing their part. By some strange means, more than two hundred bales of cotton mysteriously disappeared, and were never found. Some ten thousand dollars in commercial notes left with a bank the day on which Garland was arrested, to be used as collateral for a loan to be granted the next day, vanished; and the bank that issued the eight thousand dollar cashier's check for the same amount of currency, claimed and obtained this check in the bankrupt court. Thus that amount was lost to the creditors.

Trivial matters, such as these just related, would be too small to receive the slightest consideration had they been the work of a man of Garland's character and proclivities. But when they lay at the doors of great and reputable financial institutions, they assume an aspect of gravely serious import, and deserve attention as portraits of a shady feature of the weakness of human nature, even in quarters where evil or dubious practices should not only find no place to harbor, but should be far above suspicion.

While Garland is in prison awaiting the result of his legal destiny, a prominent attorney and member of the State Senate one day calls on him. This gentleman had served with Garland as the commanding officer of a battalion in the same brigade for four consecutive campaigns, up to the very battle in which the latter lost his arm; knew him well; and appears to remember him distinctly as Capt. Garland, and to recall the fact that he was promoted to the rank of Colonel, and at the same time transferred to a new command. They talk over their old experiences, and they meet often from this time forward.

After the lapse of five months, the creditors are forced to conclude that there is nothing for which to censure Garland but the criminal irregularities of his bank negotiations, and that these had not been designed to defraud his victims. Otherwise, there is absolutely nothing morally wrong to urge against him, and no other party takes any share in his prosecution, except the little bank that had him arrested; and the managers did this persistently at first, as a means to secure the full payment of their claim—*privately*.

Their plan was to multiply charges to an extent to render giving bail out of the question, if not impossible.

Garland is represented by fine criminal talent in the legal ranks. No attempt to give bail is ever made until after the grand jury finally disposes of the case by finding five bills of indictment. Upon these the prosecutors rely that the amount of bail will be fixed at not less than fifty thousand dollars; still, however, it is fixed at five thousand; and the comrade of the old brigade procures bondsmen.

The country customers had not paid the creditors a dollar. When Garland is liberated the cotton season is so far advanced that the prospects for collecting are poor indeed; yet still he collects about five per cent. of the amount due his late firm in the South.

He is soon in business again, for the sole purpose, so far as the present is concerned, of trying to collect for the creditors.

He makes a silent arrangement with two brothers, who put up a little money—less than one-tenth of the amount agreed—which their stipulated salaries soon absorb.

Some friends assist Garland with small sums. These melt away in the steady suction of unavoidable expenses.

Manonia returns, and they go to humble housekeeping. This she in a great measure maintains by a laundry.

A year passes. Garland is making money, handling unmerchantable cottons. For this purpose, soon he has machinery established.

But before long he is swindled by New York and Philadelphia parties on some large lots. Then the market suddenly breaks down when he has a heavy stock on hand, and takes all that he has made, leaving him a loser by several thousand dollars.

Court after Court, his case is continued at the solicitation of the creditors of the bankrupt firm. His bondsmen die or become insolvent. The prosecutors try to have him re-arrested, but the Court denies the motion. The prosecuting bank in the meantime fails.

Nearly three years elapse. The creditors, through the wasting medium of the Bankrupt Court, after all the shrinkage and loss of available assets immediately after the crash, and the loss of eighty per cent. of the Southern advances, have been paid more than fifty cents on the dollar.

Now Garland is tried and convicted. This arouses the public. The jury, the Court, and the merchants—even many of those who had always been his enemies,—the cotton presses and shipping interest, protest against the execution of sentence. In consequence of this, he is a few days thereafter pardoned without ever leaving the jail, before he is sentenced by the Court.

Had the curse of the past, which had pursued him so many years, been as effectually obliterated as the one of the present, there might have been still hope on earth for him.

About this time a cotton house fails, with some of his funds on hand; and just two weeks after his release from jail, his cotton establishment and machinery burn, only partially insured. After long and tedious delay, adjustments and settlements are made.

Now Garland arranges to re-build not only the destroyed works, but to build in addition thereto an extensive factory, all to be completed by the first of September.

While this is progressing, the largest bank in the city fails, with every dollar he has to pay his workmen. But he is assisted after some delay, and continues the work.

It was necessary to buy and store cotton to run on for three months. This is bought through advances from a few friends and a bank, with the understanding that the works will be in operation on or before September the first. Just as soon as they are prepared to start, there is a partner ready with all the money that can be used.

In August, Manonia goes on a visit to her father.

There are constant delays and disappointments about the completion of machinery. September finds the works far from completion. The September delivery of cotton arrives. Cotton begins to decline. Everything is contrary. The bank wants its money; so do some other parties.

The morning of the eighteenth of September comes. The machinists are positive that the works could start on the twenty-fifth of the month. Garland is satisfied they may start by October the first, at the farthest.

On this day—September the eighteenth—Garland is notified that the contemplated partner has reconsidered the matter, and determined not to embark in the enterprise.

This information is a death-knell to Garland, that tolls the distracting tocsin of despair, which he at once resolves to stifle in the terrible act of self-destruction.

He is now thoroughly satisfied that he can neither escape the cruel consequences of his ever-pursuing curse, nor obtain any measure of redemption from it in this world: and that, no matter what the nature of the enterprise in which he embarks, nor however true the fidelity and undeviating the honesty of purpose with which he follows, the result will be failure and ruin, let the mortal encouragment and support be what they may. He is forced to believe, and the conviction perpetually haunts him, that to this source is due all the unaccountable forces of unfriendly opposition and unnatural difficulties that he encountered in every honorable move he attempted to make in the past.

He sets about making preparations for the dark exit with methodical system.

A plan of the works is drafted, and explicit details are written. All the remainder of that day and all night he is thus employed.

He has between five and six hundred dollars, all told.

Some time previous to this, he borrowed five hundred dollars from a poor widow, and was to give her children employment when the works were completed. Early next morning, he goes, and returns her money.

He is wearing a very fine gold watch and chain, the property of Manonia, a present from her father in the prosperous age before the war, when she was a happy girl.

He seeks a friend, and borrows two hundred dollars; then he registers a chattel mortgage on his household effects in favor of that friend, and sends the money and her watch to Manonia. Now he pays to his housekeeper the small amount due her, and leaves whatever balance there is remaining in the bank. These things consume all the forenoon; now he goes home.

The afternoon he passes writing to Manonia and her family. He tells her that but for her his dreadful end would not be so painful and bitter; but expresses the hope that she may be happier with her people, whom she loves so much, than she had ever been with him. Asserts that he has been so long estranged and so widely banished from happiness that it is utterly impossible for him, under any state of circumstances, to have rendered her happy; and beyond human power for him to avoid causing her misery as unending as life itself; that he is thankful they had no children to inherit his shame; that he has made life a failure; and he entreats her to forget, as he knows that she could never forgive him. He closes this cruel letter with these pathetic and melancholy lines:

" Fare thee well—thus disunited,
Torn from every nearer tie;
Seared in heart and lone and blighted—
More than this—I scarce can die."

Sadly, tenderly, he bids the little inanimate objects about the house farewell; and just as the sun is setting, he leaves the house, with his vial of potent bane-forever. Now he hastily bends his steps in the direction of some old coal-fields just beyond the suburbs of the city, among which he had once lived, where he knows of an accessible cavern, in which he designs to find a lonely death-bed and an unknown grave.

AMID THE DARK CAVERN'S GLOOM!

This woe-begone, self-abandoned, God-forsaken wretch, by the aid of the dimly flickering light of a small waxen taper, which he lights on arriving at the mouth of the cave, penetrates to the dark and dismal recess of its dreary depths, sets the little luminary in the niche of a rock, and repeats these most impressive lines from Cato's soliloquy.

> " Eternity! thou pleasing, dreadful thought!
> Through what variety of untried being,
> Through what new scenes and changes must we pass?
> The wide, the unbounded prospect lies before me,
> But shadows, clouds, and darkness rest upon it.
> I am weary of conjectures. This must end them.
> Thus am I doubly armed; my death and life,
> *This* in a moment brings me to an end:
> But *this* informs me I shall never die.
> The soul secured in her existence smiles
> At the drawn dagger, and defies its point.
> The stars shall fade away, the sun himself
> Grow dim with age, and nature sink in years
> But thou shalt flourish in immortal youth,
> Unhurt amid the war of elements,
> The wreck of matter and the crash of worlds!"

"Oh, alas, that the remorse of the coward, Conscience, should have brought—nay, driven me to this fearful extremity! This is the last fell stroke of the Avenger's scourging lash. What a terrible penalty! What a sad expiation! All, all alone, here must I die.

"How many years I have escaped this last fiendish wrath of the curse, through prolonged and oft wellnigh intolerable torture, only ultimately to taste its poignant bitterness! How I have blindly struggled to avert the pangs of this unhallowed act, the mystic witnesses of the supernatural realms alone know!

"That heaven which I can never enter, bears me testimony that the thirsty cravings of my wretched heart have ever been to be true and good,—boons of honor and purity to me forbidden, because my life and name were perverted and false—a prolific curse, that from a little germ to a huge monster grew.

"O Earth! with all thy maddening delusions and vain strifes, thy trials, disappointments, and heart-aches; and thou, blessed Sun! that oftentimes gladdens the crushed heart; and thou, O Moon! luminary of darkness; and ye bright little stars! infallible guides to the despairing mariner adrift on the wide waste of waters, and to the wanderer astray in the trackless desert or in the pathless wilderness—and all things that are beautiful and good,—farewell! Ah, yes, farewell! forever farewell!

"My God! whither, whither shall I fly?

"O Heaven! O Saviour! Have mercy on my poor soul, that has ever abhorred my false and wayward life! Spare it, then, from the eternal doom of a never-ending hell, and let it expiate in some definite ages of purgation, I pray, for the sins of a life in which it never found delight. Lord, if it be thy good pleasure, grant me a doom less severe than I deserve!

"Thou subtile, life-severing potion! what dismal affinity the ghostly shadows of this dreary pit bear to thy dark potency. Swift be thy surceasing course, to still with speed the now feebly throbbing currents of my despairing life!

"How tasteless!—as but a harmless draught of water. But ah, my fingers and my toes tingle as though their nerves had been distended and suddenly relaxed. My heart throbs with stifling palpitation. Ah, my senses vanish! The death bells ring in my ears! I sink! It is all over! I die! Lord be merciful! Spare—spa——"

CHAPTER LXIV.

MORE EVIL FRUIT AND ITS CONSEQUENCES.

> " Retribution thus decreeth:
> What thou dost to others mete,
> Shall to thee again be meted;—
> Sowing tares, ye reap not wheat."
> —M. A. BILLINGS.

FROM the time of Samuel Van Allen's disagreeable and disastrous complication with Madam Mountjoy, resulting from his contemplated intrigue with one of her daughters, the hand of an unpropitious Destiny appeared to be ever against him. Prosperity vanished from him as a flitting shadow, which seemed perpetually reflected in mocking derision from the frowning brow of angry Fortune. His affairs became more and more straitened, and caused him continually increasing embarrassment.

At first he adopted, as an expedient, the unhealthy system of "commercial killing." This in itself was shameful business faith, closely bordering on criminal hypocrisy.

As this sickly practice invariably leads from bad to worse, it alone could not long serve his turn. Soon it became necessary for him to resort to prevarication, and grossly to misrepresent his condition, in order to strengthen that treacherous and pusillanimous support upon which he leaned, and which alone upheld the tottering walls of his failing structure.

When a merchant or other person occupying a position in the world in which public confidence is reposed, and in which public interest might be jeopardized, advances thus far on the road leading to black and damnable dishonor, he has, no matter how unconscious of the fact he is or how widely far his intentions are therefrom, become the helpless slave of circumstances, and is hopelessly shackled with all the degrading chains thereto appertaining.

Such was, in the naturally true course of events, the miserable predicament in which Van Allen found himself engulfed.

His family was as old as the city itself, and its escutcheon was untarnished by one stain of reproach. He was a churchman of high standing and influence in the very first order of congregations of the most prominent church in the great metropolis of New York. His own household was all that education, culture, refinement, social position, purity and piety could make it. To him it was devoted to the verge of a fondly cherished idolatry—an interesting, a promising, hopeful, happy little circle, which never dreamed that the husband and father was faithless to his own family, and false to that piety which he professed.

Here was a man with the priceless heritage of family honor; the most tenderly endearing ties of the present; the powerful influences of religion and public confidence to restrain him, to conjure him—nay, more: almost, as it were, to bind him with hallowed chains of golden purity, far and securely away from devious and forbidden paths, steadily, systematically, surely rushing onward, and ever nearer and nearer still, to the brink of perdition.

How could he stoop to pervert all this enviable and bounteous wealth, to subserve the masked phantom of the basest infamy? How turn away from the sweet and delicate charms of a pure and confiding wife, to bask in the cold, hollow, mocking, deceptive smiles of a heartless, imperious, unmerciful and cruel mistress? Oh, how could he thus lavish his treasure and sacrifice his honor on that deadly shrine of reeking lust? How turn his back upon that home of love and that church of redeeming salvation, to face a grim and cheerless pile of unpitying granite, and in it a living tomb behind a dreary, solitary dungeon's hope-excluding bars?

However, be all this conjecture founded as well as it may, that was, notwithstanding, the identical course pursued by Samuel Van Allen. It was but a step from conjugal infidelity and hypocrisy to crime. Soon he was a forger and an embezzler.

With this fatal step began a life of mental torture, such as only a man who has staked so much in a desperate game can know. The church, his home, and all their endearing and sacred associations, were but purgatory to him. The gilded perfumed boudoir of his mistress was an earthly hell, to which he seemed bound by adamantine chains.

Deeper and deeper grew the sucking quicksand of his thralldom.

His mind became abstracted, and his deportment listless; his face haggard and careworn—he was a hopeless wreck of his former self.

His family and friends were alarmed with fear lest there was some strange and incurable malady slowly but surely sapping his vitals. Ah, how prophetic were their conjectures; but how far from the true source of his wasting leprosy was directed so much as the shade of suspicion!

Remorse of conscience was unceasingly gnawing at his heart-strings; and the shadow of that most terrible of all spectres, "the ghost of justice," haunted him day and night. Every face he beheld on the street turned toward him as if to cast a scrutinizing glance; every step he heard on the floor seemed as if approaching his office; and every time his door-bell rang he involuntarily started, and shuddered at the bare fancy that there was the inexorable pursuer, ready to grasp him with the heavy and relentless hand of the law.

Thus hours—long, irksome, tedious hours of agonizing suspense, dragged themselves away, each in itself an age of torture, until they were multiplied into years.—What a life!

All things in this world, sooner or later, come to an end, so did this feature of Van Allen's doom of torment.

One morning he leaves home as usual. This day his long-time apprehensions are realized. The heavy hand is upon him. He finds himself, at last, fast bound in the toils of Justice. The Avenger, with his chastening rod of retribution, has overtaken him.

He is conducted to the bar of the Court without delay, to plead to indictments which have already been found against him. He pleads guilty. This evening the sun sets upon the walls of a prison, within which he is decked with the striped insignia of his shame.

But the home—ah the home! The sun sets upon a home of despair, in which the star of hope has gone down forever. The curse that follows the wrong-doer has entered, wreaking its unmitigated vengeance upon innocent heads.

The poor wife is smitten with a piercing stroke of frenzy, from which she never rallies, but becomes a raving maniac. The amiable daughter is stricken by the venomous shaft, and soon dies heart-broken; and the tidings are ere long wafted up from the asylum that the mother, too, is dead.

Then the Executive deems that the author of all this woe and death has drained the cup of retribution to the last bitter dregs, and pardons the murderer, to give him an opportunity of attending his victim's funeral. What a spectacle! What a terrible warning! Let us draw the veil over the heart-sickening scene.

———

CHAPTER LXIV.

THE WANDERER'S RETURN.

"Break, break, break,
    On thy cold, grey stones, oh sea!
But the tender grace of a day that is dead
    Will never come back to me."
                —TENNYSON.

THE blighting frosts have transformed the deep green foliage of Virginia's fair landscapes into a robe of sere and yellow, golden and brown and red—a variegated coat of many colors. The chilling winds pelt fiercely upon this fantastic mantle of the forest, and steadily rend it into shreds, covering the ground with its beauteous fragments.

Here and there may be seen, now and then, a grand old sentinel of departed centuries with his majestic limbs denuded.

Amid this solemn, impressive scene of Nature, in which all things wear the melancholy imprint of death, on the lofty summit of an old field, on a branch of the Blue Ridge Range, there might be seen, just before noon, a lone, travel-weary individual. Here, standing with head bare and the wind playing with his long hair and beard, he is gesticulating wildly and addressing the panorama which spreads in undulating waves far away all round him, until the outlines are lost in the misty curtain of blue, with that emotional vehemence that animated beings are wont to inspire. He personifies all upon which he gazes, as he thus casts his words forth upon the wings of the wind:

"Oh my own, my native blue mountains! ragged crags and heaven-ward towering peaks! And oh, ye murmuring, sleepless cascades and thundering cataracts! do I once again behold you, fondly cherished scenes of childhood's blissful dreams, with my open eyes, unchanged by wrinkles of the heavily journeying years and unscathed by war, the same as when I bid you farewell long, long years ago—long though not very many? Oh, how sad and ominous was that parting! Ten thousand times more bitter and joyless is this meeting!

"Oh mountains! here is thy long-absent and wandering son; from war's wasting flames, the perils of the deep, and Death's haunted valleys found in traversing earth, covered with shame, steeped in crime's thrice crimsoned dye, all unworthy to receive thy greeting smile. Nor man, nor thee, nor Heaven will wash from my desecrated brow its brand of burning ignominy. I left thee, young, and brave, and pure, and true. I return prematurely aged, and cringing, and defiled, and false. Times unnumbered have I pined to stand here as I stand now. Ah! in dreams, on the unfriendly shores of foreign lands, have I stood here as in the by-gone time, with a thrill of hope; but now that emotion is unknown. Would that I had not come!

"Oh! But in yonder valley, in that farm-house once dwelt my mother. My mother, oh my mother! are you there now? Like the mountains and the brooks, do you still live? or, like the leaves of the forest, have you withered and fallen?"

He now picks up his hat, and with slow and hesitating steps approaches the house.

At the house there is a crowd of the neighbors gathered, as it is Sunday—a custom much in vogue in many rural districts of the Southern States.

The stranger arrives, is invited in, and accepts a seat; but no one recognizes him.

More than sixteen years have elapsed since he left that home circle, a beardless boy. For ten years he has been mourned as dead; is really well nigh forgotten. But still he is, nevertheless, in his father's house, and beholds the well-remembered faces of both father and mother, some of his sisters, and a few of the guests.

All traces of the wild excitement of a few moments before have disappeared, and his face has assumed an expression of listless stoicism. No one would guess the wildly conflicting emotions now warring in his breast. At last one of his sisters says:

"Does no one know Garland Cloud?"

She is right. After long and silent absence, the erratic wanderer is again at the home of his tender years and unsullied innocence, whence the ebbing tidal wave has rolled him back.

The story of the past appears fraught with bitter memories, that seem to conjure up the most excruciating anguish.

He has no money, no purpose, no prospect, no hope; and is subject to fits of melancholy and despondency that often last for hours, during which time he lies on the ground in some secluded spot, thinking—thoughts that his God and himself alone will ever know.

Months, the entire winter, pass away. He is so much enfeebled that he rarely ever goes beyond his father's premises.

Garland Cloud has one unmarried sister who was a little girl when he left home. During his absence, she has bloomed to mature and charming womanhood.

His gloomy abstractions touch her tender and sympathetic heart. She yet remembers him as she saw him the last day at the Mountain Meadows, and vanishing the next morning like a spectre through the shadows of the grey twilight, a proud, true, pure, and noble youth. And she again remembers the dread story, as mild fragments of it reached her father's home through the mails, of his blighted hopes and reputed end; and her years of mourning, such as none but a sister or a mother may know, for the lost son or brother.

Also she remembered the sweet, angelic, more than sister mourner, who with her had sorrowed many days in the meek resignation of incurable despair as they again and again together mingled their tears, and each on the other's neck wept in true sisterly love—Maimie Cloud and Carrie Harman.

And she pities her brother with the keen sensation generated by a yearning to alleviate a bane for which there is no antidote—a sentiment whose only fountain is the heart of pure innocence.

In graphic strains of melting pathos she recounts to him the pitiful story of the mournful lamentations of Carrie Harman. Thus for the first time he has forced upon him the overwhelming conviction that "The Angel of Consolation," the dream of his youthful days, the idol of his shadowy manhood, the queen of his earthly hopes, and the genius of his mortal despair, had loved him with a regally royal adoration that shamed his own cowardly inconstancy that induced and permitted him to wring her heart, blast her hopes, and veil her life in a shroud of sombre sadness. This adds fresh pangs to his excruciating agonies, which were before all but unbearable.

Gradually the guileless little sister artfully seeks to draw from her disconsolate brother the story of his wanderings. For months she never permits him out of her sight many minutes at a time. Wherever he goes, she is by his side, striving to console and lure him away from the terrible thralldom in which he is a prey to his own dark mind.

After a long time, when spring has come, the flowers are on the hills, and the birds are singing in the tender foliage of the forest, he sits with his sister amid the charming sweetness of a sylvan grove, just as it has sprung from Nature, deep in the wilds of an unpruned mountain wilderness, and says:

"Ah! my sweet sister, if you knew the bitter and inexpressible sadness which entwines about the memories of the past, you would not importune me with such subtle suasion to recall and recount my untold miseries to you.

"But, oh! my sissie, with the afflicting yet thrice-blessed name of Carrie Harman is the very quintessence of my unhappy life blended. Of the cruel depth of this fearful truth, God alone in heaven can ever know the unutterable reality.

"From the moment I was rescued from my watery shroud up to this hour, go where I would, do what I might, the ghost of Carrie Harman haunted me, haunts me still, will haunt me ever.

"Life ceased to have a charm for me. There is scarcely a danger on the earth or the deep to which I have not recklessly exposed myself; yet, with rare exceptions, in maddening strifes in the battle of life, designed to benefit the human race, I thought that thus to die would be no suicide.

"But some mysterious providence seemed to preserve me. I was never sick among even the most scourging epidemics; no other danger harmed me.

"I traversed Mexico and the South American States amid brigands and savage hosts; made and lost moderate fortunes. I have been in many enterprises, and lived for many years at the same place.

"One of the saddest and most unfortunate transactions in which I became involved was getting married. Except Carrie Harman, this is the most painful memory of my distorted and ill-starred life—something that created an endless but unavailing regret.

"Why I married, I am unable to explain. I suppose I was mad. I did not love as man should love. This was impossible.

"The photograph about which you have asked me so many questions was hers. She was as good as she was beautiful—both as beautiful and as good as Carrie Harman. She loved me blindly—my lost and unhappy bride! A loss I must ever mourn; a bereavement that no words can ever portray. It is a theme much too painful to think about seriously; too agonizing to discuss. Pray spare me the torture which further details would inflict.

"Oh that I could tear this distressing memory from my mind, which is prone upon it forever to dwell.

"I beg of you, now, my good sister, do not again recall this sorrowful subject. I would forget it, forget Carrie Harman—all connected with the past—that I have ever lived, and start life over anew, if such were possible."

Cloud makes money during the summer selling goods by sample on commission.

In the fall he is selected as an advance agent for a colony.

And now once more he bids adieu to his native hills to enter upon new and varied scenes. This time, perhaps, he turns his back to the enchanting, spell-binding views of the mystic Blue Mountains forever. But his face is to the restless surge of the deep, blue Atlantic, and his frail bark is again launched on the seething waves of the tempestuous sea of life—a *mystery* to all the world—*almost* to himself.

———

CHAPTER LXVI.

WHERE THE PALMETTO BUDS AND THE MAGNOLIA
BLOOMS.

" Let us go where the wild flowers bloom,
Amid the soft dews of the night,
Where the orange dispels its perfume,
And the rose speaks of love and of light."
—SENTIMENTAL SONG.

GARLAND CLOUD soon finds himself under the genial sunshine and dreamland skies of the Italy of America—the land of the orange and the rose, where the blight of winter is unknown; where zephyrs fragrant with rare and delicate perfumes forever sip and waft odors from never-fading flowers; where plants and fruits of every clime will grow; where, in a thousand spots, may be found more than the fabled vale of Vaucluse; where, more than elsewhere, there is a paradise on earth; where blushing Nature blooms in eternal spring-time and reproduces the grand and matchless enchantments of our imaged Garden of Eden—oftentimes creating a veritable ideal oasis in the sandy waste.

Of all other spots on this continent, or on the face of the whole globe, as to that matter, nowhere else may be found a more concentrated interest for the human race—especially the invalid and the afflicted—than that belt of the United States whose shore is laved by the cooling swash of the Gulf Stream, where frost is unknown. Nowhere else has Nature left so visibly the imprint of a bounteously lavish hand that bestowed her gifts with such unmeasured prodigality.

Upon this delight-inspiring coast stands the oldest town in America, built by hands from the Old World—or, at least, the oldest whose story has been portrayed on the "pictured page" of history.

Elsewhere there may be, and more than probably are, buried ruins built by the Carthaginians, the Romans, or, yet more likely, by the Phœnicians, in times of great antiquity.

Somewhere there must be a foundation for the well-preserved legend of "The Lost Atlantis" of the Romans, who must have largely credited

16

the story, or rather, perhaps, did not doubt its authenticity.

Somewhere in the Western world, there must have been land known to the Roman navigators, which, owing to the want of compass, new men were unable again to find after some sudden vicissitude had crippled navigation until those acquainted with the distant shores were all dead.

But, however, we have unquestionable testimony to support the claim of this quaint sea-coast town to the appellation of *ancient*—the mother of towns in the United States.

This fact alone should shed upon that shore where stands this venerable place a bright ray, a refulgent halo of reverential interest worthy to be consecrated as hallowed and sacred, were there no other charms about it to bind the admiring beholder with ravishing rapture. But there are other captivating charms with thrilling fascinations entwined about them, before which, to the carnal sensibilities of mankind, this relic of the centuries pales to insignificance.

The old Fort claims the attention of tourists. Its tragic legends are familiar to the student or the reader of American history.

Along with the Fort stands the ancient Cathedral, whose lamp has been kept trimmed and uninterruptedly burning for more than two hundred years.

Farther down South, along the coast, are the ruins of the old Indigo and Sugar Works, and plantations.

Here was once maintained a serfdom rarely paralleled in the history of slavery. The unfortunate sufferers were mostly colonies lured by their ruthless masters to emigrate from Greece and the shores of the Mediterranean.

There is nothing pictured in "Uncle Tom's Cabin" to approximate the atrocities to which these hapless and helpless victims were subjected.

Their domiciles of torture were many miles from the ancient town, the residence of the Governor, with a broad river intervening.

In time, their burdens grew much and multiplied until they became unbearable; and the poor wretches conspired against their masters.

A few men worked at night, and were assisted

by others to complete their weekly tasks, in order to secure a sufficient holiday to give them time to visit, and lay their grievances before the Governor. They were obliged to swim the river, both going to and returning from the town.

The Governor graciously listened to their prayers for relief, and invited them to come at once to the town with all their people, and take up their abode under his protection.

As soon as dark, after their return, they collected their people; armed the men with wooden spears and other improvised weapons; formed them into a hollow square, so as to present a solid phalanx on either side, surrounding the old people, women and children, and marched away in bold defiance of their chagrined and menacing masters.

Thus emancipated, they became an important factor to the ancient town, where many of their descendants are to be seen to this day.

They are yet an exclusive and rather ostracized race; but unjustly, because they are a proud, an intelligent, industrious, and withal a good people. They are known as " Mornarcains."

This term usually is meant to imply contempt, inferiority, or some other indefinable slur, when employed by other races; who often aver that they are speaking of a mongrel people, whose blood is deeply tainted with that of the negro.

Nothing is more basely false. Such is due more to ignorance of the true history of this long-suffering and much-persecuted people, to current prejudice and common report, than to willful maliciousness on the part of their often slandering neighbors.

Naturally new-comers hear and believe these stories. If they casually inquire who such people are, the answer, "Oh, they are nothing but 'Mornarcains,'" usually suffices to put to rest all interested inquisitiveness.

The poor people are patient, and never resent, nor strive to counteract their injuries, which really appear to cause them no concern. Their complexion is very light Creole. Among the women are Andalusian beauties, with long black hair and large, dark, dreamy eyes.

This race is widely dispersed through the State,

and, except in the savage tribes, were for long periods of time almost its only inhabitants.

But enough of this interesting people, and something more of the country.

Few countries, and no other section of the United States, have ever been scourged, and smitten, and paralyzed in the struggling vicissitudes of the march of civilization, as this fair and smiling land of which we write.

The jealous rivals of the olden time often almost depopulated it. To its few citizens the savage hosts never ceased to be a murderous and devastating terror, until nearly the middle of the present century.

The Civil War, and the reign of terror which followed in its wake, retrogressed settlement and prosperity almost to the deplorable condition in which the savages left them.

Not until about the year 1870, did actual settlement and development set in.

Since 1876, enthusiasm, progress and "booms," have been the predominating features prevailing in this "sunny land of flowers."

In 1883, her destiny is fixed, her future more than a shadowy dream: she is the winter garden of America—the invalids' asylum of Earth.

The capital of earth to her sceptre is beginning to bow; the golden streams of the world to pour into her lap.

Her waste, howling swamps, where the screaming panther, the snarling bear, and the deep-mouthed roaring alligator have held undisputed carnivals as monarchs of the forest and the deep since Creation's dawn, are in process of transformation to blooming Edens.

Her orange-groves are rapidly becoming the wonder of the world, while all other productions of the tropics are found to flourish prolifically.

This is true of the southern belt only, below the frost line; north of this, however, the orange and other hardy fruits are quite successfully cultivated.

Many poor people are greatly deluded and swindled by "land sharks." These miscreants publish falsely colored statements to attract emigration; and then induce the unsuspecting victims to settle on unsuitable land.

The variety of soil is very great. Some sections are entirely unsuited to industries which are admirably adapted to other sections; there is much land valuable for other purposes, upon which oranges will never grow.

This fact many people learn to their disgust and sorrow, only after all their money and some years of time, have been wasted in the useless attempt to accomplish an impossibility.

This is truly the poor man's country, after he once becomes acclimated and secures a foothold. But if he lands here very poor, ignorant of the country, and a stranger to the phenomena of the climate, he may anticipate some bitter and very trying experiences during the first season, as well as some cruel disappointments. But, however, these features are steadily improving with the civilization and the prosperity of the country.

The cool winds from the Gulf Stream transform the Southern coast, which otherwise might be a torrid clime, to one of the most moderately temperate sections on the globe, where the ordinary range of the thermometer is between 60° and 85°, averaging 73° all the year round. Never is it uncomfortable in the shade at noonday, nor the use of a blanket unnecessary at night. As a place for winter residence and resort, it is nowhere rivaled.

Here it is so easy merely to live without great effort, after securing a foothold, that the term, "the lazy man's country," is apt and appropriate.

But we must desist: this charming theme is luring us far from our proper province.

Of this matchless clime and land Garland Cloud writes the most glowing letters to his constituency.

He makes very admirable arrangements for his friends; but their tardy arrival greatly mars their prospects.

This requires Cloud to make a trip to the leading sea-port, where his room is entered, chloroform administered to him, and he robbed of all his money—except some previously remitted to the East, to purchase supplies for a contemplated arrangement.

While in this city he is very nearly imperiled once more in the painful embarrassment of mistaken identity, as the sequence will demonstrate.

He meets a stranger on the street who thus accosts him:

"Are you not Mr. Garland, formerly of the 'Future City?'"

CLOUD: "No, sir; my name is Cloud; my home is in this State."

STRANGER: "I beg your pardon, sir; I readily perceive my mistake. I am a cotton merchant in that city, and you very much resemble a man whom I once knew well there by that name, but the first word you uttered convinced me of my mistake."

CLOUD: "There is often a strangely striking resemblance between two persons. Being mistaken for another man, about the close of the war, has cost me more trouble than belongs to forty average lives."

STRANGER: "Yes, sir; I have known men hung the same way. Good-day."

Garland Cloud is seriously embarrassed by the loss of his money. His health is much impaired from the effect of the powerful dose of chloroform administered to him.

He returns to the section selected for his friends. There he finds himself under the ban of suspicion. He is regarded as an impostor. It is doubted whether or not he represents a colony; and it is not believed that he lost any money.

This is a bitter ordeal; but there is no alternative but to remain and endure it. To leave, would be but to confirm the strong suspicions entertained against him.

In the meantime he loses nearly every opportunity upon which he had most relied for his friends, long before they arrive.

From this moment Cloud loses courage and hope. He recognizes the shadow of the unpitying avenger still pursuing him, and comes to believe that every member of the innocent, over-confiding colony will become enthralled in the excruciating torture of his situation, and be forced to suffer the inevitable contagion of his own proper curse.

The poor colonists work with courageous will, but nothing they touch prospers. Anxiety, over-exposure, and insufficient nourishment, together combined, prostrate every member of the colony with fever by mid-summer. Cloud alone remains out of bed and able to look after the sick, who are scattered over territory several miles in extent. These people are not acclimated. The tides are unusually high. The locality is naturally miasmatic, and the overflow renders it doubly unhealthy.

Cloud sticks to the people with fidelity. He is their only hope for a long time. His endurance during the summer and fall is incredible.

But in October he is stricken down, after the colonists are able to take care of themselves, and his life for some time despaired of—it seems that he must die. However, he rallies, gets well, and withdraws the shadow of his curse from his friends.

He goes to a prosperous town and soon forms a commercial co-partnership, which, however, proves unsatisfactory, and is in a short time dissolved.

Now he goes, with very little money, to the city where he had been robbed. Why he goes there, appears a mystery.

He is so thoroughly impressed with the conviction that the dark curse of his own rayless life had been communicated to the innocent people who had linked their destiny with his, that he now becomes a thorough and fixed convert to the faith that nothing with which he is connected can thrive, but is sure to come to grief and ruin.

This is a strange man, linked to a strange destiny. From this point he appears to enact his rôle as though following the text of a perfectly planned programme, for which he has been fully prepared by the most careful study and the most patient practice.

He still believes that he can neither escape the consequences of the curse which has pursued him every day for nearly fifteen years, while ever augmenting its pitiless severity, nor cure it; that the day has long since gone by when for it there was a remedy. And in contemplating it, as its developments steadily unfold, we are gradually forced to admit the same.

He seems to have settled down to a dormant state of stoical indifference as to himself, or to have nothing new to fear.

Can it be that there is nothing—no ghostly shadow from out the hidden stores of those years

of silent and mysterious absence—to haunt him? or is it true that there can be naught on earth worse than the present reality?

At all events, as to these things he appears to exist in tranquil composure.

CHAPTER LXVII.

SUNSHINE AND SHADOW.

" Fair clime! where summer ever smiles
   Benignant o'er thy blessed isles;
   There mildly dimpling Ocean's cheek,
   Reflects the tints of many a peak,—
   Caught by the laughing waters that lave
   These Edens of the southern wave.
   And if at times a transient breeze,
   Breaks the blue crystal of the seas,
   Or sweeps one blossom from the trees,—
   How welcome is each gentle air—
   That wakes and wafts the odors there;—
   For the Rose o'er crag or vale—
   Sultana of the nightingale—
   The maid for whom his melody,
   His thousand songs are heard on high,—
   Blooms blushing to her lover's tale."—BYRON.

THE invalid who has but once escaped from his ice-bound northern home to bask in this blessed sunshine, and to feel his languid cheek fanned and kissed by these exhilarating zephyrs, will exclaim, after reading the above lines:

"Oh, how truly well Byron has pictured that matchless clime!"

Within twenty-four hours after his arrival at the "City by the Sea," Garland Cloud is in business; in ten days, his success is assured.

In less than a month, he is the commission agent of first-class houses in more than a dozen lines—some of the first houses in the land; and is selling three-fourths of the goods in such lines purchased by the wholesale trade.

He is, moreover, planning and organizing to control the leading productions of the country.

Being a thorough master of the intricate problems of business negotiations, and a man of consummate commercial experience in every branch of the science, undoubtedly constitute the prime source whence his extraordinary success springs; because he has no influence to favor him with friendly or material assistance.

His mail propositions—the medium through which he opened the negotiations and consummated all his important business arrangements and connections, alone and unaided—led on to the results which they were designed to achieve.

A few months later, his father's family joins him, and the father and brother are associated with him in the business.

The firm is prosperous, and its future bright; or thus it appears to the world.

Garland Cloud attends church and Sunday-school; but steadily declines to accept invitations to go into society, and to be introduced to ladies, even those in the Sunday-school class with him.

As no local influence may in any way promote his business interests, and as he avoids the fair sex and shuns society, we are unable to detect any sinister motives in his church and Sabbath-school attendance. Perhaps he contemplates leading an exemplary life, and cherishes some degree of hope that in this way he may wean himself, at least partially, from the weary dream of the bitter past.

But this with him is like repentance for sins which are still retained. Although we cannot challenge his motives of the present, by which he is actuated; nor call into question the purity or the sincerity of his daily life; nor doubt his desire and resolution to make it useful, true, worthy, and noble, yet still the dark, scowling ghost of the past hovers about and haunts him. It is the hideous and menacing phantom—his insatiable curse; the unatoned penalty for wearing a mask; the skeleton shadow of all false lives—that incurable moral leprosy. Hence, it is with Garland Cloud as impossible to go smoothly and correctly down the journey of life, as it would be for mortal powers to stay the wailing breath of the tempest, or to tame the ocean's sweeping surge.

The Avenger, with unabating force, still holds the retributive scourge suspended, ready to inflict his long-deferred chastisement. This hold he will never relax; this menace never abate; will never relinquish the unpitying severity of the stern and unsympathetic executioner, until the mask has been rent and torn bodily from the transgressor's face. After this has been done, and he is left standing in the nude deformity of his veri-

table and degrading shame, a true and horrible semblance of what he has been and is; an appalling object of solemn warning for the world to contemplate, the Avenger will be satisfied for the affairs of this world. The fullness of the measure of his earthly chastisement will be meted out to the offender; then he will be left free to start a new and true life, the sole architect and creator of his own temporal redemption.

Man might, but he never will, tear away the mask with his own hands. Because he will not do this, the Avenger causes cherished plans and skillfully designed projects to be woven into a snare to bring the culprit to grief. Thus he will be misled to make the very moves which to him seem the most feasible and proper, but which, of all others he could have made are the ones, as he invariably perceives only when too late, the most certain to precipitate his discomfiture and ruin.

For Garland Cloud such is the doom laid up in the store-house of Fate, and there held subject to the dispensing hand of Destiny—the Avenger's reserve of retribution.

This mortal mystery views a struggling people crippled and retarded by the terrible blight of poverty, amid natural resources that but little capital and effort will develop to fountains whence will flow perpetual streams of wealth—such as will emancipate the country from the bondage of penury and elevate the indigent to independence.

The visions of the past and its vows of devotion to the tillers of the soil, return anew to Garland Cloud. The shadowy images of that August midnight, as he seemed to behold them beneath the deep-green foliage of the spreading walnut-tree, so many years before, again stand around him amid the purple midnight, of the "land of all-night twilights," under the mystic shadows and in the delicious perfumes of a lovely grove of orange-trees, intermingled with beds of roses.

The soft and airy images in this superstition-conjuring scene seem to rebuke him for his inert apathy.

After these extraordinary, if imaged visitations, he resolves to struggle with more intensified zeal to attain the consummation of his projects—the offsprings of uncurbed ambition, the progeny of rational madness.

The supreme obstacle which intervenes to be surmounted, is the want of an immense sum of money above the available resources and credits at his command—means beyond the ability of home banking facilities to supply : a theme which causes him deep solicitude.

He dreams of the most absurd and improbable expedient, involving both intricate and dangerous contingencies deeply shaded by dishonor and darkly fraught with crime.

But what are these considerations to a man with Garland Cloud's elastic scruples, so long as the barriers to the progress of his cherished schemes are thus cleared away ? Though there is no more in favor of their use, than a fair probability that his success might be assured, he would scarcely hesitate to employ any means, regardless of personal jeopardy. On "the field of Gettysburg" we heard him thus vowing to his father, while he was yet young, worthy, noble and true in character—before *more* than "the mask of war" had shadowed his fair and courageous brow.

The dream presents a programme as lucid as though it had been printed in glowing letters—or thus it was impressed on the memory of Garland Cloud.

It is a plan to procure over-issued securities and borrow money on them, the *modus operandi* to be executed in a great commercial centre—but so hazardous that few professional swindlers would risk the first and most simple preliminary steps requisite to a successful issue of the venturesome transactions.

He casually investigates the preliminary features, without the remotest dream that they will lure him to pursue them. He is amazed, however, to find them identically as indicated by the dream.

Now, step by step, he follows the other features without the slightest deviation, thoroughly fortifying each one against ordinary dangers of commercial detection, or even suspicion, until the negotiation for the money is actually consummated.

In less than two days after his strange dream,

he is on the way to execute its problematical revelations.

He dines at home, and takes leave of the family for a fortnight, with lightly indifferent confidence. No member of his firm or family entertains the remotest idea of the nature of his sudden trip, nor the secret purpose carried away in his heart.

His family-people gaze after his receding form, as it turns the street corner, with apprehensions not unlike those experienced as they looked at him through the misty twilight so many years before, as he was vanishing on that wave of the sea of life which was to bear him onward into the battle-storm.

The first night out, he dreams that he sees his father's family in tears of despair, and leaving home.

Had the business arrangements made in connection with his forbidden operation rested upon a legitimate and an honorable basis, few are ever consummate with advantages equal to those then promised.

SOME REMINDERS OF THE BY-GONE TIME.

On the fourth day of July, while thus sojourning in the "big city," pending his precarious enterprise, as Cloud is slowly walking under the inviting shade amid the refreshing fountains of a beautiful park, seeking relief from the oppressive heat of a super-tropical sun, he meets an unexpected and startling incident.

He is suddenly arrested by the sound of a voice—a long-forgotten but still familiar voice—calling his name. The voice of one whom he had known amid the stirring, unearthly scenes of fire, blood and death, in the dark and trying past; a voice with thrilling pathos in its tones, soul-moving music in its cadence. Turning his face in the direction whence it came, he mentally exclaims : "Shades of Uncle Jake and the fairies."

What memoirs and associations for the mind to revert to in sadness! And what an awe-inspiring theme! The early days of the war around the out-posts; the secret service and its mysteries; the actors and the actresses who were together blended in its excitements and its dangers—their shadows suddenly and unexpectedly rising up, as though from the earth, and appearing in the broad light of day in the peaceful dells of an enchanting park, is indeed a startling wonder.

There, before Cloud's open eyes, sits the veritable, ebon-faced old man, with hair and beard white as ermine—or thus it appears when contrasted with the deep black of his face—on the box of a coach, holding a spirited, restless team; and his good-natured, honest face beaming with a smile of earnest sincerity. And near him, on a bench, are those whom Cloud once knew as Cornelia Earl and Leonora Fairchild, with some bright-eyed, curly-headed children gambolling around them.

The ladies beckon to Cloud to advance. He does so. As he passes by the coach, the old man bends forward with an extended hand, which is grasped by Cloud, as he exclaims:

"Ah! Uncle Jake, it does me good to press an honest hand. But who told you it was I, before you called?"

JAKE: "Bress de Lawrd, Massa Cloud, dese ole ize ob mine, dat would no yore ize an' noze if yore hare and berde waz white, an' yore face rinkled az mine. Glad to see yor."

CLOUD: "Thank you, Uncle Jake. I appreciate your sentiments. Your memory is acute."

The ladies explain that one of them is married to a prosperous lawyer, the other to a banker; and that they have resided in the city for more than ten years.

The story of the ladies, relative to the burning of their homes, their flight into the Confederate lines, and subsequent career as hospital nurses in Richmond, is intensely interesting to Garland Cloud, and might prove equally interesting to the few friends of these ladies—friends who would be able to recognize them from reading these pages; but the circumstances and details are too much like those of many familiar and kindred stories to interest the public.

After recounting these by-gone incidents, and much other rambling conversation, Cloud excuses himself for not accepting pressing invitations to call on the ladies at their homes; and he takes leave of these friends, around whose names cluster so many reminiscences of the deadline scenes of war.

On the next Sabbath following this incident, Garland Cloud is standing in the rotunda of his hotel looking out on the street, when a man approaches him, saying: "Howday do?" repeating the words three times, extending at the same time his hand, until Cloud says:

"Pardon me, sir, but you are mistaken," and starts to turn indifferently away, when the man answers:

"I am not mistaken, sir. If you are not Garland Cloud, whom I once and long knew in Virginia, then my name is not Daño."

CLOUD: "Mr. Daño! my best friend in the dark days of yore?"

DAÑO: "Yes; and your friend in the light days or any other days, who could and would have saved you from that torturing earthly hell in which I know you have existed every hour of your life, whether waking or sleeping, for thirteen years this very month, or, perhaps, next month, and from which you may never find redemption on this side of the tomb, had you only confided to me a bare hint of the nature of the maddening reality that drove you to despair.

"I afterwards learned with amazement that all your desperation was the result of the black and damnable machinations of Walter Paulona and Charles Lorenzi: the former being actuated by a desire to remove you from between himself and the hand of Carrie Harman; the latter by a purpose to step into your business shoes."

CLOUD: "I never once suspected that their letters were basely false. It was my implicit faith in the sincerity of these men and the truthfulness of their statements that drove me mad.

"More than two years ago I accidentally met Judge R——, who told me all the heart-rending story—not then heart-rending, because my heart was lifeless to such emotions, but a story which might have saved me, had I merely imagined its existence in that dark hour of the long ago.

"Ah, my friend! to remember that I was ever induced to believe that the friendship of Carrie Harman had been suddenly estranged from me, yet provokes a pang of agony."

DaÑo: "Well, Cloud, I have pitied and sympathized with you as though you had been my brother. I have been gratified to recognize in you one among the few truly honest business men."

Cloud: "No, don't say that. I do not merit it. The want of an indomitable moral courage to enable me to fling, yes, fearlessly to tear from my life every vestige of falsehood, and to appear as I have been, as I am, and as I feel, has been my bane.

"Your conjectures as to my life are true. I have ever struggled to appear to the world in a false light, so that my life has been a lie. To every one, except myself alone, it has been, and is, a deceptive delusion."

DaÑo: "That may all be very true, yet it is not pertinent to the question in point to which I allude. I mean that the irrefutable evidence of your honesty was manifested in the act of your contriving to return the T—— banks the many thousand dollars to cover your drafts which were refused by the parties upon whom they were drawn—the fate of all your drafts presented after the publication of your supposed self-destruction—and many months after your disappearance, when the banks had given up the matter as hopelessly lost.

"Most of your agents acted badly. Paulona and Lorenzi bought up the claims of the farmers for a song, and kept the money you sent to pay such claims. Out of all that was due you, and the large stock of goods on hand, your Eastern friends never received a dollar."

Cloud: "These are painful themes to discuss or contemplate. Pray spare me the torture of talking over these scenes of folly, which I shall ever regret, but can never recall nor repair.

"As a matter of course, you would like to know all the story from then to this day. I have told you more than I intended to tell. Please refrain from asking me for fuller details."

DaÑo: "Certainly, Cloud. I would not cause you needless pain, merely to gratify my curiosity."

Cloud: "I would tell you all as freely as any one on earth, but it would do you no good and cost me much pain.

"It is my purpose to make good, sooner or later, every dollar that any one, anywhere, has ever lost on my account. If I can ever get on a true, substantial basis, this may be possible. My talents and capacities are adequate to the task, could they be properly employed in the right direction and cause.

"But somehow I feel oppressed by a superstitious apprehension that anything I undertake is fated, and will be blighted by the curse of the past, from which it seems that there is no escape in this world.

"I wish that I could detail to you all the complications of my present enterprises. Had I met you ten days earlier, I might have told you all about my prospects and wants, and secured your assistance. But it is too late now. The destiny of my future is past my control. With no failures, in my promised facilities, success seems probable. Should fair promises prove delusive, I will be stranded. This will be neither a surprising nor a new experince. I am inured to such fortune."

DaÑo: "I hope you will succeed. You deserve success. Your greatest trouble is, you cannot learn to make haste slowly. You cannot be content to take a low or intermediate position, and build from it; you must do something grand from the very start, and surpass every one about you."

Cloud: "I confess that my ambition and my will have always outstripped my ability and means."

DaÑo: "I suppose you have connections with Oglethrop, Harman & Co. I am sure that you could get large assistance there."

Cloud: "No; I have not and shall not. There is too much of the past associated with them."

For a week, these friends of the olden time are almost inseparable.

Cloud finally details to this old friend everything about his present plans, save the pending dark transaction. Had he met this friend at an earlier day, the chances are great that he never would have imbued his hand with this crime.

He felt that this meeting was one last, indefinable chance that had been afforded him to escape from his false fetters, and to enable him to return to paths of truth and honor.

After he had bidden this friend farewell late at night, and returned to his room, while the friend was speeding away for his south-western home, Cloud regrets that he had not grasped the opportunity and told him all. He once was Cloud's savior in a dark hour. Cloud might have arranged with him and through his house to do a safe and honorable business, just half as extensive as that planned in connection with the false and precarious paper; and then canceled that hazardous arrangement, and destroyed the paper. But it had passed, as had many other regretted occasions, and could not be recalled.

***

HORRORS OF THE NIGHT.

After midnight Cloud falls into a deep sleep, from exhaustion—not the refreshing slumber of quiet repose.

While thus wrapped in the arms of semi-death, Garland Cloud dreams that he is in his own sunny land in the level, open woodland country; flying with his false paper, seeking in vain for a place to hide it, unobserved by his pursuers. Finally he succeeds in eluding them, sufficiently to gain his own home, where he fancies he may burn the paper before they can arrive.

But—great horrors!—on opening and entering the front gate, a strange and powerful dog catches him by the wrist and holds him firmly, so that he finds it impossible to kick him off, or in any way to extricate his limb, which the brute every moment is mangling in a most horrible manner; and he is unable to utter one cry for assistance, while the pursuers are rapidly approaching.

Just as they arrive at the gate, he awakes with great beads of cold sweat standing all over him, and he is so weak that he can scarcely move or speak.

He stammers aloud: "Thank God! it is only a dream." But he is unable to sleep, and walks the floor of his room until morning.

When the sun at length rises, Garland Cloud's mind is made up. He has resolved that before the sun reaches the zenith, the last false bond shall be in ashes.

It will, however, be ten o'clock before the vaults in which some of the paper is deposited will be opened. He cannot endure the suspense of the intervening hours at the hotel.

Thus oppressed, he leaves the hotel and goes down town among those of his correspondents who are earliest at their places of business. He finds everything so cheerful, re-assuring and promising, that his gloomy forbodings are quickly dispelled.

Now, then, he can readily attribute his disquieting dream to a late and heavy supper, of which he partook too freely with his friend, after returning hungry from the sea-beach; and he goes to work in extraordinary and good spirits, with no purpose to abandon his unworthy transactions.

***

RAPIDLY CHANGING SCENES.

Garland Cloud returns to his room, and writes letters for some hours.

This work complete, he descends to the office, drops his letters in the box—little dreaming of the revolution about to burst upon him, or that he is at the end of the closing scene, in the last act of the widely varying vicissitudes of his strangely checkered and mysteriously eventful career.

Turning from the letter-box he takes three steps in the direction of the water-cooler, when a well-known man taps him on the shoulder—a man from his own city.

From this man Garland Cloud learns that the hounds of justice are on his track; that the menacing danger of the heavy hand of the law is hovering over his head.

After many years his final and inevitable day of retribution has come with crushing vengeance. Fate has decreed, and the guardian angels of the good and the pure have so guided, directed and disposed events as to prevent one farthing of crime-contaminated funds from being employed in connection with the honest and the innocent father and brother, and caused the masked son and brother to be severed, with his abiding curse, from them.

And furthermore, Providence ordains that he shall be precipitated into the seething eddy of the boiling, impetuous whirlpool of the horrors of an earthly hell, where the mask will be stripped from him, and he left standing in the nude deformity of his true but darkly ignoble character.

Garland Cloud is under surveillance. Instantly he comprehends the hideous reality.

From the first moment he bows in humble resignation to the Chastener's scourge. · He makes no effort to retard the operation nor to escape the penalties of justice; but he rather lends helping haste to facilitate its process.

The exposure sprang, apparently, from mere chance—an outside source separate from, and entirely independent of the commercial features of the transaction—the story of an errand boy to his family. This boy had seen some of the paper in Cloud's room. This circumstance founded the story named. After a long time it found its way to the ears of the proper party, to develop the results indicated.

Who can confute the manifest testimony here afforded, that in all this the invisible finger of some supernatural power had been the means which so influenced and directed all as to bring upon Garland Cloud his long and well-merited retribution. Nothing can be clearer or more positive. Mere chance never brought all these little points together in such harmony and unison. Such was Cloud's superstitious conclusion.

He at once delivers up all the paper, having gone in company with a detective and withdrawn it all from the parties with whom it was deposited. Not one of these parties entertained the remotest suspicion why the paper was withdrawn. Some of them canceled the transaction with reluctance.

A warrant has been in the meantime obtained by the detective for Cloud's arrest. This is served upon him as soon as the last of the paper has been taken up.

No one of the parties with whom the transaction had been made will prosecute him.

However, he waives examination, demands immediate indictment, pleads guilty, and is sentenced to a term of years imprisonment, notwithstanding the fact that able legal talent maintains the "criminal intent" could not be sufficiently established to sustain conviction.

As he is entering the corridor of the jail he receives some distressing letters from home.

While reading these letters an involuntary moan escapes the lips of this wretch, as he slowly paces the dark and gloomy recess of a condemned cell, and he soliloquizes:

"Ah, at last I am now draining to the dregs the cup of bitterness! I have wrung other hearts; now it comes home to me in the piteous wails of the members of my poor father's family. It is *their* suffering and not my own, that lashes me now with such stinging blows.

"Now must the dark secrets of my life come to light."

CHAPTER LXVIII.

THE MEETING OF THE BLUE AND THE GREY UNDER A CLOUD.

" Of all sad words of tongue or pen,
 The saddest are these—it might have been."
—WHITTIER.

LET us shift the staging a bit, in order to permit two of our early characters to step forth and develop some features of their ill-fated rôles.

On a sultry Sabbath morning, a few weeks after Garland Cloud's arrival at his prison home, he obtains permission from his keeper to cross the yard for some purpose.

When turning the corner of a building on the way he suddenly runs almost against another fellow-unfortunate coming in haste from the opposite direction. Both stop as if transfixed as dumb statues to the spots where they stand.

Where? when? or under what circumstances have we before met, are questions which each is mentally asking himself, while they thus remain gazing at each other in speechless wonderment.

Up to this moment, Cloud has been persuaded that there is not one man in the prison domain who had ever known him personally in the other life.

Such is precisely the fancied conviction of the other man.

But now each is forced to realize the certainty that he is recognized by some one who had been more than a merely casual acquaintance of the past. Still, however, they both feel that such acquaintance had been of some nature blended with the terrible or the tragic so closely as to imprint upon the memory of each indelible recollections not to be forgotten.

Time, with obliterating furrows, had ploughed and defaced the countenance, yet the sharp outlines of the well-remembered features still remain to haunt the two men with momentary and mystifying suspense. At length Cloud gasps: "Lawrence Pleasington!"

LAWRENCE: "Garland Cloud!"

It is a fact. The two proud and daring horsemen have met again, after more than fifteen years since they last met and parted in the spectral darkness of the lugubrious pine forests of North Carolina, amid the ghostly death-scene preparation, with poor Pleasington—as it appeared and as he believed—in the launched ferry on the bosom of the dark river. Yes, they have met again amid the dark and dreary shadows of a living tomb—a scene more terrible than that in which they last parted—for them the grave of every earthly hope. They are woeful wrecks of the past; walking skeletons of their former selves; the sad remains of two young and handsome soldiers.

We saw them pure, true and innocent as the forest-bespangling, silvery dew-drops which gleamed like pearly gems in the brilliant rays of the "early, early morning's" summer-sunshine of that July Sabbath, as they rushed with flushed cheeks, with hearts wildly buoyant with youth and hope, and with souls on fire across the fatal plains of Manassas, into the iron jaws of flaming death.

Poor wretches! With what longing fondness their minds travel back to rest in envy on that spot where slumber, in blissful peace and tranquil repose, the crumbling bones of so many who then with them moved, but fell and died, to be buried in the bloody shroud of honor—the soldier's glorious winding-sheet and heroic tomb, so dear to the memory of every true and noble heart.

What a contrast these two relics of that time now present! Here they are engulfed in the seething eddy of the deepest social damnation. Cloud, a self-sacrificed victim of circumstances on the unhallowed altar of dark Ambition; Pleas-

ington, the innocent and pitiable victim of the fiendish machinations of a diabolical conspiracy, and the most cruel and heartless treachery, that consigned him to sixteen years in the rayless gloom of a dungeon life.

Tongue may never depict, pen may never picture the nameless torture endured by this hapless, ill-fated young man during all those long days of trying agony and weary nights of tedious torment, each in itself an age of living death.

Think of this, oh ye ministering powers! and beware being made the dupes of wicked plotters. How often is justice perverted, and thus led to manacle and scourge the innocent! Thus are they entangled so cunningly in the meshes of deceptive falsehood that their seeming guilt appears more overwhelming, clear and positive than truth rarely ever clothes testimony. So thoroughly convincing does such evidence seem, that it is wholly beyond the ken of mortal man for the victim to attempt to establish innocence, with the ghost of a chance to succeed. Truly, he might not induce any one to entertain the bare idea that there could exist a possibility of the accusation being false.

Oh ye pure and honest hearts, who love the human race, and would save your young men from ruin and despair! Here are now before you two characters who afford the material substance out of which lessons of incalculable value may be drawn, with which many a wayward man may be warned of the great and terrible danger in which he must expect to find himself enthralled unless he changes his course.

Those who cannot be deterred from going onward in the road to this earthly hell, by the appealing voices—the echoes of their wail of woe —sent forth into the world by these two men, to be borne onward by the swift wings of sweet freedom's wind, are lost indeed.

Among all the thousands of the condemned here in the dread rôle of paying penalties for the abuse of that heritage bequeathed to them by Nature's divine and equitable law, there have been few others who approach Garland Cloud and Lawrence Pleasington as objects that furnish subject-matter coming exclusively from the heart and the mind. But they afford material to make a true picture of that torture which is distinctly and widely separated from mere penal inconvenience and physical pain. This is a picture, such as will appeal to refined hearts and lofty minds: those we now so much desire to reach and move with awe and alarm at the contemplation of the realities of a state in which flesh and blood exist, that is so dreadful and terrible as to beggar the power of language.

As Pleasington is an innocent victim, his suffering, as a matter of course, is different from Cloud's, and is not, therefore, as forcibly instructive a lesson to stay the erring in their mad career and cause them to reflect. His case is the exception, not the rule; for men from reputable walks of life rarely find themselves in prison without cause. For this reason we shall present a much larger part of Cloud's experience—very largely in *verbatim* copies of his own letters.

After another embarrassing pause, Pleasington speaks: "Garland, in Heaven's name! Then it is you! I heard that a Garland Cloud from the semi-tropical South was here, but never dreamed that he was my once enemy-friend.

"I am not here under my true name. You are the only man here who ever has recognized me; and there are very few who ever knew me. Please never mention my name.

"Next Sunday, if you are willing, I will obtain permission to spend the day with you in your cell, when I will tell you all. We dare not stand here."

CLOUD: "Nothing else could happen, Lawrence, that would afford me more pleasure here than to spend a day with you. Come by all means. Until then, adieu."

LAWRENCE: "I will not disappoint you. Good-day."

This is a privilege often granted men of long continued good record: to spend a Sunday or other holiday in the cell of a friend until just before the night-watchmen come on duty, when the visitors return to their own cells to be locked up for the night.

When the day arrives, and the two ex-officers of the Blue and the Grey are caged together, Cloud gives Pleasington a hasty sketch of his career down to his fall and final doom. Then Pleasington proceeds to reciprocate.

"Well, Garland," he says, with a deep drawn sigh, "for the first time I now open my mouth to speak a word, either directly or indirectly, about the true nature of my own bitter and nameless woe within the hearing of mortal ears.

"My first day of convict-life satisfied me that I was in an earthly hell—with demons and fiends, as a rule, for companions, who were more likely to mock me with low, profane and vulgar jeers than to sympathize with me in my great and terrible affliction and suffering, which I then thought would drive me to the desperation of a raving maniac. I resolved to keep to myself, and remain aloof from other men—a course from which I have never departed.

"With my early trouble, affliction and cruel bereavement, you are familiar, for which I am really thankful, as it will spare me the pain of recounting them to you.

"What a burden of misery the information you have just imparted to me, that Oglethrop and his wife know that I am innocent, lifts from my crushed mind. Ah! but Garland, the mischief can never be mended—it is irreparably and eternally sealed in its fixed destiny by the cruel sods of the grave.

"Nothing on this earth, nor in the blackest realms of the Infernal world, was ever perpetrated on man or fiend more cruel and diabolical than the vengeance wreaked upon me.

"For years my brain was forever in a feverish state, as though molten lead was being poured into it. The pangs of my heart were incessantly, whether sleeping or waking, as acutely excruciating as though it was being steadily pierced by the point of a revolving dagger.

"Thus I lived without hope, or anything else to look forward to as a source of relief, but death; which, though the heavily-journeying years quietly and tediously plodded along, would not come.

"But for the deep and uneffaceable imprint of the blessed training of my sainted mother, which kept me in the paths of honor and truth throughout the demoralizing vicissitudes of the war, I should have committed suicide. Yet I never thought of it only with a thrill of shuddering horror, that was, if possible, more painful than my untold anguish of soul and racking torture of mind.

" I at length became, not reconciled and insensible to my cureless malady, but I taught myself, with great and patient effort, to be resigned to my fate and to acquiesce in the hard decree that forced me to endure what could not be cured.

" I resolved to live for the great Hereafter, as I have lived, am continuing to live, and shall ever live until the blessed end comes at last, with the fidelity and pious devotion of a most zealous hermit.

" Don't smile incredulously, Garland ; from the depths of my soul, I mean it. This is my only source of comfort; and it has so soothed my intense wretchedness as to render existence less intolerable.

" Ah, Garland, there is no other place in this world where a man can—alone with himself and the spirit-consoling communion which he may enjoy both day and night in the dirty shop and the loathsome cell, in defiance of walls and bars, with the Great Eternal—lead a life as pure and blameless as it is possible for him to do in the soul-trying position and experience of a State prison, far removed as he is from the world and its evil influences and temptations. Especially true is this of those, who, like me, have not one glimmering, flickering ray of hope beyond their prison walls.

" I am speaking from experience and realities that should appall you. Five thousand seven hundred days and nights, with three hundred and fifty yet to be added ! Think of it a moment!

" That night of trial and agony through which I passed, under the scourge of that cruel rod which was forced into your reluctant hand in the North Carolina pine-woods, was rapture of bliss compared with the same number of hours in any one of all my dreary thousands of days of prison life.

" Oh Garland Cloud! from the moment that I found I was uninjured, when the deafening shock of the blinding volley had passed away, up to the moment when I was arrested and confronted with that awful charge, there was no hour nor employment of my life so sacred but what I should have embraced you with all the ardent enthusiasm that I cherished for, or could have manifested to, the dearest objects of my heart. I well knew that you had deliberately spared my life by loading the guns with *blank* cartridges, at the risk of forfeiting your own for willful disobedience of orders. But since that more cruel tocsin sounded the knell to my last hope, I have often, often reproached you most bitterly.

" Had I then thus perished a sacrifice on my Country's altar, she would have inscribed an epitaph of honor to my memory. I would have been mourned by fondly loving hearts ; esteemed by all who knew me as worthy of one pious teardrop, such as is merited only by the true and the brave—with which the stranger-soldier's grave is often bathed by strangers' eyes in a foreign land.

" Oh, but now—but now, Cloud ! Pardon my rising tears and my choking voice's huskiness. I am a vagabond-outcast, with that dear country's brand of infamy stamped upon my degraded brow, that has faced the battle-storm so many times in supporting the cause I loved so well. And oh, those loving hearts! rent in twain, shivered, sundered—all these hopeless years have they been moldering beneath the sods of the grave! And the eyes that would have then bathed my grave, and the kind and tender hearts that would have mourned my loss, would now but coldly gaze upon me with unpitying contempt, and spurn me with unfeeling disdain. Such have been the fiery torture and gloom of my terrible life; such is the cheerlessness of its unpromising future.

" But I have run partly ahead of my narrative, or at least its proper order.

" I have observed your delicacy in abstaining from asking me how I came to be here, after the expiration of my ten years' term in another State, yet I will now tell you.

" The morning that I left the gloom of that dreary prison-tomb behind me, and emerged into the bright glare of the sun of liberty, which for me had no more cheering anticipations nor comforting assurances than those bleak scenes of hopelessness out of which I had passed, a man, elegantly attired, of refined deportment and gentlemanly appearance, took the seat by my side in the car, bound for my destination, whither I was going without object, money, or friends.

"He at once entered into conversation with me, and informed me that he knew of the sad history of my case and of my innocence, and had come over expressly to meet me. He claimed to be an importer, and that he had valuable employment for me in connection with his large and rapidly increasing Southern trade. As a matter of course, I realized that I must seek work, and I at once seized this opportunity as a God-send.

"This man carried me to his suite of rooms, in one of the first hotels of the city, and rigged me out in a handsome and stylish business suit of clothing.

"That night he carried me out to sundry places of resort for business men, necessitating a very large extent of walking, which much fatigued me.

"Just before midnight, we returned to his room, where he assigned me one of the beds. Being weary, I at once retired, and was soon soundly sleeping.

"I awoke after daylight. It was a violent shaking by a policeman that awoke me. I found myself a prisoner. The interested importer was gone. A great robbery had been committed in the hotel. Some burglars' tools and articles of the stolen property were in the room with me. The hotel people knew nothing about me, or that I was an occupant of the room.

"The theory was that I had been prostrated from inhaling the chloroform which had been administered to the victims of the robbery, and thus rendered unable to make good my escape with my alleged accomplices. The case and proof were clear against me.

"At nine o'clock the previous morning, I had been liberated. At the same hour on the morning of which I am speaking, I occupied a cell in the jail. I did not have one day of liberty.

"The man furnished me with employment—steady employment for six years and seven months—the net time I was doomed to serve in this prison.

"This is the whole story. I cannot but imagine it was the guiding finger of Providence that brought this about, by so directing events as to

cause them to produce this result, for some purpose entirely hidden from me in the impenetrable obscurity of the deepest mystery, but yet which still must be for some wisely good purpose, and all for the best. Viewing it as such, I have acquiesced in it with patient and uncomplaining resignation."

CLOUD: "Oh, Heavens! the execrable villain! He was either specially employed by the active participants in the first diabolisms perpetrated against you, who were interested in putting you out of the way, or he was merely seeking for a victim unknown in the city, and chanced to strike you.

"But, Pleasington, we have now consumed half the time you are permitted to remain with me in recounting our mutual woes—the bitter and trying realities of life which we have each known and are now experiencing since the interruption of our occasionally spasmodic relations, which grew out of our strange acquaintance and were maintained by our stranger ties of sympathy. But, my dear fellow-miserable, those are things of the lamentable and deplorable past—things that are now buried in the grave of our hopes, with the irreclaimable days that cannot be recalled—those mournful days that are dead. With them what have we now to do? Oh, my poor friend, it is of the gloomy present and the cheerless future that we should think! Let us talk and counsel together of them.

"As to ourselves, for ourselves, we are as dead as those friends whom we once loved so well. The early broken ties that severed our connection and communion with them, which we have mourned so long, are no wider sundered than the ties which linked us to earthly happiness and to mortal hope. But for our country—our reunited and regenerated country—let us live and work.

"In our youth's summer—yes, from its latter spring-time to its mid-summer days—we offered up those tender, promising, hopeful, loving young lives, that had never known a breath of sorrow's wrecking winds, nor felt a pinch from despair's blighting frosts, a sacrifice—yes, a daily sacrifice—throughout the dark and trying years of that long and wasting war, upon its unhallowed altar of blood. Then this was demanded of us—this truly noble sacrifice.

"Now let us devote our bitterly unhappy and most undesirable lives—lives upon which we place not one poor, crooked, blunt-pointed pin's value—to that same country, whether she will have the sacrifices, which she may deem too unworthy, or no. We can do this. We can commence now and here to wage war, relentless and uncompromising war, upon that monster enemy of our race, Crime. That destroys and damns all whom it can seduce from honor's paths or virtue's thrones.

"Oh, let us send out from here—from this our prison home, this veritable, earthly hell, and the foster child of that eternal hell—into that world of liberty where the pure and uncontaminated air fans with its fragrant breezes and cools with its soft and balmy zephyrs the feverish brow and the care-wrecked brain; and where the beauteous sun shines in resplendent brilliancy, undimmed by the darksome shadows and mystic gloom of prison walls, such a startling and piercing wail of woe that it will enter deep, down deep, into the depth of men's souls."

LAWRENCE: "Ah, Cloud! Let me take your hand in both my hands, while I tell you that on this question our hearts beat in unison, and that heart and soul, mind and body, I am with you in anything, in all things, that we can do, or attempt to do, in this grand cause; which, if properly advocated and appropriately construed, rivals the cause and the works of Divine grace itself. For upon the radical principles contained in this criminal question—the principles which should be, and are, the ingredients from which might be compounded a potent antidote that would largely counteract its baneful influences—rest all social order and security, all law and all religion. But how may we best promote its advancement?"

CLOUD: "By writing letters to the utmost extent. Then there is a man in the world partially known to you, and somewhat better known to me, who designs writing a book on this subject. He already has a large part of the essentially material facts collected and arranged in order. To these he is constantly adding more,

either to fill up discrepancies or to extend the scope of his design.

"He knows something of the outlines of the stories of our personal experience, and that of those who have been more or less blended with us—such as have been, either directly or indirectly, the means that effected ours, or those who, in their turn, have been effected by us. In a general, crude, imperfect way, he knows these mere fragmentary sketches. Let us supply the deficiencies.

"From time to time I will send you a memorandum of the feature of information that you can furnish, that is necessary to complete a link with mine, which you can fill in with abbreviated answers to the questions, in the spaces left between them for that purpose, on the sheet of brown paper which can pass to and fro between us by the trusty hands of our mutual friend, 'The Old Man'; and I will revise and supply our consolidated reminiscences to the architect of the work.

"Both your identity and my own, together with that of our friends, as well as that of our enemies, shall be sacredly guarded against detection, for which I will be personally accountable to you here and hereafter. I now most solemnly pledge myself never to expose nor to reveal to any one, in the most indefinite and indirect manner, anything whatever relative to your true personality."

LAWRENCE: "All right, Cloud. If any man on this earth could trust you with his very soul's salvation, I am that man."

CLOUD: "Now, then, we have disposed of that part of our problematical question which relates to the present. Yet the most serious of all still remains to be considered: that part which relates to the future."

LAWRENCE: "Ah! of all the sad features of life with me, that is by far the saddest—my dreadful, gloomy future. What am I to do to sustain life and promote the cause which we have resolved to espouse, and to which we have mutually pledged ourselves to devote our unpromising lives? This is a question that puzzles and staggers me so much, is so appalling, that its bare contemplation makes me shudder, and feel that it would be a blessing if I could never pass out beyond this terrible portal except as inanimate clay. Yet I fancy to me that great mercy is a boon that will be denied."

CLOUD: "You must confide all to Oglethrop, who is, with his wife, your unchanged and changeless friend. They together know your former innocence, and the damnable nature of your persecution, which they deplore most sincerely. They sympathize with you with all their hearts. Your last calamity will but serve to strengthen their friendship and to increase their solicitude for you. You must contrive to get one letter to him over the 'underground mail route, telling him all. After that, you can correspond with him with impunity, and directly, under the name by which you are known here.

"Harman and Flowers will have the same degree of sympathetic fidelity for you as your youthful and faithful comrade Oglethrop.

"And again, there still is that fatherly friend now sinking beneath the weight of years and the burdensome cares of an active business life, Silas Worthington, who is superior to all uncharitableness and conventional compunctions, will take you by the hand and reēnshrine you in his noble heart, that never yet has thrilled with. an unworthy impulse, nor rankled with the pangs inflicted by that stinging lash—*remorse of conscience.*

"These good people will send you into active usefulness, to be regenerated by the benignant influence of the mellow rays of sunshine; the soothing freshness of perfume-laden zephyrs exhaled by never-fading flowers; and a thousand other enchanting charms of bounteously generous nature, to be found nowhere save in that earthly Paradise that can exist but beneath 'Southern dream-land skies.'"

LAWRENCE: "You have pertinent reason, Cloud; a will that nothing can tame; a courage that nothing can subdue. I believed that this course might possibly be open to me; but I wanted courage and faith. I never should have attempted to avail myself of the great benefits that it might promise to bestow. But now I shall try it with a hope that it may enable me to spend the remainder of my sad days in promoting the welfare and advancing the interests of humanity.

"Now, what of yourself? Whither tend your masterful experience and your all but matchless talents?"

CLOUD: "Oh, my friend, that is a question deeply fraught with the problematical and mysterious unknown. If as I will, in the same pathway, amid the same blessed scenes as those indicated to you.

"But I am not as you—innocent, and pure, and true, and good. My one puny hand is reeking with crime to stain a thousand hands with indelible infamy. My wretched life—little, if any, less hopeless, and almost as utterly a stranger to happiness as yours has been, from the very day upon which I beheld the battle flag of my idolatrously cherished Confederacy struck for the last time: the same trying moment when I yielded up that sword forever, that had flashed so often and so long amid smoke and flame on blood-slippery fields in her vain and fruitless defense—has been, throughout the tediously weary hours of every day of its existence, naught but *a masked lie.* And from its enslaving chains I have never, with all my mortal courage, been able to extricate myself, nor to emancipate my shackled nature.

"Oh, Pleasington! the greatest curse on this sin-polluted earth is moral cowardice, and that has been mine.

"Before the charged cannon's mouth I could stand and face certain death unmoved, or suffer the anguish of having my body hacked to pieces with sabres, without uttering a groan.

"Yet I have fled, and still keep flying and seeking to hide away from a mythical shadow, which, if promptly and properly met in the very onset, at the first indication of its approach, could not have been, in the most serious form that it could have possibly assumed, under no circumstances, a matter of greater consequence than that of occupying a vedette's post on but one stormy, wintry night.

"It has plunged me deeper and deeper still into the mazy labyrinths of perplexing, maddening difficulty, until of late I have neither been swayed nor led, but driven, absolutely driven, by the force of concentrated and inexplicable circumstances, directed by some mysterious and supernatural hand.

"But here is a letter from an able minister, in answer to one written him from the jail, in which I intimated what I desired to attempt for suffering humanity. Read it aloud, Pleasington, I desire to hear it."

LAWRENCE: "Poor Cloud! How I pity you! But I will read what the good man has to say. Perchance it may edify and console us in our gloomy captivity."

CLOUD: "But wait a moment, Pleasington. I have a letter here written last Sunday and Sunday night, in answer to the one you hold now in your hand. It is addressed to the Sabbath-school of that minister's church.

"I was a member of the Bible-class, and the recitations of the lesson were always so fascinating and interesting as to absorb me for one hour into soothing obliviousness of the past, and to wean me from the weary and haunting dream of its ever-crushing bitterness.

"Oh that I could have thus lived on, or that I could have then expired before the last echoes of the closing line of the parting song died away, and left me relapsing back into the consciousness of the cruel yet merited reality that I was merely merging into the soothing influence of the care-beguiling opiate of a broken spell!

"To-morrow this letter will be mailed. I wish you to read it after you have read the other, as it is a pen picture of what I dream is, should be, and will be true, in a great measure, in the lives of all men who wander down from the high road of truth and honor into devious and forbidden paths. And it is, moreover, my true self, as nearly as it is consistent with the harmony of things for me to be identified with truth."

LAWRENCE: "Oh, my God, Cloud! you have doubtless been in one perpetual earthly hell beyond the shadow of these dreary walls, no less terrible than the one you are now in. But to read the letters. I am nervous with anxiety to devour their contents.

"'SUMMERVILLE, S. C., 1880.

"'COL. GARLAND CLOUD:

"'My Dear Sir:

"'In consequence of my absence from the City by the Sea, your letter of the 1st inst. was not seen by me until several days after its publication: hence my delay in replying to it. If you have therefore attributed my silence to any other cause, I beg you no longer to entertain the thought that, under any other circumstances, I would have been so long in giving you the assurance that I deeply feel for you in the terrible misfortune which has befallen you.

"'The first intelligence that I received of your downfall was a severe shock and sore disappointment to me. It was a thing that I could not under any circumstances have thought it possible for you to do. Imagine, then, how great must have been the shock when I read in the paper that you had fallen a victim to the subtle tempter's deceitful allurements and enticements, which set before you in a flattering manner the certain and speedy way of acquiring riches. My mind immediately reverted to that passage of Scripture which says: 'Make not haste to become rich.' And I thought that you had certainly forgotten that 'there is nothing hid which shall not be revealed; for, the eyes of the Lord are in every place, beholding the good and the evil.'

"'I am perfectly aware of the fact, however, that there are moments and hours in which the minds of men are ready to seize upon anything which promises a relief to their perplexed souls; and that these times are such as are fraught with the greatest temptations and the strongest enticements to do wrong. These are the greatest burdens of men's souls, and require more than ordinary courage to resist and vanquish. The strongest men often fall victims to these allurements, and sometimes the best men—those who are known and respected for their high Christian character—have fallen into the clutches of the deceiver and tempter. Hence I do not think that it is charitable to censure and blame too severely those who in an unguarded moment yield to the dulcet song of the siren and the flattering deceits of the tempter. I give you, therefore, the assurance that, notwithstanding the greatness of the surprise and the severeness of the disappointment which I felt when I learned of your unfortunate, and, I must say, vain and sinful attempt to deceive and do wrong, I felt no lack of interest in you, no decrease of solicitude for you, and no want of pity for you.

Your case incited within me mingled feelings of commiseration and compassion. I actually grieved over your downfall, and wished a thousand times over that such had not been your case.

"'Since reading your letter, I think I speak truly when I say to you, that my pity for you has grown stronger and my sorrow has become deeper; for I see, from the view which you have given of the temptations by which you were assailed, how strong and great were the difficulties which you had to encounter. And just here let me thank you for that letter. I am glad that you wrote it; for it sets before the world the experience of one tried by temptation, and shows how the tempter entices those whom he desires to entrap. I believe that its publication will have a beneficial effect upon the lives of many young men, and that the characters and souls of many who read it will be saved from ignoble deeds and irretrievable disgrace and degradation.

"'I am not certain but that your misfortune and serious calamity may prove to you a greater blessing than your conduct has proved a loss. God in his providence may have permitted you to become the victim of the tempter in order to make you the instrument of warning and turning others from the ways of evil. I doubt not but that great and important issues hinge upon the temptations to which you yielded.

"'The ways of God are mysterious, and He uses various agents to accomplish His purposes; and who knows but what He has permitted your good name to become disreputable among men, and your honorable character to become stained with the pollution of a great crime, in order that you may be a prominently striking object of warning to arrest others now on the same road to ruin, as well as for the especial purpose of bringing you to a sense of your own danger, and of making you a sharer in the blessings of his salvation? You have not, therefore, such a great loss to deplore, as it may now seem to you that you have, if you should benefit the human race and gain a title to an inheritance of God's salvation in heaven, which it is not impossible for you to do, though you may consider yourself the greatest of sinners.

"'Come now, and let us reason together;

'though your sins be as scarlet, they shall be white as snow.' I would not then encourage you in the idea which you entertain of your spiritual condition. I do not believe that the offense of which you have been guilty is the greatest iniquity that you could have committed, though it be great enough to cause you disgrace among men, and great enough to damn you to destruction, yet not great enough so that the mercy of God cannot reach it, nor so great that the charity of men cannot condone and palliate it. Others in the world have been guilty of more atrocious crimes and have perpetrated fouler deeds, and yet they found mercy and obtained pardon, and experienced peace. I would, therefore, counsel and encourage you not to give way to despondent or despairing feelings as regards your future destiny. Do thyself, therefore, no harm, but be faithful to yourself; to the cause of humanity, which you are well qualified and able to render inestimable service in the very way indicated in your letter; and to the cause of honor, right and truth, and all will end for the best.

"'Let me now assure you that you have my sincere sympathy, and that my prayers daily ascend to God in your behalf.

"'Now, a few words in reference to your father's family. It will give me great pleasure when I return to my charge to do all that I can to console and comfort them. I will also use every effort to prevent them from being made the objects of unjust proscription and persecution. So far as I am able, I will endeavor to extend to them that charity and sympathy which are due them in their distressed and sad circumstances, and to have others do the same.

"'I am glad to learn that your term of confinement is to be comparatively short. It is enough, however, I think, to satisfy the demands of justice.

"'Please let me hear from you, if you are able to write, and give me anything you can say that may be used as a weapon against that alluring cause that brought you to grief and ruin.

"'With many prayers for your welfare and safety, I remain, your true friend and sincere sympathizer,

"'W. HENRY D——,

"'Minister Presbyterian Church.'

"Ah, Garland, that is one manly and noble Christian letter."

CLOUD: "Yes, sir; I have taken that letter for my anchor of faith, by which I am resolved to seek to cling ever in all the relations with the affairs of this life that it is possible for me to hold with mankind.

"It is this letter that has confirmed me in a fixed and changeless resolution as to my course, in a line of duty while here, that is now perfectly clear to me, but about which I before wavered and hesitated. But that I shall now strive to follow, come weal, come woe, in the direction in which you are pledged to accompany and assist me. For my part of all this, that letter is the strengthening support to a hitherto unsolid and unsteady foundation.

"The answer to the other letter, which you are now to read, may have much to do with my plans for the future, because I fancy that it must elicit some good and practical advice worthy to be incorporated in my general plan—possibly to modify, if not to model, its predominating features. What the nature of that answer will be cannot, as a matter of course, be anticipated by the vague and uncertain deductions of mere conjecture. Assuming that it will be of the most discouraging character, or of the most inappropriate forms of precepts, then it would in no wise effect the main bent of my purpose, which has been already rather crudely mapped out, subject to necessary modifications.

"After you have read my letter, we will then discuss that feature a bit. Please read to me. I want to hear it in another voice than my own, in order that I may the better judge of its merits."

LAWRENCE: "I perceive that you are deeply laying the plans for a universal and most glorious campaign. May it be successful. I will now proceed to read your letter.

"'Sunday, October, 1880.

"'NEWNAN-STREET PRESBYTERIAN SABBATH-SCHOOL, CITY BY THE SEA.

"'*Friends of other days:*

"'Words have no adequate power to fulfill the mission of conveying to you the thoughts and feelings of my mind and heart: the vivid, realistic picture which they would outline and paint, and which I desire to transmit and suspend to your view in a light of transparent brilliancy, and to impress it on the tablets of your memories in glowing and indelible letters.

"'As an example to man, it stands out in bold, distorted, hideous relief, heralding in every tint and shade of its grim, ghastly, glaring, fiendish visage, the shrill, discordant, piercing notes of warning—which would to God they could resound from every house-top, from every hill, and in every valley throughout this vast and mighty land!

"'To you, good people, they would be only idle, meaningless sounds. Good to-day, and you think that you are forever safe. Alas, that forever!

"'Be not over self-confident. Experience forces the conviction that the men are few who, under some extraordinary force of circumstance and peculiar temptation, goaded to madness either by *distress*, by *pride*, or by *ambition*, might not be influenced to take some rash step that would cause the vibrations of the heart ever after to thrill and tremble with regret, and burning shame to blight life's fondest hopes and embitter its every joy, demanding the pathetic exclamation of old mother Eve: 'Oh, unexpected stroke, worse than of death!' Creating a pang of deeper sorrow than the wail above the dead! Hopelessly wrecking life on the dreary stream of Time.

"'What lesson is so unerring as that of experience? Of what other benefit to mankind can I now ever be, but to give them mine? What other duty remains for me to perform in this world? What else to live for, so much as a day?

"'This duty to my race performed, then the dark and lonely grave, where alone there can be found blissful quietude and endless repose.

"'All this alone is of no consequence to the social world; but the lessons which my dark chapters teach are full of grave import. They teach that man is ever in danger of falling, and the inestimable cost of such a fall.

"'Furthermore, they contain a theme fraught with the deepest interest to society: the momentous problem of the after lives of the fallen. Whether there exists a possibility for their reformation and redemption; whether they will be permitted to return to lives of usefulness and honor;

what will be the path of duty society will expect them to follow? or whether they may not be regarded as dangerous outlaws, and thus be driven to become confirmed enemies of society, contaminating others, increasing the records of crime, undermining the safety and peace of society, so that it must ever rest on the brittle, treacherous crust of a smoldering volcano?

"'This is a subject which I have resolved to investigate with a tireless zeal and an impartial, unselfish philosophy, and to bestow upon mankind, in some shape or other, all the benefit that is contained in the sad lessons which this painful subject teaches, whose lightest burden to me a the doleful echo of that terrible word, Ruin!

"'Again and again I take a calm, retrospective review of the past, and seek to find in all the course of my tempest-tossed life a true solution of the cause or causes that led me on and down to a fate like this. It must have been self-confident, self-willed ambition; and, perhaps added to this was the blunting of the finer sensibilities of nature by long-continued and unparalleled misfortunes. Ambition in war induced reckless exposure to secure promotion. In business, it enslaved me.

"'For fifteen years I was a stranger to recreation, pleasure, social intercourse, and influence; caring far less for gain than for rank and position acquired from the fame of my transactions; and from the renown of the extraordinary capacity required to handle them. I was in no way intemperate; and I was unknown in the haunts of vice, mostly from disinclination, and partly because both were fatal to my ambitious schemes.

"'An early social disappointment refused to be healed by distance and time.

"'I sought the unfriendly shores of a foreign land, and there eagerly plunged into the maddening crowd, without finding a soothing balm.

"'After many years of toil from dawn until midnight, I acquired hoards of gold; but a sudden revolutionary crisis swept it away, almost in a day.

"'Then, a broken, hopeless man, I sought an asylum on your genial and friendly shores.

"'The first year was an unbroken chapter of sore trials and losses.

"'After this period, so bitterly painful, had passed away, I found an opening for a road to wealth and influence, but distant a few years.

"'Then came the temptation promising this brilliant success, with the stroke of a single season's business, that hurled me down the yawning abyss into a gulf of cruel and unmitigated despair.

"'For the past and the present, I neither deserve nor do I desire pity.

"'I am not an ignorant, inexperienced man. The experience of an average life-time has been crowded into the space of twenty years. My commercial education is consummate, and fixes upon me the grave responsibility of having capacity to be among the representative men in any sphere of business. My talents, which even when 'unmerciful disaster followed fast, and followed faster' with crushing blows, should have been only a shining light to guide the inexperienced, have stooped to the basest infamy. Had success crowned the hapless effort, it would not, with all its motives of purity, have been fairly acquired. Under ordinary circumstances, and a natural state of mind, this would have been clear; but Ambition drew her veil over my eyes; the dulcet notes of the siren lulled my doubts and scruples to slumber. I have my reward; and I acquiesce in all its hardships uncomplainingly. I alone am to blame.

"'This untold misery is not bodily suffering, nor is it physical pain. The present is nothing, nothing, nothing, only in the relation that it bears to the past and the future. The future contains everything: the daily torture of meeting, in the broad sunlight of liberty, the life-long scorn and the endless contempt of mankind—and no struggle can ever redeem me from the crushing odium of its impending thraldom; for

'There is a secret proneness in man that no charm can
    tame,
Of loudly proclaiming his neighbor's shame.'

"'As to social restitution, I know that between me and it there rolls a fathomless and an impassable gulf. I think of it only as a fated impossibility. No charity, no forbearance that may exist for me, can ever remove from my life its cup of unmeasured bitterness.

"'My repentance has not been fierce and demonstrative. Dry sorrow steadily drinks the blood. The wells of the heart are empty and closed; each shadowy picture of the dim future pierces deeper the incisions of its cureless wounds —a bane for which there is no antidote.

"'I have been where the fiercest raging billows that ever heaved the bosom of a storm-rid ocean were sweeping the helpless, unmanned ship like a shrouded ghost through the dark and dreary midnight. I have been in a plague-stricken city, where the epidemic raged like a merciless demon, and the King of Terrors appeared to reign supreme—yes, and I have been again and again in the leaden tempest of battle, where thousands were dying around me. Gladly, without a moment's hesitation, would I brave all these dangers over anew rather than bide this indelible stain, this eternal disgrace—my inseparable heritage; a thraldom from which nothing but death can bring relief.

"'I know that it is base ingratitude and gross impiety; yet from the depths of my soul do I wish that the ball that carried away my arm had shattered my body, and stilled my proud heart in death while it yet beat buoyant with youth and hope, leaving with the numberless dead a spotless name; but I am 'nameless now forevermore.'

"'The days of the week fly with wondrous rapidity, amid the thundering hum of factory machinery; the broad river and the surrounding country plainly visible; forfeited liberty so near. At night, weary nature forces grateful repose.

"'Even this light shade of the picture should startle any one, and deter him from taking the dangerous, fatal road leading to ruin.

"'This, coming now whence it comes, may provoke smiles of contempt. Pray do not despise it, but guard well your careers; for who can penetrate that obscure veil, and glance but for a moment at Futurity's picture—so varied, yet oh, how true?

"'Every human being is in this drama of life: his stage the world. Quickly shifting and widely varying are the scenes. It is but a step from the sweetest bliss to the bitterest woe. Often a faint voice of the slightest warning would stay the horrible transition from which there is no redemption, and for which no repentance can ever atone.

"'Danger may be far away in the dim vista of coming years, or it may be nightly crouching on the pillow where the weary head slumbers in innocent repose, whispering into the ear words of infection. Should tangible danger never come, the watchful vigils provoked by its anticipated approach will neither mar nor blight the beauties and the joys of life.

"'I recount to you in this semblance of warning, dangers and disasters real as life, true as the purest gospel. How eagerly would you pause with bated breath, to catch the faintest echo of a voice from the grave! This voice which I waft to you from beyond the confines of the dreary, dismal shadow of prison walls, is from the dread allegory of the real grave, where living death is no vague and fancy dream, but an untold reality.

"'Now we come to the long and lonely Sabbath, filled with memories and associations of yore.

"'During its early hours, from this uninviting seclusion my thoughts travel back over the vicissitudes of by-gone times—twenty years now buried with the dead ages of the past. The war cloud looming up in the northern sky; the shouts and tumult of embattled hosts on blood-crimsoned fields; the death and the grave of the *Lost Cause;* the after years of a wanderer on the devious, cheerless road, and in the unequal struggle in the battle of life—ultimate victory at length crowning years of toil; then swift disaster, beneath the tropical sun and dream-land skies of a foreign land; then the precipitate velocity down the slippery steep, terminating *here.* Reflections that conjure up scenes of inexpressible sadness, more bitter than sweet; mementoes of the past; ungainly visitors mocking my misery, crowd themselves with me every Sabbath day into the deep recess, narrow confines, and dark, sombre gloom of this cheerless, solitary cell, whither the rays of the sun never penetrate, and where, literally, comfort and hope never enter.

"'As the day advances, and the shadows of evening begin to fall, visions of your school and the Bible-class appear painfully impressive to the imagination at the hour you meet. The pleasing, joyous faces; the harmonious notes of the music; the very words of the songs you used to sing; the venerated teacher propounding questions; answers taking their round; the tiny envelope gliding from hand to hand—I hear and see, or seem to see and hear, as clearly, as distinctly, as when they were no illusion. But when the spell is broken, it is a crushing delusion.

" 'Yet still disdaining restraint, the spirit—the better, the purer, the nobler impulses of life—will ever continue to soar away on the pinions of fancy, swift as thought, each Sabbath eve to take its wonted part in your angelic devotions; leaving its polluted tenement of clay to the fires of purgation, whither its soul-grieving degradation caused its consignment.

" 'The hours spent with you were among the few truly happy ones that I have known in twenty years; yet there are none that I now so deeply regret having enjoyed.

" 'What changes may be wrought by the relentless hand of Time ere my unworthy form darkens the door of your sanctuary.

> 'Some in the old church-yard will be laid,
> Others may sleep beneath the sea;
> And few may be left, of your good class,
> Who once knew and respected me.'

" 'The mental misery, anguish and torture of the present, no tongue, no pen, no words can unfold. Add to this, mere forfeiture of simple physical liberty, the appalling disasters it entails; the utter annihilation of all the tender and endearing ties of nature, present and prospective; the blighting, withering curse to the future, inevitably following, ever haunting, shadowing and darkening like a spectral ghost the pathway of life down to the grave. Then come with me just a little while, in the hushed, dreary, darksome, awful silence of the Sabbath-midnight hour, when nature is not weary; when balmy slumbers and delightful dreams do not come into the little, lonely cell; when the elements without are raging; when the wild wind wails and moans as if chanting a requiem for the lost; when the memories of the past, the companions of the day, are gone, and other companions, more terrible and merciless, have taken their place. Vision of going from here down to darkness and death, alone and friendless, in the last sad and trying hour; with no pitying eye to watch over the lowly cot; no gentle hand to smooth the rude pillow, and soothe the aching, feverish brow; no sympathetic, tender voice to whisper loving words of comfort to cheer the departing spirit on its dread journey to the unknown world, and you will have a picture but faintly outlining the reality, before which you can but stand aghast. Contemplate it; pause and consider it; look upon it as you will, and it reflects, in some uncertain, figurative similitude, the suffering of the lost soul, doomed without hope to the realms of eternal darkness.

" 'Yet a few fleeting months and the supreme moment of my nameless woe will come, when I will be set adrift on life's tempestuous sea in the frailest craft ever launched on unfriendly waves, with no rudder to steer me; no breeze to speed me onward; nothing to buoy me up; nowhere to go; no resting place; no home in all the wide world—a lone, friendless, blighted man. My enfeebled frame maimed and covered with the scars of battle; my heart mangled by the shafts of dire misfortune; my brow decked with burning shame, not unlike the mark of Cain—for I have murdered hope. The avenues of life for gaining daily bread closed against me, I drift with the tide until a sandy beach rises out of the waves; I am gazing on your fair Southland's genial shores.

" 'As I approach, the sweet native flowers blushingly turn their pretty little faces away; and the birds cease to chant their sweet refrain.

" 'This is enough; I drift back with the tide, and the echoes of the surf on the beach, gradually receding in the distance, seem to reverberate the dirge of 'never more, never more,' and no other shore has a charm for me.

" 'Now, good people, in the consecrated name of your true Christian charity—in the name of that Heaven we all adore—if there exists a definable duty for me in this life, if there be a pathway of duty open to me, let me conjure you in some way to indicate where it may be found and how I may know it, so my willing footsteps may seek it, and that I may begin to educate myself to be prepared to pursue it faithfully.

" 'I am, if sinful, still a fellow being. The purest Anglo-saxon blood courses in my veins; my heart is not hopelessly dead and utterly insensible to every pure and noble impulse. I cannot be worse than he whom Christ blessed on the cross. If Christ would do this at the last moment, surely you can condescend to vouchsafe me a little advice—whether there be balm in Gilead for me. I crave no sympathy, no blessing other than that asked above.

"'I have no prospects of finding an early grave, and I will in no way hasten it, unless the mere pressure of mental distress causes vitality to ebb out. And never again will I, under any state of circumstances, swerve from the path of rectitude and duty, should I ever find it more.

"'A little reflection, a mere passing thought, suffices to satisfy the most sensitive, however reluctantly the truth is admitted, that we are all tending toward, and that, ere many years more have been marked by the dial of Time, we will have passed to one common level—*the grave;* where weal and woe, pleasure and pain, joy and sorrow, will blend in silent harmony, undisturbed by disdainful smiles.

"'I have recalled in vain all I ever heard or read on this subject, to find something more truly appropriate than the lines:

'Can storied urn or animated bust,
    Back to its mansion call the fleeting breath?
Can Honor's voice provoke the silent dust,
    Or Flattery soothe the dull, cold ear of death?
  *   *   *   *   *   *   *
The boast of heraldry, the pomp of power,
    All that beauty, all that wealth e'er gave,
Await alike the inevitable hour—
    The paths of glory lead but to the grave.'

"'In bidding you a long and, to me, painful farewell, I know nothing that is more consonant with the anguish of the cureless wounds in my wretched heart than that which flowed from the agonized soul of the primitive red man, long ago, when he exclaimed:

'Oft shall glowing hope expire,
Oft shall wearied love retire,
Oft shall death and sorrow reign,
Ere we all shall meet again.
When the dreams of life are fled,
When its wasted lamps are dead,
When in cold oblivion's shade,
Beauty, fame, and wealth are laid,
Where immortal spirits reign,
There may we all meet again.'

"'May your good guardian angels ever direct your steps throughout life's treacherous journey, and shield you from the many dangers lurking beside it, and from all harm.

'Adieu!   Once again, farewell!

"'Your wretched example,

"'GARLAND CLOUD.'

"Ah, Garland, this is truly the outpourings of a heart full of wretchedness. What a sad reflection on human nature and its proneness to depravity, that men capable of cherishing such fine sentiments as are embodied in this letter, will take chances that will render them liable to become subject to such disastrous and ruinous consequences as have overtaken and crushed you."

CLOUD: "Of all that is incomprehensible in this world, that is the most puzzling to explain or understand. In my own case, I cannot try to define why it was thus with me; yet mysterious as it is to myself, still it is none the less sadly true."

LAWRENCE: "Now, Garland, my time with you is rapidly drawing to a close. Let us talk over the other features of your personal plans, as you intimated having them outlined, in order that I may see how far they may be applied to my own case."

CLOUD: "Well, Lawrence, partly they will apply to your case, but largely they cannot, owing to the wide difference that must obtain between the condition in our after situations and relations in life—assuming that you will be under the protecting influence of powerful friends.

"The first step, the base of the foundation of all my future plans, no matter how much their general features of construction may be effected by the influence of any outside order of circumstances that transpire, is to complete the mastery of the French, the German, the Spanish, and the Italian languages while here, under a thoroughly theoretical and practical system, some of which I am already well advanced in, as to the primary principles of their radical construction. This qualification, added to my commercial experience and most consummate knowledge of human nature, will guarantee me employment as a commission salesman, to travel in the interest of the first houses of the land, on the express condition of '*No results, no pay*,' and of States desirous of obtaining emigration in and from those islands, provinces and countries where these tongues are spoken.

"Thus I expect to earn money to pay any just commercial claims against me, and to reinstate myself in whatever sphere from which there is a feasible prospect of my being able the most advantageously to benefit the human race. Thus I hope to atone, against the reserved wrath of the hereafter, for the transgressions of my erratic life—the only evidence of reformation, the only voucher for repentance, the only offering for atonement, in which I have one particle of faith. Being sorry for the past, merely in consequence of the penalties it entails, without a thorough revolution in the natural bent of the inclinations, and the established current of the lives of men who have gone astray, the deep and solid foundations of which changes must be firmly laid while they are writhing under the scourging lash of their stern and unpitying Retribution, upon which the structure of their after lives must be erected with undeviating correctness and precise accuracy, is of no more value, socially or morally, than the cries of a miserable hound from the blows received for trespassing on the culinary premises of his master, which he will repeat again the first opportunity.

"While I am engaged in the occupations of my after life, I am resolved to write some lines for the press, to say a word in private, and to deliver a free public lecture as often as it is practicable and consistent with the nature of the circumstances under which I may be placed with reference to my travels and labors, for the express purpose of turning men from paths that lead to this or a similar hell on earth.

"And in addition to this, I am fully determined, after harvest and crop laying-by time of each year, to devote two months of my lonely life in the rural districts of some section of country to teaching ten-day free schools, in order there, in each community, to lay the foundation of a simple system of self-education, such as I have learned in the hard school of experience is

both efficacious and practical, and which will enable any clod-hopper, at a cost of two dollars and without the loss of a single hour from his labor, to acquire a fair average business education. The two dollars will supply the books that are absolutely indispensable.

"Should I be able to accomplish these things, I am persuaded that the inexorable voice of stern duty could demand no more of me in this dreary life. All the latter part you can easily reduce to practice."

LAWRENCE: "Yes, I can, and I will, to the extent of my ability."

"Now, Garland, my time with you is up. God knows whether we shall be able to speak to each other again or not before my term expires, perhaps never.

"Let us, therefore, as a parting salutation, here amid the thickening gloom of this dreary cell, solemnly vow, and call upon these grim and sombre walls to witness, that to the ends of our lives we will be true and faithful to our mutual pledges made to-day. Give me your hand."

CLOUD: "With all my heart. May health and peace be yours."

LAWRENCE: "God bless you, Garland, and deliver you from the spectral shadow that haunts your life."

Thus met and parted these two strangely-fated characters, as widely different from each other as the icy pole is separated from the torrid clime. Innocent Pleasington is, however, a thinker much of the same order as sinful Cloud, whose logical theories have always been philosophically sound; while the current of his practice has been perpetually muddy with error and crime.

To Garland Cloud and Lawrence Pleasington are we indebted for the ground-work of most of the chapters in this volume—and especially to the interview which we have just recorded—because without concert of action on their part, it would have been a moral impossibility to get at the essential facts absolutely indispensable to our purpose—facts which one of them alone never could have supplied. But one was always able to furnish the connecting links which were wanting on the part of the other.

This interview occurred sufficiently long ago to

have been placed as the introductory chapter; but we preferred to keep it in the back-ground, to take its place in the regular order of events, just as they transpired, believing that it was a matter of little or no consequence when we explained exactly how we came in possession of the information thus acquired.

As to the copies of letters introduced, they are as authentically genuine as the same number of words copied from the pages of the Bible would be, even to the name of the minister and the Sabbath-school. The letter written by Cloud from the county prison would have appeared, but we failed to procure a copy of it.

The letter to the Sabbath-school was shown by the chaplain, as it was going through his department's routine for the mail, to a prominent gentleman, as a marvel of a pen-picture of a prison life to a sensitively intelligent mind. This gentleman had a copy made of the letter. Months after he informed Cloud that he had this copy, which he had read again and again to crowds of people, upon whose minds it had produced a grave impression. He requested Cloud to take the letter and see whether or not the copy was correct. It was in this way that we obtained our copy; Cloud had not retained a copy of a single sentence of the original. Since that time, those of his letters that appear were copied for us from the originals before they were sent to the chaplain to mail. All letters from outside parties have been, and will be, copied from the originals directly into our pages.

We produce the letters because they reflect in as clear and forcible a light the features of our purpose to which they refer, as anything that we could possibly write might approximately attain the same result; and because we are not so egotistical as to flatter ourselves that we could so touchingly appeal to the hearts of mankind, while addressing all men of intelligence, as those writers have appealed when pouring out their sad hearts' keenly felt emotion to their personal friends—or to those whom *they dreamed were friends*.

CHAPTER LXIX.

UNMASKED AND STANDING IN NUDE DEFORMITY.

" What stings
Are theirs! One breast laid open was a school
Which would unteach mankind the lust to shine or
rule."
—BYRON.

ABOUT two weeks after the interview between Cloud and Pleasington, the former enters his cell at night, weary from standing all day in the shop, and feeling unusually depressed and despondent. For a week past his dreams have been torturingly unpleasant, causing sleep to be a horrible nightmare, from which he often has awoke with beaded drops of cold perspiration standing upon his brow. Throughout the day his mind has darkly brooded over these dreary visions, and lapsed into gloomy forebodings that they were premonitory omens of some great and impending calamity about to be visited upon his father's innocent family as a direct result of his own misdeeds and crimes. Ah, but how little he dreamed of its true nature!

On this particular evening, immediately after his lamp is lighted—the next thing in order after closing the iron door—a letter is passed in to him through the grating. It is in the well-known characters of his brother, a fair and promising young man, whose life is now marred and his prospects blighted by the wreck and ruin caused by the catastrophe which terminated the erring brother's career and consigned him to his present doom. Some ten days previously he had received a letter from this same brother that reproached him bitterly; and he involuntarily shudders as he draws this latter letter from its covering preparatory to reading it. A death-warrant would be preferable. It runs:

"CITY BY THE SEA, October, 1880.

"*My Lost Brother:*

"It becomes my painful duty to inform you that some startling developments, referring to yourself, have been published here this morning, that rendered me speechless with amazement, and stupefied me with shocking horror. They brand the vague intimations which you have made as to the past seven of your ten years of mysterious and silent wanderings—silent, at least, to us—as miserable fabrications. More than this, they locate you definitely and unquestionably for every day of that period in Louisiana and the 'Future City,' where you were known as Nube Garland, and lived a married life with a most estimable lady, the daughter of a cotton planter, Eldred Donné. Furthermore, they demonstrate that the magnitude of your transactions had startled the commercial community, and that the unscrupulous audacity of your financiering had made the banking interest tremble to its foundation with alarm in the 'Future City.'

"Ah! my wayward brother, the deep mystery of your disconsolate and miserable life is now unfolded. I can now understand why it was not possible for you ever to be happy or cheerful; and why that life had no charms for you.

"Is it possible that you again attempted to commit suicide at the 'Future City,' and fled because you failed? It must be true. This accounts for the pitiable plight you were in when you reached home.

"In your first flight you had no cause to change your name; a name of which you are the first one ever to be ashamed, and a name that you are the first one to dishonor. Why merely transpose your name by placing your true Christian as your surname, and using a word in a strange language, of the same meaning as your true surname, for your Christian name? Why not call yourself Garland Cloud, just as well as Cloud Garland? Of all the strange people in this world you are one of the strangest!

"That you would change your name and continue to do business with the same cities, and the same houses even, and to visit those cities where you were known by hundreds of people under your true name; that you would locate in the 'Future City,' where there lived those who knew you well; and that you should establish yourself here and open up direct relations with houses in that city with which you had transactions under your assumed name, appears too incredible to believe. Yet, as I understand it, such are the facts.

"You know what you have done. I do not know all—and regret that I have life in me now and know so much.

"As I understand it, a merchant of the ·'Future City,' who had been a warm friend to, and taken a deep interest in, you, read·an account of your shame in a paper where your trouble occurred, and his attention was attracted by the fact that your Christian name was the same as the surname of the party whom he at once made up his mind that you must be; and he wrote to Louisiana for the photograph of that man to be sent to the chief of police of this city.

"Accordingly, Mrs. Manonia Garland sent the photograph. Capt. C——showed it to me and asked me if I was able to place it. It did not look like you did since I can remember you; but it was the same as one you gave sissie, and by the same artist in New Orleans; so I at once told him it was my brother. The captain did not intimate the truth to me then.

"The publication was a letter from the 'Future City' merchant, and another from Eldred Donné, both addressed to the mayor of this city, and evidently not intended for the Press; yet the mayor gave them to the papers.

"This completes my commercial damnation. Henceforth I shall devote my life to the profession of civil engineering, in building railroads in miasmatic swamps where life is short. But for the home folks, who are now almost delirious with trouble, I would not live until morning.

"Your letter, covering a note to Rev. W. H. D——, and a lengthy address to the Sabbath-school, has been received. Your request to deliver the same will not be complied with. They will never be delivered.

"I am writing this letter down town without the knowledge and contrary to the wish of the family.

"Your unhappy brother,
                                    "J——."

The letter drops from Cloud's hand; and he stands as if transfixed to the spot—an image as grim and motionless as the encircling walls of granite that environ him so closely. There is no perspiration standing on the swarthy forehead; no labored breathing; no change in the pale and haggard features which naturally are ghastly as a spectre, in the ghostly glimmer of the flickering lamplight. What is the matter?

Is he paralyzed with terror and dumb with amazement? Ah, no! This is foreign to that neutrality of nature that could rally such forces of self-control, and command such masterful and seemingly indifferent composure in the supreme moment of a great crisis.

He had arrived at that point on the stage of his checkered career where no wonder awaited him, and where, for himself alone, he recked not what might befall him.

He is absorbed in rapidly active thought. In a moment he slowly raises his bowed head, and pressing his hand on his forehead, soliloquizes:

"Garland Cloud — Nube Garland — hunted down, amalgamated, re-united! Falsehood and truth—Oh Truth, thy victorious sceptre prevails at last; may it forever reign! Blessed Truth, thou has rent in twain and torn in tattered shreds from my life its ingloriously ignominious and damnably enslaving mask! Unmasked! Unmasked! Unmasked!

"Free once more from the thraldom of the demon's curse.—But before the world I stand in the nude deformity of my horrible infamy and unutterable shame.

"What of it? Where stood I before? Avaunt! execrable fiend! I will no more with thy hellish sway.' Speak 'not, whisper not, approach not my grated door! Away with thy damnable hope-crushing, life-blighting mask! I have worn it long, but with rebellious reluctance that has taxed thy wily craftiness to its utmost cunning to retain it upon me. One stroke of moral courage, to assist me at any moment and in open defiance, I was free. Truth has kindly shattered thy fetters and broken thy spell. I am thy slave no more. On the swift wings of freedom's wind my song of liberty shall go. And my curse be upon thy curse. In the name of truth, the odious loathsomeness of thy cruel service, and the shocking story of its bitter penalties will I proclaim. In thine own sub-realm, one victim thou hast lost. From thine own relay-house thy late but now emancipated slave will wage war—uncompromising, relentless war—upon thee and thy detestable cause ; fearlessly hurling defiance in thy teeth and those of thy surrounding minions. I know

thee and thine from the reality of terrible experience. I am one of them no more.

"Oh ye delivering powers of truth, defend me! Keep me free and far from the mask and the terrors of a masked life! Rather give me forever the dismal horrors of a dungeon's gloom, free from those haunting spectres that are ever hovering around the mask. Let me now remain as I am known : my veritable self, with all my shame and degradation proclaimed to the world. Anything, everything, but the mask again that will transform a palace into an unmitigated hell. And oh! what then can I call it—what name must it mérit, in a lone dungeon's life? Words fail, language recoils from the task.

"Alas for those hearts that have bled and those lives that are blighted from the contagious destruction wrought alone by my false life! But the evil has been done—past cure, past redemption. Regrets are unavailing ; and brooding over what might have been can afford me no relief. So let me turn my thoughts to, and train my mind for, works of usefulness."

For many days after this experience, Garland Cloud is notably a changed man. He appears exhausted, as a traveler after a long and toilsome journey under a heavy burden; but, like this man, after he has arrived at his destination, laid aside his burden, he rests calmly, with a quiet and placid mind. Cloud seems to be easier, reposing visibly conscious that he is greatly relieved, and feeling, no doubt, that a second great crisis in his life has arrived and is passed.

In this relation, in a point of mortal view pertaining to this life only, as compared with the immortal vision of spiritual existence, we can but think of Bunyan's Christian, as we contemplate him and his condition after the burden has been severed and rolled from his shoulders, while we are considering Cloud in his emancipated state. Not going beyond this life, leaving the spiritual consequences entirely out of the question, and the burden of this man's curse was as grievous and terrible as that of Bunyan's character, and the import of his delivery from its thraldom of slavery no less a lesson of grave value to mankind.

Of all things in this world, from the secret

longings of his heart, there is no doubt but Cloud most desired to be free from the dark terrors of his masked life, which he had long recognized as a pursuing curse that blighted all that he attempted, and from which he could neither escape nor hide away; and that with the influence of its power, he was unable to cope. Yet he lacked the moral courage to tear the mask away with his own hand and say to the world, "*There* is what I have seemed to be; *here* is what I have been and what I now am." This courage he never could have found, but would have continued drifting on from bad to worse until he drifted into the grave.

Tearing away the mask from the lives of men is as essentially necessary for their peace of mind in this world, and their deliverance from a haunting terror that is truly maddening—as important to an earthly existence that is not almost utterly intolerable, as the confessional, repentance and the cross are the only means by which a sinner may attain theological salvation. For all these reasons, then, Cloud received the greatest earthly blessing that could possibly have been bestowed upon him, and the only one that he had received for more than twenty years.

Now he may be true. What he undertakes, henceforth, provided he thus wills it, can be true, and real, and good; while, before the mask was torn from him and his true character revealed to the world, it was morally impossible for any permanent good to be associated with his life, which was but an unmitigated lie.

When he returned to his true name, his kindred and his native land, it was with a deeply-fixed determination to live true and good. So far as all the days of his past life, passed under his true name, were concerned, this might then have been possible, as the cause which first induced him to assume the mask was known.

Ah! but there was the mysterious, missing link of the unexplained and untold years of the mad and fierce career of Nube Garland still to pursue him with the pangs of undying remorse. The Avenger, scourge of retribution in hand, yet held this meed of penalty in reserve for infliction, from which, for Garland Cloud, there was no escape.

For nearly three years his life, as to anything even bordering on crime, was correct; and he struggled as man rarely ever struggles, but in vain. Destiny had prepared a doom and led him on blindly to meet and fulfill it. Obedience to this stern decree will continue to demand and require much of him throughout the remainder of his unworthy life.

For fifteen years he had incessantly acted a lie; for fifteen years he had been driven thereby, deeper and deeper into devious paths of black dishonor and infamous crime.

We observe that, although Cloud otherwise persuaded himself, being brought to grief and public shame under his true name served not to sever him from his chain of enslaving error. Still he struggled to conceal the relation of his identity with Nube Garland.

It appears, with this exception, that he at once returned to true principles and good resolutions.

He entered upon the payment of his doom with a well-defined determination to atone to society and the world with more elaborate offerings than the mere legal forfeitures, and these atonements he voluntarily rendered. But what could this ever avail him behind the horrible pall of darkening deception?

We have witnessed his vain struggles with a trifling cause of deception that ultimately severed him from his adored fatality, Carrie Harman. Some years later we beheld him merging upon the stage, at the Donné homestead, under the deceptive guise of Nube Garland. Now not only the ghost of the old deception, but also the spectre of a false name and the haunting shadows of suicide—impressions left on the minds of his friends as a withering blight to the fondest hopes of Carrie Harman—augmented his curse, the ignoble heritage of a false and treacherous life. We have seen his struggles, with the hallowed support of Manonia's pure and divine influence to strengthen and encourage his efforts, and his failures and his despair.

Again we saw him return to his true name under the fixed determination to live true and honorable. But now was added to his curse the wrongs of Manonia. We have seen him overtaken and overwhelmed by the thraldom of his accumulated sins. His letter to the minister was a grand effort, had it told all the story. Grander still was that of the letter to the Sabbath-school and his plans outlined to Lawrence Pleasington. But the curse of damnable deception and diabolical concealment shrouds all their charming beauties and admirable brilliancy in the sombre gloom of the midnight of despair. He was farther from the pathway of right and truth, deeper engulfed in the whirlpool of destruction, than ever before in his erratic and ill-breeding life.

What a wonderful and startling career! Thus to pass from one character to another under an assumed name, and then again to resume the first; coming in direct contact with people who knew him under his true colors while sailing under false ones. Then, after he was once again Garland Cloud, coming repeatedly in contact, and actually boldly doing business with people who knew him once under his false colors as Nube Garland.

Thus he lived for thirteen years without ever being detected, and but twice imperfectly and only momentarily recognized. The first time was on board a palace-car, by friends of his early years. But he quickly and successfully misled them by assuming the rôle of a Frenchman. The second time was in the "City by the Sea," by the "Future City" merchant, recorded in the chapter "Where the palmetto buds and the magnolia blooms." This merchant knew Nube Garland as well as he knew any man on the Cotton Exchange. But Cloud had become so much emaciated and careworn that the merchant was easily satisfied that he was mistaken, when first impressed with the idea that he had recognized Nube Garland.

While in the city where he consummated his final and fatal transaction, Cloud daily met and recognized men from the "Future City," and repeatedly passed them indifferently, without receiving as much as a suspicious glance from any one of them.

Then, after he had been consigned to the deep, remote seclusion of confinement for nearly three months, more than a thousand miles away from the scenes in which he had been an actor under an assumed name, a brief newspaper paragraph led to his identification and the open exposure which unmasked him. Thus he was left standing before the contemptuous gaze of the world, a nude reality. In this character he received a penalty which he had long anticipated, and which he had ever known that he justly merited.

Such were his crimes, such were his sufferings, and such was his retribution.

For his return to the paths of honor and duty he is now entitled to no degree of credit. He was driven back; voluntarily, he never would have returned.

CHAPTER LXX.

THE NOBLE PHILANTHROPIST.

"The great men may be those whose name
Is written high for worldly eyes:
The *greatest* men are those whose fame
Reach up and live beyond the skies—
Whoso lives live out the grand old plan:
God's noblest work, a noble man."

—M. A. BILLINGS.

ABOUT the year 1840, in the great shadows of the White Mountains, there was a lad at a country boarding-school. At the same small village where this school was situated, there were two or three stores. Near the same place there was a foundry. For the work performed in this establishment the men employed received high wages. With their pockets and hands full of money they went to the village to trade in the stores, where our young student observed them, their prodigal expenditures, and learned something of the nature of their trade. Fascinated with a calling that yielded money in such lavish profusion, he determined to abandon his studies and enter the foundry as an apprentice, which he promptly did.

In due time he mastered the trade, saved some money, and set out with the "Star of Empire" on its "Westward way."

After traveling a considerable distance by stage, he arrived on the banks of a majestic river, where he designed to embark, and where there was an extensive stove factory. While waiting for the boat he learned that there was a great demand for moulders, at high wages.

Quickly he observed that he was a superior moulder to any one engaged in the foundry.

These facts decided him to remain.

Thus prompted he set out to seek a boarding-house. On his way to accomplish this preliminary negotiation to a residence in a strange city, he crossed over a high hill, whence he looked down upon the works of his new employers.

From this elevation it was easy for a young mind, buoyant with hope and sanguine with a laudable ambition, to ascend yet higher; to mount in imagination to the lofty pinnacle of the temple of Fame. He dreamed wildly, as it would seem to a casual, dispassionate observer; yes, he dreamed, and not only dreamed, but he resolved to do something. With his noble, guileless, pure young heart on glowing fire, and his soul thrilling with rapturous ecstacies of brilliant anticipations for the vague prospects concealed behind the mysterious veil of the future, he reared his air-castle which, seemingly, had no claim to anything more substantial or probable than the pure visionary, yet he was in sober earnest. Thus early he realized in his nature the spark destined to kindle the spirit of indomitable will, and a germ in his soul pregnant with genius.

This recognition of his capabilities, together with the inspiration of the moment, the situation and its well defined and palpable possibilities, developed the innate bent of his inclination; established the secure foundation of his life, and indicated the road to its successful prosperity.

Could every young man or young woman thus understand himself or herself, and appreciate the possibilities and the duties of life when embarking on its voyage, while the heart is yet pure and innocent, how many more would reach the temple of Fame, or their destined goal of earthly usefulness, if not of glory, than ever reach the plane even of their aspirations!

But, ah! those who slip, stumble and fall! These are the waifs of shadowy despair. Their conceptions are obscured by mad infatuations. Blindly they gaze at the temple of Fame or the goal of glory. Upward they seek to rush. They pay no heed to their feet. They ignore the admonition that the path is narrow and rugged. They forget that it winds up slippery steeps.

They perceive not the pit of Infamy yawning beneath.

How few, alas, comparatively, early ascertain their legitimate spheres and properly set out to achieve their attainment!

Our young friend was not one of this hapless crew. Looking down from the hill, as we have seen him, upon the great manufacturing establishment in which he was to labor on the moulding floor as an humble and then a friendless employee among strangers, he resolved:

"I will be the foreman and a partner in that manufactory."

This was a grand conception. To create it required some elasticity of imagination.

The conception was nothing, however, compared with the task of its execution. This involved long years of slow, tedious, patient toil. What a nerve, what courage, what a will, must have been required to make the attempt!

But this admirable young man had faith in himself; implicitly trusted the feasibility of his ambitious designs, and worked and waited.

Self-confidence, combined with true manhood and honest motives, is a beautiful component of sterling character—something to provoke admiration and envy. This buoys up the friendless on the lone and cheerless voyage of life, and gives them courage and strength to weather adverse gales, and to stem the buffeting tides of its angry sea.

Our courageous and self-confident young friend possessed these requisites in superabundance. He also found his proper sphere, and entered upon it from the true starting point where the road begins—at the *foot*, content to rise by slow and steady stages. He was resolved to mount, step by step, making sure of his footing, rather than seek to fly upward at one wild bound.

How many thus start blinded by visionary and erroneous conceptions of duty and the road it should indicate, only to find their delusion has lured them on to failure, if not to ruin!

Half of many lives, naturally endowed with brilliant talents, and actuated by worthy motives, are thus wasted. After all this reckless prodigality of the best days of their lives, the poor

THE NOBLE PHILANTHROPIST.

dupes find that they have been all these years on the wrong road. That they mistook their calling, and must, at last, start in some other at the bottom, and ascend slowly or else never rise, but grope and grovel ever in the lowly planes of life.

This estimable young man made not these mistakes. He started right. He had learned his calling. He was its master. He went to work with a will.

No other work in the establishment compared with his—did not even approach its perfection.

Soon he is placed in the position as instructor to all the other workmen, much to the disgust of old mechanics who are "wedded to their idols." But he weans them from their prejudices. They soon recognize the value of his first detested innovation. From a spirit disposed to persecute him, they quickly change to his willing pupils.

From this position he soon rises to that of book-keeper. Here he finds latitude for the development of other features of his talents in the ascending scale. This opportunity paves the way to other advances in his life battle-lines.

Some years pass. A change comes over the spirit of his dream and life. A new light dawns and sheds a gleam of brightness across his pathway, and kindles an emotion of strange and blissful hope in his breast. It is something refining, elevating, ennobling—that influence which brings man upward and exalts him far above his normal nature. It is the witching fascination of a young lady of finished education and brilliant accomplishments—a member of an estimable family. She is Nature's sweet princess. Gracious goodness is her attribute—her dowry from the realms of the blessed.

For him to fall in love with this fair creature was not unreasonable. That she reciprocated, but proves her good taste and discriminating judgment; for who else in ten thousand had more treasure of Nature's priceless jewels to lay at a good woman's feet? Who could promise her more of true happiness to lighten the burdens to be borne on the journey of life?

Their courtship was the dream of blissful fairyland romance. No crosses marred its beauty, no disappointments its sweets, and no sorrows blighted its joys. With them true love flowed in its course gently, smoothly, enchantingly.

But why delay the truth? They married. For some time Fortune smiled propitiously upon this promising young couple, and he steadily advanced up the hill.

At length a change came; a shadow crossed the threshold of his prospects; he met a very unpromising check in his upward career. His employers failed in the panic of 1857.

They, however, made arrangements to start again, provided they could raise a certain sum of money.

After exhausting all their efforts, only a part of the requisite amount could be raised; and they were on the point of relinquishing the enterprise in despair.

Now, to their amazement, our young friend steps forward, and hands them his check for the needed sum or deficiency. This is nearly all his savings during the long years he had passed in their employment. They never dreamed that he had saved such a sum.

He had faith in them and their business. He did not despair when they failed.

Long had he bided his opportune time to make one grand stride upward toward the goal he early set out to win. It came at last. The very circumstance that seemed to be the knell to his every hope tending in that direction, afforded him that desired opportunity.

After this, he went to work with new life. For seven years he went on the road, and thus built up a stupendous business.

Then he returned to the office as a full partner, and assumed the arduous duties of managing the correspondence, the credits, and the finances of his firm.

Now does his talent begin to develop and his genius to shine. He puts life, as if by magic, into every department of his business. He becomes its very soul and creator. Onward and upward he moves it. The vision which his fancy created so many years ago, when looking down from the hill on the works below—that phantom ship of airy imagination—is now a reality before his open eyes. He treads her decks in the proud dignity of her captain, and stands at her helm as her guiding pilot.

Patient builder! courageous captain! matchless pilot of thy own ship and voyage, ever ready for gale or storm!

Upon the appearance of the first harbinger of the panic of 1873; he at once began to prepare for it. When its darkest hours came and paralyzed the great commercial centres of the country, he was perfectly easy, with a large surplus of available cash in bank.

He has raised his house and business to be the first, in its line, in the world.

Ultimately he became the regenerator, the uplifter, and the redeemer of Garland Cloud. By a strange dispensation of mysterious destiny, he learned the wild story of Cloud's antithetical career and stormy life. He concluded that Garland Cloud was worth saving; that there was usefulness in his nature and being that might be rendered available to the world; and he resolved to save him.

With the exception of Cloud's unscrupulousness, generated by the indiscretion of early deception and concealment—his double-life folly that led him deeper and deeper into devious paths—these were kindred spirits.

By nature, Garland Cloud possessed the fine sentiments and noble aspirations of true greatness in a degree equally as grand as his new-found friend. But Garland Cloud got on the wrong track, and thus grew to be unscrupulous. The war was his bane. There dark ambition, tinged with a hue of the art of deception, became his ruling passion.

After the war, the influence of this evil tendency fastened its hold upon him in the peaceful pursuits of life, and drove him perpetually and deeper into devious paths, and on to earthly destruction and social damnation.

Thus was he enthralled when the good man found and resolved to help and to rescue him.

This good man did not proclaim to the world that he purposed to save Garland Cloud; but he talked to the object of his solicitude instead. He was an acute judge of human nature, and he soon learned to read Garland Cloud, and read him analytically.

He found in Cloud's being a deeply-rooted melancholy; a tendency to brood gloomily over the unpromising future, and to despair of life for himself.

These were maladies he resolved to cure or abate. His remedy was the philosophy of common sense. He appealed to the lethargic manhood of Cloud, in substance about as follows:

"You are," he said, "laboring under an erroneous delusion. It is not all over with you in this world—far from it. Life is worth living to you. To abandon and shirk its duties is cowardice too far beneath your nature and true character to be possible for you to yield to such unmanly predispositions. I want to help—I mean to save you. But you must help me.

"Place yourself on the broad and solid foundation of truth; stick to and build upon it, guaging your structure by the rule of honor, and modeling it by the draft of integrity.

"If you are hesitating—yield in the slightest degree to shuffling duplicity and the baneful influence of deception, you are lost indeed.

"Your reputation as a soldier of the 'Lost Cause' is beautiful as a brave and intrepid man. But you must now summons to your aid a grander courage than any that ever swayed the soldier in the wild fury of the charge, or nerved him to stand and meet death at his post—a sublime, moral courage.

"This is the only antidote for 'MORAL COWARDICE;' what you admit has for many years been your bane.

"Know and conquer thyself, my despondent friend, and you will gain the grandest victory of life.

"This has been my hardest conflict—the ceaseless war with myself to subdue my convulsing passions, and to curb my inordinate ambition.

"Had I been persecuted and tempted as you have been, I shudder at the bare contemplation of what might have been the consequences.

"You can live for humanity, but not truly after you abandon yourself. Self-forsaken people are the most desolate waifs of the earth.

"He who ceases to be a friend to himself, can little expect to attract or retain the friendship of others. No more can he who respects not himself hope for respect from other people.

"Rise up, and be superior to your weakness, your misgivings, and your most sad want of faith in yourself!

"Many men are guilty of greater wrongs than you have ever committed, and never suffer the least reproach.

"All men make mistakes, greater or smaller; mistakes that are really not crimes. Your faults are of this character. Your mistakes are grave; but it is the consequences which they entailed, rather than the acts themselves, that constitute the most serious phase of your distress.

"To any logical mind, it is clear that your mind has never been criminal. Your ambition and your fanaticism on the subject of helping the poor tillers of the soil of your fair and sunny land, drove you to the desperation of deeming that the end to be attained abundantly justified the means.

"This rendered you unscrupulous. From this ebbed state of moral compunctions it was but an easy and a natural step to mistakes.

"Your motives were high and noble. You had gigantic undertakings to promote. These required vast sums of money, which you did not have, and could not legitimately command.

"While your enterprises were feasible and entitled to charitable consideration, they were not shaped so as to attract the financial aid they deserved. Their basis could not be recognized in the light of approved security, when presented to the close and critical scrutiny of money lenders. You had faith in yourself and your enterprises. More than this, you believed that you should have received the encouragement and the assistance wanted. The disappointment in not receiving these embittered your mind and soured your disposition.

"Now you had reached that point when it was easy for you to conclude that to obtain the money with deceptive security was no serious wrong. You reasoned that you would be excusable for obtaining the same money by strategy which you believed you had failed to obtain legitimately.

"But here was your mortal mistake. Nothing could justify the wrong thus committed. No sort of deception will thrive forever. Sooner or later it must come to grief and, most likely, ruin its in-

fatuated votary, no matter what the nature of his artifice may be, nor how prominent his own character and position in society and business.

"Had your masked character remained unexposed, this awful experience and terrible lesson to you would have been in vain. It would have been simply as impossible for you to return to paths of honor, and to steer your course with the helm of integrity and duty, as it is to turn the current of a mighty river back towards its source.

"You were wrong, and nothing could ever put you right short of full confession or open exposure. The first you wanted the moral courage to make. Mercifully, the last was made for you. Thus are you placed right. Easily now may you fulfill a high and noble destiny. To assist you to do this shall be my earnest solicitude and special province."

Through this friend Garland Cloud became acquainted with other prominent people, who were of great importance to his future and the plans of life mapped out and designed by him to be followed.

Could every weak and hesitating man, "who has sinned, and suffered for his sin," have a similar friendly and helping hand extended to him at the opportune moment, many would be uplifted, regenerated and redeemed who ever continue to drift down the muddy current of the maelstrom of life, to the seething eddy and destructive whirlpool of hopeless perdition. Probably Garland Cloud might not have thus continued to drift, had he never met this friend of destiny, as his mind had become settled and his plans been formed, as to the future, many months before the first meeting with this friend; yet certain it is that he would have had much less to cheer and sustain him in the unequal and discouraging struggles, with the almost insurmountable obstacles thickly interposed to intercept his course, in the correct voyage of life. Many years longer would it have taken him to reach the haven which he set out to gain, had he never known and received the friendship of THE NOBLE PHILANTHROPIST.

CHAPTER LXXI.

LETTERS OF COMFORT AND WARNING.

" The quality of mercy is not strained:
It droppeth as the gentle rain from Heaven,
Upon the place beneath : It is twice bless'd;
It blesses him that gives and him that takes;
It is enthroned in the hearts of kings;
It is an attribute to God himself."
—SHAKSPEARE.

A MONTH after the Sabbath-day's interview between Cloud and Pleasington, the former receives from the latter, by the trusty hand of their mutual courier, a note with a letter and its enclosure received by Pleasington from the friends of his early years, or their representative, in answer to the one sent them, in pursuance to the resolution formed during the interview with Cloud. Both letters had passed over the contraband underground mail route. The enclosure was in a doubly sealed envelope and addressed in well remembered lady characters :

" COL. GARLAND CLOUD.

" *In durance of distress.*"

This Cloud carefully lays aside, as if touched by a thrill of pious awe at beholding it—a sad and painful reminiscence of the days that are dead—and takes up Pleasington's letter, which is in a neat, but unknown lady's hand. It is as follows :

"—— SQUARE, NEW YORK, Nov., 1880.

" MAJOR LAWRENCE PLEASINGTON :

" *My long mourned and esteemed Friend:*

" Your most unexpected yet thrice welcome letter, which is held in unspeakable and indescribable appreciation, came duly to hand in Orlando's absence on a Southern business tour, which will be prolonged for many weeks to come. In accordance with his parting instruction relative to all letters received to his private address, yours was opened by me.

"Oh! when I saw that it was from you, our long-sought friend whom we have mourned for these six years as dead or lost to us forever, and of whom we have sought the country over, in every quarter without the gloomy confines of prison walls, information, or a clue that might lead to it, I cannot attempt to describe to you the rapturous ecstacies of joy that I experienced; let it suffice to say that it was supremely full.

"Your sad and cruel fate, for peculiarly serious reasons, has been excruciatingly painful to us, and has enshrined you in our hearts with all the sanctity of endearing affection that can be claimed as a Divine attribute appertaining to kindred ties and blood. What stronger assurance can I offer you of our constant friendship and undying love ?

"The odium of your dungeon life, of which you write so feelingly and pathetically, may apply to the heartless, unfeeling and unthinking world, but it is foreign to any degree of relation to us, who are not the world, but your friends who hold you as sacredly dear as our own sweet lives.

"How sad is this last cruel ordeal through which you are passing; and what strange workings brought it about !

"But for his train arriving an hour behind time, Orlando would have received you in his own arms when you emerged from the dreary prison. When he called at the door you were gone—whither the officials could not tell.

"From that moment we have had no tidings from you, until this propitious day dawned to light the way for your letter to break in upon us a grateful surprise, and dispel the corroding suspense of our melancholy despair; and, furthermore, to re-inspire us with assuring hope, that the gratifying reality of again beholding your face and feeling the warm and re-animated clasp of your hand, will yet be ours; and that we may experience the comforting consolation which will accrue to us from being able to repair the cruel wrongs of which you have been the hapless victim, so far as such may be within the scope of human power to accomplish.

"How we all join with you in pitying your strange friend, Col. Cloud, through whom, as a fortuitous medium, you will be restored to us. How fortunate that he knew of your innocence, and how providential that he should be thrown with you to tell you about it, as such a sad fate was destined to be his; but for which circumstance, as you write us, we should never have heard from you again.

"We have held a family meeting of all the families of the members of Orlando's firm—I, as the representative of ours—and talked over your affairs, and the result is that I have been commissioned to write to you that you will be placed in charge of most important Southern interests, on ten times more favorable terms than those which you seek; that you will be supplied with a proper suit of clothing in which to pass the portal of the prison; and that a carriage will be in waiting to speed you away to safety and friends the moment you have crossed the cruel, forbidding threshold of that dreary, unhallowed habitation.

"Please hand or send the enclosure by safe conveyance to Col. Cloud.

"Now, my poor friend, what more can I say to you?

"I shall forward your letter to Orlando, from whom you may expect a letter before he returns home.

"You must write to us often; and we, on our part, will not neglect to write you, nor to do everything else in our power that we deem might comfort or cheer you in your lone way.

"Your true and sympathetic friend,

"EVA OGLETHORP."

This letter read, Cloud folds and returns it to its envelope, lays it aside, and then taking up the other one, which he proceeds to open with a hand trembling like the aspen leaf in the wind, while his lips are pale as salt, he slowly reads with stifled emotion:

"—— SQUARE, NEW YORK, Nov., 1880.
"COL. CLOUD:

"*My unforgotten and never forsaken friend:*

"Let me conjure you, in the name of the memory of the dark and trying times in which our young friendship was born, out of which sprung the 'Soldier's Family Relief Association,' and which inspired you with that strange fancy to christen me 'The Angel of Consolation,'—though unworthy that I was and am, to have be-

stowed upon me a name that caused you to commit sacrilege when you first associated it with me, yet still to this day it remains an undiminished incentive with me to continue to strive more earnestly to become worthier of it, by dispensing all the charity I can in missions of mercy—do not unkindly and unjustly censure my seeming impropriety in overstepping the prescribed bounds of etiquette so far as to venture to indict a letter to you. My excuse must plead in extenuation for my fault, should you deem me guilty of a serious one.

"Circumstances which I knew that embittered your life; some things I have recently heard relative to your checkered career, extending over a period of ten years of wandering, and a sketch in Major Pleasington's letter describing your present gloomy and painful state of mind, relative to your personality for yourself alone, prompt and actuate me with the purest motives of unselfish charity to write you this letter, because I feel that I am thus much indebted to you.

"Alas! that I must ever feel that but for me—I who was designed to be your evil genius—all the trying scenes through which you have passed during those dreary, tedious years, and through which you are now passing; the marks of wrong that you have left strewn along your backward track; your suffering and your woes, would never have been. Yet God in Heaven knows that on my part it was not willful. Of all persons on this earth, not of my own house and heart, you would have been the last whom I would have caused pain or led into difficulties and trouble.

"To me it matters not what you have been since we last met, what you are now, or what you may be hereafter—I shall remember only what you were then, and what you had been previous to that time; which was the cruel and fatal crisis in your life; which was brought upon you by the basest and the most fiendish treachery and falsehood ever perpetrated upon an inoffensive victim within the compass of my knowledge. I can think of you only to be impressed anew with the overwhelming conviction that but for that cruel stab of Envy's envenomed dagger, you would ever have remained true and noble and good, because I know that all of wrong that you have done has been contrary to your nature. But enough of this, and something more of the true subject matter of my letter.

"Our family owes you an enormous debt of gratitude, with its accrued and compounded interest of now nearly twenty years, not one iota of which has ever been paid. The time has now come, or is near at hand, when we can offer to discharge a portion of it with a degree of confidential propriety so impressively and manifestly appropriate as scarcely to admit the excuse for hesitating on the ground of fear that such action on our part would or might give you offence, or wound the sensitive impulses of your unconquerable pride, which we hope, and which, permit me to entreat, that you will accept, leaving the matter entirely with us to arrange. Assure me that you will do this, and I will then unfold to you all our plans.

"I am exceedingly anxious to have from you the true outlines of the story of your life through the trials of those ten years while we supposed you dead; and most especially those features relative to your attempted suicide at the time of your disappearance from the 'Future City.' With that exception I have had a version of most of the features of the sad narrative as supplied by other people. I should like to know what relation your plans for the future of this sad life bear to the life of that period of ten years. If you will condescend to take the trouble upon yourself and endure the pain which it will inflict, please furnish it to me in sacred confidence, if you wish. Please, I beg of you, do me this favor on the score of old friendship which, though ill-fated it was to you, is still with me as lasting as life itself.

"While you were in the world of liberty, after your return to your native region, I should have written to you, but I never was able to learn your proper address. Had we been at home while you were in jail, we should have come to see you, whether you were willing or not.

"It was a sad disappointment to us all when we received your message informing us that you would neither receive our visits nor our tokens of friendship in the form of little articles to mitigate the rigorous severity and the stern hardships of prison life, and that you forbid us to write you one letter, and refused to write a line to us. Now let me appeal to the youthful tenderness and the noble magnanimity of Garland Cloud's heart—Garland Cloud, the soldier boy—as it was from the 'Plains of Manassas' to the 'Hills of Gettysburg.' Was not this cruel treatment to friends whose hearts beat for you in tender sympathy, and were filled with emotions of true and zealous interest in you and your welfare?

"I feel a deep and solicitous interest in and for the success of the work which Major Pleasington wrote that you and he were engaged in assisting some author to compile. This, I know, might be so wrought as to be the means of producing much good in the world. I should not have so far transgressed against your most emphatic injunction, as to write you this or any other letter while your sojourn continues in that lonesome prison-house, had I not met with this opportunity to send it to you without being subjected to the scrutiny of other eyes before it would be greeted by yours. The officer of the prison, who was the bearer of Major Pleasington's letter, boldly made the proposition to Mrs. Oglethorp to perform similar services between the local post-office of the village and the prison, for a money consideration, which was accepted. You can write to us and we to you under cover of the same arrangement, provided that you are willing. I cannot imagine that you could be so cruel as to object. I know that if you do, it would not be your true self, nor the natural promptings of your heart, that you will be obeying. I cannot believe, though you were to tell me so a thousand times over, and all the world would bear you witness that it is so, that all the true and the good impulses that once were yours have been utterly and hopelessly crushed out of your being.

"Then you will write a line, if but one, to say that cruel *farewell* which you did not even vouchsafe in that by-gone time of bitterness to

"Your ever changeless friend,

"CARRIE V. FLOWERS."

In reply to this pressing letter Cloud wrote:

"November, 1880.

" Mrs. Carrie V. Flowers:

" *Friendly object of my vanished dreams:*

" I shall not attempt to describe to you the emotions that thrilled my being when I merely glanced at the long and distinctly well-remembered characters of the address on the envelope covering your letter. What, then, can I say of the letter itself? Silence most eloquently answers this question.

" I write briefly, merely to say, with reference to your letter, that it is impossible for me to answer it now, but that I shall do so, and fully, by Pleasington, when he goes hence, and to make a reciprocal request of you.

" Should the letter which I wrote you in the winter of 1861, relative to the outpost and scouting service, by any chance have survived the lapse of time among the rubbish of the old homestead, and may now be found, I should be under lasting obligations if you would write and have it sent to you, and then send it to me. I want some data which it contains to supply a deficiency in the early chapters of the work to which you referred in your letter.

" Pray, then, consider this letter as being purely of an informal business character; and please write me one solely upon the subject to which it refers.

" In conclusion, I beg to assure you that I am not insensible to a feeling of gratitude for the rich benevolence of your true friendship, and that my appreciation of the generous charity manifested in bestowing upon me so much lavish sympathy, is not indifferently wanting.

" Thanking you for your extreme kindness, and your compassionate solicitude to and for me and my welfare, I am, with shameful regret, " Your lost friend,

" Garland Cloud."

By an early mail came this reply:

" December, 1880.

" Col. Cloud:

" *My Reclaimed Friend:*

" I have partially complied with your request, contained in your much-appreciated letter, which is proof positive, that though crushed beneath the merciless force of circumstances and the cruel weight of misfortune, you are still enough your former self to concede to the petitions of your friends what they solicit, but in your own way and time. But I will refrain from quarreling with you about it.

" You do me much injustice to imagine that the correspondence to which you refer had either been lost, destroyed, or left among the castaway rubbish of the dear old Valley Mansion—those sad letters, solemn reminiscences of those anxious days, those trying weeks, those tedious months and those weary years. While I live and retain one keepsake or one treasured jewel of my tender years, those historical sheets of paper will remain preserved among them. Remember that the hand that traced their lines by the wintry bivouac fire, though the bleeding heart that prompted its motion still beats on, has been long years mingling with its mother dust.

" No; you can't have that letter. It is yellow with age, and marked and streaked and blurred with traces of my maiden tear-drops—the first that ever man, not related to me by kindred ties of blood, caused me to shed. Then, again, the tears of mature womanhood were rained upon it; and now, to-day, those of the wife—the faithful and devoted wife—have once more moistened its pages.

" I have made you a faithful copy of that letter, together with two or three of my own to you and one or two others of yours to me, all of about the same date, which I trust will serve your purpose just as well as the originals. Upon these no other eye than mine has ever gazed since first I looked at them. They will continue to be held thus sacred, as though they were mementoes of the dead, so long as I retain my faculties and sight. They recall youthful dreams associated with a young friendship, and remind me of a new friend who was then sober, grave, serious and true.

" Should it be in my power to give, or to obtain for you, any other information, to aid the work which you have become enlisted in, please let me know what it is.

" I am much gratified to know that you have formed a resolution to devote your life to good work; to promote the cause of humanity, which is *the* course to pursue to atone for the errors and the crimes of the past; to redeem your clouded life upon the earth, and to secure salvation for the life eternal. To do all the good that we can and the least ill that is possible in this life, is life's great duty and supreme object; and doing good consists in alleviating suffering, soothing sorrow, striving to influence the good to remain so, or to become better for the sake of the reward it will give in this world; to induce the vicious and the criminal to turn from their forbidden ways, for the sake of escaping the pain of the penalties to which they lead in this life; instructing the ignorant; encouraging the despondent; comforting the sick and the distressed; declaiming against the errors and the deceptions of society; and, in a word, raising the moral tone and sentiment of those with whom we come in contact in the walks of daily life, by our conversation and example in all that we say and do. Whether they be our inferiors, our equals, or our superiors, this matters not; it is always possible for us to leave some good impression, however small it may be, upon the minds of the wisest and the best of them, that, not infrequently, amounts to actual influence, and promoting the cause and advancing the interest of humanity. Such are what I deem true principles of religion, and I tremble for the professors of the Christain faith and character who neglect to practice the same.

"Since the first wintry morning, now nineteen years ago, that I quitted the cheerful hearth of my father's mansion to face the driven snow and the northern storm blast, on a mission in my espoused cause, to 'The Mountain Cabins,' I have never once let the sun go down without having tried to accomplish some good, or to gladden some heart, and to my latest day I crave to be able to continue to do the same.

"Now I want to say to you that this briny, tear-stained, time-yellowed letter of yours, of which I have made you the copy, was the influence that led to this, as well as to the revolutionizing of the lives of two families and the blending of them together—my father's and that of 'The Angels of the mountain.' I know of other influences and examples in your poor sad-fated

life that have produced as much good as this just named; and I doubt not, that among your seeds of blighting error and damning crime you have sown some good seeds that are producing fruits.

"How heart-rending to think that you should have ever sown any bad seed, as well as to know your awful fate!

"Oh, my hapless friend! look upon these pages all blotted by the blinding tears—yes, humble tears, of once proud and haughty, disdainful, scornful, aristocratic Carrie Harman, and remember that she was converted to the cause of humanity and usefulness by the influence of the distant acts and the then provokingly indifferent letters of an humble mountain boy; a boy upon whom, she now blushes to admit, before that time she would have looked down with stunning contempt: yes, with far more uncharitableness than she would now look upon the most degraded and abandoned wretch as he emerges from your stern and merciless prison walls; for she could, without the least reluctance, take him by the hand and say, ' my friend, come forth, go into better ways, let me intreat you, and be a man.' Then I beg of you, that with all your well matured experience and the consummate lessons of life that it has taught you in its hard schools, you do not despair of doing good even while you are thus shut out from the world, nor of doing more good hereafter than you have ever done or than you ever could have done but for your misfortunes. Now convert them into blessings for the human race; return to your true self and let your natural impulses rule your life and be once again Garland Cloud.

"This will smooth your rugged pathway and strew along its desolate margins a few cheering flowers. It will last but a little time, the sorrowful journey will be a short one and soon over; at most, fifty years will end it:—a little more than twice the time that has elapsed since first we were friends. Oh! then, my disconsolate friend, take courage and be brave again as of yore. But not that youthful courage that defied the sabre's menacing blade and the cannon's frown of death. No, but that moral courage—something higher and nobler—that can stand unmoved before the scornful uncharitableness of the unthinking world and there dare to perform an unpleasant and an unthankful duty.

"How impatiently I shall await that promised letter. Please reward my anxious suspense by opening to me your heart—'to a friend that not forsakes.'

"In conclusion, I pray that you will remember the beautiful sentiment and the sublime truths contained in the closing lines of your favorite song, which I often sing, and think of you:

"'But there is a future, Oh, thank God,
Of life this is so small a part:
'Tis dust to dust beneath the sod,
But there, up there, 'tis heart to heart.'

"Your true and devoted friend,

"CARRIE V. FLOWERS."

On the last night of the year 1880, Lawrence Pleasington wrote the following to enclose in a letter to one of his friends:

"WATCHING WITH THE DYING YEAR IN A DUNGEON'S GLOOM.

"DEATH is a sad contemplation—the death of friends and the death of hope—because the places of the departed must be re-supplied by objects that are new and untried; the former by persons perchance less kind and more inconstant, and the latter by despair.

"To-night I am keeping a solitary vigil in my lonely, cheerless cell, watching the departure of one, and the arrival of another friend—the death of the old and the birth of the new year.

"With me, each dying year has been much the same as those that had long since been passing away before it—born in despair, and dying without bringing me a hope for this world. But lately I have espied a faint gleam of hope low down on the horizon of my benighted sky, which will cause the new year to dawn with a shade of brightness such as I had never before dared to dream would again be known to me. Now I cherish a shade of hope that I may yet be of some service to the human race.

"Midnight in a dungeon's spectral and haunted confines is a terrible thing; a reality of which no one on this earth can ever form an adequate conception, save alone those with polished breasts and refined sensibilities, who have proved it by

the test of bitter experience—and they can never tell to the world, though they may not all conceal, what its horrors are, for such things are untold.

"But a new year's midnight, when the ghostly spirits of the victims of crime are permitted to burst the cerements of the dead and come forth from their barred and shadowy realm of the mystic unknown, to walk these dismal halls and haunt the cells of their despoilers and their murderers; until, in fancy, their tufted foot-falls may be heard by ears of flesh and blood—it is then that the blood runs cold, the breathing is bated and suspended, and the startled heart beats with echoing thuds that sound as the measured strokes of some mighty forge-hammer. No stories of a haunted house, nor yet of the traditional church-yard, where grim and menacing spirits are supposed to walk and haunt the night, are half so terrible to timid minds as would be, and is, this seeming reality. Then the minions of hell that are ever here, almost perceptible to the naked eye and palpable to the touch of mortal fingers, mingle freely in the scenes, to work upon the terror-stricken minds of the haunted, after their ghostly tormentors have fled back to their futurity-veiled sphere.

"This is a New Year's watch-meeting, *solus*, to a mind and heart that have not been polluted by the contagion of debauching poison, nor rendered callous by self-abandonment in the veritable experience of a dungeon life.

"It is now dead midnight; the lights burn blue. The dying year, with its hopes and despair, its anticipations and disappointments, its joys and sorrows, its festivities and deaths, vanishes—now it is gone forever. Hark, list! It is but the mournful notes of the village bells, tolling, tolling, tolling, their knell of death. How they startle and pierce the still and icy air!   •

"Farewell, old year, that has measured me one mark less on the dial of time—one less of sorrow and suffering!

"I am, in not ungrateful memory,

"LAWRENCE PLEASINGTON."

We have many other letters written by Cloud and Pleasington and their friends, but deem it needless to transcribe more of them into these pages. Several of these letters are from Cloud to the minister, and from the latter to the former.

But Cloud's last letter to the good man remains unanswered. For some strange and inexplicable cause, the man of God abandoned his partially-reclaimed charge to his fate.

This seems more strange and unaccountable, when we come to consider the solicitude which the minister manifested for Cloud in his early days of suffering, and which continued long after the relation was definitely established between him and Nube Garland. To the minister, Cloud's darkest chapters were intimately known months before his last cheering letters were penned. Cloud grieved over the loss of this friend, but ceased not to treasure the precepts and assurances contained in his letters, nor to regard them as an anchor of faith and hope.

CHAPTER LXXII.

THE FAREWELL.

" Farewell! 'tis a lonely sound,
    And oftimes brings a sigh ;
But give to me that better word,
    That comes from the heart, 'Good-by,'
'Good-by, good-by,' will do for the gay,
    When Pleasure's throng is nigh,
But the heart feels most when the lips move not,
    And the eyes speak the gentle ' Good-by.' "
                    —OLD SONG.

LAWRENCE : " Well, Cloud, my friend, I obtained leave for a few moments, and a pass, to run over to say good-by, as I knew you are not under the galling scrutiny of the sleepless gaze of an officer; and that, therefore, we could have a quiet chat. To-morrow, you know, the end of this will come for me, after sixteen years and seven months, besides the few weeks—I almost forget how long—spent in jail.

" I am sorry to leave you here, so sorry that, was such a thing possible, I would take half your time upon myself in order to have you go away with me into the other life; but, since that cannot be, I must leave you behind and go out into the untried realities of a new existence."

" CLOUD : " Ah ! my magnanimous fellow, though you be the only friend I have wearing the stripes, and though I know I shall miss the little voiceless tokens of that true and unselfish friendship which have often caused me to repeat intuitively and aloud the lines,

' 'Tis death to be parted, yet near thee
    'Tis woe, irretrievable woe,'

more than fancy can image or words can depict, yet from the depths of my soul, I rejoice to bid you adieu."

LAWRENCE : " So would I rejoice to bid you adieu, were you going instead of staying ; but let us not quarrel about the inevitable. Moments are too few and precious."

" What of the commissions, with which you desire to entrust me, the first thing ?"

CLOUD : " I have a long letter on tissue-paper, put up in two shoe-sole shaped packages and pressed until they are no thicker than brown paper. I want you to put one under each false sole in your shoes, and thus carry them to Mrs. Flowers, who will expect a letter by your hand and will, therefore, make such an opportunity for you to deliver it as suits her fancy. Please wait for her to indicate this before even intimating to her that you have a letter for her; and, as to others, keep your own counsel, as I am unadvised as to her pleasure on the subject. This is all, Lawrence, except to thank all the good friends for their kind interest and charitable solicitude in and for me; and to express to them my regrets that circumstances over which I exercise no control, should have so cruelly precluded me from accepting their magnanimous offices and friendly visits, so generously tendered to me."

LAWRENCE : " Well, Garland, that shades all the shrewd ingenuity to pass out a letter that I have ever heard of in the long and varied catalogue of State prison prolific and inventive expedients. I will carry it and keep silent. I owe you a letter-carrying debt now twenty years old. I shall faithfully attend to your other requests.

" Col. Worthington and Oglethrop, with their ladies, were here to see me yesterday, and expressed their mortification at not being able to see you when they were so near you. The old gentleman has changed very little since last I saw him. Oglethrop is the perfect picture of manhood and health.

THE SUICIDE.
"THE VISION OF DEATH, AND BEYOND."—See page 282.

"It is definitely settled that I am to go to the Southern seaboard, to take charge of an important interest—the same port that I wrote you the note about some time ago. Do you still think that we must not correspond while you remain here?"

CLOUD: "Oh, yes, I do, and decidedly, for the same reasons advanced before. This letter that goes out by you is the last one that I shall ever send that does not pass through the regular channel. It does not contain one contraband word. It is merely something that I do not care to be made the subject of prison gossip just now; for I know that the letter would be copied before it went forward. Our mutual friend has a copy of it to be used in his work."

PLEASINGTON: "I guess you are right, Cloud. I never should have used the forbidden route but for the peculiar position in which I was placed. I have not used it to pass one word that could injure the prison or prejudice the interests of the State."

CLOUD: "Has Arnold Noel never yet suspicioned your identity?"

PLEASINGTON: "Not in the least. I have often been so near him, I could have taken him by the throat. He never knew me very well, and never met me after the second year of the war. Since then time has changed me so much that few of those who then knew me most intimately would recognize me now. Even Col. Worthington and Oglethrop say they would not have recognized me, not though they had been seeking me, while Noel continues to appear about the same image as when a boy."

CLOUD: "Well, Lawrence, I trust that you may find such repose and comfort of body, and quiet and peace of mind throughout the remainder of your life, as will soften and alleviate the cruel memories of the past, to an extent to render existence even more placidly serene than you now dare to dream that it will prove."

LAWRENCE: "Oh, well, Garland! I have taught myself, resignation in all these years of effort, to bow in meekness before the Chastener, that has enabled me to endure *this*, and which I believe will assist me to continue to bear my cross uncomplainingly, and to do my duty to my race

in a purer atmosphere, under more congenial skies, amid surroundings and scenes that are less diabolical and more brightly cheering. Pray do not forget me, nor to remember our mutual pledges. I shall think of you, and pray for you every day, while I await your greeting letter of friendship and liberty.

"Now, Garland, one changeless friend must leave you. My blessing remains with you; and may God bless and spare you to your friends and our cause of usefulness, in which, I hope, we may meet again and together work. So thus we must part. Farewell."

CLOUD: "God bless and spare you to humanity, Lawrence. I will be faithful and constant in all things, and will never forget you. My friend, farewell."

CHAPTER LXXIII.

"FAITHFUL HEARTS THAT NOT FORSAKE."

"And thus the heart will break, yet brokenly live on;
Even as a broken mirror, which the glass
In every fragment multiplies, and makes
A thousand images of one that was,
The same and still the more, the more it breaks,
And thus the heart will do which not forsakes;
Living in shattered guise, and still, and cold,
And bloodless, in its sleepless sorrow aches,
Yet withers on till all without is old,
Showing no visible sign, for such things are untold."
—BYRON.

"Sept., 1881.

"MRS. CARRIE V. FLOWERS:

"*My best and truest friend:*

"The intervening months between the receipt of your last sublime letter and this moment, that I then deemed so long, and that appeared so far distant, have one after another rolled past, and as I to-night gaze out over the wake of the backward track of time, I fancy that it was not more than a week ago when that letter first gladdened and grieved mine eye. Yet still, however, the time is here now when my promise to you is due—when that sad, sad letter, of which I have shuddered and dreaded to think, and hesitated so long to commence, must be written. I no less now dread the task than at any time in the past—a task from which I would gladly shrink; a subject of which I would a thousand times over prefer never to think, much less broach. However, it is a theme and duty to which I am fated—am bound with more than admantine chains. So, being thus irretrievably condemned, I will proceed to acquit myself of the letter portion of the penalty by its fulfillment.

"To attempt to answer your letter, especially the last one, with the spectral ghost of one feature of the subject of which your first letter demands of me to render an account, haunting my mind, and causing a thrill of terror to pervade my being, would be more than folly—it would be madness.

"Of the darkest chapter of my ignoble career, I shall assume that you have a version sufficiently authentic both to gratify the demands of curiosity and to satisfy the solicitude of interested friendship. Surely, this is ample as to all particulars, save that blank and mysterious missing .link between the evening on which I disappeared from the 'Future City,' and the day on which I reappeared at my father's home. There my presence was as much a surprise to the family and the neighbors, who were there on that occasion, as though they had witnessed me rise up out of the ground. This is one feature of that subject that is so painful and terrible to contemplate that I have never written one syllable upon it; about it I have never breathed one word—have been as silent as the grave; nor have I dared think of it aloud in the presence of any one. If ever the most horrible of all horrors was revealed to mortal man upon this earth, if ever the vision of judgment, of death and hell, the grim-visaged terrors of their appearance to the approaching spirits of the lost and the damned, were a veritable reality, divested of every semblance of imaginary coloring and feature of superstitious fancy, that experience was then mine.

"We have all been taught a divine maxim, that 'Confession is good for the soul'—then why not for the body and the mind as well? Implicitly trusting to the efficacy of the doctrine as being applicable alike to the one and to the other, I shall proceed to a practical test of the force of the virtues of this antidote as an operative agent to counteract the mortal malady. I shall,

therefore, make to you an *honest* confession of that deep, dark, and long-guarded secret, before taking up any other point of the promiscuous features of information which your letter demands. I do this with a hope that my mind will thereby experience some relief from the torturing rack of painful distress and acute remorse to which it is perpetually exposed. Therefore, without further preliminary cringing, I will free my mind by opening my heart and laying bare to you the fearful story that lies therein concealed.

"*The pangs of suicide; the vision of death and beyond!*

"After swallowing the potent and venomous drug, there was a strange sensation instantaneously creeping through my being. The healthful currents of life were being sapped and curdled, and were becoming stagnate and clogged and dormant in their wonted channels. The heart, in consequence, labored heavily to perform its functions, but was gradually stifled, as the pure blood which its pulsations expelled from the reservoir of its great fountain-head, and started out on its vitalizing course, flowed prematurely back upon its supplying source, as yet but slightly impregnated with the deadly bane. This was swiftly permeating the smaller branches, and there leaving its work of destruction behind it complete, as it proceeded on with unabated force to encroach upon the heart itself. The great rotary pumping-engine of the heart was rapidly submerged and flooded and disabled; its struggles grew feebler and more feeble still. Upon each failing effort, the submerging currents rushed back, yet more deeply impregnated with that wasting agent of death. Finally, the faint struggles were barely perceptible, as they steadily and ever continued to decline. The fingers and the toes tingled. The eye-balls quivered in their sockets. The muscles of the neck and face twitched convulsively. The head grew dizzier and dizzier, until it seemed that I was on some wheel that might have been making a million of revolutions per minute. There was a roaring sound in the ears resembling the thunder of a monster cataract.

"Now the heart surceased to beat. Then there was a moment of painful suspense not unlike, nor yet was it just the same sensation as that experienced in the last instant of consciousness when passing under the influence of chloroform. The ebbing faculties of vitality were yet able to realize that their annihilation was drawing its work rapidly nearer and nearer to its final consummation.

"Then followed a period of deeper blank between this latter state and a profoundly unconscious sleep, during which, could the act which had produced it have then been recalled, no mental anguish, no suffering, no bereavement, no sorrow, no disappointment, no misfortune, no loss, no shame, no fear of all the combined terrors and tortures that ever afflicted, scourged, tormented, slew, or consumed man upon this trouble-stricken earth, could have ever tempted, induced, or driven me to fly from *them* and seek refuge in *this!*

"But oh, my God! even in that horrid dream on the very mystic borders of death, I yet was able to realize that it was forever too late, forever past recalling; and that I was swiftly passing into the mysterious realities of the great Hereafter and of the terrible Unknown. This was the most awful moment ever experienced by mortal mind or spirit ken, without the dreadful reality of that infernal torment of which the preacher sometimes tells us in startling words.

"Now all the ties of consciousness, that had bound together the relations of mind and nature, were severed; and I passed into a state far more vivid than the most impressively realistic dream. While thus enthralled in suspense, all the thread of my life unfolded, and every act thereof, both great and small, passed in solemn array before my startled and wondering vision. But I could not awake, as from some horrid night-mare dream. The bright spots of life; the clean pages of its history, together with the dark, the stained, and the blurred ones, continued to pass before me, until they came down to this last and final scene, where all was still, on one page of black and rayless blank. This I comprehended to be a token of my everlasting doom. I seemed to feel, but as yet vaguely, that my spirit was free and on the bordering confines of the spirit world, or about to fly thitherward. It seemed that separation had actually taken place, and that my poor, long-suffering body was left stark and stiff and tenantless, to moulder in the unknown depths of that lone-

some, subterranean vault, while its late tenant was hastening to an existence which it then appeared to realize in conscious conviction was ten thousand times more awful and terrible than it has been or ever can be named.

"From this uncertain state of semi-stupefaction, the spirit suddenly awoke to a keen sensibility and deep realization of its immortal force of glowing penetration. It could survey, at will, with its spirit eye, the most distant sphere of the spirit world in all stages, all states, all forms, and in all time. Thus it understood that its own station was fixed with the hopeless and the damned. Though yet with its clay tenement in the dark vault of earth unflown, its sealed doom was clear, whither it could discern the grim messenger coming swiftly through space, on the speedy wings of thought, to guard it hence to its home of terror.

"Poor soul! it shuddered and shrunk back upon itself, and would have then flown alone for some blessed station of visible glory, but it was transfixed and bound by the magic spell of its approaching master. It had forfeited those bright realms of peace which spread out before its longing gaze in boundless, endless sublimity.

"There myriads upon myriads of numberless happy spirits appeared in tranquil blissfulness. In semblance they were as near as an earthly picture of comparison can be drawn to approximate the reality of this vision, as I yet retain its impression, which now sinks far below its then forcible perfectness—much the same as joyous, happy girls of meekly modest and innocent purity, whose hopes have never been embittered by one cruel disappointment, and whose lives have never been clouded by one sorrow, when mingling together in some sociably pleasing reunion. Thus appeared the perfect peace, tranquil contentment, and supreme happiness of those who had not, like me, forfeited their inheritance to a home in that bright world of beatific glory. To my spirit's eye they did not appear just what in fancy we have been taught to picture angel forms; nor was their wide and varied realms of bliss the same as our imaged Heaven. But they appeared as worlds on worlds, each particular orb, both visible and invisible to science's magic eye, in the vast era and boundless expanse of the starry plain—being a happy spirit world bordering on limpid rivers and crystal seas, upon the opposite margins of which were other worlds, until thus all were together entwined in one continuous and endless chain of perfect and symmetrical beauty. Those happy beings appeared in form and beauty much the same as the most exquisite model of the sculptor's art, yet a thousand times more pleasing to the eye; and they bore the full bloom and deep imprint ' of immortal youth,' that had been, was, and was to continue to be, eternally changeless, with unabatable faculties and tastes for the fullness of enjoyment of the delicious pleasures of their benignant clime, and the delightful communion of social intercourse and love, which care, nor sorrow, nor pain can never mar.

"Their glorious realms of unalloyable happiness appeared to be diversified into numberless and perpetually varying scenes of bliss-promoting wonders and rapture-inspiring features, whose genial influences lived on ever new. There were shady groves and enchanting gardens resplendent with unfading flowers and replete with immortal fruits. There were hill and dale and valley and plain decked in living green and beauteous flowers, interspersed ever and anon with murmuring, musical streams, and rippling cascades of living water, covered with groups and communities and villas and cities of their happy habitants, employed in many ways.

"Beyond and above all this, there appeared to be wrapped in a mystic veil of cloud the angelic Heaven, of which we cherish a vague conception, within the thrice consecrated precincts of which was located the throne of God, whence was dispensed blessings and mercy and grace, to His surrounding dominions.

"How terrible to gaze with longing admiration upon the beauties and the glories of those blessed abodes of the redeemed and happy spirits, and know that their consoling peace is fortified—that one is debarred from their enjoyment forever—and to realize, as I did then, that the last act of life by which the self-freed soul was liberated from its house of clay was the capital offence which had incurred the liability to that dread

penalty. Oh, that was one trying moment of indescribable bitterness and supreme anguish to the hope-exiled soul!

"Ah! but there was yet one scene wanting to complete the consummation of the trembling, terror-stricken spirit's torturing agony; to survey the waste howling realms of the damned in torment—that horrible sphere of endless darkness, blank and eternal despair; the awful home of my shrinking, frightened soul that was about to be conducted thitherward forevermore to dwell. Here was grim-visaged terror, the mere vision of whose yet untried realities created, each twinkle of an eye, deeper pangs of suffering than all that I had ever experienced in my natural life, could it have been combined into one piercing pang and thrust at one instantaneous stroke of woe into the mortal heart. To eyes and ears of flesh and blood, a true picture and a true story of the dread reality of that terrible moment, could art's coloring paint or the paucity of words depict it as it was then seen and felt by my crushed soul's acute sensibility, would be a sight, a theme of terrifying horrors to drive mankind to frenzied madness. One glimpse, one pang would suffice to stay any desperate hand raised in armed strife, arrayed against itself for self-destruction.

"That burning Hell, with its blue sulphurous flames, I did not behold; yet worse than that, by far, then to my astounded vision was revealed. I saw the lost and the damned suffering in the purple darkness of their eternal midnight, in unnumbered forms and endless degrees, in their worlds of chaotic waste. They were exposed on icy rocks, in boggy fens, and upon the crested billows of raging seas, to the pelting storms and the relentless lash of contending elements. Driven by the waves; dashed upon the rocks; caught up by the whirlwind; spun through space by the hurricane; sitting pensively absorbed in silent despair, wringing the hands; rushing frantically to and fro in wild panic, as the terrified passengers on a sinking ship, or moaning piteously, as the last survivor of a family laid low by the fell plague in one dreadful night. Then, in their stern realms of grim terrors, ghastly shadows, woeful horrors, unmitigated despair and endless pain, the realms of bliss, with all their alluring delights and fascinating joys, burst forth, ever in dazzling splendors upon the hungry view of the damned, causing them continually to pine with ceaseless yet vain desire. Thus, perpetually consumed by hunger and thirst, yet not able to die—powerless to cease to be—their longing suspense, their doom of fate, is fixed, unmeasured by years, uncheered by one distant gleam of hope.

"Such was 'that wide, that boundless prospect' that then opened up before my despairing soul. Oh Heaven! how I then longed to be back in my late esteemed intolerable existence, with all its wretchedness increased a thousand fold. I would have flown from it again, never; but would rather have embraced it as a boon of bliss.

"Now my guide and guard from those dark and infernal shores drew near, to take charge of my spirit and hasten it onward through space to its dread doom. But just as the fiendish messenger was about to enter the dark vault's dismal mouth and rayless gloom, like a flash of light, with flaming sword in hand, a bright angel intercepted his approach and bid him stand at bay. The baffled fiend protested and urged his time-honored right to the forfeited soul. The angel rebuked him for thus hastily pressing his claim before it was due, before the spirit and nature were fully parted; and informed him that while in law and custom the parted soul, when free, was his forfeited right, the Great Judge had in mercy decreed to judge that soul—had then dispatched his swift and holy messenger to guard it from farther harm, until its final doom was fixed. Murmuringly the fiend turned away and sped him back towards his ghostly realm, while gradually my spirit sunk back into a state of blank unconsciousness. Thus I passed through the sleep of death and fully experienced 'what dreams may come,' such as are the suicide's appalling terror.

"At last I came back to conscious life; but for some time I could not realize, nor yet believe, that such was true. When, finally, I did comprehend the situation, and was well assured that I still lived in the flesh, I at first, and for a

long time—I could not tell how long, though it seemed ages to me then—was unable to move or speak. I was paralyzed and stiff and cold; and a raging thirst seemed to be devouring me as a consuming flame. My head and limbs ached as though they were ready to burst into shattered fragments. I believed that I was doomed to die there, helplessly.

"However, by desperate and persistently continued efforts, I moved, and at length succeeded in getting my hand to my head. There was a perceptible indication of moisture on my forehead, which my constant exertions to move caused gradually to spread, until, probably in the course of an hour, I was perspiring and able to rise to a sitting posture; but it was much like Rip Van Winkle rising from his fabled sleep of twenty years. The popping of my joints echoed lugubriously sad through that dark and terrible vault.

"Sometime later I was once more under the starry canopy of Heaven, much refreshed from drinking some water from a little brooklet and washing my hand and face. It was about two o'clock in the morning. But what morning? I was unable to tell. I walked with much difficulty and great pain.

"Now a crisis was upon me. I was confronted by that great and momentous problem and its menacing question—'What are you going to do?' I was weak and feeble, and still suffering the agonizing tortures of torment. I was in a dilemma of irresolution and perplexing doubt, while I fancied there was a stern voice of command ringing in my ears. 'Fly! fly! from Nube Garland and his irredeemable curse, back to Garland Cloud and truth and duty.'

"I had more will to go than inclination to stay. How could I now return to those scenes and experiences from which I had been driven to attempt an everlasting flight? Would not the reproach of that attempt be worse to bear than all that had induced it? So far as all the world who had ever known me as Nube Garland was concerned, my relation would only be the same as it would have remained had I never returned to life. All the pangs of anguish and feelings of disappointment that my rash act would cause in the world, had already been most cruelly inflicted—past recalling, past cure; wounds which my reappearance would but aggravate. Thus influenced, I resolved to fly; but I had no money, and what to do I could not tell.

"Directly I remembered where Milton Land had lived ten years before, about forty miles away. I was about one mile from a point on a railroad leading to that place—a point at which an out-going freight train would stop at a few minutes past three o'clock in the morning. If I could catch that, and prevail on the conductor to pass me to Milton Land's station, I might there obtain money to carry me back to my native blue mountains, where I then dreamed I would pass my remaining days, be they many or few, in almost hermetical seclusion, far from the seething, surging strifes of life in which I had suffered such sorrow, endured so much pain.

"Taking from my pocket a large linen handkerchief, and tying the corners together, I then slipped it tightly over the top of my head, and under my chin, to form the semblance of a huge bandage. This concealed my side features and covered my lower beard. This done, I set out to reach the railroad. Never in my life have I performed any physical effort that was accomplished with so much difficulty and at the cost of so much bodily pain.

"However, I reached the desired point in time, and the conductor, who happened to be intimately acquainted with Milton, passed me without a word of objection, and landed me at my destination before the sun peeped over the neighboring hill-tops. The conductor pointed out to me the residence of Milton Land.

"I was met at the door by Milton, who never would have recognized me. He was loth to believe at first I was not some imposter, as he had been informed ten years before that I had committed suicide by drowning in the Tennessee river, but that my body had never been found. Yet, however, I quickly satisfied him as to my identity, and told him that I had been drugged nearly to death at the 'Future City,' was thus left penniless; and that I had sought him in my dire extremity with a hope that I could obtain assistance to enable me to get to my native land. This

he promptly assured me I could have. Then he conducted me into a room in order that I might wash and comb before meeting the family. He left me there alone for a few minutes.

"After washing, I went to the glass to comb. At the first glimpse I started back aghast. My hair and beard were nearly half grey, and every hair on my neck was as white as wool. My eyes were sunken, with great black circles under them; and my features were contracted and haggard. With the evidence of my missing arm concealed, I could have walked the active thoroughfares of the 'Future City,' with impunity, with no fear of being recognized.

"As to the meeting and day spent with the family—just imagine it! That night I bid them adieu and took passage on a mail train that swiftly widened the distance between me and the city with which were associated so many sadly bitter memories, and the dark vault for seventy-six hours my tomb.

"After I was at my father's house the first evening and night, I found that the phantom of Garland Cloud, which had haunted me so many years, was gone; but that there was still, and more horrible to contemplate, the ghost of Nube Garland with me, destined to be and to remain ever present.

"The horrors of that sleep of death and its frightful dreams weighed heavily upon my desponding mind, creating pangs which my enfeebled frame was little able to sustain.

"Then, added to this, was the keen knife of remorse, cutting the lacerated mass and pulp of my crushed heart. Remorse for my act—that act of horror that had more than miraculously failed, for the drug was pure and of the most potent known, and had been taken in the accurately measured proportion prescribed by science to dispatch a man of my natural strength and powerful constitution, and it did its work well and finally, had not a super-human power intervened and stayed its fatal influence before the work of destruction was complete—and for my commercial brigandage, do you think? Ah, no; but it was for the poor forsaken Manonia, whom I should never see any more, that I wept; and for whom my heart began to bleed ever again anew. I had beheld her grief, that nearly broke her heart; and now I could not rest one moment, either sleeping or waking, for the haunting image of her pitiful despair. She had been devoted to me to a degree to rival anything I ever read in the most fabulously colored descriptions of romanticly imaged conjugal affection. She was, for a time, happy; but between her father's family and I her heart was about equally divided, with my half rather in the preponderance. When she was with me, temptation never assailed me; but her frequent and protracted visits to her family proved my bane.

"Had she been with me when the emergency came to force a decision, whether I would abandon my sinking craft of commerce and let her go down with her over burthen, honorably, or buoy her up by casting honor overboard and calling to my assistance those most disreputable of piratical sloops, Deception and Crime, my ship would have been submerged beneath the encroaching and disastrous waves of misfortune. But, poor Manonia! she was not there with her angelic influence to counteract and disarm the power of the Tempter, whose slave I was and had been for so many years, whenever I was alone unguarded by some soul of purity which he dared not approach; or, had she been with me in that last great crisis of supreme trial, I had never known that sleep of death with its dreams of horror.

"Could I recall that step—that nameless wrong that linked her fate with the burden of my curse—I would, to have that it had not been, go back again to that sleep of death, as I was when the angel came, never more to wake. Is this not proof of my remorse?

"I struggled hard, but all in vain, to resist the spell that forged the links of that fatal chain that bound her to me, and enslaved her hopes in the direful thraldom of a cruel despair.

"Ah, my true friend, before the charm of that magic and enchanting spell, I was as powerless to exercise my own free will as I was while under the baneful influence of that potent drug. It has been, is, and ever will be, a mystery too deep for the penetration of my dark mind. Some strange power, unrevealed, decreed—some

invisible hand of destiny directed, that I should be her fell fatality. "Before her pure chain of love had bound me fast, your image, my true young heart's idol—the first, the last, the only shrine of love upon which, in all truth and sincerity, all its incense, with no reserve, was sacrificed, and but for that fiendish lie that told me how base slander's envenomed whisper, that lied so as to seem true, had alienated your good friendship from me, for with you, friendship, true friendship, was all that it ever could have been—I would have mourned, and felt the same keen remorse for your sake that I have known for poor Manonia in her desolate lot.

"Against the spell that linked my soul to you I fought long and well, and was oft and truly warned. Few are the men, with ambition's fire glowing in their hearts, who would not have a fair angel, adored by seraphs and all the world, for a friend, though he knew that nearer he could never be than for distant, unseen smiles and far-sent messages of approbation to cheer him on with tireless courage to stem the opposing tides and brave the adverse storms that would dispute his daring course. I was that aspirant, you the angel, then when you proffered friendship I embraced it with a secret vow, a mental oath, that beyond that safe line of propriety's bounds I would never attempt, nor seek to go, nor dream of going.

"My unwhispered plans of ambition to rise were deeply formed before my proud young heart bounded, with one wild and enthusiastic thrill, when first I gazed upon the tented field. But I realized the want of an inspiration, and that your name proved to be to me, a name which I learned to cherish with holy reverence, and to consecrate as my guiding star and my consoling angel, without one selfish thought or one future hope, save such as were far away removed beyond an earthly love, the same as I do now. Had I never met you under the mystic influence of that cave-guarded spring, or had you then met me more coldly formal, and proved afterwards less warmly friendly, my sentiments had ever remained unchanged; I had never dreamed that fatal dream of love, for I trembled when I thought of the pangs of a hopeless love.

"When that decoy letter, that sent me on the wild and tempestuous voyage around the shores of death and hell, reached me, could I then but have known that your true friendship still remained unshaken, I would have returned, defied all their reptile crew, faced the whole world, and confessed to you as I confess now. But this was not to be ; upon it rested the interdiction of Fate, and your guardian angel watched over you and shielded 'The Angel of Consolation' from all harm, and gave to you the purest and the truest Christian man that I ever knew. So, thus, were you doubly blessed.

"How truly well all ended, and would be now, had not that hapless dove, the forlorn Manonia, been drawn upon the stage as an actress, to perform the saddest rôle in the sadly cruel scenes.

"After my return, I spent one night in that town where once you dwelt, where we first met and last parted.

"In the early summer morning, before the sun rose, I walked over the well-remembered pathway to the cave spring ; looked around and thought backwards to another morning in May, long years ago. The limpid spring, the arching of the cave, the moss-covered spring-house, the venerable shade-tree, and the gravelly walk up the gently sloping declivity to the mansion, were there unchanged by time, but Carrie Harman was nowhere to be seen. Then I walked pensively up to the stile, and sat down upon it, where you once sat by my side, when you would not let me sing some lines of that pathetic song, 'I am Sitting on the Stile Mary,' as I wanted to transpose them ; yet oh! how prophetic they were. This last morning I sang alone, in a humming, husky voice :

> ' I am sitting on the stile, Carrie,
>   Where we sat side by side
> One bright May morning long ago,
>   When you were my joy and pride.
> The corn was springing fresh and green,
>   The lark sang loud and high,
> The red was on your lip, Carrie,
>   The love-light in your eye.'

"I could go no farther. I looked over at the closed windows of the deserted mansion, and of the parlor where last I lightly, and with a hope,

bade you good-night. 'The graveyard' did not lie between, Carrie,' but there was one lonely, neglected, unknown grave there, and to bow in meekness at its shrine I had made a pilgrimage. It was ' *The grave of my hopes.*'

      *   *   *   *

"Your grateful, yet unworthy friend,
      "GARLAND CLOUD."

Half of this letter is omitted, as the answer indicates its nature.

"——— SQUARE, NEW YORK, Jan., 1882.

"COL. GARLAND CLOUD:

"*My unhappy and much pitied friend :*

"Your compassion-eliciting, heartrending, soul-stirring letter, by the friendly hand of our mutual and esteemed friend, Major Pleasington, has been read and re-read, again and again, with feelings of mingled sorrow, pity and awe. Who lives, with heart and soul so dead, as to be unmoved by that letter ?

"Of that terrible experience in the closing scene of your relation to Nube Garland, which terminated your career and residence in the 'Future City,' I care to say but little—the less the better ; because nothing could be so appropriate, in the presence of such a frightful and horrible subject as silent awe.

"I am truly gratified to know that it has been the means of effectually curing you of that baneful proneness to commit suicide, with which your mind had been so long and so sadly infected ; that this distemper has been thereby so thoroughly eradicated that you have never since even dreamed of self-destruction, except with a shocking thrill of inexpressible horror that drove you yet farther away from this distressing danger. Also, let me say that I am, furthermore, thankful that your present experience has cured you of that fatal and erroneous principle that caused you to reason that to commit a wrong with pure motives, designed to promote a good cause that would directly benefit many thousands of the laboring poor or produce good, was not a crime. I rejoice that you take the view of it that you do ; that your fearful penalty was necessary as the only remedy that would have fully effected this much-to-be-desired result; and that, therefore, you regard those two appalling experiences as being the chief and only blessing that you have received since you first strayed from the path of true honor. Thus they must be, as they have set you back in it again, freed from the galling slavery into which the spell—that fatal spell of the magic mask—had plunged and there held you bound. Now you are a wiser and may be a better man.

"I now have abiding faith and boundless confidence in your future career, believing that you are yet destined to be the agent and instrument through and with whom the Divine benefactor of mankind designs to dispense inestimable temporal blessings upon the human race, by inspiring your purposes and directing your efforts so that they will become the means of saving many thousands from a career of crime, and their near ones and their dear ones from the cruel pangs wrought by the criminal's disgraceful ruin.

"Throughout the wild vicissitudes of your strangely checkered career, I can trace the finger of a mysterious Destiny, guiding you from stage to stage, through scene after scene, as he brought you on to this final point of preparation for his great work, else why or how has all this been? What you designed—desired, was not to be; and what you dreamed not of, has been—is yours.

"Viewing the situation from your standpoint, that you are a hopeless outcast and a friendless exile from the benignant atmosphere of the only social sphere in which you would dream of attempting to exist, and which will, therefore, doom you to a lonely life of cheerless desolation, I can but stand, as it were, transfixed with admiration at beholding the meek resignation and unselfish courage with which you devote your life to the cause of that social world in which you are unlikely to find, for yourself, much benevolence grafted on charity, and where you may expect to meet small personal encouragement.

"Long years ago, when our bright Southern skies were overcast with darkly portentious gloom, and Dixie's children of the mountain and the vale from day to day, in trembling suspense, whispered with white lips, 'The foe—they come, they come!' I admired the youthful, mountain soldier-boy, Garland Cloud, for his unselfish devotion to those who had ill-treated him;·and for his temperate life of purity, that the corruptions of the camp could not infect.

"Then, you confess to having been an ambitious aspirant to have entwined upon your youthful brow the trophied laurels of cruel war, man's wasting scourge—that universal and destructive pestilence—and to having enshrined me as an inspiration in your proud heart. It was a pleasing duty with me to cheer you on.

"Now, again, with your pursuing odium of the past, and crushing ignominy of the present, I admire you—and more, a thousand times, with no springing hope of selfishness as then enflamed my young and romantic heart, but with a nobler, higher hope for the human weal of all hearts—Garland Cloud, regenerated and redeemed; matured in years; ripe with knowledge acquired from lessons taught in Experience's cruel school; a stern veteran and courageous soldier, brandishing in bold defiance the unsheathed sword drawn in a far more glorious war against the enemy of all mankind, that monster enemy—Crime!

"Was I worthy, in that other wasting war, to be your inspiration, I am a thousand times more worthy to be so now. Then, in this long struggle in that dark hour that may be coming on, let me be your inspiring and consoling friend. I speak now of your work—the duty of your life. I am yet to speak of yourself, and life for yourself alone.

"As to the cureless wrongs of your lost and much-regretted Manonia, I am unable to see how you can do better than to let them remain just as they would have been had you never awoke from that horrible sleep of death, except that in the future you may now contribute whatever you can towards her support and temporal comfort; because, for her, mental remedy you have none. Evidently, it would be worse than madness, under the circumstances now existing, for you to think of attempting to return and live with her people. It would be, assuming that the last lingering spark of her affection for you has not been wholly extinguished, a cruelty to tear her away from her family again, almost as bad as the other wrongs which she has suffered, even granting that she would consent to such an arrangement. This is highly improbable; for now she, doubtless, hates you as cordially as she once loved you passionately, and is, most likely, divorced, if not married again.

"I think her deplorable and pitiful lot is but the natural consequence and penalty resulting from the most indiscreet imprudence on her part and that of her family. Had she maintained towards you that retiring reserve and caution that should always be meted out to unvouched-for strangers by all ladies; or, even before making the final leap into the darkness, had her family done what custom inexorably demand that they should have done—called on you for references, from whom your credentials could be obtained, you would have never married her. You should not, however, have been induced to marry her. While censuring her imprudence, I am not excusing you. I noted in your letter that you actually reproached me for the extreme warmth with which I manifested my friendship to you, even after our long-continued and most intimate relations. Certainly, Manonia was no less retiring.

"Now, it becomes me to make my confession to you—to do which I am compelled to repeat something of the story of the past which I have never told save to myself alone, but to myself so oft that it will be repeating to tell it to you. But in reflecting upon this theme the lines from our once mutually admired 'Poet of the passions,' and, I doubt not, now thrice in harmony with your emotions, involuntarily rush into my mind:

'Since my young days of passion, joy or pain,
Perchance my heart and harp have lost a string,
And both may jar.'

"And thus out of time, the discord of my story must grate harshly in contrast with the present situation, to which it bears a distant relation.

"My interest in Garland Cloud, after the sentiments of gratitude which sprung from the depths of pure, sisterly love, were selfish. From gratitude the gradations upward can be ascended with rapid facility, and the steps are few to the highest emotions and the purest sentiment of the human heart—that of the most intensified love.

"When I received definite reports from the army as to how the young gentlemen of my own social class were utterly failing to stand the moral, crucible test to which they were subjected in camp life, and drinking, gambling, and otherwise conducting themselves in an ungentlemanly manner, I experienced a feeling of inexpressible disappointment, because, from this class I had been educated to understand that I was to draw my prize in the lottery of life.

"Stories of Garland Cloud's temperate life and unselfish devotion as a soldier, both to his country and his unkind aristocratic comrades, constantly reached me; and coming, as they did come, from those companions themselves, greatly enhanced these qualities and acts in my estimation. I decided in my own mind, that there was a young man in the lowest ranks of the army that would outstrip all of his comrades, with their greater advantages of education, and the powerful influence of wealthy and official friends against him, alone by his own personal exertions, unaided and unbefriended; and, though belonging to a lower sphere of life, that in moral character and natural talents he was the superior of any one of my personal young friends in the army, my own dear and idolized brother not excepted. From the moment that this conviction became positively fixed in my mind, I resolved that he should be the prize for me in the lottery of life, unless the blood of his pure young heart was sacrificed on the altar of his country. From that wild December day, until that evening of your last goodnight, every thought, every action of my life, that bore the most distant relation to you, was aimed to tend to promote the progress, or to hasten the consummation of that result. I dreamed and deemed that it would be an easy conquest, a struggle in which you would, without opposition, surrender at discretion. Alas! how soon and how painfully I learned my mistake!

"I wrote you letters couched in such warmly expressed terms as to be nothing more nor less than advances, at which my maidenly pride blushed, and against which my true woman's nature revolted. Then I waited on tip-toe of expectation for the reply, after mailing one after another of my numerous and often voluminous letters, containing exhaustive reports of the work in which I was engaged, but which, even as to this feature, were simply love-letters. Your replies were always tardy, and thus in ill-harmony with the anxiety of my watching heart. Then, when at last they did come—cruel things that they were—in the studied reserve of your guarded coldness I was unable to find just one little word of encouragement for which my hungry, thirsty heart was pining, whose expressive force was not so modified by some qualifying term as to destroy all possibility of placing upon it the least semblance of a favorable construction. As I read these letters, I could feel the sensation of an icy tremor creeping through my veins and penetrating to my heart, mingled with provoking despair. I was baffled and foiled.

"Then, finally, I concluded that you must be engaged to some mountain beauty; for methought that a mountain rose would be more enticingly preferable than a lily of the valley, especially to a mountain boy; because, if otherwise, I could not dream that you could be indifferent to that then self-esteemed, treasured jewel, Carrie Harman, and I wept—and wept most bitterly. The thought never once entered my head, I was so honestly sincere and so intensely in earnest, that all this time you were dreading and shunning a coquettish flirtation—something of which I was as incapable of being guilty, and which was as foreign to my nature, as the most degrading vices.

"After long years of waiting, when at last we met, my woman's heart soon discerned that yours, though distant and apparently indifferent and cold, could be won. When you came to the point of declaring your love, it was then that I experienced the ecstacies of success, of a crowning triumph, which, in that glad hour, I thought compensated for all the cruel anxiety and bitter disappointments of the past. Ah! but these were ecstacies of bliss too fierce—too fierce to last.

"You bade me good-night for evermore, with my heart a stranger to you, and its sentiments struggling so hard to be free that I could scarcely stifle them. Had I then confessed as I do now!— The sad, sad lines in your old song are appropriate here:

'And what we might have been, Lorena,
Had but our lovings prospered well!'

"But they were doomed by the stern and merciless interdiction of Fate.

"Oh, my God! that I could be spared the memory, much more the repetition, of another syllable of this story. Your regretted Manonia, nor any other woman who was a wife, never mourned more bitterly than I mourned. Oh! cruel, cruel man that you were, in order to escape slander's venomously pointed dagger, to wring a heart so truly yours, and blight the one fond hope of a long-suffering life—that had suffered for you alone! Had you then known my heart, I never could have forgiven you.

"After my full two years of mourning and retirement from society, the question of marrying was a bitter one. I looked upon the clause of a letter—a farewell letter—you wrote to your father, as a positive will that I should marry Jesse Flowers; and that you designed to make me the executrix of that will, and I married—devoted my life as a sacrifice upon the altar of duty. It was, on my part, but meekly bowing in resignation at the shrine of duty; then, farther than this, my heart—poor, crushed and mangled heart—was not in it. Jesse knew this; I told him that, had you remained, I should have been your wife.

"But I have since taught myself loving devotion, and am as happy as any one can be in a second love, after the heart has once bled; and here the lines of our poet come again:

'Oh! thyself deceive not;
Love may sink by slow decay;
But by sudden wrench believe not,
Hearts may thus be torn away.

'Still thine own its life retaineth;
Still must mine, though bleeding, beat;
And the undying thought which paineth,
Is that we no more may meet.'

"Now, as to your future: I admire your resolution to start the new life on the foundation laid in prison, and commend your desire to prove to the world what is possible for fallen men to do. But I do not think you are right in declining to accept assistance from true friends, who are so anxious to pay you something on their great debt of gratitude. If you think that it will be too painful to call at the house, pray see the men in business.

"Now, my friend, one last request: All the woman's heart that I have is wholly and truly devoted to Jesse Flowers. But I have a sister's heart and a sister's boundless love—half of these are yours.

"When I look at my dear brother, in his supreme happiness with his mountain Rose, and think that but for you, a poor, all but friendless prisoner, languishing all these long and bitter wintry nights in the murky damp of a granite tomb, his bones would now be bleaching or mouldering to dust on the banks of the Potomac, I forget that you have ever been Nube Garland, or that there are crime stains on the solitary hand—stains that I would wash away in briny tears—and say, 'He is my BROTHER!' Yes, Garland, I am your sister; and a sister's tender solicitude and pure love shall be yours, the same as Edgar's. Think of me, then, please, and write to me when you are once more on the great sea of life, as you do of and to your own little sister away down yonder in 'The city by the Southern sea,' and I will write to you; advise; cheer you onward; help you every way I can.

"Be true, be good, be constant to your purposes, and live the remainder of your cheerless, sorrowful days, for the good of your race, and for yourself in the great Hereafter. God bless you, my poor brother; I shall think of and pray for you every night. Do not, I entreat you, do not forget

"Your devoted sister-friend,

"CARRIE V. FLOWERS."

CHAPTER LXXIV.

THE ATONEMENT OFFERING.

"I, who have sinned, and suffered for my sin,
A wanderer far from hope forever now,
A life whose dirge will be, 'It might have been!'
Before thy altar, Oh my country, bow.
I watch the suns of others rise and set,
I know that mine has set for evermore;
But this I give thee; what remaineth yet
Of future unto me, whate'er its store,
Labor, life itself, is thine till life is o'er."
—M. A. BILLINGS.

WITH the term "atonement" are associated both the beautiful and the terrible. The beautiful obtains when the offering is a free-will one, joyously made, and secures the full and perfect blessing of forgiveness as its reward. The ter-

rible is shadowed forth to startle reflective contemplation when the atonement is compulsory and wreaked in the horrible semblance of unmitigated vengeance.

About the earliest account we recall of "atonement offerings," made with the free will, bears close relevancy to the immediate exiles from the Garden of Eden—their "Lost Paradise." Almost as ancient, also, is the idea of "atonement" in the typical form of vengeance, often unrighteously wreaked, as in the tragic case of Abel. But such cases as this can hardly be classed under that head. To the punishment of crime does the term, thus qualified, more appropriately apply.

In this guise we last beheld Garland Cloud, the erratic wanderer, shuddering at the uninviting prospect of his unpromising future.

Now, once more we take up the thread of his story. We find him again embarked on the voyage of the "new life." As he met and faced death so many times in the early years of his first voyage, now does he meet the world and face the stern behests of duty with unfaltering courage. The high standard of moral courage which he imaged in the secluded solitude of his doomed atonement's shadows, has proved more than a dream—a mere mythical delusion. That courage is his. Strengthened by it, he dares to speak and battle for the right. Far more has he accomplished within the pale of the first year than he had any right to anticipate that he might accomplish in less than five years. Without the slightest modification or abatement, he has redeemed his pledges in every direction—he continues to redeem them every day of his life.

Through the press has his poignant phrases assailed crime, as no other erring man of the age has ever before openly and defiantly arrayed himself on the side and in the suffering interests of society, after he has paid a legal atonement.

From his letters transcribed herein some idea may be formed of the nature of his articles made public. More than this, too, he did: he went onto the platform, before large audiences, as a free lecturer in the interest of society. Thus he tendered his "Atonement offering." From notes of one of these lectures we are able to make some extracts, such as might interest many per-

sons—lovers of the true and the right. He said:
" I stand in your presence, this evening, in the semblance of an object of warning, to address you on the grand problems of human life—PEACE and HAPPINESS in this world. Beyond this, my province as a teacher does not extend.

" I stand here aghast at the bare contemplation of my descent from your sphere of blissfulness, where ebb and flow the eternal springs of hope, down the yawning abyss to the isolated bog of despair—dangers and penalties against which it becomes my hapless duty to warn you.

" Between your sphere and mine there seems to roll a fathomless and an impassable gulf, at least to me. You might not pass it without imperiling that thrice-blessed birthright, which yet is yours to enjoy, to cherish, to treasure as the most sacred and priceless jewel in this world; so precious that, after it has once been lost, all the gold of Ophir, and all the diamonds of Golconda, would not suffice to restore it again.

" Oh, young people! those of you whose hearts are yet buoyant with youthful hope, I am here to talk to you. I still cling to one link of the broken chain—that tie which once bound me to the past, and yet keeps alive in my heart one quenchless spark of reverence for the true and the right, now cherished as sacred, in memory of ' the loved and the lost.' Against this fate I earnestly desire to warn you.

" Nothing else could induce me to assume this painful responsibility, and to endure the ordeal of trial which it imposes. Oh, that I could imprint upon each young heart, now under the sound of my voice, impressions of my story, so they might there remain in deathless memory !

" Shudderingly, I glance along my backward track, so thickly strewn with wrecks of hope, reeking in the groaning blood of aching hearts, until, far beyond all these ruins and all this woe, I behold that young summer of my youth, as I then stood on the same plane of life where your stations are now. My brow was then wreathed with hopeful honor. Courageously I gazed up the slippery steep leading to the pinnacle of Fame. With the fiery glow of inordinate ambition igniting a flame of desperation in my heart that would one day dare to tempt even Fate

itself, there I stood. Ah! had I then gazed with equal intensity at the pit of Infamy beneath, I would not be here to tell my dread story.

" To one who falls from your sphere of life, crime is living death, the dungeon's solitude, a living tomb. My own case is an enigma to the philosophy of crime. But, either in a greater or in a less degree, it is the same form the danger may most likely assume to menace some one of you. Human nature is frail and weak, or perverse and willful.

" But had I never suffered shipwreck of fortune, nor received a legal brand, I would be to-day none the less an orphan of the heart. I would be a moral leper in disguise—respected by the world, but loathsome to myself. For myself, I prefer my present degradation, with nothing concealed and nothing to fear. Reputation and public esteem do not make our true character, and are of little intrinsic value, when we know that the unveiled truth would shroud them in the thraldom of the blackest social damnation.

" I have no purpose to enlist your sympathy for myself. But my whole nature, so long inertly rusting in stagnation, is thoroughly aroused and fired with a glowing desire and a desperate determination to awaken sympathy for yourselves and yours, that may cause you to shun and save you from the odium of that nameless curse which makes joy and me strangers for evermore.

" I assure you, and most earnestly, too, that my mind had never before been so acutely perceptive, or so infallibly tenacious, as it was amid shadows of the dungeon's solitude. Do you desire to know why this was so? My mind was cured of its fallacious aberrations. My heart was free from the malady of moral leprosy. The immortal mind, thus purified, elevated my being above its surroundings, and taught me to abominate crime, because of the loathsome degradation to which it sinks mankind, and in which it holds its pitiable victims so hopelessly enthralled.

" The majesty of the mind defies the dungeon's bars; and, scorning its non-restraining environments of brick and granite, flies away to commune with virtuous purity, and drink ambrosial nectar from Nature's crystal fountains. It is the pure diamond that passes through the fiery crucible unscorched, and comes from the test shining in augmented lustre. The mind must rise or sink. If it wills to rise, all the powers of vice, crime, and hell—the triune genius that wields the supreme sway in abandoned hearts—cannot drag it down, nor stay its triumph.

"Do not, good people, I implore you, do not despise these humble reflections because they are of dungeon birth. Truth, my friends, seeks a dwelling place amid the inhospitable confines of dungeon walls, whenever they hold in their chilling embrace *a human heart!* Wherever the heart of man pulsates, there truth, like death, enters and delivers her message, but does not, like death, take forcible possession. She pleadingly, lovingly, sues for entertainment.

"Before you, my friends, I stand this evening enrobed in the habiliments of truth, to live in disguise nevermore. No gold, no prospective friendship, no anticipations of love, could lure me to attempt to conceal what I have been or who I am, no matter where I go. Now, one of the highest elements of my duty is to deter other people from descending from the throne of honor.

"Oh! do not deceive yourselves. When you part with the path of honor, and cast away the lamp-light of truth, you enter alone and helpless upon the dark and tempestuous sea of crime, exposed to all its entangling nets and storms of wrecking contention. It is as if you inhale the contagious breath of the pestilence, and pass on, unconscious that the germ of early death is in your being—yet it is there, subtly developing its life-blighting forces. Suddenly and unexpectedly, these smite you, sap and poison the fountains of vitality, and spread to the anxious and loving ones standing beside that couch of untimely death. Ah! but this is as nothing to the paralytical stroke of moral leprosy, that breaks, yet stills not the heart. Alas! for the innocent hearts that are thus broken and lacerated, to bleed in silent sorrow and pine with the blight of irretrievable woe. The paths of honor and shame start out side by side. It is but a step from the one to the other. One may move for a time, with a foot in each path, until finally they abruptly part.

"Good people, in the affairs of life and duty in this world, independent of all spiritual considerations, there are but two ways for the traveler to pursue; the one is the right, the other the wrong way. And beyond the scope of all controversy you are, each of you, assuredly and unquestionably in one of these ways—you are right or you are wrong. If wrong, you are subject to all the dangers which beset the sinister ways of life, and liable to incur all the fearful penalties which they entail. From the forbidden path there is very rarely a voluntary return, and a full and free confession. Partial returns, with hidden crimes that remain unatoned, are worse yet than the dungeon's haunted gloom. Every moment, whatever is designed for the sweetest bliss of life, is transformed to the bitterest woe. The shadow of an imaginary pursuer haunts the charming joys of the most delightful entertainment with pleasant friends, disturbs the most soothing slumbers, and embitters the purest fountains of love.

"These are tortures from which there is no escape, for which there is no remedy, but to tear away the mask of deception and confess the truth to some trusty friends. Thus may the potent charm of that fatal spell be broken; a spell so aptly depicted by the poet in the lines—

'And like the bird whose pinions quake,
But cannot fly the gazing snake.'

"Oh my friends! be there one of you in any stage of this hope-wasting slavery, in the name of all that is lovable, dear and sacred in this life, let me conjuringly implore you to break its galling chains without delay. Shut your eyes and rend these fetters, regardless of imaginary consequences. Call around you your dearest ones and nearest friends, and have the gentle tenderness of loving and friendly hands to extricate you from the subtle embrace of the destroying mask, the baneful curse of all false lives. Could you realize what it is to have the mask of life, the curse of earth, torn away by the rude and pitiless hand of the law, not one of you would ever experience these nameless pangs. But beware of the mask in its mildest and most seemingly innocent form, because it leads its victims into the clutches of the law or drives them beneath the sods of premature graves.

"Ladies, this cruel truth applies to you with more crushing and overwhelming force than it does to men—not always because of your own errors so much as ou account of the false lives of deceitful men. Forlorn and desolate, indeed, is that man's lot, in the realm of bright life, for whose waywardness no true woman's heart would bleed. Each of you can fight intemperance and vice by becoming the guardian angel of your husband, your brother, your cousin, your childhood's friend, or your sweetheart. Such is the magnetism of a pure woman's power of influence, so skillful her devices for exercising it, when thoroughly determined to win the sway over the conduct of man, that one word, a glance of the eye, even, will tame a man for whom the law's unrelenting scourge has no restraining terrors, and sever him from a proneness to stray in devious paths. The wisest, the bravest of men, despots and conquerors, each have been vanquished and tamed by one little woman. You are Nature's queens, destined to reign over society, over the home circle, and over the hearts of men. By demanding these rights and ruling over them with gentle despotism, the only sovereignty you would willingly maintain, you would not be usurping; the world would become better; many bitter tears would never be wept—woman's despairing midnight tears.

"Oh merciful Heaven! what silent wretchedness the mask has caused! Were but half its buried secrets known; were the silent groanings of all the despairing hearts that are lacerated, crushed and rent by the cruel tyranny of its hopeless slavery, sent forth upon the wings· of the wind for but one night, so that all the world might hear them, those who knew not the cause would tremble in speechless terror and stand appalled, under the conviction that the ministers of doom's-day were on earth, ready to sound the awful judgment knell.

"Blessed are those who are strangers to this unutterable damnation, that turns the fondest hopes to dust, the brightest dreams of life to the most desolate despair; thrice blessed will be those who pass down to the shores of the dark river,

and over into the great Unknown, without having experienced the mysteries of this relentless curse.

"Well may the ministers of God startle the souls of the wicked with their warning notes of 'woe! woe!' if *that* doom be as dreadful for spirits as *this* is for flesh and blood, when it goes not beyond the purgatory of liberty, and buries the mortal secrets of shame beneath the sods of the grave, without the stigma of a legal brand. Then, oh merciful God! what can I say of those who go down to the darkest depths of an earthly hell? Where, where are the words adequate to the power of expressive coloring requisite to paint this frightful reality? Unknown to mortal man. No words can depict, no artist could portray the woeful despair and haunted gloom that pervade the dread precincts of a living tomb. I have passed through both this purgatory and this hell on earth; and I swear to you, by the sacred memory of all that I have loved, and all that I have lost, and by the untold memory of all that I have suffered, that they are no vague and fancy dreams, coined by a distempered mind, but realities as true as the blessed sun that gladdens the world, and as stern as the decree that dooms all mankind to death.

"Ah! good people, these frightful lessons of experience, drawn from sources so broad, so deep, and so terrible, what startling memories cluster about them! Oh, that you could but see and realize them for a moment, in the cruel terrors of their actual existence! May not one of you ever be nearer the reality than you are now. Could I, fifteen years ago, heard what you have just heard, or its purport, I would not be standing here to tell my story as a warning to others. Ponder it well. Go through it in imagination, because the reality is immedicable ruin.

"Those of you who have loved ones, love them better. If any of them be wayward, do not spurn and cast them off, but strive to win them back to duty and to love—for the natural channels of kindred ties and blood are such that nothing can stay them; no matter how grievous the cause be that dries them up for a season, some time they will re-flow again over the lapse of years, the breadth of the world, or the sods of the grave. Better, a thousand times better, that they re-flow over the sods of the grave, than over prison walls and a living tomb.

"Such, my friends, is my *atonement offering*. Deign to accept and treasure it. Its waned lustre may serve to keep your life-jewels bright. Its value is in this fearful contrast."

Cloud made a retrospective picture of his own career and experience in harrowing colors; a mere outline of what has been so elaborately portrayed in this volume. It made a deep impression on the minds of his auditors, and led to earnest discussion.

The stand he has taken, the labors he has rendered, and the enterprises in which he is engaged, seem to promise that Garland Cloud is yet destined to do much for the human race, and truly and honorably redeem his vows made under the shadows of the war-cloud, and in the shades of the dungeon's gloom. There appears to be every plausible reason to support the presumption that he will pursue the course upon which he has entered, and little in favor of a suspicion that he will be lured or driven to abandon it for anything less noble. There is every reasonable prospect that he may now be many fold more valuable to the world than he ever could have been had be never suffered; and the world seems disposed to use him. If his experience has not been consummate in deceptive arts, and the consequences of such indiscretion amply terrible to constitute lessons of warning, it would be hard to find either a devotee or a victim possessing these features of the shady characteristics of erratic life.

Garland Cloud has declined every overture, coming from friends of the olden time, tendering him assistance, or soliciting him to embark in commercial enterprises. He claims that he is hopelessly exiled from the world of commerce, and that he is weaned from the desire to enter the conflict there again, where his rashness cost him so many scars, and where, necessarily, he would labor under so many incalculable disadvantages. Perhaps he is right. Men with fair names and ample capital find a hard struggle to stem the commercial tide and hold their own in a business voyage in 1883, and many go under. What then could a man do without such potent requi-

sites? Absolutely nothing. But Garland Cloud can do much in other fields, those in which he has undertaken to devote himself.

Garland Cloud's greatest and most perplexing problem is concentrated in that one characteristic word—"Manonia." In this fair name and sad memory obtains the one remaining spectre which yet continues to haunt his cheerless life. Back to her his mind ever wanders, to linger in longing fondness, and to pine with the agony of unavailing regrets. Upon all other subjects he expresses himself with unreserved freedom. About her he speaks rarely, and with guarded brevity. To Carrie Flowers he has said:

"I can express no intention as to Manonia; she is my lost, my regretted, my ever mourned bride. That I am severed from her—simply the cruel reality of separation—adds little, never has added much to my pangs. But the true nature of that fatal and broken chain which once bound her to me, the fearful manner in which t was rent in twain, her awful wrongs and her wretched suffering—it is the thought of these things that is unbearable."

CARRIE: "Have you any tidings from her since your last letter on this subject was mailed to me?"

CLOUD: "No, my friend; I know nothing whatever, save the meagre part, presented in connection with her name that led to unmasking me. I do not know her feelings; I have no means of learning them."

CARRIE: "Do you mean ever to write to her?"

CLOUD: "This question I am unable to answer. I could hope that she detests me; yet I have not the courage to ask her. Her reproaches would drive me mad. Could I learn her sentiments and fate from others than her or hers, without their knowledge, I might make the attempt. But to know that she still cherishes for me any degree of that endearing devotion which 'not time, nor sorrow, nor pain,' can ever stifle in my being, would but add to my present suffering."

CARRIE: "What do you regard as your duty in this respect, and other social relations of life?"

CLOUD: "I know not my duty to poor Manonia; I think it silent absence. In no other way can I imagine it possible to pay her due reverence, for my greeting or my appearance would but add to outrageous wrong, more aggravated insult. As to social duties, I have none, more than to mend my ways, and strive to do good to others; I am a social waif."

CARRIE: "I do not see any other feasible course open for you, as to Manonia, but that which you have intimated as the probable one to be adopted and pursued. Were I in her place it would be preferable to me. Her wrongs are irreparable; her wounds may never heal. Fresh and forcible reminders of you could but probe anew her long-festering punctures of unmerciful sorrow. But to society, to your race and line, you yet owe a duty. Your marriage with Manonia is a nullity. You owe it to yourself and the world to get married, and to cease to be an aimless wanderer. In no other way can you ever fully atone for the past. This is the true incense of your offerings, without which they are tendered in vain."

CLOUD: "Oh Carrie! are you the victim of frenzied madness, or are you laboring under the delusion of a deceptive hallucination? Do you imagine that I am capable of marrying while Manonia lives single in her great sorrow? I am debased, perhaps, beyond redemption, but I have not yet descended to that stage of detestable degradation. I am, if still human, yet Garland Cloud. The same wretch upon whom you now gaze is wedded to Manonia—she is his hapless bride, no matter about the false nature or delusive name. I cannot, I will not marry again. The idea is preposterous. No lady is so blind as to marry wretchedness. I am not so unmanly as to seek such a victim. I was the despoiler of Manonia, but if false to her, I will yet be true to her memory. 'Sweet Angel of the South,' hover over me now and stay the luring fascination of tempting dangers—snares that destroyed thy dreamy bliss!"

CARRIE: "Garland, I am not mad. Your devotion is noble and manly. Doubly does this demonstrate your duty. To you, Manonia is dead. You will be no less true to her memory than you were to mine when you married her. There was no barrier between us. In Heaven I am as much your bride as you are her husband. You deserted me without any cause. In obedience to your heartless will I sacrificed a cherished memory—

truer than any ever held in imaged sacredness by you—upon the altar of duty, and married. I have never regretted, do not regret that step. Now I demand of you the same sacrifice. I have a right to expect compliance. Return to Manonia, and throw yourself at her feet, or renounce your allegiance to her forever. Such is your duty to society, the world, yourself and your God. You have no more right to allow your manhood to run to waste from the blight of an unavailing regret than you have to commit suicide. You have rendered two true and devoted women miserable. Now you owe it to womenkind to make one good woman happy."

CLOUD: "Carrie, all words are idle to me, and meaningless on this subject. I confess, with shame, that I owe you much more than my life itself for the pain I caused you. But instead of giving a good woman her meed of happiness, I would but doom her to wretchedness. Joy will dwell not with me. My shadowy existence would dim its lustre, and then extinguish its feebly-flickering rays forever, and another fair woman would become the mournful victim of disappointed love. To the plausible argument of Manonia, whose bent of mind ran much as yours runs now, I once yielded. You know the sequence of that surrender. What good and rational woman could wed such inevitable misery as I could but promise? Ah, Carrie, this is wasted breath we are employing. I shall never offer a trusting woman my hope-devouring curse."

CARRIE: "Garland, you amaze me! Your obdurate will no disappointment, no sorrow, no loss, no bereavement, no pain can tame. The unyielding young trooper stands before me now unchanged and changeless, in proud defiance to the gentle authority of his most solicitous friend, as he stood then in rebellion against the fondest wish of his admiring genius, cruelly denying poor infatuated Carrie Harman the maddening dream of her life. Now he as stubbornly denies recognition to his duty, and turns a deaf ear to its admonitory mandates. Oh, Garland! I am despairing of you. There is no hope for you. You are lost—lost!"

CLOUD: "Whom would you have me victimize? Suppose you were free, and met a man, now the first time—a man who might seek to win your hand and heart—and you early learned that his life was shrouded in odious shame, what would you do?"

CARRIE: "Marry him—if his name was Garland Cloud."

CLOUD: "Ah, Carrie! but remember all ladies are not Carrie Flowers."

CARRIE: "I do; and that all men are not Garland Cloud. I know a lady, beautiful as day, pure as crystal, wise as a sage, and wealthy as—well, as even quite extravagant ideas could desire—ready to marry Garland Cloud. She knows his story. I am to introduce her to you this evening. Your suffering, as depicted to her by me, has won her ere you greet her and are greeted by her smile, which, I am sure, will gently touch your heart."

CLOUD: "In this arrangement, it occurs to my mind that you prematurely reckoned on one insignificant yet rather important personage, and answered for him without authority. When your fair lady arrives, you may introduce her to my vacant place in the room. I shall not be here to receive her smile, nor to give her mine—that could be but a deceptive lie. Carrie, yours is 'love's labor lost.'"

CARRIE: "Garland, you inexorable ingrate! Go back to Manonia. Such devotion should not be cherished in vain. Rarely has such severed love lingered with this abiding constancy. It should—it shall be re-united."

CLOUD: "Again are you hasty. Our severance—rendered thus by her wrongs from me—may be eternal. I deserve it; cannot ask it otherwise; yet it precludes the possibility of other tender ties ever existing between any charming angel of earth and I. No, Carrie; your anxious solicitude, your care, and your trouble have been bestowed but to reward you with fierce disappointment. I would rather pass my days in a dungeon, with Manonia's voiceless portrait, than in a palace with a fairy queen. Good night."

          *   *   *   *

Far down in a little valley in the heart of Louisiana, the sun has set. The crimson fires that its going down had kindled in the west,

have died away, and from their ashes has sprung, phœnix-like, one solitary evening star.

Purple shadows shroud the distant hills; now and then, across the dewy air, the drowsy chirp of some discontented songster, half asleep, is heard. For the rest, there is the dewy silence, and still repose, and ineffable peace of night.

Where the shadows fall the darkest, in the door of an old plantation homestead set down almost in the midst of a grove of oaks and hickories and pines, a woman stands. She holds in her hand a spray of honeysuckle, which she has pulled down from the festooned arch above her head. Her face shows indistinctly through the gloom—beautiful, even with the white seal of sorrow and suffering set upon it. Her eyes, with the wistful sadness of years of waiting in their depths, are fixed upon the distant hills.

A step upon the walk arouses her from a reverie that holds no happiness in its dream. A figure, coming slowly through the grey twilight, causes her to run down the steps to meet it. It stops as she approaches, and lays a wrinkled, brown hand upon her shoulder. She slips it through her arm, and they walk thus up the path and into the house.

"You are late, to-night, father," she says.

ELDRED DONNE: "Yes, Manonia; yes, I am late."

He sits in his arm-chair, watching his daughter as she busies herself about the room. For the beautiful, sad woman, in the dress of plain and simple black, with the eyes that have looked upon more days of sorrow than they have years of life, is Manonia—Garland Cloud's ill-fated bride.

Eldred Donné is changed also. Time has not spared him. She has seamed his face with wrinkles; she has bent his once erect form, and enfeebled his once firm step, and the snows of her many winters rest thickly upon his head.

Presently Manonia comes and sits beside him; then his eyes, that have been fixed upon her musingly, betoken a sudden recollection.

DONNE: "I have a letter for you, Manonia. I had quite forgotten it. Here it is."

MANONIA: "From whom can it have come? I am certain that I never saw that handwriting before."

Manonia breaks the seal, moving, as she does so, nearer the light in the centre of the room, so that her face is quite hidden from her father.

There is a long, long silence, so long that Eldred Donné several times looked at his daughter inquiringly. Surely it was not a letter that should take so much time to read. At length he speaks.

"Manonia."

There is no answer; she does not even turn her head; not when he speaks a second time does she look up. At length he rises and goes softly to her side.

The letter has fallen in her lap; she sits with her hands clasped across it. The pallor of her face has deepened, and her eyes have the far-away look of one who sees, past the light of this sphere, the visions of a world beyond.

Donné: "Manonia, my child, speak to me. What is the matter?"

Manonia: "My father, you have called me back from among the dead. Ghosts of days that are gone forever; memories over whose grave the grasses have long been growing; voices, tones—ah! my father, *this* has brought them from their sepulchres, unlocked them from their fast-bound sleep."

She unfolds the letter as she speaks, and while the old man listens with attention and wonder, she reads:

"'—— Place, New York, June —, 18—.

"'Mrs. Manonia Garland,
"'Rural Rest, La.:

"'Madam:—One who is unknown to you, but whose heart has ached over the story of your wrongs, and whose eyes have dimmed in sympathy with your sorrows, has a short story to tell you, and craves your pardon should its telling prove tedious or unwelcome.

"'Sixteen years ago a woman listened, one night, to a tale that is as old as the first-created hills, but to all ears, at some first time of its telling, is new, and sweet, and very precious. This woman loved the man who told it. You—forgive me if my pen deals a blow here—have also loved, and know what sweet music this story was to the listener's ears.

"'But a mistaken motive and a false pride, sealed her lips—kept back from their utterance words that her heart wildly longed to speak; and while from the depths of her soul she cried, "I love you," her lips said, "Wait, I must yet consider."

"'Miserable procrastination! to what did it not lead? Hollow, blighting pride, what untold sorrow did she not store up for herself in listening to its delusive counsels! But pardon me my digression. I resume my story.

"'The breath of slander, fanned into life by envious hate and bitter jealousy, assailed this man. Deluded into the belief that all who heard its lying tongue believed it the voice of truth, and—bitterest blow of all, which her own hand had aided in striking—deeming that the woman he loved listened implicitly to its poisoned tale, he determined upon self-destruction, and left her to mourn him as dead.

"'There is a break in my story here which I deem it unnecessary to close. He drifted out of *her* life, but not, through Heaven's merciful intervention, from life itself.

"'Another woman met him and loved him. Ah, my sister in sorrow, *I* know truly how well—how bitterly, sorrowfully well!

"'And he married her. Of her wrongs and sorrows, her anguish in the bitter after-time, her weary, slow-creeping days of pain, her sleepless, tardily-dragging nights of misery, your heart knows the full completeness, and mine pities.

"'This man's life has been one long night. In its time of summer the frosts of winter blighted it, and her thick-falling snows buried its blossoms of joy in an icy shroud.

"'The measure of his life holds many sins, "full, overflowing, running over." And a retributive Power has meted out to him, for his many misdeeds, a penance likewise. Truly has it been "measure for measure."

"'Disaster has pursued, misfortune has overtaken him. The dreary walls of a prison-tomb have witnessed his repentance, and within the narrow confines of his cell Remorse has been an ever-constant guest. In the still, slow hours of dragging midnights, he has heard the "never, never" whispered by the phantom years, and the ceaseless whisper of a sleepless conscience has sounded ever in his ears, "It might have been!"

"'Oh, is not she whose wrongs and sorrows will pursue him to his grave, and whose mournful face will haunt him until death—is she not avenged?

"'Some time ago he was urged by one who held his welfare of great interest, to marry. These are his words: "Do you imagine me capable of marrying while Manonia lives single in her great sorrow? I am debased, perhaps, beyond redemption, but I have not yet descended to that stage of detested degradation. I am, if still human, yet Garland Cloud. * * * I was the despoiler of Manonia. But if false to her, I will yet be true to her name."

"'Interrogated by this same friend as to his duty to the woman he had so cruelly wronged, he replied, "I know not my duty to poor Manonia. I think it silent absence; in no other way can I imagine it possible to pay her due reverence."

"'Need I say more? Does not the heart of the woman to whom I am writing know the rest? Is it so cruelly broken that it has no thrill of pity for one who, sinning much, has suffered more? She who loved him once, and whose lips have drank deep from the bitter cup which you have drained to the dregs, has forgiven him. Do other wrongs require fuller vengeance? Are we better than He who would forgive—aye, "seventy times seven?"

"'My story is done—but a word more remains. He is conscious that his sins have been so great that he dare not ask her sinned against for pardon. He is in New York. He does not know or dream of this thing I have done. If you can forgive him, send him hope.

"'Your sister in suffering,

"'CARRIE FLOWERS.'"

DONNE: "So Garland Cloud is heard from at last. A fine letter, that, fine—in words. How does it run? 'If you can forgive him.' And after the best years of his life have been squandered, he would gather up the pitiful remainder as an atonement to the life he has wrecked. After the sorrow, and the misery, and the des-

pair—heartless man—that he has caused, he would ask his victim——"

MANONIA: "Father, my father, I have suffered enough. Spare me!"

She has suffered in meekness, and borne her sorrows in silence. The great patience which Heaven sometimes vouchsafes its stricken children, has been her endowment. Like unto Him who was reviled by men and jeered at by priests, she whose sweet dreams of happiness Fate has laughed to scorn, at the mockings of the fickle goddess, has "answered not a word." But now, as those old memories come back to her—those bittersweet recollections of the long ago—the pain of her bitterness and the joy of their sweetness once more thrills her heart. She bows her head upon the table, and her eyes grow dim with tears.

The old man's voice falters, and his eyes grow dim. That he should add one stab to the cureless wounds already inflicted in the heart of his daughter, unmans him. His head bows, and his rough, hard hand gently strokes her hair, as he says:

"There, there, Manonia, don't mind me. I'm old, you know, and I get easily upset. There, there, you shall do as you like. I never meant—Suppose we let it drop? Yes. Good night."

MANONIA: "Good night, my father. Alone—Ah, no, not alone. I cannot be that—never. What memories! What sweet dead dreams! The man I loved so long ago—My husband once. He who embittered my life; furrowed my brow with lines of care; dimmed my eyes with tears—bitter blinding tears of sorrow—Why should I pity him who had none for me? And yet, and yet—ah me! a woman's heart is hard to read."

The darkness falls with silent wings. Its swiftly descending shadows shut out the dim outlines of the far mountains, the misty hills, the valleys between. The wind chants its lullaby to the sleeping world, through the thick branches of the green old pines; and only the stars, gazing down upon silence, see the white, troubled face of the woman who is striving to read her own heart—her beautiful sad eyes lifted wistfully upward to the light of their sleepless and eternal glory.

CHAPTER LXXV.

THE DAWN FROM A LONG AND GLOOMY NIGHT.

"For lives that hold no pain are held in earthly prison
    bars,
    And griefs are often wings whereby our souls can
    reach the stars,
For in the fire the dross is burned, the gold stands pure
    and good,
    And she who suffers wears the best, the crown of
    womanhood."
                            —M. A. BILLINGS.

MRS. CARRIE FLOWERS, in accordance with the polite fiction that society allows, is "not at home," although the convenient precaution is, in this case, scarcely necessary, for few would feel inclined to be abroad—even for the seeking of Mrs. Carrie Flowers—on such a night, one dark and stormy, with the rain coming down in fitful gusts, dashing against the windows, not at all well pleased to find itself so securely barred from the mischief it contemplates and vainly strives to execute.

She is alone, with the curtains pulled down, and the light falling across the easy chair in which she is snugly ensconced. She is thinking, with a little running commentary upon her thoughts, which, judging from the expression of her dissatisfied face, and the disconnected sentences which fall from her lips, are neither very pleasing nor yet instructive.

"Two, three—no, *four* weeks, and I have heard not a word. It was foolish of me to write that letter—I cannot imagine what Garland would think of me. And some women do not easily forgive. I am sure I—but then, I am not Manonia, Mrs. Garland Cloud.

"However, I need not proclaim my foolishness from the housetop. I am certain that I shall entertain no one with that tale of folly. As for Garland, there is no shaking his firm resolution. It is a pity; he has caused her much misery, it is true, and it is properly wise that she should do as she does and pay no heed to my reckless letter; yet—oh, why could she not be foolish, and forgive him?"

Thus, Carrie Flowers, deeply buried in her own thoughts, and absorbed in the puzzling maze of her own perplexities, fails to hear the sound of carriage wheels, that, driving hastily up, stop at her door; fails, likewise, to hear the ring at the bell, until the entrance of a servant rouses her to a sense of the present realities of life.

CARRIE: "I am 'not at home,' I told you—stay, let me see the card. What! is it possible? Who would have thought it? Show the visitor up, directly."

For several moments after the departure of the bewildered servant, Carrie Flowers waits, eager impatience manifest in every feature; at the end of that time, a soft rustle is heard without, the door opens, she takes one eager step forward, and beholds—Manonia.

At last these two women, so widely severed yet so closely united, who have suffered the same sorrows and borne the same griefs; who have laid, in the long ago, at the feet of one man the richest treasures of their hearts, to gather up again, in weary bitterness, their shattered fragments—these two, in all their lives as far apart as the river from the sea, yet united by the one bond that makes all the world kin—the bond of suffering—stand face to face.

Something else stands with them. The memories of the long ago rise and confront them. Their long past dreams, their hopes, their sorrows—with one man's face, and one man's voice, and the bittersweet recollections of one man's memory, and what it has been to each.

It is too much. All barriers are swept away, all distance removed—sisters in suffering, companions in sorrow, the arms of one open, and the weary, tired head of the other finds a resting-place upon her breast.

CARRIE: "My poor sister! There is no need for me to tell you how I feel for you—when hearts speak to hearts, the lips can remain silent."

MANONIA: "Oh, thank you—thank you! I did not expect this welcome. I was afraid I had not done wisely in coming. It may mean ——"

CARRIE: "That you, in your loving-kindness, would not *send* hope, but *brought* it. That the man who fancies his sin so grievous that it is past pardon—who has so bitterly crushed a woman's heart that he would deem it folly and madness to ask that woman ever to find a place in that heart again for him—will bless her to the last hour of the last day of the life that God will give him, and, if she can trust him once more, will render her reward as great as he has rendered her sufferings—this is what it means."

MANONIA: "Ah, if I could but believe it! But so many dreams of mine have been shattered; so many foundation stones of hope have fallen, that I am afraid—afraid to build again. I have been in the night so long, that the light which you tell me is so near, blinds me. I cannot believe that the world, for me, holds any light."

CARRIE: "Ah, but, my sister, the radiance is glorious. No shadows of the past are so dark that its gleam will not dispel them, its bright beams warm them—the light that 'never yet was on sea or land'—God's light of love."

MANONIA: "If he but loves me—ah, a woman can forgive so much when she loves, and knows that the sinner holds her dear!"

CARRIE: "If he were but here now, you should doubt no longer. Oh, if he were but here! Hark, what is that? Oh, joy, it is his ring; I know it! He is coming up. Quick, quick; hide behind this curtain. You will know when to reveal yourself. Oh! was Fortune ever more propitious? What a blessed, blessed night this stormy eve will prove!"

As Garland Cloud enters the room, Carrie Flowers re-seats herself in the easy chair as composedly as the nature of the circumstances will allow, at the same time saying: "This is indeed an agreeable surprise. I did not dream that I was to be rendered happy by a call from you this evening."

CLOUD: "And I did not dream of coming, but —— well, I am afraid, Carrie, that I have the blues, and —— "

CARRIE: "You thought of me as an antidote. Quite right; I shall exert myself to the utmost. If you are not cheered to-night, I shall despair of your ever being rendered happy in this life, since you so absolutely refuse the only other available means offered."

CLOUD: "Carrie, I beg of you, do not broach that topic. I do not desire to listen, will not listen.

I have multiplied wrong with wrong, and my life has been one long catalogue of errors, but I will not add this great evil-doing to the list."

CARRIE: "Then you obstinately refuse to seek comfort in the smiles of any woman?"

CLOUD: "No woman's smiles can comfort me while I remember Manonia's tears. And to the day of my death, the memory of those bitter drops my evil life and many sins have caused to flow, will not forsake me.

—When we hold a woman's heart in our hands, and crush it and fling it from us, leaving it bleeding among the thorns on the dusty road-side of life; when we guide her ship of happiness among the breakers, and set it adrift on a boundless sea that has no haven of peace nor shores of safety, what man can go back to a woman then and say: 'Forgive me; your heart is broken; your life is wrecked; your peace destroyed, but forgive me?'"

CARRIE: "Where a woman loves, it is easy to forgive."

CLOUD: "But where the hope, the happiness, the heart, is dead, love perishes among the ruins."

"And rises from the ruins, and lives—forever!"

This last sentence was uttered by an invisible speaker, or one who was thus when Cloud entered the room. At the sound of another voice, a voice often heard, bitterly mourned, well remembered, Garland Cloud turns. Is it a dream? Standing before him, her hands extended toward him, her beautiful eyes gleaming with the brightness of unshed tears, her pale, sad face turned to greet him in mute appeal, divine forgiveness, pathetic loveliness, is Manonia.

He stands as if transfixed to the spot, dazed by a wonder that he cannot fathom, fearing to speak lest the vision might vanish; and the vision, taking one nearer step to him, softly says: "I have come to tell you that I forgive you. I have come to give my life into your hands as trustingly as I once gave it in the long ago. Ah, Garland, the heart I gave you then was young and untried, and the one I offer you now is crushed and broken, but it is yours; take it, or reject it, what you will."

CLOUD: "Manonia—my wife!"

As his arm closes about her, and her head finds the resting-place it never should have lost, that, through weal or woe, in all the life to come, it will never lose again, Carrie Flowers, the woman who loved this man once, and who suffered for his sake, rises and moves softly from the room.

All is forgiven; we have waited long
And suffered much—yet all is for the best;
And Love can pardon many a grievous wrong,
And lay its trust in Heaven for the rest.

CHAPTER LXXVI.

EIGHTEEN YEARS AFTER.

" My task is done, my song hath ceased, my theme
Has died into an echo; it is fit
The spell should break of this protracted dream;
The torch shall be extinguished which hath lit
My midnight lamp, and what is writ is writ;
Would that it was worthier; but I am not now
That which I have been, and my visions flit
Less palpably before me; and the glow
Which in my spirit dwelt, is fluttering low.
    *   *   *   *   *
Farewell! a word that must be, and hath been;
A sound which makes us linger; yet—Farewell!"
                    —BYRON.

EIGHTEEN years after! What a deep and significant meaning this term implies! What memories it conjures up before the minds of Americans! How the thoughts travel back to dwell upon that by-gone time! What sad days of emotions, mingling with sorrow, rejoicing and mourning, of discord, desolation, poverty and despair! The South, mourning over her baffled zeal, her "LOST CAUSE," her perished hopes, her ruined homes, her fallen sons! The victorious legions of the vanquishers, and the triumphant North, rejoicing over the success of the Government cause. A nation mourning over the bier of her "Martyred President!"

Eighteen years after the Civil War; eighteen years after the deluging torrents of human blood —a country's mad attempt at fratricide; and eighteen years after the fiendish severing of Lawrence Pleasington and Effie Edelstein.

Since then, the sweeping surge of time has rolled on, and submerged, in eternal oblivion, much that vexed and troubled mankind in that trying time of " the long ago." As we look back upon the hideous aspect of that ghastly picture—

now gaze, half doubting we are dreaming, at the portrait standing out before us in bold relief to-day—we are dumb with amazement and paralyzed with electrifying admiration.

What wonderful changes the hand of Time has wrought! Astonishing has been the healing powers of the antidote administered by this silent physician!

How it has soothed and cured the rankling hate, the devastating ravages, the aching hearts, and the gaping wounds of war!

" Oh, Time! thou beautifier of the dead;
    Adorner of the ruin, comforter,
    And only healer when the heart hath bled;
    Time—the corrector, where our judgments err—
    Test of truth, love, sole philosopher—"

To-day, we glance back at the ruined walls and the broken columns of strife, decaying and crumbling to dust. Amid these vanishing monuments of mortal combat, which once " shadowed forth their glory," may be seen, now and then, a feeble, tottering, grim sentinel, still guarding his cherished prejudices and his treasured hate. But these misguided minds the benignant hand of Time is steadily relieving from the onerous posts of their fond and self-chosen charge—mistaken duty's non-definable trust. Around these discordant characters a new generation has sprung up, to whom the war is a legendary story, and upon whom their influence makes not the slightest impression in the direction of keeping alive the fire-brands of hate. The battle storm-rent plains and fields of this once distracted country are again verdant, blooming, and fruitful over the dreary wastes of brooding desolation and ensanguined destruction.

From this general declaration, we reserve one exception; and we are constrained to admit that it is appropriate that this should exist. We seek in vain for brightness or loveliness on the threshold, or within the arena, where was ushered forth the first world-startling scene in the tragic drama. These cheering rays illuminate not the sombre ruins of FORT SUMTER. Forever should it stand enveloped in its ghastly shroud—a waste howling wilderness of eternal desolation—as an admonitory monument to posterity, in commemoration of the scourging curse of civil war. The unpropitious cradle of the Confederacy, it should ever remain her solitary grave. Above these sea-girt, sand-capped ruins of once frowning battlements, the plaintive wave murmurs its sad refrain, the curlew chants her mournful melody in discordant strains—meet music for this desolate relic of the Atlantic's once-dreaded child.

But from *this*, we follow the wild course of the bloody conflict, as it rushed onward over the country in one engulfing wave of destruction, and find little remaining to indicate the traces of its ravages, save alone those mournful "Cities of the Dead," where,

> " On Fame's eternal camping ground,
> Our nightly tents are spread;
> And Silence guards with solemn round,
> The bivouac of the dead."

The wasted fences have been replaced; the orchards replanted; the fields restocked with their lowing herds; the ruined homesteads resurrected from their smoldering ashes; the destroyed cities rebuilt. Long-flown prosperity has returned to hover again in benign graciousness over the valleys, and to rest once more in blessed peace upon the misty summits of the mountains. The yawning, bloody chasm, that once appeared so fathomless and impassable, has been bridged by fraternal bonds, cemented with the adhesive tenacity of common interest and brotherhood.

> From Plymouth's gale-lashed spray
> To San Francisco's placid bay;
> From Biscayene's tropic sand
> To Alaska's frozen strand,

good will, prosperity and peace reign over a regenerated and an everlasting Union—a free and mighty people. Even the fierce animosity growing out of the petty bickerings and blunders of reconstruction folly, has yielded to, and been dissipated by, the harmonizing influence of more intimate relations and a closer acquaintance between the people of the once antagonistical sections.

The great exhibitions and fairs, together with numerous military visits, have done much in the direction of restoring fraternal harmony and mutual confidence between the people of the North and the South. The attractions of the Southern climate, as a refuge from the cold blasts of a Northern winter, have exercised a wonderful in-

fluence, tending to generate a spirit of conciliation between the people of the former hostile sections, thus happily drawn together. Each visitor carries back with him to his Northern home a more favorable impression of his hosts and their country than he entertained before his sojourn beneath their sunny skies. This sentiment he disseminates among his friends, and thus are seeds of pacification quietly, imperceptibly, but steadily and surely sown; and noiselessly they produce and mature their fruits. All these good works deserve to be extended, fostered, and encouraged; because they create the fraternal and accordant bonds of a common, re-united country.

The greatest misfortune that yet remains to disturb the placid serenity of the peaceful waters, is the malignant misrepresentations made by scheming and unscrupulous politicians in the heated turmoil and fanatical excitement of an active campaign. Thus are false impressions of a damaging character scattered broadcast over the land. As a rule these stories are utterly unworthy of credit. At such seasons, honest and impartial missionaries should be sent into the Southern States to procure and publish the legitimate truth.

In this way might much needless discord and bitterness be averted. Between the great masses of the two sections of this once distracted country an ardent desire for harmony has long existed. Wrangling politicians alone marred and delayed the happy consummation of this most desirable state of tranquility. But the day has gone by when they enjoyed unlimited creative powers of mischief. Their influence must grow less as the years vanish.

The wearers of the Grey, if mistaken, were honest in their convictions. They staked their principles in the desperate game of war, and lost. Thus they proved their professions. They are none the less honest now; none the less have they forcibly demonstrated their abiding fidelity to the Union and the principles maintained by the wearers of the Blue—their magnanimous foemen—by their zealous efforts to fill up and bridge over the bloody chasm. Beneath the dreamland skies of the South no traitors dwell.

The wearers of the Blue never pursued the

wearers of the Grey beyond the battlefield; never stooped to persecute the vanquished with needless oppression. These antagonists alone, undisturbed by "bomb-proof" politicians of the "*stay at home corps*," could have settled the difficult problem in short order at any time, had it been submitted to them as peaceable arbitrators. They are now, and have been for many years, thus settling it through the influence of organized intercourse in the semblance of formal and most appropriate military visits, and in many other ways, laying the broad foundation for everlasting friendship. Thus have a nation's woes and a nation's rankling hate been alleviated and neutralized.

The "fire-eaters" and the fanatics who kindled that red flame of war are rapidly making their final exits from the stage; and their ultra doctrines are giving place to equitable ideas of pacific moderation. Implacable enemies of the early days of reconstruction are amicable friends. As the people of the two great sections come to know and understand one another better, the more still will their fraternal bonds be strengthened. Every week, almost, ushers in some new era of influences or associations, tending to promote good feeling and to generate solid and enduring friendship among the people of the "NEW UNION."

The terms "The Solid South" and "The New South" are misconstrued and misunderstood: in the first instance, by designing sycophants; in the second, by the great masses of the Northern people. A broad and liberal construction of the true definition implies simply "A New and Solid Union." Where would rest the secure foundation of this nation's hope without "A New and Solid South?" *On treacherous quicksands.* In "The New South" the emancipated slave and the master of the olden time dwell and labor in mutual harmony. Thus is the supreme object of the war attained — the ultimate principles of abolitionism secured. That this was the real bone of contention over which the spirit of war was generated, no intelligent and well-informed mind can hesitate to admit; that, sooner or later, it must have inevitably led to open hostilities, there is no room to doubt; and that it was infinitely better for these to have developed when

they did, rather than to have been reserved for a future age and a more numerous people, there is still less reason in favor of a judgment. Hence, therefore, we conclude that the war, under the peculiar nature of the circumstances, was an evil that could not have been averted; a thing necessary to preserve and indissolubly cement the accordant ties of the UNION.

Now the grand object and the supreme solicitude of the people of this nation should be to secure the utmost fruits of their gigantic sacrifices, and to make doubly sure that such fruits are not blighted or destroyed. No effort should be spared that promises to promote their cultivation. Increased intercourse and more intimate relations between the sections once so widely severed by the scourge of murderous strife, would most tend to secure this desirable and happy consummation. Thorough acquaintance with the South and her people are too important considerations to be approximately estimated. Equally important is it for the Southern to know their Northern countrymen. These, all the citizens of the Union should mutually, carefully and patiently study, learn duly to understand, and strive properly to appreciate. By such means would the trophies of triumph be secured, and the laureled wreath and olive branch of peace entwined and established *for evermore.*

The witching magnetism of the fertile fields and the salubrious enchantment of the matchless clime of the South are attracting myriads of people away from their ice-bound winters of the North. Fascinated by these charming beauties and wondrous bounties of lavishly generous nature, many become permanently domiciled in this lovely land, and induce friends to join them in their semi-Paradise on earth.

As the South is the land of flowers, so is it the cradle of love. And those who winter there or migrate thither to remain, are sure to fall in love with the climate and the country, and hence, too, with the people. They too, in their turn, learn to love their Northern visitors and neighbors. Thus, this intermingling is welding the links of a fraternal chain as solid and as durable as adamant.

Let those who wish to know the "True South," "The New South" and "The Solid

South," of 1883, vividly contrasted with "the decimated, the desolate, the ruined South of 1865," enter the Valley of Virginia—the garden spot of America—and proceed South to Salem; then traverse the majestic mountains to the blue hills of the Southwest, return to Lynchburg, and travel down the James River to Richmond and Norfolk.

From this point penetrate North Carolina to Ashville, amid the misty peaks of the Blue Ridge. Thence scan the smiling gardens and the rice plantations of South Carolina; the mystic mountains and magic vales of Tennessee. Now look over the cotton wonderlands of Alabama and Mississippi, of Louisiana and Arkansas, with their sugar, rice and wheat fields; the prodigious amazements of Texas, too vast and too diversified to be enumerated or indicated.

Then go to Atlanta, and gaze down in admiration upon the astonishing panorama of Georgia, —the New England, the Empire State of the South, in enterprise—elaborately dispersed. and in material prosperity. Thence go to Florida, the winter garden of the North, the Italy of America.

If, in all this vast and varied domain, nothing has been found to attract emigration and to induce settlement as permanent residents, the tastes of the seekers would be too fastidious to be satisfied anywhere in this world.

The known resources of the South are too formidable to be computed; the undeveloped ones are too incredible to be comprehended. Hence, she offers unparalleled inducements to emigrants from all sections of the Union, and from every quarter of the globe. People the South, develop her resources, and there will be the mainspring of prosperity, the mighty right arm of the Nation.

A beautiful example of reconciliation is afforded by the devoted relations and boundless friendship early established and uninterruptedly maintained among Edgar Harman, Jesse Flowers, Orlando Oglethrop, their wives, Lawrence Pleasington and some of their friends.

These reflections lead us back again in the direction of the thread of romance in our story. Our rambles away have merely led over much of the same ground upon which our early and progressive scenes developed—simply a casual and somewhat informal review of the transformation wrought by these changing scenes, and the magic touch of the hand of Time. Out of the war and in its wake, as resultant sequences, grew most of the features of our story: then, therefore, it can hardly be deemed inappropriate that we have sketched various outlines of its material effects, beyond the individuality of our legitimate characters. Whatever effected these, as to their ordinary affairs of life, operated in a greater or a less degree, or might have thus influenced many other persons—the generality of the masses of the American people.

We have wandered over a romantic country, the stage of wild and tragic scenes. The vicissitudes of recuperation through which the Southern States and people have passed, are replete with startling and pathetic romance—struggling with dire poverty amid the sombre shadows of despair, cheered on and strengthened by self-abnegating devotion, alone, and seemingly estranged forever from the realm of Hope.

Ah, what treasures of romance, in real life. those distressed old mountains and desolate valleys, as they were in those dark days of yore, hold hidden away in their secret vaults of mysteries! Some day we may enter and explore a few of these musty recesses, bring to the light of the sun their guarded treasures, and portray their mystic wonders. Until then, indulgent friends, we crave your forbearance for having made any semblance of digression. Pray attribute this to our zeal in the cause of reconciliation, and our overweening desire to promote national harmony between the people of the North and South. We deem it the duty of every one to put forth some effort, however feeble, in this direction; hence our simple attempt.

We now glance in retrospection, along the backward track, over the course of our story, in its tortuous meanderings, briefly to summarize; bind the fibres broken now and then, under the pressure of the concentrated friction of time and circumstance; resume the readjusted thread of our vanishing theme and pursue it to that scene which is to be its last.

This might not be be thus, were our chronicles posted up to 1893, instead of 1883. But to the latter epoch has it led us; beyond this fate interposes the stern interdiction that says, "No farther." Here must we halt. We dare not conjecture even what scenes are yet behind the mysterious curtain of futurity, that may develop sometime, with one or more of our characters as participating actors on the stage where they have played so long. Earnestly do we wish that we could seize the prophet's divining ken, and read but this once the future pages of some lives. Alas! we cannot; nor can we trust the perversity of human nature sufficiently to imagine what these singular charac⁺ .rs may yet demonstrate, to startle and shock, or to excite admiration in the minds of mankind. We must, therefore, rest satisfied, or not, with what we have, and submit simply what has been and is in our portrait. The inquisitive and the captious can expect no more.

Following each individual feature, as it is traced along its course, and gauging it by the most rigid rules of the philosophy of "cause and effect," we find we have advanced nothing that these do not imperatively demand. If we have erred in this respect, it has not been on the side of over-elaborate outlining, but rather in the direction of concession. Our aim has been to keep ideas of personality of the author in the back-ground, and to demonstrate absolute developments. Hence, will be observed our often abrupt transition of scenes, with almost no preliminary comments

We are most sensible that this is a departure from the beaten tract—what many style "out of the common;" yet we are persuaded that it will prove a not unacceptable departure, with the majority of readers of refined taste. Such readers, as a rule, if interested in a work at all, find their interest, not in the author nor in his abstract opinions, but in his characters, and what they do and say. The description of characters, often most elaborate delineations, even, may be quite acceptable to the average reader of refinement, when the author's egotistical opinion simply, to the same extent, in the same direction, might prove a reading extremely irksome.

In unmeasured terms, sometimes, have we denounced or praised; but not usually have we thus indulged at great length; and almost always, these efforts were more than semi-descriptive of features of vice or virtue, or their fruits, inseparable from the rôles and the lives of our characters.

We have been unable to resist the temptation, when some intensified scenes were nearing, or had seemingly reached their climax, to suspend their ultimate sequences in abeyance; but in no instance have we failed to develop these in a later period.

Thus have we sought to hold in reserve some unexpected surprises. How far we have been successful in this direction, the reader alone must render a verdict.

As to other irregularities and imperfections, we can offer no special apology. We have meant to instruct, with pictured lessons from carnate life, rather than to amuse with a pleasing vein of humor. We make no sort of pretentions to a claim of literary merit for this work. Such would be absurd. We have tried to tell our story with simplicity, as we progressed with timid inexperience, If we have moderately succeeded in the direction of rendering it intelligible, our utmost dreams are attained.

First upon the stage was Garland Cloud, the obscure and youthful mountaineer, the scout and the erratic wanderer. In him were the natural characteristics requisite to assume the hazard of adventure, and to blend with the mysterious and the romantic. His alloted rôle led him into startling scenes, where these attributes of nature together commingled in wondrous harmony.

But in reviewing the complete career of this strange and incomprehensible character, in his intensely adhesive relations with the strongest features of romance in our antithetical portrait of real life, we must not ignore the potent influences which thus bound and held him so inseparably.

Uncle Jake, the old Virginia, common-place, rollicking log-cabin darkey, was the supreme genius, the peculiar founder, the wonderful architect and the untutored creator from whom, directly, or indirectly, as resultant elements of the developing theme, in the inexplicable order of progression, all this masterful combination of complot sprung. Here starts the mysteriously unfolding thread of our singular story. This is the primitive source of "The Secret Service League" of the border. Without Uncle Jake, this particular organization would never have existed; without Uncle Jake, Garland Cloud never would have attracted important attention as a scout.

The meeting of Garland Cloud and Jesse Flowers on the field of Manassas, was an event that shadowed forth in importance second only to Jake.

The finding and caring for Lawrence Pleasington by those children of the mountain, were simply in seeming obedience to the directing finger of Destiny. In this relation, as to Pleasington's letters, Jake again became an indispensable actor. To these circumstances is due the gratitude on the part of Pleasington, that generated the strange sympathy and peculiar friendship between him and Cloud; that swayed them so strongly while they were yet armed in hostility, and influenced them so powerfully on other occasions. Thus were many features of this volume developed.

Cloud's service as a scout and kindness to Edgar Harman, were auxiliary but necessary circumstances, required to bring Carrie Harman upon the stage. This, and Jessie Flowers' relations with Cloud, were indispensable to unfold the pathetic and startling events developed in the thrilling story of Gertrude Flowers. Thus was she re-united with the long severed links of the broken chain of the past; thus was cast a distant gleam of uncertain light upon the shadowy visage of Helen Mountjoy, and her mysterious relations with Ira Atkinson and Adam Stringfellow; and, moreover, thus was the unity of relations among these strong characters re-established, and the true nature of the wonderful romance of Mountjoy House revealed.

From the very first moment when she comes into the scene, until her last appearance, Carrie Harman is a star of matchless magnetism and powerful influence. At once she becomes the inspiration, the genius, the destiny of Garland Cloud, and, in turn, passes, herself, under the spell of his unschooled diplomacy. Gratitude, and a spirit of pure romance, superinduced her admiration and esteem so inordinately cherished for the plebeian soldier boy.

She, as we have just demonstrated, became blended in the plot as a direct sequence of Uncle Jake, in the legitimate line of offspring—the veritable progeny issuing in strict pursuance of the thread of fairy tale. Beyond, then, obtains indirect fruits from Jake's primitive plant of creation. Carrie Harman becomes a creative genius of thrilling vicissitudes. She propagates, cultivates, and develops, in a high degree, what Jake planted in such simple crudeness. Her aspirations were lofty and noble; her motives and actions were swayed and controlled by the most worthy impulses in this world.

What she was in the rôle of purity and goodness, Helen Mountjoy was in that of deceit and wickedness. To many persons Carrie Harman was a good angel—to many persons Helen Mountjoy was an evil spirit, a fatal curse. Her first victim was Gertrude Flowers. Carrie Harman proved to be a ministress of mercy and blessing to the poor widow and her children. Next we find Helen Mountjoy victimizing her own family, and some of her not over-scrupulous friends. Finally, we witness her culminating atrocity, wreaked with fiendish fury, upon poor Lawrence Pleasington and confiding Effie Edelstein. Then the retribution of stricken conscience ultimately overtakes and drives her to the desperation of self-destruction.

Garland Cloud, through indiscretion, under the fell sway of unscrupulous impulses, was led and driven into paths of error, whence the charming potency of Carrie Harman's enchanting influence failed to beguile him. Thus he bequeathed to her the disconsolate heritage of life-long disappointment and unavailing regret.

From this wreck of that phantom ship of Carrie Harman's cherished dreams and the grave of Garland Cloud's fondest hope, starts that ill-starred thread of Manonin's fatality.

From the severance of this thread springs that one which leads on to Garland Cloud's retribution and exposure, and Lawrence Pleasington's restoration to the friends of his early years—yes, and to more: Thus emerged to the light of day the material subject matter from which this volume was produced. Without the mutual reminiscences of Garland Cloud and Lawrence Pleasington, the thread of their story and its peculiar relations never could have been obtained. Without the meeting of these prominent characters "Under a Cloud," Lawrence Pleasington never would have learned that his most devoted friends possessed the secret of his innocence, and still remained forever constant to him; and hence he would never have been restored to them. Thus to Lawrence Pleasington this last act of friendship, received from Cloud, became the most important of any of those acts so highly prized in the past, because it conveyed an assurance more precious than life itself, which had before been rescued from jeopardy—it assured him that his fair name was redeemed from the unjust stigma of shame.

The evil fruits springing from Arnold Noel have been sufficiently outlined. They were simply the direct or the indirect productions of Helen Mountjoy's scheming baseness, and untoward influence. With his innate propensities for devious conduct stimulated and encouraged by the evil counsels of his wicked aunt, it was no difficult matter for this young villain to engage in anything diabolical. His third time in prison for the long term now hangs heavily with the weight of long and dreary years over his head. His father, mother, and two of his sisters have been borne to' the silent churchyard, victims of the broken heart, caused by his yet unabatable perversity.

The mischief wrought by Helen Mountjoy should be a lesson to unscrupulous wives and mothers, who scheme to consummate ignoble designs without compunction or pity for their acts or their victims.

The career of Garland Cloud should be a lesson to every young and ambitious man. Some phases of his distorted portrait are admirable examples worthy of emulation; others are fearful lessons of terrible warning. All of these, in both relations, have been amply defined—how they were heterogeneously and antithetically compounded from the noblest and the basest influences.

The simple meeting, as if by hazard, of Jake and Cloud, of Cloud and Flowers, and of these and Pleasington, insignificant in themselves, assume great importance when traced to their resultant developments. They led to Currie Harman; they led to Gertrude Flowers and Rosalia; they led to Mountjoy House and the discovery of its mysteries and their associate relations; they led to Silas Worthington; they led to the romantic, woeful and sadly-fated love between Cloud and Carrie Harman; they led to Cloud's strange complications; they led to the restoration of her fortune to Gertrude Flowers, and the marriage of herself and Rosalia; they led to the formation of the firm of Oglethrop, Harman & Co.; they led to Garland Cloud's downfall, flight and checkered career; they led to the union between Jesse Flowers and Carrie Harman; and, finally, they led to the foundation of most of these chapters, and to the composition of them all.

Before passing definitely on to the resumé of the incompleted thread of our narrative, let us pause a moment in final review.

Look back at Gertrude Flowers, preparing to leave her palatial home; harken to the lonely widow's pitiful moans of desolate despair, borne, on many a cold and dreary night, from her lonely mountain cabin home, upon the tempest's breath, to the Avenger's ear; think of Maud Pleasington's overpowering agony, and Effie Edelstein's mournful despair, as you, in fancy, follow Lawrence Pleasington through his dreary years of hopeless wretchedness; behold frail Beatrice and Rosalind flying from the ghost of their shame to the protective seclusion of a convent, in obedience to the advice of Cassandra, their conscience-stricken sister; then turn to the desolate home of Samuel Van Allen, and see the despair of the dying wife and daughter; now look back at the slow torture of Norman Mountjoy, and stand again with him a moment in that chamber of death, before taking a last, lingering gaze at the authoress of all this woe and premature death—Helen Mountjoy—as she, in terror, is confessing to her daughter Evalina.

From these scenes of death-producing misery, turn to Garland Cloud's last Sabbath evening in his "Future City" mansion; then to his dream of death; now to the nameless despair of Manonia; then, again, to the lonely cell in which he finds that the mask has been torn from his face and life. Think a moment of the heart-aches he has left behind him in traversing the earth, and those he has borne onward with himself. Contrast all these with the rewards of virtue and truth reaped by Harman, Flowers and Oglethrop, with their angelic wives, and conclude which are the most desirable to pursue and to possess.

Again we resume the thread of our story. To this, Lawrence Pleasington still clings, or, perhaps, it adheres to him. His rôle is yet incomplete. We have to follow him into some undeveloped scenes—scenes which should be clothed with absorbing interest.

Lawrence Pleasington has been a not uninteresting character. Lawrence Pleasington is the more than ideal character—he is the sublime hero, matchless, unapproachable, admirable man! Unrivaled child of resignation, constancy, and devotion! To thee we can impute no fault, lay no stigma upon thy untarnished name. Pleasing, at last, becomes our task, to bring thee forward, free from and untrammeled by the machinations of evil influence, secure from their menace, and place thee upon the stage in thy own element of truth and purity.

How beautiful, how noble, how exemplary the life of this man has ever been, amid trial, persecution, and temptation that were overwhelming. Upon his well-poised mind and disciplined virtue, the intoxicating whirl and black demoralization that ran riot in the mad excitement of war, made no impressions, but those of loathing and abhorrence. When the blighting pall of suspicion, misfortune, and despair overshadowed him, and hope fled, seemingly, forever, he yet remains a true man. Courageously he braves the worst and the most dreadful fate ever wreaked upon an innocent man, to which death, in any form of torture, slow or swift, would have been a welcome mercy —an inestimable blessing.

After all that he has endured, he certainly deserves a meritorious reward. If this be not accorded—if the perversity of Fate interdicts and withholds this well-earned trophy—where will hold the faith that patient virtue shall be richly compensated, no matter howsoever long the boon be deferred? Beyond any question, this would shake our abiding confidence in the doctrine of ultimate remuneration.

But we find, during the latter days of his bitter chastisement, the inexorable hand of Destiny relenting and relaxing its unpitying hold; and once more the goddess grows propitious. A ray of hope breaks in, and reflects a gleam to re-illuminate his long despair-benighted mind. From out the deep gloom of utter hopelessness, amid the storm-lashed billows, on the troubled sea of earthly perdition, he descries a glimmering light—a beacon, perchance, on some distant headland, some unknown promontory. How eagerly he gazes upon it! What strangely intense emotion thrills his being, as he watches this unexpected indication of some haven on that long-dreamed shoreless sea! What wild conflicts convulse his breast, as he peers through the spectral gloom out over the desolate waste! Is it a land-light, or a transient meteor? Is it a light to guide the drifting, hope-bereft mariner to safety, or a treacherous delusion, placed high up on inaccessible crags, to warn the voyager of dangerous breakers on a rock-bound coast?

Poor Pleasington! he had cause to tremble, to hesitate and to doubt. Once before a seemingly friendly, but destructively deceptive light, had lured him to swift disaster, after he had passed safely the perils of the Charybdis despair.

But now it is plainer. The sharply defined outlines of a practicable shore rise up against a smiling horizon. It is—it is a light upon the land! How invitingly it beams at last! How brightly it glows in a peaceful haven. Behold now, around it, the friends of yore beckoning invitingly and calling, "Come—come!" Blessed friends! What enchantments to lure our long suffering voyager from the sea of despair! Friends, did we say? Yes, and truly; that changeless, constant friendship that remains unshaken forever, that no misfortune, no envenomed breath of slander can ever chill. Friendship, Heaven's own attribute!

Lawrence Pleasington was taken at once into the bosoms of the families of his friends. Col. Worthington, Orlando Oglethrop, Edgar Harman, and Jesse Flowers vied with one another in claiming him as their permanent guest during his temporary sojourn in New York. But at last they compromised, on the basis that his time should be equally divided among them.

Carrie Flowers and Rosalia Harman were equally as sympathetic and kind as were Cassandra Worthington and Evalina Oglethrop, his long ago intimate and admiring friends. Of all these, Carrie manifested the most attentive solicitude. Often, when alone with him, in the parlor of her own mansion, she conversed with him in a tremulous voice and with moistening eyes. Why this was true, she, probably, might have vaguely imagined, but certainly she never explained, nor did any one question her on the subject. Pleasington alone observed it. To all others, her emotions were an unrevealed mystery, because they were never visible when a third person was present.

Perhaps these symptoms of pitying sympathy thrilled the being of Carrie Flowers, because she was better able to realize and to appreciate the depth of Pleasington's nameless woe than any other of his good friends. She had beheld mortal suffering that sickens the soul, and she had endured that silent sorrow that never reveals its wretchedness to the world. But then she was not unmindful of the fact that he was a secure link that connected the thread of romance which bound her family and the family of "the Angels of the Mountain" into one, or mated each one of three persons in the one to each in the other family. Thus she had received the only balm of consolation, after her own heart had bled, that mortal powers could bestow—the unsullied jewel of Jesse Flowers' spotless character and pure devotion.

It might have been, too, that, as she gazed upon the traces of care so deeply imprinted on the fair features and noble brow of Pleasington, while she reflected that he was the victim of Helen Mountjoy, she recalled the scene in which she had mingled on that bitter winter day in "The Mountain Cabin," twenty years before, when she first heard the plaintive story of Gertrude Flowers. She recognized that the day on which the thread of her own life became inextricably entangled and forever blended with

that of our story, as the once brightest and the saddest of its varying years.

Yet, moreover, who can divine if there was not still another association, almost inseparably entwined with the name and life of Lawrence Pleasington, and certainly so with the relations which these bear to this story, to which the mind of Carrie Flowers reverted in such sadness as to conjure up in her heart the deepest sentiments of pure womanly compassion? Innate sympathy for Pleasington, and undying pity for that association, linked, perhaps, with a lingering regret, were ample incentives, despite all dissembling arts and powers of self-control, to stir with intense emotion the depths of her soul.

However, be all or any of these conjectures well founded, or without a shade of claim to validity the result was nevertheless important to Lawrence Pleasington. In Carrie Flowers he found a constant and devoted friend, a source of comforting sympathy which he sorely needed. To him she became, in all the queenly majesty of the zealous and transcendent grandeur of her tender years, "The Angel of Consolation." With her he delighted to linger. At her home he often called on days when his company was due to other friends. With eager avidity he listened to her cheering words, which pictured hope-dawning happiness for the near future, so clearly, that it seemed as though he might grasp the reality with his outstretched hand as a tangible substance; yet he was unable to realize in it more than the beguiling delusion of a pleasing dream—simply the creation of imaginary fancy, springing spontaneously, as the abortive result of the overwrought solicitude of a highly romantic mind.

At that day, Carrie Flowers was fully conscious that the pages of this story were slowly growing. Well did she know to what extent she had contributed to their foundation. Truly she was advised of the character and purport of their contents, up to the last chapter before the present one we are now unfolding. More than ever was she intensely anxious to be instrumental in shaping events out of which the suspended chapter was to form and be unfolded before the reader's eyes. Hence, partly, at least, her boundless interest in Lawrence Pleasington; her uncontrollable desire to bring his life under the sway of her influence. For this she had an all-absorbing motive. But to him this was as incomprehensible and mysterious as the silent secrets of the grave wherein he had buried his fondest, his last, his only earthly hopes—the cherished object of his youthful dreams, the idolized adoration of his laurel-wreathed manhood, slumbering and mouldering to dust for so many mournful years. Then, he turned away from the enchanting portrait of a new hope, shuddering, doubting.

In sadness his mind wandered back into the desolate shadows of the bitter past, to dwell with fondness upon the treasured memory of one vanished form; to recall in sorrowful cadence and with tender reverence the mournful accents of one saintly name. With nothing earthly was Lawrence Pleasington able to associate the idea of the remote dream of dimly imagined Hope, save alone the name and life of Effie Edelstein—that loved one for whom he had suffered so much unabatable sorrow, who had suffered such untold anguish for him, in the consecration of her self-sacrificing devotion. Long years before, the news had reached him in his gloomy seclusion that his lost Effie had been borne from her saintly retirement to the peaceful repose of the silent church-yard. Hence, thus he mourned her.

To Carrie Flowers, and Pleasington's other friends, this latter fact was known; but to her at least, this may not have been accepted as conclusive and overwhelming testimony that Effie's place might not be re-supplied in his heart. She well knew, from the most consummate experience, the flexible nature of the human heart, and its proneness to yield to the healing antidotes of time and the soothing lullaby of gentle influence.

Probably she did not conceive that Pleasington might be an exception to the rule, nor believe that his heart was more abidingly true than her own had been devotedly constant.

However, Pleasington never mentioned the name that still remained so dear to him, nor did his friends ever allude to it in his presence. Thus was poor, persecuted. Effie's memory seemingly buried in the bosoms of her friends. It was en-

shrined in the heart of Lawrence Pleasington so deeply that time could never weaken its hold, could never dim the brightness of its long cherished remembrance.

Oglethrop, Harman & Co. had a branch house in a commercial centre of the South. At the same place they had a palatial residence, where some one of them, with his family, and usually the families of the other two, spent the winter.

Already had it been previously arranged that Lawrence Pleasington was to be domiciled at this home and instructed in the routine of the business, so that he might become qualified to assume the management in the interest of the firm of his confiding friends.

After a reasonable sojourn in New York, he gladly took his departure for his new home, amid other scenes more pleasing, leaving behind him associations from which painful reflections were inseparable. These were the shades of his blighted life, the grave of his Hope.

Once installed in his new sphere, accumulating duties and gigantic responsibilities devolved upon him with such amazing rapidity, that his mind and time became so much absorbed as measurably to wean him from the weary dream of the past. He was in his legitimate latitude. He recognized fully, and duly appreciated, the wonderful opportunities for unlimited usefulness thus placed at his disposal. At once he became intensely interested in his labors. Rapidly he mastered their intricacies. Soon his friends had unmistakable indications of his developing ability.

Early and thoroughly disciplined training received at the Military School, the stern and precise duties of an active commander in the field, and the long years of practical experience as an accountant—as he was employed during most of the darkest days of his life of trial—had admirably qualified and fitted him for the position to which he was assigned in his new calling. His first care and pride were to meet the expectations of his patrons; his second to gain information for himself. In all these directions he far outstripped the most sanguine anticipations of both himself and friends; he succeeded rapidly and admirably.

With his benefactors the terrible secrets of his hapless life securely reposed. No one at his new home knew aught concerning his history, except his war record, and that he was a confidential friend of Oglethrop, Harman & Co. His sorrows and his sufferings were yet unrevealed mysteries.

He gained friends, and grew in business and social popularity with surprising rapidity. Carrie Flowers was an ornament and a favorite in the society of that Southern city of Pleasington's adoption. To her influence was his special and speedy advancement largely due. Her vivid portrayal of his many virtues and high order of talents—the veritable nobility of character and true manhood everywhere admired—awakened extraordinary interest in him.

Not many months elapsed before he had unconsciously and unintentionally made a deep impression on the heart of more than one young lady. Quickly the wiles of Cupid were devising subtly constructed meshes of a cunning net, designed to entangle him in the toils of love. No unfair means, however, were employed to entrap him. The ladies did not overstep the bounds of strict propriety. They rather brought into requisition the attractions of their natal charms, the spell of their graceful beauty, and the winning enchantment of their modest virtue. Many of them were the reigning belles of the social kingdoms in which they held their sway. They were the admired of all admirers. At any moment could they, at will, have accepted a heart from scores of those of the first young men of the city, figuratively cast in confusing multiplicity around their fair feet, entreatingly appealing to be chosen. That Pleasington would thus come to sue there could be little doubt. Thus reasoned the young ladies and their intimate friend, Carrie Flowers.

As to Pleasington he met and treated all with that courteous consideration so natural to an educated officer of the United States army, especially of the old school, to which he had belonged. He was too refined to manifest indifference. In fact, no man of appreciative sensibilities could remain in such company and not be interested, if not fascinated. He esteemed the young ladies, not only because they were the friends of Carrie Flowers, but also because they were worthy of admiration. But the most perplexing feature was that he appeared to have no preference—that he seemed equally to admire and enjoy the society of them all.

Of all other persons, Carrie Flowers watched the progress of these social conflicts with the most intense interest. She believed that Lawrence Pleasington could be weaned from the dream of his hopeless love, and won by some other fair daughter of Eve. She had little faith in the abiding constancy of the heart of man, after he has been severed forever from the object of his transitory affections. She had, herself, received ample proof to sustain her skepticism. That Lawrence Pleasington had proved true and faithful to his first love for so many years, there were, to her mind, abundant reasons in the insurmountable barrier of interposing circumstances over which he exercised no power of control. In her opinion his constancy would not last one-tenth the same length of time amid the surroundings in which she then beheld him, exposed, as he was, to the captivating allurement of beauty, under the spell of the most refined social influence that ever swayed the heart of man. Positive was she that no susceptible heart could resist the encouraging temptation perpetually offering to that of Pleasington to be vitally impressed. Resolved was she to see it put to the utmost test to which social strategy and woman's witching graces could reduce the love engendering science.

Pleasington's persistent coyness as to the love-making feature of his social relations with his fair friends, was a marvel to the fascinating enchantresses themselves, and none the less an incomprehensible surprise to Carrie Flowers. Between her and the young ladies there existed, as to this subject, the most unreserved confidence. Each fair strategist understood that, upon the slightest indication of a preference on the part of Pleasington, Mrs. Flowers would do everything in her power to encourage the cultivation of the sentiment; all understood that her utmost skill was employed to induce him to choose among them some object as a favorite. They could rely implicitly on her discretion and prudence as to what she would disclose to him.

Her inference was that he feared the fate which

he was assured many of the admirers of the fair creatures were constantly receiving—a cold and unpitying decision that declined to accept and reciprocate their passionately proffered love. For a long time she could not, with propriety, attempt to disabuse his mind in this direction, or, perhaps, this course might have been adverse to her well defined policy. She did all in the bounds of consistency by arranging to throw Pleasington constantly in the company of some one of the young ladies. Thus was he placed constantly under circumstances the most favorable to ignite a spark and kindle the flame of love. His was one ceaseless round of social ovations. If he had vanity that delighted in admiration, it certainly was flattered to an extent sufficient to gratify the most inordinate desire. Whatever may have been her wishes in the premises, Mrs. Flowers manifested no disposition to disturb the natural tenor of the course of events.

In the height of this season, she admitted to us that the goal of her ambition was to force us to place Lawrence Pleasington where we had assumed the audacity, already, to place herself—in the innumerable category of "the hearts that heal." She assured us, with complacent and confiding *sangfroid*, that the siege was progressing most successfully; that while all approaches, to outward appearance, seemed invulnerable, there were, unquestionably, deep internal rents and breaches, steadily making inroads to, and undermining, his stronghold of resistance; and that it was only a matter of a little time before he would surrender at discretion. She claimed that he was weaned from the binding spell of his dream of early love; that his broken heart was virtually healed; and that the bitter memory of his great sorrows and fearful suffering was rapidly dissipating under the potent influence of pleasing associations. Earnestly did she importune us to await the development of the scene of romance in which Lawrence Pleasington would be one of the attractive characters. That this scene would unfold, on a select social stage, within a year, she was absolutely confident. She doubted not that this would revolutionize one prospective feature, at least, of our romance, as originally mapped out, in accordance with problematical anticipations of what was likely to be the inevitable.

We, as a matter of course, desired the final social scene in the rôle of Lawrence Pleasington. His station in the battle of life was amply established to meet the requirements of our purpose. He was earnestly engaged in many good works. This was in strict accord with the natural bent of his inclination. His intimate relations with Carrie Flowers would have thus enlisted him, no matter how he was disposed; and these stimulated and encouraged his efforts very materially. We could, therefore, do no better than to wait. One year would soon roll round on the wheel of time. And then, it would be cruel to deny the entreating appeal to "The Angel of Consolation," to be allowed to model this last scene, since she had modeled and wrought so many of those left in the wake of the past.

As Lawrence Pleasington was leisurely walking along the main promenade of the city, one lonely evening, he was suddenly confronted and addressed by an unique individual. The voice seemed familiar, but the features were a blank in his memory. "It must be some phantom of the by-gone time," he thought, as he gazed in wonderment upon the unearthly-appearing visage standing before him. He was puzzled and troubled. At last, he shook his head, and said: "You are too hard for me, old man. I am unable to place you."

With a twinkle in his bright eye—something Pleasington fancied he had seen many times before—he said:

"Think a bit, Massa Pleasington."

Suddenly a flash of light appeared to dawn before Pleasington's mind, as he said slowly, and with visible emotion, at the same time extending his hand:

"Ghostly shadow of UNCLE JAKE."

It was a fact. There stood the venerable form of the old man of another age—superannuated, with locks seemingly more snowy and skin more ebon-hued than in former days, when Pleasington knew him so well, and met him so often, amid many varying and exciting scenes.

JAKE: "Yes, sah; Massa Pleasington, I spects youze putty nigh right; dis am berry close ter ole Jake's ghost. De ole man am mighty nigh ter de land ob ghosts. But Ize 'ticular gladt er see you."

PLEASINGTON: "I am delighted to see you, Jake; but ashamed that I had entirely forgotten, so that I should never have recognized you on the street."

JAKE: "But I hadn't forgot you. Youze older and stouter; but de ize and de feturs am de same."

PLEASINGTON: "But how do you happen to be away here?"

JAKE: "Oh, sah; dat am eazce 'splained. Missus and Miss Carnelia, aze use ter be, when you uzed ter kno' her, comze here eberry winter, an' I comze wid dem. But, Massa Pleasington, de ole manze not comin' manne timze mo'."

Jake's voice was husky with emotion, and Pleasington hung his head in mute meditation.

This circumstance—the casual and unexpected meeting with Uncle Jake—afforded subject matter to Pleasington for reflection. It recalled some stirring reminiscences of the dark days of the war, and the young and hopeful summer of his life.

PLEASINGTON: "I had just left my office, Jake, but come with me. I will return. I want to talk with you."

The two men walked slowly back to the office. Pleasington looked upon Jake with reverence. Jake gazed up at Pleasington's face with an air of simple and childish affection.

The old man's mind was acutely tenacious. He recalled with surprising accuracy many incidents which had long since passed to oblivion in Pleasington's mind. He detailed, with astonishing rapidity, the vicissitudes through which he had passed since he left the smouldering ruins of the old homestead mansion and his own "cabin in the lane." When referring to this circumstance, Jake wept like a broken-hearted child. Poor old man! Nature's child he was; he is a child again by reason of his dotage.

Pleasington was missing that evening from his accustomed place in the gay and festive social circle, so uniformly graced by his presence; he was with Leonoria, Cornelia and Jake. The old man brought forth the traditional banjo, and thrilled his friends with the memory of days that were dead, and the dear "voices that were forever still."

When the shadows of the next evening spread their balmy wings over the beautiful city, Carrie Flowers had met Pleasington's fair friends of the "out-post days," and the renowned Jake, whose romantic and pathetic story she had heard so many times—whose thrilling experiences in their active and exciting lives she had oftener envied and sighed in vain to emulate.

Among other incidents related to Pleasington by Jake, at various times, the former was much interested in some features of the reminiscences of Gen. E——, with which the old man seemed to be singularly familiar. He pictured most vividly the General's flight, disguise, escape from the country at the close of the war, and long residence, with its innumerable hardships and privations, in a foreign land. Some of these features Pleasington often recounts with unfeigned gusto.

To some of his friends he said:

"It seems that there was a famous doctor in the Valley of Virginia, wealthy, and the owner of numerous slaves before the war. This doctor was a member of the Virginia Convention, and denounced E—— with all the opprobrious epithets in the language, owing to his masterful opposition to secession. The doctor's favorite hobby was his rights in the Territories. With this doctrine he assailed E—— continually, whenever he had the floor. The latter retorted with his usual unanswerable philippics—the ghastly portrait of a civil war and ruin of the South. Time rolled on apace. Sheridan was devastating the Valley of Virginia; Gen. E—— advancing to meet him. The latter was well up to the front, reconnoitering. Citizens were flying pell-mell before the Federal advance, leaving their burning homesteads behind them. One wagon, driven by an over-excited white man, containing a woman, two children, and some odd household effects, specially attracted the attention of the General. He recognized the doctor in the driver. This was the nearest the doctor had ever been to the war. The General had waited long and patiently. He saw at last his supreme opportunity. Memories of the hot debates in the Convention rushed up before his mind. For the moment he forgot the advancing enemy and the flying missiles of death. Standing straight in his stirrups he shouted:

"'Hallo! Hold on there, Doctor. Where are you going, Doctor?'

"Doctor: 'I don't know, General. My house is in flames. I am ruined. Everything I have left is in the wagon. I don't know what to do, nor where I am going.'

"Gen. E—: 'I know where you are going, doctor!'

"Doctor: 'Where am I going, General?'

"Gen. E—: 'To hunt for your rights in the Territories, sir.'

"The old General had his revenge, and rode on apparently gratified.

"During his wanderings, while an exile, a Major-General of the United States Army—a native of the Old Dominion—recognized the General's name on the register of a hotel. Now if there was any one thing which the old General hated more cordially than everything else, that object was a native and resident Virginian who had served against her during the war. The United States officer had never met Gen. E—— personally, and hence was unable to recognize him among the guests of the hotel. He, therefore, applied to the landlord for an introduction. The latter, by this time, knew the uncouth old General pretty well. He very politely declined to make the introduction desired; and, at the same time, informed the applicant that his rank justified him to introduce himself to a fellow-countryman in a strange land. He pointed out the old Confederate commander. The latter, with his broad-brimmed slouch hat well down over his eyes, and his hands behind his back, was leisurely promenading back and forth along the grand piazza of the hotel. Approaching him, the United States officer, Gen. H——, said courteously:

"'Gen. E——, I presume. I am Gen. H——, of the United States Army. We met rather unpleasantly in the Valley of Virginia and elsewhere; but I hope we may be friends now. I am glad to meet you.'

"Pausing abruptly and eyeing the elegantly dressed soldier carefully, he said slowly and with sententious sarcasm:

"'Yes, it used to be Gen. E——, and I was there, sir.'

"After an embarrassing pause, Gen. H—— expatiated on the vicissitudes of the war, and ultimately wound up by displaying a beautiful gold medal, which he explained had been presented to him by the officers of his division for gallant and meritorious service on the battlefield. The old general remained silent for some moments, and then said:

"'Yes, I see it.'

"Then, brooding reflectively for some time, as he slowly paced the floor, he again paused and said:

"'Times have greatly changed.'

"Gen. H——grasped the situation, and doubtless imagining that the rancorous old rebel was warming up, to some extent, at least, in the direction of appreciation, he boldly launched out in a beautiful little speech, most appropriately worded, to pave the way for a lavish compliment from his late antagonist. The latter paused and faced the speaker, when the climax of the peroration was reached, and the harmonious cadences of that musical voice had died away. Thus standing, he made one herculean effort to raise his stooping, decrepit form to the towering dignity of his vanished grandeur, and said in tones of inimitable sarcasm:

"'Yes, in the good old days of Christ, they used to hang thieves on crosses, but now they hang all the crosses on thieves.'

"The old man had wreaked his revenge, and he then resumed his walk with composed indifference."

We might fill a chapter with the quaint speeches of this eccentric and unreconstructed old man, whose prejudices and hatreds neither time nor circumstance has tended to abate; who never forsakes a friend, and never forgives an enemy in his native State. For the people of the Northern States, who proved their professions, by facing the battle-storm, he cherishes no animosity. These he esteems. But the public distractors he detests. He is a marvel of sincerity—never dissembling—and the unbending soul of honor. A man of unflinching courage, a mind replete with inexhaustible stores of wit, and immeasurable acumen of cool and tenacious judgment, it is to be regretted that his all but matchless talents and overpowering eloquence

were not early employed in the cause of reconciliation and in restoring the ruined fortunes of
the South. But the contumely cast upon his
name by his own people, because of his desperate zeal and determinate efforts in the tireless
struggles to avert the inevitable disasters which
he so clearly foresaw and so truly predicted for
his hot-headed countrymen, and the cause that
banished him so long from his native land, after
the end came, doubtless soured his disposition
and embittered his life, to an extent estranging
his affections from what might have proved
otherwise a pleasing enterprise.

With lingering reluctance we leave this interesting character, who has moved for more than
eighty winters in the dreamy shades of fairy-
tale realities. His whole life has been almost one
unbroken chain of thrilling vicissitudes, many
of which the creators of fiction might strive in
vain to rival in imagery. We have, all along,
regretted that so little of his war rôle would
blend with the thread of our story—that our
characters were not more intimately associated
with him. In the camp, on the parade-ground,
on the march, and on the battlefield, he transformed the sober duties of the commander to a
pleasing vein of witty or sarcastic romance.

Was it possible to disguise his identity beyond
the peradventure of recognition, his life and its
varied relations would make a romance of deeply
thrilling interest.

Here, too, are we constrained to part with
Uncle Jake—nature's romantic child. Largely
would the latter journey of his life blend with
that of the old general in a new story, with these
peculiar men as prominent characters. Jake
admired the old general; the latter esteemed and
appreciated Jake for his intrinsic merit, sincerity,
and, above all, his natal honesty.

In conclusion, it must suffice to say, as an
explanation of these relations, that Leonoria Fairchild was a near relative of Gen. E——.

Leonoria and Cornelia must also disappear.
Their rôles, as direct participants in our scenes,
terminated away back in the early months of
the war. They have since passed through many
varied experiences, but these would not harmonize with our story. Only twice have they

casually and but slightly re-entered in the long
and tortuous course of its unfolding. Now they
must leave it—and forever.

The gay season amid the sylvan bowers of the
Southern Eden, in which Lawrence Pleasington
met such varying experiences, drew towards its
close. The day was fixed on which his good
angel, Carrie Flowers, would leave him and retire to her Northern home. The time was near
when his fair friends, the witching daughters of
Dixie, would take their departure for the festive
conquests of summer watering resorts. Soon
Lawrence would be left a prey to the monotony
of the dull business season of a Southern city,
and the lonely occupant of the charming mansion
of his friends.

To him these were not, probably, altogether
pleasing reflections, yet they were the inevitable.
He had no inclination to visit the land of his
nativity and of his sorrows. To his Southern trust
he was enslaved, but it was a pleasing bondage
to him.

Here he had an opportunity to do good. At
his disposal a special fund was placed by Carrie
Flowers, to be employed in such charities as he
might deem best. Many were the sad and despairing hearts by him gladdened and cheered.

The scenes through which he had passed during the winter were wonderful. The transfor-
mations wrought by one short season, which was
far spent before he was known in the brilliant
circles in which he moved and where he had met
such appreciative favor, were astonishing. He
could hardly realize that he was not in the beguiling delusion of a fairy dreamland—in the
hallucination of a deceptive delusion, as he had
been so many times in the sad, sad visions of the
past.

Might it be at all strange if he wondered what
another season would develop among scenes so
charming and under influences so captivating?
Certainly there was no telling; this was far
beyond the latitude of conjecture. There were
many chances in favor of the doctrine of Carrie
Flowers, that the seemingly extinct embers would
again be ignited, and from their smouldering ashes
rise again, phœnix-like, the glorious blessing of a
happier love. There could be no question but

that the shadows of gloom were vanishing, and refulgent rays of brightness were dawning in their stead. Nature was asserting her sway; Time was administering her antidotes; the malady of a settled melancholy, with its "serpent's tooth" of hopeless despair, was steadily and surely yielding to the soothing influences of these potent remedies. Lawrence Pleasington was becoming the new creature of a metamorphosed life. He himself doubted whither these influences were leading or driving him.

Pleasington's good friend, Carrie Flowers, had been extremely indulgent. She never alluded to any serious sentiments, on his part, in relation to his social complications. Never did she intimate to him that she imagined it possible for him to become entangled in the meshes of Cupid's ensnaring net. She rather tended her efforts in the direction of impressing his mind with the idea that the solicitous esteem manifested for himself by the blushing Roses of the South, was but the natural spontaneity of the boundless sociability and exuberant friendship inherent with the genial people of their sunny land. Earnestly she desired Destiny to take its course undisturbed. Eagerly she watched its wavering progress.

But as the day drew near for her departure, she decided to speak to him. Perhaps she was thus impelled by the promptings of her woman's irrepressible curiosity, or may be she had another and a subtler motive. At all events, she desired to bear off with her an intimation of his sentiments. And she said to him:

"Now, Lawrence, my good friend, I have a favor to ask of you. Will you grant it? It shall be a matter of sacred confidence, if you prefer."

Pleasington: "Certainly, I will grant any favor you can ask, to my life itself. Such is my gratitude."

Carrie: "Don't talk to me about gratitude. I have simply discharged a debt to humanity, in my solicitude for your welfare, comfort and happiness. I have merely sought to win you back to the brightness of life again. I earnestly hope I am succeeding."

Pleasington: "You are succeeding far beyond the bounds of reasonable possibility, or what I dreamed might ever prove a reality."

Carrie: "I want to know with whom of your fair friends you are now most favorably impressed?"

Pleasington: "I esteem and appreciate them all very much. I think I have not the slightest preference. Really, I have never given the subject a thought. I could like any one of them as a sister. Beyond this, my inclination is not prone to venture."

Carrie: "I am really disappointed. I felt sure that ere now you would have selected a favorite flower from the pretty group."

Pleasington: "I have never for one moment indulged a dream—not even as the remotest possibility. The young ladies are the admired of many admirers. Many sore hearts are exiled supplicants from their disappointing shrines. Had I an emotional fount capable of being thus victimized, I know too truly and remember too well the pangs of social discomfiture to jeopardize it where I clearly perceive the baffled expectations of others stranded as helpless wrecks."

Carrie: "But I can assure you, from my consummate knowledge of human nature, that you would meet no such experience. I am positive, without, however, having the slightest expressed intimation on the subject, that any of them would be pleased to meet a serious proposition from you half way. Rarely have I observed a gentleman so encouragingly received in society."

Pleasington: "I prize the fact more than I am able to express to you. But, frankly, my good friend, were there no questions about the results, I could not entertain the idea, without a heart in the enterprise; and this I cannot have—it would be impossible."

Carrie: "But, my friend, you must educate yourself for this responsibility. It is your duty. You owe it to society, to humanity, to your race and line. 'Life is short and time is fleeing.' You have been robbed of much of these heritages. Now you are in the prime of manhood. You cannot afford to incur the risk of a penalty for shirking the palpable demands of divine and moral law. There is too much nobility of natural character in you to be sacrificed on the dreary altar of Disconsolation. Once I felt as you now feel. But the dark phantom of stern duty rose up before and haunted me perpetually. Its voice was too imperative to be disregarded. My melancholy compunctions yielded to its urgent commands. And thus, my friend, I desire to persuade you, is your remedy to be secured."

PLEASINGTON: "Probably you are right. Your arguments appear to be unanswerable. But it will require time for me to reconcile myself to their application. I shall reflect upon the subject, because you urge me to adopt its practical principles. Still, however, otherwise I feel not the slightest interest in the probable or, perhaps, more properly speaking, the problematical issue of its consideration."

CARRIE: "Well, I shall not further press the question. Beauty, wealth, and the highest excellence of womanly virtue, are, figuratively speaking, kneeling at your feet. I can depend on your good judgment to bid them rise in their sublime majesty and receive your blessing. I know that, ultimately, you will accept them considerately and graciously—nay, earnestly sue for their smiling bestowal."

PLEASINGTON: "I recognize the burden of duty which devolves upon me. Whenever I can experience a harmonizing emotion of inclination, I shall apprize you that I am vanquished. This may be next winter; it might be—NEVER. Matrimony is a question too serious to be lightly esteemed."

To Pleasington the summer and fall were long and monotonous seasons. Business activity did not appear until late in November. From his friends in New York he learned that none of them would join him until Christmas-eve. During these long and lonesome months he had considered seriously the important subject discussed with Carrie Flowers.

Early in the fall his fair friends of the past winter, returned to the sunny land of their birth, to gladden it with their smiles, and fill its fragrant zephyrs with the melody of their voices. But they saw much less of Lawrence Pleasington than they had formerly seen when Carrie Flowers was present to display her delicate feats of social strategy. Why it was, he could not explain nor understand, but instinctively he shrunk from the responsibility of acting on her advice. December found him with his relations no more

intimate with any lady than they were when the gay season closed—rather tended his proneness in the direction of retrogression than that of advancement. Thus he unbosomed himself to his absent friend:

"December 2, 1882.

"MRS. CARRIE V. FLOWERS, NEW YORK:

"*My much appreciated friend:*

"It is my duty to acknowledge and answer your esteemed letter of the 28th ult., which reached me this evening. How sad to reflect that twenty-two more long days and nights must dawn and wane ere I am to be blessed with your genial greeting. I am very lonesome, and miss you beyond expression. No other can supply your absent company.

"But, since I want to see you so much, I must still frankly admit, that I dread to meet you. Undutifully have I disregarded your injunction. My social status and inclination remain unchanged, except, perhaps, I view the subject with more disfavor than I viewed it when we parted. I regret to tell you this. I am pained to disappoint you. Gladly would I make great sacrifices to meet your wishes, in any other direction. But in this they are too serious. I cannot make them. They involve questions of too much import.

"A lady expects, with an offer of marriage, a profession of love. This is her right. Without it, made in manifest sincerity, I could not respect the lady who would accept such a suitor. This would be my predicament: I should be that uninviting wooer. How could I ask one of your friends, whose fair and impulsive nature is passionate, exacting devotion personified, to be my bride? With what could I reward her affection, if bestowed? With nothing but the hollow mockery of dissimulation forced from the sterile cavities of my desolate heart. I cannot, I will not, attempt such base deception. My chivalrous instincts of soldierly gallantry, and the promptings of true manhood, revolt at the bare contemplation. Your friends are adorable. Had I the inestimable treasures of love to bestow I should at once lay them entreatingly at the feet of some one of these sweet daughters of the South. I once have loved, but, with me, love is at an end. I cannot pretend that I feel an emotion to which I am an utter stranger.

"With great and patient effort have I tried to reconcile my conscience to a course that might ultimately lead to your expectation.

"In your grand old parlor have I brooded over this question, amid the purple gloom and haunted loneliness of many a midnight: yes, haunted by a spirit that forsakes me not. There, before me, stood the ideal image of that fair young life, whose broken heart once beat for me alone—a devotion unsurpassed in this world. Think of the bitter abnegation of its sacrifice, voluntarily rendered. A blighting curse on my very thought of inconstancy! Well might the phantom spectre rebuke my musings. It should have paralyzed my reflective faculties. Your own case, my gracious friend, offers no parallel to mine. You were forsaken—no matter if you had been laboring under no delusion as to the fate of the object of your adoration. This abundantly justifies your doctrine as to your course. But I should have nothing to console me, as an extenuating excuse. It would be monstrous ingratitude to a sacred memory.

"I have refrained from intimating this mournful subject to you. I have been thankful that your charitable consideration restrained you from alluding to this sad theme. I should not recall it now—nor never—was I not driven to this desperate extremity, in self-defence, of apparent ingratitude to you. A proper reverence strictly enjoins silence. No other expression could be so eloquently appropriate. I trust there may be no occasion again to disturb the quietude of its repose—that should be eternal.

"Pray abandon your social projects for me. I appreciate your solicitude, but no pleasing influence, nor associations, in this world, could ever compensate for the pain the continued endeavor to consummate your plans would inflict.

"I trust you may be able to appreciate my position. I hope you will pardon my seeming ingratitude, and that this may be the last expression you will ever exact of me on this subject.

"I am, gratefully, your friend,

"LAWRENCE PLEASINGTON."

In due course of time he received the following reply:

"——PLACE, NEW YORK, Dec. 10, 1882.

"MAJOR LAWRENCE PLEASINGTON!

"*My Esteemed Friend:*

"Your late letter has been read with interested surprise. It amazes me. Admiration is no adequate term to express my emotion. I am constrained to confess that I am vanquished, and must exclaim 'Eureka!' Yes, I have found what I verily believed did not exist—*a man of constant devotion*, whom time, circumstance, nor temptation could never change. The romancer's ideal dream, at last! Well have you acted your part! How subtly have you played to his fancy! Is it conspiracy to refute and overwhelm my cherished doctrines? For this once, I am baffled.

"I shall not, however, abandon my purpose. I shall speak of it with deeper meaning than ever, and teach you speedily to dwell on it with delight. Before the season closes, I shall witness you in love, bowing meekly at Cupid's shrine, and standing blushingly at the altar of matrimony, sealing your plighted vows with one of Eve's fairest daughters. Then your long mourned Effie will be no more regretted.

"Your constant friend,

"CARRIE V. FLOWERS."

The twenty-fourth of December came, and with it, Pleasington's friends, Harman, Oglethrop, and Flowers, with their families.

The grand double parlors were aglow with the mellow brightness of the chandeliers. All within was perfumed by Southern flowers, and beautiful in artful appointments and the assembled company.

But stifled anticipation seemed to pervade the apartments, except as to Pleasington, who alone was tranquil, and unable to divine the cause of the perceptible flutter of restless expectation among his friends. A few moments sufficed to reveal the mystery.

Robed in bridal splendor, appeared and stood before him, in queenly majesty, witching modesty, and blooming loveliness, the graceful form of EFFIE EDELSTEIN—*his long lost love, his resurrected bride!*

Lawrence Pleasington turned deathly pale and trembled violently. For the moment the shrouded ghost of so many nights became, to his mind, a tangible reality. But there were the heaving bosom, the love-lit eye of the dreamy past. Was it a resemblance so striking that he could not perceive the deception, designed to delude him, or was it a spirit? Equally discomposed was the faithful woman of so many sorrowful years. She stood convulsed with emotion too deep for utterance, too sacred for mortal appreciation. Adorable heroine!

She was the first to speak.

EFFIE: "Lawrence, don't you know me?"

Her voice sent a current of electric magnetism through his being. The red glow of long-forgotten joy remounted to his cheek. With one impulsive bound he clasped her to his bosom; pressed eagerly "the touch of a vanished hand."

LAWRENCE: "Effie, my long mourned love! This is more than a fleeting dream!"

EFFIE: "Yes, Lawrence, there are no shadowy delusions here. The ecstacies of this blessed moment compensate for all I have suffered!"

CARRIE: "My prophecy is fulfilled. Your mourned Effie is no longer regretted. Here is a queenly reward for constant devotion. I proved you. I weighed you in love's sensitive scales, and found you not wanting in its sublime attributes. I rejoice with you. I shall have the unutterable pleasure of witnessing, in this sunny land of love, the happy consummation of the blissful dream of your manhood's years."

EVALIA: "Effie and Lawrence, my re-united friends! Words cannot express the joy I feel."

ROSALIA: "God bless you, my friends! I am happy. At last your broken hearts have found their healing balm."

OGLETHROP: "Lawrence, behold thy admirable marvel of devotion! Effie, I often told him all the world could never estrange you from him. This is pleasure to me beyond fiction's image."

FLOWERS: "I thank God that I have lived to see the light of this day, which dawned to illuminate the way to so much mortal happiness, and that I am here as a participating witness."

HARMAN: "My thrice fortunate friends! I am thrilled with your boundless delights. May your

21

future paths be strewn with flowers, and may you never know a sorrow."

CARRIE: "This occasion is too sacred for eyes and ears of flesh and blood. Let us retire. When the Christmas bells chime midnight, we will return with the holy man."

Left alone to the rapture of their own society, Lawrence and Effie, the faithful, the devoted, the true, found themselves genuine children of love, reborn to a realization of its fascinations. He was the first to speak.

LAWRENCE: "Tell me, darling, how this all came to be? Many years I have mourned you dead. Why has no one sooner undeceived me?"

EFFIE: "The story is long and complicated. The pleasure of this hour should scarcely be shadowed by its gloomy recital, but since this propitious Christmas-eve meeting is the result, we may be yet thankful for and bless the otherwise uninviting theme. We will, therefore, pass that feature now, and leave it in the desolate grave of our resurrected hopes.

"You remember that sad, sad Christmas of 1865—a day on which the doleful notes of woe, borne in those melancholy words, 'It might have been!' brought so much of mournful distress to our despairing hearts. This, which you now behold, was the bridal robe I should have worn on that glad day. I prepared it in the joyous month of May, when we were so happy together over our re-union, that of our long distracted country, and your safe delivery from the dark valleys of death. Yes, we were, in confiding simplicity, existing in dreams of blissfulness. Poor visions! they were too sweet to last. All those sorrowful years I kept this robe, jealously treasured it— my ill-fated bridal raiment—for the burial shroud of my perished hope.

"Ah, Lawrence! the memory of those disconsolate days, those cheerless nights, waiting for the summons to come, makes my heart sick. I sank to the borders of the tomb. For months my life was considered the prey of Death; for forty hours all indications of its lamp were extinct. I was reported gone to the land of 'the Hereafter.' To you this solemn news was wafted. When, at last, I rallied and vanquished the destroying enemy, it was many weeks before

I became rational. There were no lucid intervals in my delirium. My attendants believed I must die. It was deemed best to leave you thinking my sorrows were at an end. When I did return to conscious responsibility, I realized that you had already suffered the pangs of bereavement—if aught on earth could add to your agony—and were wedded to the loneliness of a hopeless melancholy. I was satisfied my days were yet few and numbered. I esteemed it cruel to tell you I lived, when, in a little while, you must again hear the story of my long repose in the solitude of the grave. I insisted that it would be merciful to leave you under the impression that I was no more. After I was able to rise from my bed, I still considered it better to leave the subject, as to you, undisturbed. I did not expect to live long.

"As the years plodded on in their slow and monotonous track, I gained strength, and experienced a perceptible emotion of hope that we might meet again. This stimulated my desire for life. Rapidly I recuperated. My eager consent was granted that you should know the truth and see me the first day circumstances admitted.

"But oh, Lawrence, cruel Fate! As the days passed, after this anticipated reality might have been, to multiply weeks and months and years, that 'hope deferred' which 'maketh the heart sick,' was mine with a pitiless vengeance. I could never forgive myself that I had not earlier apprised you that I was not dead. I concluded that you had gone to some secluded spot to hide away from the eyes of the world; and that I was doomed to pass, at last, from my gloomy retirement to the silent loneliness of the grave. The bridal dress was again returned to its recess of guarded treasures, to await that solemn ceremony; and I grew resigned to the inevitable.

"At length, however, after hope was only a vanished dream, Mrs. Flowers, the good angel, came to tell me that she had pressed your hand and looked into your honest eyes. This was not until after you had departed for the South, and she was on the eve of starting to join you. She importuned me to aid her in developing a thrilling surprise. She desired to prove your constancy. Urgently she implored me to come forth from the convent and remain with my friends, very quietly, until time to arrive here for this gladsome season and its precious compliments—thrice blessed to us. From that day it has all been her affair. To-night its sequel unfolded before your open eyes. I know your sad story—never mention it again in the future.

"This night, seventeen years ago, I expected to be with you, attired as I am now. How long since then! But the infallible doctrine that patient virtue and unyielding honor will ultimately receive their meritorious reward, those heavily journeying years have abundantly demonstrated to us, tedious as they have been, and hopeless as they have seemed. I thought it well that you should thus see me, the first time after our mournful severance, as I should have then appeared, save alone these deep and defacing imprints of care, time and sorrow. I am delighted to see that these wasting agents of youth and life have dealt no more severely with you."

LAWRENCE: "My poor, long-suffering darling, you are as young and fair to me as then, and thrice precious for the fidelity cherished for silent absence, amounting to seeming neglect. How thankful I am for this reserved surprise and the opportunity it has afforded me to prove my constancy. I thought Mrs. Flowers was in serious earnest about her social plans."

EFFIE: "No, she was not. But her faith in the fidelity of mankind in general was less than mine in you individually. She would have discouraged you on the first symptom of a disposition on your part to yield to the fascinating temptation with which you were tried. I was constantly and fully advised all the time. I should not have blamed you had you surrendered; but I appreciate you all the more that you were faithful to my memory."

LAWRENCE: "We are agreed on all these points. Now you wear the blessed robe, and the sacred season is here again. At last, after the long and relentless interdiction of time, I implore you, my resurrected darling, let us never permit time to have the latitude to play her fickle freaks, until the birth of another day, to dissever us. Before the morning dawns let us be united for aye. Mrs. Flowers said something about the Christmas chimes and the holy man."

EFFIE: "My plighted vows were yours in the bright days of yore; they have been constantly yours in the darkest days of my bitter affliction; they remain none the less yours to night. I have ever been as ready to seal and consecrate them on the holy altar of pure love as I am now. Mrs. Flowers has all that arranged. When the bells toll midnight, she will come upon the stage with her supporting train—the unrivaled star in the scene. In that solemn hour, amid these sacred associations, here beneath the genial skies of this benignant clime, I shall reward your constant devotion with the treasured love of a heart which has ever thrilled with the reverberating emotions of the pulsating notes, unceasingly chanted, 'Truly thine!'"

LAWRENCE: "I wonder if there will be many present, beside our mutual friends."

EFFIE: "All of the reigning belles, and some of their admiring gallants, in the social circles where you are known, are to come. But to them the affair is a profound mystery. They will meet a surprise as startling, comparatively, as that which paralyzed you with sudden amazement. Mrs. Flowers has her plot highly wrought. She desires the scene to be clothed with a halo of pleasing sensation. Her very being is enveloped in the quintessence of passionate and creative natural romance in real life. Under its magic spell has she lived and moved all her days. She is one of God's noblest works, and none the less 'The Angel of Consolation' to-night, than when she was the guardian spirit of the children of the mountain forest. Our cause is her special charge—our happiness her zealous solicitude.

"You are a full partner with your late confiding employers and much appreciative friends. This lovely mansion is ours exclusively. Here are we to dwell. Such is my wish. I desire never to be nearer the scenes of our sorrows and suffering."

LAWRENCE: "God bless her! To her more than to all our other friends combined, are we indebted for this blessed occasion and our promising future."

EFFIE: "That is true. She knows how to pity us. It would move a heart of stone to hear her pathetic recitals of her own bitter experience and silent suffering, as she sometimes confidingly recounted them to me."

LAWRENCE: "It is both wonderful and mysterious—the devoted and unselfish interest she has taken in our behalf, and more especially mine. I am unable to understand what so powerfully influenced her in our favor. I can attribute it to nothing but charitable sympathy and immeasurable philanthrophy, that superinduce such boundless compassion for distressed, afflicted, suffering humanity."

EFFIE: "That is the cause in the main, on general principles, perhaps sufficient to have prompted her to do all she has done for us. But, ah, Lawrence! there has been, and is, a more powerful incentive that has actuated and still controls her impulsive nature: it is a cherished phantom of the past—the hallowed memory of associations, as these were when, and soon after, your name first became with them blended. Oh, Lawrence! it is the spell of that influence—that nothing can ever subdue until Carrie Flowers passes beneath the sods of the grave—that makes her interest in us as lasting as life itself. She has been requested to make our weal her own, by one whose slightest intimation is, with her, an imperative injunction she would no more disregard than she would break the most sacred commandment. Lawrence, it is gratitude—that divinest of all mortal influences and attributes, so rarely found in its sublime perfection in this non-appreciative world—that prompts Carrie Flowers to be to us a ministering comfortress; gratitude to one whom she mournfully realizes is lost to her for evermore."

The great clock in the library strikes the first knell of midnight. Instantaneously a thousand bells chime in discordant chorus, and send their startling echoes floating away, in mingling reverberations, on the soft and balmy air—such odoriferous zephyrs as can be found on Christmas-eve nowhere else on earth, save alone under the dreamy skies of some fair and sunny land, such as this is where the re-union of Lawrence and Effie is consummated. It is the greeting of a Southern metropolis to the festive season—the chant of *peace and good will.*

But, ah! to those loving hearts, what a thrill of ecstasy the gladsome tocsins send! What a greeting they usher in unto Lawrence and

Effie! A charming procession of the gayest of the gay and the fairest of the fair, beside adoring admirers, file into the main parlor. "The beauty and the chivalry" of this "Southern Queen" are assembled now. To Lawrence, there is no stranger in this merry throng. But amazement is clearly depicted on each face when the lovely woman by his side is observed.

Gracefully Mrs. Flowers presides over the ceremony of introduction. She is beaming with the satisfaction of delight—with the anticipation of the crowning triumph of her cherished surprise. Lawrence is greeted without reserve, and with manifest and undisguised admiration.

If the presence of Effie created surprise, the approach of an eminent divine, in his sacredotal robes, provokes wonderment that no words can describe. The introduction of the "man of God" to Effie, and his greeting to the other members of the company over, Mrs. Flowers steps a few paces from the group, turns, faces her guests and friends, and bows. Silence reigns supreme in the appartments. Breathless suspense pervades her audience. Some mysterious scene is about to develop. All realize that such is true. Mrs. Flowers says:

"MY GOOD FRIENDS: I have called you here after much coaxing importunity, to witness an occasion replete with fascinating surprise. Had I sooner intimated its nature there would have been no necessity to entreat you to come; but then the pleasure of this moment would not be mine: that of beholding you on the tip-toe of expectation. Before you now, my friends, is unfolding the final scene in a drama of baffled love that has crept on its slow and mournful course through the winding vicissitudes of almost eighteen years. For nearly seventeen years your friend here has grieved for his fair companion as one who stands by the bier of a departed loved one. For years she has borne in her heart that sorrow known to those only, to whom the certainty comes, that the dearest object of earth is lost forever. To-night they met for the first time in all those sad and suffering years. To-night you are to see the realization of the romancer's dream, in actual life. Immediately now, before your open eyes, here, in this Paradise of Love, you are to see them married.

"My fair friends, don't be envious. You have had every opportunity to estrange his lingering affection from the memory of, to him, the dead. You failed. He is her rewarding treasure; she is his consecrated jewel. Behold two admirable marvels of devotion! Bestow upon them your smiles. Vouchsafe them your blessing. They are worthy."

She then names the conventional and assisting couples, as attendants in the sacred ceremony, and invites the minister to proceed with its solemnization.

The ceremony is that of the Episcopal Church. This completed, the venerable man says:

"My Children: I know the pathetic story of your sorrows and your suffering. These you endured with patient fortitude and virtuous resignation. In this pleasing moment you realize your well earned reward. It gladdens my heart to bestow upon you Christ's blessing.

"Now, in this beautiful land and delicious clime —the home of love—from this, your sylvan bower of enchantment, you may glance back over the sterile waste left behind you, and complacently smile, while the magic of true love revivifies your long blighted hopes, heals your once broken hearts, and envelopes you in a halo of *supreme happiness.*"

"My task is done, my song hath ceased, my theme
　　Has died into an echo; it is fit
The spell should break of this protracted dream;
　　The torch shall be extinguished which hath lit
My midnight lamp, and what is writ is writ;
　　Would that it was worthier; but I am not now
That which I have been, and my visions flit
　　Less palpably before me; and the glow
Which in my spirit dwelt, is fluttering faint and low.
　　*　　　*　　　*　　　*
　　　　" Mine be the pain,
If such there was; yours the moral of this strain.
　　*　　　*　　　*　　　*
" Farewell! a word that must be, and hath been:
　　A sound which makes us linger; yet—FAREWELL!

THE END.